Annotations to the Front Cover

1   Jane Austen's sister, Cassandra, painted this picture of
their niece, Fanny Austen Knight. Fanny's surname resulted
from her father's adoption by distant relations named Knight
who left their estate to him. This reasonably common procedure could explain the difference in name of Mr. Bennet
and Mr. Collins in the novel, despite their common paternal
ancestry.

2   Fanny was very close to Austen, often asking her advice
about love and marriage. In her replies, Austen acknowledges
the economic benefits of marriage for women but also argues
firmly, in words she repeats almost verbatim in *Pride and Prejudice*, that one should never marry without love.

3   Fanny's sketching, like Cassandra's execution of this picture, suggests how many ladies drew or painted at that time.
Such accomplishments were highly valued in young ladies;
the Bennet girls are criticized for their inability to draw.

4   Fanny's dress is typical of period fashions, which favored
high waists, soft flowing fabrics, and light colors.

The Annotated
PRIDE AND PREJUDICE

Annotated and Edited by
DAVID M. SHAPARD

———

David Shapard graduated with a Ph.D. in European History from the University of California at Berkeley; his specialty was the eighteenth century. Since then he has taught at several colleges. He lives in upstate New York.

The Annotated

PRIDE

AND

PREJUDICE

Jane Austen's House Chawton M

The cottage at Chawton, Hampshire. This was where Jane Austen lived in the last part of her life, and where she wrote most of her novels.

[From Mary Augusta Austen-Leigh, *Personal Aspects of Jane Austen* (New York, 1920), p. 112]

The Annotated

PRIDE

AND

PREJUDICE

―――――

JANE AUSTEN

Annotated and Edited, with an Introduction, by

DAVID M. SHAPARD

ANCHOR BOOKS

A Division of Random House, Inc.

New York

FIRST ANCHOR BOOKS EDITION, MARCH 2007

Anchor and colophon are registered trademarks
of Random House, Inc.

Library of Congress Cataloging-in-Publication Data
Austen, Jane, 1775–1817.
[Pride and Prejudice]
The annotated Pride and prejudice / Jane Austen ; annotated
and edited, with an introduction, by David M. Shapard.
p.   cm.
Includes bibliographical references and index.
1. Austen, Jane, 1775–1817. Pride and prejudice. 2. Social
classes—Fiction. 3. Young women—Fiction. 4. Courtship—
Fiction. 5. Sisters—Fiction. 6. England—Fiction.
7. Domestic fiction. I. Shapard, David M. II. Title.
PR4034.P7 2007   823'.7—dc22   2006049949

Anchor ISBN: 978-0-307-27810-4

Book design by Rebecca Aidlin

www.anchorbooks.com

Printed in the United States of America
20 19 18 17 16 15 14 13 12 11

Contents

PRIDE AND PREJUDICE

VOLUME I

(Note: The following chapter headings are not found in the novel.
They are added here by the editor to assist the reader.)

VOLUME II

Notes to the Reader

The Annotated Pride and Prejudice contains several features
that the reader should be aware of:

Plot disclosures: a number of annotations allude to later developments in the story, as does the introduction. Such allusions are
essential to making a variety of points, but they can spoil the surprise for anyone unfamilar with the story. First-time readers might
therefore prefer to read the text of the novel first, and then to read
the annotations and introduction.

Literary interpretations: the comments on the techniques and
themes of the novel, more than other types of entries, represent
the personal views and interpretations of the editor. Such views
have been carefully considered, but nevertheless they will inevitably provoke disagreement among some readers. I can only hope
that even in those cases, the opinions expressed provide useful
food for thought.

Differences of meaning: many words then, like many words now,
had multiple meanings. The meaning of a word that is given at
any particular place is intended only to apply to the way the word
is used at that point in the text; it does not represent a complete
definition of the word in the language of the time. Thus some
words are defined differently at different points, while many
words are only defined in certain places, since in other places
they are used in ways that remain familiar today.

Repetitions: this book has been designed so it can be used as a reference. For this reason many entries refer the reader to other pages where more complete information about a topic exists. This, however, is not practical for definitions of words, so definitions of the same word are repeated at each appropriate point, except in cases when such definitions are extremely close together.

Acknowledgments

I would first like to thank my mother and my sister and brother-in-law, Mara and Steven Elliott, whose many kind offices have proved invaluable in the preparation of the manuscript and the completion of this project.

I would also like to thank the citizens of the Republic of Pemberley, who formed one of the inspirations for my decision to embark on the project in the first place, and whose questions and discussions concerning Jane Austen and *Pride and Prejudice* have stimulated my thinking and helped direct me to issues and points in the novel that deserve explanation or commentary.

Finally, I would like to thank the staff of the Bethlehem Public Library and the New York State Library, who have helped me procure many of the materials essential for my research.

Introduction

Pride and Prejudice has always held a special place among Jane Austen's novels. She herself called it "my own darling child," an endearment that goes beyond what she said about any of her other works. It is the work that attained the greatest popularity in her own day, that became known as the quintessential Jane Austen novel as her reputation grew, and that is still her most widely-read book.

Its roots lie in the writings of Jane Austen's youth. She was born on December 16, 1775 in the English county of Hampshire, just west of London. Her father, George Austen, was a clergyman, and her mother, Cassandra Leigh Austen, came from a family of landed gentry and clergy. Jane was the seventh of eight children, six of whom were boys. The family was one that valued education highly and loved books, and that always encouraged Jane Austen's own literary efforts, which commenced at thirteen with short, highly comical sketches. As she matured she wrote longer fictional pieces, including unfinished fragments of novels, that reveal her interest in human character. In 1795, at the age of 19, she wrote her first complete novel, *Elinor and Marianne* (the later *Sense and Sensibility*). This was followed in 1796–97 by *First Impressions* (the first version of *Pride and Prejudice*): it pleased her and her family enough that they sent it to a publisher; he, however, rejected it. No copy of *First Impressions* exists, so it is impossible to know its exact character, but the generally light-hearted spirit of *Pride and Prejudice* suggests that *First Impressions* bore strong traces of the playfulness and high comedy of her early writings. Such elements are certainly prominent in her next writing, *Susan* (the later *Northanger Abbey*), composed in 1798–99.

It would be a number of years, however, before these initial efforts bore fruit in actual published works, including *Pride and Prejudice*. In 1800 Jane Austen experienced a major disruption in her life when her father retired from his clerical position and moved to the city of Bath. This introduced a less settled period in Jane Austen's life, one that included her father's death in 1805 and further changes of abode and that saw her write less. It was also a period when she turned down her one known offer of marriage; there are hints of other possible lovers in her earlier life, as well as evidence in her letters of interest in men, but nothing that ever led to any serious entanglements. Eventually, in 1809 she, her mother, and her sister moved into a house, owned by her brother Edward, in the small Hampshire town of Chawton. The quiet of her new circumstances allowed Jane Austen to return to her writing with renewed vigor. Her first effort was *Sense and Sensibility*, crafted from the earlier *Elinor and Marianne*; it was finished in 1810 and published in the latter part of 1811. She then turned to *First Impressions*, and during 1811–1812 transformed it into *Pride and Prejudice*.

The novel appeared in early 1813 and soon attracted a wide audience, becoming one of the literary sensations of the year. Jane Austen was gratified by this reception, as she was also by the money she earned from the novel, which gave her far more personal wealth than she had ever known. The book earned her the notice of some of the leading literary figures of the day, but she showed little interest in this reward, shying away from publicity and remaining aloof from any literary circles. Instead she devoted her energies to further writings, and in 1814 and 1815 she published *Mansfield Park* and *Emma*, both of which attained a degree of success but not that of *Pride and Prejudice*. Work on another novel, *Persuasion*, began, but unfortunately in 1816 she became increasingly ill. Although able to finish *Persuasion* later that year, and even to begin work on a new novel, *Sanditon*, her worsening physical condition forced her to abandon all her efforts during the spring of 1817. Some researchers have diagnosed her ailment as what is now called Addison's Disease, though this is not certain. On July 18, 1817, Jane Austen died. Shortly afterwards *Persuasion* was published, accompanied by an unpublished earlier novel, *Northanger Abbey*. Her reputation grew slowly after her death, and during the second half of the nineteenth century she attained, both among critics and the general public, the status of one of the great English novelists, a status she has maintained ever since.

Pride and Prejudice, like the rest of Jane Austen's writings, has its roots in the novels of the eighteenth century, a time when the novel first emerged as a major literary genre. One of the distinguishing features of this new genre, pointed out by many commentators of the time, was its relative realism: in contrast to the exotic and often fantastical romances of earlier periods, its stories were generally set in the current world, with characters such as one might encounter in daily life and incidents that might happen to ordinary people. Over the course of the century a continuous stream of such stories poured forth from the presses, proving an ideal literary stimulus for Jane Austen. She, like the rest of her family, was an avid reader of novels; throughout her letters she refers frequently to incidents and characters from novels, with the evident expectation that her correspondent will readily catch the reference. These novels influenced her in different ways, providing both positive examples to emulate and negative examples to avoid; in fact, much of her earlier writing involves satires of the various absurdities she perceived in many novels.

The novelists of the eighteenth century who exercised the greatest influence on Jane Austen were Samuel Richardson and Fanny Burney. Richardson, who wrote in the 1740's and 1750's, was the century's most influential novelist in general, the man whose efforts did more than anyone's to establish the novel as a genre deserving serious aesthetic and moral evaluation. His three novels—*Pamela, Clarissa,* and *Sir Charles Grandison* (the last of which was Jane Austen's particular favorite)—are distinguished by a deep insight into the intricacies of human psychology, vividness and realism in the presentation of scenes and dialogue, and an engagement throughout with vital issues of morality. Such qualities are undoubtedly what attracted Jane Austen, whose works display them as well. Fanny Burney wrote in the later decades of the century, producing three novels—*Evelina, Cecilia,* and *Camilla*—that provide the closest model for Jane Austen's efforts: they are all generally humorous novels, centering around the romantic tribulations and choices of a young heroine and offering in addition a series of supporting figures who provide both comic relief and a picture of various social and personality types. Jane Austen alludes to Burney's novels often in her letters and draws on elements of them in her own works; in fact, the title of *Pride and Prejudice* probably derives from a critical passage in *Cecilia,* whose hero's relationship to the heroine has some affinities with Darcy's relationship to Elizabeth.

At the same time, Jane Austen departs from these two novelists in crucial ways. Her satirical sketches ridicule the very features that most frequently mar their novels: strong doses of sentimentality and melodrama, overly perfect heroes and heroines, preachiness and sententiousness in the exposition of moral points, the use of improbable coincidences and contrivances to advance the plot (a feature especially marked in Fanny Burney), and extreme prolixity (a particular problem for Richardson, whose second and third novels are both over 2000 pages long). Jane Austen attempts to avoid each of these flaws in her own work. Her stories are carefully constructed and reasonably compact. They also maintain a restrained tone throughout, avoiding ardent appeals to the reader's emotions and allowing the moral themes and messages to emerge naturally from the story. Finally, her stories always strive to be true to life: her protagonists, while virtuous, are not superhumanly so, and the actions of the characters fall within the range of normal probability. An ideal of verisimilitude was already an important aspect of the new novel genre, but, as in the cases of Richardson and Burney, many authors' interest in providing drama and excitement or in espousing certain ideals made them, amidst their ostensible stories of real life, introduce people and incidents that would rarely if ever be found in reality. In contrast, Jane Austen shows, both in her novels and in the comments on novel writing in her letters, a consistent commitment to creating stories that, down to the smallest details, correspond to life as it actually occurs.

The basic situation Jane Austen uses for each of her works allows her to fulfill that demand for realism, while also crafting a plot that gives shape to the novel and keeps the reader's attention. Essentially each of her novels centers around a group of unmarried young men and women, gathered in the same place, who will experience various attractions, rivalries, and misunderstandings before at some point being matched with a suitable partner. The situation is one that, while not found everywhere, is common enough, and it provides many opportunities for plot developments. She further focuses the action by centering attention on one of the young women (except in *Sense and Sensibility*, which has two heroines), and presenting the romantic dilemmas or choices facing this woman. In each case, though a man exists who is ideally suited to her, some barrier impedes the joining of these two until the end of the story. Some have argued that the ubiquity of such a barrier in Jane Austen's plots suggests a belief in the inherent difficulty of establishing a solid love or intimate relationship between two people. But there is no clear hint of that in her novels: she presents a number of couples in supporting roles whose love and marriage seem to have been accomplished, sometimes before the novel commences, without any hitches. The more obvious reason why Jane Austen always entangles her main characters in difficulties is the same one that has spurred countless writers of romantic stories not to show the course of true love running smooth—namely, that two lovers who quickly perceive their compatibility and then marry happily provide a dull basis for any but the briefest tale.

Jane Austen also follows a consistent pattern in the choice of difficulties for her principal lovers. While family quarrels, differences in social background, forces of circumstance, or the

machinations of other characters sometimes play a role in imped-
ing her lovers, neither these nor any other external factors determine the story as they do in so many romantic tales. Jane Austen
always shows her characters operating with relative freedom: they
are subject to certain pressures and restraints, but they are able to
make crucial decisions, especially decisions about love and marriage, on their own. This emphasis on freedom stems in part from
her realism, for much of the evidence from her own life and letters and the lives of those around her indicates that people of the
class she wrote about usually enjoyed a fair degree of liberty in
making their marital choices. The emphasis also reflects her
strong interest in moral questions. Jane Austen is a writer who
consistently judges her characters by a firm set of ethical standards; she is particularly concerned to judge her principal characters, and to explore both the merits or flaws of the actions they
take and the motivations behind those actions. To do this it is
vital to allow her principals freedom of choice, and thereby to
make them ultimately responsible for whatever good or bad they
experience. Thus it is always the mistaken choices of either the
hero or heroine that create the difficulties they suffer, and these
mistakes in turn that shape the main outline of the plot.

It is in this last aspect that *Pride and Prejudice* stands out from
Jane Austen's other novels. In the central romantic plots in her
other novels, the error that prevents the consummation of the
principals' love—whether it be a commitment to an unworthy
lover, an indulgence in a foolish fantasy, or an unwarranted hostility or resentment toward the other—comes primarily from one
of the principals. In three cases—*Northanger Abbey*, the Marianne plot of *Sense and Sensibility*, and *Emma*—it comes from the
heroine. In three others—the Elinor plot of *Sense and Sensibility*,
Mansfield Park, and *Persuasion*—it comes from the hero (in the
last case the heroine also made a crucial error in earlier refusing
the hero, but that error took place long before the action of the
novel and no longer forms a barrier on her side). But in *Pride and
Prejudice* both hero and heroine are in the wrong on important
matters, and both bear a significant responsibility for the estrange-

ment that lasts for most of the novel. Furthermore, their mutual errors and mutual misunderstandings create an antagonism between the two principals exceeding that of any other novel. Other Jane Austen romantic pairs tend to like each other throughout the story, however much something keeps them apart romantically; at worst, one of the two stands aloof from the other. In contrast, *Pride and Prejudice*'s hero is both aloof at times toward the heroine and frequently uncomprehending of her, while its heroine develops a positive loathing for the hero, and informs him fully of this feeling.

These two distinct features of *Pride and Prejudice* offer a number of advantages. First, the hostility between the two protagonists allows the novel to present a running battle of wits and intellects between the two. This battle lets them both display vividly their distinctive characters; it also provides a particular thrill for the reader through the presentation of two combatants who are actually made for each other and who will both end up having to eat many of their words. This is a long established formula, perhaps seen most memorably in the sparring of Beatrice and Benedick in Shakespeare's *Much Ado about Nothing*. It is even possible that Shakespeare's play influenced *Pride and Prejudice*, for Jane Austen was familiar with Shakespeare, though there is no evidence indicating she drew on that source. Second, the mutuality of error gives the story a neat symmetry and equality, for both the hero and heroine are forced to reform and learn lessons, and neither enjoys a clear advantage over the other. Third, the sharp estrangement of the protagonists allows for a highly dramatic reversal of fortune, in which for a long while all looks hopeless and then in the end all turns out right.

Finally, the many plot developments necessarily involved in such a sharp reversal of fortune mean that much, both good and bad, occurs between the hero and heroine, which allows the novel to focus continual attention on their relationship. This is another unique characteristic of *Pride and Prejudice*. In no other Jane Austen novel does the romance between the hero and heroine occupy such center stage (except for the slight *Northanger*

Abbey): in *Sense and Sensibility* and *Persuasion* the pairs of lovers have only limited contact with each other over the course of the novel; in *Mansfield Park* and *Emma* they have extensive contact, but until the end it is only in the capacity of friends. In contrast, Elizabeth and Darcy have frequent contacts, and the issue of love between them is almost always on at least one of their minds. Such focusing of attention has obvious advantages in a novel whose main subject is this very love.

Along with offering such advantages, these distinctive features of *Pride and Prejudice* also pose a critical challenge, one that determines the nature of the story and that leads to difficulties of its own. The challenge is how to reconcile two conflicting imperatives, that of showing a strong enough compatibility between the hero and heroine to make their eventual union both believable and satisfying, and that of also making plausible a severe rupture between two such compatible souls. In other words, how can two who are destined to love and comprehend each other so deeply, stumble instead into hating or misunderstanding so strongly? For writers of a romantic stamp, who dwell on extreme passions, often of a type that can easily change into other extreme passions, and who emphasize the mysteriousness or unpredictability or perversity of the human heart, such reversal of sentiment would not present a serious problem, or even perhaps a need for much explanation. But it does for Jane Austen, who has a strong commitment to clear and rational explanations and whose novels depict people acting in ways that, while often irrational, are still comprehensible.

One way she reconciles these conflicting imperatives is through the differing social positions she provides for the hero and heroine. In all her novels Jane Austen concentrates almost exclusively on the class to which she and her family belonged, and which she knew best, the class generally known as the gentry. The gentry meant the broad mass of those who were considered genteel, which in effect meant moderately wealthy landowners along with the clergy and most military officers. Above it stood the aristocracy or nobility (though the line between it and the gentry was not a firm one), the class of those with privileged titles, tremendous wealth in land, and great political power. Below the gentry stood a generally urban middle class, consisting of merchants and manufacturers as well as the members of most professions. *Pride and Prejudice* is distinctive for focusing more on these other two classes than any other Jane Austen novel. Darcy, the grandson of an earl and the possessor of wealth comparable to many titled lords, is almost part of the aristocracy; his relatives Lady Catherine and Colonel Fitzwilliam, both the children of earls, are certainly part of it. Elizabeth, in contrast, has a mother who, as the daughter of an attorney, definitely comes from the middle class, and a pair of aunts and uncles who remain in that class; her initial love interest, Wickham, is also someone of middle-class origin. Moreover, Elizabeth's lack of almost any inheritance creates the prospect that she might have to marry someone of that level, and thereby lose her own membership in the gentry (since a woman's position derived from that of her husband).

The resulting social gulf between Darcy and Elizabeth plays a critical role in keeping them apart, despite the compatibility of their personalities. Initially it keeps Darcy from even considering marriage to Elizabeth, regardless of her attractions; in fact, his fear of becoming attracted to her motivates him at times to be even more aloof than usual in his conduct toward her. Moreover, Darcy's social superiority to Elizabeth, as well as to those around her, encourages his early arrogant behavior, as well as his actions to separate Bingley and Jane. Even when he does decide to pursue Elizabeth, his superior position makes him assume she would welcome any offer of marriage from him, and thus reduces any incentive for him to behave more agreeably or to propose more courteously. On Elizabeth's side, awareness of his high position makes her unwilling to imagine he could be interested in her, which in turn makes her misinterpret his behavior, and it makes Wickham's slanders against Darcy more believable, since a powerful man could more easily have caused the great harm that Wickham alleges.

Yet even as it thereby alienates Elizabeth and Darcy, the gulf between them does not rule out ultimate union. Prevailing norms were not so rigid as to keep people from disregarding social differences at times; nor are Elizabeth and Darcy so far apart socially, for they ultimately belong to the same class, even if they stand on opposite edges of it. In addition, because a degree of social pride was perfectly acceptable in this society, outward expressions of it like Darcy's do not necessarily indicate a bad character. What this means for the story is that it is possible for Darcy to behave in ways that severely offend and alienate Elizabeth, even while being a fundamentally decent man who will prove worthy of her in the end.

Jane Austen also accomplishes her dual imperatives of estranging and reconciling the protagonists through the mechanics of the plot, which assume a particular prominence in this novel. Several plot devices further the estrangement of the two. The first, and most important, is Darcy and Elizabeth's being such total strangers to each other. This plays an essential role in her misassessment of him, for when she perceives unpleasant behavior in him, and hears a bad report of him, she has no good means of receiving a truer picture of his character. It is highly unlikely that an intelligent person like Elizabeth would have judged so wrongly, had Darcy lived long in her neighborhood, or shared important acquaintances or relations with her; instead, the first contact she has with him is when she hears him utter insulting words about herself. The second device is the love affair between Darcy's best friend and Elizabeth's sister, which gives Elizabeth greater reason to dislike Darcy when she learns of his role in separating the two lovers. The third is the introduction of a character, Wickham, who has a coincidental relationship with, and grudge against, the hero; when he also proves attractive to the heroine, she is led to believe terrible slanders about the hero. Here again Elizabeth's lack of acquaintance or connection with Darcy plays a vital role, for it means she has no alternative source of knowledge for learning the real truth of Wickham's charges.

All this provides a good basis for antagonism between the principals; the difficulty is that such antagonism, along with the lack of personal connections between the two, gives them little reason to interact with one another, and it is such interaction that moves the plot along and provides much of the interest of the novel. It thus become essential for the author, even while keeping Elizabeth and Darcy estranged from each other, to arrange reasons for their continued meeting. One means for this is provided by the situation of Jane and Bingley, for the former's illness while visiting the latter's residence prompts Elizabeth, against her wishes, to spend many days in the same house with Darcy; the resulting several days of exchanges and disputes between the two are one of the highlights of the novel. Another means, one that leads to even more significant meetings between them, is the introduction of characters, Mr. Collins along with Mr. and Mrs. Gardiner, who have coincidental links to both hero and heroine. Mr. Collins, through his ties to Darcy's aunt along with Elizabeth's visit to him after his marriage to her best friend, provides a basis for a meeting between Elizabeth and Darcy after his departure from Netherfield seemed to ensure they would never see each other again. Mr. and Mrs. Gardiner, thanks to her former residence near Darcy's home, give Elizabeth occasion to encounter Darcy at a time when she, while no longer disliking him, still prefers to avoid him, and when he, having been badly burned in his proposal, is not likely to seek her out.

Coincidences like this, in fact, loom large in the whole development of the plot. Elizabeth's and Darcy's time together at the Collinses and Lady Catherine's occurs not only because of their mutual connection to one of those households, but also because Darcy's two to three week visit there happens to fall in the middle of Elizabeth's six week visit. Elizabeth's vehemence in rejecting Darcy, which in turn helps spur his crucial letter to her and his ultimate reformation, is exacerbated because it was that very day that she learned of his role in separating Bingley and Jane. Elizabeth's encounter with Darcy at Pemberley is especially dependent on chance: they only meet because he was scheduled to arrive the following day, which makes her think it safe to visit, but he in fact advances his plans and arrives during her visit. Finally, in addition to the coincidence of Wickham's running off with

Elizabeth's sister, the essential development of Darcy's learning of the affair, without which Lydia would probably have been ruined and Elizabeth in consequence too tainted socially to marry him, happens only because he arrives at Elizabeth's room at the moment when she, having just finished reading about Wickham and Lydia, is in too agitated a state to maintain normal discretion about a terrible family secret.

These various coincidences serve the novel in many ways: by repeatedly connecting the various characters, by ensuring that important characters like Wickham can continue to play a major role, and by allowing all the main story lines to be neatly wrapped up. Yet the repeated use of coincidence conflicts with one of Jane Austen's most cherished literary values, fidelity to real life, a life in which coincidence normally plays a far smaller role than it does in this novel. This feature of the work does not destroy the general realism of its presentation of people and society, but it does give it some affinity to the earlier novels that Jane Austen had ridiculed for their reliance on unexpected encounters and improbable connections.

This affinity to earlier novels appears in various aspects of *Pride and Prejudice*, which is the last completed, and the best, of Jane Austen's early novels, the ones that she started in the 1790's and that bear the strongest traces of the fiction she had absorbed in her youth. In contrast, her later novels—*Mansfield Park, Emma,* and *Persuasion*—possess a slightly different manner, one that includes a lesser reliance on coincidence or highly dramatic events in the plot, and a greater restraint and realism in the characterization and language. The early novels present characters who are almost larger than life, and who at times resemble the "types"—i.e., deliberately exaggerated representatives of specific emotions or propensities—who dominate much of eighteenth-century literature. Lady Catherine, Mrs. Bennet, and Mr. Collins (especially the last) are the strongest examples of this in *Pride and Prejudice*, characters who are memorable in part because they border on caricature.

Similarly, the language and dialogue of the early novels tends

to be more pointed and emphatic. *Pride and Prejudice* in particular is distinguished by the lapidary polish of its prose. Jane Austen
spoke in a letter of having "lopt & cropt" the novel, and it does
seem to be the most carefully edited and reworked of her novels.
She also wrote of the "playfulness and Epigrammatism of its general stile [sic]," a feature seen in its many clever epigrams and
specimens of wit that come from both the narrators and the characters, especially the main character of Elizabeth. This gives the
novel tremendous stylistic force, but at the cost of a little artificial-
ity, for it is hard to imagine that the type of ordinary people who
populate the novel would ever be so quick with so many ingenious and pithily phrased rejoinders to one another. This may be a
reason why Jane Austen, just before mentioning this "Epigrammatism," wonders if the novel is "too light & bright & sparkling."

   None of this means, however, that the novel should be judged
negatively. Any work of literature has to choose between different
imperatives, not all of which can be satisfied. *Pride and Prejudice*
may lack some of the subtlety and profundity of her later novels,
but it has a brilliancy that in many respects surpasses those works.
Its dialogue is not as consistently close to that of real life as the
dialogue of her later novels, but that also means it avoids the tendency of these later novels to present speeches and exchanges
that are sometimes as long-winded, or even occasionally as tedious, as those found in real life. Mr. Collins is a more exaggerated
character than any of those in the later novels; but those exaggerated features make him probably the funniest character in all
Jane Austen's novels.

   As for *Pride and Prejudice*'s plot, while it may occasionally border on the improbable in its coincidences, it achieves, in part
through those coincidences, a distinctive harmony and symmetry
in its structure. Both the early and later parts of the novel contain
important and dramatic developments, ensuring that reader
interest never flags and that the overall story is well-balanced;
such balance is emphasized by having both the critical marriage proposal, and the heroine's realization of her errors, occur at
the exact center point of the novel. The story also proceeds by a

careful alternation of sections focusing on Elizabeth and Darcy's relationship with intervals when they are not together, which means that the main plot is never too long absent, but that it also never absorbs so much attention that other elements in the story are forgotten. Moreover, the intervals prepare the ground for the next development in the main plot. The final lengthy one, the affair of Wickham and Lydia, has a particularly resonant relationship to the main plot, for it both appears, while it is happening, to rule out a happy resolution of Darcy and Elizabeth's romance, while in fact it gives Darcy his best opportunity to prove his love for her and overcome any doubts she may still harbor. The last section of the book exhibits a similar aptness, for in it the major romantic tangles are resolved in ascending order of both their importance for the plot and the worth of the participants—i.e., Lydia and Wickham, then Jane and Bingley, and finally Elizabeth and Darcy.

Pride and Prejudice also achieves a particular deftness and sparkle in the person of its heroine, Elizabeth Bennet. Jane Austen called her, "as delightful a creature as ever appeared in print," and legions of readers have felt similarly. Her psychology is not explored with the depth and intensity of the heroines of the next two novels, *Mansfield Park* and *Emma*, but the charm and humor of her character make her equally memorable, and an ideal embodiment of the general wit and buoyancy of the novel. Her character in fact represents a departure from the usual pattern of novels—seen consistently in such predecessors as Samuel Richardson and Fanny Burney and more often than not in Jane Austen—whereby the romantic principals are presented mostly in a serious mode, and supporting figures are relied upon for any comedy that exists. In fact, Elizabeth's strongest literary affinity is probably with a character who is a mostly humorous supporting figure: Charlotte Grandison, the sister of the hero in Richardson's *Sir Charles Grandison*, and in many ways the most interesting and vital figure in that novel. The interest she held for Jane Austen is signaled by a short dramatic adaptation she did of Richardson's novel, in which she gives Charlotte more than twice the lines of any other character. Charlotte is a character who combines a brilliant wit, high intelligence, and fundamental decency with a refusal to take anything seriously, which in turn causes her, even with her many charms, to antagonize those around her and nearly to destroy her marriage before she finally accepts the need to check some of her constant teasing and ridicule of others.

Elizabeth's exhibition of similar qualities, though in a less extreme form, allows Jane Austen to develop a similar lesson, and, because of Elizabeth's central role, to give it even greater prominence. More generally, the presence of a humorous heroine means that the book can unite in one character two of the author's most cherished purposes: amusing the reader and imparting serious moral points. The danger is that attempting such a dual purpose may cause the comedy to undermine or distract from the moral seriousness; Jane Austen's worries about the novel's being too "light & bright & sparkling" may stem partly from that concern. Several elements of the story, however, keep this danger from being realized, at least to any significant degree. One is that Elizabeth is never the almost purely comic figure that some of the secondary characters are; her actions and difficulties are treated seriously, and Elizabeth herself usually knows (unlike her father) what matters are not fit subjects for laughter. Another element helping to maintain an equilibrium between humor and seriousness is the mutual capacity for error of the hero and heroine and their mutual responsibility for the difficulties they suffer: were the heroine a person who does not make any significant errors, she would serve almost inevitably as the exemplar of the novel's moral principles or ideals; were the heroine someone whose flaws or mistakes formed the main determinant of the plot, she would stand as the representative of what the novel warns against; in either case, too much humor in her characterization would threaten to dilute the seriousness of the positive or negative example she is designed to present. Finally, the balance of the novel is greatly assisted by the person of the hero, whose gravity forms an ideal contrast to the playfulness of the heroine.

This contrast and juxtaposition of hero and heroine appears in other ways, and forms another aspect of the novel's symmetry. Their actions exhibit strong parallels, for they both commit serious errors in the first half of the story, and then learn and reform in the second half. In their personalities they display both similarities and differences. The similarities serve the valuable purpose of signaling the ultimate compatibility of their personalities and thus the aptness of their marriage. The differences, such as Darcy's much greater seriousness, suggest at the same time that their marriage will not simply be one in which two like-minded souls reinforce their shared tendencies, as Bingley and Jane's marriage will probably do, but will be a union in which the partners can complement and impart unique benefits to each other. It is this exact sort of marriage that Jane Austen consistently upholds as her ideal; it is also one that receives particular emphasis in *Pride and Prejudice* through being foreshadowed in the parallel reformations Darcy and Elizabeth undergo before their marriage in response to each other.

A further dialectic of similarity and difference appears in the arguments between hero and heroine that play such a prominent role in the novel. Crucial shared traits—keen intelligence, outspokenness, independence of judgment, and forcefulness of expression—make them both inclined to argue, and able to do so with eloquence, even as differences in other areas ensure that they frequently argue in favor of opposing positions. The resulting disputes serve in turn both to sharpen their immediate antagonism, and to lay a foundation of respect for the other's abilities that later comes to the fore. The disputes serve the additional purpose of allowing the author to emphasize a number of issues crucial to the novel by having them be matters of direct debate between the two protagonists. These issues include the relative value of seriousness and humor, the right degree of amenability toward others, the best way to avoid mistaken or prejudicial judgments, and the appropriateness of pride.

These last two issues, of course, relate directly to the novel's central theme of pride and prejudice. This theme appears most obviously in the contrast between Darcy's pride—in his social position, his intelligence, his scrupulousness of behavior—and Elizabeth's prejudice against him, a contrast that is underlined by the way his proud behavior feeds much of her prejudice. But the theme is not confined to this contrast, in part because pride is not confined to Darcy nor prejudice to Elizabeth. Darcy's social pride is itself fed by his prejudice against people of her rank, while Elizabeth's pride in her judgment and wit spurs her dislike of Darcy, both through her offense at his scorn of her and his general air of superiority, and through her enjoyment of the opportunity to exercise her cleverness and wit by abusing such a tempting target as Darcy. In their respective reformations they also must each shed both pride and prejudice. He must acknowledge, and alter, his improper arrogance, while learning, through his experience with people like Elizabeth and the Gardiners, that those of a lower social rank can be superior in their sense and behavior. She must admit the error of her judgments, and must absorb the need to be less hasty and confident, and to be a little less eager to seize opportunities for witty repartee.

Nor do pride and prejudice pertain solely to the two central characters; a host of supporting figures display their own forms of one or the other. In fact, pride and prejudice are such ubiquitous features of human personality and behavior that a novel centering around them will have ample opportunity to highlight and reinforce its main theme. At the same time, such a novel may not break significant intellectual ground, for it will to a great extent be restating simple and familiar truths. This is probably why *Pride and Prejudice* does not involve as much examination of complex social or philosophical issues as many other novels, including *Sense and Sensibility* and *Mansfield Park*, and why, unlike these last two, it has not stirred as much disagreement or commentary regarding its ultimate meaning. But a familiar truth may be just as important as a novel or controversial one, and to make the former a vital part of a lengthy story, and keep it from seeming tiresome in its familiarity, constitutes a significant achievement in itself. This choice of theme also constitutes one more factor allowing the novel, and its heroine, to be infused with a high degree of comedy without losing a claim to seriousness, for a simple and venerable message is one that neither needs the sort of lengthy exposition that could overwhelm the comic aspects of the story, nor stands in danger of being forgotten or misunderstood if not subject to such exposition. In this respect pride and prejudice forms the perfect theme for a novel that, among great works of literature, is almost unsurpassed for combining the imperatives of entertainment and of art.

The Annotated

PRIDE

AND

PREJUDICE

VOLUME ONE

Chapter One

*I*t is a truth universally acknowledged, that a single man in possession of a good fortune, must be in want of a wife.[1]

However little known the feelings or views of such a man may be on his first entering a neighbourhood, this truth is so well fixed in the minds of the surrounding families, that he is considered as the rightful property of some one or other of their daughters.

"My dear Mr. Bennet," said his lady[2] to him one day, "have you heard that Netherfield Park is let at last?"[3]

Mr. Bennet replied that he had not.[4]

"But it is," returned she; "for Mrs. Long has just been here, and she told me all about it."

Mr. Bennet made no answer.

"Do not you want to know who has taken it?" cried his wife impatiently.

"*You* want to tell me, and I have no objection to hearing it."

This was invitation enough.

"Why, my dear, you must know, Mrs. Long says that Netherfield is taken by a young man of large fortune from the north of England; that he came down on Monday in a chaise and four[5] to see the place, and was so much delighted with it, that he agreed with Mr. Morris immediately; that he is to take possession before Michaelmas,[6] and some of his servants are to be in the house by the end of next week."[7]

"What is his name?"

"Bingley."

"Is he married or single?"

1. The famous opening line, with wonderful economy, accomplishes two main purposes. It indicates the novel's central subject of marriage, along with the financial considerations usually involved in it. It also sets the tone of irony that will pervade the book, for in fact, as we immediately see, it is the single women in this society who are truly in want, or need, of a man of large fortune. The term "acknowledged" adds to this effect, for it suggests the possibility that this supposed truth about single men may be more valid in people's beliefs than in reality.

2. *his lady*: his wife.

3. Netherfield Park is the name for a home in the Bennets' neighborhood. It was common for houses, if grand enough, to be given a name, often with words such as park in them to indicate their attractive and rustic character.

It was not unusual for large houses to be rented out, for it cost a substantial amount of money to staff and maintain a grand home, and many landowners might find themselves unable to afford it. In Jane Austen's *Persuasion* the heroine's family, thanks to the father's extravagant spending habits, is forced to let their house and move into apartments in the resort city of Bath.

4. Until its concluding paragraph, the entire rest of the chapter consists of dialogue between Mr. and Mrs. Bennet. Dialogue occupies much of Jane Austen's novels, and presentation of character through dialogue is one of her fortes as a novelist. In this case, Mrs. Bennet's excitable exclamations and exaggerated phrasing reveal her flightiness and impetuousness, while Mr. Bennet's terseness and irony reveal his cool detachment.

5. *chaise and four*: chaise is a type of carriage; it seated three people, all facing forward, and was enclosed (see illustration on p. 397). Four refers to the number of horses pulling it. A chaise was a popular vehicle for long-distance travel, so it would be a logical one for someone coming from far away to use (in this case, as we find out later, it happens to be the carriage Mr. Bingley owns and uses regularly).

6. *Michaelmas*: September 29. It was one of the four days used to divide the year into quarters; the other three were Christmas, Lady Day (March 25), and Midsummer Day (June 24). The action of the novel, which is carefully worked out chronologically, will terminate around Michaelmas of the following year; most of Jane Austen's novels transpire over an approximate period of one year.

7. It was common for servants to precede their masters in order to prepare a house for the latter's arrival.

"Oh! single, my dear, to be sure! A single man of large fortune; four or five thousand a year.[8] What a fine thing for our girls!"

"How so? how can it affect them?"

"My dear Mr. Bennet," replied his wife, "how can you be so tiresome! You must know that I am thinking of his marrying one of them."

"Is that his design in settling here?"

"Design! nonsense, how can you talk so! But it is very likely that he *may* fall in love with one of them, and therefore you must visit him as soon as he comes."

"I see no occasion for that. You and the girls may go, or you may send them by themselves, which perhaps will be still better, for as you are as handsome as any of them, Mr. Bingley might like you the best of the party."

"My dear, you flatter me. I certainly *have* had my share of beauty, but I do not pretend to be any thing extraordinary now. When a woman has five grown up daughters, she ought to give over thinking of her own beauty."

"In such cases, a woman has not often much beauty to think of."

"But, my dear, you must indeed go and see Mr. Bingley when he comes into the neighbourhood."

"It is more than I engage for, I assure you."

"But consider your daughters. Only think what an establishment[9] it would be for one of them. Sir William and Lady Lucas[10] are determined to go, merely on that account, for in general, you know, they visit no new comers. Indeed you must go, for it will be impossible for *us* to visit him if you do not."[11]

"You are over scrupulous, surely. I dare say Mr. Bingley will be very glad to see you; and I will send a few lines by you to assure him of my hearty consent to his marrying which ever he chuses of the girls; though I must throw in a good word for my little Lizzy."

"I desire you will do no such thing. Lizzy is not a bit better than the others; and I am sure she is not half so handsome as Jane, nor half so good humoured as Lydia. But you are always giving *her* the preference."

8. *four or five thousand a year*: his annual income in pounds. This is the way Jane Austen usually describes men's wealth; the income would normally come from the agricultural profits on land or from other property and investments (in Bingley's case it turns out to be the latter). It is not easy to translate incomes of the time into today's money. By some calculations, the effects of inflation mean that a pound in Jane Austen's time has the same value as almost forty pounds today; if so, Bingley's income would be the equivalent of 150,000 to 200,000 a year in today's pounds (or around $250,000–$300,000 in current U.S. money). Altered economic condition, however, make estimates like this tricky: for example, goods tended to be much dearer at that time, in relative terms, while labor tended to be much cheaper. In addition, average incomes in this period, even when adjusted for inflation, were much lower than today, so Bingley's income represents a far sharper deviation from the prevailing norm than its current equivalent would be.

Another way to look at the issue is to note that in *Sense and Sensibility* a mother is able to support herself and three daughters in reasonable comfort in a nice home she has rented, and with a staff of three servants, on five hundred a year. Jane Austen herself lived most of her life on less than that. The Bennets themselves have an income of 2,000 a year (to which should be added a house and its contents). Hence Bingley, however one calculates it, is a truly rich man, which is why he is such a desirable matrimonial prospect.

Mrs. Bennet's statement about Bingley's income, uttered before he has even arrived, reveals the speed with which vital information about people could circulate. The principal means for this is local gossip, which plays a central role in this society. The gossip would be greatly assisted by the many servants in employment, for the servants in one household could tell its secrets to servants in other households, who could in turn tell their employers. This process is mentioned later in this novel, as it is in other Jane Austen novels, most notably in *Emma*.

9. *establishment*: marriage.

10. *Sir William and Lady Lucas*: William Lucas, as is shortly revealed, was knighted. This means that he is now called Sir William Lucas, or just Sir William, and his wife is Lady Lucas.

11. In this society there are strict rules for visiting people one does not know. In the case being discussed here, since Mr. Bingley is a man, Mr. Bennet should make the acquaintance first (Mrs. Bennet worries about both Sir William and Lady Lucas visiting, but in fact only Sir William goes—see p. 14). Mr. Bennet certainly knows this, and is simply pretending not to know in order to tease his wife. His teasing goes still further in his earlier suggestion that the daughters go without even their mother, for young unmarried women would never visit an unmarried and unrelated young man on their own, even in cases, unlike the present one, where they were already acquainted with him.

"They have none of them much to recommend them," replied he; "they are all silly and ignorant like other girls; but Lizzy has something more of quickness than her sisters."[12]

"Mr. Bennet, how can you abuse your own children in such a way? You take delight in vexing me. You have no compassion on my poor nerves."[13]

"You mistake me, my dear. I have a high respect for your nerves. They are my old friends. I have heard you mention them with consideration these twenty years at least."

"Ah! you do not know what I suffer."

"But I hope you will get over it, and live to see many young men of four thousand a year come into the neighbourhood."

"It will be no use to us, if twenty such should come since you will not visit them."

"Depend upon it, my dear, that when there are twenty, I will visit them all."[14]

Mr. Bennet was so odd a mixture of quick parts,[15] sarcastic humour, reserve, and caprice, that the experience of three and twenty years had been insufficient to make his wife understand his character. *Her* mind[16] was less difficult to develope.[17] She was a woman of mean understanding,[18] little information,[19] and uncertain temper.[20] When she was discontented, she fancied herself nervous.[21] The business of her life was to get her daughters married; its solace was visiting and news.[22]

12. Lizzy's being the first to be mentioned, as well as her being the first to speak in the next chapter, indicates her prominence in the story. This exchange also gives a hint of her affinity with her father, and of the quickness, or mental sharpness, that is one of her defining features.

13. During the century preceding this novel, nerves had become one of the dominant ways of explaining bodily processes (they often replaced earlier theories revolving around "humours"). A whole variety of diseases or ailments were commonly ascribed to nervous disorders or to nervousness; one medical writer of the time, Thomas Trotter, declared that "nervous diseases make up two-thirds of the whole with which civilized society is infested." Nerves also had the advantage for hypochondriacs of being intangible and invisible, which meant that their aggravation or distress could not be easily disputed. This made poor nerves a popular self-diagnosis for those such as Mrs. Bennet who liked to complain about their health.

14. The indifference Mr. Bennet professes throughout this scene toward his daughters' marital prospects is meant humorously, but it also suggests what will become more apparent later, that he, while possessing many good qualities, is irresponsible as a father. Mrs. Bennet's obsessive husband-hunting clearly goes too far, but it has a basis in the dire economic consequences suffered by young women in this society who fail to find husbands. Since, as is revealed later, the Bennet girls' financial situation is particularly desperate, their need for husbands is even more acute.

15. *parts:* qualities or attributes.

16. *mind:* mental and emotional character. The word had a less purely intellectual connotation then than it does now.

17. *develope:* discover, understand.

18. *mean understanding:* inferior intelligence or judgment.

19. *information:* education or knowledge.

20. *uncertain temper:* unsteady or capricious temperament.

21. *nervous:* suffering from nervous disorders.

22. *news:* news or gossip about the neighborhood (not news of national affairs).

Chapter Two

Mr. Bennet was among the earliest of those who waited on[1] Mr. Bingley. He had always intended to visit him, though to the last always assuring his wife that he should not go; and till the evening after the visit was paid, she had no knowledge of it. It was then disclosed in the following manner. Observing his second daughter employed in trimming a hat,[2] he suddenly addressed her with,

"I hope Mr. Bingley will like it Lizzy."

"We are not in a way to know *what* Mr. Bingley likes," said her mother resentfully, "since we are not to visit."

"But you forget, mama," said Elizabeth, "that we shall meet him at the assemblies,[3] and that Mrs. Long has promised to introduce him."

"I do not believe Mrs. Long will do any such thing. She has two neices of her own. She is a selfish, hypocritical woman, and I have no opinion of her."[4]

"No more have I," said Mr. Bennet; "and I am glad to find that you do not depend on her serving you."

Mrs. Bennet deigned not to make any reply; but unable to contain herself, began scolding one of her daughters.

"Don't keep coughing so, Kitty, for heaven's sake! Have a little compassion on my nerves. You tear them to pieces."

"Kitty has no discretion in her coughs," said her father; "she times them ill."

"I do not cough for my own amusement," replied Kitty fretfully.

"When is your next ball to be, Lizzy?"[5]

"To-morrow fortnight."[6]

"Aye, so it is," cried her mother, "and Mrs. Long does not come back till the day before; so, it will be impossible for her to introduce him, for she will not know him herself."

1. *waited on*: called upon.

2. *trimming a hat*: decorating a hat, usually by attaching ribbons or feathers or other items to it. Adding decorations to hats, as well as to other articles of dress, was a common practice at the time. Sometimes the trimmings or decorations could cost more than the hat. Jane Austen refers, with evident pleasure, to trimming a hat on numerous occasions in her letters; in one she wonders about, and asks her sister's opinion on, whether flowers or fruit would look better on a hat, making sure to mention that the flowers would cost less (June 11, 1799).

3. *assemblies*: general social gatherings with dancing and other amusements. They had become popular during the eighteenth century, and by the time of the novel almost every town, except for the very smallest, had assembly rooms built for the specific purpose of accommodating them. Assemblies were generally public, i.e., open to whichever families or individuals could afford to buy tickets or subscriptions.

The public nature of assemblies means that, in contrast to the case with an initial formal visit to a strange man, Mrs. Bennet and her daughters can go without Mr. Bennet (in fact, he does not accompany them to the assembly when it occurs). Thus they will not be impeded by Mr. Bennet's apparent reluctance to make Bingley's acquaintance.

4. *I have no opinion of her*: I have no good opinion of her. Mrs. Bennet fears that Mrs. Long will not introduce them in order to preserve Mr. Bingley for her nieces. This competitive suspicion of Mrs. Bennet, revealed also in her fears about Lady Lucas visiting Mr. Bingley, has its foundation in a reality mentioned by Jane Austen at the beginning of *Mansfield Park*: "there certainly are not so many men of large fortune in the world, as there are pretty women to deserve them."

5. The speaker is probably Mr. Bennet. The question seems too calm to be asked by the agitated Mrs. Bennet; in addition, she would probably know when the next ball would happen since, unlike her husband, she likes balls and will attend this one. Jane Austen omits explicit identification of the speaker at other points in the novel. She herself commented on this in a letter concerning *Pride and Prejudice*: "a 'said he' or a 'said she' would sometimes make the Dialogue more immediately clear—but 'I do not write for such dull Elves'" (January 29, 1813). Her quotation alludes to a concluding passage from Sir Walter Scott's poem "Marmion": "I do not rhyme to that dull elf/Who cannot imagine to himself, . . ."

6. *To-morrow fortnight*: two weeks from tomorrow.

"Then, my dear, you may have the advantage of your friend, and introduce Mr. Bingley to *her*."

"Impossible, Mr. Bennet, impossible, when I am not acquainted with him myself; how can you be so teazing?"[7]

"I honour your circumspection. A fortnight's acquaintance is certainly very little. One cannot know what a man really is by the end of a fortnight. But if *we* do not venture, somebody else will; and after all, Mrs. Long and her neices must stand their chance; and therefore, as she will think it an act of kindness, if you decline the office,[8] I will take it on myself."

The girls stared at their father. Mrs. Bennet said only, "Nonsense, nonsense!"

"What can be the meaning of that emphatic exclamation?" cried he. "Do you consider the forms of introduction, and the stress that is laid on them, as nonsense? I cannot quite agree with you *there*.[9] What say you, Mary? for you are a young lady of deep reflection I know, and read great[10] books, and make extracts."[11]

Mary wished to say something very sensible, but knew not how.[12]

"While Mary is adjusting her ideas,"[13] he continued, "let us return to Mr. Bingley."

"I am sick of Mr. Bingley," cried his wife.

"I am sorry to hear *that*; but why did not you tell me so before? If I had known as much this morning, I certainly would not have called on him. It is very unlucky; but as I have actually paid the visit, we cannot escape the acquaintance now."

The astonishment of the ladies was just what he wished; that of Mrs. Bennet perhaps surpassing the rest; though when the first tumult of joy was over, she began to declare that it was what she had expected all the while.

"How good it was in you, my dear Mr. Bennet! But I knew I should persuade you at last. I was sure you loved your girls too well to neglect such an acquaintance. Well, how pleased I am! and it is such a good joke, too, that you should have gone this morning, and never said a word about it till now."

7. *teazing*: teasing, or annoying, irritating.

8. *office*: duty, service to another.

9. Mr. Bennet's professed scrupulousness here about the forms of introduction stands in humorous contrast to his professed indifference to them in the last chapter, when he suggested that his wife or daughters visit Mr. Bingley on their own.

10. *great*: large, weighty, important. The description suggests nothing of the quality of the books, for "great" had not yet developed the meaning of extremely good; in fact, Mr. Bennet is probably mocking Mary for the pretentiousness of her reading.

11. *make extracts*: copy out passages from books. The *Encyclopaedia Britannica* of the time defines an extract as "something copied or collected from a book or paper." Such copying would be done as an aid to learning. That Mary appears to do it regularly hints at her character, for much of her conversation consists of mechanical repetitions of phrases and passages she has read, ones that she may have memorized through her making of extracts.

12. This, the first glimpse we have of Mary, provides an excellent summary of her character, for throughout the novel she will strive to speak wisely, and generally fail.

With Mary, all five Bennet girls have been mentioned. They are, from oldest to youngest: Jane, Elizabeth, Mary, Catherine/Kitty, and Lydia. At later points in the novel Jane is said to be 22, Elizabeth 20, and Lydia 15; the ages of Mary and Kitty are never stated specifically, but at one point Kitty says she is two years older than Lydia, which would make her 17 and make Mary either 18 or 19.

The names of all five girls are thoroughly ordinary. This is also true of the last names mentioned so far: Bennet, Bingley, Morris, Lucas, Long. Unlike many novelists who try to express their characters' natures through unusual or symbolic names, Jane Austen always selects those names most likely to be found in normal life. This reflects her commitment to strict realism in all social details.

13. *ideas*: thoughts.

"Now, Kitty, you may cough as much as you chuse," said Mr. Bennet; and, as he spoke, he left the room, fatigued with the raptures of his wife.

"What an excellent father you have, girls," said she, when the door was shut. "I do not know how you will ever make him amends for his kindness; or me either, for that matter. At our time of life, it is not so pleasant I can tell you, to be making new acquaintance every day; but for your sakes, we would do any thing. Lydia, my love, though you *are* the youngest, I dare say Mr. Bingley will dance with you at the next ball."

"Oh!" said Lydia stoutly, "I am not afraid; for though I *am* the youngest, I'm the tallest."[14]

The rest of the evening was spent in conjecturing how soon he would return Mr. Bennet's visit, and determining when they should ask him to dinner.[15]

14. This is the first appearance of Lydia, who will later play a crucial role in the novel. The confidence and assertiveness that help determine her later behavior are already evident here.

15. This reveals some of the ritual of social introductions. Mr. Bennet has visited Mr. Bingley (the established inhabitant, rather than the newcomer, making the first overture); Mr. Bingley is expected to return the visit; after that he can be asked to dinner, the initial visits being only brief calls. Jane Austen insisted on getting such matters right: in a letter criticizing a niece's draft of a novel, she focuses on the niece's failure to have her characters adhere to standard social proprieties, particularly as regards rules about visiting (Sept. 9, 1814).

Fashions of the period. See also p. 15, note 3.

[From Iris Brooke, *Western European Costume, Seventeenth to Mid-Nineteenth Century* (New York, 1940), p. 131]

Chapter Three

Not all that Mrs. Bennet, however, with the assistance of her five daughters, could ask on the subject was sufficient to draw from her husband any satisfactory description of Mr. Bingley. They attacked him in various ways; with barefaced questions, ingenious suppositions, and distant surmises; but he eluded the skill of them all; and they were at last obliged to accept the second-hand intelligence of their neighbour Lady Lucas. Her report was highly favourable. Sir William had been delighted with him. He was quite young, wonderfully handsome, extremely agreeable, and to crown the whole, he meant to be at the next assembly with a large party. Nothing could be more delightful! To be fond of dancing was a certain step towards falling in love; and very lively hopes of Mr. Bingley's heart were entertained.

"If I can but see one of my daughters happily settled at Netherfield," said Mrs. Bennet to her husband, "and all the others equally well married, I shall have nothing to wish for."

In a few days Mr. Bingley returned Mr. Bennet's visit, and sat about ten minutes with him in his library.[1] He had entertained hopes of being admitted to a sight of the young ladies, of whose beauty he had heard much; but he saw only the father.[2] The ladies were somewhat more fortunate, for they had the advantage of ascertaining from an upper window, that he wore a blue coat[3] and rode a black horse.

An invitation to dinner was soon afterwards dispatched; and already had Mrs. Bennet planned the courses that were to do credit to her housekeeping, when an answer arrived which deferred it all. Mr. Bingley was obliged to be in town[4] the following day, and consequently unable to accept the honour of their invitation, &c.[5] Mrs. Bennet was quite disconcerted. She could not imagine what business he could have in town so soon after his arrival in Hertfordshire;[6] and she began to fear that he might be

1.   Libraries, which had become a standard feature of wealthy families' houses during the eighteenth century, were usually sitting rooms as well as places for books and reading.

2.   Mr. Bingley, as a man, would call on the father of the family; it would then be up to the father to decide whether to introduce the visitor to the rest of the family at this time.

3.   *blue coat*: blue was considered fashionable. It was during this period that darker, more sober colors were coming to be considered preferable for men's attire. In letters written when she was near the Bennet sisters' age, Jane Austen jokes that a man who admired her had a morning coat that was "a great deal too light," and that she will refuse any marriage offer from him "unless he promises to give away his white Coat" (January 9 and 14, 1796). For an example of men's clothing from this period, including the sort of coat at issue, see p. 13.

4.   *town*: London.

5.   *&c.*: etc. This is a way of abbreviating the standard apologies and courtesies that Bingley would include in his note.

6.   *Hertfordshire:* the county in England where the action is taking place (see maps on pp. 742 and 745). Its not being mentioned until this point, and now only in passing, indicates its relative lack of importance for the story. Place matters little to Jane Austen compared to many novelists; she sets her novels in various parts of England, but the characters rarely, if ever, exhibit any particular regional characteristics. In part this reflects the reality among the class of people she portrays, for an important trend over the century preceding her novels was for regional differences among the wealthy classes in England to diminish or disappear, thanks to such factors as improved communication and transportation and the increased size and influence of London.

     In choosing a setting for her stories, Jane Austen's main consideration seems to be how the geographic position of the place, particularly its proximity to other places, facilitates the plot. In this case, Hertfordshire, which is immediately north of London, may have been chosen in part because it allows a number of characters, such as Mr. Bingley, to travel easily to and from the capital (for another possible source of the Hertfordshire setting, see p. 51, note 8).

always flying about from one place to another, and never settled at Netherfield as he ought to be. Lady Lucas quieted her fears a little by starting the idea of his being gone to London only to get a large party for the ball; and a report soon followed that Mr. Bingley was to bring twelve ladies and seven gentlemen with him to the assembly. The girls grieved over such a number of ladies; but were comforted the day before the ball by hearing, that instead of twelve, he had brought only six with him from London, his five sisters and a cousin. And when the party entered the assembly room, it consisted of only five altogether; Mr. Bingley, his two sisters, the husband of the eldest, and another young man.[7]

Mr. Bingley was good looking and gentlemanlike; he had a pleasant countenance, and easy, unaffected manners. His sisters were fine[8] women, with an air of decided fashion.[9] His brother-in-law, Mr. Hurst, merely looked the gentleman; but his friend Mr. Darcy soon drew the attention of the room by his fine, tall person, handsome features, noble mien; and the report which was in general circulation within five minutes after his entrance, of his having ten thousand a year.[10] The gentlemen[11] pronounced him to be a fine figure of a man, the ladies declared he was much handsomer than Mr. Bingley, and he was looked at with great admiration for about half the evening, till his manners gave a disgust[12] which turned the tide of his popularity; for he was discovered to be proud, to be above his company, and above being pleased; and not all his large estate in Derbyshire[13] could then save him from having a most forbidding, disagreeable countenance, and being unworthy to be compared with his friend.

Mr. Bingley had soon made himself acquainted with all the principal people in the room; he was lively and unreserved, danced every dance, was angry that the ball closed so early, and talked of giving one himself at Netherfield. Such amiable qualities must speak for themselves. What a contrast between him and his friend! Mr. Darcy danced only once with Mrs. Hurst and once with Miss Bingley, declined being introduced to any other lady, and spent the rest of the evening in walking about the room, speaking occasionally to one of his own party. His character was decided.[14] He

7. The inaccuracy of these initial rumors about Mr. Bingley's party gives the first glimpse of the fickleness and unreliability of public opinion, something that will be seen frequently in the novel. It also indicates the general danger of relying on initial impressions, which is one of the main themes of the book (the earliest version of the novel was entitled *First Impressions*).

8. *fine*: elegant, refined.

9. *fashion*: high social standing. It could also mean the expected elegant behavior and demeanor of those belonging to upper-class society. The word will be used often in the novel, almost always with these meanings.

10. *ten thousand a year*: a sum that places him among the one or two hundred wealthiest men in England then. Since he also possesses a lavish house, with its grounds and contents, he may have at least three times the wealth of Bingley.

11. *gentlemen*: this is the third use of gentlemen/man in this paragraph. The term and its corollaries "genteel" and "gentility," along with the concepts behind the terms, play a significant role in the novel, as they did in the society and culture of the time. In her letters Jane Austen frequently judges people by how genteel they are. The terms have both a social and a moral meaning.

Socially (and "gentle" was originally used in a social rather than a moral sense), a gentleman is someone wealthy enough not to have to work, or able to work in a profession considered genteel, the main ones being military officer or clergyman. That is what is meant by this third use of "gentlemen"—though the term is here being used generously, since assemblies tended to include men whose professions were not quite genteel. The division between those who are genteel, which would include the wives and children of gentlemen, and everyone else, forms the crucial social distinction in the book.

Morally, a gentleman is someone who possesses certain virtues, such as courtesy, refinement, honesty, and generosity. The description of Mr. Bingley as gentlemanlike signals his possession of these qualities. Ideally all those who are gentlemen in a social sense would also be gentlemen in a moral sense, but in reality this is not always the case. Mr. Hurst, who "merely looked the gentleman" (and thus lacks the true character of one), is an example of this.

The terms "gentlewoman" and "lady" have similar meanings, though "lady," the most popular of the two terms, could refer to slightly broader categories of women, and would not be used as often for moral judgments.

12. *gave a disgust*: produced a distaste or dislike.

13. *Derbyshire*: a county in the northern half of England; see map, p. 742.

14. *His character was decided*: the general opinion of him was established.

was the proudest, most disagreeable man in the world, and every body hoped that he would never come there again.[15] Amongst the most violent against him was Mrs. Bennet, whose dislike of his general behaviour, was sharpened into particular resentment, by his having slighted one of her daughters.

Elizabeth Bennet had been obliged, by the scarcity of gentlemen, to sit down for two dances; and during part of that time, Mr. Darcy had been standing near enough for her to overhear a conversation between him and Mr. Bingley, who came from the dance for a few minutes, to press his friend to join it.[16]

"Come, Darcy," said he, "I must have you dance. I hate to see you standing about by yourself in this stupid[17] manner. You had much better dance."

"I certainly shall not. You know how I detest it, unless I am particularly acquainted with my partner. At such an assembly as this, it would be insupportable. Your sisters are engaged, and there is not another woman in the room, whom it would not be a punishment to me to stand up[18] with."[19]

"I would not be so fastidious as you are," cried Bingley, "for a kingdom! Upon my honour, I never met with so many pleasant girls in my life, as I have this evening; and there are several of them you see uncommonly pretty."

"*You* are dancing with the only handsome[20] girl in the room," said Mr. Darcy, looking at the eldest Miss Bennet.[21]

"Oh! she is the most beautiful creature I ever beheld! But there is one of her sisters sitting down just behind you, who is very pretty, and I dare say, very agreeable. Do let me ask my partner to introduce you."

"Which do you mean?" and turning round, he looked for a moment at Elizabeth, till catching her eye, he withdrew his own and coldly said, "She is tolerable; but not handsome enough to tempt *me*; and I am in no humour[22] at present to give consequence[23] to young ladies who are slighted by other men. You had better return to your partner and enjoy her smiles, for you are wasting your time with me."[24]

Mr. Bingley followed his advice. Mr. Darcy walked off; and

15. Jane Austen means to present an initial negative impression of Darcy, but by having the public, already shown as fickle, condemn him in such extreme terms, she suggests the possible defects of that impression.

16. Significantly, it is only at this point, when the question of her relationship with Darcy arises, that Elizabeth emerges as a central character. This foreshadows the focus of the story.

17. *stupid*: dull, tiresome.

18. *stand up*: dance.

19. This exchange between Bingley and Darcy, the first time either of them is seen speaking, displays the first man's enthusiasm and fondness for everyone and the second man's reserve and critical eye, a contrast between them that will persist throughout the novel.

20. *handsome*: a term often used for women in the novel; it had no particular masculine connotation at the time.

21. This is Jane, who is consistently described as beautiful. But no further information about her appearance is ever provided. In general, Jane Austen offers little or no physical descriptions of her characters. This is not because she lacks any notion of how they look: in a letter she describes seeing a picture that exactly resembled Jane, in "size, shaped face, features & sweetness," and even says the picture confirms her supposition that "green was a favourite color with her" (May 24, 1813). But in her novels she omits all this, for it does not serve her artistic purposes.

22. *humour*: mood

23. *consequence*: importance or dignity. In other words, being asked to dance would raise Elizabeth's standing, after she has been slighted by other men. Darcy may also mean that dancing with him would confer a special dignity upon her, an opinion in line with his high estimation of himself.

24. These insulting words play a significant role in the story. Though Darcy is not addressing Elizabeth, he presumably is in a position to anticipate that she will overhear him. His defense would probably be that he is engaged in a private conversation that she has no business hearing, and thus strictly speaking he has not violated any rule of etiquette. Yet his behavior shows a clear disregard for others. The early part of the novel will show additional instances where Darcy, while generally remaining in the letter of the law as regards politeness, exhibits frequent disdain for the general spirit of courtesy, especially as it involves kindness and consideration toward others.

Elizabeth remained with no very cordial feelings towards him. She told the story however with great spirit among her friends; for she had a lively, playful disposition, which delighted in any thing ridiculous.[25]

The evening altogether passed off pleasantly to the whole family. Mrs. Bennet had seen her eldest daughter much admired by the Netherfield party. Mr. Bingley had danced with her twice, and she had been distinguished[26] by his sisters. Jane was as much gratified by this, as her mother could be, though in a quieter way. Elizabeth felt Jane's pleasure. Mary had heard herself mentioned to Miss Bingley as the most accomplished girl in the neighbourhood;[27] and Catherine and Lydia had been fortunate enough to be never without partners, which was all that they had yet learnt to care for at a ball. They returned therefore in good spirits to Longbourn, the village where they lived, and of which they were the principal inhabitants.[28] They found Mr. Bennet still up. With a book he was regardless of time; and on the present occasion he had a good deal of curiosity as to the event[29] of an evening which had raised such splendid expectations. He had rather hoped that all his wife's views[30] on the stranger would be disappointed; but he soon found that he had a very different story to hear.

"Oh! my dear Mr. Bennet," as she entered the room, "we have had a most delightful evening, a most excellent ball. I wish you had been there. Jane was so admired, nothing could be like it. Every body said how well she looked; and Mr. Bingley thought her quite beautiful, and danced with her twice. Only think of *that* my dear; he actually danced with her twice; and she was the only creature in the room that he asked a second time. First of all, he asked Miss Lucas. I was so vexed to see him stand up with her; but, however, he did not admire her at all: indeed, nobody can, you know; and he seemed quite struck with Jane as she was going down the dance.[31] So, he enquired who she was, and got introduced, and asked her for the two next.[32] Then, the two third he danced with Miss King, and the two fourth with Maria Lucas, and the two fifth with Jane again, and the two sixth with Lizzy, and the Boulanger——"[33]

25. This is the first time that Elizabeth is shown in action, and her response to Darcy's words gives a good sense of her general character, as well as of her future relationship with him. The term "lively," which is often used to describe Elizabeth, means not only vigorous or animated, but also light-hearted or merry. Her possession of these latter qualities is one of the main ways she contrasts with the serious Darcy.

26. *distinguished*: singled out for notice or attention.

27. Young women were often praised for being accomplished. For what this meant, see the discussion on pp. 68 and 70, and the notes to those pages.

28. *principal inhabitants*: the family of the highest social position in the village. A village is defined by the *Encyclopaedia Britannica* of the time as "an assemblage of houses inhabited chiefly by peasants and farmers, and having no market, whereby it is distinguished from a town." In the case of Long-bourn the other residents are all too low socially for the Bennet family ever to socialize with them; it is probable that many of them work on the Bennets' farm. This social gap, along with the absence of a market, is what causes many of the Bennets to venture so frequently to the town of Meryton, which contains shops as well as people of a higher social level.

29. *event*: outcome.

30. *views*: expectations.

31. *going down the dance*: moving down the row of dancers. At this time the most popular dances were the so-called longways country dances, in which two rows of dancers, one male and one female, would face each other, and each couple would proceed in turn down the rows while the others watched. The latter could thus get a good look at those proceeding down the rows, as Bingley does with Jane. During these years the waltz, in which each couple keeps to itself, was starting to become popular at the highest social levels; its eventual triumph can be seen as a move toward greater individualism, and away from the more communal spirit represented by the country dances.

32. *two next*: people normally had the same partner for a pair of dances (Elizabeth was described as sitting down for two dances). Hence Mrs. Bennet's list—two third, two fourth, etc.—relates to the succeeding pairs of dances that Bingley shared with someone. Each pair of dances would generally last around half an hour.

33. *Boulanger*: a dance imported from France. Jane Austen refers to dancing it at a ball she attended (September 5, 1796). In a collection of her music, one piece is entitled "boulangerie." It is a moderately lively piece, and one that would be appropriate for dancing.

"If he had had any compassion for *me*," cried her husband impatiently, "he would not have danced half so much! For God's sake, say no more of his partners. Oh! that he had sprained his ancle in the first dance!"

"Oh! my dear," continued Mrs. Bennet, "I am quite delighted with him. He is so excessively handsome! and his sisters are charming women. I never in my life saw any thing more elegant than their dresses. I dare say the lace upon Mrs. Hurst's gown——"

Here she was interrupted again. Mr. Bennet protested against any description of finery. She was therefore obliged to seek another branch of the subject, and related, with much bitterness of spirit and some exaggeration, the shocking rudeness of Mr. Darcy.

"But I can assure you," she added, "that Lizzy does not lose much by not suiting *his* fancy; for he is a most disagreeable, horrid man, not at all worth pleasing. So high[34] and so conceited that there was no enduring him![35] He walked here, and he walked there, fancying himself so very great![36] Not handsome enough to dance with! I wish you had been there, my dear, to have given him one of your set downs.[37] I quite detest the man."

34. *high*: haughty.

35. *no enduring him!*: such an exaggerated expression, coming on top of others like "so excessively handsome!," "never in my life," and "horrid," indicates Mrs. Bennet's shallowness. Jane Austen often has her more foolish characters speak in such a way. Having as unreliable a judge as Mrs. Bennet condemn Darcy in such harsh terms also underlines the potential inaccuracy of everyone's initial negative verdict on him.

36. *great*: important, especially in a social sense.

37. *set downs*: humiliating rebuffs. Mrs. Bennet's wish has a particular significance, for over the course of the novel Elizabeth, who shares many characteristics with her father, will give Darcy a number of "set downs," and this will play a central role in the story.

Chapter Four

When Jane and Elizabeth were alone, the former, who had been cautious in her praise of Mr. Bingley before, expressed to her sister how very much she admired him.

"He is just what a young man ought to be," said she, "sensible, good humoured, lively; and I never saw such happy manners! — so much ease,[1] with such perfect good breeding!"[2]

"He is also handsome," replied Elizabeth, "which a young man ought likewise to be, if he possibly can. His character is thereby complete."

"I was very much flattered by his asking me to dance a second time. I did not expect such a compliment."

"Did not you? *I* did for you. But that is one great difference between us. Compliments always take *you* by surprise, and *me* never. What could be more natural than his asking you again? He could not help seeing that you were about five times as pretty as every other woman in the room. No thanks to his gallantry[3] for that. Well, he certainly is very agreeable, and I give you leave to like him. You have liked many a stupider person."

"Dear Lizzy!"[4]

"Oh! you are a great deal too apt you know, to like people in general.[5] You never see a fault in any body. All the world are good and agreeable in your eyes. I never heard you speak ill of a human being in my life."

"I would wish not to be hasty in censuring any one; but I always speak what I think."

"I know you do; and it is *that* which makes the wonder. With *your* good sense, to be so honestly blind to the follies and non-sense of others! Affectation of candour[6] is common enough; — one meets it every where. But to be candid without ostentation or design — to take the good of every body's character and make it

1. *ease:* amiability, openness—i.e., the quality of getting along easily with others.

2. *good breeding:* good manners (considered to result from being bred well).

3. *gallantry:* courtesy or consideration toward women.

4. This is the first conversation between Elizabeth and Jane, whose close relationship is central to the book. Jane Austen's previous novel, *Sense and Sensibility*, revolved even more around a relationship between two sisters. Her use of this element had strong personal roots, for throughout her life Jane Austen was closer to her elder sister Cassandra than to any other person. In this case, the two sisters' closeness is indicated by, among other things, Elizabeth's frequent teasing of Jane without causing any offense.

The two sisters also furnish an important contrast of personality, one revealed in this very discussion: Jane is inclined to think well of everyone, to the point of naivety, and Elizabeth is more critical of others and far more sharp-tongued. Jane Austen often illuminates character through such contrasts; in a letter commenting on a niece's draft of a novel, she commends her niece for having created two characters (apparently sisters) whose dispositions are "very well opposed" (September 9, 1814).

5. This echoes a line in Jane Austen's letters, that a recent acquaintance "seems to like people rather too easily" (September 14, 1804). As the novel progresses the different outlooks of Elizabeth and Jane will illuminate important moral issues, and each will suffer problems from her respective tendency to judge too harshly or too leniently. Yet, consistent with the line from the letter, it will be Elizabeth's more critical perspective that proves wiser overall.

6. *candour:* innocence, generosity, or—especially—a favorable disposition toward others and tendency always to think well of them. Elizabeth's point is that while many affect, or pretend, to have this quality, Jane is unique in really being so candid.

One source for the observation given by the author to Elizabeth could have been a periodical written by Jane Austen's brother James, *The Loiterer*. In one of its essays he discusses the types of affectation to be found among different people, and identifies the most common type among women to be affectation of candour. He also declares the next most popular female affectation to be that of proclaiming fervent affection or friendship for others, an affectation that the very women under discussion here, Bingley's sisters, will display at several points.

still better, and say nothing of the bad—belongs to you alone.
And so, you like this man's sisters too, do you? Their manners[7] are
not equal to his."

"Certainly not; at first. But they are very pleasing women when
you converse with them. Miss Bingley is to live with her brother
and keep his house;[8] and I am much mistaken if we shall not find
a very charming neighbour in her."

Elizabeth listened in silence, but was not convinced; their
behaviour at the assembly had not been calculated to please in
general; and with more quickness of observation and less pliancy
of temper than her sister, and with a judgment too unassailed[9] by
any attention to herself, she was very little disposed to approve
them. They were in fact very fine ladies; not deficient in good
humour when they were pleased, nor in the power of being agreeable where they chose it; but proud and conceited. They were
rather handsome, had been educated in one of the first private
seminaries in town,[10] had a fortune of twenty thousand pounds,
were in the habit of spending more than they ought, and of associating with people of rank;[11] and were therefore in every respect
entitled to think well of themselves, and meanly[12] of others. They
were of a respectable family in the north of England; a circumstance more deeply impressed on their memories than that their
brother's fortune and their own had been acquired by trade.[13]

Mr. Bingley inherited property to the amount of nearly an hundred thousand pounds from his father,[14] who had intended to purchase an estate, but did not live to do it.—Mr. Bingley intended it
likewise, and sometimes made choice of his county; but as he was
now provided with a good house and the liberty of a manor,[15] it
was doubtful to many of those who best knew the easiness of his
temper, whether he might not spend the remainder of his days at
Netherfield, and leave the next generation to purchase.

His sisters were very anxious for his having an estate of his
own;[16] but though he was now established only as a tenant, Miss
Bingley was by no means unwilling to preside at his table, nor
was Mrs. Hurst, who had married a man of more fashion than fortune,[17] less disposed to consider his house as her home when it

7. *manners:* behavior; disposition toward others. The term had a broader meaning then, referring not just to matters of etiquette and courtesy.

8. *keep his house:* manage the household. This was a central function of upper-class women of the time. Most single men would try to have a female relative live with them to perform this function. Such an arrangement also served the woman's interests, for it was considered very improper for young unmarried women like Miss Bingley to live alone.

9. *unassailed:* unaffected.

10. *private seminaries in town:* London boarding schools for girls. Seminaries were the most prestigious type of female education; London ones had the extra advantage of helping students shed undesirable provincial accents.

11. *of rank:* of high rank. Excessive spending was a frequent habit among those at this level.

12. *meanly:* poorly, disdainfully. Jane Austen is clearly being ironic about their being entitled to this attitude.

13. Money from trade was not genteel in the way that money from land was.

14. His having almost five times the fortune of his sisters is typical for this society, in which men inherited most of the family wealth. It is this fortune that gives him four to five thousand pounds a year in income, for 5% was the most common annual rate of return on property or investments.

15. *liberty of a manor:* the right to kill game on the lands he is renting. Strict game laws in force at the time confined this right to the wealthy.

16. This is the critical requirement for attaining true gentility. The Bingley family presents a standard example of social climbing. Earlier generations have attained wealth through trade; this generation uses it to gain acceptance among the elite. The expensive schooling of Bingley's sisters, which Bingley probably had also, was a principal means for this, for it enabled its recipients to learn the habits of genteel people and to form friendships with them.

17. *more fashion than fortune:* more social status than wealth. People like that often married those, like the Bingleys, trying to rise in society. One side gained status, the other money—though in this case, even with Mrs. Hurst's 20,000 pounds, the Hursts are needy enough to prefer living off Bingley.

suited her. Mr. Bingley had not been of age two years,[18] when he was tempted by an accidental[19] recommendation to look at Netherfield House. He did look at it and into it for half an hour, was pleased with the situation[20] and the principal rooms, satisfied with what the owner said in its praise, and took it immediately.[21]

Between him and Darcy there was a very steady friendship, in spite of a great opposition of character. — Bingley was endeared to Darcy by the easiness, openness, ductility of his temper, though no disposition could offer a greater contrast to his own, and though with his own he never appeared dissatisfied. On the strength of Darcy's regard Bingley had the firmest reliance, and of his judgment the highest opinion.[22] In understanding[23] Darcy was the superior. Bingley was by no means deficient, but Darcy was clever. He was at the same time haughty, reserved, and fastidious,[24] and his manners, though well bred, were not inviting.[25] In that respect his friend had greatly the advantage. Bingley was sure of being liked wherever he appeared, Darcy was continually giving offence.

The manner in which they spoke of the Meryton assembly was sufficiently characteristic. Bingley had never met with pleasanter people or prettier girls in his life; every body had been most kind and attentive to him, there had been no formality, no stiffness, he had soon felt acquainted with all the room; and as to Miss Bennet,[26] he could not conceive an angel more beautiful. Darcy, on the contrary, had seen a collection of people in whom there was little beauty and no fashion, for none of whom he had felt the smallest interest, and from none received either attention or pleasure. Miss Bennet he acknowledged to be pretty, but she smiled too much.

Mrs. Hurst and her sister allowed it to be so — but still they admired her and liked her, and pronounced her to be a sweet girl, and one whom they should not object to know more of.[27] Miss Bennet was therefore established as a sweet girl, and their brother felt authorised by such commendation to think of her as he chose.

18. One came of age, and legally became an adult, at twenty-one. Hence Bingley, having done so less than two years ago, is twenty-two.

19. *accidental*: chance, fortuitous.

20. *situation*: position or location (especially in relation to its surroundings).

21. Bingley's hastiness and willingness to accept another's word are two of his main characteristics; they will play an important role in the later action, specifically in facilitating Darcy's interference in his affairs.

   Bingley's interest in a house in Hertfordshire would be consistent with his position, for those trying to rise socially tended to prefer country houses near London, the main venue for social life and meeting with the elite.

22. No precise information is ever given on how Bingley and Darcy originally became friends. They would not have met at school, since Darcy is in fact six or seven years older. Since they both come from northern England, they presumably met at a social function or through a mutual acquaintance.

23. *understanding*: intelligence, judgment.

24. *fastidious*: disdainful, difficult to please.

25. This means Darcy's manners are polite, but also cold and distant.

26. *Miss Bennet*: Jane Bennet. "Miss + last name" always means the eldest daughter of a family, or at least the eldest unmarried one. For younger daughters a first name is also used; thus Elizabeth is called Miss Elizabeth Bennet.

27. *not object to know more of*: these words indicate their lack of any real interest in Jane.

Chapter Five

Within a short walk of Longbourn lived a family with whom the Bennets were particularly intimate. Sir William Lucas had been formerly in trade in Meryton,[1] where he had made a tolerable fortune and risen to the honour of knighthood by an address to the King,[2] during his mayoralty.[3] The distinction had perhaps been felt too strongly. It had given him a disgust to his business and to his residence in a small market town; and quitting them both, he had removed with his family to a house about a mile from Meryton, denominated from that period Lucas Lodge,[4] where he could think with pleasure of his own importance, and unshackled by business, occupy himself solely in being civil to all the world. For though elated[5] by his rank, it did not render him supercilious; on the contrary, he was all attention to every body. By nature inoffensive, friendly and obliging, his presentation at St. James's[6] had made him courteous.[7]

Lady Lucas was a very good kind of woman, not too clever to be a valuable neighbour to Mrs. Bennet.—They had several children. The eldest of them, a sensible, intelligent young woman, about twenty-seven, was Elizabeth's intimate friend.

That the Miss Lucases and the Miss Bennets should meet to talk over a ball was absolutely necessary; and the morning after the assembly brought the former to Longbourn to hear and to communicate.

"*You* began the evening well, Charlotte," said Mrs. Bennet with civil self-command[8] to Miss Lucas. "*You* were Mr. Bingley's first choice."

"Yes;—but he seemed to like his second better."[9]

"Oh!—you mean Jane, I suppose—because he danced with her twice. To be sure that *did* seem as if he admired her—indeed

1.   *Meryton:* the main town in the area. The assembly would have been at Meryton.

2.   *the King:* King George III, who reigned from 1760 to 1820, though in 1811 mental incapacity caused his son to become Regent and thus effectively the ruler.

3.   The mayor was the head of the municipal corporation, the body that governed most towns at the time. The corporation was normally in the hands of the leading citizens of the town, who often would be merchants, so it would make sense for one of their number to be mayor. Knighthood is an honor conferred by the monarch for some meritorious service; an address to the monarch, which meant a formal speech of respect or thanks, was a frequent means then of attaining the honor. During the time when Jane Austen lived the number of new knighthoods increased significantly, with a particular flood in the years 1811–1815, the period when the novel was published.

4.   Giving their home such a name is a sign of pretentiousness. The Bennets, who appear to be wealthier than the Lucases, seem not to have given a special name to their residence, though on occasion it is called Longbourn House by the narrator on account of the village where it is located.

5.   *elated:* puffed up, raised in pride.

6.   *St. James's:* the royal court. The ceremony of being knighted involved being presented there.

7.   In some respects this course of action conformed to the current ideal of the gentleman, who was considered to be able to cultivate superior qualities, such as courtesy, precisely because he was free from the sordid tasks of making money and getting ahead. Sir William, however, represents a rather silly example of this ideal, for he is described here as being "solely" devoted to the one virtue of being civil, and in fact he never displays any other virtue over the course of the novel.

8.   *civil self-command:* a polite willingness to compliment Charlotte Lucas rather than her own daughters. It takes very little to make Mrs. Bennet drop such self-command.

9.   Once again a character's first lines are revealing. Here Charlotte, by willingly recalling Bingley's preference for Jane over herself, displays the matter of fact and unillusioned attitude that will characterize her throughout the novel.

I rather believe he *did*—I heard something about it—but I hardly know what—something about Mr. Robinson."

"Perhaps you mean what I overheard between him and Mr. Robinson; did not I mention it to you? Mr. Robinson's asking him how he liked our Meryton assemblies, and whether he did not think there were a great many pretty women in the room, and *which* he thought the prettiest? and his answering immediately to the last question—Oh! the eldest Miss Bennet beyond a doubt, there cannot be two opinions on that point."[10]

"Upon my word!—Well, that was very decided indeed—that does seem as if—but however, it may all come to nothing you know."

"*My* overhearings were more to the purpose than *yours*, Eliza," said Charlotte. "Mr. Darcy is not so well worth listening to as his friend, is he?—Poor Eliza!—to be only just *tolerable*."

"I beg you would not put it into Lizzy's head to be vexed by his ill-treatment; for he is such a disagreeable man that it would be quite a misfortune to be liked by him. Mrs. Long told me last night that he sat close to her for half an hour without once opening his lips."

"Are you quite sure, Ma'am?—is not there a little mistake?" said Jane.—"I certainly saw Mr. Darcy speaking to her."

"Aye—because she asked him at last how he liked Netherfield, and he could not help answering her;—but she said he seemed very angry at being spoke to."

"Miss Bingley told me," said Jane, "that he never speaks much unless among his intimate acquaintance. With *them* he is remarkably agreeable."[11]

"I do not believe a word of it, my dear. If he had been so very agreeable he would have talked to Mrs. Long. But I can guess how it was; every body says that he is ate up with pride, and I dare say he had heard somehow that Mrs. Long does not keep a carriage, and had come to the ball in a hack chaise."[12]

"I do not mind his not talking to Mrs. Long," said Miss Lucas, "but I wish he had danced with Eliza."

"Another time, Lizzy," said her mother, "I would not dance with *him*, if I were you."

10. This suggests the frequency of overhearings in a ball room, and thus shows that Darcy had good reason to expect that Elizabeth would hear his dismissive words about her.

11. Jane's defense of Darcy signals the possible limits of everyone else's negative verdict, especially since she provides an explanation for his behavior, discomfort with strangers, to supplement the obvious explanation of pride. At the same time, Jane's description of him as "remarkably agreeable" goes too far, based on what we will see of Darcy's behavior among his companions; it reflects Jane's own naive faith in everyone, as well as possibly, to the degree she derived this description from Miss Bingley, the latter's partiality for Darcy.

12. *hack chaise:* a hired, or rented, chaise. Mrs. Long had to use one because she does not keep her own carriage. A chaise was the most popular carriage for rental, and many, including those who were well off, hired them for long distance travel; Elizabeth does that later in the novel. Hiring one for local travel, however, indicates lower social status, and thus would be a reason for someone snobbish not to speak to her.

The term "hack" is an abbreviation of "hackney," which started as a term for an ordinary, workaday horse, then was extended to mean a hired horse as well, and finally was applied to hired carriages. London at the time was full of hackney-coaches, which were essentially horse-drawn taxis — "hack" as slang for taxi derives from this usage.

"I believe, Ma'am, I may safely promise you *never* to dance with him."

"His pride," said Miss Lucas, "does not offend *me* so much as pride often does, because there is an excuse for it. One cannot wonder that so very fine a young man, with family, fortune, every thing in his favour, should think highly of himself. If I may so express it, he has a *right* to be proud."[13]

"That is very true," replied Elizabeth, "and I could easily forgive *his* pride, if he had not mortified *mine*."[14]

"Pride," observed Mary, who piqued[15] herself upon the solidity of her reflections, "is a very common failing I believe. By all that I have ever read, I am convinced that it is very common indeed, that human nature is particularly prone to it, and that there are very few of us who do not cherish a feeling of self-complacency on the score of some quality or other, real or imaginary. Vanity and pride are different things, though the words are often used synonimously. A person may be proud without being vain. Pride relates more to our opinion of ourselves, vanity to what we would have others think of us."[16]

"If I were as rich as Mr. Darcy," cried a young Lucas who came with his sisters, "I should not care how proud I was. I would keep a pack of foxhounds,[17] and drink a bottle of wine every day."[18]

"Then you would drink a great deal more than you ought," said Mrs. Bennet; "and if I were to see you at it I should take away your bottle directly."[19]

The boy protested that she should not; she continued to declare that she would, and the argument ended only with the visit.[20]

13. Charlotte, whose pragmatic nature has already been shown, now reveals a strong regard for rank and fortune, something that will later influence her own marital choice.

14. A critical line, which indicates that the "pride" of the novel's title does not apply only to Darcy.

15. *piqued:* prided.

16. Mary's words here, as elsewhere, echo statements in books. One source could be Hugh Blair's influential *Lectures on Rhetoric and Belles Lettres,* which is referred to by Jane Austen in *Northanger Abbey.* Blair, in discussing precise distinctions between various words, declares, "Pride, makes us esteem ourselves; Vanity, makes us desire the esteem of others. It is just to say, as Dean Swift has done, that a man is too proud to be vain." Another source could be a frequently reprinted female conduct book of the day, Hester Chapone's *Letters on the Improvement of the Mind,* which has a passage making almost the identical point. Both are books that Mary, pedantic about both language and conduct, would have been likely to read.

It is not certain if Jane Austen intended to endorse this precise distinction between vanity and pride. She would, however, certainly agree with Mary's affirmation of the prevalence of pride in humanity, for that is a central point of the novel. This point is in fact underlined here, by the manner in which the person speaking is oblivious to the way that her own pride in her reflections demonstrates the very "self-complacency on the score of some quality or other" that she is discussing.

17. *foxhounds:* dogs for foxhunting, which had emerged in the preceding century as a leading rural sport.

18. In *Northanger Abbey* a foolish young man, John Thorpe, speaks of this as the desirable amount of liquor for a man to consume.

19. *directly:* immediately.

20. Mrs. Bennet reveals herself further by her willingness to persist in such a fruitless argument with a mere boy.

Chapter Six

The ladies of Longbourn soon waited on[1] those of Nether-field. The visit was returned in due form.[2] Miss Bennet's pleasing manners grew on the good will of Mrs. Hurst and Miss Bingley; and though the mother was found to be intolerable and the younger sisters not worth speaking to, a wish of being better acquainted with *them*, was expressed towards the two eldest. By Jane this attention was received with the greatest pleasure; but Elizabeth still saw superciliousness in their treatment of every body, hardly excepting even her sister, and could not like them; though their kindness to Jane, such as it was, had a value as aris-ing in all probability from the influence of their brother's admira-tion.[3] It was generally evident whenever they met, that he *did* admire her; and to *her* it was equally evident that Jane was yield-ing to the preference which she had begun to entertain for him from the first, and was in a way to be very much in love; but she considered with pleasure that it was not likely to be discovered by the world in general, since Jane united with great strength of feeling, a composure of temper and a uniform cheerfulness of manner, which would guard her from the suspicions of the impertinent.[4] She mentioned this to her friend Miss Lucas.[5]

"It may perhaps be pleasant," replied Charlotte, "to be able to impose on the public in such a case; but it is sometimes a disad-vantage to be so very guarded. If a woman conceals her affection with the same skill from the object of it, she may lose the opportu-nity of fixing him;[6] and it will then be but poor consolation to believe the world equally in the dark. There is so much of grati-tude or vanity in almost every attachment,[7] that it is not safe to leave any to itself. We can all *begin* freely—a slight preference is natural enough; but there are very few of us who have heart enough to be really in love without encouragement.[8] In nine

1. *waited on*: visited (often in a formal way).

2. Such reciprocal visiting was part of the standard etiquette of the day. Visiting represented an important function of the ladies of the genteel classes.

3. In fact, it is when Bingley's sisters become convinced that he really is in love with Jane that they work to separate the two. Thus Elizabeth's judgment here is a little off. This chapter presents the first examples of some errors on Elizabeth's part; the ones here are mostly minor errors, but they foreshadow more significant mistakes later.

4. *the impertinent*: the intrusive or presumptuous; those inclined to meddle with what does not pertain to them. The idea is that Elizabeth does not want such people to gossip about Jane or poke their noses into her affairs.

5. The following exchange between Elizabeth and Charlotte Lucas parallels in some respects that between Elizabeth and Jane of two chapters ago. In both cases, someone who is close to Elizabeth, and who shares her general intelligence and goodness, differs from Elizabeth in critical ways that help illuminate the latter's character.

6. *fixing him*: securing his affections.

7. *attachment*: condition of affection between people.

8. This sober and realistic analysis of love and its development corresponds to how Jane Austen often presents love. In some of her youthful sketches she ridicules the common literary convention in which lovers always swoon for each other at first sight. In *Northanger Abbey* she says, regarding how the hero fell in love with the heroine, "I must confess that his affection originated in nothing better than gratitude, or, in other words, that a persuasion of her partiality for him had been the only cause of giving her a serious thought. It is a new circumstance in romance, I acknowledge, and dreadfully derogatory of an heroine's dignity; but if it be as new in common life, the credit of a wild imagination will at least be all my own." It is obvious that Jane Austen did not in fact believe such a circumstance to be unknown in common (i.e., ordinary) life, and since it is that type of life that she portrays, she often shows love developing in such prosaic and incremental ways.

cases out of ten, a woman had better shew *more* affection than she feels. Bingley likes your sister undoubtedly; but he may never do more than like her, if she does not help him on."

"But she does help him on, as much as her nature will allow. If *I* can perceive her regard for him, he must be a simpleton indeed not to discover it too."[9]

"Remember, Eliza, that he does not know Jane's disposition as you do."

"But if a woman is partial to a man, and does not endeavour to conceal it, he must find it out."

"Perhaps he must, if he sees enough of her. But though Bingley and Jane meet tolerably often, it is never for many hours together; and as they always see each other in large mixed parties, it is impossible that every moment should be employed in conversing together. Jane should therefore make the most of every half hour in which she can command his attention. When she is secure of him,[10] there will be leisure for falling in love as much as she chuses."

"Your plan is a good one," replied Elizabeth, "where nothing is in question but the desire of being well married; and if I were determined to get a rich husband, or any husband, I dare say I should adopt it.[11] But these are not Jane's feelings; she is not acting by design. As yet, she cannot even be certain of the degree of her own regard, nor of its reasonableness. She has known him only a fortnight. She danced four dances with him at Meryton; she saw him one morning at his own house, and has since dined in company with him four times.[12] This is not quite enough to make her understand his character."

"Not as you represent it. Had she merely *dined* with him, she might only have discovered whether he had a good appetite; but you must remember that four evenings have been also spent together—and four evenings may do a great deal."

"Yes; these four evenings have enabled them to ascertain[13] that they both like Vingt-un better than Commerce;[14] but with respect to any other leading characteristic, I do not imagine that much has been unfolded."

9.   Elizabeth's point is presumably that Bingley, since he is the one in close contact with Jane and the object of her regard, should notice it better than anyone. But, as Charlotte points out, Bingley's lack of familiarity with Jane can make it hard for him to perceive her true feelings; it certainly is unreasonable of Elizabeth to say that only a simpleton in such a situation would fail in perception.

10.   *is secure of him:* has secured him as her husband. The idea of a woman trying to secure a man, often by whatever means are necessary, is standard in this society. It reflects, among other things, the precarious economic position of women.

11.   Elizabeth and Charlotte's difference of opinion on how much a woman's actions should be directed toward getting a husband, especially a rich one, is a difference that will later appear in their respective actions regarding marriage proposals.

12.   Thus in two weeks there have been at least five social gatherings for dancing or dinner (all of these have probably involved a number of families). This indicates the high level of socializing in this society, especially when newcomers enter the neighborhood. Bingley has not seen Jane at her house because, as stated at the start of the chapter, only the ladies of Netherfield returned the visit of the Bennet ladies.

13.   *ascertain:* make certain, become convinced.

14.   *Vingt-un . . . Commerce:* two popular card games of the time. Vingt-un is Twenty-one, or Blackjack ("Vingt-et-un" means twenty-one in French; why the "et" is ungrammatically omitted for the card game is unclear). Commerce is a game in which players exchange cards in an attempt to obtain a hand with better combinations. Both are good social games, as they usually involve betting, do not demand complex strategy or great skill, and work best with a large number of players. In her letters Jane Austen often writes of playing them, especially Commerce.

"Well," said Charlotte, "I wish Jane success with all my heart; and if she were married to him to-morrow, I should think she had as good a chance of happiness as if she were to be studying his character for a twelvemonth. Happiness in marriage is entirely a matter of chance. If the dispositions[15] of the parties are ever so well known to each other, or ever so similar before-hand, it does not advance their felicity in the least. They always continue to grow sufficiently unlike afterwards to have their share of vexation; and it is better to know as little as possible of the defects of the person with whom you are to pass your life."

"You make me laugh, Charlotte; but it is not sound. You know it is not sound, and that you would never act in this way your-self."[16]

Occupied in observing Mr. Bingley's attentions to her sister, Elizabeth was far from suspecting that she was herself becoming an object of some interest in the eyes of his friend. Mr. Darcy had at first scarcely allowed her to be pretty; he had looked at her without admiration at the ball; and when they next met, he looked at her only to criticise. But no sooner had he made it clear to himself and his friends that she had hardly a good feature in her face, than he began to find it was rendered uncommonly intelligent by the beautiful expression of her dark eyes.[17] To this discovery succeeded some others equally mortifying. Though he had detected with a critical eye more than one failure of perfect symmetry in her form, he was forced to acknowledge her figure to be light and pleasing; and in spite of his asserting that her man-ners were not those of the fashionable world,[18] he was caught by their easy[19] playfulness.[20] Of this she was perfectly unaware;—to her he was only the man who made himself agreeable no where, and who had not thought her handsome enough to dance with.

He began to wish to know more of her, and as a step towards conversing with her himself, attended to her conversation with others. His doing so drew her notice. It was at Sir William Lucas's, where a large party were assembled.

"What does Mr. Darcy mean," said she to Charlotte, "by listen-ing to my conversation with Colonel Forster?"

15. *dispositions:* characters. Disposition then referred more to the whole character, including inner moral qualities, than it does now.

16. Elizabeth refuses to think that Charlotte could be serious in her cynical opinion of marriage, even though this opinion is consistent with Charlotte's general outlook. Presumably Elizabeth does not wish to believe that opinions she regards as thoroughly wrong could in fact be held by her best friend. She is helped in her dismissal of her friend's words by her own tendency to laugh at things.

17. This type of precise examination and evaluation of a woman's physical attributes is something often found in Jane Austen's novels, both among male and female characters. It also appears in her letters (where it is sometimes applied to men as well). Darcy's initial evaluation of Elizabeth's face gives a sense of how sharp he can be in his judgments.

18. *the fashionable world:* elite society.

19. *easy:* relaxed, easy-going.

20. These glimpses into Darcy's thinking, which will be repeated in the early part of the novel, are virtually the only times the reader sees the inner thoughts of anyone besides Elizabeth; they also go beyond what is revealed about the inner thoughts of any other hero in Jane Austen's novels. The glimpses are necessary in this novel to reveal Darcy's growing interest in Elizabeth, since throughout this stage of the novel that interest is only occasionally revealed by his actions.

This passage also hints at two of Darcy's central traits, his scrupulousness and his sense of his own importance. He is very concerned to arrive at the correct verdict on this question—hence his thorough examination and his mortification at finding that his initial judgment had erred. He also considers his verdict a matter of great significance, one that deserves to be shared with others.

"That is a question which Mr. Darcy only can answer."

"But if he does it any more I shall certainly let him know that I see what he is about. He has a very satirical[21] eye, and if I do not begin by being impertinent myself, I shall soon grow afraid of him."[22]

On his approaching them soon afterwards, though without seeming to have any intention of speaking, Miss Lucas defied her friend to mention such a subject to him, which immediately provoking Elizabeth to do it, she turned to him and said,

"Did not you think, Mr. Darcy, that I expressed myself uncommonly well just now, when I was teazing Colonel Forster to give us a ball at Meryton?"

"With great energy;—but it is a subject which always makes a lady energetic."[23]

"You are severe on us."

"It will be *her* turn soon to be teazed," said Miss Lucas. "I am going to open the instrument,[24] Eliza, and you know what follows."

"You are a very strange creature by way of a friend!—always wanting me to play and sing before any body and every body!—If my vanity had taken a musical turn, you would have been invaluable, but as it is, I would really rather not sit down before those who must be in the habit of hearing the very best performers." On Miss Lucas's persevering, however, she added, "Very well; if it must be so, it must." And gravely glancing at Mr. Darcy, "There is a fine old saying, which every body here is of course familiar with—'Keep your breath to cool your porridge,'[25]—and I shall keep mine to swell my song."

Her performance was pleasing, though by no means capital. After a song or two, and before she could reply to the entreaties of several that she would sing again, she was eagerly succeeded at the instrument by her sister Mary,[26] who having, in consequence of being the only plain one in the family, worked hard for knowledge and accomplishments, was always impatient for display.

Mary had neither genius[27] nor taste; and though vanity had given her application,[28] it had given her likewise a pedantic air and conceited manner, which would have injured a higher degree

21. *satirical:* censorious. She thinks that Darcy looks at her very critically. While she complains of this quality in him, she often shows a strong satirical side herself.

22. This statement reveals her competitive and defiant spirit, as well as how it shapes her initial treatment of Darcy. One can imagine that she, who appears to be quicker and cleverer than almost everyone she knows, has until now probably encountered few people who have looked at her with the satirical eye she perceives in him. Her further perception, as she sees him more, of his intelligence and of his frequently critical opinions will only increase her sense of defiance.

23. Dancing was often seen as an amusement more popular among women. Men's lesser interest in dancing was at times lamented in writings praising dance, and in a description of a ball in *Emma* Jane Austen refers to the "husbands, and fathers, and whist players" who stood aloof from dancing.

24. *the instrument:* the piano. It had grown in popularity in the period preceding this novel, becoming the most common instrument played (that is probably why Charlotte can simply refer to it that way). Jane Austen played the piano, and was devoted enough to practice on it every day. Playing music was common at social events; it was one of the only ways at this time for people to enjoy music. For an example of an instrument of the time, see p. 319.

25. Elizabeth's use of a common colloquial expression (something Darcy never does), as well as the mock gravity she adopts in uttering it, demonstrates the playful and irreverent character that will end up attracting Darcy.

26. Mary and Elizabeth are the only ones who appear to play; though this is the Lucas's instrument, none of their girls ever seem to use it. This was not unusual: pianos had become such a symbol of affluence by this time that families would wish to own one regardless of whether it was actually used.

27. *genius:* natural aptitude.

28. *application:* diligence of effort (in practicing music).

of excellence than she had reached. Elizabeth, easy and unaffected, had been listened to with much more pleasure, though
not playing half so well; and Mary, at the end of a long concerto,
was glad to purchase praise and gratitude by Scotch and Irish
airs,[29] at the request of her younger sisters, who with some of the
Lucases and two or three officers joined eagerly in dancing at one
end of the room.

Mr. Darcy stood near them in silent indignation at such a
mode of passing the evening, to the exclusion of all conversation,
and was too much engrossed by his own thoughts to perceive that
Sir William Lucas was his neighbour, till Sir William thus began.

"What a charming amusement for young people this is, Mr.
Darcy!—There is nothing like dancing after all.—I consider it as
one of the first refinements of polished societies."[30]

"Certainly, Sir;—and it has the advantage also of being in
vogue amongst the less polished societies of the world.—Every
savage can dance."[31]

Sir William only smiled. "Your friend performs delightfully;"
he continued after a pause, on seeing Bingley join the group;—
"and I doubt not that you are an adept in the science[32] yourself,
Mr. Darcy."

"You saw me dance at Meryton, I believe, Sir."

"Yes, indeed, and received no inconsiderable pleasure from the
sight. Do you often dance at St. James's?"[33]

"Never, sir."[34]

"Do you not think it would be a proper compliment to the
place?"

"It is a compliment which I never pay to any place if I can
avoid it."

"You have a house in town,[35] I conclude?"

Mr. Darcy bowed.

"I had once some thoughts of fixing in town myself[36]—for I am
fond of superior society; but I did not feel quite certain that the air
of London would agree with Lady Lucas."[37]

He paused in hopes of an answer; but his companion was not
disposed to make any; and Elizabeth at that instant moving

29. *concerto . . . Scotch and Irish airs:* a concerto is a more formal and difficult piece of music, one that Mary, eager to show her musical sophistication, would naturally start off playing; that this is her motive is signaled by its being a long concerto. Scotch and Irish airs are folk tunes that would be more suitable for dancing. Scotch and Irish music, especially the former, had become extremely popular in England in the decades preceding this novel.

30. Such praise of dancing was a platitude of the time, for dancing was commonly celebrated as a sign of, and stimulus to, elegance and refinement. "Polished societies" was a common term, often seen among social thinkers and historians, to denote more advanced and refined societies; hence Darcy, in his reply, makes reference to savages, who would be the opposite of polished.

31. The sharpness of Darcy's response to Sir William's innocuous statement, like Darcy's earlier stricture on ladies before Elizabeth, indicates a characteristic he will display continually, even in his conversations with his best friend Bingley. Though generally silent and reserved, he is also outspoken and blunt in response to others' statements or questions.

32. *science:* science of dancing. Many books existed on dancing then, giving precise instructions as to its theory and practice, so calling it a science would seem natural.

33. *St. James's:* the royal court. Sir William presumes that Darcy's high social position would give him access there, an access that the snobbish Sir William values very highly.

34. Darcy's repeated use of "sir" shows his formality. He is one of the only characters who uses this designation frequently.

35. *house in town:* a house in London. Thanks to its many and growing amusements, London had become an increasingly popular residence for the wealthy, although those who could afford it, such as Darcy, also maintained a country house.

36. Sir William, not having Darcy's wealth, would have to make London his sole home if he moved there.

37. Presumably it would not be good for her health. Medical opinion of the time attributed many ailments to bad air, and city air was considered especially unhealthy.

towards them, he was struck with the notion of doing a very gallant thing, and called out to her,

"My dear Miss Eliza, why are not you dancing?—Mr. Darcy, you must allow me to present this young lady to you as a very desirable partner.—You cannot refuse to dance, I am sure, when so much beauty is before you." And taking her hand, he would have given it to Mr. Darcy, who, though extremely surprised, was not unwilling to receive it, when she instantly drew back, and said with some discomposure to Sir William,

"Indeed, Sir, I have not the least intention of dancing.—I entreat you not to suppose that I moved this way in order to beg for a partner."

Mr. Darcy with grave propriety requested to be allowed the honour of her hand; but in vain. Elizabeth was determined; nor did Sir William at all shake her purpose by his attempt at persuasion.[38]

"You excel so much in the dance, Miss Eliza, that it is cruel to deny me the happiness of seeing you; and though this gentleman dislikes the amusement in general, he can have no objection, I am sure, to oblige us for one half hour."

"Mr. Darcy is all politeness,"[39] said Elizabeth, smiling.

"He is indeed—but considering the inducement, my dear Miss Eliza, we cannot wonder at his complaisance;[40] for who would object to such a partner?"

Elizabeth looked archly,[41] and turned away. Her resistance had not injured her with the gentleman, and he was thinking of her with some complacency,[42] when thus accosted by Miss Bingley,

"I can guess the subject of your reverie."

"I should imagine not."

"You are considering how insupportable it would be to pass many evenings in this manner—in such society; and indeed I am quite of your opinion. I was never more annoyed! The insipidity and yet the noise; the nothingness and yet the self-importance of all these people![43]—What would I give to hear your strictures on them!"[44]

38. Elizabeth's steadfast refusal is interesting, for otherwise she never shows any disinclination to dance. It may stem from the concern suggested in her comment that she does not wish to be supposed to be angling for a partner; in fact, she consistently avoids any maneuvers designed to attract or snare men, something that distinguishes her from Miss Bingley and that ends up being part of her attraction to Darcy. It is possible that her refusal is the first indication, albeit a mild one, of her hostility to Darcy, a hostility that presumably stems from her sense of his satirical eye as well as her remembrance of his earlier disparagement of her.

39. Elizabeth's words of refusal may be intended as a criticism of Darcy. On a specific level, she could be implying that he only asked her to dance out of politeness, under the influence of Sir William's pleas, and not from any real interest in dancing with her. On a general level, she could mean to label him as all politeness because she sees him only upholding the outward forms of etiquette, without infusing them with any genuine friendliness or consideration for others.

40. *complaisance*: obligingness, desire to please.

41. *archly*: in a playful, saucy, or mischievous manner.

42. *complacency*: pleasure, satisfaction.

43. *the nothingness and yet the self-importance of all these people*: they are nothing in a social sense (from Miss Bingley's fashionable London perspective), but they think of themselves as important (presumably because of their prominence in local society).

44. One sees Miss Bingley, who knows Darcy well, expecting sharp or critical comments from him.

"Your conjecture is totally wrong, I assure you. My mind was more agreeably engaged. I have been meditating on the very great pleasure which a pair of fine eyes in the face of a pretty woman can bestow."

Miss Bingley immediately fixed her eyes on his face,[45] and desired he would tell her what lady had the credit of inspiring such reflections. Mr. Darcy replied with great intrepidity,

"Miss Elizabeth Bennet."

"Miss Elizabeth Bennet!" repeated Miss Bingley. "I am all astonishment. How long has she been such a favourite?—and pray when am I to wish you joy?"[46]

"That is exactly the question which I expected you to ask. A lady's imagination is very rapid; it jumps from admiration to love, from love to matrimony in a moment. I knew you would be wishing me joy."

"Nay, if you are so serious about it, I shall consider the matter as absolutely settled. You will have a charming mother-in-law, indeed, and of course she will be always at Pemberley with you."[47]

He listened to her with perfect indifference, while she chose to entertain herself in this manner, and as his composure convinced her that all was safe, her wit flowed long.

45. The first indication of her interest in Darcy, and her jealousy of any possible rival.

46. *wish you joy*: a commonly used expression for congratulating someone on their marriage or engagement.

47. Miss Bingley, eager to discredit Elizabeth in Darcy's opinion, focuses immediately on what will be Elizabeth's, as well as Jane's, principal marital handicap—her family, especially her mother.

Chapter Seven

Mr. Bennet's property consisted almost entirely in an estate of two thousand a year, which, unfortunately for his daughters, was entailed in default of heirs male,[1] on a distant relation; and their mother's fortune, though ample for her situation in life, could but ill supply[2] the deficiency of his. Her father had been an attorney[3] in Meryton, and had left her four thousand pounds.

She had a sister married to a Mr. Philips, who had been a clerk to their father, and succeeded him in the business,[4] and a brother settled in London in a respectable[5] line of trade.

The village of Longbourn was only one mile from Meryton; a most convenient distance for the young ladies, who were usually tempted thither three or four times a week, to pay their duty to their aunt and to a milliner's shop[6] just over the way. The two youngest of the family, Catherine and Lydia, were particularly frequent in these attentions; their minds were more vacant than their sisters', and when nothing better offered, a walk to Meryton was necessary to amuse[7] their morning hours and furnish conversation for the evening; and however bare of news the country in general might be, they always contrived to learn some from their aunt. At present, indeed, they were well supplied both with news and happiness by the recent arrival of a militia regiment in the neighbourhood; it was to remain the whole winter, and Meryton was the head quarters.[8]

Their visits to Mrs. Philips were now productive of the most interesting intelligence. Every day added something to their knowledge of the officers' names and connections.[9] Their lodgings were not long a secret, and at length they began to know the officers themselves. Mr. Philips visited them all, and this opened to his nieces a source of felicity unknown before.[10] They could talk of nothing but officers; and Mr. Bingley's large fortune, the

1. *entailed in default of heirs male*: an entail was a common legal device for keeping the family estate intact and under the same name (this latter purpose usually meant keeping it from women). Generally an entail specified that the current owner of the property was only a life tenant, and that after his death it would all go to the eldest son, or if there were no sons (i.e., "in default of heirs male"), to the father's next closest male relative. This means that while the Bennets live well now, the daughters will have little inheritance.

2. *ill supply*: poorly make up for.

3. *attorney*: a lawyer who handled ordinary legal business, such as property transactions, but could not try cases in court (a solicitor is the current equivalent in England). While the social prestige of attorneys had increased over the last century, it was still not considered a truly genteel profession, which means that Mrs. Bennet's social origins are lower than her husband's.

4. A clerk assisted the attorney; usually he had been apprenticed to the attorney for five years, after which he was qualified to work as an attorney. It often happened that a clerk would marry the attorney's daughter and, through the aid of this connection, succeed the attorney in the business.

5. *respectable*: socially worthy and decent, but not necessarily genteel.

6. *milliner's shop*: a shop for women's clothes, hats, and decorative articles.

7. *amuse*: occupy (with something entertaining).

8. The militia was the main part of the army concerned with home defense. The novel occurs during the Napoleonic Wars, when the fear of French invasion was strong in Britain. Jane Austen's brother served in the militia from 1793 to 1801; his duties included guarding an area of English coast not far from Hertfordshire. She also had a cousin living in a section of Hertfordshire who experienced the winter residence of the Derbyshire militia in 1794–95; one scholar, Deirdre Le Faye, suggests this event may have helped inspire the first version of this novel (written in 1796), especially since the militia officer who plays such a critical role in the novel, Wickham, is from Derbyshire.
   Militia units usually took up residence in a town for the winter, when there was little danger of invasion. They were housed in local inns; the inns were required to offer this accommodation but were paid for it by the soldiers.

9. *connections*: family background and ties. They would be very important for evaluating people, especially new acquaintances.

10. Mr. Philips's establishment of social relations with the officers is what allows his nieces to meet and talk with them.

mention of which gave animation to their mother, was worthless in their eyes when opposed to the regimentals[11] of an ensign.[12]

After listening one morning to their effusions on this subject, Mr. Bennet coolly observed,

"From all that I can collect[13] by your manner of talking, you must be two of the silliest girls in the country. I have suspected it some time, but I am now convinced."

Catherine was disconcerted, and made no answer; but Lydia, with perfect indifference, continued to express her admiration of Captain Carter, and her hope of seeing him in the course of the day, as he was going the next morning to London.

"I am astonished, my dear," said Mrs. Bennet, "that you should be so ready to think your own children silly. If I wished to think slightingly[14] of any body's children, it should not be of my own however."

"If my children are silly I must hope to be always sensible[15] of it."

"Yes—but as it happens, they are all of them very clever."

"This is the only point, I flatter myself, on which we do not agree. I had hoped that our sentiments coincided in every particular, but I must so far differ from you as to think our two youngest daughters uncommonly foolish."

"My dear Mr. Bennet, you must not expect such girls to have the sense of their father and mother.—When they get to our age I dare say they will not think about officers any more than we do. I remember the time when I liked a red coat[16] myself very well—and indeed so I do still at my heart; and if a smart[17] young colonel, with five or six thousand a year,[18] should want one of my girls, I shall not say nay to him; and I thought Colonel Forster[19] looked very becoming the other night at Sir William's in his regimentals."

"Mama," cried Lydia, "my aunt says that Colonel Forster and Captain Carter do not go so often to Miss Watson's as they did when they first came; she sees them now very often standing in Clarke's library."[20]

Mrs. Bennet was prevented replying by the entrance of the footman[21] with a note for Miss Bennet; it came from Netherfield,

11. *regimentals:* army uniforms. They were so called because each regiment, which was the basic unit of organization in the army, would have its own special features on the uniform distinguishing its members from those belonging to other units.

12. *ensign:* the lowest ranking officer in the army. Yet even he—who is as low a military man as anyone from a genteel family would associate with, since enlisted men were generally from much poorer backgrounds—looks better to Lydia and Kitty than Bingley does.

   The sexual appeal of military officers, and their uniforms, was notorious. The uniforms, which were an important inducement to recruitment, were often made more for display than for utility, being usually of a very tight fit and adorned with decorations. Officers' uniforms had the further advantage of being specially tailored for the wearer. Jane Austen speculates in a letter that a young woman's negligence in writing may stem from her being distracted by a new set of officers who have come to her town (Sept. 15, 1796).

13. *collect:* gather.

14. *slightingly:* disparagingly.

15. *sensible:* aware, conscious.

16. *red coat:* the normal color of British army uniforms.

17. *smart:* stylish, elegant.

18. *five or six thousand a year:* in fact, a colonel would usually earn one to two thousand a year. Mrs. Bennet will stretch the income of marriageable men on other occasions.

19. *Colonel Forster:* since militia regiments were normally headed by a colonel, he would be the highest-ranking officer there.

20. *library:* a circulating library. It was generally a private shop that lent books to those who paid a subscription. Circulating libraries had expanded greatly during the preceding century and had become a fixture in most towns. Libraries had originated as shops selling books as well as other items, and they continued in this period to sell a variety of goods; in Jane Austen's unfinished novel *Sanditon* a character buys things to wear at one. Libraries were also social centers. Thus the officers' going to the library regularly does not necessarily indicate any interest in books on their part.

21. *footman:* the servant who usually answers the door; his duties could also include carrying messages and waiting at table.

and the servant waited for an answer. Mrs. Bennet's eyes sparkled with pleasure, and she was eagerly calling out, while her daughter read,

"Well, Jane, who is it from? what is it about? what does he say? Well, Jane, make haste and tell us; make haste, my love."

"It is from Miss Bingley," said Jane, and then read it aloud.

My dear Friend,

If you are not so compassionate as to dine to-day with Louisa and me, we shall be in danger of hating each other for the rest of our lives, for a whole day's tête-à-tête between two women can never end without a quarrel. Come as soon as you can on the receipt of this. My brother and the gentlemen are to dine with the officers. Yours ever,

CAROLINE BINGLEY.[22]

"With the officers!" cried Lydia. "I wonder my aunt did not tell us of *that*."

"Dining out," said Mrs. Bennet, "that is very unlucky."

"Can I have the carriage?" said Jane.

"No, my dear, you had better go on horseback, because it seems likely to rain; and then you must stay all night."

"That would be a good scheme," said Elizabeth, "if you were sure that they would not offer to send her home."

"Oh! but the gentlemen will have Mr. Bingley's chaise to go to Meryton; and the Hursts have no horses to theirs."

"I had much rather go in the coach."

"But, my dear, your father cannot spare the horses, I am sure. They are wanted in the farm, Mr. Bennet, are not they?"

"They are wanted in the farm much oftener than I can get them."[23]

"But if you have got them to day," said Elizabeth, "my mother's purpose will be answered."

She did at last extort from her father an acknowledgment that the horses were engaged. Jane was therefore obliged to go on horseback, and her mother attended her to the door with many

22. The first of many letters in the novel. Some of Jane Austen's early works, possibly including the first version of this novel, consisted only of letters, as did a large number of eighteenth-century novels. While Jane Austen eventually rejected this epistolary form, she continued to employ its practice of revealing people through the manner of their correspondence. In this case, Miss Bingley's exaggerated expressions ("hating each other for the rest of our lives," "Yours ever") display her affected and insincere character. The letter also provides a strong hint that the invitation to Jane results not from any great affection for her but from the two sisters' being bored because the men are gone to dine elsewhere. Mrs. Bennet laments that absence as bad luck, but without it Jane might not be going at all.

23. This exchange, in addition to showing the extremes to which Mrs. Bennet will go in her marital scheming, gives a sense of the family's economic status. They are rich enough to have their own coach, which is a large and expensive carriage, and their own horses (unlike the Hursts). But they are not rich enough to have separate horses for the coach and for their farm, and the latter must have priority since it is the main source of the Bennets' income.

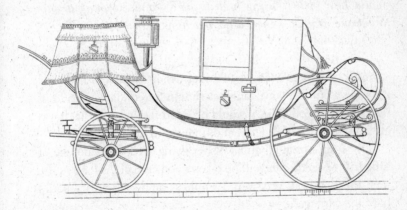

A coach. It would seat six people inside, with three facing forward and three facing backward. Not all coaches would have such fancy trimmings on the outside.

[From T. Fuller, *An Essay on Wheel Carriages* (London, 1828), Plate No. 11]

cheerful prognostics of a bad day. Her hopes were answered; Jane had not been gone long before it rained hard. Her sisters were uneasy for her, but her mother was delighted. The rain continued the whole evening without intermission; Jane certainly could not come back.

"This was a lucky idea of mine, indeed!" said Mrs. Bennet, more than once, as if the credit of making it rain were all her own. Till the next morning, however, she was not aware of all the felicity of her contrivance.[24] Breakfast was scarcely over when a servant from Netherfield brought the following note for Elizabeth:

"My dearest Lizzy,

"I find myself very unwell this morning, which, I suppose, is to be imputed to my getting wet through yesterday.[25] My kind friends will not hear of my returning home till I am better. They insist also on my seeing Mr. Jones[26]—therefore do not be alarmed if you should hear of his having been to me[27]—and excepting a sore-throat and head-ache there is not much the matter with me.[28]

"Yours, &c."[29]

"Well, my dear," said Mr. Bennet, when Elizabeth had read the note aloud, "if your daughter should have a dangerous fit of illness, if she should die, it would be a comfort to know that it was all in pursuit of Mr. Bingley, and under your orders."[30]

"Oh! I am not at all afraid of her dying. People do not die of little trifling colds. She will be taken good care of. As long as she stays there, it is all very well. I would go and see her, if I could have the carriage."

Elizabeth, feeling really anxious, was determined to go to her, though the carriage was not to be had; and as she was no horse-woman, walking was her only alternative. She declared her resolution.

"How can you be so silly," cried her mother, "as to think of such a thing, in all this dirt! You will not be fit to be seen when you get there."[31]

"I shall be very fit to see Jane—which is all I want."

24. *felicity of her contrivance:* the beauty or value of her scheme.

25. It was commonly believed then that becoming wet or chilled was the main cause of colds. Recent medical opinion has tended to dispute this.

26. *Mr. Jones:* the apothecary. See p. 61, note 41.

27. Jane's worry is justified, for her aunt Mrs. Philips will later reveal herself to have found out about Jane's recovery from her illness through her questioning of Mr. Jones's shop boy. Little in this society goes unnoticed by local gossip.

28. Jane's letter also reveals her character, in particular her tendency to look on the bright side of everything and her concern not to trouble others.

29. This often appears in the novel at the end of letters. It is probably a way for the correspondent to abbreviate the customary formal salutations at the end. Another possibility is that it is a way for Jane Austen to save space, but since she includes the full salutation in some letters, it is likely she intends the "&c" of other letters to be something from the actual letter. Such abbreviations seem to be used most often in correspondence between intimate acquaintances, who would presumably feel freer to dispense with formalities. Jane Austen employs a variety of abbreviations in her own letters.

30. Mr. Bennet's harsh words stem from his disgust at his wife's matrimonial scheming, but his expressed fear for Jane is not completely fanciful, for in this period, with limited medical care and no antibiotics, complications from even ordinary infections were potentially fatal.

31. Any of the roads or paths that Elizabeth could use would be dirt ones, so someone using them after a rainstorm would get very muddy.

"Is this a hint to me, Lizzy," said her father, "to send for the horses?"[32]

"No, indeed. I do not wish to avoid the walk. The distance is nothing, when one has a motive; only three miles. I shall be back by dinner."

"I admire the activity of your benevolence," observed Mary, "but every impulse of feeling should be guided by reason; and, in my opinion, exertion should always be in proportion to what is required."[33]

"We will go as far as Meryton with you," said Catherine and Lydia.—Elizabeth accepted their company, and the three young ladies set off together.

"If we make haste," said Lydia, as they walked along, "perhaps we may see something of Captain Carter before he goes."

In Meryton they parted; the two youngest repaired[34] to the lodgings of one of the officers' wives, and Elizabeth continued her walk alone, crossing field after field at a quick pace, jumping over stiles[35] and springing over puddles with impatient activity,[36] and finding herself at last within view of the house, with weary ancles, dirty stockings, and a face glowing with the warmth of exercise.

She was shewn into the breakfast-parlour,[37] where all but Jane were assembled, and where her appearance created a great deal of surprise.—That she should have walked three miles so early in the day, in such dirty weather, and by herself, was almost incredible to Mrs. Hurst and Miss Bingley; and Elizabeth was convinced that they held her in contempt for it.[38] She was received, however, very politely by them; and in their brother's manners there was something better than politeness; there was good humour and kindness.—Mr. Darcy said very little, and Mr. Hurst nothing at all. The former was divided between admiration of the brilliancy[39] which exercise had given to her complexion, and doubt as to the occasion's justifying her coming so far alone. The latter was thinking only of his breakfast.

Her enquiries after her sister were not very favourably answered. Miss Bennet had slept ill, and though up, was very feverish and

32. This means taking the horses away from their work on the farm so they could be used for the carriage.

33. Mary's praise of reason over feeling is an idea Jane Austen endorses in general. Here, however, it is ridiculous, for the feeling in question, Elizabeth's wish to help Jane, is wholly laudable and leads to no violation of any important principle of reason.

34. *repaired*: made their way.

35. *stiles*: sets of steps or bars that separate fields and, while allowing human passage, prevent livestock from getting through. Turnstiles are one form, although in this case, since Elizabeth jumps over them, the stiles are probably ones lower to the ground.

36. *activity*: vigor, energy.

37. *breakfast-parlour*: those at Netherfield are eating breakfast much later than the Bennets did (even the latter would probably not have eaten theirs until 9 or 10 in the morning). Later hours, both for meals and for sleep, tended to characterize those who were more wealthy and fashionable.

38. They are astonished at her coming alone because it was generally considered improper for young ladies, especially if unmarried, to venture out on their own. The main reason behind this was to prevent any sexual impropriety, for it was considered essential not just that an unmarried woman maintain her virginity, but that she avoid even the slightest suspicion of being unchaste. The rule about her being alone was thus especially firm for social or public gatherings. In this case, in which Elizabeth was walking in the country and unlikely to meet anyone, going out alone was more acceptable, though many might still frown at it. Darcy's strict sense of propriety makes him question her action also, though not as sharply as Bingley's sisters do.

39. *brilliancy*: brightness, luster.

not well enough to leave her room. Elizabeth was glad to be taken to her immediately; and Jane, who had only been withheld by the fear of giving alarm or inconvenience, from expressing in her note how much she longed for such a visit, was delighted at her entrance. She was not equal, however, to much conversation, and when Miss Bingley left them together, could attempt little beside expressions of gratitude for the extraordinary kindness she was treated with. Elizabeth silently attended her.[40]

When breakfast was over, they were joined by the sisters; and Elizabeth began to like them herself, when she saw how much affection and solicitude they shewed for Jane. The apothecary[41] came, and having examined his patient, said, as might be supposed, that she had caught a violent cold, and that they must endeavour to get the better of it; advised her to return to bed, and promised her some draughts.[42] The advice was followed readily, for the feverish symptoms increased, and her head ached acutely. Elizabeth did not quit her room for a moment, nor were the other ladies often absent; the gentlemen being out, they had in fact nothing to do elsewhere.

When the clock struck three, Elizabeth felt that she must go; and very unwillingly said so. Miss Bingley offered her the carriage, and she only wanted[43] a little pressing to accept it, when Jane testified such concern in parting with her, that Miss Bingley was obliged to convert the offer of the chaise[44] into an invitation to remain at Netherfield for the present. Elizabeth most thankfully consented, and a servant was dispatched to Longbourn to acquaint the family with her stay, and bring back a supply of clothes.

40. Elizabeth's silence hints at her not sharing Jane's belief in the others' extraordinary kindness.

41. *apothecary*: someone who dispensed drugs and who also examined and advised patients suffering from ordinary illness. Apothecaries, who generally had received only limited training, occupied the lowest rung on the medical ladder; above them ranked surgeons, who treated wounds, and physicians (see p. 73, note 44).

42. *draughts*: doses of liquid medicine.

43. *wanted*: needed, required.

44. *chaise*: a type of carriage; see p. 3, note 5.

Chapter Eight

At five o'clock the two ladies retired to dress,[1] and at half past six Elizabeth was summoned to dinner.[2] To the civil enquiries which then poured in, and amongst which she had the pleasure of distinguishing the much superior solicitude of Mr. Bingley's, she could not make a very favourable answer. Jane was by no means better. The sisters, on hearing this, repeated three or four times how much they were grieved, how shocking it was to have a bad cold, and how excessively they disliked being ill themselves;[3] and then thought no more of the matter: and their indifference towards Jane when not immediately before them, restored Elizabeth to the enjoyment of all her original dislike.[4]

Their brother, indeed, was the only one of the party whom she could regard with any complacency.[5] His anxiety for Jane was evident, and his attentions to herself most pleasing, and they prevented her feeling herself so much an intruder as she believed she was considered by the others. She had very little notice from any but him. Miss Bingley was engrossed by Mr. Darcy, her sister scarcely less so; and as for Mr. Hurst, by whom Elizabeth sat, he was an indolent man, who lived only to eat, drink, and play at cards, who when he found her prefer a plain dish to a ragout,[6] had nothing to say to her.

When dinner was over, she returned directly to Jane, and Miss Bingley began abusing her as soon as she was out of the room. Her manners were pronounced to be very bad indeed, a mixture of pride and impertinence; she had no conversation, no stile, no taste, no beauty. Mrs. Hurst thought the same, and added,

"She has nothing, in short, to recommend her, but being an excellent walker. I shall never forget her appearance this morning. She really looked almost wild."

"She did indeed, Louisa. I could hardly keep my countenance.

1. Changing into more formal wear for dinner was standard practice, especially in wealthy households. Dinner was the main meal of the day, and was generally conducted with great formality. At the same time, not everyone would take an hour and a half to dress for dinner, as Miss Bingley and Mrs. Hurst seem to be doing.

2. At this time the usual hour for dinner was four or five. Later dinner hours were starting to appear among the wealthy, especially in London, so dinner at 6:30 at Netherfield is another indication of the higher social position of its inhabitants. In a letter Jane Austen jokes that her own very early meal hours will provoke the contempt of her sister, who is currently visiting their wealthy brother and thus eating later (Dec. 18, 1798). One reason for this class difference is that preparing and eating dinner while it was still light outside would save money on candles, which would be important to those who were not wealthy.

3. The superficiality of their concern is revealed by their only repeating such standard expressions of concern, and then quickly bringing the issue around to themselves. In her youthful story "Catharine, or the Bower" Jane Austen presents a young woman whose extreme expressions of sympathy regarding a friend's ailment are joined to a complete selfish disregard of that friend.

4. Elizabeth's dislike is understandable; her enjoyment of this dislike hints at a feature of her character that will cause her problems in relation to Darcy, as she ultimately admits.

5. *complacency*: pleasure, satisfaction.

6. *ragout*: meat in a stew and highly seasoned—hence the opposite of a plain dish. Elizabeth's less fancy tastes could reflect her less affluent and more rural background; French cooking, which often involved ragouts, had become popular among the wealthy and fashionable. Appreciation of such cuisine could also be a source of snobbery, as is shown by Mr. Hurst's reaction. Elizabeth's food preferences would have been easily apparent because the custom at dinners then was to offer a number of dishes on the table and to let each person choose which ones to have, rather than to serve every person the same things.

Very nonsensical to come at all! Why must *she* be scampering about the country, because her sister had a cold? Her hair so untidy, so blowsy!"[7]

"Yes, and her petticoat; I hope you saw her petticoat, six inches deep in mud, I am absolutely certain; and the gown which had been let down to hide it, not doing its office."[8]

"Your picture may be very exact, Louisa," said Bingley; "but this was all lost upon me. I thought Miss Elizabeth Bennet looked remarkably well, when she came into the room this morning. Her dirty petticoat quite escaped my notice."

"*You* observed it, Mr. Darcy, I am sure," said Miss Bingley; "and I am inclined to think that you would not wish to see *your sister* make such an exhibition."

"Certainly not."[9]

"To walk three miles, or four miles, or five miles, or whatever it is, above her ancles in dirt, and alone, quite alone! what could she mean by it? It seems to me to shew an abominable sort of conceited independence,[10] a most country town indifference[11] to decorum."

"It shews an affection for her sister that is very pleasing," said Bingley.[12]

"I am afraid, Mr. Darcy," observed Miss Bingley, in a half whisper, "that this adventure has rather affected your admiration of her fine eyes."

"Not at all," he replied; "they were brightened by the exercise."—A short pause followed this speech, and Mrs. Hurst began again.

"I have an excessive regard for Jane Bennet, she is really a very sweet girl, and I wish with all my heart she were well settled.[13] But with such a father and mother, and such low connections,[14] I am afraid there is no chance of it."

"I think I have heard you say, that their uncle is an attorney in Meryton."

"Yes; and they have another, who lives somewhere near Cheapside."[15]

"That is capital," added her sister, and they both laughed heartily.

7. *blowsy*: disheveled.

8. *doing its office*: fulfilling its function or purpose. In some fashions of the time the gown was pinned up in some manner in order to expose the petticoat, which would be made to be seen. In such cases the petticoat would have most contact with the ground, and thus would get especially muddy. Elizabeth has presumably unpinned her gown in order to cover this mud, though not well enough to escape the critical eyes of Miss Bingley and Mrs. Hurst.

9. Since Darcy's sister is younger than Elizabeth, and he is very protective of her, his words do not necessarily indicate disapproval of Elizabeth.

10. *independence*: a word sometimes used in a pejorative sense, for too much self-assertion, or the disregarding of one's social ties and one's dependence on others, was regarded negatively.

11. *country town indifference*: the indifference of someone from a country or rural town. Urban life was often considered superior at the time, especially by those living in cities; the boorishness and crudity of rural people was a common stereotype. Many thinkers celebrated urban life for the greater politeness supposedly fostered by frequent contact with a variety of people, even as others denounced the city as a source of moral laxness and corruption. This debate, which has a long pedigree, took on particular significance during this period in England because of the spectacular growth of urban areas, especially London, and because of the growing tendency of the rural gentry to adopt urban ways. The conflict between city and countryside is a prominent theme in Jane Austen's next novel, *Mansfield Park*, and there she shows herself thoroughly on the side of the rural world.

12. Though Darcy says nothing, it is probable that he shares this sentiment, for his own strong affection for his sister would make him appreciate Elizabeth's action. In the last dialogue of the novel, he mentions Elizabeth's sisterly tenderness as an early example of her goodness that he observed.

13. *settled*: married.

14. *low connections*: relations whose social position is low.

15. *Cheapside*: a street and section in the City of London, the oldest part of London and its commercial center. Only a man engaged in trade would live there, which means that he is certainly not genteel and is thus an easy target for snobbish ridicule. Mrs. Hurst may have chosen Cheapside to add to this ridicule through the negative connotations of the word "cheap" (the actual street of this uncle, Gracechurch St., could be identified as near several sections of the City, not just near Cheapside).

"If they had uncles enough to fill *all* Cheapside," cried Bingley, "it would not make them one jot less agreeable."

"But it must very materially lessen their chance of marrying men of any consideration in the world," replied Darcy.[16]

To this speech Bingley made no answer; but his sisters gave it their hearty assent, and indulged their mirth for some time at the expense of their dear friend's vulgar[17] relations.

With a renewal of tenderness, however, they repaired[18] to her room on leaving the dining-parlour, and sat with her till summoned to coffee. She was still very poorly, and Elizabeth would not quit her at all, till late in the evening, when she had the comfort of seeing her asleep, and when it appeared to her rather right than pleasant[19] that she should go down stairs herself. On entering the drawing-room[20] she found the whole party at loo,[21] and was immediately invited to join them; but suspecting them to be playing high[22] she declined it, and making her sister the excuse, said she would amuse herself for the short time she could stay below with a book. Mr. Hurst looked at her with astonishment.

"Do you prefer reading to cards?" said he; "that is rather singular."[23]

"Miss Eliza Bennet,"[24] said Miss Bingley, "despises cards. She is a great reader and has no pleasure in anything else."

"I deserve neither such praise nor such censure,"[25] cried Elizabeth; "I am *not* a great reader, and I have pleasure in many things."

"In nursing your sister I am sure you have pleasure," said Bingley; "and I hope it will soon be increased by seeing her quite well."

Elizabeth thanked him from her heart, and then walked towards a table where a few books were lying. He immediately offered to fetch her others; all that his library afforded.

"And I wish my collection were larger for your benefit and my own credit; but I am an idle fellow, and though I have not many, I have more than I ever look into."

Elizabeth assured him that she could suit herself perfectly with those in the room.

"I am astonished," said Miss Bingley, "that my father should have left so small a collection of books.—What a delightful library you have at Pemberley, Mr. Darcy!"

16. An indication that, while Darcy does not share the two women's cruel pleasure in laughing at the low Bennet connections, he does share their regard for status. The issue of Jane or Elizabeth marrying men of any consideration (i.e. social prominence) will figure prominently in Darcy's later actions. His statement here is highly ironic in light of the outcome of the story.

17. *vulgar:* pertaining to the common people. The vehemence of Miss Bingley and Mrs. Hurst in ridiculing those lower than themselves may stem, at least in part, from their own family's recent attainment of genteel status, which could make them eager to affirm that status by denigrating those still at a lower level.

18. *repaired:* returned again.

19. *right than pleasant:* she does not want to go, but considers herself obliged to mix with her hosts. Her action shows that, while independent-spirited about many things, she has a strong sense of social obligations. She will criticize Darcy for his unwillingness to perform such duties or to accommodate others.

20. *drawing-room:* the room where people normally gathered in the evening. The word comes from the idea of people withdrawing after dinner.

21. *loo:* a card game for three to eight persons with affinities to draw poker and to bridge. It was especially popular among the wealthy at the time.

22. *playing high:* playing, or gambling, for high stakes. Playing cards for money was normal then, but Elizabeth fears that too much money might be involved here. Heavy gambling was a favorite pastime then of the rich and fashionable, so "playing high" would be a mark of elevated social position.

23. *singular:* peculiar.

24. *Miss Eliza Bennet:* the use of "Eliza" rather than "Elizabeth" is overly familiar, and thus disrespectful, according to the norms of the time (this shows the limits of Miss Bingley's superficially polished manners). Only close acquaintances would normally be authorized to use an abbreviated version of one's name.

25. Social opinion of the time praised women for being well read, and this period saw increasing support for female education. But most people frowned on truly scholarly women, especially if their learning led them to slight other pursuits. One guide to female conduct expresses criticism of bookish women for often neglecting their appearance: Miss Bingley's comment may be made in the hope that such an image of Elizabeth will fix itself in Darcy's mind.

"It ought to be good," he replied, "it has been the work of many generations."[26]

"And then you have added so much to it yourself, you are always buying books."

"I cannot comprehend the neglect of a family library in such days as these."[27]

"Neglect! I am sure you neglect nothing that can add to the beauties of that noble place. Charles, when you build your house, I wish it may be half as delightful as Pemberley."

"I wish it may."

"But I would really advise you to make your purchase in that neighbourhood, and take Pemberley for a kind of model. There is not a finer county in England than Derbyshire."

"With all my heart; I will buy Pemberley itself if Darcy will sell it."

"I am talking of possibilities, Charles."

"Upon my word, Caroline, I should think it more possible to get Pemberley by purchase than by imitation."[28]

Elizabeth was so much caught by what passed, as to leave her very little attention for her book; and soon laying it wholly aside, she drew near the card-table, and stationed herself between Mr. Bingley and his eldest sister, to observe the game.

"Is Miss Darcy much grown since the spring?" said Miss Bingley; "will she be as tall as I am?"

"I think she will. She is now about Miss Elizabeth Bennet's height, or rather taller."

"How I long to see her again! I never met with anybody who delighted me so much. Such a countenance, such manners! and so extremely accomplished for her age! Her performance on the piano-forte[29] is exquisite."

"It is amazing to me," said Bingley, "how young ladies can have patience to be so very accomplished, as they all are."

"All young ladies accomplished! My dear Charles, what do you mean?"

"Yes, all of them, I think. They all paint tables, cover skreens, and net purses.[30] I scarcely know any one who cannot do all this,

26. In this comment Darcy indicates that he comes from a family that has long been wealthy and prominent. In contrast, Bingley's small library reflects not only his own idleness, but also his family's recent arrival into a higher social rank, which means his ancestors would have lacked the resources or the educated taste to accumulate a fine collection.

27. *such days as these:* presumably this means at a time when so much is being published. The previous century had witnessed an explosion in book publishing, so those of Jane Austen's time could justly regard themselves as living at a time of unprecedented opportunity for reading and book collecting.

28. *by purchase than by imitation:* by buying it rather than by constructing something just like it. This conversation introduces the subject of Darcy's home of Pemberley, which plays such a vital role later. Its grandeur is already suggested here. We also see Elizabeth's fascination with the topic, which foreshadows her ultimate reaction upon seeing it.

29. *piano-forte:* the original name for piano ("forte-piano" was also used). Piano-forte derives from the respective Italian words for soft and loud, for the distinctive feature of the instrument was its extraordinary flexibility in playing the same notes either softly or loudly. Soon after this period the abbreviated term "piano" would become standard. For a picture, see p. 319.

30. Examples of the mostly decorative projects that women frequently engaged in. Skreens, or screens, refer to frames or boards, whether standing or handheld, that shield people from drafts or heat or light (see illustrations on p. 299). They would often be covered by elaborate embroidered pictures, an art form that was highly regarded at the time. Painting tables means painting designs or pictures on tables; a variety of household objects were decorated in this way by ladies. Netting involves looping and twisting thread with special tools in order to create a strong mesh. Making purses in this way was very popular; such purses could be useful as well as ornamental.

Two of these three activities involve needlework, which was a central occupation of women of the time. Jane Austen herself, some of whose needlework has been preserved, was skilled at it. Thus she would not look with contempt on the activities mentioned by Bingley, or the women who pursued them, though she would undoubtedly agree with Darcy's rejoinder (see next page) that only women who also engaged in more substantial, nondecorative pursuits should be considered truly accomplished.

and I am sure I never heard a young lady spoken of for the first time, without being informed that she was very accomplished."[31]

"Your list of the common extent of accomplishments," said Darcy, "has too much truth. The word is applied to many a woman who deserves it no otherwise than by netting a purse, or covering a skreen. But I am very far from agreeing with you in your estimation of ladies in general. I cannot boast of knowing more than half a dozen, in the whole range of my acquaintance, that are really accomplished."

"Nor I, I am sure," said Miss Bingley.

"Then," observed Elizabeth, "you must comprehend[32] a great deal in your idea of an accomplished woman."

"Yes; I do comprehend a great deal in it."

"Oh! certainly," cried his faithful assistant,[33] "no one can be really esteemed accomplished, who does not greatly surpass what is usually met with. A woman must have a thorough knowledge of music, singing, drawing, dancing, and the modern languages,[34] to deserve the word; and besides all this, she must possess a certain something in her air and manner of walking, the tone of her voice, her address and expressions,[35] or the word will be but half deserved."

"All this she must possess," added Darcy, "and to all this she must yet add something more substantial, in the improvement of her mind by extensive reading."[36]

"I am no longer surprised at your knowing *only* six accomplished women. I rather wonder now at your knowing *any*."

"Are you so severe upon your own sex, as to doubt the possibility of all this?"

"*I* never saw such a woman. *I* never saw such capacity, and taste, and application, and elegance, as you describe, united."[37]

Mrs. Hurst and Miss Bingley both cried out against the injustice of her implied doubt, and were both protesting that they knew many women who answered this description,[38] when Mr. Hurst called them to order, with bitter complaints of their inattention to what was going forward. As all conversation was thereby at an end, Elizabeth soon afterwards left the room.

31. Bingley's comments reveal both the popularity of praising women for their accomplishments (it is probable Jane Austen herself heard frequent repetitions of such trite praise), and his own tendency to accept as true whatever everyone else says. Darcy, in his reply below, reveals in contrast his own more critical standards and greater independence of judgment.

32. *comprehend:* include.

33. *his faithful assistant:* some have identified this as Mr. Bingley, but it is more likely Miss Bingley. If he were the speaker, he would be completely reversing the opinion he has just stated, which seems overly compliant even for him. She, in contrast, has always been Darcy's faithful assistant, ready to echo him and to say whatever she can to please him. She also would have an incentive to proclaim a high standard of female accomplishment, since she, having gone to a leading school for women, would be more likely to have acquired these abilities than Elizabeth. Finally, the concluding words about a woman's physical manner do not seem like anything Mr. Bingley would say.

34. A good list of the leading female accomplishments of the time. The modern languages would be French and Italian. Classical languages, the most prestigious area of study, were usually considered inappropriate for women.

35. *address and expressions:* way of speaking (including choice of words).

36. Darcy's addition to the list serves several functions. It reveals his respect for female intelligence, which will play a significant role in his behavior toward Elizabeth. It implicitly repudiates, perhaps intentionally, Miss Bingley's earlier scornful comment about Elizabeth being a great reader. Finally, it reveals important differences on the issue of female accomplishment. Miss Bingley focuses on the accomplishments that lend themselves well to display. This would be in line with the focus of many young women (and their parents), who saw education and accomplishment as means of attracting potential husbands. Jane Austen's story "Catharine, or the Bower" speaks mockingly of the case of a young woman in which "twelve years had been dedicated to the acquirement of Accomplishments which were now to be displayed [i.e. to get a husband] and in a few Years entirely neglected." Darcy's opinion, in contrast, echoes that of an increasing number of writers at the time who criticized the current focus on decorative accomplishments and called for girls' education to involve more serious reading and learning; these writers sometimes condemned boarding schools, such as Miss Bingley has attended, for offering only a superficial education.

37. *united:* meaning all these fine attributes joined in the same person. Elizabeth's skepticism could reflect her honesty, or her not having traveled in social circles where women had received the best educations of the day.

38. In her protest Miss Bingley contradicts her own earlier agreement with Darcy on knowing no more than a half dozen such women. Her, and her sister's, quickness in countering Elizabeth may stem in part from a sense that the latter's skepticism about accomplishments is a slap at them, whose expensive educations were designed to make them highly accomplished.

"Eliza Bennet," said Miss Bingley, when the door was closed on her, "is one of those young ladies who seek to recommend themselves to the other sex, by undervaluing their own; and with many men, I dare say, it succeeds. But, in my opinion, it is a paltry device, a very mean art."[39]

"Undoubtedly," replied Darcy, to whom this remark was chiefly addressed, "there is meanness in all the arts which ladies sometimes condescend to employ for captivation.[40] Whatever bears affinity to cunning is despicable."[41]

Miss Bingley was not so entirely satisfied with this reply as to continue the subject.

Elizabeth joined them again only to say that her sister was worse, and that she could not leave her. Bingley urged Mr. Jones's being sent for immediately; while his sisters, convinced that no country advice could be of any service, recommended an express[42] to town[43] for one of the most eminent physicians.[44] This, she would not hear of; but she was not so unwilling to comply with their brother's proposal; and it was settled that Mr. Jones should be sent for early in the morning, if Miss Bennet were not decidedly better. Bingley was quite uncomfortable; his sisters declared that they were miserable. They solaced their wretchedness, however, by duets[45] after supper,[46] while he could find no better relief to his feelings than by giving his housekeeper[47] directions that every possible attention might be paid to the sick lady and her sister.

39. *a paltry device, a very mean art:* paltry and mean both mean low or contemptible; device and art mean stratagem or cunning procedure (hence Miss Bingley, in her zeal to denounce Elizabeth, simply says the same thing twice). Her criticism stands in hypocritical contrast to her own denigration of women in her letter inviting Jane to Netherfield.

40. *condescend to employ for captivation:* stoop to use to captivate men.

41. Darcy's abhorrence of cunning and disguise is one of his most significant features, and will play an important role over the course of the novel. Elizabeth, who unlike Miss Bingley is not full of such "arts," will end up attracting Darcy in part because she never makes any special effort to do so. Miss Bingley's perception of how Darcy's words might apply to herself is presumably why she chooses not to continue the subject.

42. *express:* express message, conveyed by a special messenger.

43. *town:* London.

44. A physician was the highest ranking medical man; he was also the only one to be considered a gentleman. Physicians, who were few in number, had studied at a special college, generally resided in London or other big cities, and were consulted by the wealthy (the only people who could afford their fees) on difficult medical questions. In a letter Jane Austen mentions her brother traveling to a nearby town to consult a physician.

45. *duets:* pieces for two to play at the piano, or for two to sing. Duets were often lively, and Jane Austen is clearly using them to cast a sardonic eye on the two sisters' professed wretchedness about Jane.

46. *supper:* this is probably a cold and very light meal, if not a mere snack, for by this point it is very late in the evening. In fact, the trend in wealthy households was, as the dinner hour became later, to eliminate supper entirely.

47. *housekeeper:* the chief female servant, and often the chief servant overall, in a household.

Chapter Nine

*E*lizabeth passed the chief[1] of the night in her sister's room, and in the morning had the pleasure of being able to send a tolerable answer to the enquiries which she very early received from Mr. Bingley by a housemaid, and some time afterwards from the two elegant ladies[2] who waited on his sisters. In spite of this amendment,[3] however, she requested to have a note sent to Longbourn, desiring her mother to visit Jane, and form her own judgment of her situation. The note was immediately dispatched, and its contents as quickly complied with. Mrs. Bennet, accompanied by her two youngest girls, reached Netherfield soon after the family breakfast.

Had she found Jane in any apparent danger, Mrs. Bennet would have been very miserable; but being satisfied on seeing her that her illness was not alarming, she had no wish of her recovering immediately, as her restoration to health would probably remove her from Netherfield. She would not listen therefore to her daughter's proposal of being carried home; neither did the apothecary, who arrived about the same time, think it at all advisable.[4] After sitting a little while with Jane, on Miss Bingley's appearance and invitation, the mother and three daughters all attended her into the breakfast parlour.[5] Bingley met them with hopes that Mrs. Bennet had not found Miss Bennet worse than she expected.

"Indeed I have, Sir," was her answer. "She is a great deal too ill to be moved. Mr. Jones says we must not think of moving her. We must trespass a little longer on your kindness."

"Removed!" cried Bingley. "It must not be thought of. My sister, I am sure, will not hear of her removal."[6]

"You may depend upon it, Madam," said Miss Bingley, with cold civility, "that Miss Bennet shall receive every possible attention while she remains with us."[7]

1. *chief*: greater part.

2. *elegant ladies*: these would most likely be the two sisters' personal lady's maids. Their main function was to help dress and groom their mistresses (most likely they were performing that function before they came to Elizabeth, which is why they are much later than the maid sent by Mr. Bingley—one can see the priorities of Miss Bingley and Mrs. Hurst). Calling them ladies is a courtesy, since no servant could, socially speaking, be considered a true lady. Lady's maids, who often received special training in such tasks as dressing hair, were the highest ranking and frequently the most educated and refined of all female servants, so "ladies" could be intended to imply the relative refinement of the two in employ here.

3. *amendment*: improvement in health.

4. The universal belief that Jane must remain stems both from fear of the potential danger of any illness and from specific worries about the harmful effects of carriage rides, for such rides, due to the rough nature of roads then, could be a trying ordeal. Jane Austen's mother was made very ill once by the hardships of a coach journey.

5. *breakfast parlour*: this room was often used as a morning sitting room as well as a place to eat breakfast, which is already over.

6. As the person keeping house for her brother, Miss Bingley would be considered to have a crucial say in such matters.

7. Miss Bingley is clearly far less enthusiastic about Jane's staying, though she still knows to maintain the outward forms of politeness.

Mrs. Bennet was profuse in her acknowledgments.

"I am sure," she added, "if it was not for such good friends I do not know what would become of her, for she is very ill indeed, and suffers a vast deal, though with the greatest patience in the world, which is always the way with her, for she has, without exception, the sweetest temper I ever met with. I often tell my other girls they are nothing to *her*. You have a sweet room here, Mr. Bingley, and a charming prospect[8] over that gravel walk. I do not know a place in the country that is equal to Netherfield. You will not think of quitting it in a hurry I hope, though you have but a short lease."

"Whatever I do is done in a hurry," replied he; "and therefore if I should resolve to quit Netherfield, I should probably be off in five minutes. At present, however, I consider myself as quite fixed here."

"That is exactly what I should have supposed of you," said Elizabeth.

"You begin to comprehend me, do you?" cried he, turning towards her.

"Oh! yes—I understand you perfectly."[9]

"I wish I might take this for a compliment; but to be so easily seen through I am afraid is pitiful."

"That is as it happens. It does not necessarily follow that a deep, intricate character is more or less estimable than such a one as yours."

"Lizzy," cried her mother, "remember where you are, and do not run on in the wild manner that you are suffered[10] to do at home."

"I did not know before," continued Bingley immediately, "that you were a studier of character.[11] It must be an amusing[12] study."

"Yes; but intricate characters are the *most* amusing. They have at least that advantage."

"The country," said Darcy, "can in general supply but few subjects for such a study. In a country neighbourhood you move in a very confined and unvarying society."

"But people themselves alter so much, that there is something new to be observed in them for ever."[13]

8. *charming prospect*: charming view, particularly of the landscape outside. Having such a view was considered an essential element of fine houses, which were often sited so as to give them the best possible view of their surroundings.

9. A significant expression of overconfidence in her own intellect, and her ability to judge on the basis of initial impressions. In fact, Elizabeth will later find, to her great vexation, that on a critical point she has guessed very wrongly about Bingley.

10. *suffered*: allowed. Mrs. Bennet's words suggest a parental difference on this point, for she has already indicated that she thinks her husband is too inclined to favor Elizabeth.

11. One of the ways in which Elizabeth is clearly close to her creator, whose novels attest to her powerful interest in studying character; Jane Austen would have had innumerable opportunities to do so on social occasions exactly like this one.

12. *amusing*: interesting.

13. This statement probably expresses some of Jane Austen's own feelings, for she was able to develop her extraordinary insights into human character despite having lived most of her life in the country, and often among a limited number of acquaintances.

"Yes, indeed," cried Mrs. Bennet, offended by his manner of mentioning a country neighbourhood. "I assure you there is quite as much of *that*[14] going on in the country as in town."

Every body was surprised; and Darcy, after looking at her for a moment, turned silently away. Mrs. Bennet, who fancied she had gained a complete victory over him, continued her triumph.[15]

"I cannot see that London has any great advantage over the country for my part, except the shops and public places. The country is a vast deal pleasanter, is not it, Mr. Bingley?"

"When I am in the country," he replied, "I never wish to leave it; and when I am in town it is pretty much the same. They have each their advantages, and I can be equally happy in either."

"Aye—that is because you have the right disposition. But that gentleman," looking at Darcy, "seemed to think the country was nothing at all."

"Indeed, Mama, you are mistaken," said Elizabeth, blushing for her mother. "You quite mistook Mr. Darcy. He only meant that there were not such a variety of people to be met with in the country as in town, which you must acknowledge to be true."[16]

"Certainly, my dear, nobody said there were; but as to not meeting with many people in this neighbourhood, I believe there are few neighbourhoods larger. I know we dine with four and twenty families."[17]

Nothing but concern for Elizabeth could enable Bingley to keep his countenance. His sister was less delicate, and directed her eye towards Mr. Darcy with a very expressive smile. Elizabeth, for the sake of saying something that might turn[18] her mother's thoughts, now asked her if Charlotte Lucas had been at Longbourn since *her* coming away.

"Yes, she called yesterday with her father. What an agreeable man Sir William is, Mr. Bingley—is not he? so much the man of fashion! so genteel and so easy![19]—He has always something to say to every body.—*That* is my idea of good breeding;[20] and those persons who fancy themselves very important and never open their mouths, quite mistake the matter."

"Did Charlotte dine with you?"

14. *that*: this presumably refers to people's altering, though in fact Mrs. Bennet does not seem to have a clear idea what she means, except that she dislikes Darcy and his comment.

15. What Mrs. Bennet does not appreciate is that Darcy's turning away in silence reflects his contempt for her, and was often considered to be the way a true gentleman should react to someone who was impertinent or ridiculous. His action bears affinity to the attitude of the heroine of *Sense and Sensibility*, who, when confronted by a man expressing idiotic opinions, disdains to reply, not thinking that "he deserved the compliment of rational opposition." Darcy's paying Elizabeth such a compliment, by debating her on important matters, is one sign of his genuine regard for her.

16. An indication that, despite Mrs. Bennet's earlier denunciation of Elizabeth's outspokenness, it is the latter who has the true sense of what should and should not be said.

17. *four and twenty families*: this would presumably refer to whoever might appear at the same dinner or social event, not to intimate acquaintances. If so it represents a far smaller number than what could be claimed by those, like the inhabitants of Netherfield, who reside in London and circulate in fashionable society. Furthermore, anyone secure of their position would not need to boast about their number of social acquaintances. All this is why Mrs. Bennet's statement seems so risible to the others.

18. *turn*: divert (from the current subject).

19. *easy*: easy to get along with. Easiness was often considered the opposite of formality, so Mrs. Bennet probably intends to contrast Sir William with the formal and stiff Darcy.

20. *good breeding*: politeness.

"No, she would go home. I fancy she was wanted about the mince pies. For my part, Mr. Bingley, *I* always keep servants that can do their own work; *my* daughters are brought up differently.[21] But every body is to judge for themselves, and the Lucases are very good sort of girls, I assure you. It is a pity they are not handsome! Not that *I* think Charlotte so *very* plain—but then she is our particular friend."

"She seems a very pleasant young woman," said Bingley.

"Oh! dear, yes;—but you must own[22] she is very plain. Lady Lucas herself has often said so, and envied me Jane's beauty. I do not like to boast of my own child, but to be sure, Jane—one does not often see any body better looking. It is what every body says.[23] I do not trust my own partiality. When she was only fifteen, there was a gentleman at my brother Gardiner's in town, so much in love with her, that my sister-in-law was sure he would make her an offer before we came away.[24] But however he did not. Perhaps he thought her too young. However, he wrote some verses on her, and very pretty they were."[25]

"And so ended his affection," said Elizabeth impatiently. "There has been many a one, I fancy, overcome in the same way. I wonder who first discovered the efficacy of poetry in driving away love!"

"I have been used to consider poetry as the *food* of love,"[26] said Darcy.

"Of a fine, stout, healthy love it may. Every thing nourishes what is strong already. But if it be only a slight, thin sort of inclination, I am convinced that one good sonnet will starve it entirely away."

Darcy only smiled; and the general pause which ensued made Elizabeth tremble lest her mother should be exposing herself[27] again. She longed to speak, but could think of nothing to say; and after a short silence Mrs. Bennet began repeating her thanks to Mr. Bingley for his kindness to Jane, with an apology for troubling him also with Lizzy. Mr. Bingley was unaffectedly civil in his answer, and forced his younger sister to be civil also, and say what the occasion required. She performed her part indeed without much graciousness, but Mrs. Bennet was satisfied, and soon

21. Mrs. Bennet, trying to promote Jane's prospects with Bingley and denigrate any possible rivals, brings up Charlotte Lucas's need to help out in the kitchen. It was a sign of gentility if the daughters in the family did not have anything to do with cooking or housework, as Mrs. Bennet says is the case in her family. Jane Austen herself, living in a household of relatively modest means, had to assist a little in the kitchen, though her tasks consisted of keeping track of the stores rather than of actual cooking. It is possible that Charlotte's kitchen duties also involved such supervisory functions; many gentlewomen did that, in part because such activities, by making them familiar with the preparation of food, assisted them in directing and evaluating the efforts of their servants.

22. *own*: acknowledge.

23. The irony of all this aggressive promoting of her daughters by Mrs. Bennet is that it ends up hurting their prospects by tainting them with their mother's vulgarity.

24. *came away*: departed.

25. Writing poetry to or about one's love was a common practice then.

26. *the food of love*: a probable allusion to the opening line of Shakespeare's *Twelfth Night*, where music, which was often linked with poetry, is supposed the food of love. Darcy expresses the standard ideas of the time on the subject. Elizabeth's contrary argument is just something she is tossing out in order to divert the conversation away from her mother.

27. *exposing herself*: making an exhibition of herself, making herself look ridiculous.

afterwards ordered her carriage. Upon this signal, the youngest of her daughters put herself forward. The two girls had been whispering to each other during the whole visit, and the result of it was, that the youngest should tax[28] Mr. Bingley with having promised on his first coming into the country to give a ball at Netherfield.

Lydia was a stout,[29] well-grown girl of fifteen, with a fine complexion and good-humoured countenance; a favourite with her mother, whose affection had brought her into public at an early age. She had high animal spirits,[30] and a sort of natural[31] self-consequence,[32] which the attentions of the officers, to whom her uncle's good dinners and her own easy manners recommended her, had increased into assurance.[33] She was very equal therefore to address Mr. Bingley on the subject of the ball, and abruptly reminded him of his promise; adding, that it would be the most shameful thing in the world if he did not keep it.[34] His answer to this sudden attack was delightful to their mother's ear.[35]

"I am perfectly ready, I assure you, to keep my engagement; and when your sister is recovered, you shall if you please name the very day of the ball. But you would not wish to be dancing while she is ill."

Lydia declared herself satisfied. "Oh! yes—it would be much better to wait till Jane was well, and by that time most likely Captain Carter would be at Meryton again. And when you have given *your* ball," she added, "I shall insist on their giving one also. I shall tell Colonel Forster it will be quite a shame if he does not."

Mrs. Bennet and her daughters then departed, and Elizabeth returned instantly to Jane, leaving her own and her relations' behaviour to the remarks of the two ladies and Mr. Darcy; the latter of whom, however, could not be prevailed on to join in their censure of *her*,[36] in spite of all Miss Bingley's witticisms on *fine eyes*.

28. *tax*: call to account or take to task. In other words, Lydia is insisting that Bingley fulfill his promise.

29. *stout*: robust, healthy. The word was only beginning at this time to mean overweight, at least when applied to people, and thereby to acquire a pejorative connotation; Jane Austen does not mean it in this way. In a letter she says that someone's "figure is much improved; she is as stout again as she was" (Sept. 1, 1796).

30. *high animal spirits*: great natural vivacity or good humor. Animal as an adjective was often used to refer to those aspects of human nature that were shared by animals, i.e., the sensual or carnal parts rather than the spiritual or intellectual ones. As will be seen, it is indeed these animal parts that guide Lydia.

31. *natural*: inherent, innate.

32. *self-consequence*: self-importance.

33. *assurance*: audacity, presumptuousness. The term often had a negative connotation then.

34. It would be considered unusual for a girl of only fifteen to confront and challenge so starkly an older man whom she knew little, and who was her host.

35. *their mother's ear*: "their" presumably refers to Kitty and Lydia, though since only Lydia is mentioned speaking to Bingley, "her mother's ear" would seem more natural (the third edition of the novel in fact wrote it that way).

36. In other words, Darcy also criticizes Mrs. Bennet, and possibly the younger daughters, but he does not criticize Elizabeth.

Chapter Ten

*T*he day passed much as the day before had done. Mrs. Hurst and Miss Bingley had spent some hours of the morning with the invalid, who continued, though slowly, to mend; and in the evening[1] Elizabeth joined their party in the drawing-room. The loo table,[2] however, did not appear. Mr. Darcy was writing, and Miss Bingley, seated near him, was watching the progress of his letter, and repeatedly calling off[3] his attention by messages to his sister. Mr. Hurst and Mr. Bingley were at piquet,[4] and Mrs. Hurst was observing their game.

Elizabeth took up some needlework,[5] and was sufficiently amused[6] in attending to what passed between Darcy and his companion. The perpetual commendations of the lady either on his hand-writing, or on the evenness of his lines,[7] or on the length of his letter, with the perfect unconcern with which her praises were received, formed a curious dialogue, and was exactly in unison with her opinion of each.

"How delighted Miss Darcy will be to receive such a letter!"

He made no answer.

"You write uncommonly fast."

"You are mistaken. I write rather slowly."

"How many letters you must have occasion to write in the course of the year! Letters of business[8] too! How odious I should think them!"

"It is fortunate, then, that they fall to my lot instead of to yours."

"Pray tell your sister that I long to see her."

"I have already told her so once, by your desire."

"I am afraid you do not like your pen. Let me mend it for you. I mend pens[9] remarkably well."

"Thank you—but I always mend my own."

"How can you contrive to write so even?"

1. *morning . . . evening*: at this time, they comprised all or most of the waking hours (which is why there is little reference to afternoon in the novel). Morning lasted all the way until dinner, which was generally around four or five but is even later in this household.

2. *loo table*: this may mean a special table just for loo. Furniture of this time included a variety of tables that were specially designed to suit particular card games.

3. *calling off*: summoning away, distracting.

4. *piquet*: a complex and absorbing card game for two people in which players attempt both to create combinations in their hands and to win tricks.

5. *needlework*: an activity often done in company; it was an occupation that did not demand one's full attention and therefore allowed one to pay attention to other things as well, as Elizabeth is doing now.

6. *amused*: entertained, occupied.

7. Good handwriting was an art that was highly esteemed. It was an important subject in school, and many books existed to instruct people in better writing. One important principle was writing in even lines (there was no lined paper to help one write evenly). In *Gulliver's Travels* Swift pokes fun at women's supposed propensity to write in crooked lines.

8. *Letters of business*: probably letters concerning his house or land or investments. Owners of estates, when away from home, usually corresponded with the agents who managed the estates. This is an indication that even a gentleman of leisure would have some work to do—though Jane Austen rarely shows this aspect of their existence since doing so is unnecessary for her story.

9. *mend pens*: a frequent procedure, for the points of the quill or feather pens of the time would grow dull with usage, and would need constantly to be mended by using a pen-knife to cut away and sharpen the point. Steel pens that did not require such mending had just been invented at this time, but they did not come into widespread usage until a couple of decades later.

He was silent.

"Tell your sister I am delighted to hear of her improvement on the harp,[10] and pray let her know that I am quite in raptures with her beautiful little design for a table,[11] and I think it infinitely superior to Miss Grantley's."

"Will you give me leave to defer your raptures till I write again?—At present I have not room to do them justice."[12]

"Oh! it is of no consequence. I shall see her in January. But do you always write such charming long letters to her, Mr. Darcy?"

"They are generally long; but whether always charming, it is not for me to determine."

"It is a rule with me, that a person who can write a long letter, with ease, cannot write ill."

"That will not do for a compliment to Darcy, Caroline," cried her brother—"because he does *not* write with ease. He studies too much for words of four syllables.[13]—Do not you, Darcy?"

"My stile of writing is very different from yours."

"Oh!" cried Miss Bingley, "Charles writes in the most careless way imaginable. He leaves out half his words, and blots[14] the rest."

"My ideas flow so rapidly that I have not time to express them—by which means my letters sometimes convey no ideas[15] at all to my correspondents."

"Your humility, Mr. Bingley," said Elizabeth, "must disarm reproof."[16]

"Nothing is more deceitful," said Darcy, "than the appearance of humility. It is often only carelessness of opinion, and sometimes an indirect boast."[17]

"And which of the two do you call *my* little recent piece of modesty?"

"The indirect boast;—for you are really proud of your defects in writing, because you consider them as proceeding from a rapidity of thought and carelessness of execution, which if not estimable,[18] you think at least highly interesting. The power of doing any thing with quickness is always much prized by the possessor, and often without any attention to the imperfection of the performance. When you told Mrs. Bennet this morning that if

10. *harp*: after the piano, probably the most popular instrument for ladies. Miss Darcy's playing it along with the piano indicates that she is unusually accomplished.

11. *design for a table*: such artistic projects were a popular female pastime.

12. The sarcasm of this line, which is echoed in a few other replies to Miss Bingley, serves to suggest a side of Darcy that will be able to appreciate and value Elizabeth's wit and bantering conversation.

At the same time, Darcy's frequent sarcasm or sharpness toward Miss Bingley, which suggests that he likes her little despite her flattery of him, can lead to the question of why he spends so much time in her company. The principal answer is his close friendship with Bingley: given the importance of family ties in this society, he cannot avoid frequent contact with his friend's sister, especially since she keeps house for her brother. Another probable reason is his evident dislike of meeting strangers, which would naturally incline him toward the continued company of those familiar to him. Finally, Darcy's relatively calm manner seems to suggest that he is not one to become too perturbed by a minor annoyance like Miss Bingley.

13. The crucial letter written by Darcy to Elizabeth (see pp. 362–374) is in fact carefully studied, and full of long words.

14. *blots*: leaves blots of ink on the words, which would make them illegible. This could occur frequently with those who wrote carelessly, for the highly liquid ink used then would easily run and form blots. This became a particular problem in this period because of the introduction of smoother writing paper that, while making letters easier to form on the page, absorbed ink less and thereby increased blotting. Various materials, such as sand, were used to absorb this excess ink and prevent blots from forming.

15. *ideas*: thoughts.

16. *disarm reproof*: keep anyone from reproaching you.

17. Once again Darcy reveals his distaste for anything he perceives to be deceit or false appearances.

18. *estimable*: admirable.

you ever resolved on quitting Netherfield you should be gone in five minutes, you meant it to be a sort of panegyric, of compliment to yourself—and yet what is there so very laudable in a precipitance[19] which must leave very necessary business undone, and can be of no real advantage to yourself or any one else?"[20]

"Nay," cried Bingley, "this is too much, to remember at night all the foolish things that were said in the morning.[21] And yet, upon my honour, I believed what I said of myself to be true, and I believe it at this moment. At least, therefore, I did not assume the character of needless precipitance merely to shew off before the ladies."

"I dare say you believed it; but I am by no means convinced that you would be gone with such celerity. Your conduct would be quite as dependant on chance as that of any man I know; and if, as you were mounting your horse, a friend were to say, 'Bingley, you had better stay till next week,' you would probably do it, you would probably not go—and, at another word, might stay a month."

"You have only proved by this," cried Elizabeth, "that Mr. Bingley did not do justice to his own disposition. You have shewn him off now much more than he did himself."

"I am exceedingly gratified," said Bingley, "by your converting what my friend says into a compliment on the sweetness of my temper.[22] But I am afraid you are giving it a turn[23] which that gentleman did by no means intend; for he would certainly think the better of me, if under such a circumstance I were to give a flat denial, and ride off as fast as I could."

"Would Mr. Darcy then consider the rashness of your original intention as atoned for by your obstinacy in adhering to it?"[24]

"Upon my word I cannot exactly explain the matter, Darcy must speak for himself."

"You expect me to account for opinions which you chuse to call mine, but which I have never acknowledged. Allowing the case, however, to stand according to your representation, you must remember, Miss Bennet, that the friend who is supposed to desire his return to the house, and the delay of his plan, has merely desired it, asked it without offering one argument in favour of its propriety."

19. *precipitance:* precipitous course or action.

20. The sharpness of Darcy's criticism of Bingley, who is his best friend and has done nothing to provoke him, both illuminates Darcy's character and provides a fitting introduction to an exchange in which he will argue for not accommodating others too much, including friends.

21. Many, if not most, people would probably sympathize with Bingley's complaint.

22. *temper:* disposition.

23. *turn:* interpretation.

24. Elizabeth is, as Darcy states in his reply, distorting his argument a little. This is something she will do on other occasions.

"To yield readily—easily—to the *persuasion*[25] of a friend is no merit with you."

"To yield without conviction is no compliment to the understanding[26] of either."

"You appear to me, Mr. Darcy, to allow nothing for the influence of friendship and affection. A regard for the requester would often make one readily yield to a request, without waiting for arguments to reason one into it. I am not particularly speaking of such a case as you have supposed about Mr. Bingley. We may as well wait, perhaps, till the circumstance occurs, before we discuss the discretion[27] of his behaviour thereupon. But in general and ordinary cases between friend and friend, where one of them is desired by the other to change a resolution of no very great moment, should you think ill of that person for complying with the desire, without waiting to be argued into it?"

"Will it not be advisable, before we proceed on this subject, to arrange with rather more precision the degree of importance which is to appertain to this request, as well as the degree of intimacy subsisting between the parties?"

"By all means," cried Bingley; "let us hear all the particulars, not forgetting their comparative height and size; for that will have more weight in the argument, Miss Bennet, than you may be aware of. I assure you that if Darcy were not such a great tall fellow, in comparison with myself, I should not pay him half so much deference. I declare I do not know a more aweful[28] object than Darcy, on particular occasions, and in particular places; at his own house especially, and of a Sunday evening when he has nothing to do."

Mr. Darcy smiled; but Elizabeth thought she could perceive that he was rather offended; and therefore checked her laugh. Miss Bingley warmly resented the indignity he had received, in an expostulation with her brother for talking such nonsense.

"I see your design, Bingley," said his friend.—"You dislike an argument, and want to silence this."

"Perhaps I do. Arguments are too much like disputes. If you and Miss Bennet[29] will defer yours till I am out of the room, I shall be very thankful; and then you may say whatever you like of me."[30]

25. *persuasion:* Jane Austen's last completed novel, *Persuasion,* centers around the question of how amenable one should be to persuasion by others. It is also a central issue in this novel, which presents some characters who are too obstinate, others who are too malleable, and, in the case of Elizabeth and Darcy, two who struggle to find a sensible medium.

26. *understanding:* intelligence, judgment.

27. *discretion:* wisdom or prudence.

28. *aweful:* dreadful, imposing, tending to inspire awe.

29. *Miss Bennet:* Bingley uses this form instead of "Miss Elizabeth Bennet" because it would not be considered proper for a man who had no intimate connection with a woman to use her first name when addressing her directly.

30. The differences in the replies of Elizabeth and Bingley to Darcy not only demonstrate their differences in character, but also present contrasting examples of the very issues under discussion. Elizabeth is ready to oppose Darcy and to sustain her opposition; thus, even while disagreeing with him, she displays the very firmness and independence of character that Darcy admires. In contrast, Bingley strives to avoid direct disagreement and to divert the conversation through humor, by which behavior he ends up exhibiting some of the same pliability and lack of gravity that Darcy accused him of at the start of the discussion.

This whole conversation, in fact, is one of the best examples of Jane Austen's ability to integrate plot, character, and theme, for the exchange manages in the same brief space to advance the relationship of Darcy and Elizabeth by having them argue directly and thereby acquire a greater sense of the other person's intelligence, to reveal crucial facets of the characters of Darcy, Elizabeth, and Bingley, and to introduce the themes of persuasion and amenability.

"What you ask," said Elizabeth, "is no sacrifice on my side; and Mr. Darcy had much better finish his letter."

Mr. Darcy took her advice, and did finish his letter.

When that business was over, he applied to Miss Bingley and Elizabeth for the indulgence[31] of some music. Miss Bingley moved with alacrity to the piano-forte, and after a polite request that Elizabeth would lead the way, which the other as politely and more earnestly negatived,[32] she seated herself.

Mrs. Hurst sang with her sister, and while they were thus employed Elizabeth could not help observing as she turned over some music books that lay on the instrument, how frequently Mr. Darcy's eyes were fixed on her. She hardly knew how to suppose that she could be an object of admiration to so great a man;[33] and yet that he should look at her because he disliked her, was still more strange. She could only imagine however at last, that she drew his notice because there was a something about her more wrong and reprehensible, according to his ideas of right, than in any other person present. The supposition did not pain her. She liked him too little to care for his approbation.

After playing some Italian songs,[34] Miss Bingley varied the charm by a lively Scotch air; and soon afterwards Mr. Darcy, drawing near Elizabeth, said to her—

"Do not you feel a great inclination, Miss Bennet, to seize such an opportunity of dancing a reel?"[35]

She smiled, but made no answer. He repeated the question, with some surprise at her silence.

"Oh!" said she, "I heard you before; but I could not immediately determine what to say in reply. You wanted me, I know, to say 'Yes,' that you might have the pleasure of despising my taste;[36] but I always delight in overthrowing those kind of schemes, and cheating a person of their premeditated contempt.[37] I have therefore made up my mind to tell you, that I do not want to dance a reel at all—and now despise me if you dare."

"Indeed I do not dare."

Elizabeth, having rather expected to affront him, was amazed at his gallantry; but there was a mixture of sweetness and archness

31. *indulgence:* favor.

32. *negatived:* declined. One sees that only women are appealed to for music. While in earlier centuries in England music had been considered an important academic study, and worthy of a gentleman, by the eighteenth century it had declined in prestige and was generally practiced only by women or, in professional contexts, by foreigners.

33. *so great a man:* a man of such high social station. Elizabeth knows that her own social origins are lower, and she assumes that this would preclude Darcy's being interested in her, especially in a romantic way. This was a standard assumption in this society, and it was generally justified, for in actual fact the great majority of marriages did occur between social equals.

34. *Italian songs:* these were often performed in England at the time, especially among those who had, or pretended to have, more sophisticated tastes in music. Jane Austen had some knowledge of Italian, and played Italian songs.

35. *a reel:* a lively dance, generally associated with Scotland. Reels, like Scottish music, had become very popular at this time. Some have wondered if Darcy's offer is serious, for a reel, like almost all dances of the time, could not be danced by a single couple. But many reels involved only three people, so Darcy would have needed only one person in the room besides Elizabeth to join in the dance.

36. Reels, and the music for it, were considered common or popular in character, so people of refined and exacting taste might despise someone who enjoyed them.

37. *cheating a person of their premeditated contempt:* robbing a person of the contemptuous verdict they had formed beforehand, and hoped to see confirmed.

in her manner which made it difficult for her to affront anybody; and Darcy had never been so bewitched by any woman as he was by her. He really believed, that were it not for the inferiority of her connections, he should be in some danger.[38]

Miss Bingley saw, or suspected enough to be jealous; and her great anxiety for the recovery of her dear friend Jane, received some assistance from her desire of getting rid of Elizabeth.

She often tried to provoke Darcy into disliking her guest, by talking of their supposed marriage, and planning his happiness in such an alliance.[39]

"I hope," said she, as they were walking together in the shrubbery[40] the next day, "you will give your mother-in-law a few hints, when this desirable event takes place, as to the advantage of holding her tongue; and if you can compass[41] it, do cure the younger girls of running after the officers. — And, if I may mention so delicate a subject, endeavour to check that little something, bordering on conceit and impertinence, which your lady[42] possesses."

"Have you any thing else to propose for my domestic felicity?"

"Oh! yes. — Do let the portraits of your uncle and aunt Philips be placed in the gallery at Pemberley.[43] Put them next to your great uncle the judge. They are in the same profession, you know; only in different lines.[44] As for your Elizabeth's picture, you must not attempt to have it taken, for what painter could do justice to those beautiful eyes?"

"It would not be easy, indeed, to catch their expression, but their colour and shape, and the eye-lashes, so remarkably fine, might be copied."

At that moment they were met from another walk, by Mrs. Hurst and Elizabeth herself.

"I did not know that you intended to walk," said Miss Bingley, in some confusion, lest they had been overheard.[45]

"You used us abominably ill," answered Mrs. Hurst, "in running away without telling us that you were coming out."

Then taking the disengaged arm of Mr. Darcy,[46] she left Elizabeth to walk by herself. The path just admitted three. Mr. Darcy felt their rudeness and immediately said, —

38. *in some danger:* in danger of being infatuated enough to propose to her. The idea of a man being endangered by a woman is standard in this period, for marriage was viewed as a possible trap for the man, who would be letting the woman share in his money and social position and had no guarantee of receiving comparable benefits in return. Right now Darcy, aware of such considerations, is confident that his knowledge of Elizabeth's inferior connections, or family ties, will keep him from falling in love with her.

39. *alliance:* frequently used for marriage. Traditionally marriages were alliances between families, in which practical social considerations mattered more than romantic feeling.

40. *shrubbery:* it was standard then to have a shrubbery, often containing walkways arranged in elaborate patterns, next to a house. The Bennets have one, though they have a less grand home, and so did Jane Austen's family.

41. *compass:* contrive or accomplish.

42. *your lady:* Elizabeth, who would be Darcy's lady if he married her.

43. *gallery at Pemberley:* great houses often had galleries with pictures of family members; the gallery at Pemberley figures in a later scene.

44. *different lines:* different areas of the profession. Miss Bingley is being sarcastic in an effort to appeal to Darcy's family pride. Ostensibly Mr. Philips, as an attorney, shares the profession of the law with a judge, but in fact an enormous gulf separated the two. Only around fifteen judges existed in all of England then; they formed the pinnacle of the legal system, focusing only on certain critical matters while magistrates handled most ordinary cases. Judges were also given special legal protections and would be given titles on appointment, if they did not have one already, since it was believed that only titled rank was commensurate with the high position of a judge. In contrast, attorneys were the most common type of lawyers, numbering more than 5,000 at the time. Becoming one required merely a five years' apprenticeship, at a cost of usually one to two hundred pounds; while this made it a good path of social mobility, it also tarred attorneys as men of low origins.

45. Because shrubberies usually had intersecting walkways, and contained shrubs or trees too high to be seen over, such overhearing was a distinct possibility (though it does not seem to have occurred in this case).

46. Gentlemen normally offered their arms to ladies when walking together. Mrs. Hurst takes the arm of Darcy that is not supporting Miss Bingley.

"This walk is not wide enough for our party. We had better go into the avenue."[47]

But Elizabeth, who had not the least inclination to remain with them, laughingly answered,

"No, no; stay where you are.—You are charmingly group'd, and appear to uncommon advantage. The picturesque would be spoilt by admitting a fourth.[48] Good bye."

She then ran gaily off, rejoicing as she rambled about, in the hope of being at home again in a day or two. Jane was already so much recovered as to intend leaving her room for a couple of hours that evening.

47. *avenue*: a more main, and therefore wider, path.

48. The picturesque was a concept that had become very influential at this time. It involved a strong appreciation of natural beauty, with a particular focus on those scenes of nature that would form a good landscape painting or picture (hence the term). Elizabeth's comment is a subtle reference to the most important writer on the picturesque, William Gilpin, an author Jane Austen admired. Gilpin often used cattle when discussing his ideas of the picturesque, for cattle were a frequent subject of landscapes; one of his main principles was that three was the ideal number of cattle to form a picturesque grouping, and that the effect would be ruined by introducing a fourth. The picture below, from one of his books, is meant to demonstrate this principle: Gilpin argues that the three cows in the foreground form an attractive group, and that a fourth in the group would spoil the harmony. Of course, there is a fourth cow in the picture, but Gilpin explains that it does not detract from the scene since it is detached from the others.

It is possible that Darcy, as a reader, might catch Elizabeth's allusion to Gilpin; it is doubtful that Miss Bingley or Mrs. Hurst would.

[from William Gilpin, *Observations, on Several Parts of England, particularly the Mountains and Lakes of Cumberland and Westmoreland, relative chiefly to Picturesque Beauty, made in the Year 1772, Vol. II (London, 1808), p. 254]*

Chapter Eleven

When the ladies removed after dinner,[1] Elizabeth ran up to her sister, and seeing her well guarded from cold, attended her into the drawing-room; where she was welcomed by her two friends with many professions of pleasure; and Elizabeth had never seen them so agreeable as they were during the hour which passed before the gentlemen appeared. Their powers of conversation were considerable. They could describe an entertainment[2] with accuracy,[3] relate an anecdote with humour, and laugh at their acquaintance with spirit.[4]

But when the gentlemen entered, Jane was no longer the first object. Miss Bingley's eyes were instantly turned towards Darcy, and she had something to say to him before he had advanced many steps. He addressed himself directly to Miss Bennet, with a polite congratulation; Mr. Hurst also made her a slight bow, and said he was "very glad;" but diffuseness[5] and warmth remained for Bingley's salutation. He was full of joy and attention. The first half hour was spent in piling up the fire,[6] lest she should suffer from the change of room; and she removed at his desire to the other side of the fire-place, that she might be farther from the door.[7] He then sat down by her, and talked scarcely to any one else. Elizabeth, at work[8] in the opposite corner, saw it all with great delight.

When tea[9] was over, Mr. Hurst reminded his sister-in-law of the card-table—but in vain. She had obtained private intelligence[10] that Mr. Darcy did not wish for cards; and Mr. Hurst soon found even his open petition rejected.[11] She assured him that no one intended to play, and the silence of the whole party on the subject, seemed to justify her. Mr. Hurst had therefore nothing to do, but to stretch himself on one of the sophas and go to sleep.[12] Darcy took up a book; Miss Bingley did the same; and Mrs. Hurst,

1.   It was customary for the ladies to withdraw after dinner into the drawing room, leaving the gentlemen alone for a while. The men would generally drink further, talk about subjects like politics that were considered to be of particular interest to men, or even introduce salacious matter and jokes, something strictly forbidden in the presence of ladies.

2.   *entertainment:* used to describe not just public performances, but also social gatherings or other activities done for enjoyment.

3.   *accuracy:* precision; the word then related more to the care or exactness with which an account was rendered than to its validity or truthfulness.

4.   *spirit:* animation, vigor. The abilities of the two sisters shine particularly in the area of mockery.

5.   *diffuseness:* verboseness. In other words, Bingley spoke a great deal, in contrast to the others' conciseness.

6.   *piling up the fire:* building it up so it burns hotter, and thereby warms the room more. It is now mid-November, so warding off the outside cold would be an important issue.

7.   In an age without central heating, the temperature could vary significantly in different parts of the room. If the door leads to an unheated or less heated room, being near it would be colder, though it is implied that here the possibility exists mostly in Bingley's imagination.

8.   *work:* needlework. This usage, often seen in the novel, signals needlework's central place in women's lives then. Elizabeth, though said later not to be an eager needleworker, is shown engaged in it at several points.

9.   *tea:* this normally occurred an hour or two after dinner.

10.   *intelligence:* information.

11.   As the one keeping house, Miss Bingley would be the one to decide on bringing out the card table, which means, given her interest in Darcy, that his wishes rather than Mr. Hurst's have priority.

12.   In line with the prevailing emphasis on elegance and formality, people at the time were always encouraged to maintain an erect seating posture, with any slouching or leaning back in the chair regarded as slothful (except in the case of the sick or infirm). Hence Mr. Hurst's lying down and sleeping on a sofa would be considered a true mark of laxness or self-indulgence, especially since he does it in the presence of guests.

principally occupied in playing with her bracelets and rings, joined now and then in her brother's conversation with Miss Bennet.

Miss Bingley's attention was quite as much engaged in watching Mr. Darcy's progress through *his* book, as in reading her own; and she was perpetually either making some inquiry, or looking at his page. She could not win him, however, to any conversation; he merely answered her question, and read on. At length, quite exhausted by the attempt to be amused with her own book, which she had only chosen because it was the second volume of his,[13] she gave a great yawn and said, "How pleasant it is to spend an evening in this way! I declare after all there is no enjoyment like reading! How much sooner one tires of any thing than of a book!—When I have a house of my own, I shall be miserable if I have not an excellent library."[14]

No one made any reply. She then yawned again, threw aside her book, and cast her eyes round the room in quest of some amusement; when hearing her brother mentioning a ball to Miss Bennet, she turned suddenly towards him and said,

"By the bye, Charles, are you really serious in meditating a dance at Netherfield?—I would advise you, before you determine on it, to consult the wishes of the present party; I am much mistaken if there are not some among us to whom a ball would be rather a punishment than a pleasure."

"If you mean Darcy," cried her brother, "he may go to bed, if he chuses, before it begins—but as for the ball, it is quite a settled thing; and as soon as Nicholls has made white soup[15] enough I shall send round my cards."[16]

"I should like balls infinitely better," she replied, "if they were carried on in a different manner; but there is something insufferably tedious in the usual process of such a meeting. It would surely be much more rational if conversation instead of dancing made the order of the day."

"Much more rational, my dear Caroline, I dare say but it would not be near so much like a ball."[17]

Miss Bingley made no answer; and soon afterwards got up and walked about the room. Her figure was elegant, and she walked

13. Books then were often published in multiple volumes. This was the case with all Jane Austen's novels.

14. One sees here the hopelessness of Miss Bingley's pursuit of Darcy, for her patent insincerity runs completely contrary to his hatred of deceit, and her lack of interest in books goes against his earlier praise of extensive reading for women.

15. *white soup*: a popular soup for parties. It had a long and distinguished pedigree, having been originally part of courtly cookery; its French name was *soupe à la reine*, or "Queen's soup." Its most basic ingredients were almonds and cream; Martha Lloyd, a close family friend of the Austens, left behind a recipe for White Soup that involved almonds, cream, egg yolks, and meat gravy. Nicholls is, as we learn later, the housekeeper; it is she who would be supervising the making of the soup, rather than the cook (though occasionally the two functions were combined in the same person).

16. *cards*: invitations.

17. Bingley's reply suggests that, while often unequal to Darcy, he is more than a match for his sister; it also reveals the absurdity of her statement, and thus the lengths to which she will go in her attempt to say whatever she can that might please Darcy—in this instance she has criticized dancing at balls because he does not like dancing much.

well;[18]—but Darcy, at whom it was all aimed, was still inflexibly studious.[19] In the desperation of her feelings she resolved on one effort more; and, turning to Elizabeth, said,

"Miss Eliza Bennet, let me persuade you to follow my example, and take a turn[20] about the room.—I assure you it is very refreshing after sitting so long in one attitude."[21]

Elizabeth was surprised, but agreed to it immediately. Miss Bingley succeeded no less in the real object of her civility; Mr. Darcy looked up.[22] He was as much awake to the novelty of attention in that quarter as Elizabeth herself could be, and unconsciously closed his book. He was directly invited to join their party, but he declined it, observing, that he could imagine but two motives for their chusing to walk up and down the room together, with either of which motives his joining them would interfere. "What could he mean? she was dying to know what could be his meaning?"—and asked Elizabeth whether she could at all understand him?

"Not at all," was her answer; "but depend upon it, he means to be severe on us, and our surest way of disappointing him, will be to ask nothing about it."

Miss Bingley, however, was incapable of disappointing Mr. Darcy in any thing, and persevered therefore in requiring an explanation of his two motives.

"I have not the smallest objection to explaining them," said he, as soon as she allowed him to speak. "You either chuse this method of passing the evening because you are in each other's confidence and have secret affairs to discuss, or because you are conscious that your figures appear to the greatest advantage in walking;—if the first, I should be completely in your way;—and if the second, I can admire you much better as I sit by the fire."

"Oh! shocking!" cried Miss Bingley. "I never heard any thing so abominable. How shall we punish him for such a speech?"

"Nothing so easy, if you have but the inclination," said Elizabeth. "We can all plague and punish one another. Teaze him—laugh at him.—Intimate as you are, you must know how it is to be done."

18. Miss Bingley turns to using her physical qualities to attract Darcy's attention after she has just shown, through indifference to her book and being made to look foolish in discussion by her brother, how little she could ever hope to attract Darcy through her mental ones.

19. *studious:* devoted to books or study, or intent on a purpose. In this case, it means that Darcy is paying full attention to his book.

20. *take a turn:* walk in a circuit.

21. *attitude:* posture, position.

22. Miss Bingley may wish not only to draw Darcy's attention generally, but also to have him watch herself and Elizabeth engage in an activity in which she could hope to outshine the latter. Miss Bingley, in her earlier list of female accomplishments, said that a young woman must "possess a certain something in her air and manner of walking," and she undoubtedly believes in her own excellence in this department, especially because of her education at a leading ladies' seminary. Such schools instructed their pupils in elegant and attractive manners of standing, sitting, walking, etc.; sometimes these skills were emphasized above almost all other attainments. One of Jane Austen's sisters-in-law went to a fashionable London boarding school that offered minimal academic instruction, but did include training in how to enter and exit a carriage in a becoming manner, for which purpose it installed an actual carriage in the building to allow the students to practice. Books of advice on the best ways of walking, sitting, or performing other motions existed; they could be addressed to men as well as to women, but it was the latter who had most reason to heed them since they were the ones most likely to be noticed and evaluated in these areas.

"But upon my honour I do *not*. I do assure you that my inti-macy has not yet taught me *that*. Teaze calmness of temper and presence of mind! No, no—I feel he may defy us there. And as to laughter, we will not expose ourselves, if you please, by attempt-ing to laugh without a subject. Mr. Darcy may hug himself."[23]

"Mr. Darcy is not to be laughed at!" cried Elizabeth. "That is an uncommon advantage, and uncommon I hope it will con-tinue, for it would be a great loss to *me* to have many such acquaintance. I dearly love a laugh."[24]

"Miss Bingley," said he, "has given me credit for more than can be. The wisest and the best of men, nay, the wisest and best of their actions, may be rendered ridiculous by a person whose first object in life is a joke."

"Certainly," replied Elizabeth—"there are such people, but I hope I am not one of *them*. I hope I never ridicule what is wise or good. Follies and nonsense, whims and inconsistencies *do* divert me, I own, and I laugh at them whenever I can.—But these, I suppose, are precisely what you are without."

"Perhaps that is not possible for any one. But it has been the study of my life to avoid those weaknesses which often expose a strong understanding[25] to ridicule."[26]

"Such as vanity and pride."

"Yes, vanity is a weakness indeed. But pride—where there is a real superiority of mind,[27] pride will be always under good regula-tion."[28]

Elizabeth turned away to hide a smile.

"Your examination of Mr. Darcy is over, I presume," said Miss Bingley;—"and pray what is the result?"

"I am perfectly convinced by it that Mr. Darcy has no defect. He owns[29] it himself without disguise."

"No"—said Darcy, "I have made no such pretension. I have faults enough, but they are not, I hope, of understanding. My temper I dare not vouch for.—It is I believe too little yielding—certainly too little for the convenience of the world. I cannot for-get the follies and vices of others so soon as I ought, nor their offences against myself. My feelings are not puffed about with

23. *hug himself*: congratulate, or feel smug about, himself.

24. Another exchange between Elizabeth and Darcy that illuminates an important theme of the novel, which contains characters who err by taking themselves too seriously, and ones who err by allowing their love of a joke to make them neglect serious matters (Mr. Bennet and Lydia are both, in different ways, examples of the latter). Darcy at times commits the first error, and Elizabeth the second—a difference that mirrors their disagreement here.

This issue also has particular resonance for Jane Austen, who displays throughout her novels the same love of follies and nonsense that Elizabeth avows here, even as her novels also engage continually with serious moral issues. The one truly critical comment she makes about this novel in her correspondence is to say it is "rather too light & bright & sparkling" and might benefit from a little more serious matter (though she is somewhat playful in her suggestions as to what that serious matter might be). This may be one reason why her next novel, *Mansfield Park*, which she composed while finishing this one, is in a distinctly more serious vein.

25. *understanding*: intellect, judgment.

26. A good clue to Darcy's character: he hates weakness, he has continually endeavored to avoid it, and he takes pride in his presumed success.

27. *mind*: character.

28. *under good regulation*: Darcy probably means that such superiority of mind will ensure that a person's pride is always regulated properly and will not become unreasonable. He could also mean that pride, in a superior person, will always have some justification, i.e., conform to regulations for a good character. In either case, he refuses to admit that pride is a weakness, at least for a superior person (like himself). In condemning vanity more than pride Darcy may be relying on the idea that vanity reflects a greater concern with others' opinions (see p. 35, note 16), something Darcy always disdains.

29. *owns*: acknowledges. Elizabeth is being sarcastic, for she clearly disagrees with his defense of pride.

every attempt to move them. My temper would perhaps be called resentful.—My good opinion once lost is lost for ever."[30]

"*That* is a failing indeed!"—cried Elizabeth. "Implacable resentment is a shade[31] in a character. But you have chosen your fault well.—I really cannot *laugh* at it. You are safe from me."

"There is, I believe, in every disposition a tendency to some particular evil, a natural defect, which not even the best education can overcome."

"And *your* defect is a propensity to hate every body."

"And yours," he replied with a smile, "is wilfully to misunderstand them."[32]

"Do let us have a little music,"—cried Miss Bingley, tired of a conversation in which she had no share.[33]—"Louisa, you will not mind my waking Mr. Hurst."

Her sister made not the smallest objection, and the piano forte was opened, and Darcy, after a few moments recollection, was not sorry for it. He began to feel the danger of paying Elizabeth too much attention.

30. In supposedly admitting his flaw, Darcy actually uses language that justifies himself as much as possible. According to him, what he violates is merely the world's "convenience," what he refuses to yield to are "follies and vices" or "offences against myself" (rather than anything more benign), and what his behavior contrasts with is the behavior of those who are "puffed about with every attempt to move them." It could be said that Darcy is here giving his own example of the deceitful "appearance of humility," or "indirect boast," that he had spotted and criticized in Bingley in the previous chapter.

31. *shade:* shadow, i.e., dark or negative spot. The idea of Darcy being a man of implacable resentment is one that fixes itself firmly in Elizabeth's mind. In fact, Darcy has not exactly avowed this quality, though it could be inferred from what he says, and he later proves himself not to be such a man at all, for he does not maintain his resentment of Elizabeth after she harshly rejects him and makes unjust accusations about his character.

32. Both Elizabeth and Darcy have erred, at least partly, in their description of the other. Her description is particularly wrong (however justified her position might be in the argument), for Darcy has neither said he hates everybody, nor does he. He certainly does not hate Elizabeth. Darcy is right that she misunderstands him; where he errs is in thinking her misunderstanding to be a deliberate action or policy of hers, perhaps done in playful provocation—as his smile implies he considers her words to be. In fact, Elizabeth genuinely mistakes his character, in large part because she genuinely dislikes him. That is something he utterly fails to conceive.

33. Miss Bingley's call for music represents her acknowledgement of defeat in her scheme to engage Darcy's attention by asking Elizabeth to join her in her turn about the room, for what resulted from her scheme was a conversation that involved Darcy and Elizabeth almost exclusively, and thus only increased his focus on Elizabeth.

Chapter Twelve

*I*n consequence of an agreement between the sisters, Elizabeth wrote the next morning to her mother, to beg that the carriage[1] might be sent for them in the course of the day. But Mrs. Bennet, who had calculated on her daughters remaining at Netherfield till the following Tuesday, which would exactly finish Jane's week,[2] could not bring herself to receive them with pleasure before. Her answer, therefore, was not propitious, at least not to Elizabeth's wishes, for she was impatient to get home. Mrs. Bennet sent them word that they could not possibly have the carriage before Tuesday; and in her postscript it was added, that if Mr. Bingley and his sister pressed them to stay longer, she could spare them very well.— Against staying longer, however, Elizabeth was positively resolved— nor did she much expect it would be asked; and fearful, on the contrary, as being considered as intruding themselves needlessly long, she urged Jane to borrow Mr. Bingley's carriage immediately, and at length it was settled that their original design of leaving Netherfield that morning should be mentioned, and the request made.

The communication excited many professions of concern; and enough was said of wishing them to stay at least till the following day to work on[3] Jane; and till the morrow, their going was deferred. Miss Bingley was then sorry that she had proposed the delay, for her jealousy and dislike of one sister much exceeded her affection for the other.

The master of the house heard with real sorrow that they were to go so soon, and repeatedly tried to persuade Miss Bennet that it would not be safe for her—that she was not enough recovered; but Jane was firm where she felt herself to be right.[4]

To Mr. Darcy it was welcome intelligence[5]—Elizabeth had been at Netherfield long enough. She attracted him more than he liked—and Miss Bingley was uncivil to *her*, and more teazing[6]

1. *the carriage*: meaning the Bennets' own carriage, which could come to fetch them.

2. Jane arrived on Tuesday, and it is now Saturday; see chronology, p. 714.

3. *work on*: influence, persuade.

4. Jane reveals that there are limits even to her pliability. Significantly, it is not her own welfare but considerations of general good that inspire her to be firm.

5. *intelligence*: news.

6. *teazing*: teasing, or irritating.

than usual to himself. He wisely resolved to be particularly careful that no sign of admiration should *now* escape him, nothing
that could elevate[7] her with the hope of influencing his felicity;[8]
sensible[9] that if such an idea had been suggested, his behaviour
during the last day must have material weight[10] in confirming or
crushing[11] it. Steady to his purpose, he scarcely spoke ten words
to her through the whole of Saturday, and though they were at
one time left by themselves for half an hour, he adhered most
conscientiously to his book, and would not even look at her.

On Sunday, after morning service,[12] the separation, so agreeable to almost all, took place. Miss Bingley's civility to Elizabeth
increased at last very rapidly, as well as her affection for Jane; and
when they parted, after assuring the latter of the pleasure it would
always give her to see her either at Longbourn or Netherfield, and
embracing her most tenderly, she even shook hands with the
former. — Elizabeth took leave of the whole party in the liveliest
spirits.

They were not welcomed home very cordially by their mother.
Mrs. Bennet wondered at their coming, and thought them very
wrong to give so much trouble, and was sure Jane would have
caught cold again. — But their father, though very laconic in his
expressions of pleasure, was really glad to see them; he had felt
their importance in the family circle. The evening conversation,
when they were all assembled, had lost much of its animation,
and almost all its sense, by the absence of Jane and Elizabeth.

They found Mary, as usual, deep in the study of thorough
bass[13] and human nature; and had some new extracts to admire,
and some new observations of thread-bare morality to listen to.[14]
Catherine and Lydia had information for them of a different
sort. Much had been done, and much had been said in the regiment since the preceding Wednesday; several of the officers had
dined lately with their uncle, a private had been flogged,[15] and it
had actually been hinted that Colonel Forster was going to be
married.

7. *elevate*: inspire.

8. *influencing his felicity*: getting him to marry her, which of course would influence in some way his felicity or happiness. Darcy assumes as a matter of course that she would gladly marry him if she could because of his wealth and station. His assumption has a basis in current social realities, for many if not most women of the time would be eager to marry him solely for those reasons.

9. *sensible*: conscious, aware.

10. *material weight*: substantial importance.

11. *crushing*: the use of this term implies that Darcy believes Elizabeth's affections may be so strong that they require such a severe remedy; this in turn would indicate how much he has misread her character.

12. *morning service*: church morning service, something everyone would have attended.

13. *thorough bass*: a type of bass part or line in music. More generally, the study of musical harmony. Mary's studying music in this way is a sign of her pedantry.

14. In other words, trite sayings or messages she is repeating from books.

15. Flogging, and other types of brutal punishment, were common in the army at the time, as is signaled by the subject's simply being mentioned in passing here. Some of the reasons for this are indicated by a statement of the leading British commander of the time, the Duke of Wellington, in which he described his troops as "the very scum of the earth. People talk of their enlisting from their fine military feeling—all stuff—no such thing. Some of our men enlist from having got bastard children—some for minor offences—many more for drink." The statement is partly a true description, for serving in the ranks of the army was held in such low regard that generally only those who were desperate or in trouble, often with the law, tended to join. This produced a strong criminal atmosphere among the soldiers, one that made it hard to prevent them from misbehavior, such as looting or violence against civilians, without harsh punishments. At the same time, Wellington's words also reveal the aristocratic disdain for the men among the officers, which made them very willing to employ such punishments.

Even with all that, the period did witness increased protest against the use of flogging. Jane Austen's own view of the matter is unknown, but she probably intends at least to show the crassness and shallowness of Lydia and Catherine by having them treat a flogging as merely a choice piece of gossip.

Chapter Thirteen

I hope, my dear," said Mr. Bennet to his wife, as they were at breakfast the next morning, "that you have ordered a good dinner to-day, because I have reason to expect an addition to our family party."

"Who do you mean, my dear? I know of nobody that is coming I am sure, unless Charlotte Lucas should happen to call in, and I hope *my* dinners are good enough for her. I do not believe she often sees such at home."

"The person of whom I speak, is a gentleman and a stranger."

Mrs. Bennet's eyes sparkled. — "A gentleman and a stranger! It is Mr. Bingley I am sure. Why Jane — you never dropt a word of this; you sly[1] thing! Well, I am sure I shall be extremely glad to see Mr. Bingley. — But — good lord! how unlucky! there is not a bit of fish to be got to-day.[2] Lydia, my love, ring the bell. I must speak to Hill, this moment."[3]

"It is *not* Mr. Bingley," said her husband; "it is a person whom I never saw in the whole course of my life."

This roused a general astonishment; and he had the pleasure of being eagerly questioned by his wife and five daughters at once.

After amusing himself some time with their curiosity, he thus explained. "About a month ago I received this letter, and about a fortnight ago I answered it, for I thought it a case of some delicacy, and requiring early attention.[4] It is from my cousin, Mr. Collins, who, when I am dead, may turn you all out of this house as soon as he pleases."[5]

"Oh! my dear," cried his wife, "I cannot bear to hear that mentioned. Pray do not talk of that odious man. I do think it is the hardest thing in the world, that your estate should be entailed away from your own children; and I am sure if I had been you, I should have tried long ago to do something or other about it."

1.   *sly*: silent, uncommunicative.

2.   No fish is to be had because it is Monday. Fish that could be bought would come from the previous day's catch—lack of refrigeration would cause older fish to spoil—and fishermen would not have gone out on Sunday.

3.   Hill is the chief servant (who would be summoned by the bell); her status is indicated by her being called by her last name rather than her first name, as lower servants would be called. In clamoring to summon her at this moment, before everyone has finished breakfast, Mrs. Bennet reveals her lack of self-control and of consideration for others.

4.   *early attention*: what Mr. Bennet calls answering a letter at least two weeks after it arrived. This indicates his indolence. He has also told the others of their visitor only on the day of the visitor's arrival, though he has known of it for a month.

5.   Mr. Collins is to inherit Mr. Bennet's property, which would include the house. Mr. Collins is thus Mr. Bennet's closest male relative who has a common paternal descent (an entail that cannot pass to a woman also cannot pass through a woman, which means that Mr. Collins's claim cannot derive from a mother or grandmother). Some have therefore wondered why the two men do not have the same last name. The answer is that an ancestor of one of them must have changed his name, a relatively common procedure at the time. This could happen through marriage: a favorite novel of Jane Austen's, Fanny Burney's *Cecilia*, centers around a legal provision by which the heroine can inherit a large fortune only if any husband of hers takes her venerable family name. It also happened through adoption: Jane Austen's brother Edward (father of Fanny Austen Knight, depicted on cover), who had been adopted by very wealthy cousins, had to change his last name to theirs, Knight, in order to inherit their estate. In *Emma* an important character, Frank Churchill, has changed his name for the same reason.

Jane and Elizabeth attempted to explain to her the nature of an entail. They had often attempted it before, but it was a subject on which Mrs. Bennet was beyond the reach of reason;[6] and she continued to rail bitterly against the cruelty of settling an estate away from a family of five daughters, in favour of a man whom nobody cared anything about.

"It certainly is a most iniquitous affair," said Mr. Bennet, "and nothing can clear Mr. Collins from the guilt of inheriting Longbourn. But if you will listen to his letter, you may perhaps be a little softened by his manner of expressing himself."

"No, that I am sure I shall not; and I think it was very impertinent of him to write to you at all, and very hypocritical. I hate such false friends. Why could not he keep on quarrelling with you, as his father did before him?"

"Why, indeed, he does seem to have had some filial scruples on that head, as you will hear."

> *Hunsford, near Westerham, Kent,[7]*
> *15th October.*

DEAR SIR,

The disagreement subsisting between yourself and my late honoured father, always gave me much uneasiness, and since I have had the misfortune to lose him, I have frequently wished to heal the breach; but for some time I was kept back by my own doubts, fearing lest it might seem disrespectful to his memory for me to be on good terms with any one, with whom it had always pleased him to be at variance.—"There, Mrs. Bennet."—My mind however is now made up on the subject, for having received ordination[8] at Easter, I have been so fortunate as to be distinguished by the patronage of the Right Honourable Lady Catherine de Bourgh, widow of Sir Lewis de Bourgh,[9] whose bounty and beneficence has preferred[10] me to the valuable rectory of this parish,[11] where it shall be my earnest endeavour to demean myself with grateful respect towards her Ladyship, and be ever ready to perform those rites and ceremonies which are instituted by the Church of England. As a clergyman, moreover, I feel it my duty to promote and establish the

6.   What makes Mrs. Bennet unreasonable is that an entail was a standard legal device of the time, and there is nothing Mr. Bennet can do about it. The entail gives him only a life interest in the estate; he can enjoy its income as long as he is alive, but he can make little if any change in the character of the estate, and he cannot alter the rules for determining the next heir. A father's inability, to his regret, to make such changes forms the starting point for the plot of Jane Austen's previous novel, *Sense and Sensibility*.

7.   Kent is the county at the southeastern corner of England; Westerham is a town in northwest Kent; Hunsford is fictitious. See map, p. 745.

8.   *ordination:* as a clergyman.

9.   Sir Lewis was either a knight or a baronet (a baronet, unlike a knight, would pass on his title to a descendant). A passage later in the book suggests that he was a knight (see p. 647, note 35). His widow, however, does not derive her title from him; if so, she would be Lady De Bourgh. To include her first name in her title a woman had to be the daughter of a duke, marquess, or earl, the three highest ranks of the Peerage or nobility (it later turns out to be an earl). Since the number of such nobles was small, with only around 125 at this rank in England at the time, Lady Catherine has a very high pedigree, something in which Mr. Collins takes great pride. This pride can be seen in his calling her "the Right Honourable," for this designation was obligatory only for the earl himself or his wife, and was usually omitted for an earl's daughter, though it could be used for her. Jane Austen herself was attentive to these matters: in commenting on a draft of a novel written by her niece, she criticizes the latter for using "the Honourable" in a place it would not normally be used (Aug. 10, 1814).

10.   *preferred:* advanced, promoted.

11.   The rectory is the position as rector, or clergyman. The right to appoint someone to a clerical position, known as an advowson, was possessed by a person or institution, and could be bought and sold like other forms of property. About half of all advowsons were in the hands of wealthy landowners like Lady Catherine; other holders included individual clergymen, Church Bishops, the Crown, and the Universities.

Part of the reason for Mr. Collins's extreme gratitude and deference toward Lady Catherine is his good luck in receiving this appointment—on a mere chance recommendation, without the strong personal connections or financial transactions usually necessay—and in getting it so soon after his ordination (see p. 130, and p. 131, notes 9 and 10). Such appointments, thanks to an oversupply of clergy at the time, were hard to obtain: only 20% of clergy obtained one within five years of ordination, while almost half never got one and had to work all their lives as underpaid assistants to those with positions.

blessing of peace in all families within the reach of my influence;
and on these grounds I flatter myself that my present overtures of
good-will are highly commendable, and that the circumstance of
my being next in the entail of Longbourn estate, will be kindly over-
looked on your side, and not lead you to reject the offered olive
branch. I cannot be otherwise than concerned at being the means
of injuring your amiable daughters, and beg leave to apologise for
it, as well as to assure you of my readiness to make them every pos-
sible amends,—but of this hereafter. If you should have no objec-
tion to receive me into your house, I propose myself the satisfaction
of waiting on[12] you and your family, Monday, November 18th, by
four o'clock, and shall probably trespass on your hospitality till the
Saturday se'night[13] following, which I can do without any incon-
venience, as Lady Catherine is far from objecting to my occasional
absence on a Sunday, provided that some other clergyman is
engaged to do the duty of the day.[14] I remain, dear sir, with respect-
ful compliments to your lady and daughters, your well-wisher and
friend,

WILLIAM COLLINS.[15]

"At four o'clock, therefore, we may expect this peace-making
gentleman," said Mr. Bennet, as he folded up the letter.[16] "He
seems to be a most conscientious and polite young man, upon my
word; and I doubt not will prove a valuable acquaintance, especially if Lady Catherine should be so indulgent as to let him
come to us again."

"There is some sense in what he says about the girls however;
and if he is disposed to make them any amends, I shall not be the
person to discourage him."[17]

"Though it is difficult," said Jane, "to guess in what way he can
mean to make us the atonement he thinks our due,[18] the wish is
certainly to his credit."

Elizabeth was chiefly struck with his extraordinary deference
for Lady Catherine, and his kind intention of christening, marrying, and burying his parishioners whenever it were required.[19]

"He must be an oddity, I think," said she. "I cannot make him

12. *waiting on:* calling upon.

13. *se'night:* seven nights, i.e., one week. This term was a common one of the time, but, unlike its companion term of fortnight for two weeks, it has not survived. In his plans, Mr. Collins is proposing to stay a total of twelve days, including one Sunday.

14. *duty of the day:* the Sunday service. It was not unusual for clergy to get substitutes to perform the service. In fact, clerical absenteeism was so prevalent in this period that many clergy would not have perceived any need to explain or justify their ability to be absent.

15. This letter introduces Mr. Collins, one of the most amusing of Jane Austen's comic creations. The formal and long-winded phrasing of the letter, along with its obsequious substance, give a good hint of his character. Mr. Collins also belongs to a profession, clergyman, that figures in all of Jane Austen's novels. Clergy were a basic part of rural society, and she would know their affairs intimately since both her father and her eldest brother were clergymen. It should not be imagined, however, that she intends to satirize the clergy by making their representative in this novel so foolish, for in other novels she creates admirable clerical characters.

16. The exchange following this letter, in which the various members of the family all react in distinctive ways, is an excellent example of Jane Austen's artistic technique of having characters reveal themselves in everything they say or do, no matter how brief or trivial.

17. This is spoken by Mrs. Bennet. As the mistress of the house she would normally speak after the master; in addition, the words correspond to her way of thinking. In fact, the sequence of reactions in the family follows exactly the prevailing rules of precedence and authority, with first the father speaking, then the mother, and then the children in order of seniority.

18. *thinks our due:* Jane's wording indicates that many would not think one had to atone for benefiting from an entail, since it was such a normal procedure and nobody, unless they were as unreasonable as Mrs. Bennet, would think that a legal heir had done anything unjust.

19. These were the most essential of the Church "rites and ceremonies" that Mr. Collins says he is ready to perform. In labeling this a "kind intention" Elizabeth is being sarcastic, for Mr. Collins seemed to boast of his willingness to fulfill the basic requirements of his job, which requirements were generally very light.

out.—There is something very pompous in his stile.—And what can he mean by apologizing for being next in the entail?—We cannot suppose he would help it, if he could.—Can he be a sensible man, sir?"[20]

"No, my dear; I think not. I have great hopes of finding him quite the reverse. There is a mixture of servility and self-importance in his letter, which promises well.[21] I am impatient to see him."

"In point of composition," said Mary, "his letter does not seem defective. The idea of the olive branch perhaps is not wholly new,[22] yet I think it is well expressed."

To Catherine and Lydia, neither the letter nor its writer were in any degree interesting. It was next to impossible that their cousin should come in a scarlet coat, and it was now some weeks since they had received pleasure from the society of a man in any other colour. As for their mother, Mr. Collins's letter had done away much of her ill-will, and she was preparing to see him with a degree of composure, which astonished her husband and daughters.[23]

Mr. Collins was punctual to his time, and was received with great politeness by the whole family. Mr. Bennet indeed said little; but the ladies were ready enough to talk, and Mr. Collins seemed neither in need of encouragement, nor inclined to be silent himself. He was a tall, heavy looking young man of five and twenty. His air was grave and stately,[24] and his manners were very formal. He had not been long seated before he complimented Mrs. Bennet on having so fine a family of daughters, said he had heard much of their beauty, but that, in this instance, fame had fallen short of the truth; and added, that he did not doubt her seeing them all in due time well disposed of in marriage. This gallantry[25] was not much to the taste of some of his hearers, but Mrs. Bennet, who quarrelled with no compliments, answered most readily,

"You are very kind, sir, I am sure; and I wish with all my heart it may prove so; for else they will be destitute enough. Things are settled so oddly."

"You allude perhaps to the entail of this estate."

20. *sir*: a sign of the formal nature of the society. We will see children regularly addressing parents in this way, even when a child is as close to a parent as Elizabeth is to her father.

21. *promises well*: meaning that he promises to provide amusement for Mr. Bennet.

22. Of course, the idea of the olive branch symbolizing an offering of peace is as old and hackneyed an idea as there is.

23. There will be many other incidents in which Mrs. Bennet's mood and opinions will change quickly and completely, often with little good reason.

24. *stately*: lofty, imposing.

25. *gallantry*: his praise of women. This was a common practice of the time, and could take absurdly effusive forms. In a letter Jane Austen tells her sister that a man, speaking of two trees in their yard that were recently felled in a storm, attributed the trees' falling to their grief at the sister's absence. Jane Austen comments, with evident sarcasm, "Was not it a gallant idea?—It never occurred to me before, but I dare say it was so" (Nov. 20, 1800). In a youthful writing ("A Collection of Letters") she offers a comical version of such gallantry when she has a man say to a woman, "You are more than Mortal. You are an angel. You are Venus herself. In short Madam you are the prettiest Girl I ever saw in my Life." One can presume that in this case it is the most intelligent daughters, Elizabeth and Jane, who find Mr. Collins's gallantry least to their taste.

"Ah! sir, I do indeed. It is a grievous affair to my poor girls, you must confess. Not that I mean to find fault with *you*, for such things I know are all chance in this world. There is no knowing how estates will go when once they come to be entailed."[26]

"I am very sensible, madam, of the hardship to my fair cousins,—and could say much on the subject, but that I am cautious of appearing forward and precipitate. But I can assure the young ladies that I come prepared to admire them. At present I will not say more, but perhaps when we are better acquainted——"

He was interrupted by a summons to dinner;[27] and the girls smiled on each other. They were not the only objects of Mr. Collins's admiration. The hall, the dining-room, and all its furniture[28] were examined and praised; and his commendation of every thing would have touched Mrs. Bennet's heart, but for the mortifying supposition of his viewing it all as his own future property.[29] The dinner too in its turn was highly admired; and he begged to know to which of his fair cousins, the excellence of its cookery was owing. But here he was set right by Mrs. Bennet, who assured him with some asperity that they were very well able to keep a good cook, and that her daughters had nothing to do in the kitchen.[30] He begged pardon for having displeased her. In a softened tone she declared herself not at all offended; but he continued to apologise for about a quarter of an hour.

26. In fact, entails were in general carefully drawn up to leave little to chance, so it would not be difficult to know what resulted from them. Part of the point of the entail was to secure the family property and prevent the occurrence of anything untoward or unpredictable, such as a particular heir selling or giving it to someone outside the family.

27. This shows the Bennets' earlier dinner hours, compared to those at Netherfield. Mr. Collins has arrived at four, and there has been only a short conversation before dinner. In her own letters Jane Austen most often mentions eating dinner around five; on one occasion when she eats at six she goes on to explain the reason why it was so late (Aug. 27, 1805).

28. *furniture:* furnishings; the term then could mean anything with which the room was furnished, including items on the wall or on tables and shelves.

29. As the heir to the estate Mr. Collins will also receive the house and much of its contents.

30. Mrs. Bennet has already shown the pride she takes in her daughters not having to do anything in the kitchen. It is possible that Mr. Collins asked the question because he, thinking of a prospective wife among the Bennet girls, wishes to find out about their culinary skills. Since almost no clergyman would enjoy the two thousand a year income of Mr. Bennet, and thus be able to afford as many servants as the Bennets, it is likely that a mistress of his house would need to play some role in the kitchen. Mr. Collins's question may also reflect his own less affluent background (revealed shortly), for this would make him less accustomed to living arrangements that allowed the women of the family to avoid household tasks.

His desire to have someone to manage his household may be a central reason why, as he indicates soon, he is so eager to marry. At this time, it was difficult for a man to run his own household. This spurred men either to get a female relative to perform this function, as Bingley does, or to marry someone who would. The one exception to this could be men, like Darcy, who were wealthy enough to afford a highly professional housekeeper, but Mr. Collins is certainly not in this category.

Chapter Fourteen

*D*uring dinner, Mr. Bennet scarcely spoke at all; but when the servants were withdrawn, he thought it time to have some conversation with his guest, and therefore started a subject in which he expected him to shine,[1] by observing that he seemed very fortunate in his patroness. Lady Catherine de Bourgh's attention to his wishes, and consideration for his comfort, appeared very remarkable. Mr. Bennet could not have chosen better. Mr. Collins was eloquent in her praise. The subject elevated him to more than usual solemnity of manner, and with a most important[2] aspect[3] he protested that he had never in his life witnessed such behaviour in a person of rank[4]—such affability[5] and condescension,[6] as he had himself experienced from Lady Catherine. She had been graciously pleased to approve of both the discourses,[7] which he had already had the honour of preaching before her. She had also asked him twice to dine at Rosings, and had sent for him only the Saturday before, to make up her pool of quadrille[8] in the evening. Lady Catherine was reckoned proud by many people he knew, but he had never seen any thing but affability in her. She had always spoken to him as she would to any other gentleman; she made not the smallest objection to his joining in the society of the neighbourhood,[9] nor to his leaving his parish occasionally for a week or two, to visit his relations. She had even condescended to advise him to marry as soon as he could, provided he chose with discretion; and had once paid him a visit in his humble parsonage; where she had perfectly approved all the alterations he had been making, and had even vouchsafed[10] to suggest some herself,—some shelves in the closets[11] up stairs.

"That is all very proper and civil, I am sure," said Mrs. Bennet, "and I dare say she is a very agreeable woman. It is a pity that great ladies[12] in general are not more like her. Does she live near you, sir?"

1.   *shine:* in this case, speak foolishly or absurdly and thus be amusing to Mr. Bennet.

2.   *important:* pompous, having an air of importance.

3.   *aspect:* look or expression.

4.   *of rank:* of high rank.

5.   *affability:* courtesy, mildness — especially of a superior toward an inferior.

6.   *condescension:* this word, along with the words "condescend" and "condescending," are favorites of Mr. Collins, especially in relation to Lady Catherine. He means them as words of praise, which the words could be at this time. Originally they meant voluntary descent from superiority or even humble submission; by this time the words also denoted friendliness and attention toward those of lesser position, often combined with a continued air of superiority. In this hierarchical society, such a sense of superiority was often considered natural and right for a person of high position, so even patronizing concern for others could be admired. At the same time, even by the standards of the day condescension could be taken too far, as turns out to be the case with Lady Catherine. Mr. Collins's failure to appreciate this and his use of "condescension" purely as commendation thus signal the extent of his foolish sycophancy.

7.   *discourses:* sermons.

8.   *quadrille:* a card game with affinities to bridge; see p. 305, note 41.

9.   That is, socializing with his neighbors. He does not mean joining in rich or fashionable society; this meaning of the word "society" was only then coming into vogue.

10.   *vouchsafed:* deigned, condescended.

11.   *closets:* this probably refers to small rooms, the standard meaning of closet then. In a letter Jane Austen speaks of "a Closet full of shelves, so full indeed that there is nothing else in it, & should therefore be called a Cupboard rather than a Closet I suppose" (May 17, 1799). Her words indicate that the current meaning of closet was beginning to come into use, but was still not truly accepted.
    Normally a person of Lady Catherine's high social position would not bother to dispense advice on such a mundane subject.

12.   *great ladies:* ladies of high rank.

"The garden in which stands my humble abode,[13] is separated only by a lane from Rosings Park, her ladyship's residence."

"I think you said she was a widow, sir? has she any family?"

"She has one only daughter, the heiress of Rosings, and of very extensive property."

"Ah!" cried Mrs. Bennet, shaking her head, "then she is better off than many girls. And what sort of young lady is she? is she handsome?"

"She is a most charming young lady indeed. Lady Catherine herself says that in point of true beauty, Miss De Bourgh is far superior to the handsomest of her sex; because there is that in her features which marks the young woman of distinguished birth. She is unfortunately of a sickly constitution, which has prevented her making that progress in many accomplishments, which she could not otherwise have failed of; as I am informed by the lady who superintended her education, and who still resides with them. But she is perfectly amiable,[14] and often condescends to drive by my humble abode in her little phaeton[15] and ponies."

"Has she been presented? I do not remember her name among the ladies at court."[16]

"Her indifferent[17] state of health unhappily prevents her being in town;[18] and by that means, as I told Lady Catherine myself one day, has deprived the British court of its brightest ornament. Her ladyship seemed pleased with the idea, and you may imagine that I am happy on every occasion to offer those little delicate compliments which are always acceptable to ladies. I have more than once observed to Lady Catherine, that her charming daughter seemed born to be a duchess, and that the most elevated rank, instead of giving her consequence,[19] would be adorned by her.[20] — These are the kind of little things which please her ladyship, and it is a sort of attention which I conceive myself peculiarly[21] bound to pay."

"You judge very properly," said Mr. Bennet, "and it is happy for you that you possess the talent of flattering with delicacy. May I ask whether these pleasing attentions proceed from the impulse of the moment, or are the result of previous study?"[22]

13. *humble abode:* a favorite phrase of Mr. Collins for his home. His language abounds in clichés, a practice Jane Austen always scorns, either in her letters or her novels, and presents as a sign of foolishness. Mr. Collins also tends to repeat certain pet phrases, another sign of his mental vacuity.

14. *amiable:* a common term of praise. It had a broader meaning then, signifying general kindness and friendliness.

15. *phaeton:* a type of open carriage; see p. 293, note 27, and illustration on p. 291.

16. Being presented at court was a standard aristocratic procedure; for young women of that rank it usually happened around seventeen or eighteen and marked their entry into fashionable adult society. The presentation itself was a formal, strictly regulated ceremony that culminated in a bow or curtsy before the monarch. The names of those presented were on a Court List, which would be published and thus be accessible to curious members of the public like Mrs. Bennet.

17. *indifferent:* mediocre.

18. *town:* London. London was the location of the court, and the center of aristocratic social life.

19. *consequence:* importance, distinction.

20. His meaning is that if Miss De Bourgh were elevated to a higher rank, it would not be the rank that would raise her importance, but she who would improve or embellish the rank. This gives a taste of the overdone gallantry of Mr. Collins that was mentioned in the last chapter.

21. *peculiarly:* particularly.

22. *are the result of previous study:* have been learned or memorized beforehand. Mr. Bennet is asking such a silly question in the hope that Mr. Collins will give an even sillier answer, which he does.

"They arise chiefly from what is passing at the time, and though I sometimes amuse myself with suggesting and arranging such little elegant compliments as may be adapted to ordinary occasions, I always wish to give them as unstudied an air as possible."

Mr. Bennet's expectations were fully answered. His cousin was as absurd as he had hoped, and he listened to him with the keenest enjoyment, maintaining at the same time the most resolute composure of countenance, and except in an occasional glance at Elizabeth, requiring no partner in his pleasure.

By tea-time[23] however the dose[24] had been enough, and Mr. Bennet was glad to take his guest into the drawing-room again, and when tea was over, glad to invite him to read aloud to the ladies.[25] Mr. Collins readily assented, and a book was produced; but on beholding it, (for every thing announced it to be from a circulating library,)[26] he started back, and begging pardon, protested that he never read novels.[27] — Kitty stared at him, and Lydia exclaimed. — Other books were produced, and after some deliberation he chose Fordyce's Sermons.[28] Lydia gaped as he opened the volume, and before he had, with very monotonous solemnity, read three pages, she interrupted him with,

"Do you know, mama, that my uncle Philips talks of turning away Richard,[29] and if he does, Colonel Forster will hire him. My aunt told me so herself on Saturday. I shall walk to Meryton tomorrow to hear more about it, and to ask when Mr. Denny comes back from town."

Lydia was bid by her two eldest sisters to hold her tongue; but Mr. Collins, much offended, laid aside his book, and said,

"I have often observed how little young ladies are interested by books of a serious stamp, though written solely for their benefit. It amazes me, I confess; — for certainly, there can be nothing so advantageous to them as instruction. But I will no longer importune my young cousin."[30]

Then turning to Mr. Bennet, he offered himself as his antagonist at backgammon. Mr. Bennet accepted the challenge, observing that he acted very wisely in leaving the girls to their own trifling amusements. Mrs. Bennet and her daughters apologised most

23. *tea-time:* a normal part of the daily routine, occurring at some point after dinner. It could include other beverages such as coffee, and usually involved something light to eat as well.

24. *dose:* dose of Mr. Collins's absurdity.

25. Reading aloud was a popular means of passing the time; often the listeners would perform other activities, such as needlework. Numerous letters of Jane Austen attest to the frequency of the practice in her family. Reading aloud was also a valued skill, one that was taught in schools. In a letter Jane Austen complains that her mother, in reading *Pride and Prejudice* aloud, fails to do it justice (Feb. 4, 1813). Her brother Henry, in a biographical notice after Jane Austen's death, said, "She read aloud with very great taste and effect. Her own works, probably, were never heard to so much advantage as from her own mouth."

26. Novels, because of their popularity, were the standard fare at circulating libraries, which were commercial enterprises.

27. Novels at the time were scorned and denounced by many, either as intellectually frivolous or as morally corrupting. Denunciation of novels, with an exception sometimes made for a few better novels, is standard in almost every female conduct book of the time, even as these books praise other types of books and call for women to be well read. The charge of immorality derived particularly from novels' focus on romance and sexual passion, often presented in a sensationalist style; this would make a clergyman like Mr. Collins especially likely to shun them.

28. *Fordyce's Sermons:* James Fordyce's *Sermons to Young Women*, a widely read book of the time. Collections of sermons were often issued in book form. Such choice of material could be considered presumptuous of Mr. Collins, for he is effectively taking it upon himself to preach good conduct to his cousins, on the first evening of his acquaintance with them and in front of their father, who is supposed to be in charge of such matters.

29. *Richard:* a servant. Lower servants would be called simply by their first name, which one would never do for anyone of a higher status who was not an intimate relation or acquaintance.

30. This scene, in opposing Mr. Collins and Lydia, presents a comical contrast between two opposing extremes of character. The choice of Fordyce is appropriate, for his sermons were strongly moralistic and present a picture of ideal womanhood which stands opposed to the character of Lydia Bennet in almost every way. His sermons included a particularly vehement denunciation of novels, in which he says that certain novels, "which we are assured (for we have not read them) are in their nature so shameful, in their tendency so

civilly for Lydia's interruption, and promised that it should not occur again, if he would resume his book; but Mr. Collins, after assuring them that he bore his young cousin no ill will, and should never resent her behaviour as any affront, seated himself at another table with Mr. Bennet, and prepared for backgammon.

pestiferous, and contain such rank treason against the royalty of Virtue, such horrible violation of all decorum, that she who can bear to peruse them must in her soul be a prostitute, let her reputation in life be what it will . . ."

The choice of Fordyce may also be a subtle literary reference by Jane Austen to the popular comedy, *The Rivals* (1775), of Richard Brinsley Sheridan. Sheridan's play centers around a young woman, named Lydia, who has been infected with foolish romantic notions derived from novels (just as Lydia Bennet's later foolish conduct will be like that seen in many heroines of novels). In contrast to this character in the play stands the father of her betrothed, whose hatred of novels leads him to call the libraries that abound with them, "an evergreen tree of diabolical knowledge." In one scene Lydia, perceiving his imminent arrival and knowing his attitude, hastens to hide the many novels in her possession and instead to lay out books of a more serious stamp. The most prominent of these latter is *Fordyce's Sermons*, which (despite having had pages ripped out of it by the hairdresser) is laid open to a section called "Sobriety."

Such a rift over reading matter also has serious implications for Jane Austen, for it touches on matters close to her heart as both a writer and an avid reader. She always defended novels as a literary form, even before becoming a novelist herself. This attitude, along with her awareness of the negative attitudes toward them, appears in a letter discussing a subscription to a local library: "As an inducement to subscribe Mrs. Martin [the person in charge of the library] tells us that her Collection is not to consist only of Novels, but of every kind of Literature, &c. &c—She might have spared this pretension to *our* family, who are great Novel-readers & not ashamed of being so;—but it was necessary I suppose to the self-consequence of half her Subscribers" (Dec. 18, 1798).

Her first novel *Northanger Abbey* continues this point with a lengthy aside defending novels. She laments the denigration suffered by novelists: "Although our productions have afforded more extensive and unaffected pleasure than those of any other literary corporation in the world, no species of composition has been so much decried." She goes on to denounce many other writings and to say that novels are works "in which the greatest powers of the mind are displayed, in which the most thorough knowledge of human nature, the happiest delineation of its varieties, the liveliest effusions of wit and humour are conveyed to the world in the best chosen language."

This does not mean, however, that she shares Lydia's scorn for other types of writing. She often read, and praised, other types, including sermons or other works with religious themes. In one letter she declared, "I am very fond of Sherlock's Sermons, prefer them to almost any"—with the words "almost any" suggesting that she had sampled other books of sermons as well (Sept. 28, 1814). Her own works also show her examining the same sorts of weighty ethical issues that might be found in sermons, and thus demonstrating that moral seriousness and the novel are quite compatible.

Chapter Fifteen

 M r. Collins was not a sensible man, and the deficiency of nature[1] had been but little assisted by education or society;[2] the greatest part of his life having been spent under the guidance of an illiterate[3] and miserly father; and though he belonged to one of the universities,[4] he had merely kept the necessary terms,[5] without forming at it any useful acquaintance.[6] The subjection in which his father had brought him up, had given him originally great humility of manner, but it was now a good deal counteracted by the self-conceit of a weak head, living in retirement,[7] and the consequential feelings of early and unexpected prosperity.[8] A fortunate chance had recommended him to Lady Catherine de Bourgh when the living[9] of Hunsford was vacant; and the respect which he felt for her high rank, and his veneration for her as his patroness, mingling with a very good opinion of himself, of his authority as a clergyman, and his rights as a rector,[10] made him altogether a mixture of pride and obsequiousness, self-importance and humility.

Having now a good house and very sufficient income, he intended to marry; and in seeking a reconciliation with the Longbourn family he had a wife in view, as he meant to chuse one of the daughters, if he found them as handsome and amiable as they were represented by common report. This was his plan of amends—of atonement—for inheriting their father's estate; and he thought it an excellent one, full of eligibility[11] and suitableness, and excessively generous and disinterested on his own part.[12]

His plan did not vary on seeing them.—Miss Bennet's lovely face confirmed his views,[13] and established[14] all his strictest notions of what was due to seniority;[15] and for the first evening *she* was his settled choice. The next morning, however, made an alteration; for in a quarter of an hour's tête-à-tête with Mrs. Bennet before breakfast, a conversation beginning with his parsonage-

1. *the deficiency of nature*: his natural or innate deficiency (i.e., of sense).

2. Meaning society or education have done little to make him more sensible.

3. *illiterate*: ignorant or unlearned (rather than unable to read at all).

4. Meaning he attended either Oxford or Cambridge, the only universities in England then. Their main function was to train the Anglican clergy. They would offer scholarships to some students without money, which may be why Mr. Collins was able to go despite his miserly father.

5. That is, he only remained the number of terms needed to obtain his degree; little besides such residency was required by the universities, whose exams were very lax. A similar laxity prevailed in the Church as regards the exams for becoming ordained, which were taken after getting a University degree.

6. Meeting people who would provide valuable connections or patronage was a central element of going to university.

7. *retirement*: seclusion; it usually implied a quiet, rural life. The idea here may be that seclusion has kept his self-conceit from being challenged.

8. That is, his prosperity gave him consequential, i.e. self-important, feelings.

9. *living*: a clerical position, so called because it provided a yearly income. Most livings were bestowed through personal connections, sometimes also involving money: Jane Austen's father received his because a wealthy uncle purchased it for him. Mr. Collins seems not to have needed this, though he does repay his patroness in a sense through his extreme flattery and servility.

10. *rights as a rector*: a rector had the rights to all the tithes in his parish; a vicar, the other main type of clergymen, had rights to only some of the tithes. Thus Mr. Collins has reason to feel especially fortunate in his position.

11. *eligibility*: fitness or worthiness to be chosen.

12. It does have generous elements since Mr. Collins, a rector who will eventually inherit a good estate, could hope to find a wife with a larger fortune than the Bennet girls, though locating her would likely take more time.

13. *views*: expectations.

14. *established*: confirmed, settled.

15. It was often considered best if daughters married in order of seniority. In some families the parents might even discourage the marriage of younger daughters before an elder was married; this would be to prevent the younger ones from competing with the elder and thereby lessening her chances (of course, Mr. and Mrs. Bennet are too lax as parents to bother with such rules). A comical story from Jane Austen's youth, "Three Sisters," satirizes the competitiveness between sisters that could result from these worries; in it the eldest sister decides to marry a man she dislikes out of fear that, if she refuses,

house,[16] and leading naturally to the avowal of his hopes, that a mistress for it might be found at Longbourn, produced from her, amid very complaisant smiles and general encouragement, a caution against the very Jane he had fixed on.—"As to her *younger* daughters she could not take upon her to say—she could not positively answer—but she did not *know* of any prepossession;[17]—her *eldest* daughter, she must just mention—she felt it incumbent on her to hint, was likely to be very soon engaged."

Mr. Collins had only to change from Jane to Elizabeth—and it was soon done—done while Mrs. Bennet was stirring the fire.[18] Elizabeth, equally next to Jane in birth and beauty,[19] succeeded her of course.

Mrs. Bennet treasured up the hint, and trusted that she might soon have two daughters married; and the man whom she could not bear to speak of the day before, was now high in her good graces.

Lydia's intention of walking to Meryton was not forgotten; every sister except Mary agreed to go with her; and Mr. Collins was to attend them, at the request of Mr. Bennet, who was most anxious to get rid of him, and have his library to himself; for thither Mr. Collins had followed him after breakfast, and there he would continue, nominally engaged with one of the largest folios[20] in the collection, but really talking to Mr. Bennet, with little cessation, of his house and garden at Hunsford. Such doings discomposed Mr. Bennet exceedingly. In his library he had been always sure of leisure and tranquillity; and though prepared, as he told Elizabeth, to meet with folly and conceit in every other room in the house, he was used to be free from them there; his civility, therefore, was most prompt in inviting Mr. Collins to join his daughters in their walk; and Mr. Collins, being in fact much better fitted for a walker than a reader, was extremely well pleased to close his large book, and go.

In pompous nothings on his side, and civil assents on that of his cousins, their time passed till they entered Meryton. The attention of the younger ones was then no longer to be gained by *him*. Their eyes were immediately wandering up in the street in quest of the officers, and nothing less than a very smart bonnet indeed, or a really new muslin[21] in a shop window, could recall them.[22]

he will ask one of her younger sisters and cause one of them to be the first one married in the family.

In Mr. Collins's case, his strict adherence to the principle of seniority is reinforced by his perceiving that the eldest of the Bennet daughters is also the most beautiful.

16. *parsonage-house*: residence for a parson, or clergyman. Mr. Collins would have received this with the living. For a picture of the parsonage house of Jane Austen's father, see p. 287.

17. *prepossession*: prior inclination or feeling; in this case, it refers to an existing romantic attachment of the girls.

18. The suddenness of the switch, indicated by the reference to such a brief action as stirring the fire, testifies to the shallow character of Mr. Collins's affection.

It is also possible that the reference to stirring the fire is meant by Jane Austen to suggest—at least ironically—the flame of amorous passion. If so, it would constitute one of the only examples of symbolism in her works.

19. Meaning that Elizabeth is next oldest and next most beautiful.

20. *folios*: books consisting of sheets of paper that were folded once, thereby forming pages that were half the size of a sheet. Other books were quartos, octavos and duodecimos, in which additional folds produced, respectively, pages that were a quarter, an eighth, or a twelfth the size of a sheet. In a letter Jane Austen indicates her preference for small books by denouncing "those enormous great stupid thick quarto volumes," and instead praising an author "who condenses his thoughts into an octavo" (Feb. 9, 1813). In fact, during the preceding century folios had increasingly been displaced by smaller books, and by this point only lengthy works of reference tended to be in folio form (novels, including Jane Austen's, were usually printed in octavo form). Thus it is likely Mr. Collins chooses a folio solely because its size makes it look impressive; he shows no apparent interest in reading it.

21. *muslin*: a light cotton fabric, or a dress made from this fabric; it is probably the former in this case since shops then usually displayed pieces of fabric, which were selected by a buyer and then made into a dress specially tailored for that buyer. Muslin had become the most popular of fabrics in England starting in the 1780s, thanks to technical innovations that made the fabric inexpensive to manufacture and thus widely available (the innovations occurring in the British cotton textile industry in this period formed one of the main elements of the beginning stages of the industrial revolution). Jane Austen reveals a great fondness for muslins in her letters.

22. *recall them*: call back or divert their attention. Such window displays were a recent development, a part of the rise of permanent retail shops in the eighteenth century (prior to that most shopping, especially outside of cities,

But the attention of every lady was soon caught by a young man, whom they had never seen before, of most gentlemanlike appearance, walking with an officer on the other side of the way. The officer was the very Mr. Denny, concerning whose return from London Lydia came to inquire, and he bowed as they passed. All were struck with the stranger's air, all wondered who he could be, and Kitty and Lydia, determined if possible to find out, led the way across the street, under pretence of wanting something in an opposite shop, and fortunately had just gained the pavement[23] when the two gentlemen turning back had reached the same spot. Mr. Denny addressed them directly, and entreated permission to introduce his friend, Mr. Wickham, who had returned with him the day before from town, and he was happy to say had accepted a commission[24] in their corps. This was exactly as it should be; for the young man wanted only regimentals[25] to make him completely charming. His appearance was greatly in his favour; he had all the best part of beauty, a fine countenance, a good figure, and very pleasing address.[26] The introduction was followed up on his side by a happy readiness[27] of conversation—a readiness at the same time perfectly correct and unassuming;[28] and the whole party were still standing and talking together very agreeably, when the sound of horses drew their notice, and Darcy and Bingley were seen riding down the street. On distinguishing the ladies of the group, the two gentlemen came directly towards them, and began the usual civilities. Bingley was the principal spokesman, and Miss Bennet the principal object. He was then, he said, on his way to Longbourn on purpose to inquire after her. Mr. Darcy corroborated it with a bow, and was beginning to determine not to fix his eyes on Elizabeth, when they were suddenly arrested by the sight of the stranger, and Elizabeth happening to see the countenance of both as they looked at each other, was all astonishment at the effect of the meeting. Both changed colour, one looked white, the other red.[29] Mr. Wickham, after a few moments, touched his hat—a salutation which Mr. Darcy just deigned to return.[30] What could be the meaning of it?—It was impossible to imagine; it was impossible not to long to know.

was done at weekly fairs). Such shops formed the core of small market towns like Meryton, which served the rural world as essential shopping centers.

23. *pavement:* sidewalk.

24. *commission:* position as an officer.

25. *wanted only regimentals:* only needed a military uniform.

26. *address:* manner of speaking; general demeanor in conversation.

27. *readiness:* facility.

28. This marks the introduction of another new character into the story, Wickham, who will play an even larger role than Mr. Collins. Like Mr. Collins, Wickham has a connection to Darcy that links him to the main plot. The nature of Wickham's character is suggested by the way he is introduced, for he is described purely in terms of external qualities—good looks and ease of conversation. He represents a type who figures prominently in almost all Jane Austen's novels: a young man who is smooth, charming, and (in most cases) handsome, but is also untrustworthy in some way. This young man flirts with the heroine, and attracts her to some degree. Over the course of the story she must learn to shake off this attraction and to recognize his flaws, while appreciating the superior worth of a less outwardly charming man.

29. Who turned which color is impossible to determine. The best guess is that Wickham turned red and Darcy white, for the former turns out to have reason to be embarrassed and the latter reason to be angry; Darcy is described as becoming pale with anger in a later scene with Elizabeth.

30. Touching or tipping one's hat was a standard salutation; not returning it would be very rude.

In another minute Mr. Bingley, but without seeming to have noticed what passed, took leave and rode on with his friend.

Mr. Denny and Mr. Wickham walked with the young ladies to the door of Mr. Philips's house, and then made their bows,[31] in spite of Miss Lydia's[32] pressing entreaties that they would come in, and even in spite of Mrs. Philips' throwing up the parlour window, and loudly seconding the invitation.[33]

Mrs. Philips was always glad to see her nieces, and the two eldest, from their recent absence,[34] were particularly welcome, and she was eagerly expressing her surprise at their sudden return home, which, as their own carriage had not fetched them, she should have known nothing about, if she had not happened to see Mr. Jones's shop boy in the street, who had told her that they were not to send any more draughts[35] to Netherfield because the Miss Bennets were come away,[36] when her civility was claimed towards Mr. Collins by Jane's introduction of him. She received him with her very best politeness, which he returned with as much more, apologising for his intrusion, without any previous acquaintance with her, which he could not help flattering himself however might be justified by his relationship to the young ladies who introduced him to her notice. Mrs. Philips was quite awed by such an excess of good breeding;[37] but her contemplation of one stranger was soon put an end to by exclamations and inquiries about the other, of whom, however, she could only tell her nieces what they already knew, that Mr. Denny had brought him from London, and that he was to have a lieutenant's commission in the ——shire.[38] She had been watching him the last hour,[39] she said, as he walked up and down the street, and had Mr. Wickham appeared Kitty and Lydia would certainly have continued the occupation, but unluckily no one passed the windows now except a few of the officers, who in comparison with the stranger, were become "stupid,[40] disagreeable fellows." Some of them were to dine with the Philipses the next day, and their aunt promised to make her husband call on Mr. Wickham, and give him an invitation also, if the family from Longbourn would come in the evening.[41] This was agreed to, and Mrs. Philips protested that they would have a nice comfortable[42] noisy game of lottery tickets,[43] and

31. *made their bows:* a signal of farewell.

32. *Miss Lydia's:* the officers would use "Miss" when addressing her, for calling her only "Lydia" would be too familiar.

33. Mrs. Philips's shouting out the window shows her lack of refinement.

34. *recent absence:* i.e., at Netherfield.

35. *draughts:* medicines.

36. In other words, Mrs. Philips only knew of Jane and Elizabeth's return home from talking to the shop boy of the apothecary (whose shop would be in Meryton, the main town of the area). Had the Bennets' carriage fetched the two girls, Mrs. Philips would have known from hearing reports of its journey. This gives a sense of how much everyone knew each other's affairs in such a small community. In *Northanger Abbey* Jane Austen has a character say that in current society, "every man is surrounded by a neighbourhood of voluntary spies," and she consistently demonstrates that phenomenon, though without necessarily condemning it, in her depictions of rural communities.

37. *excess of good breeding:* Mr. Collins's extreme politeness, as seen in his strict scruples about intruding on a stranger. Mrs. Philips is easily awed.

38. ——*shire:* the name of the regiment. Each county in England was obligated to enroll a specified number of troops for the militia, who would then be formed into one or more regiments bearing the name of that county. Since most county names ended in "shire," using "——shire" allows Jane Austen to avoid specifying one particular regiment. She may have done this to avoid being wrong, for the regiment she named might happen to be elsewhere at this time, or to avoid insulting a particular regiment, since one of its officers will play a villainous role in her story. The regiment cannot be the Hertfordshire, for militia units served outside their own counties; this prevented conflicts of loyalties in case the militia had to suppress a local riot, a duty often performed.

39. Mrs. Philips's spending a whole hour just watching Wickham, a newcomer in town, gives a further sense of prevailing small town nosiness.

40. *stupid:* dull.

41. *in the evening:* meaning after dinner.

42. *comfortable:* pleasant, enjoyable.

43. *lottery tickets:* a card game for any number of players, who wager on what card will be turned up next. The game's simplicity makes it an appropriate one to be sponsored by the unsophisticated Philipses.

a little bit of hot supper afterwards.[44] The prospect of such delights was very cheering, and they parted in mutual good spirits. Mr. Collins repeated his apologies in quitting the room, and was assured with unwearying civility that they were perfectly needless.

As they walked home, Elizabeth related to Jane what she had seen pass between the two gentlemen; but though Jane would have defended either or both, had they appeared to be wrong, she could no more explain such behaviour than her sister.

Mr. Collins on his return highly gratified Mrs. Bennet by admiring Mrs. Philips's manners and politeness. He protested that except Lady Catherine and her daughter, he had never seen a more elegant woman;[45] for she had not only received him with the utmost civility, but had even pointedly included him in her invitation for the next evening, although utterly unknown to her before. Something he supposed might be attributed to his connection with them, but yet he had never met with so much attention in the whole course of his life.[46]

44. Supper, except possibly in the form of a very light meal, was passing out of fashion as dinners were being served later. Mrs. Philips's offering a hot supper, which would be a substantial meal (and at the end of the next chapter Mr. Collins talks of "all the dishes" it involved), demonstrates her lack of fashion and elegance. In Jane Austen's unfinished novel *The Watsons* a snobbish character boasts to her poorer relations, "we never eat suppers."

45. This reveals the lack of discrimination in Mr. Collins's praise, for Mrs. Philips has just been shown to be not elegant at all. This lack is further indicated by his delivering such encomiums about an ordinary evening invitation.

46. The exaggerated language of praise and delight that Mr. Collins uses, even for the most ordinary occasions, is mocked by Jane Austen in a letter to her sister, in which she concludes, after relating mundane news of the neighborhood: "I *shall* be able to send this to the post to-day, which exalts me to the utmost pinnacle of human felicity, & makes me bask in the sunshine of Prosperity, or gives me any other sensation of pleasure in studied Language which You may prefer" (Jan. 9, 1799).

A highly ornamental chimney piece. See p. 141, note 4.

[From K. Warren Clouston, *The Chippendale Period in English Furniture* (London, 1897), p. 127]

Chapter Sixteen

As no objection was made to the young people's engagement with their aunt, and all Mr. Collins's scruples of leaving Mr. and Mrs. Bennet for a single evening during his visit were most steadily resisted, the coach conveyed him and his five cousins at a suitable hour to Meryton; and the girls had the pleasure of hearing, as they entered the drawing-room, that Mr. Wickham had accepted their uncle's invitation, and was then in the house.

When this information was given, and they had all taken their seats, Mr. Collins was at leisure to look around him and admire, and he was so much struck with the size and furniture[1] of the apartment,[2] that he declared he might almost have supposed himself in the small summer breakfast parlour[3] at Rosings; a comparison that did not at first convey much gratification; but when Mrs. Philips understood from him what Rosings was, and who was its proprietor, when she had listened to the description of only one of Lady Catherine's drawing-rooms, and found that the chimney-piece alone had cost eight hundred pounds,[4] she felt all the force of the compliment, and would hardly have resented a comparison with the housekeeper's room.[5]

In describing to her all the grandeur of Lady Catherine and her mansion, with occasional digressions in praise of his own humble abode, and the improvements it was receiving, he was happily employed until the gentlemen joined them;[6] and he found in Mrs. Philips a very attentive listener, whose opinion of his consequence[7] increased with what she heard, and who was resolving to retail[8] it all among her neighbours as soon as she could. To the girls, who could not listen to their cousin, and who had nothing to do but to wish for an instrument,[9] and examine their own indifferent[10] imitations of china[11] on the mantlepiece, the interval of waiting appeared very long. It was over at last however. The gentlemen

1. *furniture*: furnishings.

2. *apartment*: room.

3. *summer breakfast parlour*: it is a sign of Lady Catherine's wealth that she has a separate breakfast parlor for summer, presumably because its position in relation to the sun makes it less warm than the regular parlor—an issue she raises when she visits the Bennets later in the novel.

4. Chimney pieces, which would go above and next to the entrance to the fireplace, were often elaborately ornamented (see p. 139 for a sample). Very few, however, were so elaborate as to cost 800 pounds; records from wealthy homes show chimney pieces generally costing less than 300 pounds, and sometimes costing less than a hundred. Lady Catherine's expenditure thus indicates not only her wealth, but also her ostentatious use of it.

5. *housekeeper's room*: the housekeeper, the chief female servant, would normally have her own sitting room, though it would not be grand even in a large house like Lady Catherine's.

6. The men were already there for dinner, and would be engaged in the standard after-dinner masculine drinking and talking. They would have the advantage of deciding when to join the ladies. Mr. Collins is with the ladies because he arrived after the men's conversation had begun.

7. *consequence*: importance.

8. *retail*: repeat, recount in detail.

9. The Philips's lack of an instrument, i.e. piano, indicates their lower social position, for owning a piano was a fundamental mark of wealth and gentility.

10. *indifferent*: mediocre.

11. *imitations of china*: copies, on another surface, of the pictures or decorations on bought china. China had become popular and widespread in England over the preceding century, as had the designs and motifs, many of Chinese origin, found on china. The desire to imitate these designs, along with the further inspiration of the fine lacquer artwork imported from China and Japan, led to the rise of what was called Japanning as a favored pastime for ladies. This pastime—often known now as decoupage—involved pasting pictures or designs onto ceramic pieces or wooden boxes or a variety of other objects, and then, sometimes after raising or highlighting certain parts of the image, carefully applying coats of varnish to it. The images themselves could be copied from other decorative objects (e.g., pieces of china), usually by

did approach; and when Mr. Wickham walked into the room, Elizabeth felt that she had neither been seeing him before, nor thinking of him since, with the smallest degree of unreasonable admiration. The officers of the ——shire were in general a very creditable,[12] gentlemanlike set, and the best of them were of the present party; but Mr. Wickham was as far beyond them all in person, countenance, air, and walk, as *they* were superior to the broad-faced stuffy uncle Philips, breathing port wine,[13] who followed them into the room.

Mr. Wickham was the happy man towards whom almost every female eye was turned, and Elizabeth was the happy woman by whom he finally seated himself;[14] and the agreeable manner in which he immediately fell into conversation, though it was only on its being a wet night, and on the probability of a rainy season, made her feel that the commonest, dullest, most threadbare topic might be rendered interesting by the skill of the speaker.

With such rivals for the notice of the fair,[15] as Mr. Wickham and the officers, Mr. Collins seemed likely to sink into insignificance; to the young ladies he certainly was nothing; but he had still at intervals a kind listener in Mrs. Philips, and was, by her watchfulness, most abundantly supplied with coffee and muffin.[16]

When the card tables were placed, he had an opportunity of obliging her in return, by sitting down to whist.[17]

"I know little of the game, at present," said he, "but I shall be glad to improve myself, for in my situation of life——" Mrs. Philips was very thankful for his compliance, but could not wait for his reason.

Mr. Wickham did not play at whist, and with ready delight was he received at the other table between Elizabeth and Lydia. At first there seemed danger of Lydia's engrossing him entirely, for she was a most determined talker; but being likewise extremely fond of lottery tickets, she soon grew too much interested in the game, too eager in making bets and exclaiming after prizes, to have attention for any one in particular.[18] Allowing for the common demands of the game, Mr. Wickham was therefore at leisure to talk to Elizabeth, and she was very willing to hear him, though

tracing the image onto thin paper. They could also be cut from drawings, including ones found in books whose purpose was to provide such cut-outs. One reason for the popularity of this activity is that, while it required some patient effort, it did not demand special artistic skills. This would make it especially suitable for the Bennet girls, who, it is revealed later, do not draw and thus could not decorate anything with their own creations (as it turns out, even this project has not produced fine results). It is possible these imitations are on the mantelpiece as a substitute for actual china, which was frequently displayed in homes as a sign of affluence and gentility; if so, that would be a further sign of the Philips's lack of affluence and gentility.

Jane Austen's work cabinet, in which she kept needlework supplies, was decorated with Chinese figures, done in black lacquer and gilt.

12. *creditable*: honorable.

13. *port wine*: a strong red wine imported from Portugal; its name derived from the main Portugese port of shipment, Oporto. Port was the most popular type of wine in Britain at that time, and it was the drink normally consumed by gentlemen, often in great quantities, after dinner. Excessive drinking was presented by many writers as a sign of uncouthness, and here Mr. Philips's indulgence in port marks him as less polished than the officers.

14. Mr. Wickham's showing particular attention to Elizabeth is critical to the story. It is uncertain whether he does so by pure chance, or because she especially attracted him, or because he perceived her keen observation of his chilly encounter with Darcy. At this point, he might regard her as a profitable matrimonial catch, for, being new to the neighborhood, he may still not know that the Bennet girls will inherit almost none of their father's wealth.

15. *the fair*: a standard designation for women (the fair sex).

16. *muffin*: this would be what is known in the U.S. as an English muffin.

17. *whist*: a card game. At this time whist was becoming the most popular card game in England, a position it would hold until ousted by bridge in the early twentieth century. It is mentioned more often than any other card game in Jane Austen's novels. Whist is essentially bridge without the bidding stage or the complicated point system.

18. Lydia's love of gambling reveals the recklessness that her later actions will manifest further, while her particular fondness for lottery tickets, a game requiring no skill at all, reveals her lack of intelligence.

what she chiefly wished to hear she could not hope to be told, the history of his acquaintance with Mr. Darcy. She dared not even mention that gentleman.[19] Her curiosity however was unexpectedly relieved. Mr. Wickham began the subject himself.[20] He inquired how far Netherfield was from Meryton; and, after receiving her answer, asked in an hesitating manner how long Mr. Darcy had been staying there.

"About a month," said Elizabeth; and then, unwilling to let the subject drop, added, "He is a man of very large property in Derbyshire, I understand."

"Yes," replied Wickham;—"his estate there is a noble[21] one. A clear ten thousand per annum. You could not have met with a person more capable of giving you certain information on that head than myself—for I have been connected with his family in a particular manner from my infancy."

Elizabeth could not but look surprised.

"You may well be surprised, Miss Bennet, at such an assertion, after seeing, as you probably might, the very cold manner of our meeting yesterday.—Are you much acquainted with Mr. Darcy?"

"As much as I ever wish to be," cried Elizabeth warmly,—"I have spent four days in the same house with him, and I think him very disagreeable."

"I have no right to give *my* opinion," said Wickham, "as to his being agreeable or otherwise. I am not qualified to form one.[22] I have known him too long and too well to be a fair judge. It is impossible for *me* to be impartial. But I believe your opinion of him would in general astonish—and perhaps you would not express it quite so strongly anywhere else.—Here you are in your own family."

"Upon my word I say no more *here* than I might say in any house in the neighbourhood, except Netherfield. He is not at all liked in Hertfordshire. Every body is disgusted with his pride. You will not find him more favourably spoken of by any one."

"I cannot pretend to be sorry," said Wickham, after a short interruption,[23] "that he or that any man should not be estimated beyond their deserts;[24] but with *him* I believe it does not often happen. The world is blinded by his fortune and consequence,[25]

19. It would be rude for her to force the subject on Wickham, since it might, judging from the strained encounter of the previous day, be painful for him.

20. It is significant that Wickham is the one who raises the topic of Darcy, as he will continue to do on other occasions. In contrast, Darcy will never discuss Wickham unless prompted to by another; such silence and discretion would be considered the more gentlemanly course when two people had quarreled. More generally, prevailing ideals of courteous behavior frowned strongly upon telling private information to a stranger, as Wickham proceeds to do now.

21. *noble:* splendid, admirable, very large (it does not necessarily mean linked to the nobility).

22. Despite this avowal, and subsequent ones along the same lines, Wickham will soon take it upon himself to deliver a series of strong, and critical, opinions concerning Darcy.

23. The interruption would allow Wickham to absorb this surprising, and to him welcome, piece of information before then deciding what to say next. This would be important for him since in general he seems to calculate carefully the effects his words will have on others.

24. *estimated beyond their deserts:* valued or admired beyond what they deserve.

25. *consequence:* importance, high social position.

or frightened by his high[26] and imposing manners, and sees him only as he chuses to be seen."

"I should take him, even on *my* slight acquaintance, to be an ill-tempered man." Wickham only shook his head.

"I wonder," said he, at the next opportunity of speaking,[27] "whether he is likely to be in this country[28] much longer."

"I do not at all know; but I *heard* nothing of his going away when I was at Netherfield. I hope your plans in favour of the ——shire will not be affected by his being in the neighbourhood."

"Oh! no—it is not for *me* to be driven away by Mr. Darcy. If *he* wishes to avoid seeing *me*, he must go. We are not on friendly terms, and it always gives me pain to meet him, but I have no reason for avoiding *him* but what I might proclaim to all the world; a sense of very great ill usage, and most painful regrets at his being what he is. His father, Miss Bennet, the late Mr. Darcy, was one of the best men that ever breathed, and the truest friend I ever had;[29] and I can never be in company with this Mr. Darcy without being grieved to the soul by a thousand tender recollections.[30] His behaviour to myself has been scandalous; but I verily believe I could forgive him any thing and every thing, rather than his disappointing the hopes and disgracing the memory of his father."

Elizabeth found the interest of the subject increase, and listened with all her heart; but the delicacy of it prevented farther inquiry.[31]

Mr. Wickham began to speak on more general topics, Meryton, the neighbourhood, the society, appearing highly pleased with all that he had yet seen, and speaking of the latter especially, with gentle but very intelligible gallantry.[32]

"It was the prospect of constant society, and good society,"[33] he added, "which was my chief inducement to enter the ——shire.[34] I knew it to be a most respectable, agreeable corps, and my friend Denny tempted me farther by his account of their present quarters, and the very great attentions and excellent acquaintance Meryton had procured them. Society, I own,[35] is necessary to me. I have been a disappointed man, and my spirits will not bear solitude. I *must* have employment and society. A military life is not

26. *high*: haughty.

27. The conversation has been interrupted again, presumably by Lydia and the lottery game, but this in no way diverts Wickham from his subject.

28. *country*: county. This was the standard meaning of country then, and it is seen in many places in the novel.

29. This praise of Darcy's father, and description of his fondness for Wickham, is one of the only points on which Wickham and Darcy will agree.

30. *grieved to the soul by a thousand tender recollections*: words that represent the kind of exaggerated, sentimental language that the author often ridicules, and places in the mouths of superficial or untrustworthy characters.

31. Elizabeth maintains her characteristic discretion and sense of decorum, for such intimate subjects were usually not introduced during two people's first meeting. Yet she completely overlooks the lack of any such discretion in Wickham.

32. Meaning that he praised particularly the women there.

33. *good society*: often used for the society of those of high social station.

34. One good reason, not mentioned by Wickham, for him to accept a commission in the militia is that, unlike other genteel careers, it offered easy entry. The militia, which was less prestigious than the regular army, had great trouble finding officers, especially lower officers like Wickham. Hence it was not strict in its standards of entry, and commissions in the militia, unlike those in the regular army, cost nothing. In consequence, many penniless adventurers joined the militia, often in the hope of later transferring to the regulars. Moreover, while each militia unit came from a specific county, Wickham would not have to be from that county himself in order to become an officer. An additional attraction of the militia is that it followed a very relaxed routine, especially by the time the novel was written (when the danger of French invasion had subsided): standards of training and drill were lax, and officers had much leisure time for other things. Thus Wickham can consider the main attraction of the militia to be the opportunity it offers for society or social life.

35. *own*: acknowledge.

what I was intended for, but circumstances have now made it eligible.[36] The church *ought* to have been my profession—I was brought up for the church, and I should at this time have been in possession of a most valuable living,[37] had it pleased the gentleman we were speaking of just now."

"Indeed!"

"Yes—the late Mr. Darcy bequeathed me the next presentation[38] of the best living in his gift.[39] He was my godfather, and excessively attached to me. I cannot do justice to his kindness. He meant to provide for me amply, and thought he had done it; but when the living fell,[40] it was given elsewhere."[41]

"Good heavens!" cried Elizabeth; "but how could *that* be?—How could his will be disregarded?—Why did not you seek legal redress?"

"There was just such an informality in the terms of the bequest as to give me no hope from law.[42] A man of honour could not have doubted the intention, but Mr. Darcy chose to doubt it—or to treat it as a merely conditional recommendation, and to assert that I had forfeited all claim to it by extravagance,[43] imprudence, in short any thing or nothing. Certain it is, that the living became vacant two years ago, exactly as I was of an age to hold it, and that it was given to another man; and no less certain is it, that I cannot accuse myself of having really done any thing to deserve to lose it. I have a warm, unguarded[44] temper,[45] and I may perhaps have sometimes spoken my opinion *of* him, and *to* him, too freely. I can recal nothing worse. But the fact is, that we are very different sort of men, and that he hates me."

"This is quite shocking!—He deserves to be publicly disgraced."[46]

"Some time or other he *will* be—but it shall not be by me. Till I can forget his father, I can never defy or expose *him*."[47]

Elizabeth honoured him for such feelings, and thought him handsomer than ever as he expressed them.

"But what," said she, after a pause, "can have been his motive?—what can have induced him to behave so cruelly?"

"A thorough, determined dislike of me—a dislike which I cannot but attribute in some measure to jealousy. Had the late

36. *eligible:* desirable.

37. *living:* clerical position.

38. *next presentation:* bestowal when it next became vacant.

39. Like Lady Catherine and other wealthy landowners, the Darcy family owned church livings. Such livings, being a form of property, could be bequeathed in a will.

40. *fell:* became vacant.

41. This would have been done by the current Mr. Darcy, who would have inherited control of the living from his father.

42. The late Mr. Darcy could have formally stipulated in his will to whom the living must go, in which case his son would have been forced to give it to that person. But, according to Wickham, the will simply recommended giving the living to him, and thus did not bind the current Mr. Darcy in a legal sense.

43. *extravagance:* wildness; unrestrained or excessive living.

44. *unguarded:* incautious.

45. *temper:* character. Such a description of himself allows Wickham to place in the best possible light any harm he has done to Darcy, of which more will be revealed later. It also allows him to contrast himself with Darcy's cold and reserved character—and Elizabeth's own fervent reactions make her seem the type to prefer a warm and unguarded person.

46. In this society, where public reputation counted tremendously, such disgrace would have been a severe punishment.

47. This vow, like his earlier one not to avoid Darcy, will soon be put to the test. Wickham has already violated this one somewhat in speaking to Elizabeth, for he does not know her character and cannot be sure that she will not spread his tale to everyone in town.

Mr. Darcy liked me less, his son might have borne with me better; but his father's uncommon attachment to me, irritated him I believe very early in life. He had not a temper to bear the sort of competition in which we stood—the sort of preference which was often given me."

"I had not thought Mr. Darcy so bad as this[48]—though I have never liked him, I had not thought so very ill of him—I had supposed him to be despising his fellow-creatures in general, but did not suspect him of descending to such malicious revenge, such injustice, such inhumanity as this!"

After a few minutes reflection, however, she continued, "I *do* remember his boasting one day, at Netherfield, of the implacability of his resentments, of his having an unforgiving temper. His disposition[49] must be dreadful."

"I will not trust myself on the subject," replied Wickham, "*I* can hardly be just to him."

Elizabeth was again deep in thought, and after a time exclaimed, "To treat in such a manner, the godson, the friend, the favourite of his father!"—She could have added, "A young man too, like *you*, whose very countenance may vouch for your being amiable"[50]—but she contented herself with, "And one, too, who had probably been his own companion from childhood, connected together, as I think you said, in the closest manner!"

"We were born in the same parish, within the same park,[51] the greatest part of our youth was passed together; inmates of the same house, sharing the same amusements, objects of the same parental care.[52] *My* father began life in the profession which your uncle, Mr. Philips, appears to do so much credit to—but he gave up every thing to be of use to the late Mr. Darcy, and devoted all his time to the care of the Pemberley property.[53] He was most highly esteemed by Mr. Darcy, a most intimate, confidential friend. Mr. Darcy often acknowledged himself to be under the greatest obligations to my father's active superintendance, and when immediately before my father's death, Mr. Darcy gave him a voluntary promise of providing for me, I am convinced that he felt it to be as much a debt of gratitude to *him*, as of affection to myself."

48. Were Wickham's account true, Elizabeth's outrage would be thoroughly justified, for in this society good career opportunities were limited, especially for those of relatively humble background like Wickham. A man denied such an opportunity might never find another that was nearly as good, and would thus suffer permanent harm.

49. *disposition*: character (especially moral character).

50. *amiable*: kind, good natured. This, like Elizabeth's earlier sense of Wickham's being "handsomer than ever" as he avows his generosity, indicates how much her eager acceptance of his story is bound up with her romantic attraction to him.

51. *park*: enclosed piece of ground; here it means the grounds surrounding a large house, which was a common usage.

52. Here and elsewhere Wickham's language is thoroughly trite, and, like his story of woe, echoes literary conventions. This signals the contrived nature of what he says.

53. Wickham's father was steward for the Darcys, which meant he supervised the running of their estate. Large estates normally had such stewards, and it was a job that required substantial skill: the steward at Pemberley would certainly have had many people working under him. During this time the status of the job was rising, as estate management became more professional; not long after this the term "steward," which had servile connotations, would be dropped in favor of "land agent." Wickham's father's background as an attorney was also standard. Financial dealings, including estate business, were central to the work of an attorney, who even acted as banker and investment adviser for many people. This made attorneys a natural choice to manage estates, especially since much of this management involved legal matters such as property transactions; smaller estates that could not afford a full-time steward would generally hire an attorney to perform the task part-time.

"How strange!" cried Elizabeth. "How abominable!—I wonder that the very pride of this Mr. Darcy has not made him just to you!—If from no better motive, that he should not have been too proud to be dishonest—for dishonesty I must call it."

"It *is* wonderful,"[54]—replied Wickham,—"for almost all his actions may be traced to pride;—and pride has often been his best friend. It has connected him nearer with virtue than any other feeling.[55] But we are none of us consistent; and in his behaviour to me, there were stronger impulses even than pride."[56]

"Can such abominable pride as his, have ever done him good?"

"Yes. It has often led him to be liberal and generous,—to give his money freely, to display hospitality, to assist his tenants, and relieve the poor.[57] Family pride, and *filial* pride, for he is very proud of what his father was, have done this. Not to appear to disgrace his family, to degenerate from the popular qualities, or lose the influence of the Pemberley House, is a powerful motive.[58] He has also *brotherly* pride, which with *some* brotherly affection, makes him a very kind and careful guardian of his sister; and you will hear him generally cried up[59] as the most attentive and best of brothers."[60]

"What sort of a girl is Miss Darcy?"

He shook his head.—"I wish I could call her amiable. It gives me pain to speak ill of a Darcy.[61] But she is too much like her brother—very, very proud.—As a child, she was affectionate and pleasing, and extremely fond of me; and I have devoted hours and hours to her amusement. But she is nothing to me now.[62] She is a handsome girl, about fifteen or sixteen, and I understand highly accomplished. Since her father's death, her home has been London, where a lady lives with her, and superintends her education."[63]

After many pauses and many trials of other subjects, Elizabeth could not help reverting once more to the first, and saying,

"I am astonished at his intimacy with Mr. Bingley! How can Mr. Bingley, who seems good humour itself, and is, I really believe, truly amiable, be in friendship with such a man? How can they suit each other?—Do you know Mr. Bingley?"

"Not at all."

54. *wonderful*: amazing, tending to provoke wonder.

55. This statement, like that by Elizabeth prompting it, constitutes an interesting suggestion that pride may have beneficial aspects. The idea is that Darcy's pride would make him wish to affirm his own high opinion of himself, and to maintain others' high opinion, by acting justly. Ironically, Elizabeth, after first posing such a notion, directly contradicts it in her next statement, so vehement is she in her wish to denounce Darcy.

56. Presumably hatred and revenge, which overrode Darcy's pride in being just.

57. Hospitality, and charity for the poor, were considered basic duties of a large landowner. The tenants would be those renting land for farming on the estate; they would normally look to their landlord for assistance, whether for personal matters or for help in improvements to the land.

58. Maintaining the traditions and good name of one's family—which was often identified with its seat, i.e., Pemberley House in this case—was considered extremely important among wealthy and aristocratic families.

59. *cried up*: praised, extolled.

60. Thus Wickham ends up acknowledging several significant good features of Darcy; he does so more than once in the dialogue. His last words hint at his possible reason: since Darcy is widely known for these features, anyone who denied them would be discredited and find his attacks on Darcy disbelieved.

61. A truly incredible statement after all he has been saying.

62. More will be revealed later about her affection for Wickham, his attentions to her, and his reasons for speaking ill of her now (see p. 372).

63. A not unusual arrangement for young ladies, especially if they lacked parents with whom to live.

"He is a sweet tempered, amiable, charming man. He cannot know what Mr. Darcy is."[64]

"Probably not;—but Mr. Darcy can please where he chuses. He does not want[65] abilities. He can be a conversible companion[66] if he thinks it worth his while. Among those who are at all his equals in consequence,[67] he is a very different man from what he is to the less prosperous. His pride never deserts him; but with the rich, he is liberal-minded,[68] just, sincere, rational, honourable, and per-haps agreeable,—allowing something for fortune and figure."[69]

The whist party soon afterwards breaking up, the players gathered round the other table, and Mr. Collins took his station between his cousin Elizabeth and Mrs. Philips.—The usual inquiries as to his success were made by the latter. It had not been very great; he had lost every point; but when Mrs. Philips began to express her concern thereupon, he assured her with much earnest gravity that it was not of the least importance, that he considered the money as a mere trifle, and begged she would not make herself uneasy.

"I know very well, madam," said he, "that when persons sit down to a card table, they must take their chance of these things,—and happily I am not in such circumstances as to make five shillings any object.[70] There are undoubtedly many who could not say the same, but thanks to Lady Catherine de Bourgh, I am removed far beyond the necessity of regarding little matters."

Mr. Wickham's attention was caught; and after observing Mr. Collins for a few moments, he asked Elizabeth in a low voice whether her relation were very intimately acquainted with the family of De Bourgh.

"Lady Catherine de Bourgh," she replied, "has very lately given him a living. I hardly know how Mr. Collins was first introduced to her notice, but he certainly has not known her long."

"You know of course that Lady Catherine de Bourgh and Lady Anne Darcy[71] were sisters; consequently that she is aunt to the present Mr. Darcy."

"No, indeed, I did not.—I knew nothing at all of Lady Cather-ine's connections.[72] I never heard of her existence till the day before yesterday."

64. Elizabeth has mentioned a powerful objection to Wickham's account, Darcy's friendship with a good man. At this point, however, Elizabeth is inclined to dismiss such an objection with the idea of Bingley's ignorance, an idea Wickham is happy to support.

65. *want:* lack.

66. *conversible companion:* a good companion in conversation.

67. *consequence:* social status.

68. *liberal-minded:* open-minded, receptive to others.

69. *figure:* social rank or importance.

70. In other words, his economic circumstances are such that five shillings is no matter to him. Five shillings is one-fourth of a pound, and thus is not a large sum of money.

71. *Lady Anne Darcy:* Darcy's mother. As with Lady Catherine, her title, specifically the use of her first name, reveals that she is the daughter of an earl or higher. Thus we are informed both of Darcy's distinguished pedigree, and of Mr. Collins's indirect connection with him.

72. *connections:* relations, family ties.

"Her daughter, Miss De Bourgh, will have a very large fortune, and it is believed that she and her cousin will unite the two estates."[73]

This information made Elizabeth smile, as she thought of poor Miss Bingley. Vain indeed must be all her attentions, vain and useless her affection for his sister and her praise of himself, if he were already self-destined[74] to another.

"Mr. Collins," said she, "speaks highly both of Lady Catherine and her daughter; but from some particulars that he has related of her ladyship, I suspect his gratitude misleads him, and that in spite of her being his patroness, she is an arrogant, conceited woman."

"I believe her to be both in a great degree," replied Wickham; "I have not seen her for many years, but I very well remember that I never liked her, and that her manners were dictatorial and insolent. She has the reputation of being remarkably sensible and clever; but I rather believe she derives part of her abilities from her rank and fortune,[75] part from her authoritative manner, and the rest from the pride of her nephew, who chuses that every one connected with him should have an understanding of the first class."[76]

Elizabeth allowed that he had given a very rational account of it, and they continued talking together with mutual satisfaction till supper put an end to cards; and gave the rest of the ladies their share of Mr. Wickham's attentions. There could be no conversation in the noise of Mrs. Philips's supper party, but his manners recommended him to every body. Whatever he said, was said well; and whatever he did, done gracefully. Elizabeth went away with her head full of him. She could think of nothing but of Mr. Wickham, and of what he had told her, all the way home; but there was not time for her even to mention his name as they went, for neither Lydia nor Mr. Collins were once silent. Lydia talked incessantly of lottery tickets, of the fish[77] she had lost and the fish she had won, and Mr. Collins, in describing the civility of Mr. and Mrs. Philips, protesting that he did not in the least regard his losses at whist,[78] enumerating all the dishes at supper, and repeatedly fearing that he crouded[79] his cousins, had more to say than he could well manage before the carriage stopped at Longbourn House.

73. *unite the two estates:* unite them through marriage. Darcy and Miss De Bourgh are first cousins, but such a marriage was completely normal and acceptable among the landed classes in this society. In *Mansfield Park* the heroine and hero are first cousins who eventually marry. The ability of such marriages to unite estates and thus increase the family wealth, as would happen in this case, was one strong reason for regarding them as acceptable. Lower down the social scale, where such reasons were less applicable and where people also had far more potential mates to choose among, marriage between first cousins was more likely to be regarded as incestuous.

74. *self-destined:* the use of "self" presumably means that Darcy has agreed to this destiny.

75. In other words, she derives her reputation for high abilities partly from her rank and fortune, for people are inclined to think better of someone possessing them.

76. Meaning that Darcy wants everyone connected with him to be considered intelligent, and helps persuade everyone else this must be true. We shall see later that while Wickham's description of Lady Catherine is correct, his assertion of Darcy's high opinion of his aunt is not.

77. *fish:* tokens or chips used in betting, which were often made in the form of a fish.

78. Mr. Collins persistent mention of this topic indicates that he may be less indifferent to his loss of money than he claims; there is certainly no indication that anyone else asks him about his losses.

79. *crouded:* crowded. As a party of six, they would be at maximum capacity in the coach.

Chapter Seventeen

*E*lizabeth related to Jane the next day, what had passed between Mr. Wickham and herself. Jane listened with astonishment and concern;—she knew not how to believe that Mr. Darcy could be so unworthy of Mr. Bingley's regard; and yet, it was not in her nature to question the veracity of a young man of such amiable appearance as Wickham.—The possibility of his having really endured such unkindness, was enough to interest all her tender feelings; and nothing therefore remained to be done, but to think well of them both, to defend the conduct of each, and throw into the account of accident or mistake,[1] whatever could not be otherwise explained.

"They have both," said she, "been deceived, I dare say, in some way or other, of which we can form no idea. Interested people[2] have perhaps misrepresented each to the other. It is, in short, impossible for us to conjecture[3] the causes or circumstances which may have alienated them, without actual blame on either side."

"Very true, indeed;—and now, my dear Jane, what have you got to say in behalf of the interested people who have probably been concerned in the business?—Do clear *them* too, or we shall be obliged to think ill of somebody."

"Laugh as much as you chuse, but you will not laugh me out of my opinion. My dearest Lizzy, do but consider in what a disgraceful light it places Mr. Darcy, to be treating his father's favourite in such a manner,—one, whom his father had promised to provide for.—It is impossible. No man of common humanity, no man who had any value for his character,[4] could be capable of it. Can his most intimate friends be so excessively deceived in him? oh! no."

"I can much more easily believe Mr. Bingley's being imposed on, than that Mr. Wickham should invent such a history of himself as he gave me last night; names, facts,[5] every thing mentioned

1.   That is, account for as a product of misfortune or error.

2.   *Interested people:* people with an interest of their own in alienating Darcy and Wickham. Jane's conjuring up such people is a sign of her desperation to avoid condemning someone.

3.   *conjecture:* guess, figure out.

4.   *who had any value for his character:* who valued his character (his public reputation) at all.

5.   Actually Wickham mentioned the names only of Darcy and his father, and was extremely vague on important facts, such as the terms of the will and the reasons Darcy gave for refusing him the living.

without ceremony.[6]—If it be not so, let Mr. Darcy contradict it.[7] Besides, there was truth in his looks."[8]

"It is difficult indeed—it is distressing.—One does not know what to think."

"I beg your pardon;—one knows exactly what to think."

But Jane could think with certainty on only one point,—that Mr. Bingley, if he *had been* imposed on, would have much to suffer when the affair became public.

The two young ladies were summoned from the shrubbery where this conversation passed, by the arrival of some of the very persons of whom they had been speaking; Mr. Bingley and his sisters came to give their personal invitation for the long expected ball at Netherfield, which was fixed for the following Tuesday. The two ladies were delighted to see their dear friend again, called it an age since they had met, and repeatedly asked what she had been doing with herself since their separation.[9] To the rest of the family they paid little attention; avoiding Mrs. Bennet as much as possible, saying not much to Elizabeth, and nothing at all to the others. They were soon gone again, rising from their seats with an activity[10] which took their brother by surprise, and hurrying off as if eager to escape from Mrs. Bennet's civilities.

The prospect of the Netherfield ball was extremely agreeable to every female of the family. Mrs. Bennet chose to consider it as given in compliment to her eldest daughter, and was particularly flattered by receiving the invitation from Mr. Bingley himself, instead of a ceremonious card. Jane pictured to herself a happy evening in the society of her two friends, and the attentions of their brother; and Elizabeth thought with pleasure of dancing a great deal with Mr. Wickham, and of seeing a confirmation of every thing in Mr. Darcy's looks and behaviour.[11] The happiness anticipated by Catherine and Lydia, depended less on any single event, or any particular person, for though they each, like Elizabeth, meant to dance half the evening with Mr. Wickham, he was by no means the only partner who could satisfy them, and a ball was at any rate, a ball. And even Mary could assure her family that she had no disinclination for it.

6. *without ceremony*: in an offhand way, without fuss or ostentation.

7. Of course, Darcy is being given no opportunity to contradict it. He would also consider it beneath himself as a gentleman.

8. A significant indicator of one of Wickham's chief assets, and of what was helping to influence Elizabeth.

9. In fact, it was not "an age," but only four days since Jane left Netherfield (see chronology, p. 714). In addition, while the two sisters profess regret at not seeing Jane, they have clearly made no effort to do so in this interval, nor will they make such an effort in the five days before the ball.

10. *activity*: energy, briskness.

11. In other words, a confirmation of all Wickham's accusations. We see how much Elizabeth is judging by appearances, for Darcy's looks or behavior are not about to give her more information on the facts of the case. We also see that dislike of Darcy is occupying her mind as well as affection for Wickham; the two emotions are obviously reinforcing one another.

"While I can have my mornings to myself," said she, "it is enough.—I think it no sacrifice to join occasionally in evening engagements. Society[12] has claims on us all; and I profess myself one of those who consider intervals of recreation and amusement as desirable for every body."

Elizabeth's spirits were so high on the occasion, that though she did not often speak unnecessarily to Mr. Collins, she could not help asking him whether he intended to accept Mr. Bingley's invitation, and if he did, whether he would think it proper to join in the evening's amusement;[13] and she was rather surprised to find that he entertained no scruple whatever on that head, and was very far from dreading a rebuke either from the Archbishop,[14] or Lady Catherine de Bourgh, by venturing to dance.

"I am by no means of opinion, I assure you," said he, "that a ball of this kind, given by a young man of character,[15] to respectable people, can have any evil tendency; and I am so far from objecting to dancing myself that I shall hope to be honoured with the hands of all my fair cousins in the course of the evening, and I take this opportunity of soliciting yours, Miss Elizabeth,[16] for the two first dances especially,—a preference which I trust my cousin Jane will attribute to the right cause, and not to any disrespect for her."[17]

Elizabeth felt herself completely taken in. She had fully proposed being engaged by Wickham for those very dances:—and to have Mr. Collins instead! her liveliness[18] had been never worse timed. There was no help for it however. Mr. Wickham's happiness and her own was per force[19] delayed a little longer, and Mr. Collins's proposal accepted with as good a grace as she could.[20] She was not the better pleased with his gallantry, from the idea it suggested of something more.—It now first struck her, that *she* was selected from among her sisters as worthy of being the mistress of Hunsford Parsonage,[21] and of assisting to form a quadrille table at Rosings, in the absence of more eligible[22] visitors. The idea soon reached to conviction, as she observed his increasing civilities toward herself, and heard his frequent attempt at a compliment on her wit and vivacity; and though more astonished

12. *Society*: the society of others, social life (it would not mean English society as a whole).

13. Elizabeth seems to be trying to amuse herself, in the manner of her father, with Mr. Collins. Since it was often considered improper for the clergy to participate in such amusements, she probably hoped to see him squirm a little in his attempts to justify his attendance.

14. The Archbishop of Canterbury, the head of the English church.

15. *of character*: of good character or reputation.

16. *Miss Elizabeth*: as a cousin Mr. Collins feels entitled to omit her last name in addressing her—though he would never dare to address her only as Elizabeth.

17. As the eldest Jane could claim such a preference, so Mr. Collins wishes to indicate that he means no disrespect.

18. *liveliness*: playfulness. The reference is to her playful, and perhaps mischievous, question to Mr. Collins that started the conversation. This is not the only time this basic quality of hers—the same quality that gives her such charm—will create difficulties for her.

19. *per force*: by force of circumstances, of necessity.

20. She is not really in a position to decline, unless she wished not to dance at all, for it was considered very impolite for a woman to refuse one man and then to accept another for the same dance. In Fanny Burney's *Evelina*, the first novel by one of Jane Austen's favorite authors, the untutored young heroine suffers embarrassment from not being aware of this principle.

21. *mistress of Hunsford Parsonage*: in other words, wife of Mr. Collins.

22. *eligible*: worthy, suitable. This is an indication that Elizabeth perceives the true nature of Mr. Collins's position with Lady Catherine: he, and any wife of his, are to be invited only when Lady Catherine cannot find better companions. Since quadrille is a card game requiring four players, it would be necessary for Lady Catherine to have some guests in order to form an adequate table.

than gratified herself, by this effect of her charms, it was not long before her mother gave her to understand that the probability of their marriage was exceedingly agreeable to *her*. Elizabeth however did not chuse to take the hint, being well aware that a serious dispute must be the consequence of any reply. Mr. Collins might never make the offer, and till he did, it was useless to quarrel about him.[23]

If there had not been a Netherfield ball to prepare for and talk of, the younger Miss Bennets would have been in a pitiable state at this time, for from the day of the invitation, to the day of the ball, there was such a succession of rain as prevented their walking to Meryton once. No aunt, no officers, no news could be sought after;—the very shoe-roses[24] for Netherfield were got by proxy. Even Elizabeth might have found some trial of her patience in weather, which totally suspended the improvement of her acquaintance with Mr. Wickham; and nothing less than a dance on Tuesday, could have made such a Friday, Saturday, Sunday and Monday, endurable to Kitty and Lydia.

23. A good example of Elizabeth's sensible and generally positive approach to life. Such an approach, combining sober acceptance of reality with the attempt always to hope for the best, is one Jane Austen consistently holds up for praise.

24. *shoe-roses:* ornamental ribbons, knotted in the form of a rose, that would be attached to the top of the shoe. They would be used on fancy occasions such as a ball.

Chapter Eighteen

*T*ill Elizabeth entered the drawing-room at Netherfield and looked in vain for Mr. Wickham among the cluster of red coats there assembled, a doubt of his being present had never occurred to her. The certainty of meeting him had not been checked by any of those recollections that might not unreasonably have alarmed her. She had dressed with more than usual care, and prepared in the highest spirits for the conquest of all that remained unsubdued of his heart, trusting that it was not more than might be won in the course of the evening.[1] But in an instant arose the dreadful suspicion of his being purposely omitted for Mr. Darcy's pleasure in the Bingleys' invitation to the officers; and though this was not exactly the case, the absolute fact of his absence was pronounced by his friend Mr. Denny, to whom Lydia eagerly applied, and who told them that Wickham had been obliged to go to town[2] on business the day before, and was not yet returned; adding, with a significant smile,

"I do not imagine his business would have called him away just now, if he had not wished to avoid a certain gentleman here."

This part of his intelligence, though unheard by Lydia, was caught by Elizabeth, and as it assured her that Darcy was not less answerable for Wickham's absence than if her first surmise had been just,[3] every feeling of displeasure against the former was so sharpened by immediate disappointment, that she could hardly reply with tolerable civility to the polite inquiries which he directly[4] afterwards approached to make.[5]—Attention, forbearance, patience with Darcy, was injury to Wickham. She was resolved against any sort of conversation with him, and turned away with a degree of ill humour, which she could not wholly surmount even in speaking to Mr. Bingley, whose blind partiality[6] provoked her.

But Elizabeth was not formed for ill-humour; and though

1.   In other words, conquering his heart was not beyond what might be achieved during the evening.

2.   *town:* London.

3.   Elizabeth shows her unreasonableness here. Wickham has been invited, and Darcy has done nothing to hinder his coming; Wickham is absent because he himself, contrary to his earlier boast to Elizabeth, has chosen to avoid Darcy.

4.   *directly:* immediately.

5.   Darcy is perhaps making a little more of an effort than previously to be friendly and polite, but if so his effort comes too late since Elizabeth's negative impression of him is already too deeply formed.

6.   *blind partiality:* partiality for Darcy as his friend; it is Elizabeth who supposes it to be blind. The irony is that it is she whose partiality for Wickham is truly blind since, unlike Bingley, she has little real acquaintance with the man she is favoring.

every prospect of her own was destroyed for the evening, it could not dwell long on her spirits; and having told all her griefs to Charlotte Lucas, whom she had not seen for a week, she was soon able to make a voluntary transition to the oddities of her cousin, and to point him out to her particular notice.[7] The two first dances, however, brought a return of distress; they were dances of mortification. Mr. Collins, awkward and solemn, apologising instead of attending, and often moving wrong without being aware of it, gave her all the shame and misery which a disagreeable partner for a couple of dances can give. The moment of her release from him was exstacy.[8]

She danced next with an officer, and had the refreshment of talking of Wickham, and of hearing that he was universally liked. When those dances were over she returned to Charlotte Lucas, and was in conversation with her, when she found herself suddenly addressed by Mr. Darcy, who took her so much by surprise in his application for her hand, that, without knowing what she did, she accepted him. He walked away again immediately, and she was left to fret over her own want of presence of mind; Charlotte tried to console her.

"I dare say you will find him very agreeable."

"Heaven forbid!—*That* would be the greatest misfortune of all!—To find a man agreeable whom one is determined to hate!—Do not wish me such an evil."[9]

When the dancing recommenced, however, and Darcy approached to claim her hand, Charlotte could not help cautioning her in a whisper not to be a simpleton and allow her fancy for Wickham to make her appear unpleasant in the eyes of a man of ten times his consequence.[10] Elizabeth made no answer, and took her place in the set, amazed at the dignity to which she was arrived in being allowed to stand opposite to Mr. Darcy, and reading in her neighbours' looks their equal amazement in beholding it.[11] They stood for some time without speaking a word; and she began to imagine that their silence was to last through the two dances, and at first was resolved not to break it; till suddenly fancying that it would be the greater punishment to

7.   This is an example of how Elizabeth's love of laughter keeps her from dwelling in resentment. It is a resource that Darcy lacks.

8.   In two different letters Jane Austen describes her own efforts to escape from dancing with a bad partner; in the second case, in which the man "danced too ill to be endured," she calls her sitting down rather than dancing with him one of her happiest actions of the evening (Jan. 9, 1796; Jan. 8, 1799).

9.   *evil:* misfortune. Elizabeth's reply is clearly playful and ironic, but it also expresses a truth about her attitude toward Darcy. Her dislike is not simply spontaneous, but is something she has decided to foster, in particular by interpreting everything concerning him in the worst light.

10.   *consequence:* importance (in a social sense). Charlotte shows her greater concern than Elizabeth for such matters.

11.   The implication is that until now Darcy has asked few women, if any, to dance aside from Bingley's sisters. In addition, he and his partner would probably, thanks to his social position and his friendship with the host, be at or near the top of the lines of dancers, a position of prestige. In Jane Austen's story "Catharine, or the Bower" the heroine arouses envy in other women because she is asked to dance by the man of highest rank present and thereby ends up leading the dance.

her partner to oblige him to talk, she made some slight observation on the dance.[12] He replied, and was again silent. After a pause of some minutes she addressed him a second time with,

"It is *your* turn to say something now, Mr. Darcy.—I talked about the dance, and *you* ought to make some kind of remark on the size of the room, or the number of couples."

He smiled, and assured her that whatever she wished him to say should be said.

"Very well.—That reply will do for the present.—Perhaps by and bye I may observe that private balls are much pleasanter than public ones.[13]—But *now* we may be silent."

"Do you talk by rule[14] then, while you are dancing?"

"Sometimes. One must speak a little, you know. It would look odd to be entirely silent for half an hour together, and yet for the advantage of *some*, conversation ought to be so arranged as that they may have the trouble of saying as little as possible."

"Are you consulting your own feelings in the present case, or do you imagine that you are gratifying mine?"[15]

"Both," replied Elizabeth archly; "for I have always seen a great similarity in the turn of our minds.[16]—We are each of an unsocial, taciturn disposition, unwilling to speak, unless we expect to say something that will amaze the whole room, and be handed down to posterity with all the eclat[17] of a proverb."[18]

"This is no very striking resemblance[19] of your own character, I am sure," said he. "How near it may be to *mine*, I cannot pretend to say.—*You* think it a faithful portrait undoubtedly."

"I must not decide on my own performance."[20]

He made no answer, and they were again silent till they had gone down the dance,[21] when he asked her if she and her sisters did not very often walk to Meryton. She answered in the affirmative, and, unable to resist the temptation, added, "When you met us there the other day, we had just been forming a new acquaintance."

The effect was immediate. A deeper shade of hauteur[22] overspread his features, but he said not a word, and Elizabeth, though blaming herself for her own weakness,[23] could not go on. At length Darcy spoke, and in a constrained manner said,

12. The most popular dances of the time involved periods of standing while others in the lines of dancers performed their movements, so one had ample opportunity to engage in conversation.

13. Public balls, like the original assembly at Meryton, are open to anyone paying a certain fee. Private balls, like this one, are open only to those personally invited. This allowed the latter to be more selective about who came, which is perhaps why Elizabeth suggests they are more pleasant. It is also why private balls became more the fashion as the century progressed and why, to accommodate such dances, more homes were built with their own ballrooms.

14. *by rule:* according to a set of rules or regulations (such as ones prescribing successive intervals of speech and silence). That the phrase, which was a standard one of the time, does not mean "as a rule" is indicated by Elizabeth's reply of "sometimes," for such a reply would not make sense if Darcy were asking if she always talked while dancing.

15. In other words, when Elizabeth suggested arranging the conversation so that the participants can say little, did she wish that for herself or was she thinking of Darcy? Her words, particularly the *some,* imply the latter, as Darcy seems to realize.

16. *turn of our minds:* inclination of our characters.

17. *eclat:* brilliance, public acclamation.

18. Elizabeth's comment is humorous, but is also a jab at Darcy. Though she says they both are unsociable and taciturn, she clearly means to point to him, for it is he, not she, who has most often acted this way. Even still, it is noteworthy that she has compared herself to Darcy, for in fact they have more in common than she cares to admit at this point.

19. *resemblance:* representation, picture.

20. *my own performance:* my performance, or achievement, in describing or portraying our characters.

21. *gone down the dance:* danced past the others to take their places again at the ends of the two lines.

22. *hauteur:* haughtiness, loftiness.

23. *own weakness:* weakness in giving in to the temptation of alluding to Wickham.

"Mr. Wickham is blessed with such happy manners as may ensure his *making* friends[24]—whether he may be equally capable of *retaining* them, is less certain."

"He has been so unlucky as to lose *your* friendship," replied Elizabeth with emphasis, "and in a manner which he is likely to suffer from all his life."

Darcy made no answer, and seemed desirous of changing the subject. At that moment Sir William Lucas appeared close to them, meaning to pass through the set[25] to the other side of the room; but on perceiving Mr. Darcy he stopt with a bow of superior[26] courtesy to compliment him on his dancing and his partner.

"I have been most highly gratified indeed, my dear Sir. Such very superior dancing is not often seen. It is evident that you belong to the first circles.[27] Allow me to say, however, that your fair partner does not disgrace you, and that I must hope to have this pleasure often repeated, especially when a certain desirable event, my dear Miss Eliza, (glancing at her sister and Bingley,) shall take place.[28] What congratulations will then flow in! I appeal to Mr. Darcy:—but let me not interrupt you, Sir.—You will not thank me for detaining you from the bewitching converse[29] of that young lady, whose bright eyes are also upbraiding me."

The latter part of this address was scarcely heard by Darcy; but Sir William's allusion to his friend seemed to strike him forcibly, and his eyes were directed with a very serious expression towards Bingley and Jane,[30] who were dancing together. Recovering himself, however, shortly, he turned to his partner, and said,

"Sir William's interruption has made me forget what we were talking of."

"I do not think we were speaking at all. Sir William could not have interrupted any two people in the room who had less to say for themselves.—We have tried two or three subjects already without success, and what we are to talk of next I cannot imagine."

"What think you of books?" said he, smiling.[31]

"Books—Oh! no.—I am sure we never read the same, or not with the same feelings."

24. Darcy obviously knows Wickham well enough to be aware of his friendly manners, and of how that allows him to win friends easily. This knowledge, however, has never spurred Darcy to try to improve his own manners.

25. *the set:* the set of dancers that includes Darcy and Elizabeth.

26. *superior:* extreme, greater than normal.

27. *first circles:* best society. Sir William's compliment, though reflecting his usual extreme courtesy, is presumably inspired by seeing Darcy and Elizabeth both exhibit excellence in dancing, which would be another sign of their compatible qualities.

28. Meaning Bingley and Jane's marriage; such an event would bring Darcy and Elizabeth together often at dances. Sir William's speculation on such a marriage indicates that its likelihood has already been guessed by people in the community, despite the limited contact between Jane and Bingley so far. One reason for this guess could be Mrs. Bennet, who is already speaking of the marriage as almost certain. Another reason is the constrained nature of courtship, in which purely private contact between the couple was usually not allowed; this meant that even modest contact and friendliness between a man and a woman could indicate love between them and thus lead to speculation about an engagement.

29. *converse:* conversation, company.

30. The significance of this will be revealed later (see p. 364 and p. 365, note 25).

31. He may be smiling at Elizabeth's now rejecting any conversation, after having earlier persisted in starting one.

"I am sorry you think so; but if that be the case, there can at least be no want of subject.—We may compare our different opinions."[32]

"No—I cannot talk of books in a ball-room; my head is always full of something else."

"The *present* always occupies you in such scenes—does it?" said he, with a look of doubt.

"Yes, always," she replied, without knowing what she said, for her thoughts had wandered far from the subject, as soon afterwards appeared by her suddenly exclaiming, "I remember hearing you once say, Mr. Darcy, that you hardly ever forgave, that your resentment once created was unappeasable.[33] You are very cautious, I suppose, as to its *being created*."

"I am," said he, with a firm voice.

"And never allow yourself to be blinded by prejudice?"

"I hope not."

"It is particularly incumbent on those who never change their opinion, to be secure of judging properly at first."

"May I ask to what these questions tend?"

"Merely to the illustration of *your* character," said she, endeavouring to shake off her gravity. "I am trying to make it out."[34]

"And what is your success?"

She shook her head. "I do not get on at all. I hear such different accounts of you as puzzle me exceedingly."

"I can readily believe," answered he gravely, "that report may vary greatly with respect to me; and I could wish, Miss Bennet, that you were not to sketch[35] my character at the present moment, as there is reason to fear that the performance would reflect no credit on either."[36]

"But if I do not take your likeness[37] now, I may never have another opportunity."

"I would by no means suspend any pleasure of yours,"[38] he coldly replied. She said no more, and they went down the other dance[39] and parted in silence; on each side dissatisfied, though not to an equal degree, for in Darcy's breast there was a tolerable powerful feeling towards her, which soon procured her pardon, and directed all his anger against another.[40]

32. Now that Elizabeth's initial comments have broken through Darcy's normal reserve, he shows himself willing, if not eager, to converse, despite being angered by her mention of Wickham.

33. Elizabeth is making Darcy's earlier statement to be harsher than it actually was. It clearly continues to stick in her mind; she mentioned it also to Wickham.

34. Though Elizabeth claims to be interested in Darcy's character, in fact she shows little real interest here in examining him, except for the purpose of confirming her existing condemnation of him. In many ways this exchange does more to illustrate her character than his.

35. *sketch:* describe generally or in outline.

36. That is, he fears that her judging him now would put both of them in a bad light—him because her verdict would be negative, her because she would turn out to be wrong.

37. *take your likeness:* form a picture of you, figure out your character.

38. Meaning that since Elizabeth seems to wish to take his likeness, i.e., study and describe his character, and fears this may be her last chance, Darcy would not force her to put off that pleasure by waiting until another time. Elizabeth's fear about another chance shows how Darcy's being a temporary resident in the neighborhood encourages her misjudgment of him.

39. *other dance:* second dance of the pair they are dancing together.

40. *another:* i.e., Wickham.

They had not long separated when Miss Bingley came towards her, and with an expression of civil disdain thus accosted her,

"So, Miss Eliza, I hear you are quite delighted with George Wickham![41]—Your sister has been talking to me about him, and asking me a thousand questions; and I find that the young man forgot to tell you, among his other communications, that he was the son of old Wickham, the late Mr. Darcy's steward.[42] Let me recommend you, however, as a friend, not to give implicit confidence to all his assertions; for as to Mr. Darcy's using him ill, it is perfectly false; for, on the contrary, he has been always remarkably kind to him, though George Wickham has treated Mr. Darcy in a most infamous manner. I do not know the particulars, but I know very well that Mr. Darcy is not in the least to blame, that he cannot bear to hear George Wickham mentioned, and that though my brother thought he could not well avoid including him in his invitation to the officers, he was excessively glad to find that he had taken himself out of the way. His coming into the country[43] at all, is a most insolent thing indeed,[44] and I wonder how he could presume to do it. I pity you, Miss Eliza, for this discovery of your favourite's guilt; but really considering his descent,[45] one could not expect much better."

"His guilt and his descent appear by your account to be the same,"[46] said Elizabeth angrily; "for I have heard you accuse him of nothing worse than of being the son of Mr. Darcy's steward,[47] and of *that*, I can assure you, he informed me himself."

"I beg your pardon," replied Miss Bingley, turning away with a sneer. "Excuse my interference.—It was kindly meant."[48]

"Insolent girl!" said Elizabeth to herself.—"You are much mistaken if you expect to influence me by such a paltry attack as this. I see nothing in it but your own wilful ignorance and the malice of Mr. Darcy."[49] She then sought her eldest sister, who had undertaken to make inquiries on the same subject of Bingley. Jane met her with a smile of such sweet complacency,[50] a glow of such happy expression, as sufficiently marked how well she was satisfied with the occurrences of the evening.—Elizabeth instantly read her feelings, and at that moment solicitude for Wickham, resentment against his enemies, and every thing else gave way before the hope of Jane's being in the fairest way for happiness.[51]

41. *George Wickham:* calling him this rather than Mr. Wickham indicates Miss Bingley's contempt for him. One would not use someone's first name, without a "Mr." or "Miss" or "Mrs.," if one considered that person a social equal, unless he or she was a family member. This snobbery toward Wickham also makes Miss Bingley mention his being the son of a steward, with the idea that this will by itself condemn him in Elizabeth's eyes. In fact, the effect of the snobbery is only to encourage Elizabeth's rejection of her words, even though Miss Bingley's opinion of Wickham is actually more accurate than Elizabeth's.

42. *steward:* a position that, while it involved many responsibilities (see p. 151, note 53), meant working in some respects as a servant, and thus could be an object of contempt for a snobbish person like Miss Bingley.

43. *the country:* this area.

44. Because it would bring him close to Darcy. In fact, it is hard to see how Wickham could have known his regiment would be stationed where Darcy happened to be visiting. Such an unreasonable criticism only undermines the rest of Miss Bingley's statement.

45. *descent:* birth, ancestry.

46. In other words, [Elizabeth says to Miss Bingley] you seem to think his having low origins is what makes him guilty.

47. In fact, Miss Bingley has accused Wickham of bad conduct as well, although her mingling of these accusations with expressions of social snobbery makes it easy for Elizabeth to dismiss her words.

48. Miss Bingley's avowal of her kind intention could be partly sincere. She may consider that she was doing Elizabeth a favor by revealing the falseness of Wickham's story and his low social rank, and thereby showing Elizabeth why she should wish to disassociate herself from him. At the same time, Miss Bingley clearly enjoys the opportunity to deliver such a correction to Elizabeth.

49. The phrase may imply that Elizabeth imagines Darcy to have spurred Miss Bingley to this attack; if so it would represent a foolish surmise on Elizabeth's part, considering all she has seen of Darcy's haughty indifference toward Miss Bingley.

50. *complacency:* pleasure, satisfaction.

51. Once again the reader is reminded of Elizabeth's basic good nature, even with her mistakes relating to Wickham and Darcy.

"I want to know," said she, with a countenance no less smiling than her sister's, "what you have learnt about Mr. Wickham. But perhaps you have been too pleasantly engaged to think of any third person; in which case you may be sure of my pardon."

"No," replied Jane, "I have not forgotten him; but I have nothing satisfactory to tell you. Mr. Bingley does not know the whole of his history, and is quite ignorant of the circumstances which have principally offended Mr. Darcy; but he will vouch for the good conduct, the probity and honour of his friend, and is perfectly convinced that Mr. Wickham has deserved much less attention from Mr. Darcy than he has received; and I am sorry to say that by his account as well as his sister's, Mr. Wickham is by no means a respectable young man. I am afraid he has been very imprudent, and has deserved to lose Mr. Darcy's regard."

"Mr. Bingley does not know Mr. Wickham himself?"

"No; he never saw him till the other morning at Meryton."

"This account then is what he has received from Mr. Darcy. I am perfectly satisfied.[52] But what does he say of the living?"

"He does not exactly recollect the circumstances, though he has heard them from Mr. Darcy more than once,[53] but he believes that it was left to him *conditionally* only."

"I have not a doubt of Mr. Bingley's sincerity," said Elizabeth warmly; "but you must excuse my not being convinced by assurances only. Mr. Bingley's defence of his friend was a very able one I dare say, but since he is unacquainted with several parts of the story, and has learnt the rest from that friend himself, I shall venture still to think of both gentlemen as I did before."

She then changed the discourse to one more gratifying to each, and on which there could be no difference of sentiment. Elizabeth listened with delight to the happy, though modest hopes which Jane entertained of Bingley's regard, and said all in her power to heighten her confidence in it. On their being joined by Mr. Bingley himself, Elizabeth withdrew to Miss Lucas; to whose inquiry after the pleasantness of her last partner she had scarcely replied, before Mr. Collins came up to them and told her with great exultation that he had just been so fortunate as to make a most important discovery.

52. *perfectly satisfied:* words indicating how much she, in asking about the case, wishes only to confirm her existing opinion, rather than really to learn more.

53. Such inability to remember details would be perfectly characteristic of Bingley. Here, it plays an important role in the story by keeping him from providing the information that might have undermined some of Elizabeth's certainty.

"I have found out," said he, "by a singular accident, that there is now in the room a near relation of my patroness. I happened to overhear the gentleman himself mentioning to the young lady who does the honours of this house[54] the names of his cousin Miss De Bourgh, and of her mother Lady Catherine. How wonderfully[55] these sort of things occur! Who would have thought of my meeting with—perhaps—a nephew of Lady Catherine de Bourgh in this assembly!—I am most thankful that the discovery is made in time for me to pay my respects to him, which I am now going to do, and trust he will excuse my not having done it before. My total ignorance of the connection must plead my apology."[56]

"You are not going to introduce yourself to Mr. Darcy?"

"Indeed I am. I shall intreat his pardon for not having done it earlier. I believe him to be Lady Catherine's *nephew*. It will be in my power to assure him that her ladyship was quite well yesterday se'nnight."[57]

Elizabeth tried hard to dissuade him from such a scheme; assuring him that Mr. Darcy would consider his addressing him without introduction as an impertinent freedom,[58] rather than a compliment to his aunt; that it was not in the least necessary there should be any notice on either side, and that if it were, it must belong to Mr. Darcy, the superior in consequence, to begin the acquaintance.[59]— Mr. Collins listened to her with the determined air of following his own inclination, and when she ceased speaking, replied thus,

"My dear Miss Elizabeth, I have the highest opinion in the world of your excellent judgment in all matters within the scope of your understanding, but permit me to say that there must be a wide difference between the established forms of ceremony amongst the laity, and those which regulate the clergy; for give me leave to observe that I consider the clerical office[60] as equal in point of dignity with the highest rank in the kingdom[61]—provided that a proper humility of behaviour is at the same time maintained. You must therefore allow me to follow the dictates of my conscience on this occasion, which leads me to perform what I look on as a point of duty. Pardon me for neglecting to profit by your advice, which on every other subject shall be my constant guide,[62]

54. *does the honours of this house:* performs the civilities or duties of a host. Thus it is Miss Bingley, who is keeping house at Netherfield. Few besides Mr. Collins would employ such a formal and long-winded designation.

55. *wonderfully:* amazingly, astonishingly.

56. *plead my apology:* provide my plea or apology, i.e., be my excuse.

57. *yesterday se'nnight:* a week ago yesterday. Mr. Collins left his home on the previous Monday, and it is now Tuesday.

58. The standard practice was to speak to someone you did not know only after a mutual acquaintance had introduced you to that person.

59. The person of higher social position (the "superior in consequence"), in this case Darcy, should have the freedom to decide whether two people should speak and become acquainted. This is a basic social rule of the time, which we will see applied elsewhere in the novel.

60. *clerical office:* position or function of being a clergyman.

61. This special exception for the clergy has no basis in current social practice. Members of the clergy were thoroughly enmeshed in the prevailing social hierarchy, and were regularly ranked in relation to people in other walks of life. Mr. Collins is here following a practice he displays elsewhere, that of proclaiming whatever principles of conduct happen to suit his convenience; in this case, the convenience involves his ambition to make himself known to a rich and powerful man. His action would be regarded by almost anyone of the time as impudent, and it stands in direct contrast to his normal professions of extreme humility.

62. An allusion to his upcoming proposal to Elizabeth, and his hope that she will soon become his wife.

though in the case before us I consider myself more fitted by education and habitual study to decide on what is right than a young lady like yourself."[63] And with a low bow he left her to attack Mr. Darcy, whose reception of his advances she eagerly watched, and whose astonishment at being so addressed was very evident. Her cousin prefaced his speech with a solemn bow, and though she could not hear a word of it, she felt as if hearing it all, and saw in the motion of his lips the words "apology," "Hunsford," and "Lady Catherine de Bourgh."—It vexed her to see him expose himself[64] to such a man. Mr. Darcy was eyeing him with unrestrained wonder, and when at last Mr. Collins allowed him time to speak, replied with an air of distant civility. Mr. Collins, however, was not discouraged from speaking again, and Mr. Darcy's contempt seemed abundantly increasing with the length of his second speech, and at the end of it he only made him a slight bow, and moved another way. Mr. Collins then returned to Elizabeth.

"I have no reason, I assure you," said he, "to be dissatisfied with my reception. Mr. Darcy seemed much pleased with the attention. He answered me with the utmost civility, and even paid me the compliment of saying, that he was so well convinced of Lady Catherine's discernment as to be certain she could never bestow a favour unworthily.[65] It was really a very handsome thought. Upon the whole, I am much pleased with him."

As Elizabeth had no longer any interest of her own to pursue, she turned her attention almost entirely on her sister and Mr. Bingley, and the train[66] of agreeable reflections which her observations gave birth to, made her perhaps almost as happy as Jane. She saw her in idea[67] settled in that very house in all the felicity which a marriage of true affection could bestow; and she felt capable under such circumstances, of endeavouring even to like Bingley's two sisters. Her mother's thoughts she plainly saw were bent the same way, and she determined not to venture near her, lest she might hear too much. When they sat down to supper, therefore, she considered it a most unlucky perverseness which placed them within one of each other;[68] and deeply was she vexed to find that her mother was talking to that one person[69] (Lady Lucas) freely,

63. In fact, Elizabeth, in addition to being far more intelligent than Mr. Collins, has grown up in superior social and economic circumstances, which would have given her a much better sense of social proprieties.

64. *expose himself*: make an exhibition of himself, make himself look ridiculous.

65. It is signifcant that Darcy's comment stays in the realm of supposition, i.e. he is sure in general that his aunt could not bestow a favor unworthily. He does not say that, judging from Mr. Collins, she appears to have bestowed it worthily in this case.

66. *train*: sequence, series.

67. *in idea*: in her mind or imagination.

68. At this time guests at parties were not assigned seats for meals, whether for supper or dinner. Seating was determined by chance, and no attempt was made to alternate men and women at the table (this last custom would only develop later in the nineteenth century). Thus Elizabeth, Lady Lucas, and Mrs. Bennet can sit one after the other.

69. *one person*: the one person between Elizabeth and Mrs. Bennet.

openly, and of nothing else but of her expectation that Jane would be soon married to Mr. Bingley.—It was an animating subject, and Mrs. Bennet seemed incapable of fatigue while enumerating the advantages of the match. His being such a charming young man, and so rich, and living but three miles from them, were the first points of self-gratulation;[70] and then it was such a comfort to think how fond the two sisters were of Jane, and to be certain that they must desire the connection as much as she could do. It was, moreover, such a promising thing for her younger daughters, as Jane's marrying so greatly[71] must throw them in the way of other rich men; and lastly, it was so pleasant at her time of life to be able to consign her single daughters to the care of their sister,[72] that she might not be obliged to go into company more than she liked. It was necessary to make this circumstance a matter of pleasure, because on such occasions it is the etiquette; but no one was less likely than Mrs. Bennet to find comfort in staying at home at any period of her life. She concluded with many good wishes that Lady Lucas might soon be equally fortunate, though evidently and triumphantly believing there was no chance of it.

In vain did Elizabeth endeavour to check the rapidity of her mother's words, or persuade her to describe her felicity in a less audible whisper; for to her inexpressible vexation, she could perceive that the chief[73] of it was overheard by Mr. Darcy, who sat opposite to them. Her mother only scolded her for being nonsensical.

"What is Mr. Darcy to me, pray, that I should be afraid of him? I am sure we owe him no such particular civility as to be obliged to say nothing *he* may not like to hear."

"For heaven's sake, madam, speak lower.—What advantage can it be to you to offend Mr. Darcy?—You will never recommend yourself to his friend by so doing."[74]

Nothing that she could say, however, had any influence. Her mother would talk of her views[75] in the same intelligible tone. Elizabeth blushed and blushed again with shame and vexation. She could not help frequently glancing her eye at Mr. Darcy, though every glance convinced her of what she dreaded; for

70. *self-gratulation*: self-congratulation.

71. *so greatly*: in such a high rank.

72. As a married woman Jane would be able to conduct her sisters into company, thereby relieving Mrs. Bennet of the necessity. Single women could not go to social occasions without being accompanied or chaperoned; even their freedom to visit others, especially where there might be eligible men, had definite limits. In Jane Austen's youthful story "Three Sisters," a sister considering marriage sees one of its benefits to be that it will allow her to chaperone the other two sisters to balls. Lydia will express a similar interest later in this novel.

73. *chief*: bulk.

74. Elizabeth has a solid basis for her worry that provoking Darcy's disdain could have unfortunate consequences with regard to Bingley. At the same time, Elizabeth's extreme concern about Darcy could also indicate that there is something about him that particularly occupies her attention and thoughts, regardless of other considerations.

75. *views*: expectations, hopes.

though he was not always looking at her mother, she was convinced that his attention was invariably fixed by her.[76] The expression of his face changed gradually from indignant contempt to a composed and steady gravity.

At length however Mrs. Bennet had no more to say; and Lady Lucas, who had been long yawning at the repetition of delights which she saw no likelihood of sharing, was left to the comforts of cold ham and chicken.[77] Elizabeth now began to revive. But not long was the interval of tranquillity; for when supper was over, singing was talked of, and she had the mortification of seeing Mary, after very little entreaty, preparing to oblige the company. By many significant looks and silent entreaties, did she endeavour to prevent such a proof of complaisance,[78]—but in vain; Mary would not understand them; such an opportunity of exhibiting was delightful to her, and she began her song. Elizabeth's eyes were fixed on her with most painful sensations; and she watched her progress through the several stanzas with an impatience which was very ill rewarded at their close; for Mary, on receiving amongst the thanks of the table, the hint of a hope that she might be prevailed on to favour them again,[79] after the pause of half a minute began another. Mary's powers were by no means fitted for such a display; her voice was weak,[80] and her manner affected.—Elizabeth was in agonies. She looked at Jane, to see how she bore it; but Jane was very composedly talking to Bingley. She looked at his two sisters, and saw them making signs of derision at each other, and at Darcy, who continued however impenetrably grave. She looked at her father to entreat his interference, lest Mary should be singing all night. He took the hint, and when Mary had finished her second song, said aloud,

"That will do extremely well, child. You have delighted us long enough. Let the other young ladies have time to exhibit."

Mary, though pretending not to hear, was somewhat disconcerted; and Elizabeth sorry for her, and sorry for her father's speech, was afraid her anxiety had done no good.[81]—Others of the party were now applied to.

"If I," said Mr. Collins, "were so fortunate as to be able to sing, I should have great pleasure, I am sure, in obliging the company

76. Elizabeth's surmise of Darcy's careful attention to Mrs. Bennet will turn out to be correct.

77. *cold ham and chicken:* since supper is a less formal meal, cold foods would be the basic fare. The supper given here at the ball might be more substantial than others mentioned in the novel, for balls ran well past midnight and those attending, especially if dancing, would certainly need nourishment. In *Emma* "a private dance, without sitting down to supper, was pronounced [by a number of characters] an infamous fraud upon the rights of men and women."

78. *complaisance:* obligingness, desire to please (here the term has a negative connotation, since it suggests excessive desire to please).

79. *favour them again:* a standard courtesy, which would not necessarily indicate any real interest in hearing her further. Since it is only a "hint of a hope" in Mary's case, it is likely that her listeners do not wish her to continue.

80. *was weak:* hence it would tire and grow worse as she kept going. Mary is almost certainly accompanying herself on the piano. Most piano playing at the time, unless it was being used for dancing, involved such accompaniment; part of the reason was that the talents of most amateur pianists were insufficient for playing purely instrumental pieces. In Mary's case the weakness of her voice means that an accompanied song hardly represents a happy alternative to an instrumental piece.

81. Meaning that the intervention by her father that she provoked turned out to be as bad as the piano-playing he stopped. The problem with Mr. Bennet's speech is that, in addition to possibly insulting Mary with its seemingly sarcastic, "You have delighted us long enough," it has certainly insulted both Mary and other musical young ladies by implying that their only reason for playing is a vain desire to exhibit before others. Furthermore, his speaking aloud, rather than walking over to her, has caused everyone to hear his sharp words and has made him look too blunt in the process. This incident is probably one of the things Darcy has in mind when he later says that even Elizabeth's father has occasionally shown impropriety.

with an air; for I consider music as a very innocent diversion, and perfectly compatible with the profession of a clergyman.[82] I do not mean however to assert that we can be justified in devoting too much of our time to music, for there are certainly other things to be attended to. The rector of a parish has much to do.—In the first place, he must make such an agreement for tythes as may be beneficial to himself and not offensive to his patron.[83] He must write his own sermons; and the time that remains will not be too much for his parish duties, and the care and improvement of his dwelling, which he cannot be excused from making as comfortable as possible. And I do not think it of light[84] importance that he should have attentive and conciliatory manners towards every body, especially towards those to whom he owes his preferment.[85] I cannot acquit him of that duty; nor could I think well of the man who should omit an occasion of testifying his respect towards any body connected with the family."[86] And with a bow to Mr. Darcy, he concluded his speech, which had been spoken so loud as to be heard by half the room.—Many stared.—Many smiled; but no one looked more amused than Mr. Bennet himself,[87] while his wife seriously commended Mr. Collins for having spoken so sensibly, and observed in a half-whisper to Lady Lucas, that he was a remarkably clever, good kind of young man.

To Elizabeth it appeared, that had her family made an agreement to expose themselves as much as they could during the evening, it would have been impossible for them to play their parts with more spirit,[88] or finer success; and happy did she think it for Bingley and her sister that some of the exhibition had escaped his notice, and that his feelings were not of a sort to be much distressed by the folly which he must have witnessed. That his two sisters and Mr. Darcy, however, should have such an opportunity of ridiculing her relations was bad enough, and she could not determine whether the silent contempt of the gentleman, or the insolent smiles of the ladies, were more intolerable.

The rest of the evening brought her little amusement. She was teazed[89] by Mr. Collins, who continued most perseveringly by her side, and though he could not prevail with her to dance with

82. More puritanical religious figures argued that music was not compatible with the profession of a clergyman, though their opinion was far from the dominant one at the time.

83. Tythes, or tithes, were a binding legal obligation on everyone in a parish to pay 10% of their gross agricultural produce to the clergyman for his support. Determing exactly what each person's produce was, and how a payment would be made, could become very complicated. It was naturally an important matter for a clergyman to arrange, and an enterprising one could try to improve his income by showing that parishioners, due perhaps to increased productivity on their land, owed more than they had heretofore been paying; this often led to disputes that had to be settled in court. Jane Austen's father improved his income that way, though he was less energetic in doing so than many. In a letter she expresses the hope that he will be able to increase his income to 600 pounds a year by raising his tithes; in another she wonders similarly whether a sparse living accepted by an acquaintance "may be improvable" (Jan. 3, 1801; Jan. 21, 1799). Thus such financial considerations were a normal part of clerical life, although most clergymen would probably not give them the prominence in a list of their duties that Mr. Collins does.

84. *light*: slight.

85. *preferment*: advancement or appointment to his post. One sees that, according to Mr. Collins, a clergyman's duty consists mostly of attending to his own comfort and interest, or of pleasing his patron—the one to whom he owes his preferment. The one real exception to this rule is his advocacy of writing his own sermons, something many clergy did not do (they used published sermons instead). It is possible that this aspiration comes from Mr. Collins's interest in cutting a figure as a speaker, an interest seen in his making such an unnecessary speech now at the ball. It is also possible Lady Catherine, who loves to lay down guidance, has expressed her belief in writing one's own sermons.

86. *the family*: the family of his patron—hence his bow to Darcy.

87. Mr. Bennet's reaction contrasts with Elizabeth's. While both derive amusement from others' absurdities, she does not see everything as an opportunity for such laughter. In this case, her concern for Jane's chances with Bingley, and for the family reputation, make her take seriously her family's follies; her concern will turn out to be justified.

88. *spirit*: zeal, vigor.

89. *teazed*: bothered with constant attention.

him again, put it out of her power to dance with others.[90] In vain did she entreat him to stand up[91] with somebody else, and offer to introduce him to any young lady in the room. He assured her that as to dancing, he was perfectly indifferent to it; that his chief object was by delicate attentions to recommend himself to her, and that he should therefore make a point of remaining close to her the whole evening. There was no arguing upon such a project. She owed her greatest relief to her friend Miss Lucas, who often joined them, and good-naturedly engaged Mr. Collins's conversation to herself.

She was at least free from the offence of Mr. Darcy's farther notice; though often standing within a very short distance of her, quite disengaged, he never came near enough to speak. She felt it to be the probable consequence of her allusions to Mr. Wickham, and rejoiced in it.[92]

The Longbourn party were the last of all the company to depart; and by a manoeuvre of Mrs. Bennet had to wait for their carriages[93] a quarter of an hour after every body else was gone,[94] which gave them time to see how heartily they were wished away by some of the family. Mrs. Hurst and her sister scarcely opened their mouths except to complain of fatigue, and were evidently impatient to have the house to themselves.[95] They repulsed every attempt of Mrs. Bennet at conversation, and by so doing, threw a languor over the whole party, which was very little relieved by the long speeches of Mr. Collins, who was complimenting Mr. Bingley and his sisters on the elegance of their entertainment, and the hospitality and politeness which had marked their behaviour to their guests. Darcy said nothing at all. Mr. Bennet, in equal silence, was enjoying the scene.[96] Mr. Bingley and Jane were standing together, a little detached from the rest, and talked only to each other. Elizabeth preserved as steady a silence as either Mrs. Hurst or Miss Bingley; and even Lydia was too much fatigued to utter more than the occasional exclamation of "Lord, how tired I am!" accompanied by a violent yawn.

When at length they arose to take leave, Mrs. Bennet was most pressingly civil in her hope of seeing the whole family soon at

90. Elizabeth could keep refusing Mr. Collins, and not be rude, only by also refusing everyone else who asked her.

91. *stand up:* dance.

92. In fact, Darcy's silence stems not from what Elizabeth supposes but from a preoccupation with other matters, ones revealed later in his letter to her (see pp. 364 and 366).

93. *carriages:* the Bennets, who now number eight including Mr. Collins, would need more than one carriage since their own vehicle, a coach, would seat only six. They have presumably hired a second, smaller one for the evening.

94. Mrs. Bennet wishes to secure as much time as possible for Jane to be with Bingley.

95. Their fatigue is understandable, for most balls ended very late. One in *Mansfield Park* goes well past 3 a.m.; in a letter Jane Austen describes a ball in which, "We began at 10, supped at 1, & were at Deane [where she was staying] before 5" (Nov. 20, 1800).

96. He presumably enjoys the spectacle of his wife being snubbed and of Mr. Collins displaying more of his foolish politeness.

Longbourn; and addressed herself particularly to Mr. Bingley, to assure him how happy he would make them, by eating a family dinner with them at any time, without the ceremony of a formal invitation. Bingley was all grateful pleasure, and he readily engaged for taking the earliest opportunity of waiting on[97] her, after his return from London, whither he was obliged to go the next day for a short time.[98]

Mrs. Bennet was perfectly satisfied; and quitted the house under the delightful persuasion that, allowing for the necessary preparations of settlements, new carriages and wedding clothes,[99] she should undoubtedly see her daughter settled at Netherfield, in the course of three or four months. Of having another daughter married to Mr. Collins, she thought with equal certainty, and with considerable, though not equal, pleasure. Elizabeth was the least dear to her of all her children; and though the man and the match were quite good enough for *her*, the worth of each was eclipsed by Mr. Bingley and Netherfield.

97. *waiting on:* calling upon.

98. Thus at this point Bingley signals every intention of seeing Jane again soon—and he does not seem one to say this without meaning it. We find out later what prevents his fulfilling his intention.

99. *settlements, new carriages, and wedding clothes:* matters to be taken care of before a wedding. Settlements were legal agreements regarding money (for further discussion, see p. 549, note 12). Agreements about new carriages were often part of this; in Jane Austen's "The Three Sisters," a marriage is almost broken off because of disagreements over settlements, with the bitterest argument between the prospective bride and groom being over the color and style of the carriage he shall purchase when they are married. Later in the novel Mrs. Bennet will reveal a strong interest in wedding clothes for a daughter about to be married.

Chapter Nineteen[1]

*T*he next day opened a new scene at Longbourn. Mr. Collins made his declaration in form.[2] Having resolved to do it without loss of time, as his leave of absence extended only to the following Saturday, and having no feelings of diffidence to make it distressing to himself even at the moment, he set about it in a very orderly manner, with all the observances which he supposed a regular part of the business.[3] On finding Mrs. Bennet, Elizabeth, and one of the younger girls together, soon after breakfast, he addressed the mother in these words,

"May I hope, Madam, for your interest[4] with your fair daughter Elizabeth, when I solicit for the honour of a private audience with her in the course of this morning?"

Before Elizabeth had time for any thing but a blush of surprise, Mrs. Bennet instantly answered,

"Oh dear!—Yes—certainly.—I am sure Lizzy will be very happy—I am sure she can have no objection.—Come, Kitty, I want you up stairs." And gathering her work[5] together, she was hastening away, when Elizabeth called out,

"Dear Ma'am, do not go.—I beg you will not go.—Mr. Collins must excuse me.—He can have nothing to say to me that any body need not hear. I am going away myself."[6]

"No, no, nonsense, Lizzy.—I desire you will stay where you are."—And upon Elizabeth's seeming really, with vexed and embarrassed looks, about to escape, she added, "Lizzy, I *insist* upon your staying and hearing Mr. Collins."

Elizabeth would not oppose such an injunction—and a moment's consideration making her also sensible[7] that it would be wisest to get it over as soon and as quietly as possible, she sat down again, and tried to conceal by incessant employment[8] the feelings which were divided between distress and diversion. Mrs.

1. This chapter marks the beginning of a section without Darcy. His relationship with Elizabeth has reached an impasse, in which he likes her but is also determined to avoid the danger of a romantic involvement, and she is determined not to like him at all. Mr. Collins's proposal offers an appropriate commencement of a new section, for it both presents a contrast to the proposal Darcy will make in the next main section, and begins the sequence of events that eventually brings Elizabeth and Darcy together again—when she visits the bride Mr. Collins chooses after her refusal—and thereby makes that proposal possible.

2. *in form*: formally, according to the prescribed rules. The contrast here is with his earlier expressions of interest in Elizabeth, unaccompanied by a formal declaration.

3. *the business*: a term that signals Mr. Collins's attitude; in fact, both in this phrase and below, he consistently follows what he considers established custom, even to the extent of using the most formulaic phrases. As for his not suffering any feelings of diffidence or nervousness, that is not difficult since he has no genuine feelings of love to distract or fluster him.

4. *interest*: influence.

5. *work*: needlework.

6. A proposal is normally made with only the two concerned present, which is why Elizabeth so earnestly wishes not to be left alone with Mr. Collins.

7. *sensible*: conscious, aware.

8. *incessant employment*: probably this means needlework.

Bennet and Kitty walked off, and as soon as they were gone Mr. Collins began.

"Believe me, my dear Miss Elizabeth, that your modesty, so far from doing you any disservice, rather adds to your other perfections.[9] You would have been less amiable in my eyes had there *not* been this little unwillingness; but allow me to assure you that I have your respected mother's permission for this address.[10] You can hardly doubt the purport[11] of my discourse, however your natural delicacy[12] may lead you to dissemble; my attentions have been too marked to be mistaken. Almost as soon as I entered the house I singled you out as the companion of my future life.[13] But before I am run away with by my feelings on this subject, perhaps it will be advisable for me to state my reasons for marrying[14]—and moreover for coming into Hertfordshire with the design of selecting a wife, as I certainly did."

The idea of Mr. Collins, with all his solemn composure, being run away with by his feelings, made Elizabeth so near laughing that she could not use the short pause he allowed in any attempt to stop him farther, and he continued:

"My reasons for marrying are, first, that I think it a right thing for every clergyman in easy[15] circumstances (like myself)[16] to set the example of matrimony in his parish. Secondly, that I am convinced it will add very greatly to my happiness; and thirdly[17]—which perhaps I ought to have mentioned earlier, that it is the particular advice and recommendation of the very noble lady whom I have the honour of calling patroness. Twice has she condescended to give me her opinion (unasked too!) on this subject;[18] and it was but the very Saturday night before I left Hunsford—between our pools at quadrille,[19] while Mrs. Jenkinson was arranging Miss De Bourgh's foot-stool, that she said, 'Mr. Collins, you must marry. A clergyman like you must marry.—Chuse properly, chuse a gentlewoman for *my* sake; and for your *own,* let her be an active, useful sort of person, not brought up high,[20] but able to make a small income go a good way. This is my advice. Find such a woman as soon as you can, bring her to Hunsford, and I will visit her.'[21] Allow me, by the way, to observe,

9.   The idea that a woman should be modest, and shy away from a proposal (even one she welcomed), was a standard one at the time, for such modesty was considered a prime feminine virtue. Female conduct books regularly counseled women not to be too forward in their dealings with men or to encourage male advances, though these books did not generally encourage the deceptive modesty that Mr. Collins will shortly attribute to Elizabeth.

10.   *address:* speech or act of courtship.

11.   *purport:* purpose.

12.   *delicacy:* modesty, sense of propriety. Mr. Collins will use this term repeatedly during his proposal.

13.   In fact, he first expressed an interest in Jane.

14.   Despite all his talk of feelings, Mr. Collins is thoroughly businesslike and orderly in how he proceeds. He forms the complete contrast with the other man who proposes to Elizabeth, Darcy. One man is full of sentimental words, but has no actual passion; the other is reticent and careful in speech, but has genuine feelings toward her. In one respect, however, the two are similar, for they both assume smugly that Elizabeth is certain to accept their proposal.

15.   *easy:* comfortable, prosperous.

16.   Mr. Collins makes sure to mention his own prosperity. He is clearly proud of it; moreover, he probably thinks that reminding Elizabeth of it will ensure her acceptance of his proposal.

17.   Other instances appear where Mr. Collins organizes his thoughts numerically. It is possible he uses a similar rhetorical device in his sermons.

18.   When talking of Lady Catherine Mr. Collins actually departs somewhat from the studied and formal phrases that he otherwise employs. This is the one subject that seems capable of exciting strong and spontaneous emotion in him.

19.   *pools at quadrille:* games of quadrille (see p. 305, note 41).

20.   *brought up high:* raised in a wealthy environment, and thus with expensive habits that would make her unsuited to live on a modest income.

21.   This suggests Lady Catherine's peremptory and dictatorial nature. Jane Austen often uses reported speech like this to reveal people's character.

my fair cousin, that I do not reckon the notice[22] and kindness of Lady Catherine de Bourgh as among the least of the advantages in my power to offer. You will find her manners beyond any thing I can describe; and your wit and vivacity I think must be acceptable to her, especially when tempered with the silence and respect which her rank will inevitably excite.[23] Thus much for my general intention in favour of matrimony; it remains to be told why my views were directed to Longbourn instead of my own neighbour-hood, where I assure you there are many amiable young women. But the fact is, that being, as I am, to inherit this estate after the death of your honoured father, (who, however, may live many years longer,) I could not satisfy myself without resolving to chuse a wife from among his daughters, that the loss to them might be as little as possible, when the melancholy event takes place—which, how-ever, as I have already said, may not be for several years.[24] This has been my motive, my fair cousin, and I flatter myself it will not sink me in your esteem.[25] And now nothing remains for me but to assure you in the most animated language of the violence of my affection.[26] To fortune I am perfectly indifferent, and shall make no demand of that nature on your father, since I am well aware that it could not be complied with; and that one thousand pounds in the 4 per cents.[27] which will not be yours till after your mother's decease, is all that you may ever be entitled to. On that head, there-fore, I shall be uniformly silent; and you may assure yourself that no ungenerous reproach shall ever pass my lips when we are married."

It was absolutely necessary to interrupt him now.

"You are too hasty, Sir," she cried. "You forget that I have made no answer. Let me do it without farther loss of time. Accept my thanks for the compliment you are paying me. I am very sensible of the honour of your proposals, but it is impossible for me to do otherwise than decline them."

"I am not now to learn," replied Mr. Collins, with a formal wave of the hand, "that it is usual with young ladies to reject the addresses of the man whom they secretly mean to accept, when he first applies for their favour; and that sometimes the refusal is repeated a second or even a third time. I am therefore by no

22. *notice:* acknowledgment, favor.

23. The clear implication is that Lady Catherine dislikes wit and vivacity. This will be confirmed once Elizabeth meets Lady Catherine; what will not be confirmed, however, is Mr. Collins's hope that this characteristic of Lady Catherine will cause Elizabeth to suppress her wit and vivacity.

24. Mr. Bennet's death, and how long it will be until then, is clearly a subject that is on Mr. Collins's mind. He has already knocked his estimate of death down, from "many years longer" to "several years."

25. It is significant that, amidst his lengthy explanations as to why he has decided to marry, Mr. Collins has said almost nothing in praise of Elizabeth herself; clearly she has little to do with his decision. All this makes his next sentence, speaking of his violent affection for her, especially ludicrous.

26. *violence of my affection:* a standard phrase in declarations of love. It is as if Mr. Collins realized that he needed at some point to speak in more emotional and personal terms—since he is proposing after all—but can only, when he finally gets to that, declare that he is using animated language, without actually doing so, and toss in the most obvious cliché available. He shows how little meaning such words have for him when he immediately moves on to discuss, in much greater detail, Elizabeth's financial condition.

27. *4 per cents.:* a type of government bond. There were also the 5 per cents. and the 3 per cents. The existence of 3 or 4 per cent. bonds does not contradict the general reality of a prevailing return on investments of approximately 5%, for bonds were normally sold at a substantial discount off their face value. For example, 3 per cent. bonds, which were the most popular type, might be sold at a 60% discount. This meant that bonds with a nominal value of 1,000 pounds would only cost 600 pounds (because they were 99-year bonds, the investor could not simply turn around and cash them in for the nominal value). This in turn would raise their effective yield: in the above example, the investor would receive an annual return of 3% of the nominal value of 1,000, i.e. 30 pounds, a sum that would represent 5% of the actual investment of 600. In the period of the novel, when the government's need for investor money was high due to the financial demands of its war with Napoleon, effective yields were often greater than 5%.

Mr. Collins's mentioning not just how much money Elizabeth has, but the specific fund in which it is invested, is unique in the novel. It places his professed indifference to fortune in an ironic light, and suggests that he might not be so silent about such matters if they were married.

means discouraged by what you have just said, and shall hope to lead you to the altar ere long."[28]

"Upon my word, Sir," cried Elizabeth, "your hope is rather an extraordinary one after my declaration. I do assure you that I am not one of those young ladies (if such young ladies there are) who are so daring as to risk their happiness on the chance of being asked a second time. I am perfectly serious in my refusal.—You could not make *me* happy, and I am convinced that I am the last woman in the world who would make *you* so.—Nay, were your friend Lady Catherine to know me, I am persuaded she would find me in every respect ill qualified for the situation."[29]

"Were it certain that Lady Catherine would think so," said Mr. Collins very gravely—"but I cannot imagine that her ladyship would at all disapprove of you. And you may be certain that when I have the honour of seeing her again I shall speak in the highest terms of your modesty, economy,[30] and other amiable qualifications."

"Indeed, Mr. Collins, all praise of me will be unnecessary. You must give me leave to judge for myself, and pay me the compliment of believing what I say. I wish you very happy and very rich, and by refusing your hand, do all in my power to prevent your being otherwise. In making me the offer, you must have satisfied the delicacy of your feelings with regard to my family, and may take possession of Longbourn estate whenever it falls,[31] without any self-reproach. This matter may be considered, therefore, as finally settled." And rising as she thus spoke, she would have quitted the room, had not Mr. Collins thus addressed her,

"When I do myself the honour of speaking to you next on this subject I shall hope to receive a more favourable answer than you have now given me; though I am far from accusing you of cruelty at present,[32] because I know it to be the established custom of your sex to reject a man on the first application, and perhaps you have even now said as much to encourage my suit as would be consistent with the true delicacy of the female character."[33]

"Really, Mr. Collins," cried Elizabeth with some warmth, "you puzzle me exceedingly. If what I have hitherto said can appear to

28. The idea of a woman initially rejecting any offer out of modesty was also a standard one, often found in novels. It was a convention Jane Austen satirized. Ironically, Elizabeth will eventually be asked a second time by the same man, but her expectation of that in no way influences her initial refusal.

29. *situation*: position as your wife.

30. *economy*: being economical. This was a trait that was often praised, though normally it would not head the list of amiable qualifications in a beloved; it is, however, something that Lady Catherine has insisted is vital in his wife, and that makes it supremely important to Mr. Collins.

31. *falls*: falls to you, i.e., when you [Mr. Collins] inherit it.

32. Female cruelty in rejecting and tormenting a lover was another convention of much romantic literature.

33. The speculative nature of this phrase, along with the absurdity of what Mr. Collins continues to assert, indicates how little his opinion of female character is based on any actual experience or observation.

you in the form of encouragement, I know not how to express my refusal in such a way as may convince you of its being one."[34]

"You must give me leave to flatter myself, my dear cousin, that your refusal of my addresses is merely words of course. My reasons for believing it are briefly these:—It does not appear to me that my hand is unworthy your acceptance, or that the establishment[35] I can offer would be any other than highly desirable. My situation in life, my connections with the family of De Bourgh, and my relationship to your own, are circumstances highly in my favour;[36] and you should take it into farther consideration that in spite of your manifold attractions, it is by no means certain that another offer of marriage may ever be made you. Your portion is unhappily so small that it will in all likelihood undo the effects of your loveliness and amiable qualifications.[37] As I must therefore conclude that you are not serious in your rejection of me, I shall chuse to attribute it to your wish of increasing my love by suspense,[38] according to the usual practice of elegant females."[39]

"I do assure you, Sir, that I have no pretension whatever to that kind of elegance which consists in tormenting a respectable man. I would rather be paid the compliment of being believed sincere. I thank you again and again for the honour you have done me in your proposals, but to accept them is absolutely impossible. My feelings in every respect forbid it. Can I speak plainer? Do not consider me now as an elegant female intending to plague you, but as a rational creature speaking the truth from her heart."[40]

"You are uniformly charming!" cried he, with an air of awkward gallantry; "and I am persuaded that when sanctioned by the express authority of both your excellent parents, my proposals will not fail of being acceptable."

To such perseverance in wilful self-deception Elizabeth would make no reply, and immediately and in silence withdrew; determined, if he persisted in considering her repeated refusals as flattering encouragement, to apply to her father, whose negative might be uttered in such a manner as must be decisive, and whose behaviour at least could not be mistaken for the affectation and coquetry of an elegant female.

34. *being one*: being an actual refusal.

35. *establishment*: settled condition or livelihood—something a woman marrying Mr. Collins would have.

36. Being motivated only by such material considerations himself, Mr. Collins undoubtedly finds it hard to imagine anyone else spurred by different motives.

37. Now that he has been thwarted in his plan, Mr. Collins begins to reveal the crassness beneath his extravagantly polite exterior.

38. *suspense*: delay, suspension of a decision—often done to maintain someone in a state of uncertainty.

39. *elegant females*: women of fashion or high social position.

40. In contrast to her later rejection of Darcy, Elizabeth always remains courteous in her language to Mr. Collins. Partly this is because Mr. Collins, even with his crassness about money and his blind persistence, does not openly insult her or speak in a truly harsh way. Partly it is because Mr. Collins is simply too ridiculous a figure to inspire any strong emotion in her besides contempt.

Chapter Twenty

Mr. Collins was not left long to the silent contemplation of his successful love; for Mrs. Bennet, having dawdled about in the vestibule to watch for the end of the conference, no sooner saw Elizabeth open the door and with quick step pass her towards the staircase, than she entered the breakfast-room, and congratulated both him and herself in warm terms on the happy prospect of their nearer connection.[1] Mr. Collins received and returned these felicitations with equal pleasure, and then proceeded to relate the particulars of their interview, with the result of which he trusted he had every reason to be satisfied, since the refusal which his cousin had stedfastly given him would naturally flow from her bashful modesty[2] and the genuine delicacy of her character.

This information, however, startled Mrs. Bennet;—she would have been glad to be equally satisfied that her daughter had meant to encourage him by protesting against his proposals, but she dared not to believe it, and could not help saying so.

"But depend upon it, Mr. Collins," she added, "that Lizzy shall be brought to reason. I will speak to her about it myself directly.[3] She is a very headstrong foolish girl, and does not know her own interest; but I will *make* her know it."

"Pardon me for interrupting you, Madam," cried Mr. Collins; "but if she is really headstrong and foolish, I know not whether she would altogether[4] be a very desirable wife to a man in my situation, who naturally looks for happiness in the marriage state. If therefore she actually persists in rejecting my suit, perhaps it were better not to force her into accepting me, because if liable to such defects of temper,[5] she could not contribute much to my felicity."

"Sir, you quite misunderstand me," said Mrs. Bennet, alarmed. "Lizzy is only headstrong in such matters as these. In every thing

1. *nearer connection*: closer connection the Bennets would have with Mr. Collins upon his marriage to Elizabeth.

2. *bashful modesty*: a description indicating the obtuseness of Mr. Collins with regard to other people, for it is hard to imagine any perceptive observer describing Elizabeth as bashful.

3. *directly*: immediately.

4. *altogether*: on the whole.

5. *temper*: character.

else she is as good natured a girl as ever lived. I will go directly to Mr. Bennet, and we shall very soon settle it with her, I am sure."

She would not give him time to reply, but hurrying instantly to her husband, called out as she entered the library,

"Oh! Mr. Bennet, you are wanted immediately; we are all in an uproar. You must come and make Lizzy marry Mr. Collins, for she vows she will not have him, and if you do not make haste he will change his mind and not have *her*."

Mr. Bennet raised his eyes from his book as she entered, and fixed them on her face with a calm unconcern which was not in the least altered by her communication.

"I have not the pleasure of understanding you," said he, when she had finished her speech. "Of what are you talking?"

"Of Mr. Collins and Lizzy. Lizzy declares she will not have Mr. Collins, and Mr. Collins begins to say that he will not have Lizzy."

"And what am I to do on the occasion?—It seems an hopeless business."

"Speak to Lizzy about it yourself. Tell her that you insist upon her marrying him."

"Let her be called down. She shall hear my opinion."

Mrs. Bennet rang the bell, and Miss Elizabeth was summoned to the library.[6]

"Come here, child," cried her father as she appeared. "I have sent for you on an affair of importance. I understand that Mr. Collins has made you an offer of marriage. Is it true?" Elizabeth replied that it was. "Very well—and this offer of marriage you have refused?"

"I have, Sir."

"Very well. We now come to the point. Your mother insists upon your accepting it. Is not it so, Mrs. Bennet?"[7]

"Yes, or I will never see her again."

"An unhappy alternative is before you, Elizabeth. From this day you must be a stranger to one of your parents.—Your mother will never see you again if you do *not* marry Mr. Collins, and I will never see you again if you *do*."[8]

6.   Mrs. Bennet would have rung for a servant to fetch Elizabeth. Houses at this time had elaborate systems of bells connected to wires: on one end were ropes, or bell-pulls, in the main rooms of the house; on the other end were bells that would ring in the servants' quarters and show in which room some-one was wanted. The summoning of a servant is indicated here by the term "Miss Elizabeth," for that is how a servant rather than her parents would nor-mally address her.

7.   *Mrs. Bennet:* one of the only times Mr. Bennet calls her this. He may do so in this case because it involves a more formal conference between them. In general he calls her simply "my dear"; Mrs. Bennet in contrast always calls him "Mr. Bennet," sometimes prefaced by "my dear." The difference in usage suggests Mr. Bennet's superior position and her respect for him, as well as possibly his condescension toward her, for "my dear" alone is most often employed in Jane Austen's novels by older people speaking to younger ones. The Bennets never call each other by their first names: this partly reflects the general formality of the society, but it also reflects Mr. and Mrs. Bennet's own lack of intimacy, for a few married couples in Jane Austen do use first names, generally with a "my dear" before the name.

8.   Mr. Bennet's mock threat forms a parody to similar melodramatic threats and menaces found in novels of the time, especially the sentimental and romantic novels Jane Austen ridiculed.

Elizabeth could not but smile at such a conclusion of such a beginning; but Mrs. Bennet, who had persuaded herself that her husband regarded the affair as she wished, was excessively disappointed.

"What do you mean, Mr. Bennet, by talking in this way? You promised me to *insist* upon her marrying him."

"My dear," replied her husband, "I have two small favours to request. First, that you will allow me the free use of my understanding on the present occasion; and secondly, of my room. I shall be glad to have the library to myself as soon as may be."[9]

Not yet, however, in spite of her disappointment in her husband, did Mrs. Bennet give up the point. She talked to Elizabeth again and again; coaxed and threatened her by turns. She endeavoured to secure Jane in her interest,[10] but Jane with all possible mildness declined interfering;—and Elizabeth sometimes with real earnestness and sometimes with playful gaiety replied to her attacks. Though her manner varied however, her determination never did.

Mr. Collins, meanwhile, was meditating in solitude on what had passed. He thought too well of himself to comprehend on what motive his cousin could refuse him; and though his pride was hurt, he suffered in no other way.[11] His regard for her was quite imaginary; and the possibility of her deserving her mother's reproach prevented his feeling any regret.

While the family were in this confusion, Charlotte Lucas came to spend the day with them. She was met in the vestibule by Lydia, who, flying to her, cried in a half whisper, "I am glad you are come, for there is such fun here!—What do you think has happened this morning?—Mr. Collins has made an offer to Lizzy, and she will not have him."[12]

Charlotte had hardly time to answer, before they were joined by Kitty, who came to tell the same news, and no sooner had they entered the breakfast-room, where Mrs. Bennet was alone, than she likewise began on the subject, calling on Miss Lucas for her compassion, and entreating her to persuade her friend Lizzy to comply with the wishes of all her family. "Pray do, my dear Miss

9. In many families the library served as a living room for all its members. Mr. Bennet, however, maintains it as a room purely for his own use, the one place where he can escape from the others.

10. *in her interest:* on her side.

11. Once again the conceit beneath Mr. Collins's surface humility appears. He contrasts here with Darcy, who, despite his genuine pride, is truly shaken by Elizabeth's refusal.

12. Lydia treats the whole episode merely as an opportunity for amusement; she will react in nearly the same way when it comes to her own marriage.

Lucas," she added in a melancholy tone, "for nobody is on my side, nobody takes part with me, I am cruelly used, nobody feels for my poor nerves."

Charlotte's reply was spared by the entrance of Jane and Elizabeth.

"Aye, there she comes," continued Mrs. Bennet, "looking as unconcerned as may be, and caring no more for us than if we were at York,[13] provided she can have her own way.—But I tell you what, Miss Lizzy,[14] if you take it into your head to go on refusing every offer of marriage in this way, you will never get a husband at all—and I am sure I do not know who is to maintain you when your father is dead.[15]—I shall not be able to keep you—and so I warn you.—I have done with you from this very day.—I told you in the library, you know, that I should never speak to you again, and you will find me as good as my word. I have no pleasure in talking to undutiful children.—Not that I have much pleasure indeed in talking to any body. People who suffer as I do from nervous complaints[16] can have no great inclination for talking. Nobody can tell what I suffer!—But it is always so. Those who do not complain are never pitied."

Her daughters listened in silence to this effusion,[17] sensible[18] that any attempt to reason with or sooth her would only increase the irritation. She talked on, therefore, without interruption from any of them till they were joined by Mr. Collins, who entered with an air more stately[19] than usual, and on perceiving whom, she said to the girls,

"Now, I do insist upon it, that you, all of you, hold your tongues, and let Mr. Collins and me have a little conversation together."

Elizabeth passed quietly out of the room, Jane and Kitty followed, but Lydia stood her ground, determined to hear all she could; and Charlotte, detained first by the civility of Mr. Collins, whose inquiries after herself and all her family were very minute,[20] and then by a little curiosity,[21] satisfied herself with walking to the window and pretending not to hear.[22] In a doleful voice Mrs. Bennet thus began the projected conversation.—"Oh! Mr. Collins!"—

13. *York:* a town in northern England, and hence far from the Bennets (see map, p. 742). Mrs. Bennet means that Elizabeth cares nothing for them.

14. *Miss Lizzy:* an unusual usage for Mrs. Bennet. Otherwise only servants or relative strangers like Mr. Collins use "Miss Lizzy" or "Miss Elizabeth." Mrs. Bennet's use of "Miss," which is generally a mark of deference, may be a sarcastic jab at Elizabeth, intended to mock what Mrs. Bennet probably perceives to be her daughter's arrogance in refusing a beneficial offer of marriage and not heeding her mother's orders.

15. This is a serious concern, however silly Mrs. Bennet may be in her expression of it. With very little inheritance, Elizabeth would be in a precarious position and dependent on the charity of her family if she were still unmarried when her father died.

16. *nervous complaints:* ailments or afflictions of the nerves. See p. 7, note 13.

17. *effusion:* pouring forth, unrestrained utterance.

18. *sensible:* aware.

19. *stately:* lofty, dignified (often in an excessive sense).

20. *minute:* detailed, precise.

21. Charlotte's curiosity could result from general nosiness, or it could indicate her already having an interest in Mr. Collins. She behaved in a very friendly manner to him at the ball, and it is possible that his current enquiries about her family reflect his return of that interest.

22. In other words, Charlotte is eavesdropping. This signals her calculating nature, and her moral limits, for it would be considered very improper to listen in purposefully on other people's conversations, especially a conversation in someone else's family and in which one of the participants had declared a wish to speak privately. In *Sense and Sensibility* the highly admirable heroine, upon finding that information she received from someone was the product of that person's listening through a keyhole, declares that because of this she wishes she had not heard it, even though the information has great importance for her. In this novel Elizabeth and Jane consistently show a similar scrupulousness.

"My dear Madam," replied he, "let us be for ever silent on this point. Far be it from me," he presently continued in a voice that marked his displeasure, "to resent the behaviour of your daughter. Resignation to inevitable evils is the duty of us all; the peculiar[23] duty of a young man who has been so fortunate as I have been in early preferment;[24] and I trust I am resigned. Perhaps not the less so from feeling a doubt of my positive happiness had my fair cousin honoured me with her hand; for I have often observed that resignation is never so perfect as when the blessing denied begins to lose somewhat of its value in our estimation.[25] You will not, I hope, consider me as shewing any disrespect to your family, my dear Madam, by thus withdrawing my pretensions to your daughter's favour, without having paid yourself and Mr. Bennet the compliment of requesting you to interpose your authority in my behalf.[26] My conduct may I fear be objectionable in having accepted my dismission[27] from your daughter's lips instead of your own. But we are all liable to error. I have certainly meant well through the whole affair. My object has been to secure an amiable companion for myself, with due consideration for the advantage of all your family, and if my *manner* has been at all reprehensible, I here beg leave to apologise."

23. *peculiar*: special, particular. Mr. Collins is saying that his good fortune makes him particularly obliged to accept setbacks with resignation.

24. *preferment*: advancement (to his church living).

25. The idea of resignation or forbearance in the face of inevitable evils was a basic principle of the time, one supported especially by Christian teaching. Mr. Collins gives it a particularly absurd twist by saying that resignation is most perfect when one has not lost anything of value, i.e., when there is no real resignation or need for forbearance.

26. It is unclear whether Mr. Collins means requesting that Mr. and Mrs. Bennet pressure, or force, Elizabeth to marry. The first was frequent practice in this society, for parents were considered rightfully to have a strong say in their children's choice of a spouse; the second was neither possible legally nor considered right morally.

27. *dismission*: dismissal. Dismission was the usual form of the word then, so this usage by Mr. Collins is not an example of pretentiousness on his part.

Chapter Twenty-One

*T*he discussion of Mr. Collins's offer was now nearly at an end, and Elizabeth had only to suffer from the uncomfortable feelings necessarily attending it, and occasionally from some peevish allusion of her mother. As for the gentleman himself, *his* feelings were chiefly expressed, not by embarrassment or dejection, or by trying to avoid her, but by stiffness of manner and resentful silence. He scarcely ever spoke to her, and the assiduous attentions which he had been so sensible of himself,[1] were transferred for the rest of the day to Miss Lucas, whose civility in listening to him, was a seasonable relief to them all, and especially to her friend.

The morrow produced no abatement of Mrs. Bennet's ill humour or ill health.[2] Mr. Collins was also in the same state of angry pride. Elizabeth had hoped that his resentment might shorten his visit, but his plan did not appear in the least affected by it. He was always to have gone on Saturday, and to Saturday he still meant to stay.

After breakfast, the girls walked to Meryton to inquire if Mr. Wickham were returned, and to lament over his absence from the Netherfield ball. He joined them on their entering the town and attended them to their aunt's, where his regret and vexation, and the concern of every body was well talked over. — To Elizabeth, however, he voluntarily acknowledged that the necessity of his absence *had* been self imposed.

"I found," said he, "as the time drew near, that I had better not meet Mr. Darcy; — that to be in the same room, the same party with him for so many hours together, might be more than I could bear, and that scenes might arise unpleasant to more than myself."[3]

She highly approved his forbearance, and they had leisure for a full discussion of it, and for all the commendation which they

1. Meaning that Mr. Collins was highly aware of having been assiduous in his attentions to Elizabeth (the implication of the phrase is that his attentiveness existed partly in his own mind, and that Elizabeth was less aware of it than he was).

2. *ill health:* meaning her claim of ill health due to her distress at Elizabeth's actions.

3. In other words, an unpleasant scene might occur between him and Darcy that would cause pain to others there.

civilly bestowed on each other, as Wickham and another officer walked back with them to Longbourn, and during the walk, he particularly attended to her.[4] His accompanying them was a double advantage; she felt all the compliment it offered to herself, and it was most acceptable as an occasion of introducing him to her father and mother.

Soon after their return, a letter was delivered to Miss Bennet; it came from Netherfield, and was opened immediately. The envelope contained a sheet of elegant, little, hot pressed paper,[5] well covered with a lady's fair, flowing[6] hand;[7] and Elizabeth saw her sister's countenance change as she read it, and saw her dwelling intently on some particular passages. Jane recollected herself soon, and putting the letter away, tried to join with her usual cheerfulness in the general conversation; but Elizabeth felt an anxiety on the subject which drew off her attention even from Wickham; and no sooner had he and his companion taken leave, than a glance from Jane invited her to follow her up stairs. When they had gained their own room, Jane taking out the letter, said,

"This is from Caroline Bingley; what it contains, has surprised me a good deal. The whole party have left Netherfield by this time, and are on their way to town; and without any intention of coming back again. You shall hear what she says."

She then read the first sentence aloud, which comprised the information of their having just resolved to follow their brother to town directly, and of their meaning to dine that day in Grosvenor street,[8] where Mr. Hurst had a house. The next was in these words. "I do not pretend to regret any thing I shall leave in Hertfordshire, except your society, my dearest friend; but we will hope at some future period, to enjoy many returns[9] of the delightful intercourse we have known, and in the mean while may lessen the pain of separation by a very frequent and most unreserved[10] correspondence. I depend on you for that." To these high flown expressions, Elizabeth listened with all the insensibility[11] of distrust; and though the suddenness of their removal surprised her, she saw nothing in it really to lament; it was not to be supposed that their absence from Netherfield would prevent Mr. Bingley's

4. Since by now Wickham presumably knows of Elizabeth's lack of fortune, his continued attention to her does not derive from any matrimonial interest. He may simply like her; he also probably appreciates someone who sympathizes so vehemently with his resentment toward Darcy.

5. *hot pressed paper:* paper that has been made smooth and glossy by being pressed between glaze boards and hot metal plates. It had been developed in the mid-eighteenth century, originally for fine books, and was noted for its brightness; a writer of Jane Austen's time (Mary Mitford) describes it as the best type of writing paper. It would thus be an appropriate choice for the wealthy and snobbish Miss Bingley (the author of the letter).

6. *flowing:* graceful, smooth.

7. Books on writing and calligraphy, of which there were many at the time, often recommended a particular species of handwriting, very graceful and ornamental, for ladies. One author declared that this hand, originally from Italy, was specially invented for use by "the fair sex." Miss Bingley, having gone to a leading girls' boarding school, was probably taught there to write this special "ladies' hand," for elegant and attractive handwriting was considered an essential accomplishment.

For a sample of Jane Austen's handwriting, which was not as fancy as that taught in many schools for ladies, see p. 221.

8. *Grosvenor street:* a very fashionable street in London; many of its houses were occupied by the nobility.

9. *returns:* repetitions, renewals.

10. *unreserved:* frank, uninhibited.

11. *insensibility:* indifference, insusceptibility to being affected. Elizabeth's mistrust of Miss Bingley's effusive professions of affection, a mistrust that will be vindicated by subsequent events, echoes that of a character in Jane Austen's story "Lesley Castle." This character, referring to a woman whose friendship she had not sought, declares, "she was so good as to conceive a violent partiality for me, which very soon settled in a downright Freindship [sic], and ended in an established correspondence."

being there; and as to the loss of their society, she was persuaded that Jane must soon cease to regard[12] it, in the enjoyment of his.

"It is unlucky," said she, after a short pause, "that you should not be able to see your friends before they leave the country. But may we not hope that the period of future happiness to which Miss Bingley looks forward, may arrive earlier than she is aware, and that the delightful intercourse you have known as friends, will be renewed with yet greater satisfaction as sisters?[13]—Mr. Bingley will not be detained in London by them."

"Caroline[14] decidedly says that none of the party will return into Hertfordshire this winter. I will read it to you—

"When my brother left us yesterday, he imagined that the business which took him to London, might be concluded in three or four days, but as we are certain it cannot be so, and at the same time convinced that when Charles gets to town, he will be in no hurry to leave it again, we have determined on following him thither, that he may not be obliged to spend his vacant hours[15] in a comfortless hotel. Many of my acquaintance are already there for the winter;[16] I wish I could hear that you, my dearest friend, had any intention of making one in the croud, but of that I despair. I sincerely hope your Christmas in Hertfordshire may abound in the gaieties which that season generally brings, and that your beaux[17] will be so numerous as to prevent your feeling the loss of the three, of whom we shall deprive you."[18]

"It is evident by this," added Jane, "that he comes back no more this winter."

"It is only evident that Miss Bingley does not mean he *should*."

"Why will you think so? It must be his own doing.—He is his own master. But you do not know *all*. I *will* read you the passage which particularly hurts me. I will have no reserves[19] from *you*."

"Mr. Darcy is impatient to see his sister, and to confess the truth, *we* are scarcely less eager to meet her again. I really do not think Georgiana Darcy has her equal for beauty, elegance, and accomplishments; and the affection she inspires in Louisa and myself, is heightened into something still more interesting,[20] from the hope we dare to entertain of her being hereafter our sister.[21] I do not

12. *regard:* care about. In other words, the company of Bingley will keep Jane from regretting the absence of his sisters.

13. Elizabeth is being sarcastic about Miss Bingley's flowery talk of bosom friendship and "delightful intercourse."

14. *Caroline:* this use of her first name indicates Jane's belief in their being close friends.

15. *his vacant hours:* his leisure time.

16. London was at its busiest during the winter. Many wealthy people who had been in the country during the summer and fall would move to London around this time.

17. *beaux:* men who admire or court a woman; also, men who are fashionable (here it includes Darcy and Mr. Hurst). The term is probably meant to signify Miss Bingley's affected character. Jane Austen rarely uses it; the one exception is her having it be the favorite word of a very vulgar young woman in *Sense and Sensibility.* Miss Bingley's use of it may also represent an effort on her part to suggest the superficial character of Jane and Bingley's attachment, for "beaux" would often be used in reference to casual flirtations.

18. This, in addition to being a conventional wish for someone, expresses Miss Bingley's hope that Jane will find other lovers and thus cease to be interested in Mr. Bingley.

19. *reserves:* secrets.

20. *interesting:* important, significant.

21. *sister:* sister-in-law. It was common custom, as can be seen at numerous points in this novel, for people to use sister or brother for someone who was married to a sibling. This usage indicates the importance in this society of family ties; it also corresponds to the virtual impossibility of divorce, which ensured that a connection by marriage was almost as permanent as a connection by blood.

know whether I ever before mentioned to you my feelings on this subject, but I will not leave the country without confiding them, and I trust you will not esteem[22] them unreasonable. My brother admires her greatly already, he will have frequent opportunity now of seeing her on the most intimate footing, her relations all wish the connection[23] as much as his own, and a sister's partiality is not misleading me, I think, when I call Charles most capable of engaging any woman's heart. With all these circumstances to favour an attachment[24] and nothing to prevent it, am I wrong, my dearest Jane, in indulging the hope of an event which will secure the happiness of so many?"

"What think you of *this* sentence, my dear Lizzy?"—said Jane as she finished it. "Is it not clear enough?—Does it not expressly declare that Caroline neither expects nor wishes me to be her sister; that she is perfectly convinced of her brother's indifference, and that if she suspects the nature of my feelings for him, she means (most kindly!) to put me on my guard? Can there be any other opinion on the subject?"

"Yes, there can; for mine is totally different.—Will you hear it?"

"Most willingly."

"You shall have it in few words. Miss Bingley sees that her brother is in love with you, and wants him to marry Miss Darcy. She follows him to town in the hope of keeping him there, and tries to persuade you that he does not care about you."

Jane shook her head.

"Indeed, Jane, you ought to believe me.—No one who has ever seen you together, can doubt his affection. Miss Bingley I am sure cannot. She is not such a simpleton. Could she have seen half as much love in Mr. Darcy for herself, she would have ordered her wedding clothes. But the case is this. We are not rich enough, or grand enough for them; and she is the more anxious to get Miss Darcy for her brother, from the notion that when there has been *one* intermarriage, she may have less trouble in achieving a second;[25] in which there is certainly some ingenuity, and I dare say it would succeed, if Miss De Bourgh were out of the way. But, my dearest Jane,[26] you cannot seriously imagine that because Miss

22. *esteem*: consider, estimate.

23. *connection*: marital connection.

24. *attachment*: attachment in love between them.

25. In other words, Miss Bingley hopes that a marriage between her brother and Miss Darcy will facilitate a marriage between herself and Mr. Darcy.

26. *my dearest Jane*: Elizabeth uses this, or similar, phrasing on other occasions. Though such usage sounds formal or pretentious to our ears, it was standard among family members at the time. Jane Austen often addresses her sister in her letters as "my dear/dearest Cassandra" (see letter below).

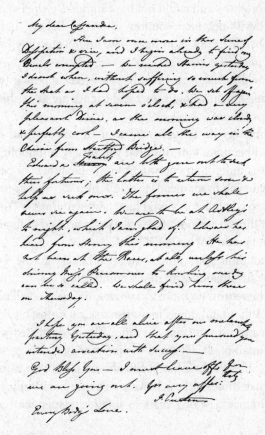

A *facsimile of Jane Austen's writing (reduced in size).*

[From Oscar Fay Adams, *The Story of Jane Austen's Life* (Boston, 1896), p. 7]

Bingley tells you her brother greatly admires Miss Darcy, he is in the smallest degree less sensible of *your* merit than when he took leave of you on Tuesday, or that it will be in her power to persuade him that instead of being in love with you, he is very much in love with her friend."

"If we thought alike of Miss Bingley," replied Jane, "your representation of all this, might make me quite easy. But I know the foundation is unjust. Caroline is incapable of wilfully deceiving any one; and all that I can hope in this case is, that she is deceived herself."[27]

"That is right.—You could not have started a more happy idea, since you will not take comfort in mine. Believe her to be deceived by all means. You have now done your duty by her,[28] and must fret no longer."

"But, my dear sister, can I be happy, even supposing the best, in accepting a man whose sisters and friends are all wishing him to marry elsewhere?"

"You must decide for yourself," said Elizabeth, "and if upon mature deliberation, you find that the misery of disobliging his two sisters is more than equivalent to the happiness of being his wife, I advise you by all means to refuse him."

"How can you talk so?"—said Jane faintly smiling,—"You must know that though I should be exceedingly grieved at their disapprobation, I could not hesitate."[29]

"I did not think you would;—and that being the case, I cannot consider your situation with much compassion."

"But if he returns no more this winter, my choice will never be required. A thousand things may arise in six months!"

The idea of his returning no more Elizabeth treated with the utmost contempt. It appeared to her merely the suggestion of Caroline's interested wishes,[30] and she could not for a moment suppose that those wishes, however openly or artfully spoken, could influence a young man so totally independent of every one.[31]

She represented to her sister as forcibly as possible what she felt on the subject, and had soon the pleasure of seeing its happy

27. We see here a case where Jane's refusal to think badly of someone has serious consequences, by leading her to an important misjudgment.

28. *you have now done your duty by her:* you have now fulfilled your obligation to her, as a friend, of not thinking her to be deceitful.

29. *hesitate:* hesitate to marry him.

30. *interested wishes:* wishes or hopes shaped by her interest (in keeping her brother from Jane).

31. Meaning independent financially and legally. Elizabeth's estimation of the situation is generally better than Jane's, especially about Miss Bingley, though Elizabeth ends up being mistaken about Mr. Bingley.

effect. Jane's temper[32] was not desponding,[33] and she was gradually led to hope, though the diffidence of affection[34] sometimes overcame the hope, that Bingley would return to Netherfield and answer every wish of her heart.

They agreed that Mrs. Bennet should only hear of the departure of the family, without being alarmed on the score of the gentleman's conduct; but even this partial communication gave her a great deal of concern, and she bewailed it as exceedingly unlucky that the ladies should happen to go away, just as they were all getting so intimate together. After lamenting it however at some length, she had the consolation of thinking that Mr. Bingley would be soon down again and soon dining at Longbourn, and the conclusion of all was the comfortable[35] declaration that, though he had been invited only to a family dinner, she would take care to have two full courses.[36]

32. *temper*: disposition, character.

33. *desponding*: prone to be despondent or despairing.

34. *the diffidence of affection*: misgivings about the strength of his affection.

35. *comfortable*: cheerful, encouraging.

36. *two full courses*: this would be a significant meal, for courses then did not mean a specific serving of a few items. A course involved a great variety of dishes, to be laid out on a table and selected among by those eating. Menus of the time show a single course containing enough food to satisfy most diners.

Chapter Twenty-Two

*T*he Bennets were engaged to dine with the Lucases, and again during the chief[1] of the day, was Miss Lucas so kind as to listen to Mr. Collins. Elizabeth took an opportunity of thanking her. "It keeps him in good humour," said she, "and I am more obliged to you than I can express." Charlotte assured her friend of her satisfaction in being useful, and that it amply repaid her for the little sacrifice of her time. This was very amiable, but Charlotte's kindness extended farther than Elizabeth had any conception of;—its object was nothing less, than to secure her from any return of Mr. Collins's addresses,[2] by engaging them towards herself. Such was Miss Lucas's scheme; and appearances were so favourable that when they parted at night, she would have felt almost sure of success if he had not been to leave Hertfordshire so very soon.[3] But here, she did injustice to the fire and independence[4] of his character, for it led him to escape out of Longbourn House the next morning with admirable slyness,[5] and hasten to Lucas Lodge to throw himself at her feet. He was anxious to avoid the notice of his cousins, from a conviction that if they saw him depart, they could not fail to conjecture[6] his design, and he was not willing to have the attempt known till its success could be known likewise; for though feeling almost secure, and with reason, for Charlotte had been tolerably encouraging, he was comparatively diffident[7] since the adventure of Wednesday.[8] His reception however was of the most flattering kind. Miss Lucas perceived him from an upper window as he walked towards the house, and instantly set out to meet him accidentally in the lane.[9] But little had she dared to hope that so much love and eloquence awaited her there.

In as short a time as Mr. Collins's long speeches would allow, every thing was settled between them to the satisfaction of both;

1. *chief:* greater part.

2. *addresses:* attempts at courtship.

3. It is now Thursday evening, and Mr. Collins is scheduled to leave on Saturday morning (see chronology, p. 714).

4. *independence:* meaning, most likely, his willingness to defy whatever conventions might demand a longer courtship. The term has an ironic edge, since in general Mr. Collins shows so little independence (not to mention fieriness) of spirit.

5. *admirable slyness:* surprising secrecy.

6. *conjecture:* guess.

7. *diffident:* lacking in confidence.

8. Meaning Elizabeth's rejection of him.

9. It would be considered improper for her to arrange a meeting alone with her lover, so she has to make it seem accidental by going into the lane on pretense of other business. Again Charlotte shows her calculating side. In contrast, Jane Bennet, when she is expecting a possible proposal later in the novel, makes every effort to avoid throwing herself in the way of her lover.

and as they entered the house, he earnestly entreated her to name the day that was to make him the happiest of men;[10] and though such a solicitation must be waved for the present, the lady felt no inclination to trifle with his happiness.[11] The stupidity with which he was favoured by nature,[12] must guard[13] his courtship from any charm that could make a woman wish for its continuance; and Miss Lucas, who accepted him solely from the pure and disinterested[14] desire of an establishment,[15] cared not how soon that establishment were gained.

Sir William and Lady Lucas were speedily applied to for their consent; and it was bestowed with a most joyful alacrity. Mr. Collins's present circumstances made it a most eligible[16] match for their daughter, to whom they could give little fortune; and his prospects of future wealth were exceedingly fair.[17] Lady Lucas began directly to calculate with more interest than the matter had ever excited before, how many years longer Mr. Bennet was likely to live; and Sir William gave it as his decided opinion, that whenever Mr. Collins should be in possession of the Longbourn estate, it would be highly expedient that both he and his wife should make their appearance at St. James's.[18] The whole family in short were properly overjoyed on the occasion. The younger girls formed hopes of *coming out*[19] a year or two sooner than they might otherwise have done; and the boys were relieved from their apprehension of Charlotte's dying an old maid.[20] Charlotte herself was tolerably composed. She had gained her point, and had time to consider of it. Her reflections were in general satisfactory. Mr. Collins to be sure was neither sensible nor agreeable; his society was irksome, and his attachment to her must be imaginary. But still he would be her husband.—Without thinking highly either of men or of matrimony, marriage had always been her object; it was the only honourable provision for well-educated young women of small fortune, and however uncertain of giving happiness, must be their pleasantest preservative from want. This preservative she had now obtained; and at the age of twenty-seven, without having ever been handsome, she felt all the good luck of it.[21] The least agreeable circumstance in the business, was

10. *happiest of men:* a standard phrase relating to marriage, similar to other trite ones employed by Mr. Collins.

11. Meaning that while Charlotte must put off for now his request to name a date, she is not inclined to delay it and keep him in suspense very long.

12. *with which he was favoured by nature:* that he was born with; the use of "favoured" is a sarcastic comment on this attribute.

13. *guard:* preserve.

14. *disinterested:* impartial, unprejudiced. There is irony in this use of the term since it often connotes lack of concern with one's monetary interest, and Charlotte's desire here centers around her own material benefit.

15. *establishment:* settled income and living arrangement; the term was often used in reference to marriage.

16. *eligible:* desirable.

17. His prospects are fair, or fine, because he will inherit the Bennet estate.

18. Meaning they should be presented at court, Sir William's obsession. Such presentations could happen on numerous important occasions, such as receiving a government promotion; Sir William hopes that Mr. Collins's inheriting a wealthy estate would justify the procedure for him and his wife.

19. *coming out:* being allowed to meet and socialize with eligible men. Generally younger daughters would be kept, or at least delayed, from coming out if an elder sister had not married yet; this was in order to keep the younger ones from competing with the elder for the same potential husbands.

20. *old maid:* an older woman who has never married. The boys are relieved because an old maid would have to be supported by her family, which meant, once her father was gone, by her brothers. This is what happened to Jane Austen and her sister after the death of their father: they, along with their mother, lived in a house provided by one of her brothers, while their money came from regular sums sent to them by all her brothers.

This sentence also suggests the large size of the Lucas family, which is a principal reason why they can give Charlotte little fortune. The "younger girls" mentioned would be in addition to Charlotte and to her sister Maria, who seems already "out" since she was earlier noted as dancing with Bingley (p. 20). The "boys" mentioned do not include, most likely, the boy presented earlier in argument with Mrs. Bennet (p. 34), for he seemed far too childish to be one of those worrying about having to support an elder sister in the future. Thus the family has at least four girls, and three boys.

21. Charlotte's decision is one of particular pertinence and poignancy for Jane Austen. She too had little inheritance, and she ended up never marrying. She also knew her fate by the time this novel was written, for she was in

the surprise it must occasion to Elizabeth Bennet, whose friendship she valued beyond that of any other person. Elizabeth would wonder, and probably would blame her; and though her resolution was not to be shaken, her feelings must be hurt by such disapprobation. She resolved to give her the information herself, and therefore charged Mr. Collins when he returned to Longbourn to dinner, to drop no hint of what had passed before any of the family. A promise of secrecy was of course very dutifully given, but it could not be kept without difficulty; for the curiosity excited by his long absence, burst forth in such very direct questions on his return, as required some ingenuity to evade, and he was at the same time exercising great self-denial, for he was longing to publish[22] his prosperous[23] love.

As he was to begin his journey too early on the morrow to see any of the family, the ceremony of leave-taking was performed when the ladies moved for the night;[24] and Mrs. Bennet with great politeness and cordiality said how happy they should be to see him at Longbourn again, whenever his other engagements might allow him to visit them.

"My dear Madam," he replied, "this invitation is particularly gratifying, because it is what I have been hoping to receive; and you may be very certain that I shall avail myself of it as soon as possible."

They were all astonished; and Mr. Bennet, who could by no means wish for so speedy a return, immediately said,

"But is there not danger of Lady Catherine's disapprobation here, my good sir?—You had better neglect your relations, than run the risk of offending your patroness."

"My dear sir," replied Mr. Collins, "I am particularly obliged to you for this friendly caution, and you may depend upon my not taking so material a step without her ladyship's concurrence."

"You cannot be too much on your guard. Risk any thing rather than her displeasure; and if you find it likely to be raised[25] by your coming to us again, which I should think exceedingly probable, stay quietly at home, and be satisfied that *we* shall take no offence."

her late thirties, and therefore beyond any realistic hope of marriage in the society of the time (Charlotte, at 27, is already almost past normal eligibility). Her awareness of the pains of Charlotte's situation appears in a line from a letter to her niece Fanny (see cover) advising her on whether to marry: "Single Women have a dreadful propensity for being poor—which is one very strong argument in favour of Matrimony" (Mar. 13, 1817). This awareness surfaces as well in her novels. Her unfinished novel, *The Watsons*, centers on a heroine who has been left penniless, and who will eventually (according to an outline of the story) have to choose between marrying for love and for money. *Emma* shows the extremely pinched circumstances of an elderly woman from a genteel background who has never married, Miss Bates, and her heavy dependence on the charity of her neighbors. Charlotte clearly appreciates this reality; she also knows that, given her age and lack of either fortune or good looks, Mr. Collins may be her last chance. With him, she will enjoy a comfortable income and home, the power of managing a household, and a much higher social position than she would have as a single woman.

All this does not mean, however, that Jane Austen endorses Charlotte's decision. In the letter quoted above, Jane Austen's ultimate advice is that her niece, since she has significant reservations about the man himself, should not marry him. In an earlier letter, relating to another man, she told her niece, "nothing can be compared to the misery of being bound [i.e. married] *without* love" (Nov. 30, 1814). Similarly in *The Watsons* the heroine declares, "I would rather be Teacher at a school (and I can think of nothing worse) than marry a Man I did not like." In her own life Jane Austen, only two weeks before turning the same age as Charlotte, accepted a proposal in marriage, and then changed her mind the next day due to her objections to the man— who seems to have been a little uncouth, but not nearly as bad as Mr. Collins. Her own words and conduct thus suggest that she does not consider Charlotte's move a wise one, even if it may be understandable in certain respects.

Charlotte's decision also reveals the pressures on Elizabeth, who will likely inherit even less than Charlotte, to make a financially advantageous marriage. It thus highlights Elizabeth's daring in twice rejecting men who have ample fortunes but whom she finds personally unsuitable.

22. *publish*: make publicly or generally known.

23. *prosperous*: successful.

24. *moved for the night*: this may mean that they moved to their rooms to prepare for bed—hence they must say goodbye to Mr. Collins now. I have not been able to find any other example of or reference to such an expression.

25. *raised*: aroused.

"Believe me, my dear sir, my gratitude is warmly excited by such affectionate attention; and depend upon it, you will speedily receive from me a letter of thanks for this, as well as for every other mark of your regard during my stay in Hertfordshire. As for my fair cousins, though my absence may not be long enough to render it necessary, I shall now take the liberty of wishing them health and happiness, not excepting my cousin Elizabeth."

With proper civilities the ladies then withdrew; all of them equally surprised to find that he meditated[26] a quick return. Mrs. Bennet wished to understand by it that he thought of paying his addresses to one of her younger girls, and Mary might have been prevailed on to accept him. She rated his abilities much higher than any of the others; there was a solidity in his reflections which often struck her,[27] and though by no means so clever as herself, she thought that if encouraged to read and improve himself by such an example as her's, he might become a very agreeable companion. But on the following morning, every hope of this kind was done away. Miss Lucas called soon after breakfast, and in a private conference with Elizabeth related the event of the day before.

The possibility of Mr. Collins's fancying himself in love with her friend had once occurred to Elizabeth within the last day or two; but that Charlotte could encourage him, seemed almost as far from possibility as that she could encourage him herself, and her astonishment was consequently so great as to overcome at first the bounds of decorum, and she could not help crying out,

"Engaged to Mr. Collins! my dear Charlotte,—impossible!"[28]

The steady countenance which Miss Lucas had commanded in telling her story, gave way to a momentary confusion here on receiving so direct a reproach; though, as it was no more than she expected, she soon regained her composure, and calmly replied,

"Why should you be surprised, my dear Eliza?—Do you think it incredible that Mr. Collins should be able to procure any woman's good opinion, because he was not so happy as to succeed with you?"

But Elizabeth had now recollected herself, and making a strong effort for it, was able to assure her with tolerable firmness

26. *meditated*: planned, intended.

27. She naturally thinks highly of Mr. Collins's reflections, for they contain just the sort of standard clichés that hers do.

28. The first case, soon to be followed by others, in which Elizabeth will be forced to confront a mistake in her estimation of someone around her.

that the prospect of their relationship was highly grateful to her, and that she wished her all imaginable happiness.

"I see what you are feeling," replied Charlotte,—"you must be surprised, very much surprised,—so lately as Mr. Collins was wishing to marry you. But when you have had time to think it all over, I hope you will be satisfied with what I have done. I am not romantic you know. I never was. I ask only a comfortable home; and considering Mr. Collins's character, connections, and situation in life, I am convinced that my chance of happiness with him is as fair, as most people can boast on entering the marriage state."

Elizabeth quietly answered "Undoubtedly;"—and after an awkward pause, they returned to the rest of the family. Charlotte did not stay much longer, and Elizabeth was then left to reflect on what she had heard. It was a long time before she became at all reconciled to the idea of so unsuitable a match. The strangeness of Mr. Collins's making two offers of marriage within three days, was nothing in comparison of his being now accepted. She had always felt that Charlotte's opinion of matrimony was not exactly like her own, but she could not have supposed it possible that when called into action, she would have sacrificed every better feeling to worldly advantage.[29] Charlotte the wife of Mr. Collins, was a most humiliating picture!—And to the pang of a friend disgracing herself and sunk in her esteem, was added the distressing conviction that it was impossible for that friend to be tolerably happy in the lot she had chosen.

29. Had she been more attentive, she could have seen that Charlotte, in addition to having a more cynical view of marriage, has consistently been more concerned with worldly advantage than Elizabeth.

Chapter Twenty-Three

*E*lizabeth was sitting with her mother and sisters, reflecting on what she had heard, and doubting whether she were authorised to mention it, when Sir William Lucas himself appeared, sent by his daughter to announce her engagement to the family. With many compliments to them, and much self-gratulation[1] on the prospect of a connection between the houses,[2] he unfolded the matter,—to an audience not merely wondering, but incredulous; for Mrs. Bennet, with more perseverance than politeness, protested he must be entirely mistaken, and Lydia, always unguarded and often uncivil, boisterously exclaimed,

"Good Lord! Sir William, how can you tell such a story?—Do not you know that Mr. Collins wants to marry Lizzy?"

Nothing less than the complaisance[3] of a courtier[4] could have borne without anger such treatment; but Sir William's good breeding[5] carried him through it all; and though he begged leave to be positive as to the truth of his information, he listened to all their impertinence with the most forbearing courtesy.

Elizabeth, feeling it incumbent on her to relieve him from so unpleasant a situation, now put herself forward to confirm his account, by mentioning her prior knowledge of it from Charlotte herself; and endeavoured to put a stop to the exclamations of her mother and sisters, by the earnestness of her congratulations to Sir William, in which she was readily joined by Jane, and by making a variety of remarks on the happiness that might be expected from the match, the excellent character of Mr. Collins, and the convenient distance of Hunsford from London.[6]

Mrs. Bennet was in fact too much overpowered to say a great deal while Sir William remained; but no sooner had he left them than her feelings found a rapid vent. In the first place, she persisted in disbelieving the whole of the matter; secondly, she was

1. *self-gratulation*: self-congratulation.

2. Their houses, or families, would now be connected because of Mr. Collins's being a cousin of the Bennets. Establishing such connections was an important aspect of marriage then.

3. *complaisance*: desire of pleasing, politeness.

4. *courtier*: person attending a court. It could also connote someone who possessed certain courtly virtues, such as courtesy. It is meant ironically in the case of Sir William, for though he has only appeared at court once to be knighted, he fancies himself a courtier and has cultivated exaggerated courtesy in his own behavior and demeanor.

5. *good breeding*: good manners.

6. It is only around twenty miles. Such a distance would take a few hours at the most, and from Hertfordshire it would be less than a day. Later Elizabeth will describe the overall distance as fifty miles, and Darcy will say that this takes little more than half a day's journey on good roads.

very sure that Mr. Collins had been taken in; thirdly, she trusted that they would never be happy together; and fourthly, that the match might be broken off.[7] Two inferences, however, were plainly deduced from the whole; one, that Elizabeth was the real cause of all the mischief;[8] and the other, that she herself had been barbarously used by them all; and on these two points she principally dwelt during the rest of the day. Nothing could console and nothing appease her.—Nor did that day wear out her resentment. A week elapsed before she could see Elizabeth without scolding her, a month passed away before she could speak to Sir William or Lady Lucas without being rude, and many months were gone before she could at all forgive their daughter.

Mr. Bennet's emotions were much more tranquil on the occasion, and such as he did experience he pronounced to be of a most agreeable sort; for it gratified him, he said, to discover that Charlotte Lucas, whom he had been used to think tolerably sensible, was as foolish as his wife, and more foolish than his daughter![9]

Jane confessed herself a little surprised at the match; but she said less of her astonishment than of her earnest desire for their happiness; nor could Elizabeth persuade her to consider it as improbable.[10] Kitty and Lydia were far from envying Miss Lucas, for Mr. Collins was only a clergyman; and it affected them in no other way than as a piece of news to spread at Meryton.

Lady Lucas could not be insensible[11] of triumph on being able to retort on[12] Mrs. Bennet the comfort[13] of having a daughter well married; and she called at Longbourn rather oftener than usual to say how happy she was, though Mrs. Bennet's sour looks and ill-natured remarks might have been enough to drive happiness away.[14]

Between Elizabeth and Charlotte there was a restraint which kept them mutually silent on the subject; and Elizabeth felt persuaded that no real confidence[15] could ever subsist between them again. Her disappointment in Charlotte made her turn with fonder regard to her sister, of whose rectitude and delicacy[16] she was sure her opinion could never be shaken, and for whose happiness she grew daily more anxious, as Bingley had now been gone a week, and nothing was heard of his return.

7.   Mrs. Bennet's contradictory utterances are similar to the joke about the man who, upon being accused of breaking something he has borrowed, responds that in the first place he never borrowed the item, in the second place he returned it intact, and in the third place it was already broken when he received it.

8.   *mischief*: trouble, evil.

9.   In other words, he is happy to be able to think someone else foolish and to laugh at them, an example of his particular type of enjoyment.

10.   To consider their happiness improbable (not the match).

11.   *insensible*: without a sense.

12.   *retort on*: throw back at (in retaliation).

13.   *comfort*: pleasure.

14.   Since Mrs. Bennet was earlier crowing to Lady Lucas about her presumed success in getting a daughter married, Lady Lucas is now turning the tables.

15.   *confidence*: intimacy or trust (i.e. willingness to confide in one another).

16.   *delicacy*: moral sensitivity and taste, fineness of feeling. These would ensure that she would never marry someone as crude and repugnant as Mr. Collins.

Jane had sent Caroline an early answer to her letter, and was counting the days till she might reasonably hope to hear again.[17] The promised letter of thanks from Mr. Collins arrived on Tuesday, addressed to their father, and written with all the solemnity of gratitude which a twelvemonth's abode in the family might have prompted. After discharging his conscience on that head, he proceeded to inform them, with many rapturous expressions, of his happiness in having obtained the affection of their amiable neighbour, Miss Lucas, and then explained that it was merely with the view of enjoying her society that he had been so ready to close with[18] their kind wish of seeing him again at Longbourn, whither he hoped to be able to return on Monday fortnight;[19] for Lady Catherine, he added, so heartily approved his marriage, that she wished it to take place as soon as possible, which he trusted would be an unanswerable argument with his amiable Charlotte to name an early day for making him the happiest of men.

Mr. Collins's return into Hertfordshire was no longer a matter of pleasure to Mrs. Bennet. On the contrary she was as much disposed to complain of it as her husband.—It was very strange that he should come to Longbourn instead of to Lucas Lodge; it was also very inconvenient and exceedingly troublesome.—She hated having visitors in the house while her health was so indifferent,[20] and lovers were of all people the most disagreeable. Such were the gentle murmurs of Mrs. Bennet, and they gave way only to the greater distress of Mr. Bingley's continued absence.

Neither Jane nor Elizabeth were comfortable on this subject. Day after day passed away without bringing any other tidings of him than the report which shortly prevailed in Meryton of his coming no more to Netherfield the whole winter; a report which highly incensed Mrs. Bennet, and which she never failed to contradict as a most scandalous falsehood.

Even Elizabeth began to fear—not that Bingley was indifferent—but that his sisters would be successful in keeping him away. Unwilling as she was to admit an idea so destructive of Jane's happiness, and so dishonourable to the stability[21] of her lover, she could not prevent its frequently recurring. The united efforts of

17. Jane has to depend on a correspondence with Miss Bingley, for it would be improper for her to correspond with Bingley himself, an unmarried man who is not a relation and with whom she has no engagement.

18. *close with:* agree to, accept.

19. This letter is a good symbol of Mr. Collins's character. After first ostentatiously thanking the Bennets, he proceeds to inform them directly that he is only visiting them because he wishes to see someone else—not the most polite of messages to send to one's hosts.

20. *indifferent:* mediocre.

21. *stability:* steadiness, firmness.

his two unfeeling sisters and of his overpowering friend, assisted by the attractions of Miss Darcy and the amusements of London, might be too much, she feared, for the strength of his attachment.

As for Jane, *her* anxiety under this suspense was, of course, more painful than Elizabeth's; but whatever she felt she was desirous of concealing, and between herself and Elizabeth, therefore, the subject was never alluded to. But as no such delicacy restrained her mother, an hour seldom passed in which she did not talk of Bingley, express her impatience for his arrival, or even require Jane to confess that if he did not come back, she should think herself very ill used. It needed all Jane's steady mildness to bear these attacks with tolerable tranquillity.

Mr. Collins returned most punctually on the Monday fortnight, but his reception at Longbourn was not quite so gracious as it had been on his first introduction. He was too happy, however, to need much attention; and luckily for the others, the business of love-making[22] relieved them from a great deal of his company. The chief of every day was spent by him at Lucas Lodge, and he sometimes returned to Longbourn only in time to make an apology for his absence before the family went to bed.

Mrs. Bennet was really in a most pitiable state. The very mention of any thing concerning the match threw her into an agony of ill humour, and wherever she went she was sure of hearing it talked of. The sight of Miss Lucas was odious to her. As her successor in that house, she regarded her with jealous abhorrence. Whenever Charlotte came to see them she concluded her to be anticipating the hour of possession; and whenever she spoke in a low voice to Mr. Collins, was convinced that they were talking of the Longbourn estate, and resolving to turn herself and her daughters out of the house, as soon as Mr. Bennet were dead. She complained bitterly of all this to her husband.

"Indeed, Mr. Bennet," said she, "it is very hard to think that Charlotte Lucas should ever be mistress of this house, that *I* should be forced to make way for *her*, and live to see her take my place in it!"

"My dear, do not give way to such gloomy thoughts. Let us

22. *love-making:* wooing, talking to one's beloved.

hope for better things. Let us flatter ourselves that *I* may be the survivor."[23]

This was not very consoling to Mrs. Bennet, and, therefore, instead of making any answer, she went on as before,

"I cannot bear to think that they should have all this estate. If it was not for the entail I should not mind it."

"What should not you mind?"

"I should not mind any thing at all."

"Let us be thankful that you are preserved from a state of such insensibility."[24]

"I never can be thankful, Mr. Bennet, for any thing about the entail. How any one could have the conscience to entail away an estate from one's own daughters I cannot understand; and all for the sake of Mr. Collins too![25]—Why should *he* have it more than anybody else?"

"I leave it to yourself to determine," said Mr. Bennet.

23. Which would mean that Mrs. Bennet, having died before her husband, would never experience being turned out of their house.

24. *insensibility*: inability to feel or be affected by anything.

25. Since in fact it would not be Mr. Bennet, but the man from whom he inherited (probably his father), who would have framed the entail then in force, such a framer would not have been entailing the property away from his own daughters (but only, possibly, from his granddaughters). This framer also could not have known that Mr. Collins would be the ultimate beneficiary of the entail.

VOLUME TWO[1]

Chapter One

*M*iss Bingley's letter arrived, and put an end to doubt. The very first sentence conveyed the assurance of their being all settled in London for the winter, and concluded with her brother's regret at not having had time to pay his respects to his friends in Hertfordshire before he left the country.

Hope was over, entirely over; and when Jane could attend to the rest of the letter, she found little, except the professed affection of the writer, that could give her any comfort. Miss Darcy's praise occupied the chief of it. Her many attractions were again dwelt on, and Caroline boasted joyfully of their increasing intimacy, and ventured to predict the accomplishment of the wishes which had been unfolded in her former letter. She wrote also with great pleasure of her brother's being an inmate[2] of Mr. Darcy's house, and mentioned with raptures, some plans of the latter with regard to new furniture.

Elizabeth, to whom Jane very soon communicated the chief[3] of all this, heard it in silent indignation. Her heart was divided between concern for her sister, and resentment against all the others. To Caroline's assertion of her brother's being partial to Miss Darcy she paid no credit. That he was really fond of Jane, she doubted no more than she had ever done; and much as she had always been disposed to like him, she could not think without anger, hardly without contempt, on that easiness of temper, that want of proper resolution which now made him the slave of his designing friends, and led him to sacrifice his own happiness to the caprice of their inclinations.[4] Had his own happiness, however, been the only sacrifice, he might have been allowed to sport[5]

1.   Jane Austen divides her novel into three volumes, a standard practice at the time. The division is somewhat arbitrary; this break between the first and second volumes does not occur at any special point in the story. One could argue that a more logical break would be just prior to Elizabeth's journey to visit Charlotte, which leads to the next major development in the action, though such a break would also make the three volumes very unequal in length. The strongest case for this break would be that what has just happened, Mr. Collins's engagement to Charlotte, marked the conclusion of the first stage of the action. For the next several chapters the existing situation will be reviewed and the ground laid for more dramatic future developments.

2.   *inmate*: inhabitant.

3.   *chief*: greater part.

4.   Her opinion here stands in ironic contrast to her earlier conversations with Bingley and Darcy about accommodating other people. Then she had argued, with particular reference to Bingley, for being compliant and for acceding to the wishes of a friend; now she censures him for those same qualities. She is thus closer to being able to appreciate the contrary opinion, and contrary character, of Darcy.

5.   *sport*: amuse himself.

with it in what ever manner he thought best; but her sister's was involved in it, as she thought he must be sensible[6] himself. It was a subject, in short, on which reflection would be long indulged, and must be unavailing. She could think of nothing else, and yet whether Bingley's regard had really died away, or were suppressed by his friends' interference; whether he had been aware of Jane's attachment, or whether it had escaped his observation; whichever were the case, though her opinion of him must be materially affected by the difference, her sister's situation remained the same, her peace equally wounded.

A day or two passed before Jane had courage to speak of her feelings to Elizabeth; but at last on Mrs. Bennet's leaving them together, after a longer irritation[7] than usual about Netherfield and its master, she could not help saying,

"Oh! that my dear mother had more command over herself; she can have no idea of the pain she gives me by her continual reflections on him. But I will not repine. It cannot last long. He will be forgot, and we shall all be as we were before."

Elizabeth looked at her sister with incredulous solicitude, but said nothing.

"You doubt me," cried Jane, slightly colouring;[8] "indeed you have no reason. He may live in my memory as the most amiable man of my acquaintance, but that is all. I have nothing either to hope or fear, and nothing to reproach him with.[9] Thank God! I have not *that* pain. A little time therefore.—I shall certainly try to get the better."

With a stronger voice she soon added, "I have this comfort immediately, that it has not been more than an error of fancy on my side, and that it has done no harm to any one but myself."

"My dear Jane!" exclaimed Elizabeth, "you are too good. Your sweetness and disinterestedness are really angelic; I do not know what to say to you. I feel as if I had never done you justice, or loved you as you deserve."

Miss Bennet eagerly disclaimed all extraordinary merit, and threw back the praise on her sister's warm affection.

"Nay," said Elizabeth, "this is not fair. *You* wish to think all the

6. *sensible:* aware, conscious.

7. *irritation:* state of excitement or vexation (meaning Mrs. Bennet is in such a state as she makes her denunciation).

8. *colouring:* blushing.

9. She means that he made her no offer of marriage, and thus she cannot reproach him for breaking off a promised engagement. Such a breach of promise by a man was a very serious matter and could lead to legal action against the perpetrator (as it does, for example, in Charles Dickens's *Pickwick Papers*).

world respectable, and are hurt if I speak ill of any body. *I* only
want to think *you* perfect, and you set yourself against it. Do not
be afraid of my running into any excess, of my encroaching on
your privilege of universal good will.[10] You need not. There are
few people whom I really love, and still fewer of whom I think
well. The more I see of the world, the more am I dissatisfied with
it; and every day confirms my belief of the inconsistency of all
human characters,[11] and of the little dependence that can be
placed on the appearance of either merit or sense.[12] I have met
with two instances lately; one I will not mention;[13] the other is
Charlotte's marriage. It is unaccountable! in every view it is unaccountable!"[14]

"My dear Lizzy, do not give way to such feelings as these. They
will ruin your happiness. You do not make allowance enough
for difference of situation and temper.[15] Consider Mr. Collins's respectability, and Charlotte's prudent, steady character. Remember
that she is one of a large family; that as to fortune, it is a most eligible match;[16] and be ready to believe, for every body's sake, that she
may feel something like regard and esteem for our cousin."

"To oblige you, I would try to believe almost any thing, but no
one else could be benefited by such a belief as this; for were I persuaded that Charlotte had any regard for him, I should only think
worse of her understanding,[17] than I now do of her heart. My dear
Jane, Mr. Collins is a conceited, pompous, narrow-minded,[18] silly
man; you know he is, as well as I do; and you must feel, as well as
I do, that the woman who marries him, cannot have a proper way
of thinking. You shall not defend her, though it is Charlotte
Lucas. You shall not, for the sake of one individual, change the
meaning of principle and integrity, nor endeavour to persuade
yourself or me, that selfishness is prudence, and insensibility of
danger,[19] security for happiness."[20]

"I must think your language too strong in speaking of both,"
replied Jane, "and I hope you will be convinced of it, by seeing
them happy together. But enough of this. You alluded to something else. You mentioned *two* instances. I cannot misunderstand
you, but I intreat you, dear Lizzy, not to pain me by thinking *that*

10. In other words, of being carried away, or thinking as benevolently of all the world as you do.

11. In fact, Bingley's actions are fairly consistent with the accommodating character he had shown earlier, a character that Elizabeth boasted of understanding perfectly.

12. Elizabeth's disgust with the world is significant because it contrasts with her usual good spirits; it represents an attitude Jane Austen consistently portrays in a bad light.

13. Bingley's conduct, which she does not mention to avoid upsetting Jane.

14. In fact, it is not unaccountable, for Elizabeth received clues regarding Charlotte (as she also did about Bingley) that she disregarded because they conflicted with what she wished to believe. Her miscalculations in these cases supplement her more serious miscalculations regarding Darcy and Wickham. One theme of the novel is that even very intelligent people, like Elizabeth and Darcy, can err seriously in judgment when blinded by wishes or prejudices.

15. *difference of situation and temper:* meaning differences in those areas between Charlotte and Elizabeth, differences Jane goes on to describe.

16. The match's eligibility, or desirability, in a financial sense would be especially important for someone from a large family, where each child would have to share the family fortune with many siblings.

17. *understanding:* judgment, intelligence.

18. *narrow-minded:* self-centered.

19. *insensibility of danger:* unconsciousness of danger (referring to the dangers arising from a bad marriage).

20. Elizabeth expresses here a fundamental principle for Jane Austen, that standards of good and bad have an objective validity and cannot be altered to suit individual cases. An individual who violates these standards is wrong, regardless of that person's other merits.

As concerns this case, while the author probably agrees with Jane that Elizabeth is a little harsh in her verdict and a little prone to neglect certain mitigating factors, most indications are that Jane Austen endorses Elizabeth's overall judgment.

person[21] to blame, and saying your opinion of him is sunk. We must not be so ready to fancy ourselves intentionally injured. We must not expect a lively young man to be always so guarded and circumspect. It is very often nothing but our own vanity that deceives us. Women fancy admiration means more than it does."

"And men take care that they should."[22]

"If it is designedly done, they cannot be justified; but I have no idea of there being so much design in the world as some persons imagine."

"I am far from attributing any part of Mr. Bingley's conduct to design," said Elizabeth; "but without scheming to do wrong, or to make others unhappy, there may be error, and there may be misery. Thoughtlessness, want of attention to other people's feelings, and want of resolution, will do the business."[23]

"And do you impute it to either of those?"

"Yes; to the last. But if I go on, I shall displease you by saying what I think of persons you esteem. Stop me whilst you can."

"You persist, then, in supposing his sisters influence him."

"Yes, in conjunction with his friend."

"I cannot believe it. Why should they try to influence him? They can only wish his happiness, and if he is attached to me, no other woman can secure it."

"Your first position[24] is false. They may wish many things besides his happiness; they may wish his increase of wealth and consequence;[25] they may wish him to marry a girl who has all the importance of money, great connections,[26] and pride."[27]

"Beyond a doubt, they *do* wish him to chuse Miss Darcy," replied Jane; "but this may be from better feelings than you are supposing. They have known her much longer than they have known me; no wonder if they love her better. But, whatever may be their own wishes, it is very unlikely they should have opposed their brother's. What sister would think herself at liberty to do it, unless there were something very objectionable? If they believed him attached to me, they would not try to part us; if he were so, they could not succeed. By supposing such an affection, you make every body acting unnaturally and wrong, and me most

21. *that person:* Bingley.

22. Jane Austen's works present examples of both these phenomena. Ironically, one instance of the latter is Wickham's flirtation with Elizabeth; the latter fails there to recognize some of the very male deceptiveness she identifies here—though her error in that case involves misjudging Wickham's character more than overestimating his regard for her.

23. Another phenomena frequently seen in Jane Austen. Her works contain few hardened villains, but they do contain numerous cases of people who are generally good, or at least not malicious or ill-intentioned, and who nonetheless commit serious faults or cause significant pain to others. Elizabeth herself provides one example of this, though hardly the worst.

24. *position:* proposition, assertion.

25. *consequence:* social position or importance.

26. *great connections:* high-ranking, or socially prominent, family connections.

27. Since Bingley's sisters would find their own social position enhanced by his marriage to someone who was wealthy and well-connected, they have strong personal reasons for desiring such a match.

unhappy. Do not distress me by the idea. I am not ashamed of having been mistaken—or, at least, it is slight, it is nothing in comparison of what I should feel in thinking ill of him or his sisters.[28] Let me take it in the best light, in the light in which it may be understood."

Elizabeth could not oppose such a wish; and from this time Mr. Bingley's name was scarcely ever mentioned between them.

Mrs. Bennet still continued to wonder and repine at his returning no more, and though a day seldom passed in which Elizabeth did not account for it clearly, there seemed little chance of her ever considering it with less perplexity. Her daughter endeavoured to convince her of what she did not believe herself, that his attentions to Jane had been merely the effect of a common and transient liking, which ceased when he saw her no more; but though the probability of the statement was admitted at the time, she had the same story to repeat every day. Mrs. Bennet's best comfort was that Mr. Bingley must be down again in the summer.[29]

Mr. Bennet treated the matter differently. "So, Lizzy," said he one day, "your sister is crossed in love[30] I find. I congratulate her. Next to being married, a girl likes to be crossed in love a little now and then. It is something to think of, and gives her a sort of distinction among her companions.[31] When is your turn to come? You will hardly bear to be long outdone by Jane. Now is your time. Here are officers enough at Meryton to disappoint all the young ladies in the country. Let Wickham be *your* man. He is a pleasant fellow, and would jilt you creditably."[32]

"Thank you, Sir, but a less agreeable man[33] would satisfy me. We must not all expect Jane's good fortune."[34]

"True," said Mr. Bennet, "but it is a comfort to think that, whatever of that kind may befal you, you have an affectionate mother who will always make the most of it."

Mr. Wickham's society was of material service in dispelling the gloom, which the late perverse occurrences had thrown on many of the Longbourn family. They saw him often, and to his other recommendations was now added that of general unreserve. The whole of what Elizabeth had already heard, his claims on Mr.

28. Jane's preference for thinking badly of herself rather than of others is characteristic. Jane also provides here an excellent contrast to the cynical and almost bitter attitude that Elizabeth expresses at this point, a function Jane often serves in the novel. Jane's behavior, however, does give rise to the question of how someone of her distinctive character could arise in the Bennet family, for while the other four sisters all possess at least some features to be found in one of their parents, Jane seems to have nothing in common with either. Mr. and Mrs. Bennet are both, in their distinctive ways, quick to condemn and to criticize others; both are also fundamentally selfish; neither exhibits a trace of Jane's almost angelic sweetness and naivety.

29. Since people who could afford to often went to London for the winter and spring, and returned to the country (which is what is meant by "down") during the summer, Mrs. Bennet's wish has some basis.

30. *crossed in love:* a phrase often used for a woman whose lover had abandoned or deceived her.

31. This statement sheds an even stronger, and less amusing, light on Mr. Bennet's callousness, for now his wit is directed not against unsympathetic fools like his wife or Mr. Collins, but against a good and intelligent person, one who is also his own daughter.

32. It is possible that Mr. Bennet, unlike Elizabeth, has perceived some of Wickham's untrustworthiness—he will later express his contempt for Wickham's obsequious manner—and that he is trying to warn her (the only one of his daughters he seems to care for significantly). If so, his habitual irony and humor keep the message from being taken seriously.

33. *less agreeable man:* less agreeable than Wickham.

34. The good fortune of being jilted by a very agreeable man, as Jane has been with Bingley and Elizabeth would be with Wickham. The idea is that the more agreeable the man, the harsher the rejection by him would be, and thus the greater the distinction that would be gained by the woman. Elizabeth is being sarcastic in describing this as good fortune.

Darcy, and all that he had suffered from him, was now openly acknowledged and publicly canvassed;[35] and every body was pleased to think how much they had always disliked Mr. Darcy before they had known any thing of the matter.[36]

Miss Bennet was the only creature who could suppose there might be any extenuating circumstances in the case, unknown to the society of Hertfordshire; her mild and steady candour[37] always pleaded for allowances, and urged the possibility of mistakes—but by everybody else Mr. Darcy was condemned as the worst of men.

35. *canvassed*: discussed. This action of Wickham's contradicts his earlier promise of discretion for the sake of Darcy's father.

36. A reminder of the irrationality of public opinion. Later the same public will assert its longstanding knowledge of exactly opposite truths.

37. *candour*: tendency always to think well of others.

Chapter Two

After a week spent in professions of love and schemes of felicity, Mr. Collins was called from his amiable Charlotte by the arrival of Saturday.[1] The pain of separation, however, might be alleviated on his side, by preparations for the reception of his bride, as he had reason to hope, that shortly after his next return into Hertfordshire, the day would be fixed that was to make him the happiest of men. He took leave of his relations at Longbourn with as much solemnity as before; wished his fair cousins health and happiness again, and promised their father another letter of thanks.

On the following Monday, Mrs. Bennet had the pleasure of receiving her brother and his wife, who came as usual to spend the Christmas at Longbourn. Mr. Gardiner was a sensible, gentlemanlike man, greatly superior to his sister as well by nature as by education. The Netherfield ladies would have had difficulty in believing that a man who lived by trade, and within view of his own warehouses,[2] could have been so well bred[3] and agreeable. Mrs. Gardiner, who was several years younger than Mrs. Bennet and Mrs. Philips, was an amiable, intelligent, elegant woman, and a great favourite with all her Longbourn nieces. Between the two eldest and herself especially, there subsisted a very particular regard. They had frequently been staying with her in town.

The first part of Mrs. Gardiner's business on her arrival, was to distribute her presents and describe the newest fashions.[4] When this was done she had a less active part to play. It became her turn to listen. Mrs. Bennet had many grievances to relate, and much to complain of. They had all been very ill-used since she last saw her sister. Two of her girls had been on the point of marriage, and after all there was nothing in it.

"I do not blame Jane," she continued, "for Jane would have got Mr. Bingley, if she could. But, Lizzy! Oh, sister! it is very hard to

1.   Mr. Collins would have to leave then in order to get back for the Sunday service. For the dates and sequence of events in this section of the novel, see chronology, pp. 714–715.

2.   *warehouses:* shops, especially shops selling goods that are not made on the premises. Mr. Gardiner's living next to his warehouses, and thus in the commercial part of town, is another mark against him socially. The trend at this time was for increasing numbers of merchants in the commercial section of London (the oldest part of London, often known as the City), to reside in the more fashionable, western parts of London and to commute to their places of business. An important reason was that the noise and smoke and unpleasant odors produced by the many enterprises in the commercial section made it a less pleasant place to live. Presumably Mr. Gardiner does not commute because he cannot afford to buy a residence in other parts of London—at least that would be the assumption of the Netherfield ladies.

3.   *well bred:* polite.

4.   *newest fashions:* Mrs. Gardiner would have known of these because she lived in London, which received the latest fashions before the countryside. This gap of city and country, which can often still exist, would have been exacerbated then by the slower pace of communication and transportation.

think that she might have been Mr. Collins's wife by this time, had not it been for her own perverseness. He made her an offer in this very room, and she refused him. The consequence of it is, that Lady Lucas will have a daughter married before I have, and that Longbourn estate is just as much entailed as ever.[5] The Lucases are very artful[6] people indeed, sister. They are all for what they can get. I am sorry to say it of them, but so it is. It makes me very nervous[7] and poorly,[8] to be thwarted so in my own family, and to have neighbours who think of themselves before anybody else. However, your coming just at this time is the greatest of comforts, and I am very glad to hear what you tell us, of long sleeves."[9]

Mrs. Gardiner, to whom the chief of this news had been given before, in the course of Jane and Elizabeth's correspondence with her, made her sister a slight answer, and in compassion to her nieces turned the conversation.[10]

When alone with Elizabeth afterwards, she spoke more on the subject. "It seems likely to have been a desirable match for Jane," said she. "I am sorry it went off.[11] But these things happen so often! A young man, such as you describe Mr. Bingley, so easily falls in love with a pretty girl for a few weeks, and when accident separates them, so easily forgets her, that these sort of inconstancies are very frequent."

"An excellent consolation in its way," said Elizabeth, "but it will not do for *us*. We do not suffer by *accident*. It does not often happen that the interference of friends will persuade a young man of independent fortune to think no more of a girl, whom he was violently in love with only a few days before."

"But that expression of 'violently in love' is so hackneyed, so doubtful, so indefinite, that it gives me very little idea. It is as often applied to feelings which arise from an half-hour's acquaintance, as to a real, strong attachment.[12] Pray, how *violent was* Mr. Bingley's love?"

"I never saw a more promising inclination. He was growing quite inattentive to other people, and wholly engrossed by her. Every time they met, it was more decided and remarkable. At his own ball he offended two or three young ladies, by not asking them

5. The estate would have been just as much entailed had Elizabeth accepted Mr. Collins, though in that case Elizabeth would have been one of the beneficiaries of the entail.

6. *artful*: crafty, cunning.

7. *nervous*: afflicted with nervous difficulties.

8. *poorly*: unwell, indisposed.

9. *long sleeves*: presumably a change in fashion, perhaps toward long sleeves. In letters written not long after this novel was published, Jane Austen first wonders whether long sleeves are being worn more, and then declares they are (June 14, 1814; Sept. 2, 1814). Mrs. Bennet's sudden segue to such a topic, amidst her lamentations about serious sufferings, marks her superficiality of mind.

10. *turned the conversation*: diverted it to another subject.

11. *went off*: fell through, came to failure.

12. A statement Jane Austen would certainly endorse. Mr. Collins has often used this and other hackneyed expressions, all the while feeling very little.

to dance, and I spoke to him twice myself, without receiving an answer. Could there be finer symptoms? Is not general incivility[13] the very essence of love?"

"Oh, yes!—of that kind of love which I suppose him to have felt. Poor Jane! I am sorry for her, because, with her disposition, she may not get over it immediately. It had better have happened to *you*, Lizzy; you would have laughed yourself out of it sooner. But do you think she would be prevailed on to go back with us?[14] Change of scene might be of service—and perhaps a little relief from home, may be as useful as anything."

Elizabeth was exceedingly pleased with this proposal, and felt persuaded of her sister's ready acquiescence.

"I hope," added Mrs. Gardiner, "that no consideration with regard to this young man will influence her. We live in so different a part of town, all our connections are so different, and, as you well know, we go out so little, that it is very improbable they should meet at all, unless he really comes to see her."

"And *that* is quite impossible; for he is now in the custody of his friend, and Mr. Darcy would no more suffer him to call on Jane in such a part of London! My dear aunt, how could you think of it? Mr. Darcy may perhaps have *heard* of such a place as Gracechurch Street,[15] but he would hardly think a month's ablution enough to cleanse him from its impurities, were he once to enter it;[16] and depend upon it, Mr. Bingley never stirs without him."

"So much the better. I hope they will not meet at all. But does not Jane correspond with the sister? *She* will not be able to help calling."

"She will drop the acquaintance entirely."

But in spite of the certainty in which Elizabeth affected to place this point, as well as the still more interesting[17] one of Bingley's being withheld from seeing Jane, she felt a solicitude on the subject which convinced her, on examination, that she did not consider it entirely hopeless. It was possible, and sometimes she thought it probable, that his affection might be re-animated, and the influence of his friends successfully combated by the more natural[18] influence of Jane's attractions.

Miss Bennet accepted her aunt's invitation with pleasure; and

13. *general incivility*: being uncivil to people in general, due to being absorbed in the person one loves. Significantly, Elizabeth neglects to apply this criteria to Jane, who continued to be civil and friendly toward everyone in spite of her love for Bingley; it was this behavior that, as Darcy reveals later, caused him to underestimate Jane's love.

14. For a visit.

15. *Gracechurch Street*: a street in the City, or commercial section, of London—and obviously where the Gardiners live. It was not a fashionable address.

16. It is evident that Darcy, despite his absence, is still on Elizabeth's mind. She cannot resist the opportunity of throwing in a critical comment about him, even though what she is discussing, Bingley's separation from Jane, is something she has so far ascribed mostly to his sisters (something natural for her to do since it is Miss Bingley's letter that has informed her and Jane about the separation and about Miss Bingley's hopes of a different marriage for him).

17. *interesting*: important.

18. *natural*: produced naturally; not requiring others' manipulation.

the Bingleys were no otherwise in her thoughts at the time, than as she hoped that, by Caroline's not living in the same house with her brother,[19] she might occasionally spend a morning with her, without any danger of seeing him.

The Gardiners staid a week at Longbourn; and what with the Philipses, the Lucases, and the officers, there was not a day without its engagement. Mrs. Bennet had so carefully provided for the entertainment of her brother and sister, that they did not once sit down to a family dinner.[20] When the engagement was for home, some of the officers always made part of it, of which officers Mr. Wickham was sure to be one; and on these occasions, Mrs. Gardiner, rendered suspicious by Elizabeth's warm commendation of him, narrowly observed them both. Without supposing them, from what she saw, to be very seriously in love, their preference of each other was plain enough to make her a little uneasy; and she resolved to speak to Elizabeth on the subject before she left Hertfordshire, and represent to her the imprudence of encouraging such an attachment.[21]

To Mrs. Gardiner, Wickham had one means of affording pleasure, unconnected with his general powers.[22] About ten or a dozen years ago, before her marriage, she had spent a considerable time in that very part of Derbyshire, to which he belonged. They had, therefore, many acquaintance in common; and, though Wickham had been little there since the death of Darcy's father, five years before, it was yet in his power to give her fresher intelligence of[23] her former friends, than she had been in the way of procuring.

Mrs. Gardiner had seen Pemberley, and known the late Mr. Darcy by character[24] perfectly well. Here consequently was an inexhaustible subject of discourse. In comparing her recollection of Pemberley, with the minute description which Wickham could give, and in bestowing her tribute of praise on the character of its late possessor, she was delighting both him and herself. On being made acquainted with the present Mr. Darcy's treatment of him, she tried to remember something of that gentleman's reputed disposition when quite a lad, which might agree with it, and was confident at last, that she recollected having heard Mr. Fitzwilliam Darcy formerly spoken of as a very proud, ill-natured boy.[25]

19. Since, as revealed in Miss Bingley's letters, she is staying at the Hurst's house in London and Mr. Bingley is staying with Darcy.

20. Visitors normally fit into the usual daily routine of their hosts, something seen in other cases in the novel, so Mrs. Bennet's zeal to provide special entertainments for her guests would be considered excessive. She probably sees guests as a good excuse to organize constant social gatherings, which she loves no matter what the occasion.

21. *attachment*: condition of affection between people.

22. *general powers*: powers of entertainment or amusement (such as his ease of conversation).

23. *intelligence of*: information or news about.

24. *character*: reputation.

25. The vagueness of Mrs. Gardiner's recollection, and its having been prompted by her hearing Wickham's tale (which would naturally make her want to remember those things that squared with his account), suggest that not too much stock should be placed in it—though it is certainly plausible that Darcy had a reputation as proud.

Chapter Three

*M*rs. Gardiner's caution to Elizabeth was punctually and kindly given on the first favourable opportunity of speaking to her alone; after honestly telling her what she thought, she thus went on:

"You are too sensible a girl, Lizzy, to fall in love merely because you are warned against it; and, therefore, I am not afraid of speaking openly.[1] Seriously, I would have you be on your guard. Do not involve yourself, or endeavour to involve him in an affection which the want of fortune would make so very imprudent. I have nothing to say against *him*; he is a most interesting young man; and if he had the fortune he ought to have, I should think you could not do better. But as it is—you must not let your fancy run away with you. You have sense, and we all expect you to use it.[2] Your father would depend on *your* resolution and good conduct, I am sure. You must not disappoint your father."

"My dear aunt, this is being serious indeed."

"Yes, and I hope to engage you to be serious likewise."

"Well, then, you need not be under any alarm. I will take care of myself, and of Mr. Wickham too. He shall not be in love with me, if I can prevent it."

"Elizabeth, you are not serious now."

"I beg your pardon. I will try again. At present I am not in love with Mr. Wickham; no, I certainly am not. But he is, beyond all comparison, the most agreeable man I ever saw—and if he becomes really attached to me—I believe it will be better that he should not. I see the imprudence of it.—Oh! *that* abominable Mr. Darcy![3]—My father's opinion of me does me the greatest honor; and I should be miserable to forfeit it. My father, however, is partial to Mr. Wickham.[4] In short, my dear aunt, I should be very sorry to be the means of making any of you unhappy; but

1. A common romantic convention, which Mrs. Gardiner is alluding to jokingly, is for opposition to love, especially on the part of a parent or other authority figure, to encourage that love. Examples of this abound in the literature of the time, including one in Jane Austen's favorite novel, *Sir Charles Grandison*, by Samuel Richardson. She herself plays with, and ridicules, this idea in the funniest of her youthful stories, "Love and Friendship." In it some very foolish characters, in conformity with the best romantic doctrines, pride themselves on never complying with their parents' advice, even when the parents advise them to do what they already desire. For example, one young man refuses his father's suggestion of marriage to a particular woman with the words, "Lady Dorothea is lovely and Engaging; I prefer no woman to her; but know, Sir, that I scorn to marry her in compliance with your wishes. No! Never shall it be said that I obliged my Father."

2. Mrs. Gardiner's warning has a strong basis: given Elizabeth and Wickham's mutual want, or lack, of fortune, it is difficult to see how they could support themselves. Army salaries for a lower officer like Wickham were barely enough to support the officer himself; nor could they rely on finding opportunities for making more money, for such opportunities tended to be limited in this society, especially for those lacking powerful connections. Jane Austen herself, when young, seems to have been obliged to terminate a love affair with a man because they both lacked sufficient fortunes to marry each other.

Jane Austen also indicates consistent support for such practical decisions in her writings. Her novels suggest that, while it is wrong to marry only for money and without love, it is also wrong to marry without regard to money. In *Sense and Sensibility* the sensible heroine accepts as a matter of course that she will be unable to marry the man she loves unless he can manage to secure an adequate income for them. Mrs. Gardiner's caution is thus meant to be seen as wise advice, even without regard to the issue of Wickham himself and his character.

3. Elizabeth denounces Darcy because she believes it is his injustice to Wickham that has prevented the latter from having the means to support a wife.

4. A curious statement, since all Mr. Bennet has been shown saying about Wickham is his joke about Elizabeth being jilted by him. Elizabeth may be unconsciously attributing her own preferences to her father.

since we see every day that where there is affection, young people are seldom withheld by immediate want of fortune, from entering into engagements with each other, how can I promise to be wiser than so many of my fellow creatures if I am tempted, or how am I even to know that it would be wisdom to resist?[5] All that I can promise you, therefore, is not to be in a hurry. I will not be in a hurry to believe myself his first object.[6] When I am in company with him, I will not be wishing. In short, I will do my best."

"Perhaps it will be as well, if you discourage his coming here so very often. At least, you should not *remind* your Mother of inviting him."

"As I did the other day," said Elizabeth, with a conscious[7] smile; "very true, it will be wise in me to refrain from *that*. But do not imagine that he is always here so often. It is on your account that he has been so frequently invited this week. You know my mother's ideas as to the necessity of constant company for her friends.[8] But really, and upon my honour, I will try to do what I think to be wisest; and now, I hope you are satisfied."

Her aunt assured her that she was; and Elizabeth having thanked her for the kindness of her hints, they parted; a wonderful[9] instance of advice being given on such a point, without being resented.

Mr. Collins returned into Hertfordshire soon after it had been quitted by the Gardiners and Jane; but as he took up his abode with the Lucases, his arrival was no great inconvenience to Mrs. Bennet. His marriage was now fast approaching, and she was at length so far resigned as to think it inevitable, and even repeatedly to say in an ill-natured tone that she "*wished* they might be happy." Thursday was to be the wedding day, and on Wednesday Miss Lucas paid her farewell visit; and when she rose to take leave, Elizabeth, ashamed of her mother's ungracious and reluctant good wishes, and sincerely affected[10] herself, accompanied her out of the room. As they went down stairs together, Charlotte said,

"I shall depend on hearing from you very often, Eliza."

"*That* you certainly shall."

"And I have another favour to ask. Will you come and see me?"

"We shall often meet, I hope, in Hertfordshire."

5.   Elizabeth's words reveal the difficulty in accepting such sensible but painful advice as her aunt has offered, for after first agreeing that it would be wise to resist the temptation of falling in love, she then suggests doubt about that conclusion. The statement indicates her honesty about herself—in other words, she never imagines that she is immune from error. It also conforms to Jane Austen's general view of humanity, for she never supposes that any person can be perfect, and she almost never creates characters who do not have at least some weakness or failing. In a letter commenting on a man who wished for ideal heroines in novels, something found in other writers of the time, she states, "pictures of perfection as you know make me sick & wicked" (Mar. 23, 1817).

6.   *his first object*: what he seeks or strives for most.

7.   *conscious*: knowing (possibly in a guilty sense).

8.   A hint of criticism regarding Mrs. Bennet's constant invitations to others while the Gardiners are visiting.

9.   *wonderful*: extraordinary, amazing. The idea is that usually such advice is resented.

10.   *affected*: moved. It does not say whether Elizabeth is moved by feelings of happiness for Charlotte, as would be the convention, or by other feelings such as regret or pity.

"I am not likely to leave Kent for some time. Promise me, therefore, to come to Hunsford."[11]

Elizabeth could not refuse, though she foresaw little pleasure in the visit.

"My father and Maria[12] are to come to me in March," added Charlotte, "and I hope you will consent to be of the party. Indeed, Eliza, you will be as welcome to me as either of them."

The wedding took place; the bride and bridegroom set off for Kent from the church door, and every body had as much to say or to hear on the subject as usual. Elizabeth soon heard from her friend; and their correspondence was as regular and frequent as it had ever been; that it should be equally unreserved[13] was impossible. Elizabeth could never address her without feeling that all the comfort of intimacy was over, and, though determined not to slacken as a correspondent, it was for the sake of what had been, rather than what was. Charlotte's first letters were received with a good deal of eagerness; there could not but be curiosity to know how she would speak of her new home, how she would like Lady Catherine, and how happy she would dare pronounce herself to be; though, when the letters were read, Elizabeth felt that Charlotte expressed herself on every point exactly as she might have foreseen. She wrote cheerfully, seemed surrounded with comforts, and mentioned nothing which she could not praise. The house, furniture,[14] neighbourhood, and roads,[15] were all to her taste, and Lady Catherine's behaviour was most friendly and obliging. It was Mr. Collins's picture of Hunsford and Rosings rationally softened; and Elizabeth perceived that she must wait for her own visit there, to know the rest.

Jane had already written a few lines to her sister to announce their safe arrival in London; and when she wrote again, Elizabeth hoped it would be in her power to say something of the Bingleys.

Her impatience for this second letter was as well rewarded as impatience generally is. Jane had been a week in town, without either seeing or hearing from Caroline. She accounted for it, however, by supposing that her last letter to her friend from Longbourn, had by some accident been lost.

11. Such a quick invitation to visit, along with her emphatic vow of writing, indicates that Charlotte is fully aware that company other than her husband's will be desirable.

12. *Maria*: Charlotte's sister.

13. *unreserved*: frank, uninhibited.

14. *furniture*: furnishings.

15. *roads*: in this period local roads depended for their upkeep on the vigilance of the local authorities, which could vary greatly. Thus in many areas the roads were poorly maintained, and travel on them was very difficult. This made good roads something to be praised in a new neighborhood.

"My aunt," she continued, "is going to-morrow into that part of the town, and I shall take the opportunity of calling in Grosvenor-street."

She wrote again when the visit was paid, and she had seen Miss Bingley. "I did not think Caroline in spirits,"[16] were her words, "but she was very glad to see me, and reproached me for giving her no notice of my coming to London. I was right, therefore; my last letter had never reached her. I enquired after their brother, of course. He was well, but so much engaged with Mr. Darcy, that they scarcely ever saw him. I found that Miss Darcy was expected to dinner. I wish I could see her. My visit was not long, as Caroline and Mrs. Hurst were going out.[17] I dare say I shall soon see them here."

Elizabeth shook her head over this letter. It convinced her, that accident[18] only could discover[19] to Mr. Bingley her sister's being in town.

Four weeks passed away, and Jane saw nothing of him. She endeavoured to persuade herself that she did not regret it; but she could no longer be blind to Miss Bingley's inattention. After waiting at home every morning[20] for a fortnight, and inventing every evening a fresh excuse for her, the visitor did at last appear;[21] but the shortness of her stay, and yet more, the alteration of her manner, would allow Jane to deceive herself no longer. The letter which she wrote on this occasion to her sister, will prove what she felt.

My dearest Lizzy will, I am sure, be incapable of triumphing in her better judgment, at my expence, when I confess myself to have been entirely deceived in Miss Bingley's regard for me. But, my dear sister, though the event[22] has proved you right, do not think me obstinate if I still assert, that, considering what her behaviour was, my confidence was as natural as your suspicion. I do not at all comprehend her reason for wishing to be intimate with me,[23] but if the same circumstances were to happen again, I am sure I should be deceived again.[24] Caroline did not return my visit till yesterday; and not a note, not a line, did I receive in the mean time. When she did come, it was very evident that she had no pleasure in it; she made a slight, formal, apology, for not calling before, said not a

16. *in spirits*: cheerful, lively. The implication, which Jane does not allow herself to imagine but which will soon be reinforced and confirmed, is that Miss Bingley is not in spirits because she does not wish to see Jane or to continue their friendship. Before Jane's coming to London the only letters Miss Bingley seems to send her are the ones in which she tells Jane they will not be returning to Netherfield and speaks of her brother's marrying Miss Darcy—in other words, letters for the purpose of ending Jane's interest in Bingley, not letters sent out of genuine friendship.

17. It can be guessed that they wish to leave quickly in order to get rid of Jane, and that Jane's letter went unanswered because it had been disregarded, not lost. One reason they have for wishing her gone is to prevent her accidentally running into their brother, and thus alerting him to her presence in London—since, as revealed later, he has been deliberately kept from this knowledge.

18. *accident*: chance, an unforeseen event.

19. *discover*: reveal.

20. *morning*: period from the beginning of the day until dinner (usually around four or five p.m.). Thus Jane was waiting almost all of each day.

21. Standard etiquette dictated that visits, such as Jane has already made on Miss Bingley in London, be returned within a reasonably short time. Miss Bingley's violation of these norms indicates her wish to break off her acquaintance with Jane.

22. *event*: final outcome.

23. The matter is not as hard to comprehend as Jane supposes. Miss Bingley and Mrs. Hurst probably did find Jane a better companion than anyone else in the area when they were at Netherfield, and therefore away from their London friends, and when they did not fear a love between their brother and Jane. Even then, the only important action they took was to invite her to come for the day while the men were out; they never really sought the intimacy Jane imagined to be there.

24. Even in this letter Jane refuses to face up fully to the truth. This unwillingness or inability to change her excessive innocence, which will appear again when Jane learns more about this whole affair, points to a crucial difference between Jane and Elizabeth. The latter also makes serious errors, but unlike Jane she draws the full lessons from her errors and as a result changes her character for the better.

*word of wishing to see me again, and was in every respect so altered
a creature, that when she went away, I was perfectly resolved to continue the acquaintance no longer. I pity, though I cannot help
blaming her. She was very wrong in singling me out as she did; I can
safely say, that every advance to intimacy began on her side. But I
pity her, because she must feel that she has been acting wrong, and
because I am very sure that anxiety for her brother is the cause of it.
I need not explain myself farther; and though we know this anxiety
to be quite needless, yet if she feels it, it will easily account for her
behaviour to me;[25] and so deservedly dear as he is to his sister, whatever anxiety she may feel on his behalf, is natural and amiable.[26] I
cannot but wonder, however, at her having any such fears now,
because, if he had at all cared about me, we must have met long,
long ago. He knows of my being in town,[27] I am certain, from something she said herself; and yet it should seem by her manner of talking, as if she wanted to persuade herself that he is really partial to
Miss Darcy.[28] I cannot understand it. If I were not afraid of judging
harshly, I should be almost tempted to say, that there is a strong
appearance of duplicity in all this. But I will endeavour to banish
every painful thought, and think only of what will make me happy,
your affection, and the invariable kindness of my dear uncle and
aunt. Let me hear from you very soon. Miss Bingley said something
of his never returning to Netherfield again, of giving up the house,
but not with any certainty. We had better not mention it. I am
extremely glad that you have such pleasant accounts from our
friends at Hunsford. Pray go to see them, with Sir William and
Maria. I am sure you will be very comfortable there.*

Your's, &c.

This letter gave Elizabeth some pain; but her spirits returned as
she considered that Jane would no longer be duped, by the sister
at least. All expectation from the brother was now absolutely over.
She would not even wish for any renewal of his attentions. His
character sunk on every review of it; and as a punishment for him,
as well as a possible advantage to Jane, she seriously hoped he
might really soon marry Mr. Darcy's sister, as, by Wickham's

25. In other words, Jane supposes that Miss Bingley's neglect stems from her desire to keep Jane away from Bingley, and keep him from renewing his love. This is why Jane calls it needless anxiety, since she believes that Bingley does not love her anymore.

In fact, the very information Jane provides could lead to a contrary inference, for if Miss Bingley, who presumably knows her brother well and has regular contact with him, continues to harbor anxiety about his affection for Jane, then such affection may still exist. Jane, however, will not permit herself to imagine that.

26. *amiable*: kind, affectionate.

27. Later this is revealed to be untrue.

28. A clue that Bingley is not partial to Miss Darcy and that he may still like Jane.

account, she would make him abundantly regret what he had thrown away.[29]

Mrs. Gardiner about this time reminded Elizabeth of her promise concerning that gentleman, and required information; and Elizabeth had such to send as might rather give contentment to her aunt than to herself. His apparent partiality had subsided, his attentions were over, he was the admirer of some one else. Elizabeth was watchful enough to see it all, but she could see it and write of it without material pain. Her heart had been but slightly touched, and her vanity was satisfied with believing that *she* would have been his only choice, had fortune permitted it. The sudden acquisition of ten thousand pounds was the most remarkable charm of the young lady, to whom he was now rendering himself agreeable; but Elizabeth, less clear-sighted perhaps in his case than in Charlotte's,[30] did not quarrel with him for his wish of independence.[31] Nothing, on the contrary, could be more natural; and while able to suppose that it cost him a few struggles to relinquish her, she was ready to allow it a wise and desirable measure for both, and could very sincerely wish him happy.[32]

All this was acknowledged to Mrs. Gardiner; and after relating the circumstances, she thus went on: — "I am now convinced, my dear aunt, that I have never been much in love; for had I really experienced that pure and elevating passion, I should at present detest his very name, and wish him all manner of evil.[33] But my feelings are not only cordial[34] towards *him*; they are even impartial towards Miss King. I cannot find out that I hate her at all, or that I am in the least unwilling to think her a very good sort of girl. There can be no love in all this. My watchfulness has been effectual;[35] and though I should certainly be a more interesting[36] object to all my acquaintance, were I distractedly[37] in love with him, I cannot say that I regret my comparative insignificance. Importance may sometimes be purchased too dearly.[38] Kitty and Lydia take his defection much more to heart than I do. They are young in the ways of the world, and not yet open to the mortifying conviction that handsome young men must have something to live on, as well as the plain."

29. She may mean that Jane would benefit by no longer having any reason to hope for Bingley. But the sentence as written implies that it would be a benefit to Jane, as well as a punishment for Bingley, if he were made unhappy by marriage to Miss Darcy. Such thoughts—and Jane is the last person to take any pleasure in another's misery, or even to wish to have her own merit vindicated by someone's rejection of her proving to be a mistake—testify to how much disappointment and anger are distorting Elizabeth's judgment and better instincts.

30. In other words, she criticized Charlotte for marrying purely for money (and correctly so, implies the author), but fails to criticize Wickham for attempting the same thing.

31. *independence*: financial independence.

32. These words suggest that Elizabeth's attraction to Wickham may have stemmed as much from her dislike of Darcy and her pleasure at having her negative judgment of Darcy confirmed, as it stemmed from any affection for Wickham. Her main reaction to the latter's abandonment of her is not to wish it had not happened or to regret what she has lost, but to attempt to justify his actions and thereby also to justify the wisdom of her judgment of him. Thus pride regarding her judgment proves to be her strongest emotion, a characteristic of Elizabeth that appears at other points.

33. A satirical reference to romantic notions of extreme love that Jane Austen consistently ridicules.

34. *cordial*: affectionate, warm. The term implied more heartfelt and sincere benevolence than it does currently.

35. Meaning her success in avoiding a serious infatuation with Wickham.

36. *interesting*: important.

37. *distractedly*: madly.

38. In other words, the pain of losing a person one deeply loved would be too high a price to pay for the importance one would acquire among others for being such a jilted lover. Elizabeth is again referring, at least in part, to romantic conventions of love, in this case the celebration of those who are consumed, or even rendered unhappy, by madly passionate love.

Chapter Four

With no greater events than these in the Longbourn family, and otherwise diversified by little beyond the walks to Meryton, sometimes dirty and sometimes cold, did January and February pass away. March was to take Elizabeth to Hunsford. She had not at first thought very seriously of going thither; but Charlotte, she soon found, was depending on the plan, and she gradually learned to consider it herself with greater pleasure as well as greater certainty. Absence had increased her desire of seeing Charlotte again, and weakened her disgust[1] of Mr. Collins. There was novelty in the scheme, and as, with such a mother and such uncompanionable sisters, home could not be faultless, a little change was not unwelcome for its own sake. The journey would moreover give her a peep at Jane; and, in short, as the time drew near, she would have been very sorry for any delay. Every thing, however, went on smoothly, and was finally settled according to Charlotte's first sketch. She was to accompany Sir William and his second daughter. The improvement of spending a night in London was added in time,[2] and the plan became perfect as plan could be.

The only pain was in leaving her father, who would certainly miss her, and who, when it came to the point, so little liked her going, that he told her to write to him, and almost promised to answer her letter.[3]

The farewell between herself and Mr. Wickham was perfectly friendly; on his side even more. His present pursuit could not make him forget that Elizabeth had been the first to excite and to deserve his attention, the first to listen and to pity, the first to be admired; and in his manner of bidding her adieu, wishing her every enjoyment, reminding her of what she was to expect in Lady Catherine de Bourgh, and trusting their opinion of her—their opinion of every body—would always coincide, there was a solicitude, an interest

1.   *disgust*: distaste.

2.   The route from Hertfordshire to Kent would pass directly through London. The overall journey would take the better part of a day, so breaking it up by a night in London, if one had a place to stay, could make sense.

3.   Mr. Bennet's distaste for writing comes up several times.

which she felt must ever attach her to him with a most sincere
regard; and she parted from him convinced, that whether married
or single, he must always be her model of the amiable and pleasing.

Her fellow-travellers the next day, were not of a kind to make
her think him less agreeable. Sir William Lucas, and his daughter
Maria, a good humoured girl, but as empty-headed as himself, had
nothing to say that could be worth hearing, and were listened to
with about as much delight as the rattle of the chaise.[4] Elizabeth
loved absurdities, but she had known Sir William's too long. He
could tell her nothing new of the wonders of his presentation[5] and
knighthood; and his civilities were worn out like his information.

It was a journey of only twenty-four miles, and they began it so
early as to be in Gracechurch-street by noon. As they drove to Mr.
Gardiner's door, Jane was at a drawing-room window watching
their arrival; when they entered the passage she was there to welcome them, and Elizabeth, looking earnestly in her face, was
pleased to see it healthful and lovely as ever. On the stairs were a
troop of little boys and girls, whose eagerness for their cousin's
appearance would not allow them to wait in the drawing-room,
and whose shyness, as they had not seen her for a twelvemonth,[6]
prevented their coming lower. All was joy and kindness. The day
passed most pleasantly away; the morning in bustle and shopping,[7] and the evening at one of the theatres.[8]

Elizabeth then contrived to sit by her aunt.[9] Their first subject was her sister; and she was more grieved than astonished to
hear, in reply to her minute enquiries, that though Jane always
struggled to support her spirits, there were periods of dejection. It
was reasonable, however, to hope, that they would not continue
long. Mrs. Gardiner gave her the particulars also of Miss Bingley's
visit in Gracechurch-street, and repeated conversations occurring
at different times between Jane and herself, which proved that the
former had, from her heart, given up the acquaintance.

Mrs. Gardiner then rallied[10] her niece on Wickham's desertion, and complimented her on bearing it so well.

"But, my dear Elizabeth," she added, "what sort of girl is Miss
King? I should be sorry to think our friend mercenary."

4. A chaise, like other carriages, would usually rattle quite a bit, thanks to the frequent bumpiness of the roads and the limited system of shock absorbers on vehicles then.

5. *presentation:* presentation at court (in order to be knighted).

6. This line indicates that the Gardiners' children must not have accompanied them on their recent Christmas visit to the Bennets. This has caused some puzzlement to readers and commentators, but in fact Christmas was not as significant a holiday then as now: it had declined in importance in England in the seventeenth century, partly under the influence of Puritanism, and would only become a major celebration again during the middle and late nineteenth century, when many of our current Christmas traditions, including the aspects most pertinent to children, were developed or made popular. During this period it was mostly an occasion for feasting and parties, and these gatherings often involved only adults. Thus by the standards of the time the Gardiners would not be unusual or negligent in having left their children behind in London, where they would be cared for by servants.

7. *shopping:* because of the immense wealth and variety of shops in London, and the cost and difficulty of transporting goods to provincial locations, shopping was a major activity of those visiting London. Jane Austen devoted considerable time to it when she stayed there. The extended nature of "morning" then means that most of the day was being spent in bustle and shopping.

8. *theatres:* another favorite activity of Jane Austen's while in London.

9. The conversation beginning here is occurring while they are at the theatre, and we are told below that it was ended by the conclusion of the play— in other words, it occurs while the play is going on. Such conversation during a play was normal at the time. One reason was that audience sections of the theatre were lit rather than in the dark (current technological limitations in lighting made it hard otherwise to illuminate the stage adequately); this naturally kept the audience's attention from being so exclusively focused on what was happening on stage.

10. *rallied:* teased or ridiculed good-naturedly.

"Pray, my dear aunt, what is the difference in matrimonial affairs, between the mercenary and the prudent motive? Where does discretion end, and avarice begin?[11] Last Christmas you were afraid of his marrying me, because it would be imprudent; and now, because he is trying to get a girl with only ten thousand pounds, you want to find out that he is mercenary."

"If you will only tell me what sort of girl Miss King is, I shall know what to think."

"She is a very good kind of girl, I believe. I know no harm of her."

"But he paid her not the smallest attention, till her grandfather's death made her mistress of this fortune."

"No—why should he? If it was not allowable for him to gain *my* affections, because I had no money, what occasion could there be for making love[12] to a girl whom he did not care about, and who was equally poor?"

"But there seems indelicacy[13] in directing his attentions towards her, so soon after this event."[14]

"A man in distressed circumstances has not time for all those elegant decorums which other people may observe. If *she* does not object to it, why should *we*?"

"*Her* not objecting, does not justify *him*. It only shews her being deficient in something herself—sense or feeling."

"Well," cried Elizabeth, "have it as you choose. *He* shall be mercenary, and *she* shall be foolish."

"No, Lizzy, that is what I do *not* choose. I should be sorry, you know, to think ill of a young man who has lived so long in Derbyshire."

"Oh! if that is all, I have a very poor opinion of young men who live in Derbyshire;[15] and their intimate friends who live in Hertfordshire are not much better. I am sick of them all. Thank Heaven! I am going to-morrow where I shall find a man who has not one agreeable quality, who has neither manner nor sense to recommend him. Stupid men are the only ones worth knowing, after all."

"Take care, Lizzy; that speech savours strongly of disappointment."[16]

Before they were separated by the conclusion of the play, she

11. A question of great pertinence in Jane Austen's novels, where marriage and love are often tied to issues of money. The distinction she normally draws is between insisting that enough money be available in order to marry a person one genuinely cares for, which is prudent, and pursuing a person one does not love merely because he or she has money, which is mercenary. This is a distinction that Mrs. Gardiner tries to draw here, by inquiring whether Wickham has any genuine feelings for Miss King, but that Elizabeth, in her persistent partiality for Wickham, refuses to see.

12. *making love:* wooing, or professing love toward, someone. At this time it did not mean anything more than that.

13. *indelicacy:* coarseness, lack of propriety or decency.

14. *this event:* her grandfather's death and her inheritance.

15. Once again Elizabeth alludes to Darcy.

16. Meaning that her denunciation of men has the flavor of something said by someone disappointed in love, and is thus an expression of petty resentment or frustration rather than of reasoned reflection. This period in the novel marks Elizabeth's low point, for she has successively been disappointed by Charlotte, by Bingley, and by Wickham. Elizabeth's speech also shows her falling into some of her father's cynicism, which represents a potential danger for her since she shares many traits with him.

had the unexpected happiness of an invitation to accompany her uncle and aunt in a tour of pleasure which they proposed taking in the summer.

"We have not quite determined how far it shall carry us," said Mrs. Gardiner, "but perhaps to the Lakes."[17]

No scheme could have been more agreeable to Elizabeth, and her acceptance of the invitation was most ready and grateful. "My dear, dear aunt," she rapturously cried, "what delight! what felicity! You give me fresh life and vigour. Adieu to disappointment and spleen. What are men to rocks and mountains? Oh! what hours of transport[18] we shall spend! And when we *do* return, it shall not be like other travellers, without being able to give one accurate[19] idea of any thing. We *will* know where we have gone— we *will* recollect what we have seen. Lakes, mountains, and rivers, shall not be jumbled together in our imaginations; nor, when we attempt to describe any particular scene, will we begin quarrelling about its relative situation. Let *our* first effusions be less insupportable than those of the generality of travellers."[20]

17. *the Lakes*: the Lake District in northwestern England (see map, p. 742), a leading tourist area. During the eighteenth century, as transportation conditions improved and overall affluence increased, travel for pleasure emerged as a favorite leisure activity. By the end of the century the Lake District had become the most popular destination in England for such travelers, thanks in particular to its mountainous and sparsely populated character, which gave it a strong appeal to those affected by the growing romantic taste for spectacular scenery and for nature untouched by human hands. The district was also a particular favorite of the romantic poets who were writing around the same time as Jane Austen.

18. *transport*: rapture, exaltation.

19. *accurate*: precise.

20. Elizabeth may be referring to the growing genre of travel writings and guidebooks that had developed with the rise of tourism and the worship of nature. Gilpin and other writers on the picturesque had popularized this concept by their writings about the natural beauties to be found in various parts of England (see p. 97, note 48). Elizabeth's words about the "relative situation" of a scene derive from such writings; the phrase was used as a way to evaluate scenic beauty, for writers on the picturesque argued that the situation, i.e., location and position, of a place or object determined its beauty.

Jane Austen's own attitude toward the picturesque and the worship of nature was mixed. She enjoyed natural beauty and liked Gilpin, though one of her letters refers affectionately to a satire on picturesque traveling that came out around the time of the novel (March 2, 1814). In a letter mentioning her brother and nephew's trip to Scotland, she expresses interest in the beauties they saw there, wishes they could also have seen the Lakes, and mildly deprecates her nephew for failing to derive the same enjoyment from natural beauty as her brother (Sept. 25, 1813). At the same time, in line with her general hostility to many romantic attitudes, she ridicules extreme encomiums to nature. One of the heroines of *Sense and Sensibility* is mocked somewhat for this attitude, and her last work, *Sanditon*, contains a foolish character whose romantic enthusiasms—for nature, for poetry, and for love—lead him to lose almost all coherence of speech. A sense of the middle ground Jane Austen prefers can be seen in her story "Love and Friendship," which ridicules romantic sentimentality mercilessly but which also has some of its sensible characters go on a tour to Scotland inspired by Gilpin.

In the case of Elizabeth, her interest in the Lakes would be in line with the author's attitude. But her words "What are men to rocks and mountains?" express a view more extreme than any seen in Jane Austen's own discussions of nature. The excessiveness of Elizabeth's outburst is further shown by its connection to feelings of resentment and of disappointment in humanity that will cause problems for her later.

Chapter Five

*E*very object in the next day's journey was new and interesting to Elizabeth; and her spirits were in a state for enjoyment; for she had seen her sister looking so well as to banish all fear for her health, and the prospect of her northern tour was a constant source of delight.

When they left the high road[1] for the lane to Hunsford, every eye was in search of the Parsonage, and every turning expected to bring it in view. The paling[2] of Rosings Park[3] was their boundary on one side.[4] Elizabeth smiled at the recollection of all that she had heard of its inhabitants.

At length the Parsonage was discernible. The garden sloping to the road, the house standing in it, the green pales[5] and the laurel hedge, every thing declared they were arriving. Mr. Collins and Charlotte appeared at the door, and the carriage stopped at the small gate, which led by a short gravel walk to the house, amidst the nods and smiles of the whole party. In a moment they were all out of the chaise, rejoicing at the sight of each other. Mrs. Collins welcomed her friend with the liveliest pleasure, and Elizabeth was more and more satisfied with coming, when she found herself so affectionately received. She saw instantly that her cousin's manners were not altered by his marriage; his formal civility was just what it had been, and he detained her some minutes at the gate to hear and satisfy his enquiries after all her family. They were then, with no other delay than his pointing out the neatness[6] of the entrance, taken into the house; and as soon as they were in the parlour, he welcomed them a second time with ostentatious formality to his humble abode, and punctually repeated all his wife's offers of refreshment.

Elizabeth was prepared to see him in his glory; and she could not help fancying that in displaying the good proportion of the room, its aspect[7] and its furniture,[8] he addressed himself particularly to

1. *high road*: highway or main road.

2. *paling*: fence or fencing.

3. *Rosings Park*: Lady Catherine's home (often just shortened to Rosings). The home, as its name implies, includes a substantial park or grounds, which is what the fence borders. The wording of the passage, by suggesting that they traveled next to the fence for some distance, indicates the large size of Lady Catherine's grounds.

4. Thus the parsonage is adjacent to Lady Catherine's residence. This was a common arrangement, a sign of the wish to maintain a close link between the clergy and the landowning class, who were the leading figures in rural communities and generally directed community affairs.

5. *pales*: stakes driven into the ground to form a fence.

6. *neatness*: simple elegance, nice proportions.

7. *aspect*: general look or appearance; position in relation to the light from outside. Either meaning is possible here.

8. *furniture*: furnishings.

The Rectory, or Parsonage, at Steventon, Hampshire; Jane Austen was born and grew up there. Her father received it through his position as rector.

[From Mary Augusta Austen-Leigh, *Personal Aspects of Jane Austen* (New York, 1920), p. 12]

her, as if wishing to make her feel what she had lost in refusing him. But though every thing seemed neat and comfortable, she was not able to gratify him by any sigh of repentance; and rather looked with wonder at her friend that she could have so cheerful an air, with such a companion. When Mr. Collins said any thing of which his wife might reasonably be ashamed, which certainly was not unseldom,[9] she involuntarily turned her eye on Charlotte. Once or twice she could discern a faint blush; but in general Charlotte wisely did not hear. After sitting long enough to admire every article of furniture in the room, from the sideboard to the fender,[10] to give an account of their journey and of all that had happened in London, Mr. Collins invited them to take a stroll in the garden, which was large and well laid out, and to the cultivation of which he attended himself. To work in his garden was one of his most respectable pleasures; and Elizabeth admired the command of countenance[11] with which Charlotte talked of the healthfulness of the exercise, and owned[12] she encouraged it as much as possible. Here, leading the way through every walk and cross walk,[13] and scarcely allowing them an interval to utter the praises he asked for, every view was pointed out with a minuteness which left beauty entirely behind.[14] He could number the fields in every direction, and could tell how many trees there were in the most distant clump. But of all the views which his garden, or which the country,[15] or the kingdom could boast, none were to be compared with the prospect of[16] Rosings, afforded by an opening in the trees that bordered the park[17] nearly opposite the front of his house. It was a handsome modern building, well situated on rising ground.[18]

From his garden, Mr. Collins would have led them round his two meadows,[19] but the ladies not having shoes to encounter the remains of a white frost, turned back; and while Sir William accompanied him, Charlotte took her sister and friend over the house, extremely well pleased, probably, to have the opportunity of shewing it without her husband's help. It was rather small, but well built and convenient; and every thing was fitted up and arranged with a neatness and consistency of which Elizabeth gave Charlotte all the credit.[20] When Mr. Collins could be forgotten, there was really a great air of

9. *not unseldom:* not infrequently. Logically the expression should mean seldom, and therefore not frequently. But it was used as a synonym for not seldom. Hence the meaning here is that Mr. Collins often says things that might make his wife blush.

10. *fender:* fire guard; generally a low metal frame in front of the fireplace. Its purpose was to keep coals from the fire from rolling out onto the floor. Fenders were often made in a decorative design, and would be fairly prominent in a room because of the importance of the fireplace (the only source of heat).

11. *command of countenance:* in other words, her ability to keep a straight face.

12. *owned:* admitted.

13. *every walk and cross walk:* an indication of a sizable garden, and thus of Mr. Collins's relative affluence.

14. Meaning that his concern with the minute features of each scene caused him to pay no attention to questions of beauty.

15. *country:* county.

16. *prospect of:* view presented by.

17. *park:* enclosed area around the house.

18. An elevated position for a house was preferred because that would provide better views of the surroundings.

19. *two meadows:* these meadows would be part of the living Mr. Collins enjoys here. Giving such land, traditionally called glebe land, to clergymen was longstanding practice; by farming the land they could add to their income. The trend at this time was for tithes to be commuted in exchange for additional glebe land, which made the clergy more like landowners. Jane Austen's father engaged in a variety of agricultural endeavors while a clergyman, including planting vegetables and herbs and fruit in his garden, dairy farming, beekeeping, and raising pigs and sheep and different types of fowl.

20. Jane Austen gives us some sense of the Collins's house and garden—for they reveal his personality and Charlotte's adjustment to her marriage—but still describes them in vague terms. This is standard in Jane Austen's novels; her picture of the Bennets' house is even sketchier. In a letter criticizing her niece's draft of a novel she says, "your descriptions are often more minute

comfort throughout, and by Charlotte's evident enjoyment of it, Elizabeth supposed he must be often forgotten.

She had already learnt that Lady Catherine was still in the country. It was spoken of again while they were at dinner, when Mr. Collins joining in, observed,

"Yes, Miss Elizabeth, you will have the honour of seeing Lady Catherine de Bourgh on the ensuing Sunday at church, and I need not say you will be delighted with her. She is all affability and condescension,[21] and I doubt not but you will be honoured with some portion of her notice when service is over. I have scarcely any hesitation in saying that she will include you and my sister Maria in every invitation with which she honours us during your stay here. Her behaviour to my dear Charlotte is charming. We dine at Rosings twice every week, and are never allowed to walk home. Her ladyship's carriage is regularly ordered for us. I *should* say, one of her ladyship's carriages, for she has several."[22]

"Lady Catherine is a very respectable, sensible woman indeed," added Charlotte, "and a most attentive neighbour."

"Very true, my dear, that is exactly what I say. She is the sort of woman whom one cannot regard with too much deference."

The evening was spent chiefly in talking over Hertfordshire news, and telling again what had been already written; and when it closed, Elizabeth in the solitude of her chamber had to meditate upon Charlotte's degree of contentment, to understand her address[23] in guiding, and composure in bearing with her husband, and to acknowledge that it was all done very well. She had also to anticipate how her visit would pass, the quiet tenor of their usual employments, the vexatious interruptions of Mr. Collins, and the gaieties of their intercourse with Rosings. A lively imagination soon settled it all.

About the middle of the next day, as she was in her room getting ready for a walk, a sudden noise below seemed to speak[24] the whole house in confusion; and after listening a moment, she heard somebody running up stairs in a violent hurry, and calling loudly after her. She opened the door, and met Maria in the landing place,[25] who, breathless with agitation, cried out,

than will be liked. You give too many particulars of right hand & left" (Sept. 9, 1814). Her general principles of artistic economy and restraint keep her from including anything that does not serve the interests of the story, and her focus on psychology, moral issues, and social relationships means that physical descriptions of place rarely do serve that.

21. *affability and condescension:* two words Mr. Collins uses frequently in describing Lady Catherine. Both involve friendliness and courtesy toward inferiors.

22. The possession of several carriages was a sign of great wealth and status and thus was often pointed out when praising someone. Jane Austen has fun with this in an early satirical sketch, "Mr. Clifford"; in it she says that the hero, "was a very rich young man & kept a great many Carriages of which I do not recollect half. I can only remember that he had a Coach, a Chariot, a Chaise, a Landeau, a Landeaulet, a Phaeton, a Gig, a Whisky, an italian Chair, a Buggy, a Curricle & a wheelbarrow."

23. *address:* skill, dexterity.

24. *speak:* signal, reveal.

25. *landing place:* landing between stairs.

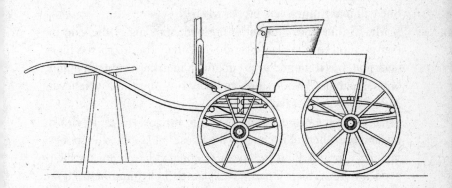

A low phaeton. See p. 293, note 27.

[From T. Fuller, *An Essay on Wheel Carriages* (London, 1828), Plate No. 11]

"Oh, my dear Eliza! pray make haste and come into the dining-room, for there is such a sight to be seen! I will not tell you what it is. Make haste, and come down this moment."

Elizabeth asked questions in vain; Maria would tell her nothing more, and down they ran into the dining-room, which fronted[26] the lane, in quest of this wonder; it was two ladies stopping in a low phaeton[27] at the garden gate.

"And is this all?" cried Elizabeth. "I expected at least that the pigs were got into the garden, and here is nothing but Lady Catherine and her daughter!"

"La! my dear," said Maria quite shocked at the mistake, "it is not Lady Catherine. The old lady is Mrs. Jenkinson,[28] who lives with them. The other is Miss De Bourgh. Only look at her. She is quite a little creature. Who would have thought she could be so thin and small!"

"She is abominably rude to keep Charlotte out of doors in all this wind. Why does she not come in?"

"Oh! Charlotte says, she hardly ever does. It is the greatest of favours when Miss De Bourgh comes in."

"I like her appearance," said Elizabeth, struck with other ideas. "She looks sickly and cross.—Yes, she will do for him very well. She will make him a very proper wife."[29]

Mr. Collins and Charlotte were both standing at the gate in conversation with the ladies; and Sir William, to Elizabeth's high diversion, was stationed in the doorway, in earnest contemplation of the greatness[30] before him, and constantly bowing[31] whenever Miss De Bourgh looked that way.[32]

At length there was nothing more to be said; the ladies drove on, and the others returned into the house. Mr. Collins no sooner saw the two girls than he began to congratulate them on their good fortune, which Charlotte explained by letting them know that the whole party was asked to dine at Rosings the next day.

26. *fronted:* faced.

27. *low phaeton:* a phaeton is a lightweight open carriage (see picture on p. 291). Its lightness made it easy to handle; this also allowed the driver to use ponies, as Mr. Collins earlier said Miss De Bourgh used, which added further to its ease of handling. At the same time, since it had four wheels, in contrast to the two of other open carriages, it was fairly stable. All this would make it ideal for one like Miss De Bourgh who was weak and sickly.

"Low" refers to the phaeton's construction. Many phaetons were made so that their riders sat far above the ground: often called "high flyers," these vehicles, popular with young men, were more exciting to ride in but also more likely to tip over; Jane Austen's story *Love and Friendship* includes an accident suffered by young men traveling in a "fashionably high Phaeton." Miss De Bourgh would naturally favor the greater steadiness of a low vehicle.

28. *Mrs. Jenkinson:* she is Miss De Bourgh's governess and attendant. A governess was in an intermediate social position, an employee but also above a normal servant. Usually governesses were women of genteel background— which would give them the education and manners to guide young ladies— whose own lack of money forced them to work. Governess, along with schoolteacher, offered almost the only decent job opportunity for such ladies. Elizabeth or her sisters, were they not to marry, might end up having to work as a governess once their father died. In a letter Jane Austen sympathizes with her nieces' new governess: "By this time I suppose she is hard at it, governing away—poor creature! I pity her, tho' they *are* my nieces" (April, 30, 1811).

29. Elizabeth is thinking, once again, of Darcy, who is supposedly destined for Miss De Bourgh.

30. *greatness:* social prominence (of the person before him).

31. *bowing:* bowing and curtsying were still normal elements of daily life at the time, but they were gradually becoming less prevalent and were mostly used on formal occasions. The only characters who frequently bow are Darcy, Mr. Collins, and Sir William, all three of whom have very formal manners. In the latter two this behavior, which is often carried to extremes, indicates their pretentiousness and silliness, as is certainly evident in this scene.

32. Elizabeth was said on the journey here to be too familiar with Sir William's absurdities to enjoy them. Now she enjoys them again. This could result from seeing them go to new extremes, for in Hertfordshire Sir William was rarely able to contemplate and bow to those as great as the De Bourghs. It could also signal an improvement in Elizabeth's mood, due to seeing a reasonably content Jane in London, learning of the trip to the Lakes, and finding out that Charlotte's situation is more tolerable than she had imagined.

Chapter Six

*M*r. Collins's triumph[1] in consequence of this invitation was complete. The power of displaying the grandeur of his patroness to his wondering visitors, and of letting them see her civility towards himself and his wife, was exactly what he had wished for; and that an opportunity of doing it should be given so soon, was such an instance of Lady Catherine's condescension as he knew not how to admire enough.

"I confess," said he, "that I should not have been at all surprised by her Ladyship's asking us on Sunday to drink tea and spend the evening at Rosings. I rather expected, from my knowledge of her affability, that it would happen. But who could have foreseen such an attention as this? Who could have imagined that we should receive an invitation to dine there (an invitation moreover including the whole party) so immediately after your arrival!"[2]

"I am the less surprised at what has happened," replied Sir William, "from that knowledge of what the manners of the great[3] really are, which my situation in life has allowed me to acquire. About the Court, such instances of elegant breeding[4] are not uncommon."

Scarcely any thing was talked of the whole day or next morning, but their visit to Rosings. Mr. Collins was carefully instructing them in what they were to expect, that the sight of such rooms, so many servants, and so splendid a dinner might not wholly overpower them.

When the ladies were separating for the toilette,[5] he said to Elizabeth,

"Do not make yourself uneasy, my dear cousin, about your apparel. Lady Catherine is far from requiring that elegance of dress in us, which becomes herself and daughter. I would advise you merely to put on whatever of your clothes is superior to the

1.   *triumph*: elation.

2.   An invitation to dine, as opposed to one to come after dinner for tea, was a greater honor.

3.   *the great*: people of high rank.

4.   *breeding*: manners, courtesy.

5.   *toilette*: process of dressing.

rest, there is no occasion for any thing more. Lady Catherine will not think the worse of you for being simply dressed. She likes to have the distinction of rank preserved."[6]

While they were dressing, he came two or three times to their different doors, to recommend their being quick, as Lady Catherine very much objected to be kept waiting for her dinner. — Such formidable accounts of her Ladyship, and her manner of living, quite frightened Maria Lucas, who had been little used to company, and she looked forward to her introduction at Rosings, with as much apprehension, as her father had done to his presentation at St. James's.

As the weather was fine, they had a pleasant walk of about half a mile across the park. — Every park has its beauty and its prospects;[7] and Elizabeth saw much to be pleased with, though she could not be in such raptures as Mr. Collins expected the scene to inspire, and was but slightly affected by his enumeration of the windows in front of the house,[8] and his relation of what the glazing[9] altogether had originally cost Sir Lewis de Bourgh.

When they ascended the steps to the hall, Maria's alarm was every moment increasing, and even Sir William did not look perfectly calm. — Elizabeth's courage did not fail her. She had heard nothing of Lady Catherine that spoke her awful[10] from any extraordinary talents or miraculous virtue, and the mere stateliness[11] of money and rank, she thought she could witness without trepidation.

From the entrance hall, of which Mr. Collins pointed out, with a rapturous air, the fine proportion and finished ornaments, they followed the servants through an anti-chamber, to the room where Lady Catherine, her daughter, and Mrs. Jenkinson were sitting. — Her Ladyship, with great condescension, arose to receive them; and as Mrs. Collins had settled it with her husband that the office of introduction[12] should be her's, it was performed in a proper manner, without any of those apologies and thanks which he would have thought necessary.

In spite of having been at St. James's,[13] Sir William was so completely awed, by the grandeur surrounding him, that he had but just courage enough to make a very low bow, and take his seat without

6. Meaning that she likes for those, like herself, who are of higher rank to be dressed more finely and elegantly. Use of clothes to denote social status was standard at the time, as was the belief in the merit of this practice. In earlier centuries there had even been laws forbidding people to wear clothing above their actual rank, for it was feared that such behavior would sow confusion and undermine the social hierarchy.

7. *prospects*: views.

8. A large number of windows was a sign of wealth. One of the taxes at the time was a window tax that was assessed according to how many windows one had in one's home. This of course made it especially impressive to have many.

9. *glazing*: installation of glass for the windows.

10. *spoke her awful*: indicated or revealed her to be worthy of awe.

11. *stateliness*: loftiness, grandeur.

12. *office of introduction*: duty or task of introducing people.

13. *St. James's*: the royal court. The reference is ironic since Sir William was only at court on one occasion, though he continually talks as if he is intimate with its ways. His lack of courage at this juncture reveals his true unfamiliarity with those of very high status.

saying a word; and his daughter, frightened almost out of her senses, sat on the edge of her chair, not knowing which way to look. Elizabeth found herself quite equal to the scene, and could observe the three ladies before her composedly.—Lady Catherine was a tall, large woman, with strongly-marked features, which might once have been handsome. Her air was not conciliating, nor was her manner of receiving them, such as to make her visitors forget their inferior rank. She was not rendered formidable by silence; but whatever she said, was spoken in so authoritative a tone, as marked her self-importance, and brought Mr. Wickham immediately to Elizabeth's mind; and from the observation of the day altogether, she believed Lady Catherine to be exactly what he had represented.

When, after examining the mother, in whose countenance and deportment she soon found some resemblance of Mr. Darcy, she turned her eyes on the daughter, she could almost have joined in Maria's astonishment, at her being so thin, and so small. There was neither in figure nor face, any likeness between the ladies. Miss De Bourgh was pale and sickly; her features, though not plain, were insignificant; and she spoke very little, except in a low voice, to Mrs. Jenkinson, in whose appearance there was nothing remarkable, and who was entirely engaged in listening to what she said, and placing a screen in the proper direction before her eyes.[14]

After sitting a few minutes, they were all sent to one of the windows, to admire the view, Mr. Collins attending them to point out its beauties, and Lady Catherine kindly informing them that it was much better worth looking at in the summer.

The dinner was exceedingly handsome,[15] and there were all the servants, and all the articles of plate[16] which Mr. Collins had promised; and, as he had likewise foretold, he took his seat at the bottom of the table,[17] by her ladyship's desire, and looked as if he felt that life could furnish nothing greater.—He carved, and ate, and praised with delighted alacrity; and every dish was commended, first by him, and then by Sir William, who was now enough recovered to echo whatever his son in law said, in a manner which Elizabeth wondered Lady Catherine could bear. But Lady Catherine seemed gratified by their excessive admiration, and gave most gracious smiles,

14. The screen would be shielding her from the light or heat of the fire. Since many screens had a small surface (see below), it was necessary to position them properly to ensure that they shielded effectively.

15. *handsome:* fine, elegant.

16. *plate:* metal utensils, often of silver or gold.

17. This would mean he had the most important position after Lady Catherine herself, for the head and foot were the places for the leading figures in the household to sit.

Examples of fire screens. The one on the right is probably embroidered.

[From K. Warren Clouston, *The Chippendale Period in English Furniture* (London, 1897), pp. 153 and 198]

especially when any dish on the table proved a novelty to them.[18] The party did not supply much conversation. Elizabeth was ready to speak whenever there was an opening, but she was seated between Charlotte and Miss De Bourgh—the former of whom was engaged in listening to Lady Catherine, and the latter said not a word to her all dinner time. Mrs. Jenkinson was chiefly employed in watching how little Miss De Bourgh ate, pressing her to try some other dish, and fearing she were indisposed. Maria thought speaking out of the question, and the gentlemen did nothing but eat and admire.

When the ladies returned to the drawing room, there was little to be done but to hear Lady Catherine talk, which she did without any intermission till coffee came in, delivering her opinion on every subject in so decisive a manner as proved that she was not used to have her judgment controverted. She enquired into Charlotte's domestic concerns familiarly and minutely, and gave her a great deal of advice, as to the management of them all; told her how every thing ought to be regulated in so small a family as her's, and instructed her as to the care of her cows and her poultry.[19] Elizabeth found that nothing was beneath this great Lady's attention, which could furnish her with an occasion of dictating to others. In the intervals of her discourse with Mrs. Collins, she addressed a variety of questions to Maria and Elizabeth, but especially to the latter, of whose connections she knew the least, and who she observed to Mrs. Collins, was a very genteel, pretty[20] kind of girl. She asked her at different times, how many sisters she had, whether they were older or younger than herself, whether any of them were likely to be married, whether they were handsome, where they had been educated, what carriage her father kept, and what had been her mother's maiden name?—Elizabeth felt all the impertinence of her questions,[21] but answered them very composedly.—Lady Catherine then observed,·

"Your father's estate is entailed on Mr. Collins, I think. For your sake," turning to Charlotte, "I am glad of it; but otherwise I see no occasion for entailing estates from the female line.—It was not thought necessary in Sir Lewis de Bourgh's family.[22]—Do you play[23] and sing, Miss Bennet?"

18. Lady Catherine's enjoyment of such sycophancy stands in sharp contrast to Darcy's indifference, if not aversion, to Miss Bingley's assiduous attentions and flattery. It indicates the considerable differences between Darcy and his aunt, despite their both being proud and of high social station.

19. *her cows and her poultry:* these would be part of the agricultural activites on the Collins's land; see p. 289, note 19.

20. *pretty:* this could mean what it does now, or it could be a more general term of praise, meaning admirable or proper or elegant.

21. It would be considered rude and impertinent to ask someone you have just met so many intimate questions, especially when unprompted. A youthful sketch of Jane Austen, "Letter the fourth," involves one character's rude attempts to force another's secrets from her and the embarrassment that results for both.

22. This is why Miss De Bourgh is to inherit the family property. The practice in the Bennet family of entailing away from the female line was more common. In the case of Miss De Bourgh, her inheritance means that if Darcy, or another man, were to marry her, he would reap tremendous financial benefits, for few women of the time had dowries that could compare with an entire wealthy estate.

23. *play:* play music, particularly the piano.

"A little."

"Oh! then—some time or other we shall be happy to hear you. Our instrument is a capital one, probably superior to[24]—— You shall try it some day.—Do your sisters play and sing?"

"One of them does."

"Why did not you all learn?—You ought all to have learned.[25] The Miss Webbs all play, and their father has not so good an income as your's.—Do you draw?"[26]

"No, not at all."

"What, none of you?"

"Not one."

"That is very strange. But I suppose you had no opportunity. Your mother should have taken you to town every spring for the benefit of masters."[27]

"My mother would have had no objection, but my father hates London."

"Has your governess left you?"

"We never had any governess."

"No governess![28] How was that possible? Five daughters brought up at home without a governess!—I never heard of such a thing. Your mother must have been quite a slave to your education."[29]

Elizabeth could hardly help smiling, as she assured her that had not been the case.

"Then, who taught you? who attended to you? Without a governess you must have been neglected."

"Compared with some families, I believe we were; but such of us as wished to learn, never wanted the means. We were always encouraged to read, and had all the masters that were necessary.[30] Those who chose to be idle, certainly might."[31]

"Aye, no doubt; but that is what a governess will prevent, and if I had known your mother, I should have advised her most strenuously to engage one. I always say that nothing is to be done in education without steady and regular instruction, and nobody but a governess can give it. It is wonderful[32] how many families I have been the means of supplying in that way. I am always glad to get a young person well placed out. Four nieces of Mrs. Jenkinson are

24. She appears about to say "superior to yours" before she checks herself.

25. The speaking style here—a succession of short, emphatic statements or questions, along with abrupt change of topics—will continue to characterize Lady Catherine. It shows how peremptory and opinionated she is.

26. The other most popular accomplishment for ladies. In the Austen family, Jane played music and her sister Cassandra drew (see cover picture); the latter's sketch of Jane is the one reliable picture we have of her. In *Sense and Sensibility*, one of the two sister heroines draws, and the other plays music.

27. *masters:* instructors in music, drawing, or other subjects. They would be found most often in London, i.e., town.

28. Lady Catherine's surprise reflects her social position, for very wealthy families would have governesses as a matter of course. The Bennets are not in that category, though they could have afforded a governess if they had wished.

29. In families that lacked governesses, the parents, especially the mother, would normally educate the children. In *Northanger Abbey* the mother is shown working hard to teach her children basic academic skills, particularly reading. Sometimes at a later age the children would be sent to a school, though this was less common for girls than for boys. Jane Austen spent only a few years at school and commented later in a letter that school mistresses were generally an "ignorant class" (Apr. 8, 1805).

30. This probably means the Bennets hired masters for specific tasks, even if they did not regularly visit London for that purpose. This arrangement also existed in Jane Austen's family when she was a girl, and in a youthful letter she refers to practicing for the sake of her music master, though in a letter from later years she criticizes the practices of a music master and says that music masters tend to be "made of too much consequence" (Sept. 1, 1796; Dec. 2, 1815).

31. Lydia and Kitty exhibit such idleness, and Lydia's later actions show the harmful results of her upbringing. Jane Austen probably considers the Bennets to be guilty of partial negligence in educating their children. She herself learned mostly at home and without a governess, but she benefited from a strong educational atmosphere since her father ran a boarding school for boys (including his own sons). Mrs. Bennet's ignorance and Mr. Bennet's indolence would mean that no such atmosphere existed in their home.

32. *wonderful:* amazing.

most delightfully situated[33] through my means; and it was but the other day, that I recommended another young person, who was merely accidentally mentioned to me, and the family are quite delighted with her.[34] Mrs. Collins, did I tell you of Lady Metcalfe's calling yesterday to thank me? She finds Miss Pope a treasure. 'Lady Catherine,' said she, 'you have given me a treasure.' Are any of your younger sisters out, Miss Bennet?"

"Yes, Ma'am, all."

"All!—What, all five out at once? Very odd![35]—And you only the second.—The younger ones out before the elder are married!—Your younger sisters must be very young?"

"Yes, my youngest is not sixteen. Perhaps *she* is full[36] young to be much in company. But really, Ma'am, I think it would be very hard upon younger sisters, that they should not have their share of society and amusement because the elder may not have the means or inclination to marry early.—The last born has as good a right to the pleasures of youth,[37] as the first. And to be kept back on *such* a motive!—I think it would not be very likely to promote sisterly affection or delicacy of mind."[38]

"Upon my word," said her Ladyship, "you give your opinion very decidedly for so young a person.—Pray, what is your age?"

"With three younger sisters grown up," replied Elizabeth smiling, "your Ladyship can hardly expect me to own it."[39]

Lady Catherine seemed quite astonished at not receiving a direct answer; and Elizabeth suspected herself to be the first creature who had ever dared to trifle with so much dignified impertinence.[40]

"You cannot be more than twenty, I am sure,—therefore you need not conceal your age."

"I am not one and twenty."

When the gentlemen had joined them, and tea was over, the card tables were placed. Lady Catherine, Sir William, and Mr. and Mrs. Collins sat down to quadrille;[41] and as Miss De Bourgh chose to play at cassino,[42] the two girls had the honour of assisting Mrs. Jenkinson to make up her party. Their table was superlatively stupid. Scarcely a syllable was uttered that did not relate to

33. *situated*: placed in situations, or positions of employment.

34. Lady Catherine's using her influence to help secure positions for those connected with her is a standard example of the patronage that was central to this society.

35. It is indeed unusual in this society.

36. *full*: very.

37. *pleasures of youth*: the main pleasures probably meant are meeting men and going to parties and balls. A girl not out would be barred from these activities, and if she had to wait until an elder sister married she might pass much of her youth without them.

38. *delicacy of mind*: sensitivity, regard for others' feelings. Elizabeth's point is that the younger sisters might dislike the elders or become jealous and spiteful if they had to wait long to come out because the elders failed to marry.

39. *own it*: admit it (her age). A woman would be considered too old for marriage at a fairly early age, and thus would have a reason not to reveal her age—though Elizabeth's age of twenty is still well below that threshold. Her reluctance to answer Lady Catherine may result from exasperation at the latter's criticising of Elizabeth's family and persistence in asking intimate questions. Some have argued that by the standards of the time Elizabeth does become a little impertinent in responding to Lady Catherine, her host and her superior in age and rank; if that is so, and it is debatable, her impertinence would be a reaction to Lady Catherine's own overbearing manner.

40. *impertinence*: rudeness, intrusiveness, tendency to speak about or interfere with what is not one's affair or has no pertinence to oneself.

41. *quadrille*: evidently Lady Catherine's favorite card game; earlier Mr. Collins referred more than once to her regularly playing it. A game similar to whist and bridge, quadrille had been very popular in the eighteenth century. Whist was in the process of displacing quadrille in public favor, in part because of the latter's complex rules, odd card values, and extensive specialized vocabulary. Lady Catherine's adherence to the game could be a function of her sex, for quadrille was reputed to be especially popular among women and whist among men; it also could reflect her strong-willed and imperious character, which leads her to continue playing the game popular in her youth instead of adapting to the new trend. The other figure in Jane Austen mentioned as playing quadrille, Mrs. Bates in *Emma*, is a very old woman.

42. *cassino*: a card game in which players attempt to form numerical combinations with cards in their hand and on the board. It involves some skill, but is also a relatively relaxed game, for it neither centers around gambling nor requires the complicated strategy and interaction of quadrille or whist. Thus

the game, except when Mrs. Jenkinson expressed her fears of Miss De Bourgh's being too hot or too cold, or having too much or too little light. A great deal more passed at the other table. Lady Catherine was generally speaking—stating the mistakes of the three others, or relating some anecdote of herself. Mr. Collins was employed in agreeing to every thing her Ladyship said, thanking her for every fish[43] he won, and apologising if he thought he won too many. Sir William did not say much. He was storing his memory with anecdotes and noble names.

When Lady Catherine and her daughter had played as long as they chose, the tables were broke up, the carriage was offered to Mrs. Collins, gratefully accepted, and immediately ordered.[44] The party then gathered round the fire to hear Lady Catherine determine what weather they were to have on the morrow. From these instructions[45] they were summoned by the arrival of the coach, and with many speeches of thankfulness on Mr. Collins's side, and as many bows on Sir William's, they departed. As soon as they had driven from the door, Elizabeth was called on by her cousin, to give her opinion of all that she had seen at Rosings, which, for Charlotte's sake, she made more favourable than it really was. But her commendation, though costing her some trouble,[46] could by no means satisfy Mr. Collins, and he was very soon obliged to take her Ladyship's praise into his own hands.

it would suit well the timid and phlegmatic Miss De Bourgh; the other figure in Jane Austen who is described as playing it is the insipid Lady Middle-
ton of *Sense and Sensibility*. Another chronicler of the manners and
behavior of the time, Mary Mitford, depicts a group of dull quiet people who
play cassino (she also mentions the popularity of quadrille—see previous
note—among some very old ladies).

43. *fish*: tokens or chips used in betting, and often made in the form of a fish.

44. Since it would now be dark, they are being driven back despite the short
distance, for the limited means of illuminating paths then would make walking at night treacherous. They would need the offer of Lady Catherine's carriage since the Collinses are not mentioned as owning any vehicle except a
gig (see below), which could never transport a party of five.

45. *determine what weather . . . instructions*: choices of words that illustrate
Lady Catherine's character. It is as if she does not merely predict the weather,
but delivers commands to the sky to make certain types of weather occur.

46. *costing her some trouble*: meaning the trouble of stretching the truth in
her praise of Lady Catherine and the dinner party.

A gig. See p. 309, note 2.

[From Marjorie and C.H.B. Quennell, *A History of Everyday Things in England*, Vol. II
(New York, 1922), p. 191]

Chapter Seven

Sir William staid only a week at Hunsford; but his visit was long enough to convince him of his daughter's being most comfortably settled, and of her possessing such a husband and such a neighbour as were not often met with. While Sir William was with them, Mr. Collins devoted his mornings[1] to driving him out in his gig,[2] and shewing him the country; but when he went away, the whole family returned to their usual employments, and Elizabeth was thankful to find that they did not see more of her cousin by the alteration, for the chief of the time between breakfast and dinner was now passed by him either at work in the garden, or in reading and writing, and looking out of window in his own book room, which fronted the road. The room in which the ladies sat was backwards.[3] Elizabeth at first had rather wondered that Charlotte should not prefer the dining parlour for common use; it was a better sized room, and had a pleasanter aspect;[4] but she soon saw that her friend had an excellent reason for what she did, for Mr. Collins would undoubtedly have been much less in his own apartment,[5] had they sat in one equally lively; and she gave Charlotte credit for the arrangement.[6]

From the drawing room they could distinguish nothing in the lane, and were indebted to Mr. Collins for the knowledge of what carriages went along, and how often especially Miss De Bourgh drove by in her phaeton,[7] which he never failed coming to inform them of, though it happened almost every day. She not unfrequently stopped at the Parsonage, and had a few minutes' conversation with Charlotte, but was scarcely ever prevailed on to get out.

Very few days passed in which Mr. Collins did not walk to Rosings, and not many in which his wife did not think it necessary to go likewise; and till Elizabeth recollected that there might be other family livings[8] to be disposed of, she could not understand the sacrifice of so many hours.[9] Now and then, they were hon-

1.   *mornings*: this would mean most of the day. Mornings lasted from breakfast until dinner, which was usually around four or five.

2.   *gig*: an open carriage drawn by only one horse (see illustration on p. 307). It was less expensive than other open carriages, which is probably why Mr. Collins has one. These long carriage rides in the country, along with other details, suggest that Mr. Collins does not have to devote heavy amounts of time to clerical duties; this was generally the case among the Anglican clergy of the period.

3.   *was backwards*: faced the back.

4.   *aspect*: appearance, or view to the outside.

5.   *apartment*: room, or section of the house.

6.   Elizabeth perceives that Charlotte's situation, while far from ideal, is better than she had imagined it could be when she first heard of Charlotte's marriage. This does not mean that she was wrong to criticize her friend's decision, but it does indicate that her immediate evaluation of the marriage did not constitute a definitive or complete verdict—as happens elsewhere with Elizabeth's immediate evaluations, or first impressions.

7.   *phaeton*: carriage; see p. 293, note 27.

8.   *family livings*: church livings or positions owned by Lady Catherine's family, and thus currently controlled by her. For more on the subject of livings, and their ownership, see p. 115, note 11.

9.   They would be hoping to receive some of these other livings. It was not unusual for clergymen to hold multiple livings: Jane Austen's father and brother both did so, and the practice had increased in the decades before the novel. Wealthy owners of many livings, like Lady Catherine, were especially likely to sponsor it. Sometimes a clergyman was given livings that were close together, which allowed him to attend to them all from one residence. If that was not feasible, he could hire a clergyman to perform the clerical duties in the additional parishes. This latter man, known as a curate, usually received a very meager salary—the oversupply of clergy guaranteed the availability of curates and kept them from demanding more money. Hence the holder of these additional livings was able to keep most of the income it produced. This system had provoked some criticism by this point, but was still generally accepted as normal and natural.

oured with a call from her Ladyship, and nothing escaped her observation that was passing in the room during these visits. She examined into their employments, looked at their work,[10] and advised them to do it differently; found fault with the arrangement of the furniture, or detected the housemaid[11] in negligence; and if she accepted any refreshment, seemed to do it only for the sake of finding out that Mrs. Collins's joints of meat were too large for her family.

Elizabeth soon perceived that though this great lady was not in the commission of the peace for the county, she was a most active magistrate in her own parish,[12] the minutest concerns of which were carried to her by Mr. Collins;[13] and whenever any of the cottagers were disposed to be quarrelsome, discontented or too poor, she sallied forth into the village to settle their differences, silence their complaints, and scold them into harmony and plenty.

The entertainment of dining at Rosings was repeated about twice a week; and, allowing for the loss of Sir William, and there being only one card table in the evening, every such entertainment was the counterpart of the first. Their other engagements were few; as the style of living of the neighbourhood in general, was beyond the Collinses' reach.[14] This however was no evil[15] to Elizabeth, and upon the whole she spent her time comfortably[16] enough; there were half hours of pleasant conversation with Charlotte, and the weather was so fine for the time of year, that she had often great enjoyment out of doors. Her favourite walk, and where she frequently went while the others were calling on Lady Catherine, was along the open grove which edged that side of the park, where there was a nice sheltered path, which no one seemed to value but herself, and where she felt beyond the reach of Lady Catherine's curiosity.[17]

In this quiet way, the first fortnight of her visit soon passed away. Easter was approaching, and the week preceding it, was to bring an addition to the family at Rosings, which in so small a circle must be important. Elizabeth had heard soon after her arrival, that Mr. Darcy was expected there in the course of a few weeks, and though there were not many of her acquaintance

10. *work*: needlework.

11. *housemaid*: the wording implies the Collinses have only one such maid. If so, it would indicate they are not that affluent, for housemaids were the most basic type of servants, and any family of means would have more than one.

12. Commission of the peace is the authority to act as justice of the peace, or magistrate, the main governing and judicial position in local communities. Its standard qualification was an estate worth more than 100 pounds a year, which meant that landowners dominated the position (often supplemented by clergy, whose incomes also counted toward the 100 pound qualification). Of those who were eligible, only a minority bothered to take the oath and pay the fee allowing them to perform the actual duties. This minority were known as active magistrates—and only some of them were truly active in the sense of carrying out these duties frequently. The description of Lady Catherine in this role is meant to be sardonic: only men can hold the commission of the peace, so she cannot be a magistrate; but she behaves like a very active one because she aggressively performs tasks, such as resolving disputes and assisting the poor, that were among the principal duties of a magistrate.

13. As the local clergyman, Mr. Collins would have reason and opportunity to know about the doings of his parishioners. It was normal for the leading landowner and the clergyman of an area to work together to run its affairs.

14. Meaning that others in the neighborhood live on too expensive a scale for the Collinses to socialize with them; "neighbourhood" here means those of the genteel class, not everyone. Many clergy were in this position since they, though part of that class, tended to enjoy much lower incomes than the landowners who dominated genteel society. Lady Catherine is different from other families of the area since she, as Mr. Collins's patroness, extends him special hospitality. One reason why Mr. Collins seeks a wife where Elizabeth lives may be his inability to socialize with genteel families in his own area, which would make it hard for him to meet a suitable woman there.

15. *evil*: misfortune.

16. *comfortably*: pleasantly, enjoyably.

17. Ideals of landscaping in this period, in line with a general increased emphasis on the value of privacy, favored the creation of such secluded paths. Elizabeth's enjoyment of country walks and scenery links her to the author, who showed a love of the countryside and its beauties throughout her life and who was a frequent walker when she lived in the country (which included the time when this novel was written). Elizabeth's appreciation of scenic beauty will play a critical role later in the novel.

whom she did not prefer, his coming would furnish one comparatively new to look at in their Rosings parties, and she might be amused[18] in seeing how hopeless Miss Bingley's designs on him were, by his behaviour to his cousin, for whom he was evidently destined by Lady Catherine; who talked of his coming with the greatest satisfaction, spoke of him in terms of the highest admiration, and seemed almost angry to find that he had already been frequently seen by Miss Lucas and herself.

His arrival was soon known at the Parsonage, for Mr. Collins was walking the whole morning within view of the lodges[19] opening into Hunsford Lane, in order to have the earliest assurance of it; and after making his bow as the carriage turned into the Park, hurried home with the great intelligence. On the following morning he hastened to Rosings to pay his respects. There were two nephews of Lady Catherine to require them, for Mr. Darcy had brought with him a Colonel Fitzwilliam, the younger son of his uncle, Lord ———[20] and to the great surprise of all the party, when Mr. Collins returned the gentlemen accompanied him. Charlotte had seen them from her husband's room, crossing the road, and immediately running into the other, told the girls what an honour they might expect,[21] adding,

"I may thank you, Eliza, for this piece of civility. Mr. Darcy would never have come so soon to wait upon me."[22]

Elizabeth had scarcely time to disclaim all right to the compliment, before their approach was announced by the door-bell, and shortly afterwards the three gentlemen entered the room. Colonel Fitzwilliam, who led the way, was about thirty, not handsome, but in person and address[23] most truly the gentleman. Mr. Darcy looked just as he had been used to look in Hertfordshire, paid his compliments, with his usual reserve, to Mrs. Collins; and whatever might be his feelings towards her friend, met her with every appearance of composure. Elizabeth merely curtseyed to him, without saying a word.

Colonel Fitzwilliam entered into conversation directly with the readiness and ease of a well-bred[24] man, and talked very pleasantly; but his cousin, after having addressed a slight observation

18. *amused*: diverted, interested.

19. *lodges*: houses or cottages near the entrance to the grounds and occupied by those who take care of or guard the grounds.

20. Lord ———: an indication that he is a peer, and thus of very high rank. He is later revealed to be an earl. Jane Austen has used a dash to avoid having to specify the name. She probably did not want to identify the character with an actual noble family, but neither did she wish to use a fictitious name. In a letter to a niece, regarding the latter's draft of a novel, she criticized the use of a name for a nobleman that was not among existing noble names (Aug. 10, 1814). It is possible that the name Fitzwilliam was suggested by a prominent political figure of the period, an earl named William Fitzwilliam. But it is doubtful that Jane Austen intended to allude to him or his family directly, for his title was Earl or Lord Fitzwilliam. In contrast, Col. Fitzwilliam's family has, like many aristocratic families, two names, one (Fitzwilliam) that existed before the acquisition of the title and that is used by all members as a normal surname, and another that goes with the title; this means that the titleholder's full name would be ——— Fitzwilliam, Earl of (or Lord) ———.

As the son of an earl Colonel Fitzwilliam can be known as the Honourable ——— Fitzwilliam. He has chosen instead to use his military title, which was distinguished in itself, for army officer was the most prestigious of all professions. It was this prestige, along with the importance of wealth and connections for determining advancement in the army (they mattered less in the Navy), that made men from aristocratic backgrounds prefer the army above other professions. Colonel Fitzwilliam's need to pursue a profession indicates he is a younger son of an earl, and not the heir (see p. 339, note 10).

21. Charlotte's excitement shows that she, while not going as far as her husband, does share his interest in the attentions of high-ranking persons.

22. Since Charlotte is of a lower social rank than Darcy, and has no particular connection to him, he would have no reason to pay her this honor immediately. His visit could indicate a persistent interest in Elizabeth, an interest that might even have been strengthened by exposure to other, less appealing women during his winter in London. But the cold manner he displays here does not suggest too much interest, even if one allows for his general coldness of manner; moreover, he will not visit her again for almost a week. It is possible that his visit is simply a courtesy he thinks should be paid to Elizabeth because of their earlier acquaintance, or that it has been prompted by the more gregarious Colonel Fitzwilliam.

23. *in person and address*: in appearance, and in speech and manners.

24. *well-bred*: polite, courteous.

on the house and garden to Mrs. Collins, sat for some time without speaking to any body. At length, however, his civility was so far awakened as to enquire of Elizabeth after the health of her family. She answered him in the usual way, and after a moment's pause, added,

"My eldest sister has been in town these three months.[25] Have you never happened to see her there?"

She was perfectly sensible[26] that he never had; but she wished to see whether he would betray any consciousness of what had passed between the Bingleys and Jane; and she thought he looked a little confused as he answered that he had never been so fortunate as to meet Miss Bennet.[27] The subject was pursued no farther, and the gentlemen soon afterwards went away.

25. *these three months:* for the last three months. Jane came to London at the very end of December; it is now early to mid-April (see chronology, pp. 715–716).

26. *sensible:* aware.

27. Later Darcy will reveal that he has a reason to look confused or be flustered by this question.

Chapter Eight

Colonel Fitzwilliam's manners were very much admired at the parsonage, and the ladies all felt that he must add considerably to the pleasure of their engagements at Rosings. It was some days, however, before they received any invitation thither, for while there were visitors in the house, they could not be necessary;[1] and it was not till Easter-day, almost a week after the gentlemen's arrival, that they were honoured by such an attention, and then they were merely asked on leaving church to come there in the evening.[2] For the last week they had seen very little of either Lady Catherine or her daughter. Colonel Fitzwilliam had called at the parsonage more than once during the time, but Mr. Darcy they had only seen at church.[3]

The invitation was accepted of course, and at a proper hour they joined the party in Lady Catherine's drawing room. Her ladyship received them civilly, but it was plain that their company was by no means so acceptable as when she could get nobody else; and she was, in fact, almost engrossed by her nephews, speaking to them, especially to Darcy, much more than to any other person in the room.

Colonel Fitzwilliam seemed really glad to see them; any thing was a welcome relief to him at Rosings; and Mrs. Collins's pretty friend had moreover caught his fancy very much. He now seated himself by her, and talked so agreeably of Kent and Hertfordshire, of travelling and staying at home, of new books and music, that Elizabeth had never been half so well entertained in that room before; and they conversed with so much spirit and flow, as to draw the attention of Lady Catherine herself, as well as of Mr. Darcy. *His* eyes had been soon and repeatedly turned towards them with a look of curiosity;[4] and that her ladyship after a while shared the feeling, was more openly acknowledged, for she did not scruple[5] to call out,

1. In other words, the Collinses and their guests would no longer be necessary to help provide diversion for Lady Catherine while she had visitors at her house.

2. This is a less important invitation than one to dinner.

3. They would almost certainly have seen him at services on Good Friday (the wording of this passage suggests that this encounter with him occurred before Easter).

Darcy's continued aloofness from Elizabeth signals either that he is not yet strongly interested in her, or that he is still successful in his struggle to suppress that interest—he will mention such a struggle when he proposes to Elizabeth, though without saying how long the struggle has gone on or when it became acute.

4. It is possible Darcy is also spurred by a sense of rivalry or jealousy as he sees Colonel Fitzwilliam charm Elizabeth.

5. *scruple*: hesitate.

"What is that you are saying, Fitzwilliam? What is it you are talking of? What are you telling Miss Bennet? Let me hear what it is."

"We are speaking of music, Madam," said he, when no longer able to avoid a reply.

"Of music! Then pray speak aloud. It is of all subjects my delight. I must have my share in the conversation, if you are speaking of music. There are few people in England, I suppose, who have more true enjoyment of music than myself, or a better natural taste. If I had ever learnt, I should have been a great proficient.[6] And so would Anne, if her health had allowed her to apply. I am confident that she would have performed delightfully. How does Georgiana get on, Darcy?"

Mr. Darcy spoke with affectionate praise of his sister's proficiency.

"I am very glad to hear such a good account of her," said Lady Catherine; "and pray tell her from me, that she cannot expect to excel, if she does not practise a great deal."

"I assure you, Madam," he replied, "that she does not need such advice. She practises very constantly."

"So much the better. It cannot be done too much; and when I next write to her, I shall charge her not to neglect it on any account. I often tell young ladies, that no excellence in music is to be acquired, without constant practice. I have told Miss Bennet several times, that she will never play really well, unless she practises more; and though Mrs. Collins has no instrument, she is very welcome, as I have often told her, to come to Rosings every day, and play on the piano forte in Mrs. Jenkinson's room. She would be in nobody's way, you know, in that part of the house."

Mr. Darcy looked a little ashamed of his aunt's ill breeding,[7] and made no answer.

When coffee was over, Colonel Fitzwilliam reminded Elizabeth of having promised to play to him; and she sat down directly to the instrument. He drew a chair near her. Lady Catherine listened to half a song, and then talked, as before, to her other nephew;[8] till the latter walked away from her, and moving with his usual deliberation towards the piano forte, stationed himself so as to command a full view of the fair performer's countenance.

6. *proficient*: one who has become very accomplished in an art.

7. *ill breeding*: rudeness. The rudeness comes in inviting Elizabeth to play only where she will be out of everyone's way. Darcy's reaction demonstrates his true sense of courtesy despite his lack of outward friendliness. He also is being placed here in a position similar to one suffered by Elizabeth, that of feeling shame at the bad behavior of a family member.

It could be asked why Darcy, given the frequently rude behavior of his aunt, continues to look snobbishly down on the bad behavior of Elizabeth's family. One possible answer is that there are substantive differences in the two cases: Lady Catherine is only one relative rather than several, she is a more distant relation to Darcy than a parent or a sister, and her behavior is never as vulgar as that of Lydia or Mrs. Bennet. Another possible answer is that Darcy, like almost everyone, is more likely to perceive others' weak points than his own. This tendency would be strengthened in his case by the inclination, normal in this society, to interpret more favorably the character and possible defects of those of higher social station like Lady Catherine.

8. A contrast to her earlier professions of love of music. Jane Austen has several instances in her novels where people's professions of musical interest are contradicted by their actions. As someone who played and liked music herself, she may have been naturally sensitive to this particular hypocrisy, and have noticed many examples of it.

A piano-forte; see p. 69, note 29. The clothes are from a slightly earlier period.

[From Marjorie and C.H.B. Quennell, A History of Everyday Things in England, Vol. II (New York, 1922), p. 179]

Elizabeth saw what he was doing, and at the first convenient pause, turned to him with an arch smile, and said,

"You mean to frighten me, Mr. Darcy, by coming in all this state[9] to hear me? But I will not be alarmed though your sister *does* play so well. There is a stubbornness about me that never can bear to be frightened at the will of others. My courage always rises with every attempt to intimidate me."[10]

"I shall not say that you are mistaken," he replied, "because you could not really believe me to entertain any design of alarming you; and I have had the pleasure of your acquaintance long enough to know, that you find great enjoyment in occasionally professing opinions which in fact are not your own."[11]

Elizabeth laughed heartily at this picture of herself, and said to Colonel Fitzwilliam, "Your cousin will give you a very pretty notion of me; and teach you not to believe a word I say. I am particularly unlucky in meeting with a person so well able to expose my real character, in a part of the world where I had hoped to pass myself off with some degree of credit.[12] Indeed, Mr. Darcy, it is very ungenerous in you to mention all that you knew to my disadvantage in Hertfordshire—and, give me leave to say, very impolitic[13] too—for it is provoking me to retaliate, and such things may come out, as will shock your relations to hear."

"I am not afraid of you," said he, smilingly.

"Pray let me hear what you have to accuse him of," cried Colonel Fitzwilliam. "I should like to know how he behaves among strangers."[14]

"You shall hear then—but prepare yourself for something very dreadful. The first time of my ever seeing him in Hertfordshire, you must know, was at a ball—and at this ball, what do you think he did? He danced only four dances![15] I am sorry to pain you—but so it was. He danced only four dances, though gentlemen were scarce; and, to my certain knowledge,[16] more than one young lady was sitting down in want of[17] a partner. Mr. Darcy, you cannot deny the fact."[18]

"I had not at that time the honour of knowing any lady in the assembly beyond my own party."

9. *state:* solemn and imposing pomp or grandeur.

10. Elizabeth's reaction, though partly playful, indicates her continued suspicion of Darcy and her sense of competitiveness with him.

11. Darcy probably has in mind a number of earlier instances in which Elizabeth spoke playfully or sarcastically or provocatively, and his words are partly accurate. What he fails to perceive is that Elizabeth was not always being playful or sarcastic; in some cases the sharp words she directed toward him were sincerely meant. This failure of perception also means that he will continue to disregard her sharp words, or perhaps even regard them as a provocative form of flirtation.

12. *some degree of credit:* a reasonably good name, a decent reputation.

13. *impolitic:* imprudent, not conducive to promoting one's interest.

14. Darcy has already been shown behaving in a somewhat friendlier manner among those he knows well.

15. He danced one pair of dances with Miss Bingley, and one pair with Mrs. Hurst.

16. *certain knowledge:* her knowledge is especially certain because she herself was one of the ladies sitting down during one pair of dances; she probably still remembers the insulting words Darcy spoke about her at this time when Bingley suggested that Darcy ask her to dance.

17. *in want of:* for lack of.

18. *fact:* action, deed.

"True; and nobody can ever be introduced in a ball room.[19] Well, Colonel Fitzwilliam, what do I play next? My fingers wait your orders."

"Perhaps," said Darcy, "I should have judged better, had I sought an introduction, but I am ill qualified to recommend myself to strangers."

"Shall we ask your cousin the reason of this?" said Elizabeth, still addressing Colonel Fitzwilliam. "Shall we ask him why a man of sense and education, and who has lived in the world,[20] is ill qualified to recommend himself to strangers?"

"I can answer your question," said Fitzwilliam, "without applying to him. It is because he will not give himself the trouble."[21]

"I certainly have not the talent which some people possess," said Darcy, "of conversing easily with those I have never seen before. I cannot catch their tone of conversation, or appear interested in their concerns, as I often see done."

"My fingers," said Elizabeth, "do not move over this instrument in the masterly manner which I see so many women's do. They have not the same force or rapidity, and do not produce the same expression. But then I have always supposed it to be my own fault—because I would not take the trouble of practising.[22] It is not that I do not believe *my* fingers as capable as any other woman's of superior execution."

Darcy smiled and said, "You are perfectly right. You have employed your time much better. No one admitted to the privilege of hearing you, can think any thing wanting. We neither of us perform to strangers."[23]

Here they were interrupted by Lady Catherine, who called out to know what they were talking of. Elizabeth immediately began playing again. Lady Catherine approached, and, after listening for a few minutes, said to Darcy,

"Miss Bennet would not play at all amiss, if she practised more, and could have the advantage of a London master. She has a very good notion of fingering,[24] though her taste is not equal to Anne's. Anne would have been a delightful performer, had her health allowed her to learn."

19. This is clear sarcasm. Sir William Lucas was shown introducing Darcy and Elizabeth at the party at the Lucases, and Bingley easily procured introductions for himself at the first dance.

20. *the world*: fashionable world, good society. The idea is that a man with such experience would have good manners.

21. Such a quick answer by Darcy's friend indicates that Darcy has behaved this way on many occasions.

22. This constitutes an important message of the book: the need to learn to perform social duties and to show regard for others, even if it does not come naturally. It is a message Darcy has yet to appreciate.

23. This is one of the most cryptic and subtle passages in the book, in part because Darcy is misinterpreting Elizabeth's previous words. By "perform to strangers" he means put on a display before others in order to win their approval or impress them. His point seems to be that, just as he does not converse with strangers for that purpose, she, unlike many women (Mary Bennet or Miss Bingley could be examples), does not waste her time putting on musical displays before large numbers of people in order to gratify her vanity. The words, "no one admitted to the privilege of hearing you," imply that her performances have been restricted as regards their audience—which in fact is not true.

All that, however, is not what Elizabeth said. She said nothing of her audience; instead, she admitted there to be something lacking in her piano playing, and attributed it to her failure to practice enough, with an implied analogy to his failure to practice the art of sociable conversation. She was offering a criticism of them both; such a tactic of criticizing oneself as well when criticizing another is a common device to make criticism more palatable and hence more effective. He, unwilling at this stage to accept serious criticism, has converted her words into a compliment to them both for their honesty and their lack of concern for others' opinions, qualities he values highly.

24. *fingering*: the action or proper method of using the fingers when playing an instrument.

Elizabeth looked at Darcy to see how cordially he assented to his cousin's praise; but neither at that moment nor at any other could she discern any symptom of love; and from the whole of his behaviour to Miss De Bourgh she derived this comfort for Miss Bingley, that he might have been just as likely to marry *her*, had she been his relation.[25]

Lady Catherine continued her remarks on Elizabeth's performance, mixing with them many instructions on execution and taste. Elizabeth received them with all the forbearance of civility;[26] and at the request of the gentlemen remained at the instrument till her Ladyship's carriage was ready to take them all home.

25. For the acceptability of love between first cousins, see p. 157, note 73.

26. *forbearance of civility:* politeness that makes her tolerate Lady Catherine's impolite remarks. Elizabeth's willingness and ability to do so helps underline the very point she was just making to Darcy about accommodating others, which he refused to perceive.

Chapter Nine

*E*lizabeth was sitting by herself the next morning, and writing to Jane, while Mrs. Collins and Maria were gone on business into the village, when she was startled by a ring at the door, the certain signal of a visitor. As she had heard no carriage, she thought it not unlikely to be Lady Catherine, and under that apprehension was putting away her half-finished letter that she might escape all impertinent[1] questions, when the door opened,[2] and to her very great surprise, Mr. Darcy, and Mr. Darcy only, entered the room.[3]

He seemed astonished too on finding her alone, and apologised for his intrusion, by letting her know that he had understood all the ladies to be within.

They then sat down, and when her enquiries after Rosings were made, seemed in danger of sinking into total silence.[4] It was absolutely necessary, therefore, to think of something, and in this emergence[5] recollecting *when* she had seen him last in Hertfordshire, and feeling curious to know what he would say on the subject of their hasty departure, she observed,

"How very suddenly you all quitted Netherfield last November, Mr. Darcy! It must have been a most agreeable surprise to Mr. Bingley to see you all after him so soon; for, if I recollect right, he went but the day before.[6] He and his sisters were well, I hope, when you left London."

"Perfectly so—I thank you."

She found that she was to receive no other answer—and, after a short pause, added,

"I think I have understood that Mr. Bingley has not much idea of ever returning to Netherfield again?"

"I have never heard him say so; but it is probable that he may spend very little of his time there in future. He has many friends,

1. *impertinent:* intrusive, meddlesome.

2. A servant would have let Darcy into the house, and then into the room containing Elizabeth.

3. This point marks the beginning of Darcy's serious interest in Elizabeth, for after this he sees her almost every day. Clearly his seeing her at Lady Catherine's the previous evening had rekindled his interest or had undermined much of his remaining reservations about pursuing her.

4. Darcy's interest in Elizabeth does not mean that his sociability or skills at conversation have improved. He clearly has given no heed to her reproach at the piano.

5. *emergence:* emergency, urgent circumstances.

6. Meaning that Mr. Bingley must have been surprised and pleased when, only a day after he had gone to London on business, the rest of his party left Netherfield to join him in London. Elizabeth is being sarcastic here, for when Mr. Bingley had left Netherfield it had been with the idea of the others staying, and his returning there. She suspects, and we in fact learn later, that his sisters and Darcy hastened to London in order to interrupt Bingley's plans and prevent his return.

and he is at a time of life when friends and engagements are continually increasing."

"If he means to be but little at Netherfield, it would be better for the neighbourhood that he should give up the place entirely, for then we might possibly get a settled family there.[7] But perhaps Mr. Bingley did not take the house so much for the convenience of the neighbourhood as for his own, and we must expect him to keep or quit it on the same principle."[8]

"I should not be surprised," said Darcy, "if he were to give it up, as soon as any eligible purchase offers."[9]

Elizabeth made no answer. She was afraid of talking longer of his friend; and, having nothing else to say, was now determined to leave the trouble of finding a subject to him.

He took the hint, and soon began with, "This seems a very comfortable house. Lady Catherine, I believe, did a great deal to it when Mr. Collins first came to Hunsford."[10]

"I believe she did—and I am sure she could not have bestowed her kindness on a more grateful object."

"Mr. Collins appears very fortunate in his choice of a wife."

"Yes, indeed; his friends may well rejoice in his having met with one of the very few sensible women who would have accepted him, or have made him happy if they had. My friend has an excellent understanding—though I am not certain that I consider her marrying Mr. Collins as the wisest thing she ever did. She seems perfectly happy, however, and in a prudential light, it is certainly a very good match for her."[11]

"It must be very agreeable to her to be settled within so easy a distance of her own family and friends."

"An easy distance do you call it? It is nearly fifty miles."[12]

"And what is fifty miles of good road? Little more than half a day's journey.[13] Yes, I call it a *very* easy distance."

"I should never have considered the distance as one of the *advantages* of the match," cried Elizabeth. "I should never have said Mrs. Collins was settled *near* her family."

"It is a proof of your own attachment to Hertfordshire. Any

7. It was considered better for a country neighborhood if those families inhabiting its grand homes, whose wealth and social standing would make them a leading force in the community, remained in the area as much as possible. Many in rural areas at the time complained of the increasing tendency of rich landowners in this period to be away from their estates for long periods, often in London or in resort towns; it was feared particularly that this would lead to neglect of the local poor, who depended heavily on charity from the wealthy.

8. Elizabeth probably intends this as a criticism of Bingley, for she is angry at his apparently selfish abandonment of Jane.

9. *eligible purchase offers*: desirable purchase presents itself or appears. In other words, when a suitable property comes along for Bingley, who is currently a renter, to buy.

10. Mr. Collins has spoken elsewhere of his parsonage and the improvements it has received. It is another sign of his good luck, and of his reasons for gratitude toward Lady Catherine. Parsonages in this period tended to be in bad shape, with some parishes not even having one. Many of the clergymen living in them lacked the money to repair or improve them, and their incentive to do so was limited by the knowledge that after they died or retired the improved parsonage would go not to their heir but to the next person filling the post. Responsibility for repair and improvement rested mainly on the landowner or other party disposing of the living, but they often did not bother since it meant spending money without receiving anything themselves. Lady Catherine, however, is not guilty of such negligence.

11. Elizabeth's criticism of Charlotte's marriage, despite its prudential or monetary advantages, indicates that she would not let considerations like that determine her own marital choice. It is a hint Darcy does not perceive.

12. The distance Elizabeth traveled to London was stated to be 24 miles; Westerham, near which the Collinses live, is a little more than 20 miles to London; thus "nearly fifty miles" would be exactly right.

13. This suggests the speed of travel. At this time, the best coaches were estimated to be able to achieve 7–8 miles per hour; private carriages, such as Darcy would certainly use, could potentially go faster. The preceding century had witnessed continual improvements in the quality of carriages and of roads, especially the latter, so that journeys, while still slow and difficult from today's perspective, were significantly faster and easier than in preceding generations.

thing beyond the very neighbourhood of Longbourn, I suppose, would appear far."

As he spoke there was a sort of smile, which Elizabeth fancied she understood; he must be supposing her to be thinking of Jane and Netherfield,[14] and she blushed as she answered,

"I do not mean to say that a woman may not be settled too near her family. The far and the near must be relative, and depend on many varying circumstances. Where there is fortune to make the expence of travelling unimportant, distance becomes no evil.[15] But that is not the case *here*. Mr. and Mrs. Collins have a comfortable income, but not such a one as will allow of frequent journeys—and I am persuaded my friend would not call herself *near* her family under less than *half* the present distance."

Mr. Darcy drew his chair a little towards her, and said, "*You* cannot have a right to such very strong local attachment. *You* cannot have been always at Longbourn."[16]

Elizabeth looked surprised. The gentleman experienced some change of feeling; he drew back his chair, took a newspaper from the table, and, glancing over it, said, in a colder voice,

"Are you pleased with Kent?"

A short dialogue on the subject of the country ensued, on either side calm and concise—and soon put an end to by the entrance of Charlotte and her sister, just returned from their walk. The tête a tête surprised them. Mr. Darcy related the mistake which had occasioned his intruding on Miss Bennet, and after sitting a few minutes longer without saying much to any body, went away.

"What can be the meaning of this!" said Charlotte, as soon as he was gone. "My dear Eliza he must be in love with you, or he would never have called on us in this familiar way."

But when Elizabeth told of his silence, it did not seem very likely, even to Charlotte's wishes, to be the case; and after various conjectures, they could at last only suppose his visit to proceed from the difficulty of finding any thing to do, which was the more probable from the time of year. All field sports were over.[17] Within doors there was Lady Catherine, books, and a billiard table, but gentlemen cannot be always within doors;[18] and in the nearness of the

14. In fact, Darcy is probably wondering about her attachment to home because of his own interest in her, for his home lies at a farther distance from her home than Kent does. Elizabeth, however, fails to perceive this, which means she unconsciously ends up fanning his hopes.

15. *evil:* great drawback or defect. Distance would not be a drawback to Darcy, who has his own carriages. The Collinses would have to hire carriages, so such travel would be harder for them. Of course, this answer would serve as an encouragement for Darcy: if "distance becomes no evil" with adequate finances, Elizabeth would have no objection on that ground to marriage with Darcy, for as his wife she would certainly have carriages enough.

16. An indication that Darcy is becoming more decided in his interest in Elizabeth, though her refusal to reciprocate his interest then makes him draw back.

17. hunting and shooting, the most popular field sports, were fall and winter activities, and it is now spring.

18. Gentlemen's need for diversion, including outdoor diversion, is often mentioned in nineteenth century novels. In contrast, ladies, often required to stay inside continuously, are pictured as more accustomed to enforced idleness, and thus less apt to chafe at it.

Parsonage, or the pleasantness of the walk to it, or of the people who lived in it, the two cousins found a temptation from this period of walking thither almost every day. They called at various times of the morning, sometimes separately, sometimes together, and now and then accompanied by their aunt.[19] It was plain to them all that Colonel Fitzwilliam came because he had pleasure in their society, a persuasion which of course recommended him still more; and Elizabeth was reminded by her own satisfaction in being with him, as well as by his evident admiration of her, of her former favourite George Wickham; and though, in comparing them, she saw there was less captivating softness in Colonel Fitzwilliam's manners, she believed he might have the best informed mind.[20]

But why Mr. Darcy came so often to the Parsonage, it was more difficult to understand. It could not be for society, as he frequently sat there ten minutes together without opening his lips; and when he did speak, it seemed the effect of necessity rather than of choice—a sacrifice to propriety, not a pleasure to himself. He seldom appeared really animated. Mrs. Collins knew not what to make of him. Colonel Fitzwilliam's occasionally laughing at his stupidity,[21] proved that he was generally different,[22] which her own knowledge of him could not have told her; and as she would have liked to believe this change the effect of love, and the object of that love, her friend Eliza, she sat herself seriously to work to find it out.—She watched him whenever they were at Rosings, and whenever he came to Hunsford; but without much success. He certainly looked at her friend a great deal, but the expression of that look was disputable. It was an earnest, steadfast gaze, but she often doubted whether there were much admiration in it, and sometimes it seemed nothing but absence of mind.

She had once or twice suggested to Elizabeth the possibility of his being partial to her, but Elizabeth always laughed at the idea; and Mrs. Collins did not think it right to press the subject, from the danger of raising expectations which might only end in disappointment; for in her opinion it admitted not of a doubt, that all her friend's dislike would vanish, if she could suppose him to be in her power.[23]

19. These visits are occurring over a ten-day period, from the Monday on which Darcy first sees Elizabeth alone at the parsonage, until the following Thursday when he proposes to her; see chronology, p. 716.

20. Elizabeth's admiration of Colonel Fitzwilliam reveals another blind spot in her judgment of Darcy, for she never stops to consider how a man whom she regards as despicable could be close friends with a worthy man such as the Colonel.

21. *stupidity*: dullness, lack of animation.

22. Another hint of additional features of Darcy, this time of not always being so proud and reserved.

23. *in her power*: in love with her. Charlotte assumes that, like herself, Elizabeth would place material advantage above personal affection in deciding on marriage, a misjudgment of Elizabeth that parallels the latter's misjudgment of her. Charlotte's perspective would be normal for the time, perhaps more normal than Elizabeth's; this is why Darcy's misplaced confidence that she would accept him has some rational basis.

In her kind schemes for Elizabeth, she sometimes planned her marrying Colonel Fitzwilliam. He was beyond comparison the pleasantest man; he certainly admired her, and his situation in life was most eligible; but, to counterbalance these advantages, Mr. Darcy had considerable patronage in the church, and his cousin could have none at all.[24]

24. This passage is one of the best examples of Jane Austen's subtle appreciation of human psychology, and its complex mixture of generous and selfish impulses. Charlotte has started her speculations about whom it would be best for Elizabeth to marry with a genuine concern for what would be best for her friend. Soon, however, she segues, almost unconsciously it seems, into wondering which choice would be best for herself and her husband—for having her best friend married to a man with great patronage in the church (and Darcy controls multiple livings) would be a significant help to her husband's career.

Chapter Ten

More than once did Elizabeth in her ramble within the Park, unexpectedly meet Mr. Darcy. — She felt all the perverseness of the mischance that should bring him where no one else was brought; and to prevent its ever happening again, took care to inform him at first, that it was a favourite haunt of hers. — How it could occur a second time therefore was very odd! — Yet it did, and even a third. It seemed like wilful ill-nature, or a voluntary penance, for on these occasions it was not merely a few formal enquiries and an awkward pause and then away, but he actually thought it necessary to turn back and walk with her. He never said a great deal, nor did she give herself the trouble of talking or of listening much; but it struck her in the course of their third rencontre[1] that he was asking some odd unconnected questions — about her pleasure in being at Hunsford, her love of solitary walks, and her opinion of Mr. and Mrs. Collins's happiness; and that in speaking of Rosings and her not perfectly understanding the house, he seemed to expect that whenever she came into Kent again she would be staying *there* too. His words seemed to imply it. Could he have Colonel Fitzwilliam in his thoughts? She supposed, if he meant any thing, he must mean an allusion to what might arise in that quarter.[2] It distressed her a little, and she was quite glad to find herself at the gate in the pales[3] opposite the Parsonage.

She was engaged one day as she walked, in re-perusing Jane's last letter, and dwelling on some passages which proved that Jane had not written in spirits,[4] when, instead of being again surprised by Mr. Darcy, she saw on looking up that Colonel Fitzwilliam was meeting her. Putting away the letter immediately and forcing a smile, she said,

"I did not know before that you ever walked this way."

"I have been making the tour of the Park,"[5] he replied, "as I

1. *rencontre*: an accidental or unexpected encounter.

2. Elizabeth perceives that he must be alluding to a possible marriage, for she would only be able to stay at Rosings if married to someone close to Lady Catherine. What is remarkable is that Elizabeth fails to perceive that Darcy might have himself in mind rather than Colonel Fitzwilliam. By now his frequent visits to the parsonage and his repeated accompaniment of her on her walks, supplemented by Charlotte's speculations about Darcy's love, should have combined to suggest at least the possibility of that love. But just as Darcy misreads Elizabeth, her prejudice against him blinds her about his intentions as well as about his character.

3. *pales*: stakes forming a fence.

4. *in spirits*: in a happy or cheerful mood. Elizabeth's perception at this point of Jane's lack of cheerfulness increases the strength of her reaction to what she is about to be told.

5. *making the tour of the Park*: going around the entire Park.

generally do every year, and intend to close it with a call at the Parsonage. Are you going much farther?"

"No, I should have turned in a moment."

And accordingly she did turn, and they walked towards the Parsonage together.

"Do you certainly leave Kent on Saturday?"[6] said she.

"Yes—if Darcy does not put it off again.[7] But I am at his disposal. He arranges the business just as he pleases."

"And if not able to please himself in the arrangement, he has at least great pleasure in the power of choice. I do not know any body who seems more to enjoy the power of doing what he likes than Mr. Darcy."

"He likes to have his own way very well," replied Colonel Fitzwilliam. "But so we all do. It is only that he has better means of having it than many others, because he is rich,[8] and many others are poor.[9] I speak feelingly. A younger son, you know, must be inured to self-denial and dependence."[10]

"In my opinion, the younger son of an Earl can know very little of either. Now, seriously, what have you ever known of self-denial and dependence? When have you been prevented by want of money from going wherever you chose, or procuring any thing you had a fancy for?"

"These are home[11] questions—and perhaps I cannot say that I have experienced many hardships of that nature. But in matters of greater weight, I may suffer from the want of money. Younger sons cannot marry where they like."[12]

"Unless where they like women of fortune, which I think they very often do."

"Our habits of expence make us too dependant,[13] and there are not many in my rank of life who can afford to marry without some attention to money."

"Is this," thought Elizabeth, "meant for me?" and she coloured[14] at the idea;[15] but, recovering herself, said in a lively[16] tone, "And pray, what is the usual price of an Earl's younger son? Unless the elder brother is very sickly, I suppose you would not ask above fifty thousand pounds."[17]

6. This day, which is when they do go, is just under three weeks after they arrived.

7. Darcy has presumably been delaying because of his interest in Elizabeth.

8. A more perceptive analysis of Darcy's character than either of them may realize. His wealth has kept him from having to accommodate others, and this has spoiled him and kept him from learning social virtues.

9. *poor*: poor in a relative sense, for Colonel Fitzwilliam seems to be counting himself as poor. There are other cases in Jane Austen's novels where characters are described as poor because they lack what is considered fundamental for a person of the genteel classes (e.g., a number of servants, a personal carriage, a spacious home), not because they truly lack material necessities.

10. This is because, under the prevailing system of inheritance, most of the family wealth, and usually all the property, went to the eldest son. Younger sons thus had to enter professions such as the Church or the military, as Colonel Fitzwilliam has done, in order to support themselves. They did generally inherit some money (as did the daughters, for whom the money served as a dowry): this money, along with family patronage and connections, helped younger sons advance in their professions, but they still were generally in a worse position than eldest sons.

11. *home*: pertinent, appropriate (i.e., ones that strike home).

12. Because they need brides with money.

13. *dependant*: dependent on money.

14. *coloured*: changed color, blushed.

15. The idea is that he is warning her that, due to her lack of fortune, he cannot consider marrying her.

16. *lively*: playful, lighthearted.

17. If the eldest son dies, the next eldest becomes the heir; thus a sickly eldest son would raise the value and marital eligibility of his younger brother.

He answered her in the same style,[18] and the subject dropped. To interrupt a silence which might make him fancy her affected with what had passed,[19] she soon afterwards said,

"I imagine your cousin brought you down with him chiefly for the sake of having somebody at his disposal. I wonder he does not marry, to secure a lasting convenience of that kind. But, perhaps his sister does as well for the present, and, as she is under his sole care, he may do what he likes with her."

"No," said Colonel Fitzwilliam, "that is an advantage which he must divide with me. I am joined with him in the guardianship of Miss Darcy."[20]

"Are you, indeed? And pray what sort of guardians do you make? Does your charge[21] give you much trouble? Young ladies of her age, are sometimes a little difficult to manage, and if she has the true Darcy spirit, she may like to have her own way."

As she spoke, she observed him looking at her earnestly, and the manner in which he immediately asked her why she supposed Miss Darcy likely to give them any uneasiness, convinced her that she had somehow or other got pretty near the truth.[22] She directly replied,

"You need not be frightened. I never heard any harm of her; and I dare say she is one of the most tractable creatures in the world. She is a very great favourite with some ladies of my acquaintance, Mrs. Hurst and Miss Bingley. I think I have heard you say that you know them."

"I know them a little. Their brother is a pleasant gentleman-like man—he is a great friend of Darcy's."

"Oh! yes," said Elizabeth drily—"Mr. Darcy is uncommonly kind to Mr. Bingley, and takes a prodigious[23] deal of care of him."

"Care of him!—Yes, I really believe Darcy *does* take care of him in those points where he most wants care. From something that he told me in our journey hither, I have reason to think Bingley very much indebted to him. But I ought to beg his pardon, for I have no right to suppose that Bingley was the person meant. It was all conjecture."

"What is it you mean?"

18. *same style*: in the same ironic and joking style Elizabeth has just used.

19. Meaning that her silence might make him think that his warning about marriage affected her emotionally, something she does not wish.

20. *guardianship of Miss Darcy*: having lost her parents, she has been placed under the guardianship of her brother and Colonel Fitzwilliam until she is twenty-one (the normal age of maturity). Her finances and education, as well as any decision to marry, would be under their legal control.

21. *charge*: the person under your care or charge.

22. As we soon find out, Colonel Fitzwilliam has a more serious reason than Elizabeth imagines for his concerned reaction, due to a recent traumatic episode involving Miss Darcy.

23. *prodigious*: Elizabeth is being ironic in using such a hyperbolic term, one that was considered colloquial at the time, and that Jane Austen usually puts in the mouth of foolish characters prone to exaggeration.

"It is a circumstance which Darcy of course would not wish to be generally known, because if it were to get round to the lady's family, it would be an unpleasant thing."

"You may depend upon my not mentioning it."[24]

"And remember that I have not much reason for supposing it to be Bingley. What he told me was merely this; that he congratulated himself on having lately saved a friend from the inconveniences of a most imprudent marriage, but without mentioning names or any other particulars, and I only suspected it to be Bingley from believing him the kind of young man to get into a scrape of that sort,[25] and from knowing them to have been together the whole of last summer."

"Did Mr. Darcy give you his reasons for this interference?"

"I understood that there were some very strong objections against the lady."

"And what arts[26] did he use to separate them?"

"He did not talk to me of his own arts," said Fitzwilliam smiling. "He only told me, what I have now told you."

Elizabeth made no answer, and walked on, her heart swelling with indignation. After watching her a little, Fitzwilliam asked her why she was so thoughtful.

"I am thinking of what you have been telling me," said she. "Your cousin's conduct does not suit my feelings. Why was he to be the judge?"

"You are rather disposed to call his interference officious?"

"I do not see what right Mr. Darcy had to decide on the propriety of his friend's inclination, or why, upon his own judgment alone, he was to determine and direct in what manner that friend was to be happy." "But," she continued, recollecting herself,[27] "as we know none of the particulars,[28] it is not fair to condemn him. It is not to be supposed that there was much affection in the case."

"That is not an unnatural surmise," said Fitzwilliam, "but it is lessening the honour of my cousin's triumph very sadly."[29]

This was spoken jestingly, but it appeared to her so just a picture of Mr. Darcy, that she would not trust herself with an answer;[30] and, therefore, abruptly changing the conversation,

24. An ironic promise, since she is a member of the family he wishes to shield from the information.

25. Bingley has already shown, through his impulsiveness and his susceptibility to others' influence, that he is in fact the sort to get in such scrapes. Colonel Fitzwilliam's words suggest that Bingley has done so before. This characteristic of Bingley's makes Darcy's interference in his affairs more understandable, even if it was mistaken in this instance.

26. *arts:* devices, pieces of cunning.

27. She naturally does not want, through her strong reaction, to reveal to him that she is sister to the lady in question.

28. *particulars:* particular facts of the case.

29. In other words, if little affection existed, separating the two lovers would have been easy, and less honor would go to Darcy for saving his friend.

30. She would not trust herself to answer calmly, and thereby keep Colonel Fitzwilliam from guessing how much she was concerned in the matter.

talked on indifferent matters till they reached the parsonage. There, shut into her own room, as soon as their visitor left them, she could think without interruption of all that she had heard. It was not to be supposed that any other people could be meant than those with whom she was connected. There could not exist in the world *two* men, over whom Mr. Darcy could have such boundless influence. That he had been concerned in the measures taken to separate Mr. Bingley and Jane, she had never doubted; but she had always attributed to Miss Bingley the principal design and arrangement of them. If his own vanity, however, did not mislead him, *he* was the cause, his pride and caprice were the cause of all that Jane had suffered, and still continued to suffer. He had ruined for a while every hope of happiness for the most affectionate, generous heart in the world; and no one could say how lasting an evil he might have inflicted.

"There were some very strong objections against the lady," were Colonel Fitzwilliam's words, and these strong objections probably were, her having one uncle who was a country attorney, and another who was in business in London.

"To Jane herself," she exclaimed, "there could be no possibility of objection. All loveliness and goodness as she is! Her understanding[31] excellent, her mind[32] improved,[33] and her manners captivating. Neither could any thing be urged against my father, who, though with some peculiarities, has abilities which Mr. Darcy himself need not disdain, and respectability which he will probably never reach."[34] When she thought of her mother indeed, her confidence gave way a little, but she would not allow that any objections *there* had material weight with Mr. Darcy, whose pride, she was convinced, would receive a deeper wound from the want of importance[35] in his friend's connections,[36] than from their want of sense;[37] and she was quite decided at last, that he had been partly governed by this worst kind of pride, and partly by the wish of retaining Mr. Bingley for his sister.[38]

The agitation and tears which the subject occasioned, brought on a headach; and it grew so much worse towards the evening that, added to her unwillingness to see Mr. Darcy, it determined

31. *understanding:* intellect.

32. *mind:* inner character.

33. *improved:* well cultivated.

34. Respectability particularly refers to his moral character, which she believes that Darcy, thanks to his supposed misdeeds and maliciousness, will never equal.

35. *importance:* social standing or consequence.

36. *connections:* relations (referring to the relations he would have if he married Jane, i.e., the Bennets)

37. Elizabeth turns out to be wrong on this point.

38. Elizabeth's final point is correct, though Darcy himself will never admit it, even after he reforms.

her not to attend[39] her cousins[40] to Rosings, where they were engaged to drink tea. Mrs. Collins, seeing that she was really unwell, did not press her to go, and as much as possible prevented her husband from pressing her, but Mr. Collins could not conceal his apprehension of Lady Catherine's being rather displeased by her staying at home.

39. *attend:* accompany.

40. *cousins:* both the Collinses, since Mrs. Collins is now Elizabeth's cousin by marriage.

Chapter Eleven[1]

W hen they were gone, Elizabeth, as if intending to exasperate herself as much as possible against Mr. Darcy, chose
for her employment the examination of all the letters which Jane
had written to her since her being in Kent. They contained no
actual complaint, nor was there any revival[2] of past occurrences,
or any communication of present suffering.[3] But in all, and in
almost every line of each, there was a want of that cheerfulness
which had been used to characterize her style, and which, proceeding from the serenity of a mind at ease with itself, and kindly
disposed towards every one, had been scarcely ever clouded. Elizabeth noticed every sentence conveying the idea of uneasiness,
with an attention which it had hardly received on the first
perusal. Mr. Darcy's shameful boast of what misery he had been
able to inflict,[4] gave her a keener sense of her sister's sufferings. It
was some consolation to think that his visit to Rosings was to end
on the day after the next, and a still greater, that in less than a fortnight she should herself be with Jane again, and enabled to contribute to the recovery of her spirits, by all that affection could do.

She could not think of Darcy's leaving Kent, without remembering that his cousin was to go with him; but Colonel Fitzwilliam
had made it clear that he had no intentions[5] at all, and agreeable
as he was, she did not mean to be unhappy about him.

While settling this point, she was suddenly roused by the sound
of the door bell, and her spirits were a little fluttered by the idea
of its being Colonel Fitzwilliam himself, who had once before
called late in the evening, and might now come to enquire particularly after her. But this idea was soon banished, and her spirits
were very differently affected, when, to her utter amazement, she
saw Mr. Darcy walk into the room. In an hurried manner he
immediately began an enquiry after her health, imputing his visit

1.   The crucial chapter in the book. It comes almost at the midway point, and marks the culmination of the first half of the book, whose principal subject has been the growth in misunderstanding between Darcy and Elizabeth, and the growth of her dislike of him.

2.   *revival:* remembering.

3.   Jane, of course, would never include such complaints in a letter of hers. She hardly even admitted to being ill in her letter informing her family of her cold.

4.   In fact, Elizabeth has no basis for believing that Darcy has boasted of inflicting misery. He only congratulated himself on helping his friend (and he soon reveals that he did not believe it would cause Jane misery). Of course, Elizabeth, after what she has heard of Darcy's actions regarding Jane, is even less disposed than before to be fair to him. This new revelation, and the extreme anger it provokes, has come at a particularly significant time, for it means that, immediately before one of the most crucial scenes in the book, she is more harshly disposed toward Darcy than she ever has been.

5.   *intentions:* intentions to marry her.

to a wish of hearing that she were better.[6] She answered him with cold civility. He sat down for a few moments, and then getting up walked about the room. Elizabeth was surprised, but said not a word. After a silence of several minutes he came towards her in an agitated manner, and thus began,

"In vain have I struggled. It will not do. My feelings will not be repressed. You must allow me to tell you how ardently I admire and love you."[7]

Elizabeth's astonishment was beyond expression. She stared, coloured,[8] doubted, and was silent.[9] This he considered sufficient encouragement, and the avowal of all that he felt and had long felt for her, immediately followed. He spoke well, but there were feelings besides those of the heart to be detailed, and he was not more eloquent on the subject of tenderness than of pride.[10] His sense of her inferiority—of its being a degradation—of the family obstacles which judgment had always opposed to inclination,[11] were dwelt on with a warmth which seemed due to the consequence he was wounding,[12] but was very unlikely to recommend his suit.[13]

In spite of her deeply-rooted dislike, she could not be insensible[14] to the compliment of such a man's affection, and though her intentions did not vary for an instant, she was at first sorry for the pain he was to receive; till, roused to resentment by his subsequent language, she lost all compassion in anger. She tried, however, to compose herself to answer him with patience, when he should have done. He concluded with representing to her the strength of that attachment which, in spite of all his endeavours, he had found impossible to conquer; and with expressing his hope that it would now be rewarded by her acceptance of his hand. As he said this, she could easily see that he had no doubt of a favourable answer. He *spoke* of apprehension and anxiety, but his countenance expressed real security.[15] Such a circumstance could only exasperate farther, and when he ceased, the colour rose into her cheeks, and she said,

"In such cases as this, it is, I believe, the established mode to express a sense of obligation for the sentiments avowed, however unequally they may be returned. It is natural that obligation should be felt, and if I could *feel* gratitude, I would now thank

6. Elizabeth's not being well provides Darcy with a good excuse to come, but his hasty manner of inquiry shows that it is only an excuse. One does not know how long before this he decided to propose to her, or was leaning in that direction, but clearly the report of Elizabeth's illness has inspired him to propose now by presenting him with an ideal opportunity.

7. *I admire and love you:* such a statement would be considered an offer of marriage, as Elizabeth immediately does consider it, for it would be highly improper for a man to speak such words to a single woman in normal conversation.

8. *coloured:* blushed.

9. *doubted, and was silent:* wondered if he were serious, until, being convinced he was, she fell silent.

10. In other words, he was as eloquent in speaking of his family pride as in offering words of tenderness to her.

11. Meaning that his reason, which told him that marriage to her would degrade him, had checked his love.

12. *consequence he was wounding:* the family position and pride he was harming (by his proposal to a woman beneath him socially).

13. *his suit:* proposal, suing for her hand. Since complimenting one's lover is such standard practice in marriage proposals, it is remarkable that a man as intelligent as Darcy would speak so insultingly. Part of the reason is undoubtedly his strong feelings of pride, along with the frankness (something he boasts of shortly) that makes him hesitate to disguise these feelings. Part of the reason is his evident confidence in being accepted, which keeps him from worrying too much about antagonizing her. Finally, it is possible that, in his myopic way, he conceives of his words as a compliment—i.e., "even though I object to your family and social position, your personal charms are so great that I am overlooking all that"—and expects her to receive them as such.

14. *insensible:* indifferent.

15. *security:* confidence or assurance (that she will accept him). Since expressing fear of not being accepted was standard form in proposals, his having done so does him little credit when it is accompanied by looks signaling such opposite feelings.

you. But I cannot—I have never desired your good opinion, and you have certainly bestowed it most unwillingly. I am sorry to have occasioned pain to any one. It has been most unconsciously done, however, and I hope will be of short duration. The feelings which, you tell me, have long prevented the acknowledgment of your regard, can have little difficulty in overcoming it after this explanation."[16]

Mr. Darcy, who was leaning against the mantle-piece with his eyes fixed on her face, seemed to catch her words with no less resentment than surprise. His complexion became pale with anger, and the disturbance of his mind was visible in every feature. He was struggling for the appearance of composure, and would not open his lips, till he believed himself to have attained it.[17] The pause was to Elizabeth's feelings dreadful. At length, in a voice of forced calmness, he said,

"And this is all the reply which I am to have the honour of expecting! I might, perhaps, wish to be informed why, with so little *endeavour* at civility, I am thus rejected.[18] But it is of small importance."

"I might as well enquire," replied she, "why with so evident a design of offending and insulting me, you chose to tell me that you liked me against your will, against your reason, and even against your character?[19] Was not this some excuse for incivility, if I *was* uncivil? But I have other provocations. You know I have. Had not my own feelings decided against you, had they been indifferent, or had they even been favourable, do you think that any consideration would tempt me to accept the man, who has been the means of ruining, perhaps for ever, the happiness of a most beloved sister?"[20]

As she pronounced these words, Mr. Darcy changed colour; but the emotion[21] was short, and he listened without attempting to interrupt her while she continued.

"I have every reason in the world to think ill of you. No motive can excuse the unjust and ungenerous[22] part you acted *there*. You dare not, you cannot deny that you have been the principal, if not the only means of dividing them from each other, of exposing one

16. Elizabeth is taking the opportunity to turn Darcy's arrogant words against him by using them as a good reason why she need not bother to speak more politely and thereby let him down more gently.

17. Even here Darcy strives to avoid weakness, in this case the weakness of losing self-control and speaking under the influence of too much emotion and anger.

18. As Elizabeth said, her reply violated the usual form of rejection, in which one politely expressed gratitude. This adds to the offense of the rejection. Of course, as Elizabeth goes on to say, he was uncivil in the way he asked her.

19. *even against your character:* even against your moral character or qualities. In other words, Elizabeth says he spoke as if asking for her hand violated his moral principles or integrity, something she naturally considers the worst implication of all in his words.

20. It could be argued that Elizabeth's mention of Jane and Bingley represents a violation of her pledge to Colonel Fitzwilliam to keep silent about what he told her of Darcy's interference in Bingley's affairs, though Colonel Fitzwilliam's main concern was to prevent the matter from becoming generally known, not to prevent Darcy himself from hearing of it again.

21. *emotion:* agitation, disturbance of mind.

22. *ungenerous:* ignominious.

to the censure of the world for caprice and instability,[23] the other to its derision for disappointed hopes,[24] and involving them both in misery of the acutest kind."

She paused, and saw with no slight indignation that he was listening with an air which proved him wholly unmoved by any feeling of remorse. He even looked at her with a smile of affected incredulity.

"Can you deny that you have done it?" she repeated.

With assumed tranquillity he then replied, "I have no wish of denying that I did every thing in my power to separate my friend from your sister, or that I rejoice in my success. Towards *him* I have been kinder than towards myself."[25]

Elizabeth disdained the appearance of noticing this civil reflection, but its meaning did not escape, nor was it likely to conciliate her.

"But it is not merely this affair," she continued, "on which my dislike is founded. Long before it had taken place, my opinion of you was decided. Your character was unfolded in the recital which I received many months ago from Mr. Wickham. On this subject, what can you have to say? In what imaginary act of friendship can you here defend yourself?[26] or under what misrepresentation, can you here impose upon[27] others?"

"You take an eager interest in that gentleman's concerns," said Darcy in a less tranquil tone, and with a heightened colour.[28]

"Who that knows what his misfortunes have been, can help feeling an interest in him?"

"His misfortunes!" repeated Darcy contemptuously; "yes, his misfortunes have been great indeed."

"And of your infliction,"[29] cried Elizabeth with energy. "You have reduced him to his present state of poverty, comparative poverty.[30] You have withheld the advantages, which you must know to have been designed for him. You have deprived the best years of his life, of that independence[31] which was no less his due than his desert.[32] You have done all this! and yet you can treat the mention of his misfortunes with contempt and ridicule."

"And this," cried Darcy, as he walked with quick steps across

23. *instability*: unsteadiness, lack of firmness.

24. Because marriage was regarded as such serious business, a man who abandoned a woman after wooing her would be harshly condemned, and a woman who was jilted would be ridiculed. In the case of Bingley and Jane, matters had not reached such a serious stage that either would suffer badly in those ways—though of course they both do suffer in another way, in their own hearts. Elizabeth's anger makes her exaggerate.

25. Meaning that, since marriage to Jane or Elizabeth would be so degrading for either of them, he has treated Bingley better than he has treated himself. It is no wonder that this "civil reflection" does not conciliate Elizabeth.

26. In other words, you [Darcy] justify your conduct with Bingley by claiming, falsely, that it was an act of friendship, but in Wickham's case even that excuse will be impossible to attempt.

27. *impose upon*: deceive.

28. We see that this subject truly angers Darcy, in contrast to the subject of Bingley and Jane.

29. *of your infliction*: inflicted by you.

30. Elizabeth corrects herself slightly, since Wickham is not actually poor.

31. *independence*: something that allows one to live comfortably. The reference is to the living Darcy denied Wickham.

32. *no less his due than his desert*: no less his legal right than his moral right. In other words, Wickham deserved the living according to the legal provisions of the will, and according to general principles of morality or fairness.

the room, "is your opinion of me! This is the estimation in which you hold me! I thank you for explaining it so fully. My faults, according to this calculation, are heavy indeed! But perhaps," added he, stopping in his walk, and turning towards her, "these offences might have been overlooked, had not your pride been hurt by my honest confession of the scruples that had long prevented my forming any serious design.[33] These bitter accusations might have been suppressed, had I with greater policy[34] concealed my struggles, and flattered you into the belief of my being impelled by unqualified, unalloyed inclination; by reason, by reflection, by every thing.[35] But disguise of every sort is my abhorrence.[36] Nor am I ashamed of the feelings I related. They were natural and just. Could you expect me to rejoice in the inferiority of your connections? To congratulate myself on the hope of relations, whose condition in life is so decidedly beneath my own?"

Elizabeth felt herself growing more angry every moment;[37] yet she tried to the utmost to speak with composure when she said,

"You are mistaken, Mr. Darcy, if you suppose that the mode of your declaration affected me in any other way, than as it spared me the concern which I might have felt in refusing you, had you behaved in a more gentleman-like manner."

She saw him start at this,[38] but he said nothing, and she continued,

"You could not have made me the offer of your hand in any possible way that would have tempted me to accept it."

Again his astonishment was obvious; and he looked at her with an expression of mingled incredulity and mortification. She went on.

"From the very beginning, from the first moment I may almost say, of my acquaintance with you, your manners impressing me with the fullest belief of your arrogance, your conceit, and your selfish disdain of the feelings of others, were such as to form that ground-work of disapprobation, on which succeeding events have built so immoveable a dislike; and I had not known you a month before I felt that you were the last man in the world whom I could ever be prevailed on to marry."

33. Darcy's accusation that Elizabeth's judgment has been distorted by pride has a particular irony, since Darcy follows it with his own proud assertions regarding his frankness and his social superiority.

34. *policy*: artfulness, shrewdness, skillful management. Darcy still cannot accept that Elizabeth is refusing him on substance, and thus tries to attribute her reaction to his style of proposing.

35. Darcy is satirizing the normal mode of proposing, with its exaggerated compliments. This mode appeared in full force in Mr. Collins's proposal.

36. A central credo of his, one that is a source of his pride. Later his aunt, Lady Catherine, will boast of a similar frankness to Elizabeth. Of course, absolute frankness is easier if, like Darcy or Lady Catherine, one is rich and powerful enough not to need others' favor and thereby not to have to worry about offending them. For Darcy this may be the first time in his adult life when he has been reduced to seeking something of great importance from someone else, especially someone not inclined to give it. He is thus placed in the position of more ordinary mortals and forced to learn some new and valuable lessons.

37. Elizabeth's growing anger may result from Darcy's reiteration of his contempt for her family and social position; it also could result from Darcy's assertion that she only rejected him because of his frankness, an assertion that implies that she is such a shallow person that she would accept a man she objected to merely because he flattered her. Whatever the reason, it is at this point that Elizabeth's anger boils over enough to inspire the truly devastating words that conclude her rejection of him.

38. Toward the end of the story the great significance of this start will be revealed, as will its relationship to the words just spoken by Elizabeth.

"You have said quite enough, madam. I perfectly comprehend your feelings, and have now only to be ashamed of what my own have been. Forgive me for having taken up so much of your time, and accept my best wishes for your health and happiness."[39]

And with these words he hastily left the room, and Elizabeth heard him the next moment open the front door and quit the house.

The tumult of her mind was now painfully great. She knew not how to support herself, and from actual weakness sat down and cried for half an hour. Her astonishment, as she reflected on what had passed, was increased by every review of it. That she should receive an offer of marriage from Mr. Darcy! that he should have been in love with her for so many months! so much in love as to wish to marry her in spite of all the objections which had made him prevent his friend's marrying her sister, and which must appear at least with equal force in his own case,[40] was almost incredible! it was gratifying to have inspired unconsciously so strong an affection.[41] But his pride, his abominable pride, his shameless avowal of what he had done with respect to Jane, his unpardonable assurance[42] in acknowledging, though he could not justify it, and the unfeeling manner in which he had mentioned Mr. Wickham, his cruelty towards whom he had not attempted to deny, soon overcame the pity which the consideration of his attachment had for a moment excited.

She continued in very agitating reflections till the sound of Lady Catherine's carriage made her feel how unequal she was to encounter Charlotte's observation, and hurried her away to her room.

39. It is significant that even after receiving such a brutal, and unexpected, rebuke, Darcy is able to depart with words of courtesy.

40. Since Darcy is wealthier and from a longer established and more highly connected family than Bingley, he would be lowering himself socially even more.

41. Elizabeth does not overlook the compliment to her own vanity in Darcy's proposal, even amidst her overall anger and agitation.

42. *assurance*: cockiness, impudence.

Chapter Twelve[1]

*E*lizabeth awoke the next morning to the same thoughts and meditations which had at length closed her eyes. She could not yet recover from the surprise of what had happened; it was impossible to think of any thing else, and totally indisposed for employment, she resolved soon after breakfast to indulge herself in[2] air and exercise. She was proceeding directly to her favourite walk, when the recollection of Mr. Darcy's sometimes coming there stopped her, and instead of entering the park, she turned up the lane, which led her farther from the turnpike road. The park paling[3] was still the boundary on one side, and she soon passed one of the gates into the ground.[4]

After walking two or three times along that part of the lane, she was tempted, by the pleasantness of the morning, to stop at the gates and look into the park. The five weeks which she had now passed in Kent, had made a great difference in the country, and every day was adding to the verdure of the early trees.[5] She was on the point of continuing her walk, when she caught a glimpse of a gentleman within the sort of grove which edged the park; he was moving that way; and fearful of its being Mr. Darcy, she was directly retreating. But the person who advanced, was now near enough to see her, and stepping forward with eagerness, pronounced her name. She had turned away, but on hearing herself called, though in a voice which proved it to be Mr. Darcy, she moved again towards the gate. He had by that time reached it also, and holding out a letter, which she instinctively took, said with a look of haughty composure,[6] "I have been walking in the grove some time in the hope of meeting you. Will you do me the honour of reading that letter?"[7]—And then, with a slight bow, turned again into the plantation,[8] and was soon out of sight.

With no expectation of pleasure, but with the strongest curiosity, Elizabeth opened the letter,[9] and to her still increasing wonder,

1. This chapter begins the second half of the book, whose principal subject is the gradual reconciliation of Elizabeth and Darcy.

2. *indulge herself in*: give herself the pleasure of. "Indulge" generally had no pejorative connotations then.

3. *paling*: fence or fencing.

4. *ground*: area of the park.

5. By this point it is almost the end of April; see chronology, p. 716.

6. This look corresponds to the proud, but also controlled, tone in which the letter is written.

7. It was considered improper for a man to correspond with an unmarried woman, unless he was engaged to her or they had a family connection. Hence Darcy cannot send a letter to Elizabeth and must deliver it by hand. Even then the letter borders on impropriety, though it could be justified in this case by the importance of the communication.

8. *plantation*: a grouping of planted items, particularly a wood of planted trees. It is almost certainly the same as the grove mentioned by Darcy, for the two words could be used interchangeably.

9. This letter constitutes one of the most dramatic developments in the novel. Some have questioned its plausibility—specifically, that a man as proud and reserved as Darcy would write on such intimate matters as he does to someone who has no connection to him. Obviously such a letter is needed for the purposes of the plot, since it changes much of Elizabeth's opinion of Darcy. Yet a basis for the letter has been established in Darcy's character. While reserved, he has also been consistently outspoken and opinionated when provoked, as he surely has been by Elizabeth's condemnation of him. Second, his pride has made him consistently hate to be wrong, or even to be thought in the wrong, so he strongly wishes to vindicate his behavior to someone whose opinion he respects.

perceived an envelope containing two sheets of letter paper, written quite through,[10] in a very close hand.[11]—The envelope itself was likewise full.[12]—Pursuing her way along the lane, she then began it. It was dated from Rosings, at eight o'clock in the morning, and was as follows:—

Be not alarmed, Madam,[13] on receiving this letter, by the apprehension of its containing any repetition of those sentiments, or renewal of those offers, which were last night so disgusting[14] to you. I write without any intention of paining you, or humbling myself, by dwelling on wishes, which, for the happiness of both, cannot be too soon forgotten; and the effort which the formation,[15] and the perusal of this letter must occasion, should have been spared, had not my character[16] required it to be written and read. You must, therefore, pardon the freedom with which I demand your attention; your feelings, I know, will bestow it unwillingly, but I demand it of your justice.[17]

"Two offences of a very different nature, and by no means of equal magnitude, you last night laid to my charge.[18] The first mentioned was, that, regardless of the sentiments of either, I had detached Mr. Bingley from your sister,—and the other, that I had, in defiance of various claims, in defiance of honour and humanity, ruined the immediate prosperity, and blasted the prospects of Mr. Wickham.—Wilfully and wantonly to have thrown off the companion of my youth, the acknowledged favourite of my father, a young man who had scarcely any other dependence[19] than on our patronage, and who had been brought up to expect its exertion,[20] would be a depravity, to which the separation of two young persons, whose affection could be the growth of only a few weeks, could bear no comparison.[21]—But from the severity of that blame which was last night so liberally bestowed,[22] respecting each circumstance, I shall hope to be in future secured, when the following account of my actions and their motives has been read.—If, in the explanation of them which is due to myself, I am under the necessity of relating feelings which may be offensive to your's, I can only say that I am sorry.—The necessity must be obeyed—and farther apology would

10. *written quite through*: completely covered with writing.

11. *a close hand*: compressed handwriting.

12. The envelope was a sheet of paper folded around the other sheets (what are now called envelopes were not widely used until the 1830s). In this case, it is also full of writing. Darcy has thus crammed his long letter into three total sheets of paper. Such economy of paper was common then, even among the wealthy, for paper was costly and postage, which was based on the weight of the letter, had become extremely high during this period. This made many strive for the close hand Darcy uses: Jane Austen laments in several letters her own inability to write in a close hand (for a sample of her writing, see p. 221).

13. *Madam*: the standard way to address a woman in a letter or in formal conversation, if one did not know her well enough to address her by name.

14. *disgusting*: distasteful. The word then had a milder meaning than now.

15. *formation*: writing, composition.

16. *character*: reputation.

17. In other words, though you will not wish to read this, your sense of fairness obliges you to do so.

18. Actually Elizabeth, in addition to the two points mentioned by Darcy here, accused him of general arrogance and selfishness. Darcy, however, is still not willing at this point to confront those charges; he prefers sticking to specific charges that he can more easily refute or explain.

19. *dependence*: resource, thing to be relied upon.

20. That is, to expect that the family patronage would be used on his behalf.

21. In describing the two cases Darcy almost exaggerates the accusation regarding Wickham, a sign of how unjust he thinks the accusation is; meanwhile he minimizes the significance of his actions regarding Bingley and Jane, a sign that he still does not take that issue very seriously.

22. *liberally bestowed*: freely and fully bestowed. Here, as in his opening words, Darcy shows his continuing resentment and bitterness. His wording also implies a criticism of Elizabeth for seeming to rate the two offenses as roughly equal, even though he considers one to be far worse than the other.

be absurd.[23]—*I had not been long in Hertfordshire, before I saw, in common with others, that Bingley preferred your eldest sister, to any other young woman in the country.—But it was not till the evening of the dance at Netherfield that I had any apprehension of his feeling a serious attachment.—I had often seen him in love before.*[24]—*At that ball, while I had the honour of dancing with you, I was first made acquainted, by Sir William Lucas's accidental information,*[25] *that Bingley's attentions to your sister had given rise to a general expectation of their marriage. He spoke of it as a certain event, of which the time alone could be undecided.*[26] *From that moment I observed my friend's behaviour attentively; and I could then perceive that his partiality for Miss Bennet was beyond what I had ever witnessed in him. Your sister I also watched.—Her look and manners were open, cheerful and engaging as ever, but without any symptom of peculiar regard,*[27] *and I remained convinced from the evening's scrutiny, that though she received his attentions with pleasure, she did not invite them by any participation of sentiment.*[28]—*If you have not been mistaken here, I must have been in an error. Your superior knowledge of your sister must make the latter probable.—If it be so, if I have been misled by such error, to inflict pain on her, your resentment has not been unreasonable. But I shall not scruple*[29] *to assert, that the serenity of your sister's countenance and air was such, as might have given the most acute observer, a conviction that, however amiable her temper,*[30] *her heart was not likely to be easily touched.*[31]—*That I was desirous of believing her indifferent is certain,—but I will venture to say that my investigations and decisions are not usually influenced by my hopes or fears.—I did not believe her to be indifferent because I wished it;—I believed it on impartial conviction, as truly as I wished it in reason.—My objections to the marriage were not merely those, which I last night acknowledged to have required the utmost force of passion to put aside, in my own case; the want of connection*[32] *could not be so great an evil*[33] *to my friend as to me.*[34]—*But there were other causes of repugnance;—causes which, though still existing, and existing to an equal degree in both instances, I had myself endeavoured to forget, because they were*

23. These words suggest how difficult the proud Darcy finds any apology.

24. A confirmation of Colonel Fitzwilliam's earlier words about Bingley's character.

25. That is, by the fortuitous or chance circumstance of being informed by Sir William Lucas.

26. Meaning that only when the event would occur was not certain.

27. *peculiar regard:* particular regard for Bingley.

28. *participation of sentiment:* similar or shared feelings. In other words, she did not share the love that Bingley felt. These lines provide a particularly strong confirmation of Bingley's earlier description of Darcy's writing as being carefully studied and full of long words, for Darcy's style is very formal, with many elaborate sentences and difficult words and phrases. In these respects it bears some resemblance to Mr. Collins's efforts. But while the latter's formal and long-winded phrases are merely verbal padding or the repetition of empty clichés, Darcy's complex phrases exist to convey complex thoughts, ones that display his intelligence, just as his careful wording displays the deliberation and scrupulousness that mark his character generally.

29. *scruple:* hesitate.

30. *temper:* disposition, temperament.

31. From what has been shown of Jane's amiability toward everyone, a quality that makes it hard for others to distinguish any particular preference on her part, Darcy has some reason for his conclusion. Elizabeth will end up admitting that in the next chapter.

32. *want of connection:* lack of good family connections.

33. *evil:* drawback, disadvantage.

34. This could be because the social gap between Bingley and the Bennets was not as great as that between Darcy and the Bennets, or because Bingley cared less about social position. Darcy's explanation runs contrary to Elizabeth's suspicion that it was this want of connection that mostly influenced Darcy.

not immediately before me.[35]—These causes must be stated, though briefly.—The situation[36] of your mother's family,[37] though objectionable, was nothing in comparison of that total want[38] of propriety so frequently, so almost uniformly betrayed by herself, by your three younger sisters, and occasionally even by your father.— Pardon me.—It pains me to offend you. But amidst your concern for the defects of your nearest relations, and your displeasure at this representation of them, let it give you consolation to consider that, to have conducted yourselves so as to avoid any share of the like censure, is praise no less generally bestowed on you and your eldest sister, than it is honourable to the sense and disposition of both.—I will only say farther, that from what passed that evening, my opinion of all parties was confirmed, and every inducement heightened, which could have led me before, to preserve my friend from what I esteemed a most unhappy connection.[39]—He left Netherfield for London, on the day following, as you, I am certain, remember, with the design of soon returning.—The part which I acted, is now to be explained.—His sisters' uneasiness had been equally excited with my own; our coincidence[40] of feeling was soon discovered; and, alike sensible that no time was to be lost in detaching their brother, we shortly resolved on joining him directly in London.—We accordingly went—and there I readily engaged in the office[41] of pointing out to my friend, the certain evils of such a choice.—I described, and enforced[42] them earnestly.—But, however this remonstrance might have staggered or delayed his determination, I do not suppose that it would ultimately have prevented the marriage, had it not been seconded by the assurance which I hesitated not in giving, of your sister's indifference.[43] He had before believed her to return his affection with sincere, if not with equal regard.—But Bingley has great natural modesty, with a stronger dependence on my judgment than on his own.—To convince him, therefore, that he had deceived himself, was no very difficult point. To persuade him against returning into Hertfordshire, when that conviction had been given, was scarcely the work of a moment.—I cannot blame myself for having done thus much. There is but one part of my conduct in the whole affair, on which I do not reflect with satisfaction;

35. Darcy touches here on an important issue, which is why his objections to the Bennet family, objections that made him warn Bingley against marrying Jane, did not also prevent his proposing to Elizabeth. His answer is that by the time of his proposal the Bennets' improprieties were distant enough to be somewhat forgettable. The implication of his phrasing is also that he tried to forget these improprieties, presumably because of his passion for Elizabeth, and this may suggest the real answer—that it was easy for him to give primacy to family considerations when advising Bingley because in that case his own amorous feelings did not influence him.

36. *situation*: social condition or position.

37. As is indicated all along, it is on this side that Elizabeth's family is considered to be lower, since her father, as the heir of a comfortable estate, is unquestionably a gentleman.

38. *want*: lack.

39. The Ball at Netherfield was where Elizabeth herself was made miserable by the behavior of her family, including her mother's talk of husband hunting, Mary's vain display on the piano, and Mr. Collins's foolish speeches. The Ball also presented Mr. Bennet's overly blunt reproof of Mary, and his tendency to see his wife's and Mr. Collins's embarrassing conduct purely as occasions for amusement; these incidents are probably at least part of what Darcy has in mind when he mentioned to Elizabeth the lack of propriety that was shown "occasionally even by your father."

40. *coincidence*: agreement, concurrence.

41. *office*: obligatory task.

42. *enforced*: emphasized, demonstrated.

43. Darcy indicates what was most crucial in alienating Bingley from Jane. Yet he does not explore the issue further, for he has already admitted that, unlike his condemnation of the Bennet family for impropriety, his evaluation of Jane was probably wrong. Hence Bingley's decision was made primarily on a dubious basis. Darcy, however, does not speak of trying to undo his work.

it is that I condescended to adopt the measures of art[44] so far as to conceal from him your sister's being in town. I knew it myself, as it was known to Miss Bingley, but her brother is even yet ignorant of it.—That they might have met without ill consequence, is perhaps probable;—but his regard did not appear to me enough extinguished for him to see her without some danger.—Perhaps this concealment, this disguise, was beneath me.—It is done, however, and it was done for the best.—On this subject I have nothing more to say, no other apology to offer. If I have wounded your sister's feelings, it was unknowingly done; and though the motives which governed me may to you very naturally appear insufficient, I have not yet learnt to condemn them.[45]—With respect to that other, more weighty accusation, of having injured Mr. Wickham, I can only refute it by laying before you the whole of his connection with my family. Of what he has particularly accused me I am ignorant; but of the truth of what I shall relate, I can summon more than one witness of undoubted veracity. Mr. Wickham is the son of a very respectable man, who had for many years the management of all the Pemberley estates;[46] and whose good conduct in the discharge of his trust,[47] naturally inclined my father to be of service to him, and on George Wickham, who was his god-son, his kindness was therefore liberally bestowed.[48] My father supported him at school, and afterwards at Cambridge;[49]—most important assistance, as his own father, always poor from the extravagance of his wife,[50] would have been unable to give him a gentleman's education.[51] My father was not only fond of this young man's society, whose manners were always engaging; he had also the highest opinion of him, and hoping the church would be his profession, intended to provide for him in it. As for myself, it is many, many years since I first began to think of him in a very different manner. The vicious[52] propensities—the want of principle which he was careful to guard from the knowledge of his best friend,[53] could not escape the observation of a young man of nearly the same age with himself, and who had opportunities of seeing him in unguarded moments, which Mr. Darcy could not have. Here again I shall give you pain—to what degree you only can tell. But whatever may be the sentiments which

44. *art:* cunning, trickery. It is characteristic that what Darcy regrets, among all his actions, is violating his own ideal of honesty and frankness. His use of "condescended" to describe his action signals his sense of its being beneath him, for one meaning of condescend was to lower oneself.

45. *not yet learnt to condemn them:* a curious phrase that indicates Darcy's divided mind. Part of him clearly sees that, given what Elizabeth has told him about Jane, he should condemn his actions. But another part of him — spurred most likely by his continued objections to the Bennet family as well as by his natural reluctance to admit to having made a serious error — recoils from that. Hence he avows his continued adherence to his position, even as he almost admits that he may, and perhaps should, learn to think differently.

46. The wording implies that several estates, or blocks of land, were connected with the Pemberley property. This was not unusual among very wealthy landowners.

47. Darcy's praise of Wickham's father is important, for it explains why his own father would have treated so favorably a bad man like Wickham.

48. The high value of a good steward, or manager of the estates, to a landowner meant that many landowners extended this kind of generous patronage to a steward and his family.

49. *Cambridge:* it is possible the Darcy family had a connection with this university, and that Darcy himself went there.

50. This helps explain Wickham's need for money; it also shows where the son of a good man could have derived his own bad features.

51. *gentleman's education:* an education that would include going to a university. It was standard for genteel young men to spend a year or two at a university, even if they were to inherit an estate and therefore, unlike those pursuing clerical careers, had no need of the degree. Such wealthy students — called, if they were not nobles, fellow or gentleman commoners — were able to pursue light courses of study and to receive honorary degrees when they left; they were usually segregated socially from other students.

52. *vicious:* immoral, corrupt. The word then did not have the connotations of ferocity or aggression that it has now.

53. *best friend:* Darcy's father. The story of Wickham and old Mr. Darcy has strong parallels with that found in one of the leading eighteenth century English novels, Henry Fielding's *Tom Jones* (1749). In both cases, an immoral but outwardly charming young man manages to deceive a good rich man as to

Mr. Wickham has created, a suspicion of their nature shall not prevent me from unfolding his real character. It adds even another motive.[54] My excellent father died about five years ago; and his attachment to Mr. Wickham was to the last so steady, that in his will he particularly recommended it to me, to promote his advancement in the best manner that his profession might allow, and if he took orders,[55] desired that a valuable family living[56] might be his as soon as it became vacant. There was also a legacy of one thousand pounds. His own father did not long survive mine, and within half a year from these events, Mr. Wickham wrote to inform me that, having finally resolved against taking orders, he hoped I should not think it unreasonable for him to expect some more immediate pecuniary advantage, in lieu of the preferment,[57] by which he could not be benefited. He had some intention, he added, of studying the law,[58] and I must be aware that the interest of one thousand pounds would be a very insufficient support therein. I rather wished, than believed him to be sincere; but at any rate, was perfectly ready to accede to his proposal. I knew that Mr. Wickham ought not to be a clergyman. The business was therefore soon settled. He resigned all claim to assistance in the church, were it possible that he could ever be in a situation to receive it, and accepted in return three thousand pounds.[59] All connection between us seemed now dissolved. I thought too ill of him, to invite him to Pemberley, or admit his society in town. In town I believe he chiefly lived, but his studying the law was a mere pretence, and being now free from all restraint, his life was a life of idleness and dissipation. For about three years I heard little of him;[60] but on the decease of the incumbent[61] of the living which had been designed for him, he applied to me again by letter for the presentation.[62] His circumstances, he assured me, and I had no difficulty in believing it, were exceedingly bad. He had found the law a most unprofitable study, and was now absolutely resolved on being ordained, if I would present him to the living in question—of which he trusted there could be little doubt, as he was well assured that I had no other person to provide for, and I could not have forgotten my revered father's intentions. You will hardly blame me for refusing to comply with this entreaty, or

his true character, and thus to secure the rich man's favor. Moreover, in both cases a good young man sees through the immoral one—though Austen's tale, unlike Fielding's, has no cataclysmic rejection of the good young man by the rich older man. It is possible that Jane Austen, whose letters indicate familiarity with *Tom Jones*, was influenced by it in this part of her novel. The episodes involving Wickham are certainly the ones that come closest to utilizing or replicating the melodramatic plot devices of other novelists.

54. The other motive, besides his main motive of vindicating himself, is his wish to make Elizabeth understand Wickham's true character and thus not be so susceptible to his charms. This could signal a continuing concern for her on Darcy's part, for he may wish to ensure that she would not marry Wickham; the phrase "the sentiments Mr. Wickham has created" indicates that Darcy suspects Wickham may have inspired some degree of love in Elizabeth.

55. *took orders:* became ordained as a clergyman.

56. *family living:* clerical position controlled by the Darcy family.

57. *preferment:* advancement to the church living or position.

58. *studying the law:* studying to be a barrister, the most prestigious type of lawyer—Wickham would not have needed to demand so much money to become an attorney, for that required at most a few hundred pounds. Barristers were the lawyers who could try cases in court; unlike attorneys, who could not try cases, barristers were considered gentlemen. Becoming a barrister required attendance at the Inns of Court in London. It was common to go there after university, and university graduates could qualify as barristers after three years of study (non-graduates required five).

59. *three thousand pounds:* this sum, a large one for the time, would make sense for someone really studying the law, since such a person normally faced several years of study, followed by many years of additional expenditure in order to establish himself in his profession and thereby attain a position where he could start earning money. One authority (Daniel Duman) estimates that between 1200 and 2600 pounds was normally needed for this.

60. Darcy would probably have heard occasional reports about Wickham from the community around Pemberley, some of whose members might have maintained enough connection with Wickham to receive news of him. This would have enabled Darcy to learn of Wickham's life of dissipation.

61. *incumbent:* clergyman who had been holding the living.

62. *presentation:* appointment to the living.

for resisting every repetition of it. His resentment was in proportion to the distress of his circumstances—and he was doubtless as violent in his abuse of me to others, as in his reproaches to myself. After this period, every appearance of acquaintance was dropt. How he lived I know not. But last summer he was again most painfully obtruded on my notice. I must now mention a circumstance which I would wish to forget myself, and which no obligation less than the present should induce me to unfold to any human being. Having said thus much, I feel no doubt of your secrecy. My sister, who is more than ten years my junior, was left to the guardianship of my mother's nephew, Colonel Fitzwilliam, and myself. About a year ago, she was taken from school, and an establishment[63] *formed for her in London; and last summer she went with the lady who presided over it, to Ramsgate;*[64] *and thither also went Mr. Wickham, undoubtedly by design; for there proved to have been a prior acquaintance between him and Mrs. Younge,*[65] *in whose character we were most unhappily deceived; and by her connivance and aid, he so far recommended himself to Georgiana, whose affectionate heart retained a strong impression of his kindness to her as a child, that she was persuaded to believe herself in love, and to consent to an elopement.*[66] *She was then but fifteen, which must be her excuse; and after stating her imprudence, I am happy to add, that I owed the knowledge of it to herself. I joined them unexpectedly a day or two before the intended elopement, and then Georgiana, unable to support the idea of grieving and offending a brother whom she almost looked up to as a father, acknowledged the whole to me. You may imagine what I felt and how I acted. Regard for my sister's credit*[67] *and feelings prevented any public exposure, but I wrote to Mr. Wickham, who left the place immediately, and Mrs. Younge was of course removed from her charge. Mr. Wickham's chief object was unquestionably my sister's fortune, which is thirty thousand pounds;*[68] *but I cannot help supposing that the hope of revenging himself on me, was a strong inducement. His revenge would have been complete indeed. This, madam, is a faithful narrative of every event in which we have been concerned together; and if you do not absolutely reject it as false,*

63. *establishment*: household, residence. Living in London, instead of returning to Pemberley, could allow Georgiana to further her education, for London would have the finest masters to tutor her; it could also allow any close friends of the family who lived in London to introduce her to more people and thereby help improve her social skills and extend her network of acquaintances.

64. *Ramsgate*: a resort town in Kent, on the southeastern coast of England (see maps, pp. 742 and 745). Thanks to their proximity to London, Ramsgate and its companion town of Margate were among the most popular seaside resorts in England at the time. Jane Austen herself visited Ramsgate. She did not, however, seem to regard it highly: in a letter she declares, regarding an acquaintance's interest in moving to Ramsgate, "Bad Taste!" (Oct. 14, 1813).

65. *Mrs. Younge*: the person in charge of Miss Darcy. A married or older woman (and "Mrs." could signal either) would normally chaperone and guide a young, unmarried one.

66. *elopement*: running off to marry. Georgiana, at her age, would not be free to marry without her guardian's consent, which of course she would not receive when the husband in question was Wickham. But if she and Wickham went to Scotland—as he and Lydia are briefly supposed to have done later—they could marry without a parent or guardian's consent, and the marriage would be legally valid in England.

67. *credit*: reputation. Public knowledge of the affair could undermine Georgiana's reputation for sexual modesty, and thus not only embarrass her, but harm her marital prospects.

68. *thirty thousand pounds*: a very large fortune for a woman at the time. Amidst the many unmarried women whose fortunes are mentioned in Jane Austen's novels, almost none possess a fortune as large as this. Such a sum would have come out of the capital of the family estate, or from family investments meant to supplement and support the estate. To make up for this loss—and it could be a serious drain if there were numerous children—it was generally expected that the heir to the estate would marry a woman who would bring a large fortune of her own to the family. Hence Darcy, if he married someone like Elizabeth whose own fortune was far less than Miss Darcy's thirty thousand, would be diminishing the capital, and thus harming somewhat the overall financial position, of his estate.

The function of women's fortunes as an addition to the capital of an estate is why their wealth is generally described by Jane Austen as a lump sum. In contrast, men's wealth is generally described in terms of an annual income, for this is what men would receive either from the estates they owned or the professional position they occupied.

you will, I hope, acquit me henceforth of cruelty towards Mr. Wickham. I know not in what manner, under what form of falsehood he has imposed on you; but his success is not perhaps to be wondered at, ignorant as you previously were of every thing concerning either. Detection could not be in your power, and suspicion certainly not in your inclination. You may possibly wonder why all this was not told you last night. But I was not then master enough of myself to know what could or ought to be revealed.[69] For the truth of every thing here related, I can appeal more particularly to the testimony of Colonel Fitzwilliam, who from our near relationship and constant intimacy, and still more as one of the executors of my father's will, has been unavoidably acquainted with every particular of these transactions. If your abhorrence of me should make my assertions valueless,[70] you cannot be prevented by the same cause from confiding in my cousin; and that there may be the possibility of consulting him, I shall endeavour to find some opportunity of putting this letter in your hands in the course of the morning. I will only add, God bless you.

FITZWILLIAM DARCY[71]

69. It is noteworthy that Darcy judges himself to have lost self-mastery on the previous night, for, given the circumstances, he controlled himself fairly well. His judgment indicates his high standards of conduct.

70. Though Darcy is much gentler here than at the beginning of his letter, his wounded feelings are still apparent.

71. FITZWILLIAM DARCY: this is one of only two times in the novel that Darcy's full name is revealed; in general, male characters are almost always identified solely by last name, both by the narrator and by other characters. Darcy's first name is his mother's maiden name (his mother having been the sister of Colonel Fitzwilliam's father). This was a common practice for eldest sons in aristocratic families, especially when, as in this case, the mother came from a titled or very wealthy family. It allowed the man himself to reveal the prominence of his descent on both sides, and it allowed the mother's family to perpetuate their own name to a degree through the female line. Sometimes the eldest son of each successive generation would continue to bear this name: thus Darcy's first son, if he has one, may also receive the name Fitzwilliam.

Chapter Thirteen

*I*f Elizabeth, when Mr. Darcy gave her the letter, did not expect it to contain a renewal of his offers, she had formed no expectation at all of its contents. But such as they were, it may be well supposed how eagerly she went through them, and what a contrariety[1] of emotion they excited. Her feelings as she read were scarcely to be defined. With amazement did she first understand that he believed any apology to be in his power; and stedfastly was she persuaded that he could have no explanation to give, which a just sense of shame would not conceal. With a strong prejudice against every thing he might say, she began his account of what had happened at Netherfield. She read, with an eagerness which hardly left her power of comprehension, and from impatience of knowing what the next sentence might bring, was incapable of attending to the sense of the one before her eyes. His belief of her sister's insensibility,[2] she instantly resolved to be false, and his account of the real, the worst objections to the match,[3] made her too angry to have any wish of doing him justice. He expressed no regret for what he had done which satisfied her; his style was not penitent, but haughty. It was all pride and insolence.

But when this subject was succeeded by his account of Mr. Wickham, when she read with somewhat clearer attention, a relation of events, which, if true, must overthrow every cherished opinion of his worth, and which bore so alarming an affinity to his own history of himself, her feelings were yet more acutely painful and more difficult of definition. Astonishment, apprehension, and even horror, oppressed[4] her. She wished to discredit it entirely, repeatedly exclaiming, "This must be false! This cannot be! This must be the grossest falsehood!"—and when she had gone through the whole letter, though scarcely knowing any thing of the last page or two, put it hastily away, protesting that she would not regard it, that she would never look in it again.

1. *contrariety*: discordance, inconsistency.

2. *insensibility*: apathy, indifference (toward Bingley).

3. The faults of Elizabeth's family.

4. *oppressed*: overwhelmed.

In this perturbed state of mind, with thoughts that could rest on nothing, she walked on; but it would not do; in half a minute the letter was unfolded again, and collecting herself as well as she could, she again began the mortifying perusal of all that related to Wickham, and commanded herself so far as to examine the meaning of every sentence. The account of his connection with the Pemberley family, was exactly what he had related himself; and the kindness of the late Mr. Darcy, though she had not before known its extent, agreed equally well with his own words. So far each recital confirmed the other: but when she came to the will, the difference was great. What Wickham had said of the living was fresh in her memory, and as she recalled his very words, it was impossible not to feel that there was gross duplicity on one side or the other; and, for a few moments, she flattered herself that her wishes did not err.[5] But when she read, and re-read with the closest attention, the particulars immediately following of Wickham's resigning all pretensions to the living, of his receiving in lieu, so considerable a sum as three thousand pounds,[6] again was she forced to hesitate. She put down the letter, weighed every circumstance with what she meant to be impartiality—deliberated on the probability of each statement—but with little success.[7] On both sides it was only assertion. Again she read on. But every line proved more clearly that the affair, which she had believed it impossible that any contrivance[8] could so represent, as to render Mr. Darcy's conduct in it less than infamous, was capable of a turn[9] which must make him entirely blameless throughout the whole.

The extravagance and general profligacy[10] which he scrupled[11] not to lay to Mr. Wickham's charge, exceedingly shocked her; the more so, as she could bring no proof of its injustice. She had never heard of him before his entrance into the ——shire Militia, in which he had engaged at the persuasion of the young man, who, on meeting him accidentally in town, had there renewed a slight acquaintance.[12] Of his former way of life, nothing had been known in Hertfordshire but what he told himself. As to his real character, had information[13] been in her power, she had never felt a wish of enquiring. His countenance, voice, and manner,

5. Meaning her wishes that Wickham's account was completely correct.

6. Since the income of the living has not been revealed, it is hard to estimate how good Wickham's deal was. On the one hand, the income from
almost all livings was less than a thousand pounds per year, often much less.
On the other hand, most generated more than the 150 per year that could be
produced by the interest on three thousand pounds. This could make Wickham's deal a poor one, except that there are obvious advantages to receiving
a lump sum in cash; moreover, it might be a number of years before Wickham could even receive the living and begin to enjoy the income from it.
Thus it is probable that three thousand pounds represented a generous compensation for him.

7. The implication is that while Elizabeth intends to be judging impartially,
and may believe that she is doing that, she is still biased toward Wickham.

8. *contrivance*: piece of ingenuity or invention (in providing an explanation).

9. *turn*: interpretation.

10. *profligacy*: extravagance, or immorality and licentiousness.

11. *scrupled*: hesitated.

12. As Darcy's account suggests, and as is shown later as well, Wickham
seems to be someone who drifts, taking little thought for the future and seizing whatever opportunity happens to befall him. Although his behavior,
including his attempt to ingratiate himself with others, is often calculating, it
never shows evidence of careful, long-term planning, whether for villainous
schemes or for anything else.

13. *information*: instruction, i.e., informing of herself about it.

had established him at once in the possession of every virtue. She tried to recollect some instance of goodness, some distinguished trait of integrity or benevolence, that might rescue him from the attacks of Mr. Darcy; or at least, by the predominance of virtue, atone for those casual errors,[14] under which she would endeavour to class, what Mr. Darcy had described as the idleness and vice of many years continuance. But no such recollection befriended her. She could see him instantly before her, in every charm of air and address;[15] but she could remember no more substantial good than the general approbation of the neighbourhood, and the regard which his social powers had gained him in the mess.[16] After pausing on this point a considerable while, she once more continued to read. But, alas! the story which followed of his designs on Miss Darcy, received some confirmation from what had passed between Colonel Fitzwilliam and herself only the morning before; and at last she was referred for the truth of every particular to Colonel Fitzwilliam himself—from whom she had previously received the information of his near concern in all his cousin's affairs, and whose character she had no reason to question. At one time she had almost resolved on applying to him, but the idea was checked by the awkwardness of the application, and at length wholly banished by the conviction that Mr. Darcy would never have hazarded such a proposal, if he had not been well assured of his cousin's corroboration.

She perfectly remembered every thing that had passed in conversation between Wickham and herself, in their first evening at Mr. Philips's. Many of his expressions[17] were still fresh in her memory. She was *now* struck with the impropriety of such communications to a stranger, and wondered it had escaped her before. She saw the indelicacy[18] of putting himself forward as he had done, and the inconsistency of his professions with his conduct. She remembered that he had boasted of having no fear of seeing Mr. Darcy—that Mr. Darcy might leave the country,[19] but that *he* should stand his ground; yet he had avoided the Netherfield ball the very next week. She remembered also, that till the Netherfield family had quitted the country, he had told his story

14. *casual errors:* accidental or chance errors; errors not reflecting premeditation or design. That is, Elizabeth would hope to explain his bad actions as the product of circumstance or of bad luck rather than of his basic character.

15. *air and address:* general presence and manner of speaking.

16. *the mess:* section of a regiment (specifically a group of officers) who eat together. It might also mean the place where meals are taken, though that meaning had not become common at this time. Officers generally formed a mess together, financed by subscriptions from the participants; it was an important means of creating solidarity in the regiment.

17. *expressions:* statements, utterances.

18. *indelicacy:* coarseness, lack of scruples or sensitivity.

19. *country:* area.

to no one but herself; but that after their removal, it had been every where discussed;[20] that he had then no reserves,[21] no scruples in sinking Mr. Darcy's character,[22] though he had assured her that respect for the father, would always prevent his exposing[23] the son.[24]

How differently did every thing now appear in which he was concerned! His attentions to Miss King were now the consequence of views[25] solely and hatefully mercenary; and the mediocrity of her fortune proved no longer the moderation of his wishes, but his eagerness to grasp at any thing.[26] His behaviour to herself could now have had no tolerable motive; he had either been deceived with regard to her fortune,[27] or had been gratifying his vanity by encouraging the preference which she believed she had most incautiously shewn. Every lingering struggle in his favour grew fainter and fainter; and in farther justification of Mr. Darcy, she could not but allow that Mr. Bingley, when questioned by Jane, had long ago asserted his blamelessness in the affair; that proud and repulsive[28] as were his manners, she had never, in the whole course of their acquaintance, an acquaintance which had latterly brought them much together, and given her a sort of intimacy with his ways, seen any thing that betrayed him to be unprincipled or unjust—any thing that spoke him of[29] irreligious or immoral[30] habits. That among his own connections he was esteemed and valued—that even Wickham had allowed him merit as a brother, and that she had often heard him speak so affectionately of his sister as to prove him capable of *some* amiable[31] feeling. That had his actions been what Wickham represented them, so gross a violation of every thing right could hardly have been concealed from the world; and that friendship between a person capable of it, and such an amiable man as Mr. Bingley, was incomprehensible.

She grew absolutely ashamed of herself.—Of neither Darcy nor Wickham could she think, without feeling that she had been blind, partial, prejudiced, absurd.

"How despicably have I acted!"[32] she cried.—"I, who have prided myself on my discernment!—I, who have valued myself

20. The obvious reason for Wickham's waiting to tell his story widely until after Darcy's departure is that if Wickham's tale were to reach Darcy's ears, the latter could step forward to contradict it.

21. *reserves*: restraint, reservations.

22. *sinking Mr. Darcy's character*: lowering others' opinion of Darcy.

23. *exposing*: laying open or holding up to censure.

24. Wickham's garrulousness contrasts with Darcy's silence. In fact, Darcy's behavior would conform to the ideal of a gentleman, who was supposed to disdain stooping to reply to unjust accusations.

25. *views*: aspirations, hopes.

26. Other examples of this willingness in Wickham will appear. It fits with the unplanned character of his conduct that is discussed in note 12 above.

27. As discussed earlier, Wickham may in fact have been deceived initially about Elizabeth's fortune because the Bennets were wealthier, as regards current income, than almost any family in the area.

28. *repulsive*: repellent, tending to repulse others.

29. *spoke him of*: indicated him to have.

30. *irreligious or immoral*: religion was almost universally considered the essential foundation of morality. Hence being irreligious was often considered synonymous with being immoral. In a letter Jane Austen says, regarding a married woman who ran off with another man, "I should not have suspected her of such a thing. She staid [sic] the Sacrament I remember, the last time that you & I did." (June 22, 1808). In other words, someone devout enough to remain for the sacrament at church would not be expected to commit such a heinous offense.

31. *amiable*: kind, affectionate.

32. Elizabeth's speech marks the crucial moment in her psychological transformation. Just as Darcy has been forced, by her rejection of him, to confront his faults, she has had to confront, through reading his letter, her own errors, ones often similar to his. The author thus achieves a fine balance between the two main characters' ordeals—though one could question whether, in rendering Elizabeth's judgment of herself, Jane Austen has made the language too formal for what are the inner thoughts of someone in a state of high agitation.

on my abilities! who have often disdained the generous candour[33] of my sister, and gratified my vanity, in useless or blameable distrust.— How humiliating is this discovery!—Yet, how just a humiliation!— Had I been in love, I could not have been more wretchedly blind. But vanity, not love, has been my folly.[34]—Pleased with the preference of one, and offended by the neglect of the other, on the very beginning of our acquaintance, I have courted prepossession[35] and ignorance, and driven reason away, where either were concerned. Till this moment, I never knew myself."[36]

From herself to Jane—from Jane to Bingley, her thoughts were in a line which soon brought to her recollection that Mr. Darcy's explanation *there*, had appeared very insufficient; and she read it again. Widely different was the effect of a second perusal.—How could she deny that credit to his assertions, in one instance, which she had been obliged to give in the other?—He declared himself to have been totally unsuspicious of her sister's attachment;—and she could not help remembering what Charlotte's opinion had always been.—Neither could she deny the justice of his description of Jane.—She felt that Jane's feelings, though fervent, were little displayed, and that there was a constant complacency in her air and manner, not often united with great sensibility.[37]

When she came to that part of the letter in which her family were mentioned, in terms of such mortifying, yet merited reproach, her sense of shame was severe. The justice of the charge struck her too forcibly for denial, and the circumstances to which he particularly alluded, as having passed at the Netherfield ball, and as confirming all his first disapprobation, could not have made a stronger impression on his mind than on hers.

The compliment to herself and her sister, was not unfelt. It soothed, but it could not console her for the contempt which had been thus self-attracted by the rest of her family;—and as she considered that Jane's disappointment had in fact been the work of her nearest relations, and reflected how materially the credit of both[38] must be hurt by such impropriety of conduct, she felt depressed beyond any thing she had ever known before.

33. *candour*: tendency always to think well of others.

34. An admission that her main fault has been the same as what she accused Darcy of, pride.

35. *prepossession*: prejudice.

36. A critical conclusion, one seen in other Jane Austen novels as well. The need to understand oneself, and in particular to acknowledge one's errors and through that knowledge to correct them, is a central theme in her work. It is often only when a heroine undergoes that process that she deserves, and is able to achieve, happiness (a similar process can sometimes be seen for the hero, though he is never as prominent in the story). The same general idea appears in one of the prayers Jane Austen wrote, in which she says, "Teach us to understand the sinfulness of our own hearts, and bring to our knowledge every fault of temper and every evil habit in which we have indulged to the discomfort of our fellow-creatures, and the danger of our own souls."

37. *sensibility*: strong feelings.

38. *credit of both*: reputation or public standing of both Jane and Elizabeth.

After wandering along the lane for two hours, giving way to every variety of thought; re-considering events, determining probabilities, and reconciling herself as well as she could, to a change so sudden and so important, fatigue, and a recollection of her long absence, made her at length return home; and she entered the house with the wish of appearing cheerful as usual, and the resolution of repressing such reflections as must make her unfit for conversation.[39]

She was immediately told, that the two gentlemen from Rosings had each called during her absence; Mr. Darcy, only for a few minutes to take leave, but that Colonel Fitzwilliam had been sitting with them at least an hour, hoping for her return, and almost resolving to walk after her till she could be found.—Elizabeth could but just *affect* concern in missing him; she really rejoiced at it. Colonel Fitzwilliam was no longer an object.[40] She could think only of her letter.

39. Elizabeth here forces herself to follow the principle she reproached Darcy for neglecting, that of being sociable and conversing well with others, even when one is not inclined to do so.

40. *an object:* an object of interest. Her indifference toward Colonel Fitzwilliam—a man she liked and who liked her greatly, as shown by his waiting an hour for her—because of her absorption in Darcy's letter suggests how much Darcy, more than any other man, is capable of occupying her thoughts.

Chapter Fourteen

The two gentlemen left Rosings the next morning; and Mr. Collins having been in waiting near the lodges,[1] to make them his parting obeisance,[2] was able to bring home the pleasing intelligence, of their appearing in very good health, and in as tolerable spirits as could be expected, after the melancholy scene so lately gone through at Rosings.[3] To Rosings he then hastened to console Lady Catherine, and her daughter; and on his return, brought back, with great satisfaction, a message from her Ladyship, importing that she felt herself so dull[4] as to make her very desirous of having them all to dine with her.[5]

Elizabeth could not see Lady Catherine without recollecting, that had she chosen it, she might by this time have been presented to her, as her future niece; nor could she think, without a smile, of what her ladyship's indignation would have been. "What would she have said?—how would she have behaved?" were questions with which she amused herself.[6]

Their first subject was the diminution of the Rosings party.—"I assure you, I feel it exceedingly," said Lady Catherine; "I believe nobody feels the loss of friends so much as I do. But I am particularly attached to these young men; and know them to be so much attached to me!—They were excessively sorry to go! But so they always are. The dear colonel rallied his spirits tolerably till just at last; but Darcy seemed to feel it most acutely, more I think than last year.[7] His attachment to Rosings, certainly increases."

Mr. Collins had a compliment, and an allusion to throw in here, which were kindly smiled on by the mother and daughter.

Lady Catherine observed, after dinner, that Miss Bennet seemed out of spirits,[8] and immediately accounting for it herself, by supposing that she did not like to go home again so soon, she added,

1. *lodges:* houses or cottages near the entrance to the grounds and occupied by those who take care of or guard the grounds.

2. *obeisance:* bow; respectful or deferential gesture.

3. The melancholy scene being their departure from Lady Catherine, which Mr. Collins assumes would distress anyone.

4. *dull:* listless, gloomy.

5. Lady Catherine's hospitality to them expands now that she again has no other guests.

6. How furious Lady Catherine would indeed have been is revealed later. Elizabeth's indulgence in such speculations is a sign that, amidst her distress, she has retained her humor and playfulness. It also shows that the idea of marriage to Darcy has not departed her mind completely.

7. The real reason for Darcy's unhappy state can be guessed: that he is far from having recovered from Elizabeth's rejection. Jane Austen often uses this technique of communicating important information about a character through someone else's casual reporting of what they have done or said.

8. *out of spirits:* downcast, in poor spirits.

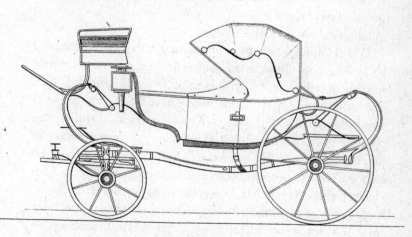

A barouche. The top can fold down to allow for an open ride. The perch on the upper left is the barouche box. See p. 391, note 11.

[From T. Fuller, *An Essay on Wheel Carriages* (London, 1828), Plate No. 6]

"But if that is the case, you must write to your mother to beg that you may stay a little longer. Mrs. Collins will be very glad of your company, I am sure."

"I am much obliged to your ladyship for your kind invitation,"[9] replied Elizabeth, "but it is not in my power to accept it.—I must be in town next Saturday."

"Why, at that rate, you will have been here only six weeks. I expected you to stay two months. I told Mrs. Collins so before you came.[10] There can be no occasion for your going so soon. Mrs. Bennet could certainly spare you for another fortnight."

"But my father cannot.—He wrote last week to hurry my return."

"Oh! your father of course may spare you, if your mother can.—Daughters are never of so much consequence to a father. And if you will stay another *month* complete, it will be in my power to take one of you as far as London, for I am going there early in June, for a week; and as Dawson does not object to the Barouche box,[11] there will be very good room for one of you— and indeed, if the weather should happen to be cool, I should not object to taking you both, as you are neither of you large."

"You are all kindness, Madam; but I believe we must abide by our original plan."

Lady Catherine seemed resigned.

"Mrs. Collins, you must send a servant with them. You know I always speak my mind, and I cannot bear the idea of two young women travelling post[12] by themselves.[13] It is highly improper. You must contrive to send somebody. I have the greatest dislike in the world to that sort of thing.—Young women should always be properly guarded and attended, according to their situation in life. When my niece Georgiana went to Ramsgate[14] last summer, I made a point of her having two men servants go with her.—Miss Darcy, the daughter of Mr. Darcy, of Pemberley, and Lady Anne, could not have appeared with propriety in a different manner.—I am excessively attentive to all those things. You must send John[15] with the young ladies, Mrs. Collins. I am glad it occurred to me to mention it; for it would really be discreditable to *you* to let them go alone."

9. Elizabeth is probably being sarcastic here, though not in such an obvious way that Lady Catherine notices, for the latter is inviting Elizabeth to stay at someone else's home.

10. Lady Catherine's confident expectation, while reflecting her belief in her own omniscience, is not unreasonable in itself. Visits this long were common in their milieu, a result both of the abundance of leisure, especially among women, and of the time and trouble involved in traveling. Jane Bennet is still in the midst of a stay of more than four months with the Gardiners. Jane Austen herself often stayed with relations for many weeks, and sometimes even for months.

11. *Barouche box:* a barouche is a fancy carriage, popular among the wealthy; Jane Austen confesses in a letter to a sense of unnatural elegance from riding in one (May 24, 1813). The box is the seat on the outside containing the driver (see picture on p. 389). Lady Catherine's idea is that Dawson, her servant, would join the driver there and free up one place inside—the barouche seats four, and the others would be Lady Catherine, her daughter, and Mrs. Jenkinson. Lady Catherine's second offer is, if it is not too warm for such crowding, to allow three people—presumably Elizabeth, Maria, and Mrs. Jenkinson—to squeeze together on one side on a seat for two. It is thus not an extremely generous offer, especially since it is only 20 miles from this area of Kent to London, so Elizabeth and Maria would receive only a short ride in return for staying an extra month.

12. *post:* the main method of traveling between towns for wealthier people. Unlike a public coach, which was used by those unable to afford better means of travel and is almost never seen in Jane Austen, traveling post involved the use of a separate, private carriage (either one's own or a rented one). The horses pulling the carriage would be rented, however, and would be changed at posts along the way (hence the name).

13. Lady Catherine's dislike of women traveling without an escort is normal for the time, for women, especially genteel unmarried women, were considered to need escorts to avoid danger as well as any possibility of sexual impropriety or scandal. Jane Austen often speaks in her letters of adjusting travel plans so that she or her sister will have a man to accompany them.

14. *Ramsgate:* a resort town—see p. 372 and p. 373, note 64. The irony is that, even with the elaborate precautions taken for Miss Darcy's journey to Ramsgate, the lack of a suitable guardian for her there almost led to disaster.

15. *John:* a lower servant, probably a footman; this is indicated by his being called by his first name (in contrast to Dawson).

"My uncle is to send a servant for us."

"Oh!—Your uncle!—He keeps a man-servant, does he?[16]—I am very glad you have somebody who thinks of those things. Where shall you change horses?[17]—Oh! Bromley,[18] of course.— If you mention my name at the Bell,[19] you will be attended to."

Lady Catherine had many other questions to ask respecting their journey, and as she did not answer them all herself, attention was necessary, which Elizabeth believed to be lucky for her; or, with a mind so occupied, she might have forgotten where she was. Reflection must be reserved for solitary hours; whenever she was alone, she gave way to it as the greatest relief; and not a day went by without a solitary walk, in which she might indulge in all the delight of unpleasant recollections.

Mr. Darcy's letter, she was in a fair way of soon knowing by heart. She studied every sentence: and her feelings towards its writer were at times widely different. When she remembered the style of his address, she was still full of indignation;[20] but when she considered how unjustly she had condemned and upbraided him, her anger was turned against herself; and his disappointed feelings became the object of compassion. His attachment excited gratitude, his general character respect; but she could not approve him; nor could she for a moment repent her refusal, or feel the slightest inclination ever to see him again.[21] In her own past behaviour, there was a constant source of vexation and regret; and in the unhappy defects of her family a subject of yet heavier chagrin.[22] They were hopeless of remedy. Her father, contented with laughing at them, would never exert himself to restrain the wild giddiness of his youngest daughters;[23] and her mother, with manners so far from right herself, was entirely insensible[24] of the evil. Elizabeth had frequently united with Jane in an endeavour to check the imprudence of Catherine and Lydia; but while they were supported by their mother's indulgence, what chance could there be of improvement? Catherine, weak-spirited, irritable, and completely under Lydia's guidance, had been always affronted by their advice; and Lydia, self-willed and careless, would scarcely give them a hearing. They were ignorant, idle, and

16. It would be a male servant because his purpose would be to escort the women, and thus prevent a situation of women traveling by themselves. Having such a servant is worthy of note for Lady Catherine because male servants cost more, both because they commanded higher salaries and because there was a special tax on them (higher than the one on female servants). Partly for these reasons the proportion of servants who were female had steadily grown over the eighteenth century; by the early 1800's it was more than 85%. All this made keeping a man-servant a mark of status.

17. *change horses*: as mentioned above, this was part of traveling post; it was necessary because horses would tire and need to rest after a certain distance. The system of post-horses was very well organized by this time, so normally each changing post had fresh sets of horses constantly on hand, and one of these sets would be immediately attached to the carriage in order to allow the travelers to continue onward with very little wait.

18. *Bromley*: a town on the road to London; it is at the approximate midpoint between the area where they are now, near Westerham, and London, and thus would be a logical stopping point. See map, p. 745.

19. *the Bell*: probably the name of the inn at Bromley; inns were usually the places where fresh horses were available. The inn could also supply refreshment for the travelers during the short time they were waiting for the horses to be changed.

20. She could be remembering his resentful references to her rejection of him or his proud refusal to acknowledge being wrong in his actions regarding Jane and Bingley.

21. This indicates the continued limits in her regard for Darcy. Much more will need to occur before they can be united.

22. *chagrin*: anxiety, melancholy.

23. This characteristic of Mr. Bennet has already been displayed; it is now that its harsh consequences for the family begin to become more apparent.

24. *insensible*: unaware.

vain. While there was an officer in Meryton, they would flirt with him; and while Meryton was within a walk of Longbourn, they would be going there for ever.

Anxiety on Jane's behalf, was another prevailing concern, and Mr. Darcy's explanation, by restoring Bingley to all her former good opinion, heightened the sense of what Jane had lost. His affection was proved to have been sincere, and his conduct cleared of all blame, unless any could attach to the implicitness of his confidence in his friend. How grievous then was the thought that, of a situation[25] so desirable in every respect, so replete with advantage, so promising for happiness, Jane had been deprived, by the folly and indecorum of her own family!

When to these recollections was added the developement[26] of Wickham's character, it may be easily believed that the happy spirits which had seldom been depressed before, were now so much affected as to make it almost impossible for her to appear tolerably cheerful.

Their engagements at Rosings were as frequent during the last week of her stay, as they had been at first. The very last evening was spent there; and her Ladyship again enquired minutely into the particulars of their journey, gave them directions as to the best method of packing, and was so urgent on the necessity of placing gowns in the only right way, that Maria thought herself obliged, on her return, to undo all the work of the morning, and pack her trunk afresh.

When they parted, Lady Catherine, with great condescension, wished them a good journey, and invited them to come to Hunsford again next year; and Miss De Bourgh exerted herself so far as to curtsey and hold out her hand to both.

25. *situation:* marital situation.

26. *developement:* disclosure, unveiling.

Chapter Fifteen

On Saturday morning Elizabeth and Mr. Collins met for breakfast a few minutes before the others appeared; and he took the opportunity of paying the parting civilities which he deemed indispensably necessary.[1]

"I know not, Miss Elizabeth," said he, "whether Mrs. Collins has yet expressed her sense of your kindness in coming to us, but I am very certain you will not leave the house without receiving her thanks for it. The favour of your company has been much felt, I assure you. We know how little there is to tempt any one to our humble abode. Our plain manner of living, our small rooms, and few domestics,[2] and the little we see of the world, must make Hunsford extremely dull to a young lady like yourself; but I hope you will believe us grateful for the condescension,[3] and that we have done every thing in our power to prevent your spending your time unpleasantly."

Elizabeth was eager with her thanks and assurances of happiness. She had spent six weeks with great enjoyment; and the pleasure of being with Charlotte, and the kind attentions she had received, must make *her* feel the obliged. Mr. Collins was gratified; and with a more smiling solemnity replied,

"It gives me the greatest pleasure to hear that you have passed your time not disagreeably. We have certainly done our best; and most fortunately having it in our power to introduce you to very superior society, and from our connection with Rosings, the frequent means of varying the humble home scene, I think we may flatter ourselves that your Hunsford visit cannot have been entirely irksome. Our situation with regard to Lady Catherine's family is indeed the sort of extraordinary advantage and blessing which few can boast. You see on what a footing we are. You see how continually we are engaged there. In truth I must acknowledge

1. *indispensably necessary*: a curious redundancy. It may be meant to convey how fervent Mr. Collins is in rendering civilities.

2. *domestics*: servants.

3. *the condescension*: the favor of lowering yourself to visit us.

A chaise, the vehicle in which Elizabeth is about to embark. The chaise pictured is a post-chaise, and thus used for traveling between towns (see p. 391, note 12); this is indicated by the position of the driver on the horse, the standard position for driving post (see p. 639, note 4). The clothing in this picture is from a slightly earlier period.

[From Marjorie and C.H.B. Quennell, A *History of Everyday Things in England*, Vol. II (New York, 1922), p. 187]

that, with all the disadvantages of this humble parsonage, I should not think any one abiding in it an object of compassion, while they are sharers of our intimacy at Rosings."

Words were insufficient for the elevation of his feelings;[4] and he was obliged to walk about the room, while Elizabeth tried to unite civility and truth in a few short sentences.[5]

"You may, in fact, carry a very favourable report of us into Hertfordshire, my dear cousin. I flatter myself at least that you will be able to do so. Lady Catherine's great attentions to Mrs. Collins you have been a daily witness of; and altogether I trust it does not appear that your friend has drawn an unfortunate—[6]but on this point it will be as well to be silent. Only let me assure you, my dear Miss Elizabeth, that I can from my heart most cordially wish you equal felicity in marriage. My dear Charlotte and I have but one mind and one way of thinking. There is in every thing a most remarkable resemblance of character and ideas between us. We seem to have been designed for each other."[7]

Elizabeth could safely say that it was a great happiness where that was the case, and with equal sincerity could add that she firmly believed and rejoiced in his domestic comforts.[8] She was not sorry, however, to have the recital of them interrupted by the entrance of the lady from whom they sprung. Poor Charlotte!—it was melancholy to leave her to such society!—But she had chosen it with her eyes open; and though evidently regretting that her visitors were to go, she did not seem to ask for compassion.[9] Her home and her housekeeping, her parish[10] and her poultry,[11] and all their dependent concerns, had not yet lost their charms.

At length the chaise[12] arrived, the trunks were fastened on, the parcels placed within, and it was pronounced to be ready. After an affectionate parting between the friends, Elizabeth was attended to the carriage by Mr. Collins, and as they walked down the garden, he was commissioning her with his best respects to all her family, not forgetting his thanks for the kindness he had received at Longbourn in the winter, and his compliments to Mr. and Mrs. Gardiner, though unknown. He then handed her in, Maria followed, and the door was on the point of being closed, when he

4. Mr. Collins's being rendered speechless, a rare occurrence, indicates how much this subject above all others moves him.

5. In other words, she tried to be civil and offer the compliments Mr. Collins desired, while also being truthful. The task would not be easy, given the truth of her feelings about Lady Catherine. Elizabeth, however, seems to succeed, at least to judge from Mr. Collins's reaction; her brevity is probably crucial to this. It signals her ability to strike a healthy balance between dishonest flattery, as seen in characters like Miss Bingley or Wickham, and inconsiderate frankness, as seen in characters like Darcy or Lady Catherine.

6. *an unfortunate—*: Mr. Collins is presumably about to say "lot" or something similar that refers to Charlotte's married position. Elizabeth's rejection of him is still on his mind, and he would probably love to have her admit that she erred, or at least to praise Charlotte's contrary decision.

7. Mr. Collins is most likely sincere in this belief. If so, it indicates how well Charlotte has managed him; obviously he has not noticed, for example, how she has arranged their daily routine so as to keep him away from her as much as possible.

8. *comforts:* felicities. Elizabeth's reply constitutes an example of her uniting of civility and truth. One notices that in her carefully crafted reply she does not say she believes in Charlotte's domestic felicity.

9. The final verdict on Charlotte's marriage remains ambiguous. She has shown a great ability to adapt to her circumstances and to make it as pleasant as possible; we never see her actively suffering or complaining. Yet her regret at Elizabeth's departure suggests the limitations of her choice.

10. *her parish:* this may refer to her assisting her husband in dealing with his parishioners or his clerical business. Her far superior intelligence and common sense would make her a valuable assistant to her husband.

11. *her poultry:* the family poultry was normally under the particular care of the woman; income from it would provide her with extra spending money. In the next chapter Lady Lucas is described as asking specifically about her daughter's poultry. Jane Austen's mother raised poultry, and Jane Austen mentions in a letter, at a time when the Austen family was leaving its home, the arrival of a group of women who wish to purchase the family's chickens.

12. *chaise:* the carriage most often used for traveling post (see picture on p. 397). It carried three people, but the only passengers would be Elizabeth, Maria, and the servant of Mr. Gardiner—mentioned in the last chapter—who is to accompany them and who has presumably brought the chaise to them.

suddenly reminded them, with some consternation, that they had hitherto forgotten to leave any message for the ladies of Rosings.

"But," he added, "you will of course wish to have your humble respects delivered to them, with your grateful thanks for their kindness to you while you have been here."

Elizabeth made no objection;—the door was then allowed to be shut, and the carriage drove off.

"Good gracious!" cried Maria, after a few minutes silence, "it seems but a day or two since we first came!—and yet how many things have happened!"

"A great many indeed," said her companion with a sigh.

"We have dined nine times at Rosings, besides drinking tea there twice![13]—How much I shall have to tell!"[14]

Elizabeth privately added, "And how much I shall have to conceal."

Their journey was performed without much conversation, or any alarm; and within four hours of their leaving Hunsford, they reached Mr. Gardiner's house, where they were to remain a few days.

Jane looked well, and Elizabeth had little opportunity of studying her spirits, amidst the various engagements which the kindness of her aunt had reserved for them. But Jane was to go home with her, and at Longbourn there would be leisure enough for observation.

It was not without an effort meanwhile that she could wait even for Longbourn, before she told her sister of Mr. Darcy's proposals. To know that she had the power of revealing what would so exceedingly astonish Jane, and must, at the same time, so highly gratify whatever of her own vanity she had not yet been able to reason away, was such a temptation to openness as nothing could have conquered, but the state of indecision in which she remained, as to the extent of what she should communicate; and her fear, if she once entered on the subject, of being hurried into repeating something of Bingley, which might only grieve her sister farther.[15]

13. The two teas happened while Darcy was there; one included his and Elizabeth's talk at the piano, while the other was the one she missed from not feeling well, and that he left in order to propose to her. The nine dinners all happened before or after Darcy's visit, and can be surmised from brief clues in the text: Elizabeth and the others dined at Lady Catherine's shortly after their arrival; they are described as dining there "about twice a week," and thus probably five more times, during the period, a little more than two weeks, until Darcy's arrival; they dined there the day he left; finally, in the week remaining, when "engagements at Rosings were as frequent" as earlier, they dined twice more, including the night before their departure. Among other things, such a chronology indicates how much less Lady Catherine bothered with those at the parsonage during the almost three weeks when Darcy and Colonel Fitzwilliam were visiting her.

14. In the original edition this speech was joined to the previous one, suggesting that it was spoken also by Elizabeth. But its tone of excitement about being entertained at Rosings, and Elizabeth's private response, indicate that it should be attributed to Maria Lucas. The third edition of the novel corrected the probable mistake by separating the two speeches.

15. In other words, she wishes to tell Jane her news about Darcy's proposal, both because it will astonish Jane and because the proposal highly gratifies Elizabeth's vanity. She has tried to reason or argue herself out of this vanity—an attempt that indicates some realization of her faults of pride—but has not fully succeeded in that. But she refrains from telling for two reasons. First, she remains uncertain about how much she should tell; her uncertainty may center around Darcy's information concerning Wickham and his sister, about which Darcy has requested her silence. Second, she fears that while speaking of the proposal and of Wickham, she might stumble into revealing information about Bingley that could cause Jane greater distress.

Chapter Sixteen[1]

*I*t was the second week in May, in which the three young ladies set out together from Gracechurch-street, for the town of —— in Hertfordshire; and, as they drew near the appointed inn where Mr. Bennet's carriage was to meet them,[2] they quickly perceived, in token of the coachman's punctuality,[3] both Kitty and Lydia looking out of a dining room upstairs. These two girls had been above an hour in the place, happily employed in visiting an opposite milliner,[4] watching the sentinel on guard, and dressing[5] a sallad[6] and cucumber.

After welcoming their sisters, they triumphantly displayed a table set out with such cold meat as an inn larder usually affords, exclaiming, "Is not this nice? is not this an agreeable surprise?"

"And we mean to treat you all," added Lydia; "but you must lend us the money, for we have just spent ours at the shop out there." Then shewing her purchases: "Look here, I have bought this bonnet. I do not think it is very pretty; but I thought I might as well buy it as not.[7] I shall pull it to pieces as soon as I get home, and see if I can make it up any better."

And when her sisters abused it as ugly, she added, with perfect unconcern, "Oh! but there were two or three much uglier in the shop; and when I have bought some prettier-coloured satin to trim it with fresh,[8] I think it will be very tolerable. Besides, it will not much signify what one wears this summer, after the ——shire have left Meryton, and they are going in a fortnight."[9]

"Are they indeed?" cried Elizabeth, with the greatest satisfaction.

"They are going to be encamped near Brighton;[10] and I do so want papa to take us all there for the summer! It would be such a delicious scheme, and I dare say would hardly cost any thing at all. Mamma would like to go too of all things! Only think what a miserable summer else we shall have!"

1. In this chapter Lydia begins to appear more than before. This is good preparation, for she is to play a central role in an upcoming section of the story.

2. Jane, Elizabeth, and Maria would have traveled from London in a hired carriage, and are now to switch to Mr. Bennet's carriage for the rest of the journey.

3. This would refer to the man driving the Bennet coach, who has brought Kitty and Lydia in plenty of time before the others' arrival.

4. *milliner*: shopkeeper selling women's hats, clothing, and decorative articles.

5. *dressing*: preparing, arranging. It would not just mean adding what is now called salad dressing.

6. *sallad*: this probably means lettuce only (since cucumber is mentioned separately). "Sallad" [sic] occasionally had that meaning.

7. This reveals Lydia's version of hospitality. She invites others to eat with her but makes them pay because she has spent her money buying a hat she did not even like much. Later she will boast to Mary of her generosity.

8. *trim it with fresh*: to put a fresh trim on it.

9. Meryton has been the militia's winter quarters. Army units normally established a camp during the warmer months, which would allow them to fight if necessary.

10. *Brighton*: a town on the southern coast of England. It was a logical place for the militia to go, since any French invasion would most likely take place in that part of England. Jane Austen's brother Henry, when he was serving in the militia, was encamped at Brighton during the summer of 1793. Brighton was also the leading seaside resort in England in this period. Its rapid growth had been spurred particularly by its being the favorite spot of the current ruler of England, the Prince Regent, who constructed an elaborate pleasure palace there. Summer was its prime season, when visitors numbered in the thousands and a multitude of entertainments were available. All this explains the eagerness of Kitty and Lydia to go there, and the fears of Elizabeth about that prospect. For its location, see maps on pp. 742 and 745.

"Yes," thought Elizabeth, "*that* would be a delightful scheme, indeed, and completely do for us at once. Good Heaven! Brighton, and a whole campful of soldiers, to us, who have been overset[11] already by one poor regiment of militia, and the monthly balls of Meryton."

"Now I have got some news for you," said Lydia, as they sat down to table. "What do you think? It is excellent news, capital news, and about a certain person that we all like."

Jane and Elizabeth looked at each other, and the waiter was told that he need not stay.[12] Lydia laughed, and said,

"Aye, that is just like your formality and discretion. You thought the waiter must not hear, as if he cared! I dare say he often hears worse things said than I am going to say. But he is an ugly fellow! I am glad he is gone. I never saw such a long chin in my life. Well, but now for my news: it is about dear Wickham; too good for the waiter, is not it? There is no danger of Wickham's marrying Mary King. There's for you! She is gone down to her uncle at Liverpool; gone to stay.[13] Wickham is safe."

"And Mary King is safe!" added Elizabeth; "safe from a connection[14] imprudent as to fortune."

"She is a great fool for going away, if she liked him."

"But I hope there is no strong attachment on either side," said Jane.

"I am sure there is not on *his*. I will answer for it he never cared three straws about her. Who *could* about such a nasty little freckled thing?"[15]

Elizabeth was shocked to think that, however incapable of such coarseness of *expression* herself, the coarseness of the *sentiment* was little other than her own breast had formerly harboured and fancied liberal![16]

As soon as all had ate, and the elder ones paid, the carriage was ordered; and after some contrivance, the whole party, with all their boxes, workbags,[17] and parcels, and the unwelcome addition of Kitty's and Lydia's purchases, were seated in it.[18]

"How nicely we are crammed in!" cried Lydia. "I am glad I bought my bonnet, if it is only for the fun of having another

11. *overset:* disturbed, thrown into disorder.

12. They do not wish the waiter to hear, in case Lydia might be revealing something important, especially relating to their family. As seen more than once in the novel, servants' gossip is a powerful force in this society. Lydia's lack of concern here with such considerations foreshadows her lack of concern later about engaging in conduct that provides tremendous ammunition for harmful gossip about the Bennets.

13. It is possible that those guarding Mary King wished to protect her from Wickham by sending her away. Liverpool is a considerable distance from Hertfordshire; see map, p. 742.

14. *connection:* marriage.

15. This is Lydia speaking. Her highly colloquial phrasing, if nothing else, indicates that.

16. Meaning that, as she is shocked to realize, she had formerly harbored similar coarse sentiments about the monetary reasons for Wickham's interest in Mary King, and had thought these sentiments to be generous or open-minded—for in earlier conversations with her aunt she had tried to justify Wickham's conduct rather than to condemn it (see pp. 280 and 282).

17. *workbags:* bags with needlework supplies.

18. A coach had seating for six and not a lot of other room, so fitting in so many items, along with the four Bennet girls and Maria Lucas, would require some arranging.

bandbox![19] Well, now let us be quite comfortable and snug, and talk and laugh all the way home. And in the first place, let us hear what has happened to you all, since you went away. Have you seen any pleasant men? Have you had any flirting?[20] I was in great hopes that one of you would have got a husband before you came back. Jane will be quite an old maid[21] soon, I declare. She is almost three and twenty! Lord, how ashamed I should be of not being married before three and twenty! My aunt Philips wants you so to get husbands, you can't think.[22] She says Lizzy had better have taken Mr. Collins; but *I* do not think there would have been any fun in it. Lord! how I should like to be married before any of you; and then I would chaperon you about to all the balls.[23] Dear me! we had such a good piece of fun the other day at Colonel Forster's. Kitty and me were to spend the day there, and Mrs. Forster promised to have a little dance in the evening; (by the bye, Mrs. Forster and me are *such* friends!) and so she asked the two Harringtons to come, but Harriet was ill, and so Pen was forced to come by herself; and then, what do you think we did? We dressed up Chamberlayne[24] in woman's clothes, on purpose to pass for a lady,[25]—only think what fun![26] Not a soul knew of it, but Col. and Mrs. Forster, and Kitty and me, except my aunt, for we were forced to borrow one of her gowns; and you cannot imagine how well he looked! When Denny, and Wickham, and Pratt, and two or three more of the men came in, they did not know him in the least. Lord! how I laughed! and so did Mrs. Forster.[27] I thought I should have died. And *that* made the men suspect something, and then they soon found out what was the matter."

With such kind of histories of their parties and good jokes, did Lydia, assisted by Kitty's hints and additions, endeavour to amuse her companions all the way to Longbourn. Elizabeth listened as little as she could, but there was no escaping the frequent mention of Wickham's name.

Their reception at home was most kind. Mrs. Bennet rejoiced to see Jane in undiminished beauty; and more than once during dinner did Mr. Bennet say voluntarily[28] to Elizabeth,

"I am glad you are come back, Lizzy."

19. *bandbox:* a lightweight, delicate box, used especially for hats. Lydia's words give a further sense of the "benefits" of her purchase and of how little she thinks of others' welfare.

20. After asking these questions, which seem to suggest an interest in the others, Lydia shows her real character and interests by not pausing a moment to hear an answer.

21. *old maid:* an older woman who has never married. A woman was considered an old maid once she passed the age of normal eligibility for marriage, which might occur by her late 20's and certainly would occur after she turned 30. Old maids were generally looked down upon and ridiculed, and were the subjects of a variety of negative stereotypes.

22. Mrs. Philips's interest in matchmaking makes her greatly resemble her sister, Mrs. Bennet. The Philipses are never mentioned as having any children of their own, so it would be natural for Mrs. Philips to take an especially strong interest in her nieces.

23. As a married woman, Lydia would have more freedom, and could act as chaperone for unmarried women, who were not supposed to attend public functions on their own.

24. *Chamberlayne:* a servant. Use of his last name indicates he is an upper servant, most likely a butler.

25. A novel of the time that Jane Austen admired, Maria Edgeworth's *Belinda*, contains several incidents in which characters demonstrate their folly or their moral irrresponsibility by dressing up in clothes of the opposite sex.

26. *what fun!:* this is the fourth time Lydia has used "fun" in this speech. It is her favorite word, and she uses it often. At this time it was still considered a slang word rather than proper English; no one else in the novel uses it. Jane Austen also has a very foolish character in the story "Catharine, or the Bower" use the word. In general, Lydia's language—her exaggerated expressions, her frequent use of exclamations, her hurried and abbreviated sentences, her rapid leaps from one thought to another, her crude choice of words—reveals perfectly her shallowness, impulsiveness, and lack of sense.

27. This gives a sense of the character of Mrs. Forster, who is shortly to be entrusted with the position of guardian for Lydia.

28. *more than once . . . voluntarily:* these represent unusual exertions for Mr. Bennet, and signal the strength of his feelings regarding Elizabeth.

Their party in the dining-room was large, for almost all the Lucases came to meet Maria and hear the news: and various were the subjects which occupied them; Lady Lucas was enquiring of Maria across the table, after the welfare and poultry of her eldest daughter; Mrs. Bennet was doubly engaged, on one hand collecting an account of the present fashions from Jane, who sat some way below her, and on the other, retailing[29] them all to the younger Miss Lucases; and Lydia, in a voice rather louder than any other person's, was enumerating the various pleasures of the morning to any body who would hear her.

"Oh! Mary," said she, "I wish you had gone with us, for we had such fun! as we went along, Kitty and me drew up all the blinds,[30] and pretended there was nobody in the coach; and I should have gone so all the way, if Kitty had not been sick;[31] and when we got to the George,[32] I do think we behaved very handsomely, for we treated the other three with the nicest cold luncheon[33] in the world, and if you would have gone, we would have treated you too. And then when we came away it was such fun! I thought we never should have got into the coach. I was ready to die of laughter. And then we were so merry all the way home! we talked and laughed so loud, that any body might have heard us ten miles off!"

To this, Mary very gravely replied, "Far be it from me, my dear sister, to depreciate such pleasures. They would doubtless be congenial with the generality of female minds.[34] But I confess they would have no charms for *me*. I should infinitely prefer a book."

But of this answer Lydia heard not a word. She seldom listened to any body for more than half a minute, and never attended to Mary at all.

In the afternoon[35] Lydia was urgent with the rest of the girls to walk to Meryton and see how every body went on; but Elizabeth steadily opposed the scheme. It should not be said, that the Miss Bennets could not be at home half a day before they were in pursuit of the officers.[36] There was another reason too for her opposition. She dreaded seeing Wickham again, and was resolved to avoid it as long as possible. The comfort to *her*, of the regiment's approaching removal, was indeed beyond expression. In a fortnight

29. *retailing:* repeating, recounting.

30. *blinds:* ones for the windows of the coach.

31. A reference to motion sickness, which would have been a problem in coaches of the time since the ride they offered tended to be bumpy.

32. *the George:* the name of the inn where they ate.

33. *luncheon:* small midday meal or snack. Lunch as a full meal had not come into fashion yet. The term "luncheon" was just coming into use.

34. The idea of female minds, or characters, being especially inclined toward silliness or frivolity is one found in a number of writings of the time, including some of the moralizing books on female conduct that Mary seems to have studied carefully.

35. *afternoon:* brief period of time from dinner until tea. This means it would usually extend from around five o'clock until around seven. Obviously the term "afternoon" makes little sense when applied to such a stretch of time; in fact, this strange usage only lasted for a brief period. Afternoon had traditionally been applied to the period from dinner (which had long been at mid-day) until evening. During the eighteenth century dinner, especially for the wealthy, gradually shifted to a later hour; as it did, the commencement of afternoon was steadily pushed back, while morning came to cover more and more of the day. It was not until later decades, after further adjustments of meal times, that afternoon reverted to its original meaning of mid-day until evening.

36. Elizabeth, like almost everyone, shows herself very concerned with society's opinion of herself and her family. Nor does it appear that the author condemns her concern. In fact, her attempts here, and elsewhere, to restrain her two youngest sisters are presented as signs of responsibility on her part, just as Mr. Bennet is clearly irresponsible not to worry about others' opinion of his family and to put his daughter in a position where she has to assume such a burden if she wants anyone to do so. This issue will be developed further two chapters later, when father and daughter clash over the issue of Lydia going to Brighton.

they were to go, and once gone, she hoped there could be nothing more to plague her on his account.

She had not been many hours at home, before she found that the Brighton scheme, of which Lydia had given them a hint at the inn, was under frequent discussion between her parents. Elizabeth saw directly[37] that her father had not the smallest intention of yielding; but his answers were at the same time so vague and equivocal, that her mother, though often disheartened, had never yet despaired of succeeding at last.

37. *directly*: immediately.

Chapter Seventeen

*E*lizabeth's impatience to acquaint Jane with what had happened could no longer be overcome; and at length resolving to suppress every particular in which her sister was concerned, and preparing her to be surprised, she related to her the next morning the chief[1] of the scene between Mr. Darcy and herself.

Miss Bennet's astonishment was soon lessened by the strong sisterly partiality which made any admiration of Elizabeth appear perfectly natural; and all surprise was shortly lost in other feelings. She was sorry that Mr. Darcy should have delivered his sentiments in a manner so little suited to recommend them; but still more was she grieved for the unhappiness which her sister's refusal must have given him.

"His being so sure of succeeding, was wrong," said she; "and certainly ought not to have appeared; but consider how much it must increase his disappointment."

"Indeed," replied Elizabeth, "I am heartily sorry for him; but he has other feelings which will probably soon drive away his regard for me.[2] You do not blame me, however, for refusing him?"

"Blame you! Oh, no."

"But you blame me for having spoken so warmly of Wickham."

"No—I do not know that you were wrong in saying what you did."

"But you *will* know it, when I have told you what happened the very next day."

She then spoke of the letter, repeating the whole of its contents as far as they concerned George Wickham. What a stroke was this for poor Jane! who would willingly have gone through the world without believing that so much wickedness existed in the whole race of mankind, as was here collected in one individual. Nor was Darcy's vindication, though grateful to her feelings, capable of

1. *chief*: greater part.

2. The other feelings are presumably Darcy's feelings of social pride along with ones of resentment toward Elizabeth.

consoling her for such discovery. Most earnestly did she labour to prove the probability of error, and seek to clear one, without involving the other.

"This will not do," said Elizabeth. "You never will be able to make both of them good for any thing. Take your choice, but you must be satisfied with only one. There is but such a quantity of merit between them; just enough to make one good sort of man; and of late it has been shifting about pretty much. For my part, I am inclined to believe it all Mr. Darcy's, but you shall do as you chuse."[3]

It was some time, however, before a smile could be extorted from Jane.

"I do not know when I have been more shocked," said she. "Wickham so very bad! It is almost past belief. And poor Mr. Darcy! dear Lizzy, only consider what he must have suffered. Such a disappointment! and with the knowledge of your ill opinion too! and having to relate such a thing of his sister! It is really too distressing. I am sure you must feel it so."

"Oh! no, my regret and compassion are all done away by seeing you so full of both. I know you will do him such ample justice, that I am growing every moment more unconcerned and indifferent. Your profusion makes me saving;[4] and if you lament over him much longer, my heart will be as light as a feather."

"Poor Wickham; there is such an expression of goodness in his countenance! such an openness and gentleness in his manner."

"There certainly was some great mismanagement in the education of those two young men. One has got all the goodness, and the other all the appearance of it."[5]

"I never thought Mr. Darcy so deficient in the *appearance* of it as you used to do."

"And yet I meant to be uncommonly clever in taking so decided a dislike to him, without any reason. It is such a spur to one's genius,[6] such an opening for wit to have a dislike of that kind. One may be continually abusive without saying any thing just; but one cannot be always laughing at a man without now and then stumbling on something witty."[7]

3. According to this speech, Elizabeth would not yet have fully decided that all the merit is on Darcy's side, and all the blame on Wickham's, though she clearly is leaning in that direction. It is possible her words are simply an ironic response to Jane's continued attempts to blame neither man and to see them both as good, and that in fact she has already made a firm decision in Darcy's favor.

4. That is, you are so profuse in your compassion and regret that it is making me be saving, or frugal, in my sympathy (since there is no need for more). Elizabeth is obviously being sardonic with regard to Jane's excessive tenderness.

5. An ingenious formulation but, as Jane's immediate response indicates, it is not exactly right. Even here, as she is admitting her faults, Elizabeth's love of clever expression leads her to be less than fully accurate.

6. *genius:* abilities, mental powers.

7. A significant acknowledgment by Elizabeth, both of her error and of the reasons for it. She admits the role of vanity and of her desire to exercise her cleverness; she also acknowledges the harm caused by her love of wit and humor. Of course, it is that very wit and playfulness that gives her such charm. But like almost any characteristic it has its dangers, especially when carried too far—Mr. Bennet provides a stark example of this. Courtesy books of the time often warned of the dangers of excessive wit and emphasized the need to join wit to delicacy and moral sensitivity, a principle that Elizabeth generally follows but that she could be judged to have violated in some of her jabs at Darcy. Jane Austen's own view of the matter is perhaps summarized in a letter to her niece Fanny (see cover) cautioning against the rejection of someone for lack of wit: "Wisdom is certainly better than Wit, & in the long run will certainly have the laugh on her side" (Nov. 18, 1814). In this novel Elizabeth always has wit; her struggle is to attain greater wisdom.

"Lizzy, when you first read that letter, I am sure you could not treat the matter as you do now."

"Indeed I could not. I was uncomfortable enough. I was very uncomfortable, I may say unhappy. And with no one to speak to, of what I felt, no Jane to comfort me and say that I had not been so very weak and vain and nonsensical as I knew I had! Oh! how I wanted you!"

"How unfortunate that you should have used such very strong expressions in speaking of Wickham to Mr. Darcy,[8] for now they *do* appear wholly undeserved."

"Certainly. But the misfortune of speaking with bitterness, is a most natural consequence of the prejudices I had been encouraging. There is one point, on which I want your advice. I want to be told whether I ought, or ought not to make our acquaintance in general understand Wickham's character."

Miss Bennet paused a little and then replied, "Surely there can be no occasion for exposing him so dreadfully. What is your own opinion?"

"That it ought not to be attempted. Mr. Darcy has not authorised me to make his communication public. On the contrary every particular relative to his sister, was meant to be kept as much as possible to myself; and if I endeavour to undeceive people as to the rest of his conduct, who will believe me? The general prejudice against Mr. Darcy is so violent, that it would be the death of half the good people in Meryton, to attempt to place him in an amiable light. I am not equal to it. Wickham will soon be gone; and therefore it will not signify to anybody here, what he really is. Sometime hence it will be all found out, and then we may laugh at their stupidity in not knowing it before. At present I will say nothing about it."[9]

"You are quite right. To have his errors made public might ruin him for ever. He is now perhaps sorry for what he has done, and anxious to re-establish a character. We must not make him desperate."[10]

The tumult of Elizabeth's mind was allayed by this conversation. She had got rid of two of the secrets which had weighed on

8. Throughout this conversation both Elizabeth and Jane simply use "Wickham"; until this point, they have always said "Mr. Wickham," just as they continue to say "Mr. Darcy." In general, people in Jane Austen's novels use "Mr." or "Mrs." or "Miss" when speaking of someone else unless that person is an intimate friend or near relation, or is a servant. Willingness to use others' names alone—in the way that Lydia has recently spoken of "Denny, and Wickham, and Pratt"—usually suggests vulgarity or excessive familiarity on the part of the speaker. In the case of Elizabeth and Jane here, their use of "Wickham" alone is probably a sign of diminished respect for him, for they certainly have not become more intimate with him.

9. Elizabeth's refusal to expose Wickham will have grave consequences, though in fairness to her, she could not really have anticipated them, especially with regard to Lydia. It is possible that one reason for her decision is that she hates having to admit in public how wrong she had been in her championing of Wickham. Such a motive might lie behind her statement, "I am not equal to it," and also behind the exaggerated nature of her prediction of how the public would react to new information concerning Darcy and Wickham.

10. In other words, Jane worries that if they expose Wickham, he would despair of ever reestablishing his character, or reputation, and thus abandon any attempts to improve himself. Jane's counsel is thoroughly naive, since Wickham has never shown any sign of repentance or of a wish to improve— nor will he after his further bad conduct.

her for a fortnight, and was certain of a willing listener in Jane, whenever she might wish to talk again of either. But there was still something lurking behind, of which prudence forbad the disclosure. She dared not relate the other half of Mr. Darcy's letter, nor explain to her sister how sincerely she had been valued by his friend. Here was knowledge in which no one could partake; and she was sensible[11] that nothing less than a perfect understanding between the parties could justify her in throwing off this last incumbrance of mystery. "And then," said she, "if that very improbable event should ever take place, I shall merely be able to tell what Bingley may tell in a much more agreeable manner himself. The liberty of communication cannot be mine till it has lost all its value!"[12]

She was now, on being settled at home, at leisure to observe the real state of her sister's spirits. Jane was not happy. She still cherished a very tender affection for Bingley. Having never even fancied herself in love before, her regard had all the warmth of first attachment, and from her age and disposition, greater steadiness than first attachments often boast; and so fervently did she value his remembrance, and prefer him to every other man, that all her good sense, and all her attention to the feelings of her friends, were requisite to check the indulgence of those regrets, which must have been injurious to her own health and their tranquillity.[13]

"Well, Lizzy," said Mrs. Bennet one day, "what is your opinion *now* of this sad business of Jane's? For my part, I am determined never to speak of it again to anybody. I told my sister Philips so the other day. But I cannot find out that Jane saw any thing of him in London. Well, he is a very undeserving young man—and I do not suppose there is the least chance in the world of her ever getting him now. There is no talk of his coming to Netherfield again in the summer; and I have enquired of every body too, who is likely to know."

"I do not believe that he will ever live at Netherfield any more."

"Oh, well! it is just as he chooses. Nobody wants him to come. Though I shall always say that he used my daughter extremely ill; and if I was her, I would not have put up with it. Well, my

11. *sensible*: conscious.

12. In other words, she says she will not be free to reveal everything until doing so will have little value, because others, particularly Jane, will already know what she can tell. She thus continues to fear that knowing the truth about Bingley could only grieve Jane further, presumably because it would increase Jane's sense of what she has lost. Elizabeth may also fear that it could lead Jane to harbor renewed hope about Bingley, a hope that might be doomed to disappointment. Even explaining part of what Elizabeth knows, such as Bingley's ignorance of Jane's presence in London during the winter, might foster these feelings in Jane, and might also lead to inquiries about the rest of the story. Hence Elizabeth prefers to avoid the whole subject.

13. The need to avoid upsetting her friends is causing Jane to abstain from indulging in regrets. Since such abstention from regrets is also good for Jane, this would be an example of how striving to accommodate others can benefit oneself.

comfort is, I am sure Jane will die of a broken heart,[14] and then he will be sorry for what he has done."

But as Elizabeth could not receive comfort from any such expectation, she made no answer.

"Well, Lizzy," continued her mother soon afterwards, "and so the Collinses live very comfortable, do they? Well, well, I only hope it will last. And what sort of table do they keep? Charlotte is an excellent manager, I dare say.[15] If she is half as sharp as her mother, she is saving[16] enough. There is nothing extravagant in *their* housekeeping, I dare say."[17]

"No, nothing at all."

"A great deal of good management, depend upon it. Yes, yes. *They* will take care not to outrun their income. *They* will never be distressed for money. Well, much good may it do them! And so, I suppose, they often talk of having Longbourn when your father is dead. They look upon it quite as their own, I dare say, whenever that happens."

"It was a subject which they could not mention before me."

"No. It would have been strange if they had. But I make no doubt, they often talk of it between themselves. Well, if they can be easy with an estate that is not lawfully their own, so much the better. *I* should be ashamed of having one that was only entailed on me."[18]

14. A common convention of the time as to the fate of spurned lovers.

15. Charlotte was shown as being a very skillful housekeeper—much better than Mrs. Bennet, whose extravagance, it is explained later, has helped ensure that her husband has never saved any money to augment their daughters' fortunes.

16. *saving*: frugal, parsimonious.

17. A dig at the Lucases for not living as comfortably or luxuriously as the Bennets. Mrs. Bennet manifests a continual need to assert her own family's superiority over the Lucases, who appear to be the closest rival to the Bennets for most prominent family in the neighborhood.

18. In fact, Mr. Bennet probably inherited Longbourn because of an entail (though if he got it from his father, he would have inherited it even without an entail). Thus Mrs. Bennet is most likely herself enjoying an estate that had been entailed on her husband. Moreover, since entails were the most popular legal device then used among the landed classes to pass on property, no one would normally regard the beneficiary of an entail as obtaining something not lawfully his own.

Chapter Eighteen

*T*he first week of their return was soon gone. The second began. It was the last of the regiment's stay in Meryton, and all the young ladies in the neighbourhood were drooping apace. The dejection was almost universal. The elder Miss Bennets alone were still able to eat, drink, and sleep, and pursue the usual course of their employments. Very frequently were they reproached for this insensibility[1] by Kitty and Lydia, whose own misery was extreme, and who could not comprehend such hard-heartedness in any of the family.

"Good Heaven! What is to become of us! What are we to do!" would they often exclaim in the bitterness of woe. "How can you be smiling so, Lizzy?"

Their affectionate mother shared all their grief; she remembered what she had herself endured on a similar occasion, five and twenty years ago.

"I am sure," said she, "I cried for two days together when Colonel Millar's regiment went away. I thought I should have broke my heart."

"I am sure I shall break *mine*," said Lydia.

"If one could but go to Brighton!" observed Mrs. Bennet.

"Oh, yes!—if one could but go to Brighton! But papa is so disagreeable."

"A little sea-bathing would set me up for ever."[2]

"And my aunt Philips is sure it would do *me* a great deal of good," added Kitty.

Such were the kind of lamentations resounding perpetually through Longbourn-house. Elizabeth tried to be diverted by them; but all sense of pleasure was lost in shame. She felt anew the justice of Mr. Darcy's objections; and never had she before been so much disposed to pardon his interference in the views of his friend.

1.   *insensibility*: lack of emotion.

2.   This line is most likely spoken by Mrs. Bennet. Sea-bathing, or swimming, had recently become popular; it was a principal reason for the growth in popularity of seaside resorts like Brighton. After a long period during which the sea was regarded with suspicion, and only entered by those who earned their livelihoods from it, attitudes toward it had changed markedly in the eighteenth century. Immersion in the sea (usually only for brief periods at a time), as well as drinking sea water, came to be regarded as cures for a variety of ailments. In a letter Jane Austen mentions an acquaintance who seems to have improved through bathing in the sea (Sept. 15, 1796). By the time of this novel people were often simply going to the sea for pleasure, though the belief in its medicinal properties continued. Sometimes reasons of health were used to justify what was primarily a simple vacation: this seems to be what Mrs. Bennet and Kitty are doing, with their talk of the good the sea would do them. Jane Austen's last writing, the unfinished novel *Sanditon*, is set in a fictional seaside resort and satirizes the increasing mania for the sea, both among those who come there for their ailments, real or imagined, and those who hope to profit from this influx of visitors.

But the gloom of Lydia's prospect was shortly cleared away; for she received an invitation from Mrs. Forster, the wife of the Colonel of the regiment, to accompany her to Brighton. This invaluable friend was a very young woman, and very lately married. A resemblance in good humour and good spirits had recommended her and Lydia to each other, and out of their *three* months' acquaintance they had been intimate *two*.[3]

The rapture of Lydia on this occasion, her adoration of Mrs. Forster, the delight of Mrs. Bennet, and the mortification of Kitty, are scarcely to be described. Wholly inattentive to her sister's feelings,[4] Lydia flew about the house in restless ecstacy, calling for every one's congratulations, and laughing and talking with more violence than ever; whilst the luckless Kitty continued in the parlour repining at her fate in terms as unreasonable as her accent[5] was peevish.

"I cannot see why Mrs. Forster should not ask *me* as well as Lydia," said she, "though I am *not* her particular friend. I have just as much right to be asked as she has, and more too, for I am two years older."

In vain did Elizabeth attempt to make her reasonable, and Jane to make her resigned. As for Elizabeth herself, this invitation was so far from exciting in her the same feelings as in her mother and Lydia, that she considered it as the death-warrant of all possibility of common sense for the latter; and detestable as such a step must make her were it known, she could not help secretly advising her father not to let her go. She represented to him all the improprieties of Lydia's general behaviour, the little advantage she could derive from the friendship of such a woman as Mrs. Forster, and the probability of her being yet more imprudent with such a companion at Brighton, where the temptations must be greater than at home.[6] He heard her attentively, and then said,

"Lydia will never be easy till she has exposed herself[7] in some public place or other, and we can never expect her to do it with so little expense or inconvenience to her family as under the present circumstances."

"If you were aware," said Elizabeth, "of the very great disadvantage to us all, which must arise from the public notice of Lydia's

3. By staying with a married couple Lydia would be able to go to Brighton without transgressing propriety. At the same time, Lydia's earlier account of her games with Mrs. Forster indicates that the latter, whatever her marital status, is hardly a mature or responsible guide. The information here, on her youth and her brief intimacy with Lydia, demonstrates further her unsuitability as a guardian.

4. An irony after her own reproaches to Elizabeth and Jane on their lack of concern for her misery.

5. *accent*: tone of voice.

6. Brighton would offer more temptations than almost any place in England. It had a reputation for licentiousness, some of it connected with the soldiers stationed there. It also had a generally raffish atmosphere, the result in part of the influence of the hedonistic Prince Regent. Jane Austen herself would be sensitive to this; in a letter written at the same time as this novel appeared she declares her hatred of the Prince, whose sexual infidelities were notorious and who was waging a bitter public quarrel with his estranged wife (Feb. 16, 1813).

7. *exposed herself*: made an exhibition of herself, attracted public attention.

unguarded[8] and imprudent manner; nay, which has already arisen from it, I am sure you would judge differently in the affair."

"Already arisen!" repeated Mr. Bennet. "What, has she frightened away some of your lovers? Poor little Lizzy! But do not be cast down. Such squeamish youths as cannot bear to be connected with a little absurdity, are not worth a regret. Come, let me see the list of the pitiful fellows who have been kept aloof by Lydia's folly."

"Indeed you are mistaken. I have no such injuries to resent. It is not of peculiar,[9] but of general evils, which I am now complaining. Our importance, our respectability in the world, must be affected by the wild volatility, the assurance[10] and disdain of all restraint which mark Lydia's character.[11] Excuse me—for I must speak plainly. If you, my dear father, will not take the trouble of checking her exuberant spirits, and of teaching her that her present pursuits are not to be the business of her life, she will soon be beyond the reach of amendment. Her character will be fixed, and she will, at sixteen, be the most determined flirt that ever made herself and her family ridiculous. A flirt too, in the worst and meanest[12] degree of flirtation; without any attraction beyond youth and a tolerable person;[13] and from the ignorance and emptiness of her mind, wholly unable to ward off any portion of that universal contempt which her rage for admiration will excite. In this danger Kitty is also comprehended.[14] She will follow wherever Lydia leads. Vain, ignorant, idle, and absolutely uncontrouled! Oh! my dear father, can you suppose it possible that they will not be censured and despised wherever they are known, and that their sisters will not be often involved in the disgrace?"

Mr. Bennet saw that her whole heart was in the subject; and affectionately taking her hand, said in reply,

"Do not make yourself uneasy, my love. Wherever[15] you and Jane are known, you must be respected and valued; and you will not appear to less advantage for having a couple of—or I may say, three very silly sisters. We shall have no peace at Longbourn if Lydia does not go to Brighton. Let her go then. Colonel Forster is a sensible man, and will keep her out of any real mischief; and she is luckily too poor to be an object of prey to any body.[16] At

8. *unguarded*: careless.

9. *peculiar*: particular.

10. *assurance*: audacity, impudence.

11. Elizabeth's passionate appeal stems from, and shows, the tremendous power and influence of the family in this society. An individual was judged to a great degree by the value of his or her family, and bad behavior on the part of one member of the family would tarnish the reputation and position of all its members. The family also largely determined one's material fate, whether that meant one's opportunities for marriage, or, in the case of a man, one's ability to pursue a career. In this case, Elizabeth knows that Darcy's opposition to a marriage of Bingley and Jane stemmed from Darcy's perception of the faults of her family, and that his attitude is a standard one that could easily affect the Bennets in future instances.

12. *meanest*: lowest, most debased.

13. *person*: physical person.

14. *comprehended*: included.

15. *Wherever*: the word was "Whenever" in the first edition of the novel. The third edition changed it to "Wherever," which seems more logical (the original word could easily have been a printer's error since "n" and "r" are so close).

16. Meaning that because Lydia has almost no fortune, she will not tempt any man who is looking to elope with a woman in order to gain money.

Brighton she will be of less importance even as a common flirt than she has been here. The officers will find women better worth their notice. Let us hope, therefore, that her being there may teach her her own insignificance. At any rate, she cannot grow many degrees worse, without authorizing us to lock her up for the rest of her life."[17]

With this answer Elizabeth was forced to be content; but her own opinion continued the same, and she left him disappointed and sorry. It was not in her nature, however, to increase her vexations, by dwelling on them. She was confident of having performed her duty, and to fret over unavoidable evils, or augment them by anxiety, was no part of her disposition.

Had Lydia and her mother known the substance of her conference with her father, their indignation would hardly have found expression in their united volubility. In Lydia's imagination, a visit to Brighton comprised every possibility of earthly happiness. She saw with the creative eye of fancy,[18] the streets of that gay bathing place covered with officers. She saw herself the object of attention, to tens and to scores of them at present unknown. She saw all the glories of the camp; its tents stretched forth in beauteous uniformity of lines,[19] crowded with the young and the gay, and dazzling with scarlet;[20] and to complete the view, she saw herself seated beneath a tent, tenderly flirting with at least six officers at once.[21]

Had she known that her sister sought to tear her from such prospects and such realities as these, what would have been her sensations? They could have been understood only by her mother, who might have felt nearly the same. Lydia's going to Brighton was all that consoled her for the melancholy conviction of her husband's never intending to go there himself.

But they were entirely ignorant of what had passed; and their raptures continued with little intermission to the very day of Lydia's leaving home.

Elizabeth was now to see Mr. Wickham for the last time. Having been frequently in company with him since her return, agitation was pretty well over; the agitations of former partiality[22]

17. Mr. Bennet's conclusion thus relies on a joke, for nobody is going to lock up Lydia. At the same time, it is still noteworthy, and a sign of his respect for Elizabeth, that he has bothered to defend his decision at such length. In general he simply announces his opinions and determinations to his family without any explanation or justification, unless it is a humorous or ironic one.

18. *the creative eye of fancy*: the creative, or imaginative, vision made by her fancy.

19. Troops were usually housed in tents in their summer encampment.

20. Scarlet from the red uniforms of the soldiers.

21. Lydia's hopes demonstrate the validity of Elizabeth's fears.

22. *agitations of former partiality*: the agitated emotions caused by her having been partial to him. The other agitations, those that still linger slightly, would be those relating to her knowledge of his bad actions and his lies to her.

entirely so. She had even learnt to detect, in the very gentleness which had first delighted her, an affectation and a sameness to disgust and weary.[23] In his present behaviour to herself, moreover, she had a fresh source of displeasure, for the inclination he soon testified of renewing those attentions which had marked the early part of their acquaintance, could only serve, after what had since passed, to provoke her. She lost all concern for him in finding herself thus selected as the object of such idle and frivolous gallantry; and while she steadily repressed it, could not but feel the reproof contained in his believing, that however long, and for whatever cause, his attentions had been withdrawn, her vanity would be gratified and her preference secured at any time by their renewal.[24]

On the very last day of the regiment's remaining in Meryton, he dined with others of the officers at Longbourn; and so little was Elizabeth disposed to part from him in good humour, that on his making some enquiry as to the manner in which her time had passed at Hunsford, she mentioned Colonel Fitzwilliam's and Mr. Darcy's having both spent three weeks at Rosings, and asked him if he were acquainted with the former.

He looked surprised, displeased, alarmed; but with a moment's recollection and a returning smile, replied, that he had formerly seen him often; and after observing that he was a very gentleman-like man, asked her how she had liked him.[25] Her answer was warmly in his favour. With an air of indifference he soon afterwards added, "How long did you say that he was at Rosings?"

"Nearly three weeks."

"And you saw him frequently?"

"Yes, almost every day."

"His manners are very different from his cousin's."

"Yes, very different. But I think Mr. Darcy improves on acquaintance."

"Indeed!" cried Wickham with a look which did not escape her. "And pray may I ask?" but checking himself, he added in a gayer tone, "Is it in address[26] that he improves? Has he deigned to add ought[27] of civility to his ordinary style?[28] for I dare not hope,"

23. *to disgust and weary:* that cause weariness and distaste.

24. Wickham's renewed interest in Elizabeth would not come from a wish for marriage with her (despite the failure of his plan to marry Miss King), for by now he would surely know of Elizabeth's lack of fortune. He is probably moved by a general love of flirtation, especially with someone as attractive and witty as Elizabeth, along with his appreciation of her supposed sympathy with his sufferings.

Elizabeth's sense of reproof stems from her earlier infatuation with him and unthinking partiality in his cause. Thus Wickham's actions here form one more link in the chain of Elizabeth's reformation.

25. Wickham would know, based on his own dealings with Miss Darcy, that Colonel Fitzwilliam was one of her guardians, and that as her guardian he would almost certainly have been informed of Wickham's attempt to elope with her. Thus Wickham has good reason to exhibit alarm at Elizabeth's mention of the other man's name.

26. *address:* manner of speaking.

27. *ought:* anything whatever.

28. *ordinary style:* normal style or manner of behaving.

he continued in a lower and more serious tone, "that he is improved in essentials."[29]

"Oh, no!" said Elizabeth. "In essentials, I believe, he is very much what he ever was."

While she spoke, Wickham looked as if scarcely knowing whether to rejoice over her words, or to distrust their meaning.[30] There was a something in her countenance which made him listen with an apprehensive and anxious attention, while she added,

"When I said that he improved on acquaintance, I did not mean that either his mind or manners[31] were in a state of improvement, but that from knowing him better, his disposition was better understood."

Wickham's alarm now appeared in a heightened complexion and agitated look; for a few minutes he was silent; till, shaking off his embarrassment, he turned to her again, and said in the gentlest of accents,

"You, who so well know my feelings towards Mr. Darcy, will readily comprehend how sincerely I must rejoice that he is wise enough to assume even the *appearance* of what is right. His pride, in that direction, may be of service, if not to himself, to many others, for it must deter him from such foul misconduct as I have suffered by. I only fear that the sort of cautiousness, to which you, I imagine, have been alluding, is merely adopted on his visits to his aunt, of whose good opinion and judgment he stands much in awe. His fear of her, has always operated, I know, when they were together; and a good deal is to be imputed to his wish of forwarding the match with Miss De Bourgh, which I am certain he has very much at heart."[32]

Elizabeth could not repress a smile at this, but she answered only by a slight inclination of the head. She saw that he wanted to engage her on the old subject of his grievances, and she was in no humour[33] to indulge him.[34] The rest of the evening passed with the *appearance*, on his side, of usual cheerfulness, but with no farther attempt to distinguish[35] Elizabeth; and they parted at last with mutual civility, and possibly a mutual desire of never meeting again.

29. *essentials:* essential elements, i.e., what is basic to his character and beneath the surface.

30. In other words, he cannot figure out whether she means that Darcy's underlying qualities remain as bad as they were, or that she now knows that, despite his outward flaws, they have always been good.

31. *mind or manners:* inner or outer character. These two words are paired to refer to a person's entire character at several points in the novel.

32. Wickham demonstrates his ability to come up with an explanation, however mendacious, for almost everything; he has undoubtedly had plenty of practice in that line. Unfortunately for him, Elizabeth has had enough exposure to Darcy's behavior around Lady Catherine and Miss De Bourgh to know the falsity of Wickham's assertions about their relationship with Darcy.

33. *humour:* mood.

34. Wickham's persistent wish to discuss his grievances is an interesting study in human psychology. One can guess that he, like many if not most of those who have acted badly, considers himself in fact to be good and believes sincerely that his distresses, as well as whatever bad reputation he has earned, stem from others' injustices against him. As Jane Austen shows throughout the novel, as well as in her other novels, few people are able or willing to perform the difficult task of recognizing their own faults. Wickham, though he has more faults to recognize than almost anyone, gives no indication of being among those few.

35. *distinguish:* single out, pay particular notice to.

When the party broke up, Lydia returned with Mrs. Forster to Meryton, from whence they were to set out early the next morning. The separation between her and her family was rather noisy than pathetic. Kitty was the only one who shed tears; but she did weep from vexation and envy. Mrs. Bennet was diffuse in her good wishes for the felicity of her daughter, and impressive[36] in her injunctions that she would not miss the opportunity of enjoying herself as much as possible; advice, which there was every reason to believe would be attended to; and in the clamorous happiness of Lydia herself in bidding farewell, the more gentle adieus of her sisters were uttered without being heard.

36. *impressive:* inclined to make an impression, capable of exciting strong feeling. In other words, Mrs. Bennet's injunctions were likely to affect the listener strongly.

Matlock (top) and Dovedale, two of the places on Elizabeth's tour to the north; see p. 440, and p. 441, note 30. It is possible Jane Austen was influenced in her choice of these places by these illustrations from Gilpin's book.

[From William Gilpin, *Observations, on Several Parts of England*, Vol. II (London, 1808), pp. 221 and 226]

Chapter Nineteen

*H*ad Elizabeth's opinion been all drawn from her own family, she could not have formed a very pleasing picture of conjugal felicity or domestic comfort. Her father captivated by youth and beauty, and that appearance of good humour, which youth and beauty generally give, had married a woman whose weak understanding[1] and illiberal[2] mind,[3] had very early in their marriage put an end to all real affection for her. Respect, esteem, and confidence,[4] had vanished for ever; and all his views[5] of domestic happiness were overthrown.[6] But Mr. Bennet was not of a disposition to seek comfort for the disappointment which his own imprudence had brought on, in any of those pleasures which too often console the unfortunate for their folly or their vice.[7] He was fond of the country and of books; and from these tastes had arisen his principal enjoyments. To his wife he was very little otherwise indebted, than as her ignorance and folly had contributed to his amusement. This is not the sort of happiness which a man would in general wish to owe to his wife; but where other powers of entertainment are wanting,[8] the true philosopher[9] will derive benefit from such as are given.

Elizabeth, however, had never been blind to the impropriety of her father's behaviour as a husband. She had always seen it with pain; but respecting his abilities, and grateful for his affectionate treatment of herself, she endeavoured to forget what she could not overlook, and to banish from her thoughts that continual breach of conjugal obligation and decorum which, in exposing his wife to the contempt of her own children, was so highly reprehensible. But she had never felt so strongly as now, the disadvantages which must attend the children of so unsuitable a marriage, nor ever been so fully aware of the evils arising from so ill-judged a direction of talents;[10] talents which rightly used, might at least have preserved the respectability of his daughters,[11] even if incapable of enlarging the mind of his wife.[12]

1. *understanding:* intellect.

2. *illiberal:* uneducated; not genteel; sordid.

3. *mind:* character.

4. *confidence:* trust, willingness to rely on someone.

5. *views:* expectations.

6. A similar case to this is Mr. Palmer of *Sense and Sensibility,* who marries a woman even sillier than Mrs. Bennet and who also takes resort in silence and in sharp or sarcastic remarks to his wife. One inspiration for these cases may have come from a passage in one of Jane Austen's favorite novels, Fanny Burney's *Camilla.* In it a woman says, regarding men's marital tastes, "They are always enchanted with something that is both pretty and silly; because they can so easily please and so soon disconcert it; . . . it [their taste] brings them a plentiful harvest of repentance, when it is their connubial criterion; the pretty flies off, and the silly remains, and a man then has a choice companion for life left on his hands!"

7. Drink, gambling, and sexual philandering are likely among those meant.

8. That is, where other means of amusement or interest are lacking.

9. *true philosopher:* a reference to the ideal of the philosopher who, thanks to his wisdom and his control over his emotions, is able to accept tranquilly all occurrences and to find means of happiness regardless of circumstances (the notion of accepting things philosophically still conveys something of that idea). This ideal, which has roots in the philosophical sects of the ancient world, was still powerful at this time, often forming the main spiritual alternative for educated people to Christianity, and sometimes being combined with a Christian perspective. Jane Austen shows traces of it in many places, especially in her admiring depiction of those who are able to rise above misfortune and to avoid despair or resentment. Here she uses the idea in a more satirical way, for seeking consolation by laughing at one's wife would not be upheld as an ideal example of philosophical virtue.

10. *ill-judged a direction of talents:* his directing his talents toward ridicule and amusement rather than toward raising his children well.

11. Mr. Bennet seems to bother little with his daughters, except occasionally with Elizabeth, even though, given Mrs. Bennet's general deference toward him, he could exercise far more influence over them than he does and thus counteract some of the effects of their mother's foolishness.

12. This discussion of the Bennet marriage, and Elizabeth's reflections on it, could be placed at many points in the novel. It fits here because it comes just before her next encounter with Darcy raises the issue of her avoiding her

When Elizabeth had rejoiced over Wickham's departure, she found little other cause for satisfaction in the loss of the regiment. Their parties abroad[13] were less varied than before; and at home she had a mother and sister whose constant repinings at the dulness of every thing around them, threw a real gloom over their domestic circle; and, though Kitty might in time regain her natural[14] degree of sense, since the disturbers of her brain were removed, her other sister, from whose disposition greater evil might be apprehended, was likely to be hardened in all her folly and assurance, by a situation of such double danger as a watering place[15] and a camp.[16] Upon the whole, therefore, she found, what has been sometimes found before, that an event to which she had looked forward with impatient desire, did not in taking place, bring all the satisfaction she had promised herself.[17] It was consequently necessary to name some other period for the commencement of actual felicity; to have some other point on which her wishes and hopes might be fixed, and by again enjoying the pleasure of anticipation, console herself for the present, and prepare for another disappointment. Her tour to the Lakes was now the object of her happiest thoughts; it was her best consolation for all the uncomfortable hours, which the discontentedness of her mother and Kitty made inevitable; and could she have included Jane in the scheme, every part of it would have been perfect.

"But it is fortunate," thought she, "that I have something to wish for. Were the whole arrangement complete, my disappointment would be certain. But here, by carrying with me one ceaseless source of regret in my sister's absence, I may reasonably hope to have all my expectations of pleasure realized. A scheme of which every part promises delight, can never be successful; and general disappointment is only warded off by the defence of some little peculiar vexation."[18]

When Lydia went away, she promised to write very often and very minutely to her mother and Kitty; but her letters were always long expected, and always very short.[19] Those to her mother, contained little else, than that they were just returned from the library, where such and such officers had attended them, and where she

father's marital errors, and before Lydia's elopement provides the strongest demonstration yet of the harmful effects of Mr. Bennet's paternal negligence.

13. *parties abroad:* social gatherings with other families, i.e., those outside the house. "Parties" then meant casual meetings as well as big occasions.

14. *natural:* normal.

15. *watering place:* fashionable spa or seaside resort. Watering places were sometimes criticized for their loose morals and tendency to lead ladies astray.

16. *camp:* military camp.

17. Of course, this is a very frequent occurrence in life; "what has been sometimes found before" is clearly a deliberate understatement. This whole passage has strong echoes of one of Jane Austen's favorite authors, Samuel Johnson, who frequently expounds upon the tendency of human beings to indulge in visions of future felicity and to suffer the disappointment of their hopes, either because their schemes went awry or because even those that succeeded ended up producing less pleasure in reality than in anticipation.

18. What Elizabeth is doing is consoling herself for the absence of Jane by reflecting that, since seemingly perfect schemes (such as a trip including Jane would be) always end in some disappointment, it is better that her trip have one flaw, for then she will not anticipate perfect pleasure and thus may experience the fulfillment rather than the disappointment of her expectations. Her reflection, though it is partly meant in a joking sense, could also be an example of the consolation of a true philosopher just mentioned in relation to Mr. Bennet. In fact, Elizabeth's way of consoling herself is more truly in line with classical philosophical ideals than her father's way, for hers neither involves underlying bitterness nor leads to irresponsible action.

19. This further reveals Lydia's thoughtlessness and selfishness. Postage, which was expensive during this period, was always paid by the recipient, so sending a very short letter would be forcing the recipient to pay much in return for little. The costs would be especially high in this case, for postage rates increased with distance, and Lydia is writing from fairly far away; rates were also higher if a letter had to be delivered to an address off the main routes, as the rural Bennet home certainly would be. In a letter Jane Austen asks pardon for not filling her final sheet of paper, and thus making the recipient pay additional postage without receiving a full page worth of news (Jan. 9, 1799). Lydia does not seem to be one who would ever suffer such pangs of conscience.

had seen such beautiful ornaments as made her quite wild;[20] that she had a new gown, or a new parasol, which she would have described more fully, but was obliged to leave off in a violent hurry, as Mrs. Forster called her, and they were going to the camp;—and from her correspondence with her sister, there was still less to be learnt—for her letters to Kitty, though rather longer, were much too full of lines under the words[21] to be made public.

After the first fortnight or three weeks of her absence, health, good humour and cheerfulness began to re-appear at Longbourn. Everything wore a happier aspect.[22] The families who had been in town for the winter came back again, and summer finery and summer engagements arose.[23] Mrs. Bennet was restored to her usual querulous serenity, and by the middle of June Kitty was so much recovered as to be able to enter Meryton without tears; an event of such happy promise as to make Elizabeth hope, that by the following Christmas, she might be so tolerably reasonable as not to mention an officer above once a day, unless by some cruel and malicious arrangement at the war-office, another regiment should be quartered in Meryton.[24]

The time fixed for the beginning of their Northern tour was now fast approaching; and a fortnight only was wanting of it,[25] when a letter arrived from Mrs. Gardiner, which at once delayed its commencement and curtailed its extent. Mr. Gardiner would be prevented by business from setting out till a fortnight later in July, and must be in London again within a month; and as that left too short a period for them to go so far, and see so much as they had proposed, or at least to see it with the leisure and comfort they had built on,[26] they were obliged to give up the Lakes, and substitute a more contracted tour;[27] and, according to the present plan, were to go no farther northward than Derbyshire.[28] In that county, there was enough to be seen, to occupy the chief of their three weeks; and to Mrs. Gardiner it had a peculiarly[29] strong attraction. The town where she had formerly passed some years of her life, and where they were now to spend a few days, was probably as great an object of her curiosity, as all the celebrated beauties of Matlock, Chatsworth, Dovedale, or the Peak.[30]

20. *wild:* filled with excitement or desire. Libraries often dealt in more than books, and could be places for meeting and socializing; see p. 53, note 20.

21. *lines under the words:* presumably this refers to secrets and special information that Lydia is sharing with Kitty, and that the former is communicating by giving special emphasis to certain words or phrases.

22. *aspect:* appearance.

23. It was normal in this period for the wealthy, after being in London for the winter and spring, to go to the country for the summer. One reason for this annual schedule was that Parliament, which was central to the lives of the leaders of elite society, was usually in session from November to June.

24. This evaluation of troop deployments with no regard to their military utility indicates the limited influence on most people's lives of the existing war, despite its being one of the longest and most trying in Britain's history; Jane Austen's other novels present a similar picture. It is one that contrasts sharply with that of the total wars of the twentieth century. Winston Churchill, who turned to *Pride and Prejudice* for relaxation while leading Britain during World War II, says the book struck him with this very contrast: "What calm lives they had, those people! No worries about the French Revolution, or the crashing struggle of the Napoleonic Wars" (*Closing the Ring,* p. 425).

25. That is, it was only two weeks away.

26. *built on:* relied or depended upon.

27. *contracted tour:* abbreviated tour. Hertfordshire is more than 200 miles from the Lake District (see map, p. 742); actual road distance would be even greater. Under prevailing travel conditions the journey would take several days each way; the mountainous and undeveloped character of the area would also make going from site to site slow, and thus further lengthen the trip.

28. The county of Derbyshire's rugged scenery made it probably the most popular tourist destination in England after the Lakes. It lies only half as far from Hertfordshire as the Lakes (see map, p. 742), and is a more settled area, so a trip there would take considerably less time. Thus Darcy's being from Derbyshire has definite advantages for the story, something Jane Austen undoubtedly had in mind when she made it his home. She herself may have toured Derbyshire when she was staying with cousins who lived nearby.

29. *peculiarly:* particularly.

30. The four principal attractions of northern Derbyshire mentioned by Gilpin (see p. 97, note 48, and p. 285, note 20) in his book on picturesque travel in that part of England. Matlock is a spa and resort area set in a river valley: Jane Austen's brother visited it, and she had characters in "Catharine, or the Bower" plan an excursion there. Chatsworth is the palatial home of

Elizabeth was excessively disappointed; she had set her heart on seeing the Lakes; and still thought there might have been time enough. But it was her business to be satisfied—and certainly her temper[31] to be happy; and all was soon right again.[32]

With the mention of Derbyshire, there were many ideas connected. It was impossible for her to see the word without thinking of Pemberley and its owner. "But surely," said she, "I may enter his county with impunity, and rob it of a few petrified spars[33] without his perceiving me."

The period of expectation was now doubled. Four weeks were to pass away before her uncle and aunt's arrival. But they did pass away, and Mr. and Mrs. Gardiner, with their four children, did at length appear at Longbourn. The children, two girls of six and eight years old, and two younger boys, were to be left under the particular care of their cousin Jane, who was the general favourite, and whose steady sense and sweetness of temper exactly adapted her for attending to them in every way—teaching them, playing with them, and loving them.

The Gardiners staid only one night at Longbourn, and set off the next morning with Elizabeth in pursuit of novelty and amusement. One enjoyment was certain—that of suitableness as companions; a suitableness which comprehended health and temper to bear inconveniences—cheerfulness to enhance every pleasure—and affection and intelligence, which might supply it among themselves if there were disappointments abroad.[34]

It is not the object of this work to give a description of Derbyshire, nor of any of the remarkable places through which their route thither lay; Oxford, Blenheim, Warwick, Kenelworth, Birmingham, &c. are sufficiently known.[35] A small part of Derbyshire is all the present concern. To the little town of Lambton, the scene of Mrs. Gardiner's former residence, and where she had lately learned that some acquaintance still remained, they bent their steps, after having seen all the principal wonders of the country; and within five miles of Lambton, Elizabeth found from her aunt, that Pemberley was situated. It was not in their direct road, nor more than a mile or two out of it. In talking over their

the Dukes of Devonshire. Dovedale is a spectacular river gorge. The Peak, a name sometimes used for the whole area, refers particularly to the rolling hills in northern Derbyshire that are currently part of Peak District National Park. For Derbyshire's position within England, and the location of these sites within it, see the maps on pp. 742 and 744. For a picture of Matlock and Dovedale from Gilpin's book, see p. 435.

31. *temper:* disposition, temperament.

32. This turn of events indicates the wisdom of her earlier reflections on the probability of disappointment; it also shows her ability to console herself.

33. *petrified spars:* pieces of fluorspar (calcium fluoride), a luminous crystalline mineral. Elizabeth would be referring particularly to a variety of fluorspar called Blue John, a purple and white stone that was popular in expensive decorative objects such as vases and urns. It was often known as Derbyshire spar because of the presence of spectacular veins of it in the many caves and mines of Derbyshire; both the spars and the caves themselves, whose convoluted shapes and many tunnels appealed to the increasing love for the mysterious and disordered in nature, were prime attractions of the area. Gilpin, the writer on the picturesque and natural beauty, spoke of the "petrified spars" of Derbyshire. Individual spars, popular as ornaments, were also sold in local stores. In Jane Austen's *Northanger Abbey*, some characters are mentioned as purchasing spars, though since they are not in Derbyshire they could be buying a different variety of spar.

34. Meaning that the affection and intelligence of Elizabeth and the Gardiners would allow them to find pleasure among themselves even if the places they visited proved disappointing or other external problems arose. Abroad refers to what is outside their home or local region.

35. Oxford is one of England's two great universities; Blenheim is the palace of the Dukes of Marlborough; Warwick and Kenelworth are both castles, the latter mostly in ruins; Birmingham is the largest city in the English Midlands, and was becoming a major manufacturing center at the time (its factories were an important tourist attraction). For all their locations, see map on p. 742.

It is perhaps significant that all of these places, as well as one of the attractions mentioned for Derbyshire, are man-made sights, rather than the purely natural ones earlier hoped for by Elizabeth.

route the evening before, Mrs. Gardiner expressed an inclination to see the place again.[36] Mr. Gardiner declared his willingness, and Elizabeth was applied to for her approbation.

"My love, should not you like to see a place of which you have heard so much?" said her aunt. "A place too, with which so many of your acquaintance are connected. Wickham passed all his youth there, you know."

Elizabeth was distressed. She felt that she had no business at Pemberley, and was obliged to assume a disinclination for seeing it. She must own[37] that she was tired of great houses; after going over so many, she really had no pleasure in fine carpets or satin curtains.

Mrs. Gardiner abused her stupidity.[38] "If it were merely a fine house richly furnished," said she, "I should not care about it myself; but the grounds are delightful. They have some of the finest woods in the country."[39]

Elizabeth said no more—but her mind could not acquiesce. The possibility of meeting Mr. Darcy, while viewing the place, instantly occurred.[40] It would be dreadful! She blushed at the very idea; and thought it would be better to speak openly to her aunt, than to run such a risk. But against this, there were objections;[41] and she finally resolved that it could be the last resource, if her private enquiries as to the absence of the family, were unfavourably answered.

Accordingly, when she retired at night, she asked the chambermaid whether Pemberley were not a very fine place, what was the name of its proprietor, and with no little alarm, whether the family were down[42] for the summer. A most welcome negative followed the last question[43]—and her alarms being now removed, she was at leisure to feel a great deal of curiosity to see the house herself; and when the subject was revived the next morning, and she was again applied to, could readily answer, and with a proper air of indifference, that she had not really any dislike to the scheme.[44]

To Pemberley, therefore, they were to go.

36. Elizabeth and the Gardiners are engaging in what had emerged as a popular tourist activity in the late eighteenth century, touring great houses; two places already mentioned in connection with their trip, Chatsworth and Blenheim, were perhaps the most visited of all such houses. The growth of this activity was one part of the general growth of tourism in this period, and country house visiting, like other forms of touring, spawned a whole series of guidebooks to assist the tourist in selecting and appreciating various houses in England. Many homes were open to visitors, and in most cases the visitors simply needed to show up, without any prior appointment. This is why the party here can decide to tour Pemberley at the last minute.

37. *own:* admit.

38. *stupidity:* dullness, lack of interest.

39. *in the country:* in the county. The grounds and gardens of great houses were important attractions for tourists as well as the interiors of the houses.

40. Since servants would normally guide visitors around the house, there was no need for the owner to be present. Some owners did like to be present for visitors, and would even help show them the house; in part this was a legacy of earlier traditions of hospitality that encouraged those who were socially prominent to accommodate guests and visitors in their homes. Many owners, however, preferred to avoid visitors. Some owners, as touring became more popular, even began to complain about the loss of privacy they suffered; this, plus the damage the contents of the house often suffered at the hands of guests, eventually led many places to impose restrictions on visitors, or at least to charge them fees.

41. These objections could be the awkwardness and the difficulties involved in telling Mrs. Gardiner of Darcy's proposal to Elizabeth, and of how wrong Elizabeth had been in her opinions of Darcy and Wickham.

42. *down:* in the country, i.e., out of London. Derbyshire is north of London, but "down" was regularly used to refer to going to places that were regarded as less important; at other points in the novel people are described as going down from London to Hertfordshire (which is north of London), or even going down to cities like Liverpool and Newcastle that are in the north of England.

43. Because a local landowning family held such prestige in the community, and would exercise great influence, socially and economically, through their activities, it would be natural for everyone living near them to know whether they were at home.

44. All developments seem to be conspiring to lead Elizabeth to Pemberley, almost as in a fairy tale.

Chapter One

*E*lizabeth, as they drove along, watched for the first appearance of Pemberley Woods with some perturbation; and
when at length they turned in at the lodge,[2] her spirits were in a
high flutter.

The park was very large, and contained great variety of ground.
They entered it in one of its lowest points, and drove for some
time through a beautiful wood, stretching over a wide extent.[3]

Elizabeth's mind was too full for conversation, but she saw and
admired every remarkable spot and point of view. They gradually
ascended for half a mile, and then found themselves at the top of a
considerable eminence, where the wood ceased, and the eye was
instantly caught by Pemberley House, situated on the opposite
side of a valley, into which the road with some abruptness wound.[4]
It was a large, handsome, stone building,[5] standing well on rising
ground, and backed by a ridge of high woody hills;—and in front,
a stream of some natural importance was swelled into greater,[6] but
without any artificial appearance. Its banks were neither formal,
nor falsely adorned. Elizabeth was delighted. She had never seen
a place for which nature had done more, or where natural beauty
had been so little counteracted by an awkward taste.[7] They were
all of them warm in their admiration; and at that moment she felt,
that to be mistress of Pemberley might be something![8]

They descended the hill, crossed the bridge, and drove to the
door; and, while examining the nearer aspect of the house,[9] all
her apprehensions of meeting its owner returned. She dreaded
lest the chambermaid had been mistaken. On applying to see the
place, they were admitted into the hall; and Elizabeth, as they

1. The third volume (much more than the second volume) begins at an obvious and natural point, for the visit to Pemberley that occurs in its first chapter is the most critical turning point in the second half of the novel.

2. *lodge*: dwelling at the entrance of the park. Also known as the gatehouse, it would be lived in and staffed by a porter, whose job was to control access, especially by carriages, into the park. It was meant to impress visitors as well, and had become more common as visiting grand homes and their grounds became more popular.

3. By the eighteenth century almost all grand homes had large parks around them ("park" meant especially the ground that had been land-scaped); the greater importance of parks was another reason for the increased building of gatehouses to guard entrance into them. The growing emphasis on personal privacy also caused wooded areas around the outer portions of parks to become standard, for this would separate the house and the more open interior sections of the grounds from the outside.

4. For the significance of the abruptness of the grounds, see note 56 on p. 461.

5. Stone had long been the preferred material for grand houses, and was associated with wealth and high status. It was especially likely to be found in houses, like this one, in the north of England because of the widespread availability there of stone suitable for construction.

6. In other words, a stream that was naturally of good size was made grander by being dammed or redirected in some manner. Landscape design-ers of the period often altered streams, for a beautiful body of water within a park was considered essential. In many cases streams were dammed to create a lake, though the lake was made to look as natural as possible.

7. This fulfills the prevailing idea of landscaping, which was to make changes that would supplement or harmonize with the natural features of a place, rather than to override these features by a purely man-made plan (as would be done in a geometric formal garden).

8. The first time Elizabeth has such an idea. Clearly the grandeur and wealth of Pemberley has impressed her, but it is more than that—after all, she already knew of Darcy's wealth. Her reaction comes just after noticing the good taste and attractiveness of Pemberley's grounds, which would be considered a reflection of the owner's character. Many owners of grand homes then were engaged in improving their grounds, but obviously not all improvements would be done with the same intelligence and eye for beauty.

9. That is, examining how the house looked from close range.

waited for the housekeeper, had leisure to wonder at her being where she was.

The housekeeper[10] came; a respectable-looking, elderly woman, much less fine,[11] and more civil, than she had any notion of finding her. They followed her into the dining-parlour. It was a large, well-proportioned room, handsomely fitted up. Elizabeth, after slightly surveying it, went to a window to enjoy its prospect.[12] The hill, crowned with wood, from which they had descended, receiving increased abruptness from the distance, was a beautiful object. Every disposition[13] of the ground was good; and she looked on the whole scene, the river, the trees scattered on its banks, and the winding of the valley, as far as she could trace it, with delight.[14] As they passed into other rooms, these objects were taking different positions; but from every window there were beauties to be seen.[15] The rooms were lofty and handsome, and their furniture[16] suitable to the fortune of their proprietor; but Elizabeth saw, with admiration of his taste, that it was neither gaudy nor uselessly fine; with less of splendor, and more real elegance, than the furniture of Rosings.[17]

"And of this place," thought she, "I might have been mistress! With these rooms I might now have been familiarly acquainted! Instead of viewing them as a stranger, I might have rejoiced in them as my own, and welcomed to them as visitors my uncle and aunt.—But no,"—recollecting herself,—"that could never be: my uncle and aunt would have been lost to me: I should not have been allowed to invite them."[18]

This was a lucky recollection—it saved her from something like regret.[19]

She longed to enquire of the housekeeper, whether her master were really absent, but had not courage for it. At length, however, the question was asked by her uncle; and she turned away with alarm, while Mrs. Reynolds replied, that he was, adding, "but we expect him tomorrow, with a large party of friends." How rejoiced was Elizabeth that their own journey had not by any circumstance been delayed a day!

Her aunt now called her to look at a picture. She approached,

10. *housekeeper:* the chief indoor servant; she would normally lead tours of the house. The standard practice was to offer her a generous tip, which would naturally make her happy to conduct such tours. Such tips were generally the only payment expected of visitors: most houses did not charge admission (and the few that did were criticized for the practice).

11. *less fine:* less showy or fancy in her appearance (i.e., with less finery). This is meant as praise. The housekeeper's lack of show, either in her appearance or her behavior, serves an important function, both in demonstrating that the Darcy family may not be as proud and pretentious as reported and in indicating that the housekeeper's praise of Darcy, seen shortly, does not result simply from pride or pretentiousness on her part.

12. *its prospect:* the view it presented.

13. *disposition:* arrangement, especially with regard to the general design.

14. These descriptions of Pemberley, which will continue through this chapter, constitute the one point in the novel where Jane Austen departs from her usual reluctance to provide detailed descriptions of place. The reason for this departure is that the physical features of Pemberley play a crucial role in the story, both because they illustrate Darcy's character and because Elizabeth's reaction to these features helps change her attitude toward Darcy.

15. Arranging for each side or window of the house to display an attractive prospect or view, both of the immediate grounds and of more distant natural scenes, was one of the main goals of the landscaping improvements of the time. Jane Austen indicates her awareness that this was a recent trend in *Emma*, when she describes a house that, thanks to "all the old neglect of prospect," has scarcely a view of the gardens and meadow and stream that are adjacent to it.

16. *furniture:* furnishings.

17. Thus Darcy contrasts with his aunt. Elizabeth's realization of the differences between the two, differences she had earlier failed to appreciate, will form an important development in the last part of the novel.

18. Because, as people in trade and thus not genteel, they would be ineligible to come as guests.

19. That is, regret at having refused Darcy.

and saw the likeness of Mr. Wickham suspended, amongst several other miniatures, over the mantlepiece. Her aunt asked her, smilingly, how she liked it. The housekeeper came forward, and told them it was the picture of a young gentleman, the son of her late master's steward,[20] who had been brought up by him at his own expence.—"He is now gone into the army," she added, "but I am afraid he has turned out very wild."

Mrs. Gardiner looked at her niece with a smile, but Elizabeth could not return it.

"And that," said Mrs. Reynolds, pointing to another of the miniatures, "is my master—and very like him. It was drawn at the same time as the other—about eight years ago."

"I have heard much of your master's fine person,"[21] said Mrs. Gardiner, looking at the picture; "it is a handsome face. But, Lizzy, you can tell us whether it is like or not."

Mrs. Reynolds's respect for Elizabeth seemed to increase on this intimation of her knowing her master.

"Does that young lady know Mr. Darcy?"

Elizabeth coloured,[22] and said—"A little."

"And do not you think him a very handsome gentleman, Ma'am?"

"Yes, very handsome."

"I am sure *I* know none so handsome; but in the gallery up stairs you will see a finer, larger picture of him than this.[23] This room was my late master's favourite room, and these miniatures are just as they used to be then. He was very fond of them."

This accounted to Elizabeth for Mr. Wickham's being among them.[24]

Mrs. Reynolds then directed their attention to one of Miss Darcy, drawn when she was only eight years old.

"And is Miss Darcy as handsome as her brother?" said Mr. Gardiner.

"Oh! yes—the handsomest young lady that ever was seen; and so accomplished!—She plays and sings all day long. In the next room is a new instrument just come down for her—a present from my master; she comes here to-morrow with him."

20. *steward:* manager of his estates; see p. 151, note 53.

21. *person:* physical person.

22. *coloured:* blushed.

23. A gallery containing family portraits was a standard feature of a grand house. A wealthy family would be able to afford the high cost of commissioning a painted portrait, and each generation's pictures would be preserved.

24. Darcy has preserved Wickham's picture, despite their mutual hatred, out of respect for his father, who was fond of Wickham. Darcy's willingness to do this indicates his lack of the implacable resentment Elizabeth accused him of earlier.

Mr. Gardiner, whose manners were easy[25] and pleasant, encouraged her communicativeness by his questions and remarks; Mrs. Reynolds, either from pride or attachment,[26] had evidently great pleasure in talking of her master and his sister.[27]

"Is your master much at Pemberley in the course of the year?"

"Not so much as I could wish, Sir; but I dare say he may spend half his time here; and Miss Darcy is always down for the summer months."

"Except," thought Elizabeth, "when she goes to Ramsgate."

"If your master would marry, you might see more of him."

"Yes, Sir; but I do not know when *that* will be. I do not know who is good enough for him."

Mr. and Mrs. Gardiner smiled. Elizabeth could not help saying, "It is very much to his credit, I am sure, that you should think so."

"I say no more than the truth, and what every body will say that knows him," replied the other. Elizabeth thought this was going pretty far; and she listened with increasing astonishment as the housekeeper added, "I have never had a cross word from him in my life, and I have known him ever since he was four years old."[28]

This was praise, of all others most extraordinary, most opposite to her ideas. That he was not a good-tempered man, had been her firmest opinion. Her keenest attention was awakened; she longed to hear more, and was grateful to her uncle for saying,

"There are very few people of whom so much can be said. You are lucky in having such a master."

"Yes, Sir, I know I am. If I was to go through the world, I could not meet with a better. But I have always observed, that they who are good-natured when children, are good-natured when they grow up; and he was always the sweetest-tempered, most generous-hearted, boy in the world."[29]

Elizabeth almost stared at her. — "Can this be Mr. Darcy!" thought she.

"His father was an excellent man," said Mrs. Gardiner.

"Yes, Ma'am, that he was indeed; and his son will be just like him—just as affable[30] to the poor."[31]

Elizabeth listened, wondered, doubted, and was impatient for

25. *easy*: relaxed, open.

26. *pride or attachment*: pride in having such a fine master, or genuine attachment to him.

27. Mrs. Reynolds' ease of communication indicates her relative refinement for a servant, as does her mostly correct speech, though her language is still a little less grammatical and more plain than that seen in most other characters. She does not use the colloquial or lower-class expressions that would mark the typical servant (and that Jane Austen shows on a few other occasions in her novels when she presents servants' speech). Since being the chief servant in as large a household as Pemberley would be a job requiring substantial skill, it is possible Mrs. Reynolds came from a higher social class than most servants. Even if she did not, her position as housekeeper would have exposed her greatly to the speech and manners of her employers, which she in turn would have picked up and imitated. This was a common phenomenon with upper servants, especially in large households where the upper servants would tend to be sharply separated, and perhaps even housed apart, from the lower servants. Mrs. Reynolds' separation from ordinary servants would be especially pronounced due to the absence of a mistress at Pemberley, which means she would effectively be running the house.

28. This is presumably an overstatement: it is hard to imagine a child never saying a cross word since the age of four—though he could have said them out of Mrs. Reynolds' hearing. Yet it may be only a slight exaggeration. Darcy, while he can be cold and haughtily silent, and can also be sharp in his replies to others, is never directly insulting (at least to people's faces); his sharp replies usually are made in the form of general statements of opinion rather than direct personal criticisms. Moreover, his reserve, and his strong self-control, would keep him in general from expressing any anger he felt, especially toward a servant, who would be unlikely to say or do anything to provoke strong emotion in him.

29. This description, which goes beyond the preceding statement that he had never uttered a harsh word, does suggest unbalanced partiality. It certainly conflicts with Darcy's own description of himself as a child toward the end of the novel.

30. *affable*: benevolent, accessible.

31. Helping the poor was an important function for one in Darcy's position. The large numbers of people in this society with meager incomes, and the fairly limited means of public support available, meant that the need for such assistance was often great, especially in years of poor harvests.

more. Mrs. Reynolds could interest her on no other point. She related the subject of the pictures, the dimensions of the rooms, and the price of the furniture, in vain. Mr. Gardiner, highly amused by the kind of family prejudice,[32] to which he attributed her excessive commendation of her master, soon led again to the subject; and she dwelt with energy on his many merits, as they proceeded together up the great staircase.[33]

"He is the best landlord, and the best master," said she, "that ever lived. Not like the wild young men now-a-days, who think of nothing but themselves. There is not one of his tenants or servants but what will give him a good name. Some people call him proud; but I am sure I never saw any thing of it. To my fancy,[34] it is only because he does not rattle away like other young men."

"In what an amiable light does this place him!" thought Elizabeth.

"This fine account of him," whispered her aunt, as they walked, "is not quite consistent with his behaviour to our poor friend."[35]

"Perhaps we might be deceived."

"That is not very likely; our authority[36] was too good."

On reaching the spacious lobby[37] above, they were shewn into a very pretty sitting-room, lately fitted up with greater elegance and lightness than the apartments below;[38] and were informed that it was but just done, to give pleasure to Miss Darcy, who had taken a liking to the room, when last at Pemberley.

"He is certainly a good brother," said Elizabeth, as she walked towards one of the windows.

Mrs. Reynolds anticipated Miss Darcy's delight, when she should enter the room. "And this is always the way with him," she added.—"Whatever can give his sister any pleasure, is sure to be done in a moment. There is nothing he would not do for her."

The picture gallery, and two or three of the principal bed-rooms, were all that remained to be shewn. In the former were many good paintings; but Elizabeth knew nothing of the art;[39] and from such as had been already visible below,[40] she had willingly turned to look at some drawings of Miss Darcy's,[41] in crayons, whose subjects were usually more interesting, and also more intelligible.[42]

32. *family prejudice*: the term family could embrace the servants of a household as well. Many servants tended, as Mrs. Reynolds clearly does, to identify strongly with the family that employed them.

33. In the period before the novel was written it became standard for grand houses to have a large, and often elaborate, central staircase.

34. *To my fancy*: from my perspective, judging by my tastes or inclinations.

35. *poor friend*: Wickham.

36. *authority*: source of information.

37. *lobby*: passage, corridor. This refers to an open area at the top of the stairs that gave access to other rooms; it was a typical feature of great houses.

38. This probably means the room has new furniture. Older furniture would frequently be kept, even by wealthy families, which is what has happened in the apartments, or rooms, below. It is the new furniture that gives the sitting room its "greater lightness and elegance:" a basic trend in furniture design over the century, or more, preceding this novel was for pieces to become lighter and thinner, something that was seen as more elegant by those living at this time. For a sample of this furniture, see illustration on p. 457.

39. *art*: art of painting. Elizabeth earlier told Lady Catherine that neither she nor any of her sisters had learned to draw.

40. *visible below*: could be seen elsewhere (and thus do not have to be looked at again by Elizabeth).

41. Her drawing as well as playing music indicates how accomplished she is.

42. The implication of this sentence is that the gallery contained other paintings besides portraits—it would be hard to imagine a portrait being unintelligible. This was not unusual in a gallery then: many wealthy people collected works of art and displayed them in their homes; a fine collection could demonstrate the taste and wealth of the owner. In fact, such galleries formed one of the main attractions for tourists to grand houses, and many accounts of tours mentioned works of great masters that had been seen.

Elizabeth's reactions to the paintings may reflect some of Jane Austen's own sentiments. She only refers occasionally to paintings in her letters and seems to have appreciated painting less than other arts. She also appears to prefer portraits above all other paintings: her main object, in one visit to a public gallery, was to search for portraits that resembled, to her mind, the Elizabeth or Jane of this novel (May 24, 1813).

In the gallery there were many family portraits, but they could have little to fix the attention of a stranger. Elizabeth walked on in quest of the only face whose features would be known to her. At last it arrested her—and she beheld a striking resemblance of Mr. Darcy, with such a smile over the face, as she remembered to have sometimes seen, when he looked at her. She stood several minutes before the picture in earnest contemplation, and returned to it again before they quitted the gallery. Mrs. Reynolds informed them, that it had been taken in his father's life time.

There was certainly at this moment, in Elizabeth's mind, a more gentle sensation towards the original, than she had ever felt in the height of their acquaintance. The commendation bestowed on him by Mrs. Reynolds was of no trifling nature. What praise is more valuable than the praise of an intelligent servant? As a brother, a landlord, a master, she considered how many people's happiness were in his guardianship!—How much of pleasure or pain it was in his power to bestow!—How much of good or evil must be done by him! Every idea that had been brought forward by the housekeeper was favourable to his character, and as she stood before the canvas, on which he was represented, and fixed his eyes upon herself, she thought of his regard[43] with a deeper sentiment of gratitude than it had ever raised before; she remembered its warmth, and softened its impropriety of expression.[44]

When all of the house that was open to general inspection had been seen, they returned down stairs, and taking leave of the housekeeper, were consigned over to the gardener,[45] who met them at the hall door.

As they walked across the lawn towards the river, Elizabeth turned back to look again; her uncle and aunt stopped also, and while the former was conjecturing as to the date of the building, the owner of it himself suddenly came forward from the road, which led behind it to the stables.[46]

They were within twenty yards of each other, and so abrupt was his appearance, that it was impossible to avoid his sight. Their eyes instantly met, and the cheeks of each were overspread with

43. *regard:* look (displayed in his picture), and affection (for her). The double meaning is intentional.

44. *impropriety of expression:* meaning its proud haughtiness.

45. *the gardener:* an upper servant. He helped implement the landscaping improvements that so many landowners pursued, which gave him a high status in the servant hierarchy. The gardener was normally the one to conduct visitors around the grounds, and he also expected to be tipped.

46. The casual nature of Darcy's entrance, one of the most important events in the novel, is remarkable. It occurs with so little fuss or fanfare that it is almost possible for the reader to miss it.

A room with the light furniture of the time. See p. 455, note 38.

[From K. Warren Clouston, *The Chippendale Period in English Furniture* (London, 1897), p. 183]

the deepest blush. He absolutely started, and for a moment seemed immoveable from surprise; but shortly recovering himself, advanced towards the party, and spoke to Elizabeth, if not in terms of perfect composure, at least of perfect civility.

She had instinctively turned away; but, stopping on his approach, received his compliments with an embarrassment impossible to be overcome. Had his first appearance, or his resemblance to the picture they had just been examining, been insufficient to assure the other two that they now saw Mr. Darcy, the gardener's expression of surprise, on beholding his master, must immediately have told it. They stood a little aloof while he was talking to their niece, who, astonished and confused, scarcely dared lift her eyes to his face, and knew not what answer she returned to his civil enquiries after her family. Amazed at the alteration in his manner since they last parted,[47] every sentence that he uttered was increasing her embarrassment; and every idea of the impropriety of her being found there, recurring to her mind, the few minutes in which they continued together, were some of the most uncomfortable of her life. Nor did he seem much more at ease; when he spoke, his accent[48] had none of its usual sedateness;[49] and he repeated his enquiries as to the time of her having left Longbourn, and of her stay in Derbyshire, so often, and in so hurried a way, as plainly spoke[50] the distraction of his thoughts.[51]

At length, every idea seemed to fail him; and, after standing a few moments without saying a word, he suddenly recollected himself, and took leave.

The others then joined her, and expressed their admiration of his figure;[52] but Elizabeth heard not a word, and, wholly engrossed by her own feelings, followed them in silence. She was overpowered by shame and vexation. Her coming there was the most unfortunate, the most ill-judged thing in the world! How strange must it appear to him! In what a disgraceful light might it not strike so vain a man![53] It might seem as if she had purposely thrown herself in his way again! Oh! why did she come? or, why did he thus come a day before he was expected? Had they been only ten minutes sooner, they should have been beyond the reach

47. Of course, Darcy was at his most angry when they last parted, since this occurred just after she had rejected him. Now he has had time to recover from that; moreover, he is on his own grounds, where he is comfortable and where he would be expected to play the host. Additional reasons for his increase in civility will soon become apparent.

48. *accent*: tone of voice.

49. *sedateness*: composure.

50. *spoke*: indicated, revealed.

51. Darcy's distraction, or confusion, suggests the continued strength of his feelings regarding Elizabeth.

52. *figure*: general appearance or form.

53. In other words, so vain a man would be likely to think she came in pursuit of him. Elizabeth has good reason to believe him vain, especially because of the smug confidence he displayed when he proposed to her.

of his discrimination,[54] for it was plain that he was that moment arrived, that moment alighted from his horse[55] or his carriage. She blushed again and again over the perverseness of the meeting. And his behaviour, so strikingly altered,—what could it mean? That he should even speak to her was amazing!—but to speak with such civility, to enquire after her family! Never in her life had she seen his manners so little dignified, never had he spoken with such gentleness as on this unexpected meeting. What a contrast did it offer to his last address in Rosings Park, when he put his letter into her hand! She knew not what to think, nor how to account for it.

They had now entered a beautiful walk by the side of the water, and every step was bringing forward a nobler fall of ground,[56] or a finer reach of the woods to which they were approaching; but it was some time before Elizabeth was sensible[57] of any of it; and, though she answered mechanically to the repeated appeals of her uncle and aunt, and seemed to direct her eyes to such objects as they pointed out, she distinguished no part of the scene. Her thoughts were all fixed on that one spot of Pemberley House, whichever it might be, where Mr. Darcy then was. She longed to know what at that moment was passing in his mind; in what manner he thought of her, and whether, in defiance of every thing, she was still dear to him. Perhaps he had been civil, only because he felt himself at ease; yet there had been *that* in his voice, which was not like ease. Whether he had felt more of pain or of pleasure in seeing her, she could not tell, but he certainly had not seen her with composure.

At length, however, the remarks of her companions on her absence of mind roused her, and she felt the necessity of appearing more like herself.[58]

They entered the woods, and bidding adieu to the river for a while, ascended some of the higher grounds; whence, in spots where the opening of the trees gave the eye power to wander, were many charming views of the valley, the opposite hills, with the long range of woods overspreading many,[59] and occasionally part of the stream. Mr. Gardiner expressed a wish of going round

54. *discrimination:* perception; noticing of them.

55. *horse:* men would sometimes travel from place to place on horseback rather than in a carriage.

56. *nobler fall of ground:* grander slope or change of elevation. Earlier passages describing Pemberley mentioned the abruptness of the landscape and of the view it presented. Abrupt rises or falls of ground were valuable according to prevailing aesthetic standards, which celebrated sharp contrasts and irregular or rough surfaces. It was also standard to design walks around parks and grounds so that people would be able to experience a variety of spectacular or beautiful views as they proceeded along. In this case, Elizabeth's experience of such views is giving her an even stronger sense of the beauties of Pemberley, and thereby adding to her perception of Darcy's good taste and of the desirability of being mistress of the place.

57. *sensible:* aware.

58. Again Elizabeth cannot let her private thoughts prevent her from performing social duties to others, in this case conversation. Moreover, as agitated as she is and as much as she wishes she were not there, the idea never occurs to her of cutting short her aunt and uncle's pleasure by asking that they all leave immediately.

59. These more distant views would still be of objects within the Pemberley grounds or park. Landscaping of the time did not aspire toward providing views of objects beyond the park such as roads or farmhouses.

A park, from a guide to landscape gardening by its leading practitioner in this period, Humphrey Repton (he is discussed in Mansfield Park*). The park embodies the prevailing ideal of sloping terrain (see note 56 above).*

[From Humphrey Repton, *The Art of Landscape Gardening* (Boston, 1907; reprint edition), p. 138.]

the whole Park, but feared it might be beyond a walk. With a triumphant smile, they were told,[60] that it was ten miles round. It settled the matter; and they pursued the accustomed circuit;[61] which brought them again, after some time, in a descent among hanging woods,[62] to the edge of the water, in one of its narrowest parts. They crossed it by a simple bridge, in character with the general air of the scene; it was a spot less adorned than any they had yet visited; and the valley, here contracted into a glen, allowed room only for the stream, and a narrow walk amidst the rough coppice-wood[63] which bordered it. Elizabeth longed to explore its windings;[64] but when they had crossed the bridge, and perceived their distance from the house, Mrs. Gardiner, who was not a great walker, could go no farther, and thought only of returning to the carriage as quickly as possible. Her niece was, therefore, obliged to submit, and they took their way towards the house on the opposite side of the river, in the nearest direction; but their progress was slow, for Mr. Gardiner, though seldom able to indulge the taste, was very fond of fishing, and was so much engaged in watching the occasional appearance of some trout in the water, and talking to the man about them, that he advanced but little.[65] Whilst wandering on in this slow manner, they were again surprised, and Elizabeth's astonishment was quite equal to what it had been at first, by the sight of Mr. Darcy approaching them, and at no great distance. The walk being here less sheltered than on the other side, allowed them to see him before they met. Elizabeth, however astonished, was at least more prepared for an interview than before, and resolved to appear and to speak with calmness, if he really intended to meet them. For a few moments, indeed, she felt that he would probably strike into some other path. This idea lasted while a turning in the walk concealed him from their view; the turning past, he was immediately before them. With a glance she saw, that he had lost none of his recent civility; and, to imitate his politeness, she began, as they met, to admire the beauty of the place; but she had not got beyond the words "delightful," and "charming," when some unlucky recollections obtruded, and she fancied that praise of Pemberley from

60. By the gardener, who would still be guiding them. His "triumphant smile" indicates that, like the housekeeper, he has a strong identification with his employers.

61. *accustomed circuit*: standard path around the grounds. During the eighteenth century the layout of grounds near a house had changed. Instead of, as earlier, having all paths radiate from a central axis (generally the house itself), landscapers moved toward circular layouts that would allow guests and visitors to traverse the entire grounds and to experience its varied beauties. Often there was a long circuit for carriage riders and a short circuit for walkers.

62. *hanging woods*: woods on a steep slope. They were called that because they would hang down. Contemporary advice on landscaping and the picturesque praised effects that could be created by such woods, especially those, such as these, that were next to water.

63. *coppice-wood*: a small woods grown in order to be cut periodically, and thereby furnish wood for fuel or other purposes. Woods and forests were becoming a more prominent feature of the grounds of grand homes during this period; this was partly because of their appeal to current aesthetic tastes, but the economic usefulness of wooded land supplied a further reason.

64. *windings*: winding or meandering paths. Winding paths constituted one of the principal elements of the natural English landscape and garden, which deliberately eschewed all straight lines. The *Encyclopaedia Britannica* of the time, in an article on gardening, states that a walk "ought to be subservient to the natural impediments (the ground, wood, and water) which fall in its way, without appearing to have any direction of its own."

65. Darcy's preservation of his trout stream, instead of making it into an artificial body of water as some landlords did, signals his restraint in his improvements. In *Mansfield Park* Jane Austen satirizes those who become excessive in their mania for improvement.

her, might be mischievously construed.[66] Her colour changed, and she said no more.

Mrs. Gardiner was standing a little behind; and on her pausing, he asked her, if she would do him the honour of introducing him to her friends. This was a stroke of civility for which she was quite unprepared; and she could hardly suppress a smile, at his being now seeking the acquaintance of some of those very people, against whom his pride had revolted, in his offer to herself. "What will be his surprise," thought she, "when he knows who they are! He takes them now for people of fashion."[67]

The introduction, however, was immediately made; and as she named their relationship to herself, she stole a sly[68] look at him, to see how he bore it; and was not without the expectation of his decamping[69] as fast as he could from such disgraceful companions. That he was *surprised* by the connexion[70] was evident; he sustained it however with fortitude,[71] and so far from going away, turned back with them, and entered into conversation with Mr. Gardiner. Elizabeth could not but be pleased, could not but triumph. It was consoling, that he should know she had some relations for whom there was no need to blush. She listened most attentively to all that passed between them, and gloried in every expression, every sentence of her uncle, which marked his intelligence, his taste, or his good manners.[72]

The conversation soon turned upon fishing, and she heard Mr. Darcy invite him, with the greatest civility, to fish there as often as he chose, while he continued in the neighbourhood, offering at the same time to supply him with fishing tackle, and pointing out those parts of the stream where there was usually most sport. Mrs. Gardiner, who was walking arm in arm with Elizabeth, gave her a look expressive of her wonder. Elizabeth said nothing, but it gratified her exceedingly; the compliment must be all for herself. Her astonishment, however, was extreme; and continually was she repeating, "Why is he so altered? From what can it proceed? It cannot be for *me*, it cannot be for *my* sake that his manners are thus softened. My reproofs at Hunsford could not work such a change as this. It is impossible that he should still love me."

66. *mischievously construed*: interpreted in a mischievous or negative way, or as something mischievous. In other words, she fears that Darcy might think she is indicating her interest in Pemberley as part of a scheme to recover the opportunity of becoming its mistress.

67. *fashion*: high social standing.

68. *sly*: secretive, furtive.

69. *decamping*: scurrying away.

70. *connexion*: relationship; in other words, connection to the Gardiners. Darcy already spoke, in his letter to Elizabeth, of his knowing the situation of her mother's family; thus, he is presumably not surprised that she has such an uncle and aunt. His surprise probably stems from his expectation that she, as a person of a higher class than the Gardiners, would not wish for them to be her traveling companions.

71. Meaning that he bore with fortitude having to meet people of lower social position. His reaction foreshadows his eventual acceptance of the rest of Elizabeth's family.

72. This contrasts sharply with Darcy's last encounter with members of Elizabeth's family, at the Ball at Netherfield. The difference results partly from an improvement in him, but it also stems from an improvement in the representatives of Elizabeth's family. In his letter explaining his objections to Bingley's match with Jane, Darcy asserted the Bennet family's improper behavior to be a greater drawback than their lower social connections, and the Gardiners exhibit none of this behavior. Darcy's conduct here also contradicts Elizabeth's earlier reflection that she would have had to renounce the Gardiners if she had accepted Darcy's proposal.

After walking some time in this way, the two ladies in front, the two gentlemen behind, on resuming their places, after descending to the brink of the river for the better inspection of some curious water-plant, there chanced to be a little alteration.[73] It originated in Mrs. Gardiner, who, fatigued by the exercise of the morning, found Elizabeth's arm inadequate to her support, and consequently preferred her husband's. Mr. Darcy took her place by her niece, and they walked on together. After a short silence, the lady first spoke. She wished him to know that she had been assured of his absence before she came to the place, and accordingly began by observing, that his arrival had been very unexpected—"for your housekeeper," she added, "informed us that you would certainly not be here till to-morrow; and indeed, before we left Bakewell,[74] we understood that you were not immediately expected in the country." He acknowledged the truth of it all; and said that business with his steward had occasioned his coming forward a few hours before the rest of the party with whom he had been travelling.[75] "They will join me early to-morrow," he continued, "and among them are some who will claim an acquaintance with you,—Mr. Bingley and his sisters."

Elizabeth answered only by a slight bow. Her thoughts were instantly driven back to the time when Mr. Bingley's name had been last mentioned between them; and if she might judge from his complexion, *his* mind was not very differently engaged.

"There is also one other person in the party," he continued after a pause, "who more particularly wishes to be known to you,—Will you allow me, or do I ask too much, to introduce my sister to your acquaintance during your stay at Lambton?"

The surprise of such an application was great indeed; it was too great for her to know in what manner she acceded to it. She immediately felt that whatever desire Miss Darcy might have of being acquainted with her, must be the work of her brother,[76] and without looking farther, it was satisfactory; it was gratifying to know that his resentment had not made him think really ill of her.

They now walked on in silence; each of them deep in thought. Elizabeth was not comfortable; that was impossible; but she was

73. They had departed from their positions in the walk when they moved toward the river bank; they had initially resumed those positions—the two ladies followed by the two gentlemen—upon returning to the walk, but had then switched to the new arrangement described in the next sentences.

74. *Bakewell:* a historic town in Derbyshire, one also recommended in contemporary travel writings. The sentence implies that it was there that Elizabeth and the Gardiners were staying the previous night, which would mean that Lambton and Pemberley were imagined to be very close to Bakewell (see maps, pp. 742 and 744).

75. This statement indicates how much this crucial meeting depends on coincidence. Had Darcy already been at Pemberley, or been scheduled to arrive this day, Elizabeth and the Gardiners never would have visited. Had Darcy arrived at Pemberley the next day as the visitors were told he would, he could not have encountered Elizabeth. Only the unlikely event of an arrival planned for the following day, but advanced to this day by Darcy without anyone's knowledge, permits the existing sequence of events.

76. Since Darcy showed only limited interest in Elizabeth before the visit to Kent during which he proposed to her, and afterwards had every reason to think he would never see her again, it is unlikely that at any point he would have said much to his sister about Elizabeth.

flattered and pleased. His wish of introducing his sister to her, was a compliment of the highest kind.[77] They soon outstripped the others, and when they had reached the carriage, Mr. and Mrs. Gardiner were half a quarter of a mile behind.

He then asked her to walk into the house—but she declared herself not tired, and they stood together on the lawn. At such a time, much might have been said, and silence was very awkward. She wanted to talk, but there seemed an embargo[78] on every subject. At last she recollected that she had been travelling, and they talked of Matlock and Dove Dale[79] with great perseverance. Yet time and her aunt moved slowly—and her patience and her ideas[80] were nearly worn out before the tete-a-tete was over. On Mr. and Mrs. Gardiner's coming up, they were all pressed to go into the house and take some refreshment; but this was declined, and they parted on each side with the utmost politeness. Mr. Darcy handed the ladies into the carriage, and when it drove off, Elizabeth saw him walking slowly towards the house.

The observations of her uncle and aunt now began; and each of them pronounced him to be infinitely superior to any thing they had expected. "He is perfectly well behaved, polite, and unassuming," said her uncle.

"There *is* something a little stately[81] in him to be sure," replied her aunt, "but it is confined to his air, and is not unbecoming. I can now say with the housekeeper, that though some people may call him proud, *I* have seen nothing of it."

"I was never more surprised than by his behaviour to us. It was more than civil; it was really attentive; and there was no necessity for such attention. His acquaintance with Elizabeth was very trifling."

"To be sure, Lizzy," said her aunt, "he is not so handsome as Wickham; or rather he has not Wickham's countenance,[82] for his features are perfectly good. But how came you to tell us that he was so disagreeable?"

Elizabeth excused herself as well as she could; said that she had liked him better when they met in Kent than before, and that she had never seen him so pleasant as this morning.

77. Girls of Miss Darcy's age and social position were often very sheltered—and Miss Darcy's recent near-elopement with Wickham would give her brother reason to be especially protective of her. In such cases they would normally be introduced only to good friends of the family.

78. *embargo:* prohibition. Since neither of them knows where they stand regarding the other, they find it almost impossible to talk about personal subjects.

79. Tourist sites in Derbyshire; see p. 441, note 30.

80. *ideas:* thoughts (i.e., things to say).

81. *stately:* high, imposing.

82. *countenance:* expression or look. This is a reference to Wickham's friendly manners and demeanor, which make him look more attractive than Darcy even if the physical features of his face are no better.

"But perhaps he may be a little whimsical in his civilities," replied her uncle. "Your great men[83] often are; and therefore I shall not take him at his word about fishing, as he might change his mind another day, and warn me off his grounds."

Elizabeth felt that they had entirely mistaken his character, but said nothing.

"From what we have seen of him," continued Mrs. Gardiner, "I really should not have thought that he could have behaved in so cruel a way by any body, as he has done by poor Wickham. He has not an ill-natured look. On the contrary, there is something pleasing about his mouth when he speaks. And there is something of dignity in his countenance, that would not give one an unfavourable idea of his heart. But to be sure, the good lady who shewed us the house, did give him a most flaming character![84] I could hardly help laughing aloud sometimes. But he is a liberal[85] master, I suppose, and *that* in the eye of a servant comprehends every virtue."[86]

Elizabeth here felt herself called on to say something in vindication of his behaviour to Wickham; and therefore gave them to understand, in as guarded a manner as she could, that by what she had heard from his relations in Kent, his actions were capable of a very different construction;[87] and that his character was by no means so faulty, nor Wickham's so amiable,[88] as they had been considered in Hertfordshire. In confirmation of this, she related the particulars of all the pecuniary transactions in which they had been connected, without actually naming her authority, but stating it to be such as might be relied on.

Mrs. Gardiner was surprised and concerned; but as they were now approaching the scene of her former pleasures,[89] every idea gave way to the charm of recollection; and she was too much engaged in pointing out to her husband all the interesting spots in its environs, to think of any thing else. Fatigued as she had been by the morning's walk, they had no sooner dined than she set off again in quest of her former acquaintance, and the evening was spent in the satisfactions of an intercourse renewed after many years discontinuance.

83. *great men:* men of high social position. Such men's power would give them the opportunity to be whimsical or capricious if they chose, and their power also meant that any such behavior would be noticed by people in general.

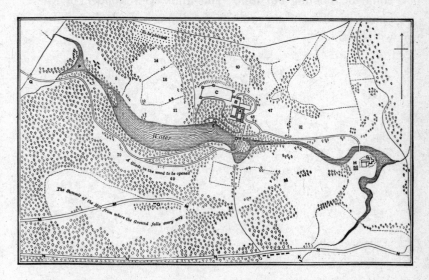

Map of an estate from The Art of Landscape Gardening, *by Humphrey Repton (see caption to illustration on p. 461). The landscape exhibits a number of the features popular at the time, including channeled water, the emphasis on woods, and a summit that is clear to provide a good view.*

[From p. 210]

84. *flaming character:* extravagantly glowing character. In other words, she was wild or extreme in her praise of him. Mrs. Gardiner's statement has an ironic twist, for a character, i.e. a testament of worthiness, was normally what a master gave a servant when the latter was seeking other employment. Here it is the servant who is testifying to the master's good qualities.

85. *liberal:* generous (in a financial sense).

86. In other words, a master's financial generosity is so important to a servant that the latter will consider such a master to be virtuous in every respect.

87. *construction:* explanation, interpretation. In other words, they could be explained very differently.

88. *amiable:* kind, good-natured.

89. Meaning the exact places where she had lived before.

The occurrences of the day were too full of interest to leave Elizabeth much attention for any of these new friends; and she could do nothing but think, and think with wonder, of Mr. Darcy's civility, and above all, of his wishing her to be acquainted with his sister.[90]

90. This would be especially important, since Darcy's wish could indicate that he hopes to continue seeing Elizabeth, whether as friends or as something else.

Chapter Two

*E*lizabeth had settled it that Mr. Darcy would bring his sister to visit her, the very day after her reaching Pemberley; and was consequently resolved not to be out of sight of the inn the whole of that morning. But her conclusion was false; for on the very morning after their own arrival at Lambton, these visitors came.[1] They had been walking about the place with some of their new friends, and were just returned to the inn to dress themselves for dining with the same family, when the sound of a carriage drew them to a window, and they saw a gentleman and lady in a curricle,[2] driving up the street. Elizabeth immediately recognising the livery,[3] guessed what it meant, and imparted no small degree of surprise to her relations, by acquainting them with the honour which she expected. Her uncle and aunt were all amazement; and the embarrassment of her manner as she spoke, joined to the circumstance itself, and many of the circumstances of the preceding day, opened to them a new idea on the business. Nothing had ever suggested it before, but they now felt that there was no other way of accounting for such attentions from such a quarter, than by supposing a partiality for their niece.[4] While these newly-born notions were passing in their heads, the perturbation of Elizabeth's feelings was every moment increasing. She was quite amazed at her own discomposure; but amongst other causes of disquiet, she dreaded lest the partiality of the brother should have said too much in her favour;[5] and more than commonly anxious to please, she naturally suspected that every power of pleasing would fail her.

She retreated from the window, fearful of being seen; and as she walked up and down the room, endeavouring to compose herself, saw such looks of enquiring surprise in her uncle and aunt, as made every thing worse.[6]

Miss Darcy and her brother appeared, and this formidable intro-

1.   Elizabeth and the Gardiners arrived in Lambton, and toured Pemberley, on a Tuesday (see chronology, p. 717 for the reasons for this). Miss Darcy was to arrive the next day, and Elizabeth expected to be visited the day after Miss Darcy's arrival, i.e. Thursday, and thus planned to remain near the inn on that day. But Miss Darcy actually came to visit on the Wednesday, the first day after Elizabeth's arrival.

The significance of this for the story is that Miss Darcy, by coming the day of her own arrival rather than a day later, shows her eagerness, or at least the eagerness of her brother, to call upon Elizabeth.

2.   *curricle*: an open carriage—which makes it good for summer—with two horses. It would closely resemble a gig (see illustration on p. 307).

3.   *livery*: a distinctive uniform or insignia worn by servants that would identify which family they worked for. Thus Darcy and his sister are being driven by a servant.

4.   A partiality, or romantic interest, of Darcy's.

5.   In other words, she feared that Darcy's partiality to her might have made him praise Elizabeth so much to his sister that the latter would be disappointed when she actually met Elizabeth.

6.   Of course, Elizabeth's agitation would only increase their suspicions concerning a romantic attachment.

duction took place. With astonishment did Elizabeth see, that her new acquaintance was at least as much embarrassed as herself. Since her being at Lambton, she had heard that Miss Darcy was exceedingly proud; but the observation of a very few minutes convinced her, that she was only exceedingly shy.[7] She found it difficult to obtain even a word from her beyond a monosyllable.

Miss Darcy was tall, and on a larger scale than Elizabeth; and, though little more than sixteen, her figure was formed, and her appearance womanly and graceful. She was less handsome than her brother, but there was sense and good humour in her face, and her manners were perfectly unassuming and gentle.[8] Elizabeth, who had expected to find in her as acute and unembarrassed an observer as ever Mr. Darcy had been, was much relieved by discerning such different feelings.[9]

They had not been long together, before Darcy told her that Bingley was also coming to wait on her; and she had barely time to express her satisfaction, and prepare for such a visitor, when Bingley's quick step was heard on the stairs, and in a moment he entered the room. All Elizabeth's anger against him had been long done away; but, had she still felt any, it could hardly have stood its ground against the unaffected cordiality[10] with which he expressed himself, on seeing her again. He enquired in a friendly, though general way, after her family, and looked and spoke with the same good-humoured ease that he had ever done.

To Mr. and Mrs. Gardiner he was scarcely a less interesting personage than to herself. They had long wished to see him. The whole party before them, indeed, excited a lively attention. The suspicions which had just arisen of Mr. Darcy and their niece, directed their observation towards each with an earnest, though guarded, enquiry; and they soon drew from those enquiries the full conviction that one of them at least knew what it was to love. Of the lady's sensations they remained a little in doubt; but that the gentleman was overflowing with admiration was evident enough.

Elizabeth, on her side, had much to do. She wanted to ascertain[11] the feelings of each of her visitors, she wanted to compose her own, and to make herself agreeable to all; and in the latter

7.   Miss Darcy's extreme shyness has given rise to the speculation that shyness is also the explanation for Darcy's reserved and haughty behavior. It is true that Darcy is uncomfortable, and less friendly, in the presence of strangers, and that does account for some of his behavior. But he also never exhibits any difficulty in speaking out, often forcefully, when he wishes; he certainly never displays the absolute inability to speak, even when surrounded by friendly people, that his sister shows.

8.   This passage provides the first glimpse of Miss Darcy, a character about whom many things have already been said. Some commentators have wondered why she has not appeared sooner; in particular, she could have accompanied her brother to Netherfield. From the point of view of the plot, her absence from Netherfield has several advantages. Her presence would have made Wickham's lies easier for Elizabeth to detect; it might even have spurred Darcy, in order to protect his sister, to step forward and contradict Wickham's story. In addition, her presence would have revealed a more affectionate and admirable side of Darcy, thus undermining some of the basis for Elizabeth's prejudice against him. Finally, an earlier meeting of Elizabeth and Miss Darcy at Netherfield would prevent Darcy from making the significant gesture of introducing his sister to Elizabeth at this point.

The one question is whether it is realistic for Miss Darcy to have stayed away from Netherfield. On the one hand, her coming to Netherfield might have interrupted her education, something Darcy values highly; while she could have brought her governess with her, she would have been separated from any masters who were instructing her in London. On the other hand, Darcy would have good reasons for bringing his sister with him: his concern for her after her recent near-elopement with Wickham should make him wish to keep her with him as much as possible, while his desire for a marriage between his sister and Bingley should make him wish to bring the two together as much as possible. Therefore, one could argue that this is one of the rare occasions when Jane Austen sacrifices, at least to a small degree, plausibility of behavior to the needs of the plot.

9.   An indication of the difference between Darcy and his sister. He, even when not speaking, could observe others with a sharp and unembarrassed eye; she is clearly too timid for that.

10.   *cordiality*: warmth, affection.

11.   *ascertain*: figure out with certainty.

object, where she feared most to fail, she was most sure of success, for those to whom she endeavoured to give pleasure were prepossessed[12] in her favour. Bingley was ready, Georgiana was eager, and Darcy determined, to be pleased.

In seeing Bingley, her thoughts naturally flew to her sister; and oh! how ardently did she long to know, whether any of his were directed in a like manner. Sometimes she could fancy, that he talked less than on former occasions, and once or twice pleased herself with the notion that as he looked at her, he was trying to trace a resemblance. But, though this might be imaginary, she could not be deceived as to his behaviour to Miss Darcy, who had been set up as a rival of Jane. No look appeared on either side that spoke particular regard.[13] Nothing occurred between them that could justify the hopes of his sister. On this point she was soon satisfied; and two or three little circumstances occurred ere they parted, which, in her anxious interpretation, denoted a recollection of Jane, not untinctured by tenderness, and a wish of saying more that might lead to the mention of her, had he dared. He observed to her, at a moment when the others were talking together, and in a tone which had something of real regret, that it "was a very long time since he had had the pleasure of seeing her;" and, before she could reply, he added, "It is above eight months. We have not met since the 26th of November, when we were all dancing together at Netherfield."[14]

Elizabeth was pleased to find his memory so exact; and he afterwards took occasion to ask her, when unattended to by any of the rest, whether *all* her sisters were at Longbourn. There was not much in the question, nor in the preceding remark, but there was a look and a manner which gave them meaning.

It was not often that she could turn her eyes on Mr. Darcy himself; but, whenever she did catch a glimpse, she saw an expression of general complaisance,[15] and in all that he said, she heard an accent[16] so far removed from hauteur or disdain of his companions, as convinced her that the improvement of manners which she had yesterday witnessed, however temporary its existence might prove, had at least outlived one day. When she saw him thus seeking the acquaintance, and courting the good opinion of people, with

12. *prepossessed*: prejudiced, already inclined.

13. *spoke particular regard*: indicated any particular affection between them.

14. This line helps date this encounter to the beginning of August; for more on the dates, see chronology, p. 717.

15. *complaisance*: obligingness, desire to please.

16. *accent*: tone.

whom any intercourse a few months ago would have been a disgrace; when she saw him thus civil, not only to herself, but to the very relations whom he had openly disdained, and recollected their last lively scene in Hunsford Parsonage, the difference, the change was so great, and struck so forcibly on her mind, that she could hardly restrain her astonishment from being visible. Never, even in the company of his dear friends at Netherfield, or his dignified relations at Rosings, had she seen him so desirous to please, so free from self-consequence,[17] or unbending reserve as now, when no importance[18] could result from the success of his endeavours, and when even the acquaintance of those to whom his attentions were addressed, would draw down the ridicule and censure of the ladies both of Netherfield and Rosings.

Their visitors staid with them above half an hour,[19] and when they arose to depart, Mr. Darcy called on his sister to join him in expressing their wish of seeing Mr. and Mrs. Gardiner, and Miss Bennet, to dinner at Pemberley, before they left the country.[20] Miss Darcy, though with a diffidence which marked her little in the habit of giving invitations, readily obeyed. Mrs. Gardiner looked at her niece, desirous of knowing how *she*, whom the invitation most concerned, felt disposed as to its acceptance, but Elizabeth had turned away her head. Presuming, however, that this studied avoidance spoke rather a momentary embarrassment, than any dislike of the proposal, and seeing in her husband, who was fond of society, a perfect willingness to accept it, she ventured to engage for her attendance, and the day after the next was fixed on.

Bingley expressed great pleasure in the certainty of seeing Elizabeth again, having still a great deal to say to her, and many enquiries to make after all their Hertfordshire friends. Elizabeth, construing all this into a wish of hearing her speak of her sister, was pleased; and on this account, as well as some others, found herself, when their visitors left them, capable of considering the last half hour with some satisfaction, though while it was passing, the enjoyment of it had been little. Eager to be alone, and fearful of enquiries or hints from her uncle and aunt, she staid with them only long enough to hear their favourable opinion of Bingley, and then hurried away to dress.[21]

17. *self-consequence*: self-importance.

18. *no importance*: nothing of consequence, no advantage.

19. This is a long time, for a normal visit of introduction lasted fifteen minutes. The longer time indicates the interest of the visitors in Elizabeth.

20. *country*: area.

21. Elizabeth's silence on this occasion contrasts with her earlier outspokenness in delivering her opinion after first meeting someone. There are various reasons for the contrast, but one is that she has learned to be more careful about pronouncing judgments. This tendency will manifest itself in various ways in the later part of the novel.

But she had no reason to fear Mr. and Mrs. Gardiner's curiosity; it was not their wish to force her communication. It was evident that she was much better acquainted with Mr. Darcy than they had before any idea of; it was evident that he was very much in love with her. They saw much to interest, but nothing to justify enquiry.

Of Mr. Darcy it was now a matter of anxiety to think well; and, as far as their acquaintance reached, there was no fault to find. They could not be untouched by his politeness, and had they drawn his character[22] from their own feelings, and his servant's report, without any reference to any other account, the circle in Hertfordshire to which he was known, would not have recognised it for Mr. Darcy. There was now an interest, however, in believing the housekeeper; and they soon became sensible,[23] that the authority of a servant who had known him since he was four years old, and whose own manners indicated respectability, was not to be hastily rejected. Neither had any thing occurred in the intelligence[24] of their Lambton friends, that could materially lessen its weight. They had nothing to accuse him of but pride; pride he probably had, and if not, it would certainly be imputed by the inhabitants of a small market-town,[25] where the family did not visit.[26] It was acknowledged, however, that he was a liberal man, and did much good among the poor.

With respect to Wickham, the travellers soon found that he was not held there in much estimation; for though the chief[27] of his concerns, with the son of his patron, were imperfectly understood, it was yet a well known fact that, on his quitting Derbyshire, he had left many debts behind him, which Mr. Darcy afterwards discharged.

As for Elizabeth, her thoughts were at Pemberley this evening more than the last; and the evening, though as it passed it seemed long, was not long enough to determine her feelings towards *one* in that mansion; and she lay awake two whole hours, endeavouring to make them out. She certainly did not hate him. No; hatred had vanished long ago, and she had almost as long been ashamed of ever feeling a dislike against him, that could be so called. The respect created by the conviction of his valuable qualities, though at first unwillingly admitted, had for some time ceased to be

22. *drawn his character:* developed or established their opinion of him.

23. *sensible:* conscious, aware.

24. *intelligence:* communication of information.

25. *market-town:* a town in a rural locale whose main function was to provide shopping and trade for the surrounding area.

26. *visit:* maintain social or friendly intercourse with the inhabitants. The Darcy family likely remained apart because a market town, which would mostly be inhabited by the families of merchants or artisans or manual laborers, would contain few if any people of the Darcy family's social level. Such avoidance of the people of the town could cause resentment and lead to accusations of pride.

27. *chief:* greater part.

repugnant to her feelings;[28] and it was now heightened into somewhat of a friendlier nature, by the testimony so highly in his favour,
and bringing forward his disposition in so amiable a light, which
yesterday had produced. But above all, above respect and esteem,
there was a motive within her of good will which could not be overlooked. It was gratitude.[29]—Gratitude, not merely for having once
loved her, but for loving her still well enough, to forgive all the
petulance and acrimony of her manner in rejecting him, and all
the unjust accusations accompanying her rejection. He who, she
had been persuaded, would avoid her as his greatest enemy,
seemed, on this accidental meeting, most eager to preserve the
acquaintance, and without any indelicate display of regard, or any
peculiarity of manner,[30] where their two selves only were concerned, was soliciting the good opinion of her friends, and bent on
making her known to his sister. Such a change in a man of so much
pride, excited not only astonishment but gratitude[31]—for to love,
ardent love, it must be attributed; and as such its impression on her
was of a sort to be encouraged, as by no means unpleasing, though
it could not be exactly defined. She respected, she esteemed, she
was grateful to him, she felt a real interest in his welfare; and she
only wanted to know how far she wished that welfare to depend
upon herself,[32] and how far it would be for the happiness of both
that she should employ the power, which her fancy told her she
still possessed, of bringing on the renewal of his addresses.[33]

It had been settled in the evening, between the aunt and niece,
that such a striking civility as Miss Darcy's, in coming to them on
the very day of her arrival at Pemberley, for she had reached it
only to a late breakfast,[34] ought to be imitated, though it could
not be equalled, by some exertion of politeness on their side; and,
consequently, that it would be highly expedient to wait on her at
Pemberley the following morning. They were, therefore, to go.—
Elizabeth was pleased, though, when she asked herself the reason, she had very little to say in reply.

Mr. Gardiner left them soon after breakfast. The fishing scheme
had been renewed the day before, and a positive engagement made
of his meeting some of the gentlemen at Pemberley by noon.

28. A reference to the time when, because of her partiality for Wickham and her belief in the correctness of her judgment regarding Darcy, she found admitting him to have good qualities to be repugnant.

29. This passage, in detailing the step by step development of Elizabeth's feelings toward Darcy, reveals how precise Jane Austen is in presenting the emotional evolution of the heroine. Elizabeth has not reached love yet, but she has already taken a number of steps in that direction. This picture of love developing gradually, and being influenced by such factors as gratitude or esteem, corresponds to the author's generally realistic and down-to-earth view of love (see especially p. 37, note 8).

30. *peculiarity of manner*: special or particular attention to Elizabeth (to the exclusion of others). This would be considered impolite, even among those in love.

31. In other words, she was especially gratified because she knew that someone so proud would have a harder time overcoming his resentment at being rejected.

32. A reference to a renewed proposal by him, which of course would make his welfare depend very much on her reaction.

33. *addresses*: courtship attempts or proposals.

34. Since breakfast normally did not take place until around ten (and sometimes after that for those who followed the fashionable trend of later hours), a late breakfast would probably be near mid-day.

Chapter Three

Convinced as Elizabeth now was that Miss Bingley's dislike of her had originated in jealousy,[1] she could not help feeling how very unwelcome her appearance at Pemberley must be to her, and was curious to know with how much civility on that lady's side, the acquaintance would now be renewed.

On reaching the house, they were shewn through the hall into the saloon,[2] whose northern aspect[3] rendered it delightful for summer. Its windows opening to the ground, admitted a most refreshing view of the high woody hills behind the house, and of the beautiful oaks and Spanish chesnuts which were scattered over the intermediate lawn.[4]

In this room they were received by Miss Darcy, who was sitting there with Mrs. Hurst and Miss Bingley, and the lady with whom she lived in London.[5] Georgiana's reception of them was very civil; but attended with all that embarrassment which, though proceeding from shyness and the fear of doing wrong, would easily give to those who felt themselves inferior, the belief of her being proud and reserved.[6] Mrs. Gardiner and her niece, however, did her justice, and pitied her.

By Mrs. Hurst and Miss Bingley, they were noticed only by a curtsey; and on their being seated, a pause, awkward as such pauses must always be, succeeded for a few moments. It was first broken by Mrs. Annesley,[7] a genteel, agreeable-looking woman, whose endeavour to introduce some kind of discourse, proved her to be more truly well bred[8] than either of the others; and between her and Mrs. Gardiner, with occasional help from Elizabeth, the conversation was carried on. Miss Darcy looked as if she wished for courage enough to join in it; and sometimes did venture a short sentence, when there was least danger of its being heard.

Elizabeth soon saw that she was herself closely watched by

1. It was made apparent to the reader early on that Miss Bingley's dislike of Elizabeth stemmed from jealousy; Elizabeth, however, had not perceived Darcy's interest in her when they were at Netherfield, and thus she ascribed Miss Bingley's dislike to general unfriendliness or snobbery.

2. *saloon:* a large room, which could serve various purposes depending on the house. It was often used to receive guests.

3. *northern aspect:* position facing north.

4. Hence Pemberley has, at least on this side, only a lawn and trees adjacent to it, rather than a garden. This is in line with prevailing ideas of landscaping, which condemned having a formal garden next to the house. A principal reason was that such a garden was believed to interfere with the view out the house windows; owners of grand houses were in fact most likely to retain gardens created by earlier generations if the gardens were off to the side and thus did not interfere with the view.

5. Their party is thus all-female; the men are outside engaging in sport. In the second half of the nineteenth century ladies would begin to participate widely in sports, but at this time walking and perhaps horseback-riding were the only standard outdoor activities for women of this class.

6. *reserved:* uncommunicative, unfriendly. The word had a stronger negative connotation then than now.

7. *Mrs. Annesley:* the lady just mentioned who lives with Georgiana. She would have replaced the woman who tried to help Wickham elope with Georgiana.

8. *well bred:* polite. "Well bred" has a particular significance here, for the term's origin lay in the idea that being bred properly, or coming from the right background, was the key to politeness. In this case, Mrs. Annesley, though less well bred than Miss Bingley and Mrs. Hurst in terms of her background or social origin, is more well bred when judged by her behavior.

Miss Bingley, and that she could not speak a word, especially to Miss Darcy, without calling her attention. This observation would not have prevented her from trying to talk to the latter, had they not been seated at an inconvenient distance; but she was not sorry to be spared the necessity of saying much. Her own thoughts were employing her. She expected every moment that some of the gentlemen would enter the room. She wished, she feared that the master of the house might be amongst them; and whether she wished or feared it most, she could scarcely determine. After sitting in this manner a quarter of an hour, without hearing Miss Bingley's voice, Elizabeth was roused by receiving from her a cold enquiry after the health of her family. She answered with equal indifference and brevity, and the other said no more.

The next variation which their visit afforded was produced by the entrance of servants with cold meat, cake, and a variety of all the finest fruits in season;[9] but this did not take place till after many a significant look and smile from Mrs. Annesley to Miss Darcy had been given, to remind her of her post.[10] There was now employment for the whole party; for though they could not all talk, they could all eat; and the beautiful pyramids of grapes, nectarines, and peaches,[11] soon collected them round the table.

While thus engaged, Elizabeth had a fair opportunity of deciding whether she most feared or wished for the appearance of Mr. Darcy, by the feelings which prevailed on his entering the room; and then, though but a moment before she had believed her wishes to predominate, she began to regret that he came.

He had been some time with Mr. Gardiner, who, with two or three other gentlemen from the house, was engaged by the river, and had left him only on learning that the ladies of the family intended a visit to Georgiana that morning. No sooner did he appear, than Elizabeth wisely resolved to be perfectly easy and unembarrassed;—a resolution the more necessary to be made, but perhaps not the more easily kept, because she saw that the suspicions of the whole party were awakened against them,[12] and that there was scarcely an eye which did not watch his behaviour when he first came into the room. In no countenance was attentive

9.   Some kind of snack or light meal during the day was normal at the time because of the long interval between breakfast and dinner.

10.   *her post:* her position or duty as hostess.

11.   The presence of these fruits, which would have almost certainly been grown on Darcy's estate, indicates his wealth. All three fruits, which had become more popular over the eighteenth century, tended to be grown by the wealthy, for they do best in warmer climates and thus in Britain they generally need to be grown under glass or next to heated walls, which adds to the cost of their cultivation. That Darcy used such methods is further indicated by having these fruits be in season (i.e., in prime eating condition) at a time of year, the beginning of August, before they would have attained this state naturally (according to an authority of the time on the normal growing season of the varieties cultivated then). Artificial heat would be essential to making the fruit ripen earlier. Improved methods of fruit cultivation, like other agricultural innovations, were pursued by many landowners during this period.

12.   In other words, because everyone was watching to see what happened between Darcy and Elizabeth, it was even more essential for Elizabeth to remain calm; yet that same universal curiosity made calmness more difficult for her.

curiosity so strongly marked as in Miss Bingley's, in spite of the smiles which overspread her face whenever she spoke to one of its objects;[13] for jealousy had not yet made her desperate, and her attentions to Mr. Darcy were by no means over. Miss Darcy, on her brother's entrance, exerted herself much more to talk; and Elizabeth saw that he was anxious for his sister and herself to get acquainted, and forwarded, as much as possible, every attempt at conversation on either side. Miss Bingley saw all this likewise; and, in the imprudence of anger, took the first opportunity of saying, with sneering civility,

"Pray, Miss Eliza, are not the —— shire militia removed from Meryton? They must be a great loss to *your* family."

In Darcy's presence she dared not mention Wickham's name; but Elizabeth instantly comprehended that he was uppermost in her thoughts; and the various recollections connected with him gave her a moment's distress; but, exerting herself vigorously to repel the ill-natured attack, she presently answered the question in a tolerably disengaged tone. While she spoke, an involuntary glance shewed her Darcy with an heightened complexion,[14] earnestly looking at her, and his sister overcome with confusion, and unable to lift up her eyes.[15] Had Miss Bingley known what pain she was then giving her beloved friend,[16] she undoubtedly would have refrained from the hint; but she had merely intended to discompose Elizabeth, by bringing forward the idea of a man to whom she believed her partial, to make her betray a sensibility[17] which might injure her in Darcy's opinion, and perhaps to remind the latter of all the follies and absurdities, by which some part of her family were connected with that corps. Not a syllable had ever reached her of Miss Darcy's meditated elopement. To no creature had it been revealed, where secrecy was possible, except to Elizabeth; and from all Bingley's connections her brother was particularly anxious to conceal it, from that very wish which Elizabeth had long ago attributed to him, of their becoming hereafter her own.[18] He had certainly formed such a plan, and without meaning that it should affect his endeavour to separate him from Miss Bennet, it is probable that it might add something to his lively concern for the welfare of his friend.[19]

13. *objects:* objects of her curiosity, i.e., Darcy and Elizabeth. Miss Bingley is interested in both, but she only smiles when speaking to one of the objects, Darcy.

14. Darcy's agitation shows why Miss Bingley's attack on Elizabeth was imprudent, for she can never hope to win Darcy's favor by bringing up the subject of Wickham in conversation.

15. Such an allusion to Wickham would naturally discompose Miss Darcy.

16. *beloved friend:* a sarcastic reference to Miss Bingley's professions of extravagant affection for Miss Darcy, seen both in earlier conversations and in her letters to Jane. Despite these professions, Miss Bingley seems to pay no attention to Miss Darcy throughout this scene, the only time the two are together in the novel.

17. *sensibility:* consciousness, awareness.

18. That is, Darcy has wished for his sister to marry Bingley, which would make the latter's connections also her connections, and this wish has made him particularly anxious to keep Bingley and his family from knowing of Miss Darcy's near-elopement with Wickham, for such an act could discredit her in Bingley's eyes.

19. In other words, Darcy's strong concern for Bingley's welfare, i.e., his separation of Bingley from Jane, was probably influenced by his hope for a marriage between Bingley and his sister. Thus Darcy's motives in this action were not quite as disinterested as he avowed; furthermore, by refusing ever to admit to such an interested motive, Darcy reveals that even his genuinely strict honesty has its limits.

Elizabeth's collected behaviour, however, soon quieted his emotion;[20] and as Miss Bingley, vexed and disappointed,[21] dared not approach nearer to Wickham, Georgiana also recovered in time, though not enough to be able to speak any more. Her brother, whose eye she feared to meet, scarcely recollected her interest in the affair,[22] and the very circumstance which had been designed to turn his thoughts from Elizabeth, seemed to have fixed them on her more, and more cheerfully.

Their visit did not continue long after the question and answer above-mentioned; and while Mr. Darcy was attending them to their carriage, Miss Bingley was venting her feelings in criticisms on Elizabeth's person, behaviour, and dress. But Georgiana would not join her. Her brother's recommendation was enough to ensure her favour: his judgment could not err, and he had spoken in such terms of Elizabeth, as to leave Georgiana without the power of finding her otherwise than lovely and amiable. When Darcy returned to the saloon, Miss Bingley could not help repeating to him some part of what she had been saying to his sister.

"How very ill Eliza Bennet looks this morning, Mr. Darcy," she cried; "I never in my life saw any one so much altered as she is since the winter. She is grown so brown and coarse! Louisa and I were agreeing that we should not have known her again."

However little Mr. Darcy might have liked such an address, he contented himself with coolly replying, that he perceived no other alteration than her being rather tanned,[23] — no miraculous consequence of travelling in the summer.

"For my own part," she rejoined, "I must confess that I never could see any beauty in her. Her face is too thin; her complexion has no brilliancy;[24] and her features are not at all handsome. Her nose wants[25] character; there is nothing marked in its lines. Her teeth are tolerable, but not out of the common way;[26] and as for her eyes, which have sometimes been called so fine, I never could perceive any thing extraordinary in them. They have a sharp, shrewish look, which I do not like at all; and in her air altogether, there is a self-sufficiency[27] without fashion, which is intolerable."

20. *emotion*: agitation, disturbance of mind.

21. Disappointed that she was not able to discompose or embarrass Elizabeth.

22. A curious statement, for it implies that Georgiana's brother, i.e Darcy, scarcely remembered her affair with Wickham, which other incidents show to be untrue. What seems to be meant is that Darcy does not recall his sister's affair at this moment since his thoughts are so completely turned toward Elizabeth, who of course has her own link with Wickham.

23. At this time, being tanned was considered highly unattractive. The ideal was to have as white a skin as possible, which is why Miss Bingley is so eager to call Elizabeth brown.

24. *brilliancy*: luster.

25. *wants*: lacks.

26. Evaluating someone's teeth as part of a judgment of appearance was normal at this time, for the absence of good dentistry, not to mention orthodontics, meant that a wide variation existed in the quality of people's teeth.

27. *self-sufficiency*: self-confidence or a high opinion of oneself—the term could have pejorative connotations then. Miss Bingley's charge is that Elizabeth has this high opinion of herself even though, not being a person of fashion or having fashionable manners, she has no basis for such an opinion.

Persuaded as Miss Bingley was that Darcy admired Elizabeth, this was not the best method of recommending herself; but angry people are not always wise; and in seeing him at last look somewhat nettled, she had all the success she expected. He was resolutely silent however; and, from a determination of making him speak, she continued,

"I remember, when we first knew her in Hertfordshire, how amazed we all were to find that she was a reputed beauty; and I particularly recollect your saying one night, after they had been dining at Netherfield, '*She* a beauty!—I should as soon call her mother a wit.'[28] But afterwards she seemed to improve on you, and I believe you thought her rather pretty at one time."

"Yes," replied Darcy, who could contain himself no longer, "but *that* was only when I first knew her, for it is many months since I have considered her as[29] one of the handsomest[30] women of my acquaintance."[31]

He then went away, and Miss Bingley was left to all the satisfaction of having forced him to say what gave no one any pain but herself.

Mrs. Gardiner and Elizabeth talked of all that had occurred, during their visit, as they returned, except what had particularly interested them both. The looks and behaviour of every body they had seen were discussed, except of the person who had mostly engaged their attention. They talked of his sister, his friends, his house, his fruit, of every thing but himself; yet Elizabeth was longing to know what Mrs. Gardiner thought of him, and Mrs. Gardiner would have been highly gratified by her niece's beginning the subject.[32]

28. Miss Bingley refers to an episode, when the Bennets apparently dined at Netherfield, that was not presented earlier in the novel. There is a reference to it, however, when Elizabeth says to Charlotte (on p. 38) that Jane has "dined in company with him [Bingley] four times." Presumably one of those times was at Netherfield; the words "in company" imply that the dinner included other guests besides the Bennets. Just after that Darcy is said, during this same period, to have "made it clear to himself and his friends that she [Elizabeth] had hardly a good feature in her face." The statement that Miss Bingley cites was undoubtedly part of the critical verdict he was rendering at that point. Miss Bingley would not be referring to the time when Jane and Elizabeth were staying at Netherfield, for by then Darcy was praising the latter's fine eyes.

29. *it is many months since I have considered her as:* I have considered her for many months to be.

30. *handsomest:* most attractive. The term "handsome" was used regularly to describe women then, and had no masculine connotation.

31. Darcy's praise of Elizabeth comes at a particularly appropriate point: it forms a fitting coda to a set of chapters in which his and Elizabeth's relationship has advanced significantly; in addition, by coming just before a new plot development that will temporarily overshadow their romance and threaten to derail it, his praise of Elizabeth encourages the reader to trust that eventually their romance will return to the fore and will triumph.

32. Elizabeth and Mrs. Gardiner's reticence, which continues during their time together, plays an important role later, for it allows Mrs. Gardiner to suppose more than exists between Elizabeth and Darcy, which in turn makes her more willing to accept his interference in a family matter (see p. 582, and p. 583, note 4).

Chapter Four

*E*lizabeth had been a good deal disappointed in not finding a
letter from Jane, on their first arrival at Lambton;[1] and this
disappointment had been renewed on each of the mornings that
had now been spent there; but on the third, her repining was
over, and her sister justified by the receipt of two letters from her
at once, on one of which was marked that it had been missent
elsewhere. Elizabeth was not surprised at it, as Jane had written
the direction[2] remarkably ill.[3]

They had just been preparing to walk as the letters came in;
and her uncle and aunt, leaving her to enjoy them in quiet, set off
by themselves. The one missent must be first attended to; it had
been written five days ago.[4] The beginning contained an account
of all their little parties and engagements, with such news as the
country afforded;[5] but the latter half, which was dated a day later,
and written in evident agitation, gave more important intelligence.[6] It was to this effect:

*Since writing the above, dearest Lizzy, something has occurred
of a most unexpected and serious nature; but I am afraid of alarming you—be assured that we are all well. What I have to say relates
to poor Lydia. An express[7] came at twelve last night, just as we were
all gone to bed, from Colonel Forster, to inform us that she was
gone off to Scotland with one of his officers;[8] to own the truth, with
Wickham!—Imagine our surprise. To Kitty, however, it does not
seem so wholly unexpected.[9] I am very, very sorry. So imprudent a
match on both sides!—But I am willing to hope the best, and that
his character has been misunderstood. Thoughtless and indiscreet I
can easily believe him, but this step (and let us rejoice over it)[10]
marks nothing bad at heart.[11] His choice is disinterested at least,
for he must know my father can give her nothing.[12] Our poor*

1. Her expectation of a letter indicates they must have had a fixed itinerary, at least for the last part of the trip where they were visiting Mrs. Gardiner's former residence; this would allow others to know where to send the letters.

2. *direction:* address.

3. Jane's bad writing would be explained by agitation, the reason for which shortly becomes apparent. This delay in the letter is another of the accidents that assist the story. Had the first letter arrived earlier, Elizabeth and the Gardiners would have had to leave the area before seeing Darcy, or after seeing him only briefly. Had only the first letter, with its more limited news, come at this point, Elizabeth would not have been as shocked by what she read, and thus not as likely to reveal her distress to Darcy.

The arrival of the two letters together also adds to the drama of the moment, and marks a more thorough transition to a new section of the novel, in which the relationship of Elizabeth and Darcy again leaves center stage.

4. For the correspondence between the days and events mentioned in Jane's letters, and those in Elizabeth's visit to Pemberley and Lambton, see chronology, pp. 717–718.

5. A large proportion of Jane Austen's own surviving letters contain just such a record of ordinary events in the country.

6. *intelligence:* information, news.

7. *express:* express message conveyed by a special messenger (someone hired just to carry this message), or the messenger himself.

8. This would be to marry, since only in Scotland could someone under 21 marry without parental consent.

9. The underlined words that were mentioned earlier as part of the letters of Lydia to Kitty suggest that the two shared many secrets (see p. 440).

10. Jane presumably means they should rejoice because it is their sister's marriage, and there is no use lamenting what cannot be prevented now.

11. It indicates nothing bad at heart because marriage, even an imprudent one, is an honorable course of action. Jane, as always, attempts to place the most favorable interpretation on everything; this is something she will find especially difficult to do in the case of Wickham and Lydia.

12. Since Lydia has almost no dowry, and Mr. Bennet is in no position to add to it, Wickham's choice of her does not stem from monetary interest.

mother is sadly grieved. My father bears it better. How thankful am I, that we never let them know what has been said against him; we must forget it ourselves. They were off Saturday night about twelve, as is conjectured, but were not missed till yesterday morning at eight. The express was sent off directly.[13] *My dear Lizzy, they must have passed within ten miles of us.*[14] *Colonel Forster gives us reason to expect him here soon. Lydia left a few lines for his wife, informing her of their intention. I must conclude, for I cannot be long from my poor mother. I am afraid you will not be able to make it out, but I hardly know what I have written.*[15]

Without allowing herself time for consideration, and scarcely knowing what she felt, Elizabeth on finishing this letter, instantly seized the other, and opening it with the utmost impatience, read as follows: it had been written a day later than the conclusion of the first.

By this time, my dearest sister, you have received my hurried letter; I wish this may be more intelligible, but though not confined[16] *for time, my head is so bewildered that I cannot answer for being coherent.*[17] *Dearest Lizzy, I hardly know what I would write, but I have bad news for you, and it cannot be delayed. Imprudent as a marriage between Mr. Wickham and our poor Lydia would be, we are now anxious to be assured it has taken place, for there is but too much reason to fear they are not gone to Scotland. Colonel Forster came yesterday, having left Brighton the day before, not many hours after the express. Though Lydia's short letter to Mrs. F. gave them to understand that they were going to Gretna Green,*[18] *something was dropped by Denny expressing his belief that W. never intended to go there, or to marry Lydia at all, which was repeated to Colonel F. who instantly taking the alarm, set off from B.*[19] *intending to trace their route. He did trace them easily to Clapham,*[20] *but no farther; for on entering that place they removed into a hackney-coach*[21] *and dismissed the chaise that brought them from Epsom.*[22] *All that is known after this is, that they were seen to continue the London road.*[23] *I know not what to think. After making every possible*

13. *directly*: immediately.

14. Hertfordshire is just north of London, so the road to Scotland would pass through it; one of the towns mentioned below, Hatfield, is in Hertfordshire.

15. Wickham and Lydia's elopement is the most dramatic, if not melodramatic, episode in the novel. Many have questioned its appropriateness, for in many ways it has greater affinities with the romances Jane Austen satirizes than with the social comedy and realism of her works—this may be one reason why she does not present the elopement directly, but has it be referred to and summarized by others. It is also not strictly required for the plot, for Darcy and Elizabeth are already moving toward reconciliation and love without it.

The episode does, however, aid that reconciliation ultimately, and it allows for a further demonstration of Darcy's good qualities and devotion to Elizabeth. In addition, it helps underline some important themes of the novel, in particular by revealing even more the error of Elizabeth's judgment of Wickham, and by providing an example of a bad love and marriage that contrasts with the better ones that conclude the story. Finally, while the episode has its melodramatic aspects, it has been carefully prepared by what has already been shown of the characters of Wickham and Lydia.

16. *confined*: pressed.

17. *answer for being coherent*: guarantee that I will be coherent.

18. *Gretna Green*: the Scottish town that was the first encountered after crossing the border with England on the main road (see map, p. 742). It was where English people wishing to marry in Scotland normally went, and it built up a substantial business in such marriages. In a novel Jane Austen knew extremely well, Fanny Burney's *Camilla*, the sister of the heroine elopes with an unscrupulous fortune hunter and marries him in Gretna Green.

19. *B.*: Brighton. The frequent use in this letter of capital letters to stand for persons and places is something also found in Jane Austen's correspondence.

20. *Clapham*: a south London neighborhood; hence their last stop before reaching the main part of London.

21. *hackney-coach*: a hired coach, similar to a cab, for transport around town. Their switching to it, away from the chaise that was being used for intercity transport, indicates an intention to stay in London.

22. *Epsom*: a town between Brighton and London. See map, p. 745.

23. *London road*: road into London.

enquiry on that side London,[24] Colonel F. came on into Hertford-shire, anxiously renewing them at all the turnpikes,[25] and at the inns in Barnet and Hatfield,[26] but without any success, no such people had been seen to pass through. With the kindest concern he came on to Longbourn, and broke his apprehensions to us in a manner most creditable to his heart. I am sincerely grieved for him and Mrs. F. but no one can throw any blame on them.[27] Our dis-tress, my dear Lizzy, is very great. My father and mother believe the worst, but I cannot think so ill of him. Many circumstances might make it more eligible[28] for them to be married privately in town[29] than to pursue their first plan; and even if he could form such a design against a young woman of Lydia's connections, which is not likely, can I suppose her so lost to every thing? — Impossible. I grieve to find, however, that Colonel F. is not disposed to depend upon their marriage; he shook his head when I expressed my hopes, and said he feared W. was not a man to be trusted. My poor mother is really ill and keeps[30] her room. Could she exert herself it would be better, but this is not to be expected; and as to my father,[31] I never in my life saw him so affected.[32] Poor Kitty has anger[33] for having concealed their attachment; but as it was a matter of confi-dence one cannot wonder. I am truly glad, dearest Lizzy, that you have been spared something of these distressing scenes; but now as the first shock is over, shall I own[34] that I long for your return? I am not so selfish, however, as to press for it, if inconvenient. Adieu. I take up my pen again to do, what I have just told you I would not, but circumstances are such, that I cannot help earnestly begging you all to come here, as soon as possible. I know my dear uncle and aunt so well, that I am not afraid of requesting it, though I have still something more to ask of the former. My father is going to Lon-don with Colonel Forster instantly, to try to discover her. What he means to do, I am sure I know not; but his excessive distress will not allow him to pursue any measure in the best and safest way, and Colonel Forster is obliged to be at Brighton again tomorrow eve-ning. In such an exigence[35] my uncle's advice and assistance would be every thing in the world; he will immediately comprehend what I must feel, and I rely upon his goodness.

24. *side London:* side of London, i.e., southern London.

25. *turnpikes:* barriers where people using a road would have to stop and pay tolls. To improve its long-distance roads the English government had granted authority to turnpike trusts, private enterprises that built new roads and then garnered the income generated by tolls on travelers.

26. *Barnet and Hatfield:* towns north of London (see map, p. 745). Inns are where travelers would stop to change horses, as well as to eat or refresh themselves. If Wickham and Lydia were continuing north to Scotland they could have been seen at one of these stops, or by a toll collector at a turnpike.

27. In fact, most people would blame them, since, as the hosts of a young unmarried girl, they had a strict responsibility to supervise her.

28. *eligible:* desirable, suitable.

29. *married privately in town:* married secretly in London; this was another way of marrying without parental consent. It involved the use of the banns, which were public notices of an impending marriage announced on three successive Sundays in church. If no one stepped forward to show legal reasons for stopping the marriage, it could then take place. Because of the enormous growth of population in London and other cities, and the Church of England's failure to increase the number of churches and clergy serving this population, many urban clergy had extremely large parishes and thus far too many marriages on their hands to verify whether each couple requesting marriage really fulfilled the legal requirements of age and residency. Furthermore, if the couple were from outside the city their families were unlikely to hear of the marriage in time to step forward and prevent it.

30. *keeps:* keeps to, remains in.

31. *my father:* this phrase and its equivalents—"my mother," "my aunt," etc.—are used throughout the novel, even when, as is true here, one sister is talking to the other and thus could logically use "our" rather than "my" (as she does occasionally). It is clearly a convention of the time: in her own letters to her sister Jane Austen also speaks of "my mother" and "my father."

32. A significant event, given Mr. Bennet's usual aloof indifference.

33. *has anger:* is the object of others' anger.

34. *own:* confess.

35. *exigence:* exigency, urgent circumstances.

"Oh! where, where is my uncle?" cried Elizabeth, darting from her seat as she finished the letter, in eagerness to follow him, without losing a moment of the time so precious; but as she reached the door, it was opened by a servant, and Mr. Darcy appeared. Her pale face and impetuous[36] manner made him start, and before he could recover himself enough to speak, she, in whose mind every idea was superseded by Lydia's situation, hastily exclaimed, "I beg your pardon, but I must leave you. I must find Mr. Gardiner this moment, on business that cannot be delayed; I have not an instant to lose."

"Good God! what is the matter?" cried he, with more feeling than politeness;[37] then recollecting himself, "I will not detain you a minute, but let me, or let the servant, go after Mr. and Mrs. Gardiner. You are not well enough;—you cannot go yourself."

Elizabeth hesitated, but her knees trembled under her, and she felt how little would be gained by her attempting to pursue them. Calling back the servant, therefore, she commissioned him, though in so breathless an accent as made her almost unintelligible, to fetch his master and mistress home, instantly.

On his quitting the room, she sat down, unable to support herself, and looking so miserably ill, that it was impossible for Darcy to leave her, or to refrain from saying, in a tone of gentleness and commiseration, "Let me call your maid.[38] Is there nothing you could take, to give you present relief?—A glass of wine;[39]—shall I get you one?—You are very ill."

"No, I thank you;" she replied, endeavouring to recover herself. "There is nothing the matter with me. I am quite well. I am only distressed by some dreadful news which I have just received from Longbourn."

She burst into tears as she alluded to it, and for a few minutes could not speak another word. Darcy, in wretched suspense, could only say something indistinctly of his concern, and observe her in compassionate silence. At length, she spoke again. "I have just had a letter from Jane, with such dreadful news. It cannot be concealed from any one. My youngest sister has left all her friends—has eloped;—has thrown herself into the power of—of Mr.

36. *impetuous*: violent, vehement.

37. Politeness would dictate letting her pass without interruption, but his feelings of concern overcome that. Such a rare occurrence for the formal Darcy indicates his affection for Elizabeth, as well as her highly agitated state.

38. It was normal for ladies to travel with a maid to help them with dressing, grooming, packing, etc. A later incident indicates that Elizabeth does not have her own personal maid (see p. 624, and p. 625, note 5). It is possible that one maid came from either the Bennets or the Gardiners to serve both Elizabeth and Mrs. Gardiner. It is also possible that Darcy is just assuming, incorrectly, that Elizabeth has a personal maid, for that would certainly be the norm in the wealthy social circles that he is accustomed to; each of Bingley's sisters has already been described as having her own maid.

39. Wine was generally considered to have medicinal properties, so people were often offered wine if they were in need of physical relief or revival.

Wickham. They are gone off together from Brighton. *You* know him too well to doubt the rest. She has no money, no connections,[40] nothing that can tempt him to—[41]she is lost for ever."[42]

Darcy was fixed in astonishment. "When I consider," she added, in a yet more agitated voice, "that *I* might have prevented it!—*I* who knew what he was. Had I but explained some part of it only—some part of what I learnt,[43] to my own family! Had his character been known, this could not have happened. But it is all, all too late now."

"I am grieved, indeed," cried Darcy; "grieved—shocked. But is it certain, absolutely certain?"

"Oh yes!—They left Brighton together on Sunday night,[44] and were traced almost to London, but not beyond; they are certainly not gone to Scotland."

"And what has been done, what has been attempted, to recover her?"

"My father is gone to London, and Jane has written to beg my uncle's immediate assistance, and we shall be off, I hope, in half an hour. But nothing can be done; I know very well that nothing can be done. How is such a man to be worked on?[45] How are they even to be discovered?[46] I have not the smallest hope. It is every way horrible!"

Darcy shook his head in silent acquiesence.

"When *my* eyes were opened to his real character.—Oh! had I known what I ought, what I dared, to do! But I knew not—I was afraid of doing too much. Wretched, wretched, mistake!"[47]

Darcy made no answer. He seemed scarcely to hear her, and was walking up and down the room in earnest meditation; his brow contracted, his air gloomy. Elizabeth soon observed, and instantly understood it.[48] Her power[49] was sinking; every thing *must* sink under such a proof of family weakness, such an assurance of the deepest disgrace. She could neither wonder nor condemn, but the belief of his self-conquest[50] brought nothing consolatory to her bosom, afforded no palliation of her distress. It was, on the contrary, exactly calculated to make her understand

40. *no connections:* no family connections of importance. Good family connections could give Wickham an incentive to marry her.

41. Tempt him to marry her. Elizabeth's failure to finish the thought signals her agitation; she may also prefer not even to mention the idea of marriage, since such an outcome seems too unlikely to hope for at this juncture.

42. Elizabeth's extreme reaction would be normal for the time. For a young woman to run off and live with a man without marriage was considered almost the worst sin she could commit, and it was one that would forever taint her and probably prevent her from ever marrying anyone respectable or entering decent society. It is this particularly that makes her "lost for ever" (though the term also could mean lost forever in a moral sense).

43. Meaning what she learned from Darcy about Wickham and Miss Darcy—something of course that Darcy entreated her not to tell to others.

44. *Sunday night:* it was actually on Saturday night according to Jane's letter, though since they left around midnight their journey would have mostly occurred during the early hours of Sunday morning.

45. *worked on:* influenced, persuaded (to marry Lydia).

46. London by this time was an enormous city; the census of 1811, just before this novel appeared, showed it containing more than a million people. Hence it would be an easy place to escape discovery.

47. Elizabeth's berating of herself for her secrecy about Wickham has a particular importance, one that she, in her agitated state, probably cannot guess. Since her listener is the one ultimately responsible for this secrecy, he would have even more reason to feel at fault for what occurred. Later he does reproach himself for this, and adduce it as his reason for coming to Lydia's rescue. It is likely that Elizabeth's words here help prompt him to blame himself, at least partly, for what has occurred and to decide he must remedy it.

48. The reasons for Darcy's being so pensive and serious, reasons very different from what Elizabeth supposes, are revealed later (see p. 674).

49. *Her power:* her power of attraction over him.

50. *self-conquest:* conquering his love for her, which he would do because of this family disgrace.

her own wishes; and never had she so honestly felt that she could have loved him, as now, when all love must be vain.[51]

But self, though it would intrude, could not engross her. Lydia—the humiliation, the misery, she was bringing on them all, soon swallowed up every private care; and covering her face with her handkerchief, Elizabeth was soon lost to every thing else; and, after a pause of several minutes, was only recalled to a sense of her situation by the voice of her companion, who, in a manner, which though it spoke compassion,[52] spoke likewise restraint, said, "I am afraid you have been long desiring my absence, nor have I any thing to plead in excuse of my stay, but real, though unavailing, concern. Would to heaven that any thing could be either said or done on my part, that might offer consolation to such distress.— But I will not torment you with vain wishes, which may seem purposely to ask for your thanks.[53] This unfortunate affair will, I fear, prevent my sister's having the pleasure of seeing you at Pemberley to day."

"Oh, yes. Be so kind as to apologize for us to Miss Darcy. Say that urgent business calls us home immediately. Conceal the unhappy truth as long as it is possible.—I know it cannot be long."

He readily assured her of his secrecy—again expressed his sorrow for her distress, wished it a happier conclusion than there was at present reason to hope, and leaving his compliments for her relations, with only one serious, parting, look, went away.

As he quitted the room, Elizabeth felt how improbable it was that they should ever see each other again on such terms of cordiality as had marked their several meetings in Derbyshire; and as she threw a retrospective glance over the whole of their acquaintance, so full of contradictions and varieties,[54] sighed at the perverseness of those feelings which would now have promoted its continuance, and would formerly have rejoiced in its termination.[55]

If gratitude and esteem are good foundations of affection, Elizabeth's change of sentiment will be neither improbable nor faulty. But if otherwise, if the regard springing from such sources is unreasonable or unnatural, in comparison of what is so often described as arising on a first interview with its object, and even

51. This is the first time that Elizabeth has spoken, to herself or others, of actual love for Darcy. In another novel, *Emma*, the heroine, one who is also guilty of serious errors of judgment, comes to realize and acknowledge her love of the hero only at the moment when she receives information suggesting he may marry someone else. In both cases, it seems a necessary penance for the heroine, one that gives her greater appreciation for the hero and for her own earlier errors and that makes their eventual union even deeper and more satisfying.

In this case, Lydia's affair also reinforces the two main points Darcy made in his letter to Elizabeth, the wickedness of Wickham and the failings of her family. Hence he has been further vindicated, although he never expresses any sign of that to her.

52. *spoke compassion:* revealed or manifested compassionate feelings.

53. Darcy's disinclination to seek thanks or gratitude for himself will appear more strongly in his later course of action regarding this whole matter.

54. *varieties:* variations, changes of fortune.

55. That is, the continuance or termination of her acquaintance with Darcy.

56. In other words, compared to the common idea, so often described, of love at first sight. This passage represents an ironic jab at one of the author's favorite targets, the cult of immediate and impulsive love. This cult was widespread in the literature of the time, and Jane Austen attacks it with particular fervor in youthful stories such as "Love and Friendship." Her favorite novel, Samuel Richardson's *Sir Charles Grandison*, includes similar attacks, along with a celebration of love that is based on strong moral principles and on a solid knowledge of the beloved. This novel's examples of impulsive love—Elizabeth's infatuation with Wickham and Lydia's current elopement with him—provide strong support for a similar position.

before two words have been exchanged,[56] nothing can be said in her defence, except that she had given somewhat of a trial to the latter method, in her partiality for Wickham, and that its ill-success might perhaps authorise her to seek the other less interesting mode of attachment.[57] Be that as it may, she saw him go with regret; and in this early example of what Lydia's infamy must produce, found additional anguish as she reflected on that wretched business. Never, since reading Jane's second letter, had she entertained a hope of Wickham's meaning to marry her. No one but Jane, she thought, could flatter herself with such an expectation. Surprise was the least of her feelings on this developement.[58] While the contents of the first letter remained on her mind, she was all surprise—all astonishment that Wickham should marry a girl, whom it was impossible he could marry for money; and how Lydia could ever have attached him, had appeared incomprehensible. But now it was all too natural. For such an attachment as this, she might have sufficient charms;[59] and though she did not suppose Lydia to be deliberately engaging in an elopement, without the intention of marriage, she had no difficulty in believing that neither her virtue[60] nor her understanding would preserve her from falling an easy prey.

She had never perceived, while the regiment was in Hertfordshire, that Lydia had any partiality for him, but she was convinced that Lydia had wanted only encouragement to attach herself to any body. Sometimes one officer, sometimes another had been her favourite, as their attentions raised them in her opinion.[61] Her affections had been continually fluctuating, but never without an object. The mischief[62] of neglect and mistaken indulgence towards such a girl.—Oh! how acutely did she now feel it.

She was wild[63] to be at home—to hear, to see, to be upon the spot, to share with Jane in the cares that must now fall wholly upon her, in a family so deranged;[64] a father absent, a mother incapable of exertion, and requiring constant attendance; and though almost persuaded that nothing could be done for Lydia, her uncle's interference seemed of the utmost importance, and till he entered the room, the misery of her impatience was severe.

57. This other mode of attachment is love that develops gradually and rationally, the kind of love that Jane Austen generally extolls.

58. *developement*: disclosure or revelation of information.

59. This brings up the question of why Wickham runs away with Lydia, when he has no intention of marrying her. The explanation Elizabeth offers here is the one that will ultimately be confirmed (see pp. 574 and 576), which is that Wickham, already running off for reasons of his own, was happy to bring along as a companion a pretty girl who adored him. At this time, an unmarried man who wanted sexual companionship usually had to resort to prostitutes; Lydia would offer something better than that for Wickham.

Some have wondered if Wickham might have hoped to revenge himself on Darcy by ruining the sister of his beloved. But Wickham has no reason to know of Darcy's interest in Elizabeth: he has never been told of the proposal; he believes Darcy to be destined for Miss De Bourgh; and his belief in Darcy's social pride would make him doubt that Darcy would marry a woman of lower birth and wealth like Elizabeth. Nor would Wickham have reason to believe Elizabeth to be interested in Darcy, for all she told him during their last conversation was that she had come to understand Darcy better, without saying that she liked him or providing any more specifics. Finally, it is doubtful if Wickham, being as self-centered as he is, spends much time speculating about anyone's affairs but his own.

Thus Wickham's choice of Lydia, a choice that plays such an important role in the action of the book, is fundamentally a coincidence. But it is not too extreme a coincidence. Lydia had been residing with the commander of the regiment, which would have given her frequent contacts with the regiment's officers; Wickham has already been described as by far the most charming and handsome of the officers; thus, given Lydia's flirtatiousness and strong interest in men, it is in no way remarkable that she fell in love with him, and that he reciprocated enough to accept her as a temporary companion.

60. *virtue*: during this time virtue, for women, normally meant sexual virtue or chastity. In this context, it especially means virtuousness, i.e. the inner character that would make a woman preserve her chastity.

61. Lydia's essential flightiness has already been displayed in a number of ways. The implication here is that her affection for Wickham was a recent development.

62. *mischief*: harm, evil.

63. *wild*: passionately eager or desirous.

64. *deranged*: disarranged, thrown into disorder.

Mr. and Mrs. Gardiner had hurried back in alarm, supposing, by the servant's account, that their niece was taken suddenly ill; —but satisfying them instantly on that head, she eagerly communicated the cause of their summons, reading the two letters aloud, and dwelling on the postscript of the last, with trembling energy.— Though Lydia had never been a favourite with them, Mr. and Mrs. Gardiner could not but be deeply affected. Not Lydia only, but all were concerned in it;[65] and after the first exclamations of surprise and horror, Mr. Gardiner readily promised every assistance in his power.—Elizabeth, though expecting no less, thanked him with tears of gratitude; and all three being actuated by one spirit, every thing relating to their journey was speedily settled. They were to be off as soon as possible. "But what is to be done about Pemberley?" cried Mrs. Gardiner. "John[66] told us Mr. Darcy was here when you sent for us;—was it so?"

"Yes; and I told him we should not be able to keep our engagement. *That* is all settled."

"That is all settled;" repeated the other, as she ran into her room to prepare. "And are they upon such terms as for her to disclose the real truth! Oh, that I knew how it was!"

But wishes were vain; or at best could serve only to amuse her in the hurry and confusion of the following hour. Had Elizabeth been at leisure to be idle, she would have remained certain that all employment was impossible to one so wretched as herself; but she had her share of business as well as her aunt, and amongst the rest there were notes to be written to all their friends in Lambton, with false excuses for their sudden departure. An hour, however, saw the whole completed; and Mr. Gardiner meanwhile having settled his account at the inn, nothing remained to be done but to go; and Elizabeth, after all the misery of the morning, found herself, in a shorter space of time than she could have supposed, seated in the carriage, and on the road to Longbourn.

65. As stated above, and as will be underlined in later passages, Lydia's disgrace would bring humiliation upon the entire family. The improper behavior and lower social origins of the Bennets have already played a critical role in Bingley's decision (guided by Darcy) to break off his ties with Jane. A sexual scandal like this would have far more severe effects on the family and on the marital prospects of the other daughters.

66. *John:* the servant commissioned by Elizabeth to summon the Gardiners.

Chapter Five

I have been thinking it over again, Elizabeth," said her uncle, as they drove from the town; "and really, upon serious consideration, I am much more inclined than I was to judge as your eldest sister does of the matter. It appears to me so very unlikely, that any young man should form such a design against a girl who is by no means unprotected or friendless, and who was actually staying in his colonel's family, that I am strongly inclined to hope the best. Could he expect that her friends would not step forward?[1] Could he expect to be noticed[2] again by the regiment, after such an affront to Colonel Forster?[3] His temptation is not adequate to the risk."

"Do you really think so?" cried Elizabeth, brightening up for a moment.

"Upon my word," said Mrs. Gardiner, "I begin to be of your uncle's opinion. It is really too great a violation of decency, honour, and interest, for him to be guilty of it. I cannot think so very ill of Wickham. Can you, yourself, Lizzy, so wholly give him up, as to believe him capable of it?"

"Not perhaps of neglecting his own interest. But of every other neglect I can believe him capable. If, indeed, it should be so! But I dare not hope it. Why should they not go on to Scotland, if that had been the case?"

"In the first place," replied Mr. Gardiner, "there is no absolute proof that they are not gone to Scotland."

"Oh! but their removing from the chaise into an hackney coach is such a presumption![4] And, besides, no traces of them were to be found on the Barnet road."[5]

"Well, then—supposing them to be in London. They may be there, though for the purpose of concealment, for no more exceptionable purpose. It is not likely that money should be very abundant on either side; and it might strike them that they could be

1. It was still common at this time, when a man had seduced and thereby ruined a woman, for a close relation, or even a close friend, of the woman to step forward and challenge the man to a duel (a duel resulting from this cause occurs in *Sense and Sensibility*). The death or injury that might result from the duel was considered a just punishment for the terrible wrong the man had committed. That duels occurred reasonably often is indicated by a letter of Jane Austen, in which she discusses a neighbor who suffered a bullet wound while traveling, and takes pains to explain why it must have been an accidental shooting and not the result of a duel (Nov. 8, 1800).

2. *noticed:* acknowledged, accepted.

3. This might be a significant deterrent to Wickham, except that, as is revealed shortly, he has decided to abandon the regiment. This would only require him to resign his commission, which could be done without any particular difficulty—or any financial penalty for him since he did not have to purchase his commission initially. Partly for this reason, the militia suffered from the frequent departure of its officers. Nor does Wickham, before any such resignation took effect, have to worry much about being charged with desertion, for in this period army discipline of officers tended to be lax and officers were often away without leave for extended periods.

4. *presumption:* ground for believing it. As indicated in the previous chapter, this presumption stems from the chaise being a standard vehicle for travel between towns and a hackney-coach being purely a vehicle for transportation within London.

5. Since Barnet is north of London, this would be the road they would take to go to Scotland. See p. 501, note 26, and map, p. 745.

more economically, though less expeditiously, married in London, than in Scotland."6

"But why all this secrecy? Why any fear of detection? Why must their marriage be private? Oh! no, no, this is not likely. His most particular friend, you see by Jane's account, was persuaded of his never intending to marry her. Wickham will never marry a woman without some money. He cannot afford it. And what claims has Lydia, what attractions has she beyond youth, health, and good humour, that could make him for her sake, forego every chance of benefiting himself by marrying well?7 As to what restraint the apprehension of disgrace in the corps might throw on a dishonourable elopement with her, I am not able to judge; for I know nothing of the effects that such a step might produce. But as to your other objection, I am afraid it will hardly hold good. Lydia has no brothers to step forward;8 and he might imagine, from my father's behaviour, from his indolence and the little attention he has ever seemed to give to what was going forward in his family, that *he* would do as little, and think as little about it, as any father could do, in such a matter."

"But can you think that Lydia is so lost to every thing but love of him, as to consent to live with him on any other terms than marriage?"

"It does seem, and it is most shocking indeed," replied Elizabeth, with tears in her eyes, "that a sister's sense of decency and virtue in such a point should admit of doubt.9 But, really, I know not what to say. Perhaps I am not doing her justice. But she is very young; she has never been taught to think on serious subjects; and for the last half year, nay, for a twelvemonth, she has been given up to nothing but amusement and vanity. She has been allowed to dispose of her time in the most idle and frivolous manner, and to adopt any opinions that came in her way. Since the ——shire were first quartered in Meryton, nothing but love, flirtation, and officers, have been in her head. She has been doing every thing in her power by thinking and talking on the subject, to give greater—what shall I call it? susceptibility to her feelings;10 which are naturally lively11 enough. And we all know

6. Mrs. Gardiner refers to the device of private marriage already mentioned by Jane (see p. 500 and p. 501, note 29). This method would be more economical than going to Scotland because of the lower travel expenses; it would be less expeditious because it could only happen after more than three weeks, for it required a week's notice to the parish priest followed by three Sundays of banns-reading before it could occur.

7. Divorce was almost impossible at this time, especially for those who lacked great wealth. Hence Wickham, by marrying Lydia, could not make a more advantageous marriage in the future unless she happened to die.

8. Brothers, as young men and therefore better fighters, would be the logical candidates to challenge a seducer to a duel. Elizabeth's comment alludes to one of the main justifications of dueling, which is that the threat of a duel could deter a man from behaving dishonorably, or, in cases where it was too late for that, frighten him into trying to remedy the wrong. In cases of seduction, the remedy would be to marry the woman and thereby save her from ruin. In this instance, however, with Mr. Bennet as the only one to pose the threat of a duel, Wickham has little to force him into taking such a remedial step.

9. One sees that Elizabeth and the Gardiners, like everyone else, accepts completely the idea that Lydia's actions would constitute a terrible sin. Jane Austen gives every indication of sharing the idea herself: making Lydia such a foolish character is one piece of evidence for that. In her next novel, *Mansfield Park*, a female character will abandon her husband and will be similarly condemned by the other characters and by the author. In none of her novels does Jane Austen, in the manner of some later novelists, try to excuse, or even elicit sympathy for, a female character who loses her chastity before marriage or who commits adultery (a young woman who has been ruined by a seducer is mentioned in *Sense and Sensibility*, and with some degree of pity, but the character herself is never shown nor is any plea offered in her defense).

10. *susceptibility to her feelings*: Elizabeth's hesitation before choosing this phrase indicates that she is trying to find a relatively mild way of describing Lydia's lack of restraint.

11. *lively*: playful and lighthearted, as well as animated. This is a quality that also marks Elizabeth; Lydia, who refuses to be serious about anything, reveals the dangers of carrying it too far.

that Wickham has every charm of person[12] and address[13] that can captivate a woman."[14]

"But you see that Jane," said her aunt, "does not think so ill of Wickham, as to believe him capable of the attempt."

"Of whom does Jane ever think ill? And who is there, whatever might be their former conduct, that she would believe capable of such an attempt, till it were proved against them? But Jane knows, as well as I do, what Wickham really is. We both know that he has been profligate[15] in every sense of the word. That he has neither integrity nor honour. That he is as false and deceitful, as he is insinuating."

"And do you really know all this?" cried Mrs. Gardiner, whose curiosity as to the mode of her intelligence[16] was all alive.[17]

"I do, indeed," replied Elizabeth, colouring.[18] "I told you the other day, of his infamous behaviour to Mr. Darcy; and you, yourself, when last at Longbourn, heard in what manner he spoke of the man, who had behaved with such forbearance and liberality towards him. And there are other circumstances which I am not at liberty—which it is not worth while to relate; but his lies about the whole Pemberley family are endless. From what he said of Miss Darcy, I was thoroughly prepared to see a proud, reserved, disagreeable girl. Yet he knew to the contrary himself. He must know that she was as amiable and unpretending as we have found her."

"But does Lydia know nothing of this? Can she be ignorant of what you and Jane seem so well to understand?"

"Oh, yes!—that, that is the worst of all. Till I was in Kent, and saw so much both of Mr. Darcy and his relation, Colonel Fitzwilliam, I was ignorant of the truth myself. And when I returned home, the ——shire was to leave Meryton in a week or fortnight's time. As that was the case, neither Jane, to whom I related the whole, nor I, thought it necessary to make our knowledge public; for of what use could it apparently be to any one, that the good opinion which all the neighbourhood had of him, should then be overthrown? And even when it was settled that Lydia should go with Mrs. Forster, the necessity of opening her eyes to his character never occurred to me. That *she* could be in

12. *person:* physical appearance.

13. *address:* manner of speaking.

14. Elizabeth is obviously thinking of herself. Lydia's action thus helps reinforce Elizabeth's sense of her own folly in being so captivated by Wickham earlier.

15. *profligate:* abandoned to vice.

16. *mode of her intelligence:* source of her information.

17. *all alive:* fully aroused.

18. *colouring:* blushing. Elizabeth's embarrassment presumably stems from her consciousness of knowing the whole story of Wickham's dealings with Darcy and Miss Darcy, and of not having informed the Gardiners of it.

any danger from the deception never entered my head. That such a consequence as *this* should ensue, you may easily believe was far enough from my thoughts."

"When they all removed to Brighton, therefore, you had no reason, I suppose, to believe them fond of each other."

"Not the slightest. I can remember no symptom of affection on either side; and had any thing of the kind been perceptible, you must be aware that ours is not a family, on which it could be thrown away.[19] When first he entered the corps, she was ready enough to admire him; but so we all were. Every girl in, or near Meryton, was out of her senses about him for the first two months; but he never distinguished *her* by any particular attention, and, consequently, after a moderate period of extravagant and wild admiration, her fancy for him gave way, and others of the regiment, who treated her with more distinction, again became her favourites."

* * *

It may be easily believed, that however little of novelty could be added to their fears, hopes, and conjectures, on this interesting[20] subject, by its repeated discussion, no other could detain them from it long, during the whole of the journey. From Elizabeth's thoughts it was never absent. Fixed there by the keenest of all anguish, self reproach, she could find no interval of ease or forgetfulness.

They travelled as expeditiously as possible; and sleeping one night on the road, reached Longbourn by dinner-time the next day.[21] It was a comfort to Elizabeth to consider that Jane could not have been wearied by long expectations.

The little Gardiners, attracted by the sight of a chaise,[22] were standing on the steps of the house, as they entered the paddock;[23] and when the carriage drove up to the door, the joyful surprise that lighted up their faces, and displayed itself over their whole bodies, in a variety of capers and frisks, was the first pleasing earnest[24] of their welcome.

Elizabeth jumped out; and, after giving each of them an hasty

19. Because Mrs. Bennet in particular is so eager to seize on any hint of a possible marriage for one of her daughters, and because the indiscretion of herself and some of her daughters means that any such hint would soon be the subject of gossip.

20. *interesting*: important.

21. This gives a sense of travel speeds. The distance, on roads existing then, would be approximately 140 to 150 miles, and they traveled from sometime in the middle of the previous day to around four or five o'clock on this day. Thus, assuming their stop for the night was relatively short, they would have averaged 7–8 miles per hour, which was close to the best speed of the time. Jane Austen always takes great pains to ensure that details of this sort are correct. In a letter commenting on a niece's novel, she declares that certain characters "must be *two* days going from Dawlish to Bath; they are nearly 100 miles apart" (Aug. 17, 1814).

22. Since a chaise, unlike other carriages, was normally used for long-distance travel, its sight would be especially likely to draw attention.

23. *paddock*: enclosed field or lawn, usually grazed by livestock, next to a house.

24. *earnest*: indication or pledge of what is to come.

kiss, hurried into the vestibule, where Jane, who came running down stairs from her mother's apartment,[25] immediately met her.

Elizabeth, as she affectionately embraced her, whilst tears filled the eyes of both, lost not a moment in asking whether any thing had been heard of the fugitives.

"Not yet," replied Jane. "But now that my dear uncle is come, I hope every thing will be well."

"Is my father in town?"

"Yes, he went on Tuesday as I wrote you word."

"And have you heard from him often?"

"We have heard only once. He wrote me a few lines on Wednesday, to say that he had arrived in safety, and to give me his directions,[26] which I particularly begged him to do. He merely added, that he should not write again, till he had something of importance to mention."[27]

"And my mother—How is she? How are you all?"

"My mother is tolerably well, I trust; though her spirits are greatly shaken. She is up stairs, and will have great satisfaction in seeing you all. She does not yet leave her dressing-room. Mary and Kitty, thank Heaven! are quite well."

"But you—How are you?" cried Elizabeth. "You look pale. How much you must have gone through!"

Her sister, however, assured her, of her being perfectly well; and their conversation, which had been passing while Mr. and Mrs. Gardiner were engaged with their children, was now put an end to, by the approach of the whole party. Jane ran to her uncle and aunt, and welcomed and thanked them both, with alternate smiles and tears.

When they were all in the drawing room, the questions which Elizabeth had already asked, were of course repeated by the others, and they soon found that Jane had no intelligence[28] to give. The sanguine hope of good, however, which the benevolence of her heart suggested, had not yet deserted her; she still expected that it would all end well, and that every morning would bring some letter, either from Lydia or her father, to explain their proceedings, and perhaps announce the marriage.

25. *apartment:* room or set of rooms. "Apartment" frequently meant a combination bedroom and dressing room.

26. *his directions:* his addresses.

27. Mr. Bennet's dislike of writing has already been made clear. In this case, despite the gravity of the situation, he does no more than send one brief note giving the most basic information, something he has been particularly begged to do.

28. *intelligence:* news.

Mrs. Bennet, to whose apartment they all repaired,[29] after a few minutes conversation together, received them exactly as might be expected; with tears and lamentations of regret, invectives against the villanous conduct of Wickham, and complaints of her own sufferings and ill usage; blaming every body but the person to whose ill judging indulgence the errors of her daughter must be principally owing.

"If I had been able," said she, "to carry my point of going to Brighton, with all my family, *this* would not have happened; but poor dear Lydia had nobody to take care of her. Why did the Forsters ever let her go out of their sight? I am sure there was some great neglect or other on their side, for she is not the kind of girl to do such a thing, if she had been well looked after. I always thought they were very unfit to have the charge of her; but I was over-ruled, as I always am. Poor dear child! And now here's Mr. Bennet gone away, and I know he will fight Wickham, wherever he meets him, and then he will be killed,[30] and what is to become of us all? The Collinses will turn us out, before he is cold in his grave; and if you are not kind to us, brother, I do not know what we shall do."

They all exclaimed against such terrific[31] ideas; and Mr. Gardiner, after general assurances of his affection for her and all her family, told her that he meant to be in London the very next day, and would assist Mr. Bennet in every endeavour for recovering Lydia.

"Do not give way to useless alarm," added he, "though it is right to be prepared for the worst, there is no occasion to look on it as certain. It is not quite a week since they left Brighton. In a few days more, we may gain some news of them, and till we know that they are not married, and have no design of marrying, do not let us give the matter over as lost. As soon as I get to town, I shall go to my brother, and make him come home with me to Gracechurch Street, and then we may consult together as to what is to be done."

"Oh! my dear brother," replied Mrs. Bennet, "that is exactly what I could most wish for. And now do, when you get to town, find them out, wherever they may be; and if they are not married already, *make* them marry. And as for wedding clothes, do not let

29. *repaired:* proceeded, made their way.

30. The prospect of a duel is also on Mrs. Bennet's mind. In fact, only a small portion of those who fought duels were killed or wounded, but it was still a possibility.

31. *terrific:* dreadful.

them wait for that, but tell Lydia she shall have as much money as she chuses, to buy them, after they are married. And, above all things, keep Mr. Bennet from fighting. Tell him what a dreadful state I am in,—that I am frightened out of my wits; and have such tremblings, such flutterings, all over me, such spasms in my side, and pains in my head, and such beatings at heart, that I can get no rest by night nor by day.[32] And tell my dear Lydia, not to give any directions about her clothes, till she has seen me, for she does not know which are the best warehouses.[33] Oh, brother, how kind you are! I know you will contrive it all."

But Mr. Gardiner, though he assured her again of his earnest endeavours in the cause, could not avoid recommending moderation to her, as well in her hopes as her fears; and, after talking with her in this manner till dinner was on table, they left her to vent all her feelings on the housekeeper, who attended, in the absence of her daughters.

Though her brother and sister were persuaded that there was no real occasion for such a seclusion from the family, they did not attempt to oppose it, for they knew that she had not prudence enough to hold her tongue before the servants, while they waited at table, and judged it better that *one* only of the household, and the one whom they could most trust, should comprehend all her fears and solicitude on the subject.[34]

In the dining-room they were soon joined by Mary and Kitty, who had been too busily engaged in their separate apartments, to make their appearance before. One came from her books, and the other from her toilette.[35] The faces of both, however, were tolerably calm; and no change was visible in either, except that the loss of her favourite sister, or the anger which she had herself incurred in the business, had given something more of fretfulness than usual, to the accents[36] of Kitty. As for Mary, she was mistress enough of herself to whisper to Elizabeth with a countenance of grave reflection, soon after they were seated at table,

"This is a most unfortunate affair; and will probably be much talked of. But we must stem the tide of malice, and pour into the wounded bosoms of each other, the balm of sisterly consolation."

32. All the symptoms listed here are ones that were ascribed by medical writers to the nervous disorders Mrs. Bennet likes to complain of having. The tendency, seen so vividly in Mrs. Bennet, to complain about ailments or to fancy oneself ill, often as a way to draw attention or sympathy, is a frequent target of Jane Austen's satire. In her story "Catharine, or the Bower" a woman imagines, after being out briefly at night in July, that her exposure to the night air will cause her to remain ill until the following May. *Emma* and *Persuasion* both have important characters who worry excessively about their health, and her last writing, *Sanditon* (written while she was gravely ill herself), includes a trio of siblings for whom hypochondria is a way of life. Her letters also include a number of acerbic comments about people imagining themselves to be unwell; her own mother appears at times to have been of their number. In one letter she describes (though she admits it is an "ill-natured [sic] sentiment") a woman who bears some resemblance to Mrs. Bennet: "the sort of woman who gives me the idea of being determined never to be well—& who likes her spasms & nervousness & the consequence they give her, better than anything else" (Sept. 25, 1813). In her own case Jane Austen seems to have lived up to her aversion to such attitudes and behavior, for her letters from the final, illness-racked year of her life show her maintaining an air of stoical calm, and trying to put the best face on matters to avoid distressing others.

33. *warehouses*: shops.

34. Only one servant of the household, presumably the housekeeper, is with Mrs. Bennet. Since servants are a prime means of spreading gossip, the absence of the other servants makes it less likely that bad family news divulged by Mrs. Bennet will make its way to others in the neighborhood.

35. *her toilette*: getting dressed.

36. *accents*: tones, ways of speaking.

Then, perceiving in Elizabeth no inclination of replying, she added, "Unhappy as the event must be for Lydia, we may draw from it this useful lesson; that loss of virtue[37] in a female is irretrievable—that one false step involves her in endless ruin—that her reputation is no less brittle than it is beautiful,[38]—and that she cannot be too much guarded in her behaviour towards the undeserving of the other sex."

Elizabeth lifted up her eyes in amazement, but was too much oppressed[39] to make any reply. Mary, however, continued to console herself with such kind of moral extractions from the evil[40] before them.

In the afternoon,[41] the two elder Miss Bennets were able to be for half an hour by themselves; and Elizabeth instantly availed herself of the opportunity of making many enquiries, which Jane was equally eager to satisfy. After joining in general lamentations over the dreadful sequel of this event, which Elizabeth considered as all but certain, and Miss Bennet could not assert to be wholly impossible; the former continued the subject, by saying, "But tell me all and every thing about it, which I have not already heard. Give me farther particulars. What did Colonel Forster say? Had they no apprehension of any thing before the elopement took place? They must have seen them together for ever."

"Colonel Forster did own that he had often suspected some partiality, especially on Lydia's side, but nothing to give him any alarm. I am so grieved for him. His behaviour was attentive and kind to the utmost. He *was* coming to us, in order to assure us of his concern, before he had any idea of their not being gone to Scotland: when that apprehension first got abroad,[42] it hastened his journey."[43]

"And was Denny convinced that Wickham would not marry? Did he know of their intending to go off? Had Colonel Forster seen Denny himself?"

"Yes; but when questioned by *him* Denny denied knowing any thing of their plan, and would not give his real opinion about it. He did not repeat his persuasion of their not marrying—and from *that*, I am inclined to hope, he might have been misunderstood before."[44]

37 *virtue*: sexual chastity, considered the supreme virtue for a woman.

38. This last line derives from the novel *Evelina* by Fanny Burney, in which a wise character describes female virtue as being both brittle and beautiful. Jane Austen, who admired Fanny Burney, is not necessarily intending to criticize this idea by putting it in Mary's mouth. Her main point is to show Mary once again spouting clichés and repeating phrases and ideas from books, without any appreciation of how inappropriate her words are to the situation. She is obviously providing no sisterly consolation to Elizabeth by seeing a family tragedy as merely an opportunity to draw a useful lesson, a lesson that in fact everyone knows already since it was a commonplace of the time. The repetitiveness of Mary's language is also revealing: she is clearly engaged in padding because she actually has little to say.

39. *oppressed*: overwhelmed, depressed.

40. *evil*: misfortune, mischief, trouble. "Evil" generally had a less strong connotation than today.

41. *afternoon*: this would be after dinner.

42. *got abroad*: became generally or publicly known.

43. A person less innocent and forgiving than Jane could think of a less generous interpretation of Colonel Forster's, namely that his and his wife's negligence allowed the affair to develop but that, despite his probably suspecting something between Lydia and Wickham, he took no action until it was too late.

44. Of course, since Denny was not giving his real opinion of the matter, it does not make sense to base hopes upon what he said then. Denny could naturally fear the anger of his commanding officer, and therefore be inclined to downplay or deny whatever unpleasant truths he knew about a man whom he himself had introduced into the regiment.

"And till Colonel Forster came himself, not one of you entertained a doubt, I suppose, of their being really married?"

"How was it possible that such an idea should enter our brains! I felt a little uneasy—a little fearful of my sister's happiness with him in marriage, because I knew that his conduct had not been always quite right. My father and mother knew nothing of that, they only felt how imprudent a match it must be. Kitty then owned,[45] with a very natural triumph on knowing more than the rest of us, that in Lydia's last letter, she had prepared her for such a step. She had known, it seems, of their being in love with each other, many weeks."

"But not before they went to Brighton?"

"No, I believe not."

"And did Colonel Forster appear to think ill of Wickham himself? Does he know his real character?"

"I must confess that he did not speak so well of Wickham as he formerly did. He believed him to be imprudent and extravagant. And since this sad affair has taken place, it is said, that he left Meryton greatly in debt; but I hope this may be false."

"Oh, Jane, had we been less secret, had we told what we knew of him, this could not have happened!"

"Perhaps it would have been better;" replied her sister. "But to expose the former faults of any person, without knowing what their present feelings were, seemed unjustifiable. We acted with the best intentions."[46]

"Could Colonel Forster repeat the particulars of Lydia's note to his wife?"

"He brought it with him for us to see."

Jane then took it from her pocket-book,[47] and gave it to Elizabeth. These were the contents:

MY DEAR HARRIET,[48]

You will laugh when you know where I am gone, and I cannot help laughing myself at your surprise to-morrow morning, as soon as I am missed. I am going to Gretna Green,[49] and if you cannot guess with who, I shall think you a simpleton, for there is but one

45. *owned*: acknowledged.

46. A statement that indicates the limitations of Jane's character, and of good intentions not guided by sound judgment. In this case, being willing to think badly of someone who deserved it, and to inform others about his character, could have put a possible check on his ability to commit similar bad actions again.

47. *pocket-book*: book for notes and papers carried in the pocket.

48. *HARRIET*: Lydia's irresponsibility is revealed by her writing only to Mrs. Forster to tell the news about such a momentous event. Even this letter seems more concerned with laughing and drawing attention to herself than with actually informing the recipient about the important matter at hand.

49. *Gretna Green*: where they could get married; see p. 499, note 18, and map on p. 742.

man in the world I love, and he is an angel. I should never be· happy without him, so think it no harm to be off. You need not send them word at Longbourn of my going, if you do not like it, for it will make the surprise the greater, when I write to them, and sign my name Lydia Wickham.[50] *What a good joke it will be! I can hardly write for laughing. Pray make my excuses to Pratt, for not keeping my engagement, and dancing with him to night. Tell him I hope he will excuse me when he knows all, and tell him I will dance with him at the next ball we meet, with great pleasure. I shall send for my clothes when I get to Longbourn; but I wish you would tell Sally to mend a great slit in my worked muslin gown,*[51] *before they are packed up. Good bye. Give my love to Colonel Forster, I hope you will drink to our good journey.*

> *Your affectionate friend,*
> LYDIA BENNET.[52]

"Oh! thoughtless, thoughtless Lydia!" cried Elizabeth when she had finished it. "What a letter is this, to be written at such a moment. But at least it shews, that *she* was serious in the object of her journey. Whatever he might afterwards persuade her to, it was not on her side a *scheme* of infamy.[53] My poor father! how he must have felt it!"

"I never saw any one so shocked. He could not speak a word for full ten minutes. My mother was taken ill immediately, and the whole house in such confusion!"

"Oh! Jane," cried Elizabeth, "was there a servant belonging to it, who did not know the whole story before the end of the day?"

"I do not know.—I hope there was.—But to be guarded at such a time, is very difficult. My mother was in hysterics, and though I endeavoured to give her every assistance in my power, I am afraid I did not do so much as I might have done! But the horror of what might possibly happen, almost took from me my faculties."

"Your attendance upon her, has been too much for you. You do not look well. Oh! that I had been with you, you have had every care and anxiety upon yourself alone."

"Mary and Kitty have been very kind, and would have shared

50. Thus Lydia almost advises against informing her family about the matter, something that in this society was the most important decision of a young woman's life, and one in which the family was supposed to be heavily involved.

51. *worked muslin gown*: muslin gown decorated with needlework.

52. Lydia's letter shows how little thought she has given the whole scheme. Engrossed by the present as usual, she bothers in such an important communication with messages about the next ball and fixing her gown—neither of which would have much significance even if she were to marry Wickham.

53. *scheme of infamy*: a plan to live together without marriage. Elizabeth rejoices that at least Lydia thought she was running away in order to marry Wickham, and therefore did not intend to do wrong.

in every fatigue, I am sure, but I did not think it right for either of them. Kitty is slight and delicate, and Mary studies so much, that her hours of repose should not be broken in on. My aunt Philips came to Longbourn on Tuesday, after my father went away; and was so good as to stay till Thursday with me.[54] She was of great use and comfort to us all, and Lady Lucas has been very kind; she walked here on Wednesday morning to condole with us, and offered her services, or any of her daughters, if they could be of use to us."

"She had better have stayed at home," cried Elizabeth; "perhaps she *meant* well, but, under such a misfortune as this, one cannot see too little of one's neighbours. Assistance is impossible; condolence, insufferable. Let them triumph over us at a distance, and be satisfied."[55]

She then proceeded to enquire into the measures which her father had intended to pursue, while in town, for the recovery of his daughter.

"He meant, I believe," replied Jane, "to go to Epsom,[56] the place where they last changed horses, see the postilions,[57] and try if any thing could be made out from them. His principal object must be, to discover the number of the hackney coach[58] which took them from Clapham.[59] It had come with a fare[60] from London; and as he thought the circumstance of a gentleman and lady's removing from one carriage into another, might be remarked,[61] he meant to make enquiries at Clapham. If he could any how discover at what house the coachman had before set down[62] his fare, he determined to make enquiries there, and hoped it might not be impossible to find out the stand[63] and number of the coach. I do not know of any other designs that he had formed: but he was in such a hurry to be gone, and his spirits so greatly discomposed, that I had difficulty in finding out even so much as this."

54. The Bennets first received the news about Lydia and Wickham on Saturday night; it is now the following Saturday (see chronology, pp. 717–718).

55. Elizabeth assumes that their neighbors wish to see them in order to look down on them and feel superior.

56. *Epsom:* a town between Brighton and London. See p. 498, and map on p. 745.

57. *postilions:* men who, for carriages traveling post, rode on one of the horses in order to guide them; they were available to be hired at the places where one changed horses.

58. *number of the hackney coach:* hackney coaches, like taxicabs today, were officially licensed, and were all given numbers.

59. *Clapham:* the south London neighborhood where Wickham and Lydia are known to have changed carriages.

60. *fare:* fare-paying passenger(s).

61. *remarked:* noticed, remarked upon. Normally two people who arrived in the London area in a chaise would continue in it until their destination—as Elizabeth and Maria Lucas do when coming from Kent. Wickham and Lydia's change of carriage would be unusual, and therefore it is possible that others at the place where they changed might remember them.

62. *set down:* dropped off.

63. *stand:* resting station for hackney coaches. Each coach was assigned to a stand.

Chapter Six

*T*he whole party were in hopes of a letter from Mr. Bennet the next morning, but the post[1] came in without bringing a single line from him. His family knew him to be on all common occasions, a most negligent and dilatory correspondent, but at such a time, they had hoped for exertion. They were forced to conclude, that he had no pleasing intelligence to send, but even of *that* they would have been glad to be certain. Mr. Gardiner had waited only for the letters before he set off.

When he was gone, they were certain at least of receiving constant information of what was going on, and their uncle promised, at parting, to prevail on Mr. Bennet to return to Longbourn, as soon as he could, to the great consolation of his sister, who considered it as the only security for her husband's not being killed in a duel.

Mrs. Gardiner and the children were to remain in Hertfordshire a few days longer, as the former thought her presence might be serviceable to her nieces. She shared in their attendance on Mrs. Bennet, and was a great comfort to them, in their hours of freedom. Their other aunt also visited them frequently, and always, as she said, with the design of cheering and heartening them up, though as she never came without reporting some fresh instance of Wickham's extravagance or irregularity,[2] she seldom went away without leaving them more dispirited than she found them.

All Meryton seemed striving to blacken the man, who, but three months before, had been almost an angel of light. He was declared to be in debt to every tradesman in the place, and his intrigues, all honoured with the title of seduction, had been extended into every tradesman's family.[3] Every body declared that he was the wickedest young man in the world; and every body began to find out, that they had always distrusted the appearance of his goodness. Elizabeth, though she did not credit above

1. *post:* mail. Daily mail service had become a basic feature of English life by this time.

2. *irregularity:* lawless or disordered behavior. Mrs. Philips's actions suggest the possible justice of Elizabeth's suspicion that others are feeling a sense of triumph from the Bennets' misfortunes.

3. Meaning that it was generally asserted that his intrigues or attempts at seduction had been extended into every family. As usual, public opinion has proved shallow and fickle.

half of what was said, believed enough to make her former assurance of her sister's ruin still more certain; and even Jane, who believed still less of it, became almost hopeless, more especially as the time was now come, when if they had gone to Scotland, which she had never before entirely despaired of, they must in all probability have gained some news of them.

Mr. Gardiner left Longbourn on Sunday; on Tuesday, his wife received a letter from him; it told them, that on his arrival, he had immediately found out[4] his brother, and persuaded him to come to Gracechurch street. That Mr. Bennet had been to Epsom and Clapham,[5] before his arrival, but without gaining any satisfactory information; and that he was now determined to enquire at all the principal hotels in town, as Mr. Bennet thought it possible they might have gone to one of them, on their first coming to London, before they procured lodgings. Mr. Gardiner himself did not expect any success from this measure, but as his brother was eager in it, he meant to assist him in pursuing it. He added, that Mr. Bennet seemed wholly disinclined at present, to leave London, and promised to write again very soon. There was also a postscript to this effect.

"I have written to Colonel Forster to desire him to find out, if possible, from some of the young man's intimates in the regiment, whether Wickham has any relations or connections, who would be likely to know in what part of the town he has now concealed himself. If there were any one, that one could apply to, with a probability of gaining such a clue as that, it might be of essential consequence. At present we have nothing to guide us. Colonel Forster will, I dare say, do every thing in his power to satisfy us on this head. But, on second thoughts, perhaps Lizzy could tell us, what relations he has now living, better than any other person."

Elizabeth was at no loss to understand from whence this deference for her authority proceeded; but it was not in her power to give any information of so satisfactory a nature, as the compliment deserved.[6]

She had never heard of his having had any relations, except a father and mother, both of whom had been dead many years.

4. *found out:* located.

5. *Epsom and Clapham:* see p. 532, and p. 499, notes 20 and 22.

6. The "compliment" concerns Elizabeth's earlier intimacy with Wickham; of course, it is more an insult than a compliment to bring up now the subject of that intimacy, and of her impulsive championing of Wickham's supposed virtues.

It was possible, however, that some of his companions in the ——shire, might be able to give more information; and, though she was not very sanguine in expecting it, the application was a something to look forward to.

Every day at Longbourn was now a day of anxiety; but the most anxious part of each was when the post was expected. The arrival of letters was the first grand object of every morning's impatience. Through letters, whatever of good or bad was to be told, would be communicated, and every succeeding day was expected to bring some news of importance.

But before they heard again from Mr. Gardiner, a letter arrived for their father, from a different quarter, from Mr. Collins; which, as Jane had received directions to open all that came for him in his absence, she accordingly read; and Elizabeth, who knew what curiosities his letters always were,[7] looked over her, and read it likewise. It was as follows:

My Dear Sir,

I feel myself called upon, by our relationship, and my situation in life, to condole with you on the grievous affliction you are now suffering under, of which we were yesterday informed by a letter from Hertfordshire.[8] Be assured, my dear Sir, that Mrs. Collins and myself sincerely sympathise with you, and all your respectable family, in your present distress, which must be of the bitterest kind, because proceeding from a cause which no time can remove.[9] No arguments shall be wanting[10] on my part, that can alleviate so severe a misfortune; or that may comfort you, under a circumstance that must be of all others most afflicting to a parent's mind. The death of your daughter would have been a blessing in comparison of this.[11] And it is the more to be lamented, because there is reason to suppose, as my dear Charlotte informs me, that this licentiousness of behaviour in your daughter, has proceeded from a faulty degree of indulgence,[12] though, at the same time, for the consolation of yourself and Mrs. Bennet, I am inclined to think that her own disposition[13] must be naturally bad, or she could not be guilty of such an enormity,[14] at so early an age. Howsoever that may be,

7.   Elizabeth is not in such despair that she has lost her taste for curiosities.

8.   Presumably from Charlotte's family.

9.   *no time can remove*: a standard phrase used in such circumstances. It was generally believed that a woman could never erase the shame of such an act. In fact, it is hard to find a writing from this period that does not argue for the absolute necessity of a woman's safeguarding her chastity.

10.   *wanting*: lacking.

11.   Another common idea of the time. It was given most memorable expression in a poem (humorously alluded to in *Emma*) by Oliver Goldsmith, from his novel *The Vicar of Wakefield*:

> When lovely woman stoops to folly
>   And finds too late that men betray
> What charm can soothe her melancholy,
>   What art can wash her guilt away?
>
> The only art her guilt to cover,
>   To hide her shame from every eye,
> To give repentance to her lover,
>   To wring his bosom—is to die.

12.   It is not clear how much Charlotte has said against the Bennets to prompt her husband's reproach. One could regard strong condemnation on her part as a betrayal of her friendship with Elizabeth, at a time when she and the Bennet family are most in need of support. At the same time, Charlotte could not have avoided giving some opinion of the case in any discussions with her husband and Lady Catherine, since she knew the Bennet family so well, and it would be hard for any honest person discussing Lydia and her upbringing to refrain from mentioning how spoiled Lydia was and how negligent her parents were. Nor would it have taken much information along those lines to inspire moral strictures on Mr. Collins's part.

   In denouncing Lydia so zealously, Mr. Collins also may be spurred by his remembrance of her rude interruption of him when he tried to read *Fordyce's Sermons* to the Bennet family. He could even be reflecting now that it would have been good for her to have attended to the lessons he was trying to impart from such a pious book.

13.   *disposition*: moral character.

14.   *enormity*: monstrous offense or crime.

you are grievously to be pitied, in which opinion I am not only joined by Mrs. Collins, but likewise by Lady Catherine and her daughter, to whom I have related the affair. They agree with me in apprehending that this false step in one daughter, will be injurious to the fortunes of all the others, for who, as Lady Catherine herself condescendingly says, will connect themselves with such a family.[15] *And this consideration leads me moreover to reflect with augmented satisfaction on a certain event of last November, for had it been otherwise, I must have been involved in all your sorrow and disgrace.*[16] *Let me advise you then, my dear Sir, to console yourself as much as possible, to throw off your unworthy child from your affection for ever, and leave her to reap the fruits of her own heinous offence.*[17]

I am, dear Sir, &c., &c.

Mr. Gardiner did not write again, till he had received an answer from Colonel Forster; and then he had nothing of a pleasant nature to send. It was not known that Wickham had a single relation, with whom he kept up any connection, and it was certain that he had no near one living. His former acquaintance had been numerous; but since he had been in the militia, it did not appear that he was on terms of particular friendship with any of them.[18] There was no one therefore who could be pointed out, as likely to give any news of him. And in the wretched state of his own finances, there was a very powerful motive for secrecy, in addition to his fear of discovery by Lydia's relations, for it had just transpired[19] that he had left gaming debts behind him, to a very considerable amount. Colonel Forster believed that more than a thousand pounds would be necessary to clear his expences at Brighton. He owed a good deal in the town, but his debts of honour[20] were still more formidable. Mr. Gardiner did not attempt to conceal these particulars from the Longbourn family; Jane heard them with horror. "A gamester!"[21] she cried. "This is wholly unexpected. I had not an idea of it."

Mr. Gardiner added in his letter, that they might expect to see their father at home on the following day, which was Saturday.

15. The consequences of Lydia's action for the other Bennet girls begin to appear, for Lady Catherine's opinion is one that would be widely shared. She herself will allude to the family disgrace of Lydia's elopement when she later confronts Elizabeth.

16. Mr. Collins congratulates himself on not having married Elizabeth, in which case he would have had to share far more in the family misfortune because of his closer connection with them.

17. Severing one's ties with such a daughter was standard practice in this society, though this often meant sending her away to live elsewhere rather than literally throwing off all affection for her as Mr. Collins advises.

18. Earlier, on p. 378, Wickham is described as having entered the militia, "at the persuasion of the young man [Denny], who, on meeting him accidentally in town [London], had there renewed a slight acquaintance." This lack of close friends hints at the flaws in Wickham's character, just as Darcy's friendship with Bingley and Colonel Fitzwilliam reveals his good character.

19. *transpired*: become known, been revealed (after being concealed).

20. *debts of honour*: debts that are not legally binding (as opposed to his debts in town, which would most likely be with merchants and thus be enforceable by law). Debts of honor generally referred to gambling debts among friends, which one was only bound by honor to pay; in this case, they come most likely from Wickham's card games with fellow officers.

21. *gamester*: gambler, especially a habitual gambler. Such a figure was often regarded with horror. A popular play of the eighteenth century, Edward Moore's *The Gamester*, depicted the ruin caused by the title character; the play is mentioned in *Mansfield Park*. In the same novel Jane Austen shows a young man, Tom Bertram, who loses a great deal of money through gambling and who, while not a villainous character, does cause severe problems for his family.

Rendered spiritless by the ill-success of all their endeavours, he had yielded to his brother-in-law's intreaty that he would return to his family, and leave it to him to do, whatever occasion might suggest to be advisable for continuing their pursuit. When Mrs. Bennet was told of this, she did not express so much satisfaction as her children expected, considering what her anxiety for his life had been before.

"What, is he coming home, and without poor Lydia!" she cried. "Sure he will not leave London before he has found them. Who is to fight Wickham, and make him marry her, if he comes away?"[22]

As Mrs. Gardiner began to wish to be at home, it was settled that she and her children should go to London, at the same time that Mr. Bennet came from it. The coach, therefore, took them the first stage of their journey, and brought its master back to Longbourn.[23]

Mrs. Gardiner went away in all the perplexity about Elizabeth and her Derbyshire friend,[24] that had attended her from that part of the world. His name had never been voluntarily mentioned before them by her niece; and the kind of half-expectation which Mrs. Gardiner had formed, of their being followed by a letter from him, had ended in nothing. Elizabeth had received none since her return, that could come from Pemberley.[25]

The present unhappy state of the family, rendered any other excuse for the lowness of her spirits unnecessary; nothing, therefore, could be fairly conjectured from *that*, though Elizabeth, who was by this time tolerably well acquainted with her own feelings, was perfectly aware, that, had she known nothing of Darcy, she could have borne the dread of Lydia's infamy somewhat better. It would have spared her, she thought, one sleepless night out of two.

When Mr. Bennet arrived, he had all the appearance of his usual philosophic composure. He said as little as he had ever been in the habit of saying; made no mention of the business that had taken him away, and it was some time before his daughters had courage to speak of it.

It was not till the afternoon,[26] when he joined them at tea, that Elizabeth ventured to introduce the subject; and then, on her briefly expressing her sorrow for what he must have endured, he

22. Mrs. Bennet's statement, in addition to exposing her usual inconsistency, indicates the widespread acceptance of dueling in public opinion of the time. Some people did denounce duels. Jane Austen's favorite novel, Samuel Richardson's *Sir Charles Grandison*, gives prominent place to its hero's renunciation of dueling; but the same novel indicates an awareness of the unusual and unpopular nature of such a renunciation. Moreover, while dueling was against the law—in fact, in a well-publicized case from 1808, just before this novel appeared, a major in the British army was executed for killing another officer in a duel—the authorities usually turned a blind eye to the practice. In 1809, two of the leading political figures in Britain, the Secretaries of War and of Foreign Affairs, fought a duel over intense differences about war policy. Dueling's general social acceptability is also indicated by the existence of books at the time that detailed the elaborate rules supposed to govern duels. One principle of the rules was that insults or injuries to ladies could be considered an especially grave offense, which would make the duel at issue here more acceptable than most.

23. It is now exactly two weeks since Lydia and Wickham first ran off together (see chronology, pp. 717–718).

24. Before the news about Lydia came, Mrs. Gardiner was in a state of suspense about Elizabeth's relationship with Darcy, suspecting something and wishing to know more, but unwilling to ask Elizabeth directly (see pp. 494 and 510).

25. This would naturally convince Elizabeth of the validity of her earlier supposition that Lydia's affair would make Darcy repudiate Elizabeth.

26. *afternoon:* after dinner. Mention of tea indicates that it is almost early evening in current terminology.

replied, "Say nothing of that. Who should suffer but myself? It has been my own doing, and I ought to feel it."[27]

"You must not be too severe upon yourself," replied Elizabeth.

"You may well warn me against such an evil. Human nature is so prone to fall into it![28] No, Lizzy, let me once in my life feel how much I have been to blame. I am not afraid of being over-powered by the impression. It will pass away soon enough."[29]

"Do you suppose them to be in London?"

"Yes; where else can they be so well concealed?"

"And Lydia used to want to go to London," added Kitty.

"She is happy, then," said her father, drily; "and her residence there will probably be of some duration."

Then, after a short silence, he continued, "Lizzy, I bear you no ill-will for being justified in your advice to me last May, which, considering the event,[30] shews some greatness of mind."[31]

They were interrupted by Miss Bennet, who came to fetch her mother's tea.

"This is a parade,"[32] cried he, "which does one good; it gives such an elegance to misfortune! Another day I will do the same; I will sit in my library, in my night cap and powdering gown,[33] and give as much trouble as I can,—or, perhaps, I may defer it, till Kitty runs away."

"I am not going to run away, Papa," said Kitty, fretfully; "if *I* should ever go to Brighton, I would behave better than Lydia."

"*You* go to Brighton!—I would not trust you so near it as East Bourne,[34] for fifty pounds! No, Kitty, I have at last learnt to be cautious, and you will feel the effects of it. No officer is ever to enter my house again, nor even to pass through the village.[35] Balls will be absolutely prohibited, unless you stand up with one of your sisters.[36] And you are never to stir out of doors, till you can prove, that you have spent ten minutes of every day in a rational manner."

Kitty, who took all these threats in a serious light, began to cry.

"Well, well," said he, "do not make yourself unhappy. If you are a good girl for the next ten years, I will take you to a review[37] at the end of them."

27. One of the only times in the book that Mr. Bennet speaks without irony or humor.

28. Mr. Bennet quickly resumes a degree of irony, since the implication of his succeeding words is that human beings are not prone to be too severe upon themselves. Certainly the novel presents far more examples of people blaming themselves too little than of people blaming themselves too much.

29. An indication of Mr. Bennet's strong self-awareness. He knows his flaws, though he is not about to make any serious effort to correct them.

30. *event*: outcome (of the whole affair).

31. An ironic statement that also shows a shrewd understanding of human nature on his, and the author's, part. In principle, people should respect and feel humbled toward someone who has been proven right; in practice, however, such a person tends to provoke resentment and anger due to others' humiliation at having been wrong. Hence Mr. Bennet boasts that, by not feeling this resentment toward Elizabeth, he is showing greatness of mind.

32. *parade*: display, piece of ostentation. Mr. Bennet intends the word as a sarcastic description of his wife's exaggerated distress.

33. *powdering gown*: gown worn over clothes to protect them while the hair was being powdered. Such types of gowns were often worn, over clothes, when people were indoors and either alone or with close family members.

34. *East Bourne* (or Eastbourne): a town along the southern coast, about 20 miles from Brighton (see maps, pp. 742 and 745). It was a small resort, and like others in the vicinity, it had emerged as a venue for those who wished to escape from Brighton's high fashion and dissoluteness. Thus it would be a far safer destination for someone like Kitty.

35. Mr. Bennet has thus resumed his normal full irony, even while expressing a serious intent regarding Kitty, for he cannot control who enters the village.

36. It was not unusual for women to dance together. Jane Austen writes in a letter of a ball where the shortage of men forced her, as well as other women, to dance a number of times with a female partner (Nov. 1, 1800).

37. *review*: public military inspection or ceremony; they originated in the practice of officers or rulers reviewing troops. By this time they had become extremely popular attractions, sometimes drawing spectators in the hundreds of thousands. Reviews would last for several hours at least: they always involved the continuous playing of military music, and could include the presentation of troops or military colors before important (even royal) figures, elaborate marches in formation, mock battles, military funerals, or the firing of guns. In a letter Jane Austen speaks of one that she will attend (June 2, 1799).

Chapter Seven

*T*wo days after Mr. Bennet's return, as Jane and Elizabeth were walking together in the shrubbery behind the house, they saw the housekeeper coming towards them, and, concluding that she came to call them to their mother, went forward to meet her; but, instead of the expected summons, when they approached her, she said to Miss Bennet,[1] "I beg your pardon, madam, for interrupting you, but I was in hopes you might have got some good news from town,[2] so I took the liberty of coming to ask."

"What do you mean, Hill?[3] We have heard nothing from town."

"Dear madam," cried Mrs. Hill, in great astonishment, "don't you know there is an express come for master from Mr. Gardiner? He has been here this half hour, and master has had a letter."[4]

Away ran the girls, too eager to get in to have time for speech. They ran through the vestibule into the breakfast room; from thence to the library;[5]—their father was in neither; and they were on the point of seeking him up stairs with their mother, when they were met by the butler,[6] who said,

"If you are looking for my master, ma'am, he is walking towards the little copse."[7]

Upon this information, they instantly passed through the hall once more, and ran across the lawn after their father, who was deliberately pursuing his way towards a small wood on one side of the paddock.[8]

Jane, who was not so light, nor so much in the habit of running as Elizabeth, soon lagged behind, while her sister, panting for breath, came up with him, and eagerly cried out,

"Oh, Papa, what news? what news? have you heard from my uncle?"

"Yes, I have had a letter from him by express."[9]

"Well, and what news does it bring? good or bad?"

1. *Miss Bennet:* what the housekeeper would call Jane.

2. *town:* London.

3. *Hill:* calling her by her last name, as opposed to her first, indicates she is an upper servant.

4. Mrs. Hill's speech is cruder and more colloquial than that of Darcy's housekeeper, Mrs. Reynolds. Mrs. Hill, as the head of a smaller household with fewer servants under her, would be more likely to come from a humble background and, while serving as the housekeeper, to spend her time with fellow servants and thus to retain their manners and speech.

5. Their running indoors, if one can assume that "ran" is meant literally, signals their eagerness, for such an action would not be considered genteel. Even the running outdoors they do was sometimes frowned upon as being unladylike.

6. *the butler:* the chief male servant within the house. Here he seems to be less important than the housekeeper, Hill, which was often not the case. His job included the important tasks of taking care of the family wines and fine utensils; he also could serve as valet to the master of the house.

7. *copse:* a small woods that is periodically cut (same as coppice).

8. *paddock:* enclosed field or lawn.

9. *express:* express messenger.

"What is there of good to be expected?" said he, taking the let-ter from his pocket; "but perhaps you would like to read it."

Elizabeth impatiently caught it from his hand. Jane now came up.

"Read it aloud," said their father, "for I hardly know myself what it is about."

Gracechurch-street, Monday, August 2.[10]

MY DEAR BROTHER,

At last I am able to send you some tidings of my niece, and such as, upon the whole, I hope will give you satisfaction. Soon after you left me on Saturday, I was fortunate enough to find out in what part of London they were.[11] The particulars, I reserve till we meet. It is enough to know they are discovered, I have seen them both——

"Then it is, as I always hoped," cried Jane; "they are married!"

Elizabeth read on;

I have seen them both. They are not married, nor can I find there was any intention of being so; but if you are willing to perform the engagements which I have ventured to make on your side, I hope it will not be long before they are. All that is required of you is, to assure to your daughter, by settlement,[12] her equal share of the five thousand pounds, secured among your children after the decease of yourself and my sister; and, moreover, to enter into an engagement of allowing her, during your life, one hundred pounds per annum. These are condi-tions, which, considering every thing, I had no hesitation in comply-ing with, as far as I thought myself privileged, for you. I shall send this by express, that no time may be lost in bringing me your answer. You will easily comprehend, from these particulars, that Mr. Wickham's circumstances are not so hopeless as they are generally believed to be. The world has been deceived in that respect; and I am happy to say, there will be some little money, even when all his debts are discharged, to settle on my niece, in addition to her own fortune. If, as I conclude will be the case, you send me full powers to act in your name, through-out the whole of this business, I will immediately give directions to Haggerston[13] for preparing a proper settlement. There will not be the smallest occasion for your coming to town again; therefore, stay

10. *August 2:* this date is a mistake—a rarity for Jane Austen. In fact, the letter must have been written approximately two weeks later. First, by this point it has been almost two weeks since Elizabeth's meeting with Bingley at Lambton, which itself must have been after July 26 since at the meeting Bingley states that the Netherfield Ball of Nov. 26 occurred more than eight months earlier and Elizabeth is "pleased to find his memory so exact" on this point. Second, the letter comes exactly two weeks before the day of Lydia's marriage—it says "She comes to us today," and later Lydia says she was at the Gardiners for two weeks (p. 576)—and the marriage occurs just before September 1 since it is not long afterwards that Mrs. Gardiner sends a letter to Elizabeth dated Sept. 6 (p. 582). Thus the date of this letter is around the middle of August.

For further information on these points, see chronology, p. 718.

11. The reason why Mr. Gardiner found out this information just after Mr. Bennet's departure is revealed a little later (see p. 586).

12. *settlement:* a marriage, especially among the wealthier classes, was normally preceded by a legally binding settlement or agreement between the family of the bride and the groom or the groom's family. The settlement would specify how much money would be given to the groom as a dowry; it would also generally establish how much personal spending money the wife would receive during the marriage, what the wife would receive if left a widow, and how much money would eventually go to the children. These last three provisions—known, respectively, as pin-money, jointure, and portions—generally represented what the groom's family was giving in response to the dowry provided by the bride's family, though in this case, because of Wickham's lack of money, nothing is coming from the groom's side.

13. *Haggerston:* probably an attorney, for one would be essential in preparing the complicated legal provisions of a settlement.

quietly at Longbourn, and depend on my diligence and care. Send back your answer as soon as you can, and be careful to write explicitly. We have judged it best, that my niece should be married from this house,[14] *of which I hope you will approve. She comes to us today. I shall write again as soon as any thing more is determined on.*

Your's, &c.
EDW. GARDINER.

"Is it possible!" cried Elizabeth, when she had finished. "Can it be possible that he will marry her?"

"Wickham is not so undeserving, then, as we have thought him;" said her sister. "My dear father, I congratulate you."

"And have you answered the letter?" said Elizabeth.

"No; but it must be done soon."

Most earnestly did she then intreat him to lose no more time before he wrote.

"Oh! my dear father," she cried, "come back, and write immediately. Consider how important every moment is, in such a case."

"Let me write for you," said Jane, "if you dislike the trouble yourself."

"I dislike it very much," he replied; "but it must be done."

And so saying, he turned back with them, and walked towards the house.

"And may I ask?" said Elizabeth, "but the terms, I suppose, must be complied with."

"Complied with! I am only ashamed of his asking so little."

"And they *must* marry! Yet he is *such* a man!"

"Yes, yes, they must marry. There is nothing else to be done.[15] But there are two things that I want very much to know:—one is, how much money your uncle has laid down, to bring it about; and the other, how I am ever to pay him."

"Money! my uncle!" cried Jane, "what do you mean, Sir?"

"I mean, that no man in his senses, would marry Lydia on so slight a temptation as one hundred a-year during my life, and fifty after I am gone."[16]

"That is very true," said Elizabeth; "though it had not occurred

14. Meaning she will stay with them until the marriage.

15. Wickham's marrying Lydia is the only course that would restore her respectability, or at least as much as could be restored at this point, for it would allow their living together to be regarded as a hasty preliminary to marriage. That would not be the case if she married someone else. Hence Wickham, despite his unworthiness, must be her husband.

16. Lydia's share of the five thousand pounds that go to the children after Mr. Bennet's death would be one-fifth, or one thousand. This would produce, at normal yields of 5%, fifty pounds a year.

to me before. His debts to be discharged,[17] and something still to remain! Oh! it must be my uncle's doings! Generous, good man, I am afraid he has distressed himself.[18] A small sum could not do all this."

"No," said her father, "Wickham's a fool, if he takes her with a farthing[19] less than ten thousand pounds. I should be sorry to think so ill of him, in the very beginning of our relationship."[20]

"Ten thousand pounds! Heaven forbid! How is half such a sum to be repaid?"[21]

Mr. Bennet made no answer, and each of them, deep in thought, continued silent till they reached the house. Their father then went to the library to write, and the girls walked into the breakfast-room.

"And they are really to be married!" cried Elizabeth, as soon as they were by themselves. "How strange this is! And for *this* we are to be thankful. That they should marry, small as is their chance of happiness, and wretched as is his character, we are forced to rejoice! Oh, Lydia!"

"I comfort myself with thinking," replied Jane, "that he certainly would not marry Lydia, if he had not a real regard for her. Though our kind uncle has done something towards clearing him, I cannot believe that ten thousand pounds, or any thing like it, has been advanced. He has children of his own, and may have more. How could he spare half ten thousand pounds?"[22]

"If we are ever able to learn what Wickham's debts have been," said Elizabeth, "and how much is settled on his side on our sister, we shall exactly know what Mr. Gardiner has done for them, because Wickham has not sixpence[23] of his own. The kindness of my uncle and aunt can never be requited. Their taking her home, and affording her their personal protection and countenance,[24] is such a sacrifice to her advantage, as years of gratitude cannot enough acknowledge. By this time she is actually with them! If such goodness does not make her miserable now, she will never deserve to be happy! What a meeting for her, when she first sees my aunt!"[25]

"We must endeavour to forget all that has passed on either side," said Jane: "I hope and trust they will yet be happy. His consenting to marry her is a proof, I will believe, that he is come to a right way

17. Already stated as more than a thousand pounds.

18. *distressed himself*: subjected himself to severe strain, exhausted himself (in a financial sense).

19. *farthing*: the smallest English unit of money; there were four farthings in a pence (see below) and 960 in a pound. The word farthing was often used, as in this case, to express the tiniest possible amount.

20. In other words, Mr. Bennet would think ill of him for not being shrewd or ruthless enough in his mercenary dealings.

21. Mr. Bennet's income is only two thousand a year, so accumulating ten thousand pounds would take years (it is soon revealed that Mr. Bennet has yet to accumulate any savings).

22. Jane's skepticism about her uncle's ability to pay such an enormous sum is justified, from what has been shown of him (a merchant who could spare that from his normal income would, for example, probably not be one who lived in sight of his own shops as Mr. Gardiner does). At the same time, her hope in Wickham's goodness is not justified. The mystery will soon be resolved.

23. *sixpence*: pence, or pennies, were the most important small units of English money. Twelve pence made a shilling. Financial records were generally kept in a combination of pounds, shilling, and pence (e.g. 12.6.8 would mean twelve pounds, six shillings, and eight pence).

24. *countenance*: support, favor.

25. Elizabeth refers to the misery Lydia will supposedly suffer because of her shame at receiving such undeserved kindness. It will soon be shown how little misery or shame Lydia actually feels.

of thinking. Their mutual affection will steady them; and I flatter myself they will settle so quietly, and live in so rational a manner, as may in time make their past imprudence forgotten."

"Their conduct has been such," replied Elizabeth, "as neither you, nor I, nor any body, can ever forget. It is useless to talk of it."

It now occurred to the girls that their mother was in all likelihood perfectly ignorant of what had happened. They went to the library, therefore, and asked their father, whether he would not wish them to make it known to her. He was writing, and, without raising his head, coolly replied,

"Just as you please."

"May we take my uncle's letter to read to her?"

"Take whatever you like, and get away."

Elizabeth took the letter from his writing table, and they went up stairs together. Mary and Kitty were both with Mrs. Bennet: one communication would, therefore, do for all. After a slight preparation for good news, the letter was read aloud. Mrs. Bennet could hardly contain herself. As soon as Jane had read Mr. Gardiner's hope of Lydia's being soon married, her joy burst forth, and every following sentence added to its exuberance. She was now in an irritation[26] as violent from delight, as she had ever been fidgetty from alarm and vexation. To know that her daughter would be married was enough. She was disturbed by no fear for her felicity, nor humbled by any remembrance of her misconduct.

"My dear, dear Lydia!" she cried: "This is delightful indeed!— She will be married!—I shall see her again!—She will be married at sixteen![27]—My good, kind brother!—I knew how it would be—I knew he would manage every thing. How I long to see her! and to see dear Wickham too! But the clothes, the wedding clothes! I will write to my sister Gardiner about them directly. Lizzy, my dear, run down to your father, and ask him how much he will give her. Stay, stay, I will go myself. Ring the bell, Kitty, for Hill. I will put on my things in a moment.[28] My dear, dear Lydia!—How merry we shall be together when we meet!"

Her eldest daughter endeavoured to give some relief to the violence of these transports,[29] by leading her thoughts to the obligations which Mr. Gardiner's behaviour laid them all under.

26. *irritation*: excitement, state of agitation.

27. An unusually early age for marriage, and hence a source of pride for Mrs. Bennet.

28. Mrs. Bennet has presumably been in her nightclothes or a dressing gown while remaining in her room; now she wishes for normal clothes, which she would need for going around the rest of the house.

29. *transports*: outbursts of ecstasy or exaltation.

Examples of the fashions of the period. The first dress is a day dress, the second is for evening wear.

[From Iris Brooke, *Western European Costume, Seventeenth to Mid-Nineteenth Century* (New York, 1940), pp. 133 and 134]

"For we must attribute this happy conclusion," she added, "in a great measure, to his kindness. We are persuaded that he has pledged himself to assist Mr. Wickham with money."

"Well," cried her mother, "it is all very right; who should do it but her own uncle? If he had not had a family of his own, I and my children must have had all his money you know,[30] and it is the first time we have ever had any thing from him, except a few presents. Well! I am so happy. In a short time, I shall have a daughter married. Mrs. Wickham! How well it sounds. And she was only sixteen last June. My dear Jane, I am in such a flutter, that I am sure I can't write; so I will dictate, and you write for me. We will settle with your father about the money afterwards; but the things[31] should be ordered immediately."

She was then proceeding to all the particulars of calico, muslin, and cambric,[32] and would shortly have dictated some very plentiful orders, had not Jane, though with some difficulty, persuaded her to wait, till her father was at leisure to be consulted.[33] One day's delay she observed, would be of small importance; and her mother was too happy, to be quite so obstinate as usual. Other schemes too came into her head.

"I will go to Meryton," said she, "as soon as I am dressed, and tell the good, good news to my sister Philips. And as I come back, I can call on Lady Lucas and Mrs. Long.[34] Kitty, run down and order the carriage. An airing would do me a great deal of good, I am sure. Girls, can I do any thing for you in Meryton? Oh! here comes Hill. My dear Hill, have you heard the good news? Miss Lydia is going to be married; and you shall all have a bowl of punch, to make merry at her wedding."[35]

Mrs. Hill began instantly to express her joy. Elizabeth received her congratulations amongst the rest, and then, sick of this folly,[36] took refuge in her own room, that she might think with freedom.

Poor Lydia's situation must, at best, be bad enough; but that it was no worse, she had need to be thankful. She felt it so; and though, in looking forward, neither rational happiness nor worldly prosperity, could be justly expected for her sister; in looking back to what they had feared, only two hours ago, she felt all the advantages of what they had gained.

30. Meaning they would have been his heirs after his death.

31. *things:* wedding clothes.

32. *calico, muslin, and cambric:* types of clothing fabric. Calico and muslin were both cottons that became popular in the late eighteenth century; calico was used particularly as a material for good dresses. Cambric was the most fashionable type of linen; it was generally white. Cambric and muslin were both light fabrics, and their widespread use contributed to the soft, flowing styles in vogue at the time. See previous page, and cover, for illustrations of these styles.

33. Jane is sensible enough to suspect, as turns out to be the case, that Mr. Bennet will be far less enthusiastic about buying wedding clothes for Lydia.

34. Mrs. Bennet will of course tell them the good news about Lydia. The constant concern in this society about what the neighbors think is again apparent.

35. Mrs. Bennet alludes to a traditional practice of allowing the servants to partake in some of the wedding celebration. That she needs to assure a servant of this, and that she only mentions a bowl of punch, could be a symptom of the general tendency in this period for weddings among the wealthy to be small-scale, intimate affairs. In fact, the decline from earlier customs of large gentry weddings, weddings that had included distributions of food to the poor, was denounced by some at the time as an abnegation of social responsibility. Later in the nineteenth century large weddings would revive. One of Jane Austen's nieces, Caroline Austen, has left a description of the wedding of another of her nieces, Anna Austen, in which the whole affair is depicted as quiet and private; Caroline Austen also mentions that the servants were given cake and punch in the evening.

36. Her mother's folly in feeling such joy, while forgetting what Lydia has done wrong.

Chapter Eight

Mr. Bennet had very often wished, before this period of his life, that, instead of spending his whole income, he had laid by an annual sum, for the better provision of his children, and of his wife, if she survived him. He now wished it more than ever. Had he done his duty in that respect, Lydia need not have been indebted to her uncle, for whatever of honour or credit could now be purchased for her.[1] The satisfaction of prevailing on one of the most worthless young men in Great Britain to be her husband, might then have rested in its proper place.

He was seriously concerned, that a cause of so little advantage to any one, should be forwarded at the sole expence of his brother-in-law, and he was determined, if possible, to find out the extent of his assistance, and to discharge the obligation as soon as he could.

When first Mr. Bennet had married, economy was held to be perfectly useless; for, of course, they were to have a son. This son was to join in cutting off the entail, as soon as he should be of age, and the widow and younger children would by that means be provided for.[2] Five daughters successively entered the world, but yet the son was to come; and Mrs. Bennet, for many years after Lydia's birth, had been certain that he would. This event had at last been despaired of, but it was then too late to be saving.[3] Mrs. Bennet had no turn for economy,[4] and her husband's love of independence[5] had alone prevented their exceeding their income.[6]

Five thousand pounds was settled by marriage articles on Mrs. Bennet and the children. But in what proportions it should be divided amongst the latter, depended on the will of the parents.[7] This was one point, with regard to Lydia at least, which was now to be settled, and Mr. Bennet could have no hesitation in acceding to the proposal before him. In terms of grateful acknowledgment for the kindness of his brother, though expressed most

1.   In other words, Lydia would still be tainted by her elopement, but she might regain some honor and credit, i.e., public reputation, through her marriage, bought by money for Wickham.

2.   When the heir to an entail came of age, if the current holder of the entail (in this case Mr. Bennet) were still alive, they could join together to break or annul the entail. They could then establish a new settlement of the property to help other members of the family. But, while Mr. Bennet could hope to get a son to agree to such a new settlement (which would mean sacrificing some of his own interest for the sake of his siblings), Mr. Bennet would have no chance with a more distant relation like Mr. Collins.

3.   *saving*: frugal.

4.   *economy*: economical management. Management of the household, including such matters as meals and shopping and servants, would be Mrs. Bennet's responsibility.

5.   *independence*: financial independence. Presumably this means that his desire to avoid going into debt, and thus becoming dependent on creditors, keeps him from being too careless.

6.   In discussing Mr. Bennet's financial failures, Jane Austen does not mention another way he could have improved his position: increasing the revenues from his estate through agricultural improvement. Such improvements were being introduced by landowners throughout England at this time and were helping to lay the foundations for her rapid economic growth and industrialization in the nineteenth century. Jane Austen refers to a landowner's improvements in *Sense and Sensibility*; she may not bother discussing them here because, given Mr. Bennet's general indolence, they may have constituted even less of a real option for him than frugal living.

7.   Marriage articles are provisions of the legally binding settlement drawn up before marriage. In this case the five thousand pounds—which would have derived from the four thousand in dowry of Mrs. Bennet (see p. 50) plus another thousand that Mr. Bennet's family would presumably have added—is a sum whose income Mr. Bennet is able to enjoy during his life, but which he cannot otherwise touch. After his death it will go to his wife or children.
    In this case there is some ambiguity as to whether the wife or the children will be the primary recipient: Mr. Gardiner's letter speaks of the money going to the children after both parents died, but Mr. Bennet then talks of Lydia receiving her thousand after his death. Normally separate provisions were drawn up for the wife, in case of her becoming a widow, and for the children, who would often receive their sum when they turned twenty-one or when they married. In this case it seems that the Bennet children may not

concisely, he then delivered on paper his perfect approbation of all that was done, and his willingness to fulfil the engagements that had been made for him. He had never before supposed that, could Wickham be prevailed on to marry his daughter, it would be done with so little inconvenience to himself, as by the present arrangement. He would scarcely be ten pounds a-year the loser, by the hundred that was to be paid them; for, what with her board and pocket allowance, and the continual presents in money, which passed to her, through her mother's hands, Lydia's expences had been very little within that sum.[8]

That it would be done with such trifling exertion on his side, too, was another very welcome surprise; for his chief wish at present, was to have as little trouble in the business as possible. When the first transports[9] of rage which had produced his activity in seeking her were over, he naturally returned to all his former indolence. His letter was soon dispatched; for though dilatory in undertaking business, he was quick in its execution. He begged to know farther particulars of what he was indebted to his brother; but was too angry with Lydia, to send any message to her.

The good news quickly spread through the house; and with proportionate speed through the neighbourhood. It was borne in the latter with decent philosophy.[10] To be sure it would have been more for the advantage of conversation,[11] had Miss Lydia Bennet[12] come upon the town;[13] or, as the happiest alternative, been secluded from the world, in some distant farm house.[14] But there was much to be talked of, in marrying her; and the good-natured wishes for her well-doing, which had proceeded before, from all the spiteful old ladies in Meryton, lost but little of their spirit[15] in this change of circumstances, because with such an husband, her misery was considered certain.[16]

It was a fortnight since Mrs. Bennet had been down stairs, but on this happy day, she again took her seat at the head of her table, and in spirits oppressively high.[17] No sentiment of shame gave a damp to her triumph. The marriage of a daughter, which had been the first object of her wishes, since Jane was sixteen, was now on the point of accomplishment, and her thoughts and her words

even receive their relatively small sum until both parents are dead, which would make their financial position even worse. The smallness of the mother's and children's inheritance, compared to that usually seen among those of this class, probably reflects the relatively weak position of Mrs. Bennet's family when the marriage articles were drawn up: since they were of lower rank than Mr. Bennet's family, they and their daughter were, socially speaking, receiving greater advantages than they were conferring; the consequent weakness of their bargaining position meant that they probably felt greater pressure to compromise.

As for the lack of a specified distribution of the sum among the children, that was more normal. This procedure was often employed because it gave the parents more power over their children by allowing them to hold out the threat, to a disobedient or misbehaving child, of allotting all the inheritance to the other children.

8. That is, she already cost him around 90 pounds a year.

9. *transports*: fits, strong emotions.

10. *decent philosophy*: philosophical resignation or acceptance (regarding something undesirable).

11. Meaning that it would have provided better talk or gossip; that is why it required "decent philosophy" for them to bear the good news.

12. *Miss Lydia Bennet*: others in the neighborhood would call her this, for just saying "Lydia Bennet" would be too familiar in speaking about someone who was not a relation and who came from a genteel family.

13. *come upon the town*: sunk into a life of dissipation or prostitution.

14. Being isolated from society, while still being given a minimum of sustenance from her family, was a common fate of women who had fallen sexually. This is what happens to the adulteress in *Mansfield Park*.

15. *spirit*: zest, vigor.

16. Jane Austen is being ironic about their "good-natured wishes," since the old ladies would have been uttering them while actually relishing Lydia's misfortunes.

17. *oppressively high*: oppressive for those around her.

ran wholly on those attendants of elegant nuptials, fine muslins, new carriages, and servants.[18] She was busily searching through the neighbourhood for a proper situation[19] for her daughter, and, without knowing or considering what their income might be,[20] rejected many as deficient in size and importance.[21]

"Haye-Park might do," said she, "if the Gouldings would quit it, or the great house at Stoke, if the drawing-room were larger; but Ashworth is too far off! I could not bear to have her ten miles from me; and as for Purvis Lodge, the attics are dreadful."

Her husband allowed her to talk on without interruption, while the servants remained.[22] But when they had withdrawn, he said to her, "Mrs. Bennet, before you take any, or all of these houses, for your son[23] and daughter, let us come to a right understanding. Into *one* house in this neighbourhood, they shall never have admittance. I will not encourage the impudence[24] of either, by receiving them at Longbourn."

A long dispute followed this declaration; but Mr. Bennet was firm: it soon led to another; and Mrs. Bennet found, with amazement and horror, that her husband would not advance a guinea[25] to buy clothes for his daughter. He protested that she should receive from him no mark of affection whatever, on the occasion. Mrs. Bennet could hardly comprehend it. That his anger could be carried to such a point of inconceivable resentment, as to refuse his daughter a privilege, without which her marriage would scarcely seem valid,[26] exceeded all that she could believe possible. She was more alive to the disgrace, which the want of new clothes must reflect on her daughter's nuptials, than to any sense of shame at her eloping and living with Wickham, a fortnight before they took place.

Elizabeth was now most heartily sorry that she had, from the distress of the moment, been led to make Mr. Darcy acquainted with their fears for her sister; for since her marriage would so shortly give the proper termination to the elopement, they might hope to conceal its unfavourable beginning,[27] from all those who were not immediately on the spot.

She had no fear of its spreading farther, through his means.[28] There were few people on whose secrecy she would have more

18. Marriage among the wealthy, i.e. elegant nuptials, would normally involve the acquisition of new carriages and new dresses—of which latter, muslins (dresses of muslin fabric) were the most popular—as well as the establishment of a new household with its servants.

19. *situation:* place to live.

20. If Wickham remains a low-ranking military officer, his and Lydia's income will be very low, far too low to enable them to rent a large home.

21. *importance:* prominence. Mrs. Bennet wants an impressive house so that Wickham and Lydia can assume a prominent place in the neighborhood.

22. He would prefer not to begin an argument with his wife in the presence of the servants, for that could undermine the respect of the latter for their employers, or lead to gossip about the argument, based on the servants' reports, spreading through the neighborhood.

23. *your son:* a son-in-law was commonly called this.

24. *impudence:* effrontery; lack of chastity or modesty. Mr. Bennet could be referring to their earlier improper sexual behavior, or to their generally shameless attitude.

25. *guinea:* a coin worth a pound and a shilling.

26. A father normally gave his daughters clothes and other presents on her wedding, so it would be a mark of shame for a father to refuse to do this; in addition, without new clothes Lydia would not be able to look as elegant at the wedding. In *Northanger Abbey* a wealthy young woman is described as having received the considerable sum of five hundred pounds in order to buy wedding clothes.

27. That is, conceal their having lived together for two weeks beforehand.

28. Meaning she has no reason to fear that Darcy, thanks to his having learned of the affair at the inn at Lambton, will tell others of it.
   It is at this point, when the crisis concerning Lydia is over, that Elizabeth can return to thinking at length about Darcy and her situation with regard to him.

confidently depended; but at the same time, there was no one, whose knowledge of a sister's frailty would have mortified her so much. Not, however, from any fear of disadvantage from it, individually to herself; for at any rate, there seemed a gulf impassable between them. Had Lydia's marriage been concluded on the most honourable terms, it was not to be supposed that Mr. Darcy would connect himself with a family, where to every other objection would now be added, an alliance and relationship of the nearest kind with the man whom he so justly scorned.[29]

From such a connection she could not wonder that he should shrink. The wish of procuring her regard, which she had assured herself of his feeling in Derbyshire, could not in rational expectation survive such a blow as this. She was humbled, she was grieved; she repented, though she hardly knew of what. She became jealous of his esteem, when she could no longer hope to be benefited by it. She wanted to hear of him, when there seemed the least chance of gaining intelligence.[30] She was convinced that she could have been happy with him; when it was no longer likely they should meet.[31]

What a triumph for him, as she often thought, could he know that the proposals which she had proudly spurned only four months ago, would now have been gladly and gratefully received! He was as generous, she doubted not, as the most generous[32] of his sex. But while he was mortal, there must be a triumph.[33]

She began now to comprehend that he was exactly the man, who, in disposition and talents, would most suit her. His understanding and temper,[34] though unlike her own, would have answered all her wishes. It was an union that must have been to the advantage of both; by her ease[35] and liveliness,[36] his mind[37] might have been softened,[38] his manners improved, and from his judgment, information,[39] and knowledge of the world, she must have received benefit of greater importance.[40]

But no such happy marriage could now teach the admiring multitude what connubial felicity really was. An union of a different tendency, and precluding the possibility of the other,[41] was soon to be formed in their family.

29. In other words, Elizabeth's regrets about Darcy's knowledge do not stem from her belief that such knowledge would make him unwilling to marry her, for she thinks that, given his hatred for Wickham, he would be unwilling to connect himself to the Bennet family regardless of the circumstances of Lydia and Wickham's marriage. Instead, Elizabeth indicates here her concern about Darcy's opinion, irrespective of the prospect of marrying him. This shows how much he has risen in her esteem.

30. *intelligence:* news, information (about him).

31. Elizabeth is thus experiencing the same pain of believing a beloved to be unattainable that Darcy experienced after she rejected him.

32. *generous:* noble, magnanimous.

33. Meaning that even the most magnanimous man would be human enough to feel some sense of triumph at such a turn of events and such a vindication of himself.

34. *understanding and temper:* mind and disposition.

35. *ease:* lack of formality or social awkwardness.

36. *liveliness:* playfulness, lightheartedness.

37. *mind:* inner character.

38. *softened:* made gentler.

39. *information:* instruction; or capacity to instruct.

40. This passages expresses what may be the central ideal in Jane Austen, that of love as a force to perfect our characters—at least when that love is a rational and sound love. Elizabeth imagines here the ways that both she and Darcy could become a better person after their marriage; the novel already demonstrates the improvements each undergoes before marriage under the influence of the other.

41. In other words, a union of a contrasting nature, one that is guaranteed to make such connubial felicity impossible. The reference is to Lydia and Wickham's match.

How Wickham and Lydia were to be supported in tolerable independence,[42] she could not imagine. But how little of permanent happiness could belong to a couple who were only brought together because their passions were stronger than their virtue, she could easily conjecture.

———

Mr. Gardiner soon wrote again to his brother. To Mr. Bennet's acknowledgments he briefly replied, with assurances of his eagerness to promote the welfare of any of his family; and concluded with intreaties that the subject might never be mentioned to him again.[43] The principal purport[44] of his letter was to inform them, that Mr. Wickham had resolved on quitting the Militia.

It was greatly my wish that he should do so, he added, *as soon as his marriage was fixed on. And I think you will agree with me, in considering a removal from that corps as highly advisable, both on his account and my niece's.*[45] *It is Mr. Wickham's intention to go into the regulars;*[46] *and, among his former friends, there are still some who are able and willing to assist him in the army.*[47] *He has the promise of an ensigncy*[48] *in General ——'s regiment,*[49] *now quartered in the North. It is an advantage to have it so far from this part of the kingdom. He promises fairly, and I hope among different people, where they may each have a character to preserve, they will both be more prudent.*[50] *I have written to Colonel Forster, to inform him of our present arrangements, and to request that he will satisfy the various creditors of Mr. Wickham in and near Brighton, with assurances of speedy payment, for which I have pledged myself. And will you give yourself the trouble of carrying similar assurances to his creditors in Meryton, of whom I shall subjoin a list, according to his information. He has given in all his debts; I hope at least he has not deceived us. Haggerston has our directions, and all will be completed in a week. They will then join his regiment, unless they are first invited to Longbourn; and I understand from Mrs. Gardiner, that my niece is very desirous of seeing you all,*

42. That is, how they would be able to support themselves in a decent manner financially.

43. The reasons for Mr. Gardiner's wish to close the subject, and to avoid receiving further thanks for his supposed rescue of Lydia, will soon be shown (pp. 586, 588).

44. *purport:* purpose.

45. Since people in Wickham's existing corps would know how he and Lydia came to be married, the two of them would probably be ridiculed and scorned.

46. *regulars:* regular units, i.e., the part of the army that, unlike the militia, would fight in wars abroad.

47. He would need assistance particularly in purchasing a commission for the regulars. See p. 589, note 29 for how it transpired.

48. *ensigncy:* the lowest officer position in the army (his main function was to carry the colors, or ensignia, of the unit). Wickham is descending in rank from his earlier position as a lieutenant, though this is balanced by his moving to the more prestigious regulars.

49. *General ——'s regiment:* as with the militia, Jane Austen prefers not to specify an actual regiment; in this case she even omits the commander's name. She was willing to name the colonel for Wickham's militia regiment, but since there were fewer generals, it would be easier for someone to say that in fact no such officer existed.

It was normal in the regular army, unlike in the militia, for the commander of a regiment to be a general (though the position of regimental command was still called a colonelcy). This was because the regular army had an abundance of generals, in contrast to the militia's frequent shortage of officers at various levels. This abundance stemmed from the practice of normally conferring automatic promotion on any colonel who had served a certain number of years, combined with the reluctance of officers to retire due to the absence of any real pension system. Thus many generals, being unable to procure one of the limited number of higher posts, remained in regimental command after promotion; at the close of the Napoleonic Wars in 1815, a mere handful of the approximately 200 regiments in the regular army were commanded by a colonel rather than by a general.

50. If other people do not know their past, something more likely if they are in a distant place, these others will consider them to have decent characters; thus Wickham and Lydia will have an incentive to act well in order to maintain those characters or reputations. Were they among those who regard them already as bad, the two would lack this incentive. The phrase "promises fairly" indicates Mr. Gardiner has at least moderate hopes that this will occur.

before she leaves the South. She is well, and begs to be dutifully
remembered to you and her mother. — Your's, &c.,

E. GARDINER.

Mr. Bennet and his daughters saw all the advantages of Wickham's removal from the ——shire, as clearly as Mr. Gardiner
could do.[51] But Mrs. Bennet was not so well pleased with it.
Lydia's being settled in the North, just when she had expected
most pleasure and pride in her company, for she had by no means
given up her plan of their residing in Hertfordshire, was a severe
disappointment; and besides, it was such a pity that Lydia should
be taken from a regiment where she was acquainted with every
body, and had so many favourites.

"She is so fond of Mrs. Forster," said she, "it will be quite
shocking to send her away! And there are several of the young
men, too, that she likes very much.[52] The officers may not be so
pleasant in General ——'s regiment."

His daughter's request, for such it might be considered, of
being admitted into her family again, before she set off for the
North, received at first an absolute negative. But Jane and Elizabeth, who agreed in wishing, for the sake of their sister's feelings
and consequence,[53] that she should be noticed[54] on her marriage
by her parents, urged him so earnestly, yet so rationally and so
mildly, to receive her and her husband at Longbourn, as soon as
they were married, that he was prevailed on to think as they
thought, and act as they wished. And their mother had the satisfaction of knowing, that she should be able to shew her married
daughter in the neighbourhood, before she was banished to the
North. When Mr. Bennet wrote again to his brother, therefore,
he sent his permission for them to come; and it was settled, that as
soon as the ceremony was over, they should proceed to Longbourn. Elizabeth was surprised, however, that Wickham should
consent to such a scheme, and, had she consulted only her own
inclination, any meeting with him would have been the last
object of her wishes.[55]

51. Their strong perception of the advantage of Lydia and Wickham's removal to a distant place may be based on more than the reason Mr. Gardiner suggested, that Wickham and Lydia might improve if among strangers. Mr. Bennet, as well as Elizabeth, may be thinking particularly of the benefits of having Wickham and Lydia far away from the rest of the family. This would allow the others to avoid their unpleasant presence; it would also mean that Kitty would be less exposed to any harmful influences emanating from the new couple. In the last chapter of the book Mr. Bennet is described, evidently for this very reason, as never allowing Kitty to visit Lydia despite the latter's frequent invitations.

52. One can imagine that Lydia frequently told her mother, while the regiment was in Meryton, of her affections for or flirtations with various officers, and that Mrs. Bennet eagerly soaked up this information.

53. *consequence:* social standing or importance.

54. *noticed:* recognized, acknowledged. A refusal of such notice by Mr. Bennet, which would be very unusual, would signal to everyone how badly they had behaved, and thus further discredit Lydia.

55. It would seem that Elizabeth hoped that, while Mr. and Mrs. Bennet would acknowledge Lydia by inviting her to come, she and Wickham would not actually accept the invitation, in part because Wickham would not be willing to face the family.

Chapter Nine

*T*heir sister's wedding day arrived; and Jane and Elizabeth felt for her probably more than she felt for herself.[1] The carriage was sent to meet them at ———,[2] and they were to return in it, by dinner-time. Their arrival was dreaded by the elder Miss Bennets; and Jane more especially, who gave Lydia the feelings which would have attended herself, had *she* been the culprit, was wretched in the thought of what her sister must endure.

They came. The family were assembled in the breakfast room, to receive them. Smiles decked the face of Mrs. Bennet, as the carriage drove up to the door; her husband looked impenetrably grave; her daughters, alarmed, anxious, uneasy.

Lydia's voice was heard in the vestibule; the door was thrown open, and she ran into the room. Her mother stepped forwards, embraced her, and welcomed her with rapture; gave her hand with an affectionate smile to Wickham, who followed his lady,[3] and wished them both joy, with an alacrity which shewed no doubt of their happiness.

Their reception from Mr. Bennet, to whom they then turned, was not quite so cordial. His countenance rather gained in austerity; and he scarcely opened his lips. The easy assurance[4] of the young couple, indeed, was enough to provoke him. Elizabeth was disgusted, and even Miss Bennet was shocked. Lydia was Lydia still; untamed, unabashed, wild, noisy, and fearless. She turned from sister to sister, demanding their congratulations, and when at length they all sat down, looked eagerly round the room, took notice of some little alteration in it, and observed, with a laugh, that it was a great while since she had been there.

Wickham was not at all more distressed than herself, but his manners were always so pleasing, that had his character and his marriage been exactly what they ought, his smiles and his easy

1. That is, they felt more shame and concern.

2. *at* —— : presumably at the church or neighborhood in London where they are getting married. The carriage would be the Bennets' own coach.

3. *his lady*: his wife.

4. *easy assurance*: uninhibited audacity or confidence; lack of embarrassment.

address,[5] while he claimed their relationship, would have delighted them all. Elizabeth had not before believed him quite equal to such assurance; but she sat down, resolving within herself, to draw no limits in future to the impudence of an impudent[6] man.[7] *She* blushed, and Jane blushed; but the cheeks of the two who caused their confusion, suffered no variation of colour.

There was no want of discourse.[8] The bride and her mother could neither of them talk fast enough; and Wickham, who happened to sit near Elizabeth, began enquiring after his acquaintance in that neighbourhood, with a good humoured ease, which she felt very unable to equal in her replies. They seemed each of them to have the happiest memories in the world. Nothing of the past was recollected with pain; and Lydia led voluntarily to subjects, which her sisters would not have alluded to for the world.

"Only think of its being three months," she cried, "since I went away; it seems but a fortnight I declare; and yet there have been things enough happened in the time. Good gracious! when I went away, I am sure I had no more idea of being married till I came back again! though I thought it would be very good fun if I was."

Her father lifted up his eyes. Jane was distressed. Elizabeth looked expressively at Lydia; but she, who never heard nor saw any thing of which she chose to be insensible,[9] gaily continued, "Oh! mamma, do the people here abouts know I am married to-day? I was afraid they might not; and we overtook William Goulding in his curricle,[10] so I was determined he should know it, and so I let down the side glass[11] next to him, and took off my glove, and let my hand just rest upon the window frame, so that he might see the ring, and then I bowed and smiled like any thing."

Elizabeth could bear it no longer. She got up, and ran out of the room; and returned no more, till she heard them passing through the hall to the dining parlour. She then joined them soon enough to see Lydia, with anxious parade,[12] walk up to her mother's right hand, and hear her say to her eldest sister, "Ah! Jane, I take your place now, and you must go lower, because I am a married woman."[13]

It was not to be supposed that time would give Lydia that

5. *easy address:* relaxed or uninhibited manner of speaking.

6. *impudence . . . impudent:* shamelessness . . . shameless.

7. This is one more example of Elizabeth's inclination to reflect upon and learn from her experiences, an inclination that few other characters in the book exhibit and that signals her worthiness as a heroine in the world of Jane Austen.

8. *want of discourse:* lack of conversation.

9. *insensible:* unaware.

10. *curricle:* an open carriage.

11. *side glass:* window of the carriage.

12. *parade:* show, ostentation.

13. Lydia refers to rules of precedence, which dictate, among other things, the order in which people should enter the dining room. Mr. and Mrs. Bennet would enter first, followed by their daughters in order of birth. A married woman, however, takes precedence over a single one, so Lydia, as she triumphantly exclaims, now moves from last position to one just behind her mother and in front of her eldest sister, Jane. Lydia's statement suggests that the Bennets follow rules of precedence as a matter of course, even for purely family dinners, a practice that reveals the formality prevailing in this society.

embarrassment, from which she had been so wholly free at first. Her ease and good spirits increased. She longed to see Mrs. Philips, the Lucases, and all their other neighbours, and to hear herself called "Mrs. Wickham," by each of them; and in the mean time, she went after dinner to shew her ring and boast of being married, to Mrs. Hill and the two housemaids.[14]

"Well, mamma," said she, when they were all returned to the breakfast room,[15] "and what do you think of my husband? Is not he a charming man? I am sure my sisters must all envy me. I only hope they may have half my good luck. They must all go to Brighton. That is the place to get husbands. What a pity it is, mamma, we did not all go."

"Very true; and if I had my will, we should. But my dear Lydia, I don't at all like your going such a way off. Must it be so?"

"Oh, lord! yes;—there is nothing in that. I shall like it of all things. You and papa, and my sisters, must come down and see us. We shall be at Newcastle[16] all the winter, and I dare say there will be some balls, and I will take care to get good partners for them all."

"I should like it beyond any thing!" said her mother.

"And then when you go away, you may leave one or two of my sisters behind you;[17] and I dare say I shall get husbands for them before the winter is over."

"I thank you for my share of the favour," said Elizabeth; "but I do not particularly like your way of getting husbands."

Their visitors were not to remain above ten days with them. Mr. Wickham had received his commission before he left London, and he was to join his regiment at the end of a fortnight.

No one but Mrs. Bennet, regretted that their stay would be so short; and she made the most of the time, by visiting about with her daughter, and having very frequent parties at home. These parties were acceptable to all; to avoid a family circle was even more desirable to such as did think,[18] than such as did not.

Wickham's affection for Lydia, was just what Elizabeth had expected to find it; not equal to Lydia's for him. She had scarcely needed her present observation to be satisfied, from the reason of

14. This passage gives the strongest clue as to the size of the staff employed by the Bennets. Besides Mrs. Hill and the two housemaids (the latter two would be responsible for cleaning the house as well as probably serving as lady's maids to the Bennet daughters), a footman and a butler have earlier been mentioned. In addition, the Bennets most likely employ a coachman to drive their coach and a gardener to take care of their grounds; the coach-man and gardener may each have a man assisting him. Finally, they almost certainly have a cook—sometimes the housekeeper could serve as a cook, but the glimpses provided of Mrs. Hill show her occupied with other things—as well as perhaps a scullery maid to assist the cook. This would result ultimately in an establishment of eight to eleven servants, which would be within the normal range for a family with their annual income.

15. *breakfast room:* this occurs after dinner, but just as a room would nor-mally be chosen for breakfast because it lets in plenty of daylight, the same room might also be used after dinner during the summer, when it is still light outside.

16. *Newcastle:* a town very far north in England, almost to Scotland. See map on p. 742.

17. As a married woman, Lydia could host her unmarried sisters.

18. That is, it was desirable to avoid being left with Lydia and Wickham and Mrs. Bennet and have to watch their foolish or irresponsible behavior.

things, that their elopement had been brought on by the strength of her love, rather than by his; and she would have wondered why, without violently caring for her, he chose to elope with her at all, had she not felt certain that his flight was rendered necessary by distress of circumstances;[19] and if that were the case, he was not the young man to resist an opportunity of having a companion.

Lydia was exceedingly fond of him. He was her dear Wickham on every occasion; no one was to be put in competition with him. He did every thing best in the world; and she was sure he would kill more birds on the first of September,[20] than any body else in the country.

One morning, soon after their arrival, as she was sitting with her two elder sisters, she said to Elizabeth,

"Lizzy, I never gave *you* an account of my wedding, I believe. You were not by, when I told mamma, and the others, all about it. Are not you curious to hear how it was managed?"

"No really," replied Elizabeth; "I think there cannot be too little said on the subject."

"La! You are so strange! But I must tell you how it went off. We were married, you know, at St. Clement's, because Wickham's lodgings were in that parish.[21] And it was settled that we should all be there by eleven o'clock. My uncle and aunt and I were to go together; and the others were to meet us at the church. Well, Monday morning[22] came, and I was in such a fuss! I was so afraid you know that something would happen to put it off, and then I should have gone quite distracted.[23] And there was my aunt, all the time I was dressing, preaching and talking away just as if she was reading a sermon.[24] However, I did not hear above one word in ten, for I was thinking, you may suppose, of my dear Wickham. I longed to know whether he would be married in his blue coat.[25]

"Well, and so we breakfasted at ten as usual; I thought it would never be over; for, by the bye, you are to understand, that my uncle and aunt were horrid[26] unpleasant all the time I was with them. If you'll believe me, I did not once put my foot out of doors, though I was there a fortnight. Not one party, or scheme,[27] or any thing. To be sure London was rather thin,[28] but however

19. *distress of circumstances:* a reference to his debts. Elizabeth's observations here about Wickham's feelings and motives confirm her earlier suppositions about why he ran away with Lydia (see p. 508).

20. *first of September:* the opening of the season for hunting game birds, particularly the main ones of partridge and pheasant. By law killing them in the period before September 1 was forbidden.

21. By law a marriage normally had to take place in the parish where either the bride or groom resided.

22. *Monday morning:* this establishes that the marriage took place just over four weeks from Lydia and Wickham's arrival in London: they ran away on a Saturday night, and arrived in London on a Sunday; it was two weeks and a day later that Mr. Gardiner wrote to say that they had been found and the marriage arranged; Lydia then stayed, as she reveals below, for two weeks at the Gardiners (for more detail on dates, see chronology, pp. 717–718). The reason for and significance of this timing is discussed in note 30 below.

23. *distracted:* mad, frantic. The term shows Lydia's tendency to exaggerate.

24. Mrs. Gardiner would of course be trying to make Lydia understand the error of her earlier conduct.

25. *blue coat:* dark colors like blue had become more fashionable for men (see p. 15, note 3).

26. *horrid:* a slang term that Jane Austen generally puts in the mouth of vulgar characters who tend to exaggerate. Lydia uses it again in this speech.

27. *scheme:* plan (of activity).

28. *thin:* sparsely populated. Many left London during the summer, and this meant there were far fewer amusements there.

the Little Theatre[29] was open. Well, and so just as the carriage came to the door, my uncle was called away upon business to that horrid man Mr. Stone.[30] And then, you know, when once they get together, there is no end of it. Well, I was so frightened I did not know what to do, for my uncle was to give me away; and if we were beyond the hour, we could not be married all day.[31] But, luckily, he came back again in ten minutes' time, and then we all set out. However, I recollected afterwards, that if he *had* been pre-vented going, the wedding need not be put off, for Mr. Darcy might have done as well."

"Mr. Darcy!" repeated Elizabeth, in utter amazement.

"Oh, yes!—he was to come there with Wickham, you know. But gracious me! I quite forgot! I ought not to have said a word about it. I promised them so faithfully![32] What will Wickham say? It was to be such a secret!"

"If it was to be secret," said Jane, "say not another word on the subject. You may depend upon my seeking no further."

"Oh! certainly," said Elizabeth, though burning with curiosity; "we will ask you no questions."

"Thank you," said Lydia, "for if you did, I should certainly tell you all, and then Wickham would be angry."

On such encouragement to ask, Elizabeth was forced to put it out of her power, by running away.[33]

But to live in ignorance on such a point was impossible; or at least it was impossible not to try for information. Mr. Darcy had been at her sister's wedding. It was exactly a scene, and exactly among people, where he had apparently least to do, and least temptation to go. Conjectures as to the meaning of it, rapid and wild, hurried into her brain; but she was satisfied with none. Those that best pleased her, as placing his conduct in the noblest light, seemed most improbable. She could not bear such sus-pense; and hastily seizing a sheet of paper, wrote a short letter to her aunt, to request an explanation of what Lydia had dropt, if it were compatible with the secrecy which had been intended.

"You may readily comprehend," she added, "what my curiosity must be to know how a person unconnected with any of us, and

29. *Little Theatre*: the "Little Theatre in the Haymarket" (so-called to distinguish it from the larger opera house, or King's Theatre, in the same location). The Licensing Act then in force permitted only three theaters in London to present spoken drama. Covent Garden and Drury Lane, the two largest, could present plays most of the year, and the Little Theatre was allowed to present plays from mid-June to mid-September, when the other two were closed.

30. *Mr. Stone*: this could be Lydia's mistaken version of "Haggerston," the man Mr. Gardiner mentioned in his letters as helping him with the marriage settlement. Whether that is the case or not, it is possible that the business he has with Mr. Gardiner is essential to the wedding, which would make Lydia's complaint about him especially ridiculous. By law a license for marriage could only be issued after one of the couple had resided in the appropriate parish for four weeks—this is why Lydia waited two weeks at the Gardiners'. Since Wickham has just fulfilled this requirement on the previous day, a Sunday (not a normal day for conducting business), there is a good chance that the purpose of the man meeting with Mr. Gardiner is to bring the marriage license.

31. By law a marriage had to be performed between 8 a.m. and noon. Lydia already stated that they were scheduled to meet at 11, so if Mr. Gardiner were detained too long, the marriage would have to be postponed until the next day.

32. *promised them so faithfully*: the hero of *Northanger Abbey*, who likes to find fault with people's use of language, ridicules the redundancy of describing someone as having "promised so faithfully": "A faithful promise!—That puzzles me.—I have heard of a faithful performance. But a faithful promise—the fidelity of promising!" In this case Lydia's use of the term signals both her lack of care in speaking, and her lack of fidelity in fulfilling her promises.

33. In other words, Elizabeth knows it would be improper to force such a secret; but since she also yearns to know, and Lydia indicates she could easily be made to tell, Elizabeth can only avoid committing such an impropriety by leaving the room.

(comparatively speaking) a stranger to our family, should have been amongst you at such a time. Pray write instantly, and let me understand it—unless it is, for very cogent reasons, to remain in the secrecy which Lydia seems to think necessary; and then I must endeavour to be satisfied with ignorance."

"Not that I *shall* though," she added to herself, as she finished the letter; "and my dear aunt, if you do not tell me in an honourable manner, I shall certainly be reduced to tricks and stratagems to find it out."[34]

Jane's delicate sense of honour would not allow her to speak to Elizabeth privately of what Lydia had let fall; Elizabeth was glad of it;—till it appeared whether her inquiries would receive any satisfaction, she had rather be without a confidante.

34. Thus even a good person like Elizabeth, who earnestly wishes not to act dishonorably, will be willing to act that way if it becomes necessary for a vital purpose. This is something often seen in Jane Austen: while she presents, and praises, good characters, she does not idealize them to the point of pretending that they are saints who would never do anything wrong or never act on a less than pure motive. Many of the novels of the time—including those by her favorite authors, Samuel Richardson and Fanny Burney—tend to present unrealistically perfect heroes and heroines, and this forms a favorite target of Jane Austen's satire. For example, in her youthful story "Evelyn" she presents a family of such absurdly pure altruism that they gladly surrender money, their house and grounds, and their daughter's hand to a stranger who happens upon them and simply requests these things. In "Plan for a Novel" she humorously outlines a possible novel that represents the absolute reverse of her literary values: it includes a hero and heroine of absolute perfection, who are so pure and refined that the hero cannot even avow his love for her until the very end, while the heroine cannot bear that anyone might propose to her without first asking her father's permission. Of this projected novel, Jane Austen says, "All the Good will be unexceptionable in every respect— and there will be no foibles or weaknesses but with the Wicked, who will be completely depraved & infamous, hardly a resemblance of Humanity left in them."

Chapter Ten

*E*lizabeth had the satisfaction of receiving an answer to her letter, as soon as she possibly could.[1] She was no sooner in possession of it, than hurrying into the little copse, where she was least likely to be interrupted, she sat down on one of the benches, and prepared to be happy; for the length of the letter convinced her that it did not contain a denial.

Gracechurch-street, Sept. 6.

MY DEAR NIECE,

I have just received your letter, and shall devote this whole morning to answering it, as I foresee that a little writing will not comprise what I have to tell you. I must confess myself surprised by your application;[2] I did not expect it from you. Don't think me angry, however, for I only mean to let you know, that I had not imagined such enquiries to be necessary on your side. If you do not choose to understand me, forgive my impertinence.[3] Your uncle is as much surprised as I am—and nothing but the belief of your being a party concerned, would have allowed him to act as he has done.[4] But if you are really innocent and ignorant, I must be more explicit. On the very day of my coming home from Longbourn, your uncle had a most unexpected visitor.[5] Mr. Darcy called, and was shut up with him several hours. It was all over before I arrived; so my curiosity was not so dreadfully racked as your's seems to have been. He came to tell Mr. Gardiner that he had found out where your sister and Mr. Wickham were, and that he had seen and talked with them both, Wickham repeatedly, Lydia once. From what I can collect,[6] he left Derbyshire only one day after ourselves, and came to town with the resolution of hunting for them. The motive professed, was his conviction of its being owing to himself that Wickham's worthlessness had not been so well known, as to make it impossible for

1. This would be within a few days of Elizabeth's having written, for mail service between London and nearby places like Hertfordshire was fast.

2. *application:* request, appeal (for information).

3. *impertinence:* interference, intrusiveness. The impertinence would come from referring to something about which Elizabeth would like to pretend ignorance.

4. Mrs. Gardiner's point is that she and her husband thought that Elizabeth, thanks to her ties of affection with Darcy, already knew about his role in the whole affair. Furthermore, if they had not believed her to be involved, they would not have allowed Darcy to interfere as he did, for it would not be right to allow a stranger to involve himself in a family matter, especially since the stranger's involvement cost him a lot of money. Thus the Gardiners' observation of Darcy's preference for Elizabeth at Pemberley, along with their uncertainty about the exact relationship between the two lovers, has facilitated Darcy's attempt to help Elizabeth and her family.

5. This would have been eight days after Elizabeth and the Gardiners left Lambton, and Darcy learned about Lydia and Wickham (see chronology, p. 718).

6. *collect:* gather.

any young woman of character to love or confide in him.[7] *He gener-ously imputed the whole to his mistaken pride, and confessed that he had before thought it beneath him, to lay his private actions open to the world. His character was to speak for itself.*[8] *He called it, therefore, his duty to step forward, and endeavour to remedy an evil, which had been brought on by himself. If he* had another *motive, I am sure it would never disgrace him.*[9] *He had been some days in town, before he was able to discover them; but he had some-thing to direct his search, which was more than we had; and the consciousness of this, was another reason for his resolving to follow us. There is a lady, it seems, a Mrs. Younge, who was some time ago governess to Miss Darcy, and was dismissed from her charge on some cause of disapprobation, though he did not say what.*[10] *She then took a large house in Edward-street,*[11] *and has since main-tained herself by letting lodgings.*[12] *This Mrs. Younge was, he knew, intimately acquainted with Wickham; and he went to her for intel-ligence of him, as soon as he got to town. But it was two or three days before he could get from her what he wanted. She would not betray her trust, I suppose, without bribery and corruption, for she really did know where her friend was to be found. Wickham indeed had gone to her, on their first arrival in London,*[13] *and had she been able to receive them into her house, they would have taken up their abode with her. At length, however, our kind friend procured the wished-for direction.*[14] *They were in —— street.*[15] *He saw Wick-ham, and afterwards insisted on seeing Lydia. His first object with her, he acknowledged, had been to persuade her to quit her present disgraceful situation, and return to her friends as soon as they could be prevailed on to receive her, offering his assistance, as far as it would go. But he found Lydia absolutely resolved on remaining where she was. She cared for none of her friends, she wanted no help of his, she would not hear of leaving Wickham. She was sure they should be married some time or other, and it did not much sig-nify when. Since such were her feelings, it only remained, he thought, to secure and expedite a marriage, which, in his very first conversation with Wickham, he easily learnt, had never been his design. He confessed himself obliged to leave the regiment, on*

7. Darcy blames himself for keeping Wickham's attempted elopement with Miss Darcy a secret from the world. Had he revealed it, Wickham would have found it difficult, if not impossible, to be accepted socially and to have gained the trust of any respectable woman (i.e., "of character"); thus he would not have been in a position to seduce Lydia.

8. That is, Darcy had disdained justifying himself on specific matters, trusting that the general soundness of his character and reputation would suffice to make people always think well of him.

9. The other motive she suspects, but that Darcy has not admitted, is his love for Elizabeth and desire to spare her the shame and misery of Lydia's ruin. He also could be wishing to preserve the respectability of her family, in case she eventually did change her mind and prove willing to marry him.

10. Hence Darcy has not told the Gardiners about his sister's misadventure; despite reproaching himself for being unwilling to reveal his secrets, he retains the same reserve and love of privacy. Similarly, in his insistence on doing everything himself (which Mrs. Gardiner mentions shortly), Darcy shows his usual imperiousness. This is a point often seen in Jane Austen: as much as she celebrates those like Darcy or Elizabeth who can change in some respects, she never imagines anyone altering their underlying personalities.

11. *Edward-Street*: it is not clear what street this means, for there were, according to a map of 1813, eight different Edward Streets in the greater London area (all of them were small, and none still bears the same name at present). Some were in prominent and fashionable areas; others were in poor or obscure areas on the outskirts of the city. One of the former is mentioned in Jane Austen's unfinished novel *Lady Susan*, in which a very wealthy couple live on an Edward Street (the most likely candidate is the present Langham Place, next to Cavendish Square). It is doubtful if Mrs. Younge, a disgraced former governess reduced to renting rooms, is meant to be inhabiting the same street. It is possible that Jane Austen had no specific street in mind.

12. This is probably the best way to make a living she could find. She would have been dismissed from Darcy's employment without a character reference, because of her dishonest collusion with Wickham, and this would make it very hard for her to find further employment as a governess.

13. Since Wickham seems to have no family, or close friends, Mrs. Younge may be the only person who could possibly help him.

14. *direction*: address.

15. —— *street*: this street is probably not specified because it is an insignificant one in an obscure corner of London.

account of some debts of honour,[16] which were very pressing; and scrupled not[17] to lay all the ill-consequences of Lydia's flight, on her own folly alone.[18] He meant to resign his commission[19] immediately; and as to his future situation, he could conjecture very little about it. He must go somewhere, but he did not know where, and he knew he should have nothing to live on.[20] Mr. Darcy asked him why he had not married your sister at once. Though Mr. Bennet was not imagined to be very rich, he would have been able to do something for him, and his situation must have been benefited by marriage. But he found, in reply to this question, that Wickham still cherished the hope of more effectually making his fortune by marriage, in some other country.[21] Under such circumstances, however, he was not likely to be proof against the temptation of immediate relief.[22] They met several times, for there was much to be discussed. Wickham of course wanted more than he could get; but at length was reduced to be reasonable.[23] Every thing being settled between them, Mr. Darcy's next step was to make your uncle acquainted with it, and he first called in Gracechurch-street the evening before I came home.[24] But Mr. Gardiner could not be seen, and Mr. Darcy found, on further enquiry, that your father was still with him, but would quit town the next morning. He did not judge your father to be a person whom he could so properly consult as your uncle, and therefore readily postponed seeing him, till after the departure of the former.[25] He did not leave his name, and till the next day, it was only known that a gentleman had called on business. On Saturday he came again. Your father was gone, your uncle at home, and, as I said before, they had a great deal of talk together. They met again on Sunday, and then I saw him too. It was not all settled before Monday: as soon as it was, the express[26] was sent off to Longbourn. But our visitor was very obstinate. I fancy, Lizzy, that obstinacy is the real defect of his character after all. He has been accused of many faults at different times; but this is the true one. Nothing was to be done that he did not do himself; though I am sure (and I do not speak it to be thanked, therefore say nothing about it,) your uncle would most readily have settled the whole. They battled it together for a long time, which was more

16. *debts of honour*: gambling debts; see p. 541, note 20.

17. *scrupled not*: did not hesitate.

18. Wickham's willingness to lay all the blame on Lydia reveals the true extent of his tenderness toward her.

19. *his commission*: his commission in the militia.

20. Wickham displays again his thoughtlessness and lack of planning. In contrast to many novelists, Jane Austen has not endowed her villain with any extraordinary cleverness or foresight or determination; instead, she has made him a man characterized by weakness as much as anything.

21. *other country*: most likely another part of England, not another nation.

22. That is, his need for immediate assistance would make it possible to tempt him to follow a course besides the pursuit of a more advantageous marriage in a different locale.

23. As shown below, Darcy ends up paying much less than the ten thousand pounds estimated by Mr. Bennet. That figure was probably always an exaggeration, a product of Mr. Bennet's frustration with the whole affair. Darcy would also have means peculiar to himself of reducing Wickham's demands; in particular, he could threaten Wickham with public exposure of some of his other misdeeds, such as his attempt to seduce Miss Darcy. Of course, it could not be known if Darcy would ever carry out such a threat, but the possibility would have to influence Wickham's calculations, for exposure of that nature would make it difficult for Wickham to pursue a different marriage, or even to advance in a new career. Darcy could also hold out the threat of using his powerful connections and influence to Wickham's detriment.

24. The total interval from Darcy's arrival until his first visit to the Gardiners was probably four days (see chronology, p. 718). This indicates Darcy's determination to settle the business quickly, for during that time he had both to locate Wickham and to negotiate a difficult agreement with him.

25. Darcy probably anticipated more potential opposition from Mr. Bennet to the interference of an outsider such as Darcy. Darcy also may have wished, by keeping Mr. Bennet in the dark, to prevent Elizabeth from learning of his role in the matter (for his possible reasons for this, see p. 665, note 2).

26. *express*: express message or messenger.

than either the gentleman or lady concerned in it deserved. But at last your uncle was forced to yield, and instead of being allowed to be of use to his niece, was forced to put up with only having the probable credit of it, which went sorely against the grain; and I really believe your letter this morning gave him great pleasure, because it required an explanation that would rob him of his borrowed feathers,[27] and give the praise where it was due. But, Lizzy, this must go no farther than yourself, or Jane at most. You know pretty well, I suppose, what has been done for the young people. His debts are to be paid, amounting, I believe, to considerably more than a thousand pounds, another thousand in addition to her own settled upon her,[28] and his commission purchased.[29] The reason why all this was to be done by him alone, was such as I have given above. It was owing to him, to his reserve,[30] and want of proper consideration,[31] that Wickham's character had been so misunderstood, and consequently that he had been received and noticed[32] as he was. Perhaps there was some truth in this; though I doubt whether his reserve, or anybody's reserve, can be answerable for the event.[33] But in spite of all this fine talking, my dear Lizzy, you may rest perfectly assured, that your uncle would never have yielded, if we had not given him credit for another interest in the affair.[34] When all this was resolved on, he returned again to his friends, who were still staying at Pemberley; but it was agreed that he should be in London once more when the wedding took place, and all money matters were then to receive the last finish. I believe I have now told you every thing. It is a relation[35] which you tell me is to give you great surprise; I hope at least it will not afford you any displeasure. Lydia came to us; and Wickham had constant admission to the house. He was exactly what he had been, when I knew him in Hertfordshire; but I would not tell you how little I was satisfied with her behaviour while she staid with us, if I had not perceived, by Jane's letter last Wednesday, that her conduct on coming home was exactly of a piece with it, and therefore what I now tell you, can give you no fresh pain. I talked to her repeatedly in the most serious manner, representing to her all the wickedness of what she had done, and all the unhappiness she had brought on her family. If she heard me, it

27. *borrowed feathers:* assumed glory or credit; something showing you off to advantage that is not yours.

28. "Her" is emphasized because settling the money specifically on Lydia means that Wickham will only have use of it as long as they are married.

29. In the more desirable regular army, unlike in the militia, a commission to be an officer had to be purchased. The official rate for Wickham's ensign commission at the time was 400 pounds, but the actual price could have been higher, for the scarcity of commissions created an active private market in which those already possessing commissions would sell them for more than the official rate. The whole system, which caused wealth often to be of greater weight than merit in determining army personnel and rank, was frequently denounced by reformers, and was eventually changed later in the century. At this time, however, it was accepted as normal, and no shame would have attached to anyone involved in it.

Jane Austen would have had a solid knowledge of these matters for her brother Henry, during a period when he was a banker, acted as an agent helping people to buy and sell army commissions.

30. *reserve:* silence, lack of openness (about Wickham and Miss Darcy).

31. *want of proper consideration:* lack of consideration about what should be done.

32. *received and noticed:* admitted and recognized socially. Had Wickham been publicly disgraced he would not have been able to mix freely with women of good family.

33. *event:* outcome, result.

34. The Gardiners would be especially likely to believe that his main interest in the affair was Elizabeth, since Darcy has not told them the details about Wickham's earlier misdeeds and thus explained the exact reason why he might blame himself for Wickham's ability to prey on Lydia.

35. *relation:* account, relation of events.

was by good luck, for I am sure she did not listen. I was sometimes quite provoked, but then I recollected my dear Elizabeth and Jane, and for their sakes had patience with her. Mr. Darcy was punctual in his return, and as Lydia informed you, attended the wedding. He dined with us the next day, and was to leave town again on Wednesday or Thursday. Will you be very angry with me, my dear Lizzy, if I take this opportunity of saying (what I was never bold enough to say before) how much I like him. His behaviour to us has, in every respect, been as pleasing as when we were in Derbyshire. His understanding[36] and opinions all please me; he wants[37] nothing but a little more liveliness, and that, if he marry prudently, his wife may teach him.[38] I thought him very sly;[39]—he hardly ever mentioned your name. But slyness seems the fashion. Pray forgive me, if I have been very presuming, or at least do not punish me so far, as to exclude me from P.[40] I shall never be quite happy till I have been all round the park.[41] A low phaeton,[42] with a nice little pair of ponies, would be the very thing. But I must write no more. The children have been wanting me this half hour. Your's, very sincerely,

M. GARDINER.

The contents of this letter threw Elizabeth into a flutter of spirits, in which it was difficult to determine whether pleasure or pain bore the greatest share. The vague and unsettled suspicions which uncertainty had produced of what Mr. Darcy might have been doing to forward her sister's match, which she had feared to encourage, as an exertion of goodness too great to be probable,[43] and at the same time dreaded to be just, from the pain of obligation,[44] were proved beyond their greatest extent to be true! He had followed them purposely to town, he had taken on himself all the trouble and mortification attendant on such a research; in which supplication had been necessary to a woman whom he must abominate and despise, and where he was reduced to meet, frequently meet, reason with, persuade, and finally bribe, the man whom he always most wished to avoid, and whose very name it was punishment to him to pronounce. He had done all this for

36. *understanding:* intellect.

37. *wants:* lacks, needs.

38. That is, marry Elizabeth. Mrs. Gardiner seconds Elizabeth in identifying greater liveliness as a principal benefit the latter could impart to Darcy. Mrs. Gardiner's use of "prudently" contains an irony, which she probably intends, for prudent, in relation to marriage, generally meant a marriage that was financially advantageous. That is how Mrs. Gardiner and Elizabeth had used the term earlier when discussing marriage (see pp. 266 and 282). Here, however, it means something very different, for Darcy, in marrying Elizabeth, would be acting not at all prudently in a financial sense, but only prudently in other ways.

39. *sly:* secretive.

40. *P:* Pemberley. She may abbreviate it because she does not want to seem presumptuous in her visions of Elizabeth's future.

41. In their earlier visit to Pemberley the Gardiners and Elizabeth took the shorter, more accustomed route that did not go around the entire park or grounds.

42. *low phaeton:* a phaeton carriage that is low to the ground (see p. 293, note 27, and illustration on p. 291). Mrs. Gardiner showed before that she was a weak walker, so a carriage would allow her to see much more of Pemberley, with an open carriage like a phaeton being especially good for that purpose. The greater steadiness of a low carriage would also suit her if, as her weakness as a walker implies, she is not robust physically.

43. That is, she feared to encourage a hope that could be dashed.

44. *pain of obligation:* pain of being in such a state of obligation (to Darcy). That is why she dreaded that her suspicions about his involvement might be just.

a girl whom he could neither regard nor esteem. Her heart did whisper, that he had done it for her.[45] But it was a hope shortly checked by other considerations, and she soon felt that even her vanity was insufficient, when required to depend on his affection for her, for a woman who had already refused him, as able to over-come a sentiment so natural as abhorrence against relationship with Wickham.[46] Brother-in-law of Wickham! Every kind of pride must revolt from the connection. He had to be sure done much. She was ashamed to think how much. But he had given a reason for his interference, which asked no extraordinary stretch of belief. It was reasonable that he should feel he had been wrong; he had liberality,[47] and he had the means of exercising it; and though she would not place herself as his principal inducement, she could, perhaps, believe, that remaining partiality for her, might assist his endeavours in a cause where her peace of mind must be materially concerned.[48] It was painful, exceedingly painful, to know that they were under obligations to a person who could never receive a return. They owed the restoration of Lydia, her character,[49] every thing to him. Oh! how heartily did she grieve over every ungracious sensation she had ever encouraged, every saucy speech she had ever directed towards him.[50] For her-self she was humbled; but she was proud of him. Proud that in a cause of compassion and honour, he had been able to get the bet-ter of himself. She read over her aunt's commendation of him again and again. It was hardly enough; but it pleased her. She was even sensible of some pleasure, though mixed with regret, on finding how steadfastly both she and her uncle had been per-suaded that affection and confidence[51] subsisted between Mr. Darcy and herself.[52]

She was roused from her seat, and her reflections, by some one's approach; and before she could strike into another path, she was overtaken by Wickham.[53]

"I am afraid I interrupt your solitary ramble, my dear sister?" said he, as he joined her.

"You certainly do," she replied with a smile; "but it does not follow that the interruption must be unwelcome."

45. *her*: Elizabeth.

46. In other words, even Elizabeth's vanity, which would make her more likely to believe that Darcy's affection was strong enough to make him wish to marry her, was insufficient to convince her of this when she considered the factors that would deter him from wishing such a marriage.

47. *liberality*: financial generosity.

48. Elizabeth hesitates to pronounce a definite judgment on the reasons for Darcy's actions. This contrasts with her earlier tendency to make quick and certain judgments of people. Now, having seen many of those judgments turn out to be wrong, she exercises greater caution.

49. *character*: reputation (restored to decent status by Darcy's actions).

50. Once more Elizabeth is forced to do penance for her earlier mistakes and bad behavior. Such penance is critical for her reformation. Darcy must undergo the same penance: one can imagine that he would often reproach himself for his proud and cold behavior toward Elizabeth, and toward others in her presence. Having to involve himself with Wickham as he has done would also be a heavy pain for him to endure. His inner ordeal, however, is alluded to rather than directly presented by the author.

51. *confidence*: intimacy.

52. Elizabeth feels regret as well as pleasure because of her conviction that Darcy will not marry her due to her being now connected with Wickham. Thus the receipt of information suggesting she may still be dear to Darcy serves to increase her sense of what she has lost due to Wickham's marriage with Lydia.

53. These would be paths in the copse where Elizabeth has been reading the letter (using one of the benches). The existence of such a wooded area, with multiple paths and benches—along with a shrubbery where people can walk (mentioned elsewhere in the novel and distinguished from the copse)—indicates that the Bennets, or the previous owners of the house, have also engaged in landscape improvements. Such improvements, though obviously most practicable among the very wealthy, were popular at various social levels. Jane Austen reveals in a letter that her family, with an income more modest than the Bennets, undertook beautifying improvements in the grounds of their home (Oct. 26, 1800).

"I should be sorry indeed, if it were. We were always good friends; and now we are better."

"True. Are the others coming out?"[54]

"I do not know. Mrs. Bennet and Lydia are going in the carriage to Meryton. And so, my dear sister, I find from our uncle and aunt, that you have actually seen Pemberley."[55]

She replied in the affirmative.

"I almost envy you the pleasure, and yet I believe it would be too much for me, or else I could take it in my way to Newcastle.[56] And you saw the old housekeeper, I suppose? Poor Reynolds, she was always very fond of me. But of course she did not mention my name to you."

"Yes, she did."

"And what did she say?"

"That you were gone into the army, and she was afraid had— not turned out well.[57] At such a distance as *that*, you know, things are strangely misrepresented."

"Certainly," he replied, biting his lips. Elizabeth hoped she had silenced him; but he soon afterwards said,

"I was surprised to see Darcy[58] in town[59] last month. We passed each other several times. I wonder what he can be doing there."

"Perhaps preparing for his marriage with Miss De Bourgh," said Elizabeth. "It must be something particular,[60] to take him there at this time of year."

"Undoubtedly. Did you see him while you were at Lambton? I thought I understood from the Gardiners that you had."

"Yes; he introduced us to his sister."

"And do you like her?"

"Very much."

"I have heard, indeed, that she is uncommonly improved within this year or two. When I last saw her, she was not very promising. I am very glad you liked her. I hope she will turn out well."

"I dare say she will; she has got over the most trying age."[61]

"Did you go by the village of Kympton?"

"I do not recollect that we did."

54. A sign that she hopes others will interrupt her conversation with Wickham.

55. Wickham introduces the topic of Pemberley presumably because, knowing of Elizabeth's recent visit there, he wishes to ascertain how much more she may have learned about his own case. Since Elizabeth is now his sister-in-law he has a particular incentive to hope that the true nature of his dealings with Darcy has not been revealed to her.

56. That is, Wickham says it would be too much for him emotionally; otherwise, he would stop there when he and Lydia traveled to Newcastle (Derbyshire would only be a little out of the way in a trip from Hertfordshire to Newcastle—see map, p. 742).

57. *not turned out well:* the housekeeper's actual words were "turned out very wild," but Elizabeth, after hesitating, softens them. In contrast to her goading of Darcy while she was championing Wickham, she now refrains from any truly harsh words towards Wickham. One obvious reason is that she has a family connection with him; another could be the way the experience of her earlier mistakes has made her delight less in witty abuse of others.

58. *Darcy:* Wickham's first use of this term; until now he has always said "Mr. Darcy." Since the two men have established no family connection at this point, Wickham's usage is a sign of over-familiarity on his part, inspired perhaps by Darcy's involvement in his affairs and assistance to him. Darcy, in contrast, uses "Mr. Wickham" throughout the novel, despite his dislike for Wickham and Wickham's lower social status.

59. *town:* London.

60. *particular:* special, unusual.

61. Meaning the age when Wickham tried to seduce her. One sees that he immediately changes the subject.

"I mention it, because it is the living[62] which I ought to have had. A most delightful place!—Excellent Parsonage House![63] It would have suited me in every respect."

"How should you have liked making sermons?"

"Exceedingly well. I should have considered it as part of my duty, and the exertion would soon have been nothing. One ought not to repine;—but, to be sure, it would have been such a thing for me! The quiet, the retirement[64] of such a life, would have answered all my ideas of happiness![65] But it was not to be. Did you ever hear Darcy mention the circumstance, when you were in Kent?"

"I *have* heard from authority, which I thought *as good*, that it was left you conditionally only, and at the will of the present patron."

"You have. Yes, there was something in *that*; I told you so from the first, you may remember."

"I *did* hear, too, that there was a time, when sermon-making was not so palatable to you as it seems to be at present; that you actually declared your resolution of never taking orders,[66] and that the business had been compromised[67] accordingly."

"You did! and it was not wholly without foundation. You may remember what I told you on that point, when first we talked of it."

They were now almost at the door of the house, for she had walked fast to get rid of him; and unwilling for her sister's sake, to provoke him, she only said in reply, with a good-humoured smile,

"Come, Mr. Wickham, we are brother and sister, you know. Do not let us quarrel about the past. In future, I hope we shall be always of one mind."

She held out her hand; he kissed it with affectionate gallantry, though he hardly knew how to look, and they entered the house.[68]

62. *living*: clerical position.

63. Many parsonage houses were in poor shape; see p. 329, note 10.

64. *retirement*: privacy, seclusion—in a positive sense.

65. Wickham's vision of clerical life involves only his own happiness of course. Mr. Collins is similar, though he does at least toss in a few hackneyed phrases about his clerical duties. In her next novel, *Mansfield Park*, Jane Austen presents in contrast a man about to be confirmed who has a true sense of the church as a moral and social calling.

66. *taking orders*: being ordained (to serve in the Church).

67. *compromised*: settled or agreed upon through mutual concession.

68. Elizabeth's holding out her hand, in addition to being a sign of amity on her part, indicates their familial relationship, for it was considered improper for a woman to shake hands with a man who was not closely connected with her. The standard procedure was for the woman to hold out her hand first (this gave her the power of deciding if she wanted to be that familiar with him), and for the man to choose whether to shake or kiss her hand. Wickham's decision to kiss it is in line with his general unctuousness; it is probable that Elizabeth was expecting him only to shake hands with her, and was not particularly pleased that he chose the more intimate response.

Chapter Eleven

Mr. Wickham was so perfectly satisfied with this conversation, that he never again distressed himself, or provoked his dear sister Elizabeth, by introducing the subject of it; and she was pleased to find that she had said enough to keep him quiet.

The day of his and Lydia's departure soon came, and Mrs. Bennet was forced to submit to a separation, which, as her husband by no means entered into her scheme of their all going to Newcastle,[1] was likely to continue at least a twelvemonth.

"Oh! my dear Lydia," she cried, "when shall we meet again?"

"Oh, lord! I don't know. Not these two or three years perhaps."

"Write to me very often, my dear."

"As often as I can. But you know married women have never much time for writing. My sisters may write to *me*. They will have nothing else to do."

Mr. Wickham's adieus were much more affectionate than his wife's. He smiled, looked handsome, and said many pretty things.

"He is as fine a fellow," said Mr. Bennet, as soon as they were out of the house, "as ever I saw. He simpers, and smirks, and makes love[2] to us all. I am prodigiously proud of him. I defy even Sir William Lucas himself, to produce a more valuable son-in-law."[3]

The loss of her daughter made Mrs. Bennet very dull[4] for several days.

"I often think," said she, "that there is nothing so bad as parting with one's friends. One seems so forlorn without them."

"This is the consequence you see, Madam, of marrying a daughter," said Elizabeth. "It must make you better satisfied that your other four are single."

"It is no such thing. Lydia does not leave me because she is married; but only because her husband's regiment happens to be so far off. If that had been nearer, she would not have gone so soon."

1. Since Mr. Bennet was unwilling to go to Brighton, which would be at most 75 miles away, it is hardly surprising that he does not wish to voyage to Newcastle, which would be at least 200 miles away—and this is not even counting his disinclination to see Wickham and Lydia.

2. *makes love*: courts, woos, professes affection.

3. Mr. Bennet's use of valuable is obviously sarcastic. In referring to Sir William Lucas he may be thinking of Sir William's own tendency toward officious courtesy, or he may be thinking of Sir William's actual son-in-law, Mr. Collins.

4. *dull*: listless, gloomy.

But the spiritless[5] condition which this event threw her into, was shortly relieved, and her mind opened again to the agitation of hope, by an article of news, which then began to be in circulation. The housekeeper at Netherfield had received orders to prepare for the arrival of her master, who was coming down in a day or two, to shoot there for several weeks.[6] Mrs. Bennet was quite in the fidgets.[7] She looked at Jane, and smiled, and shook her head by turns.

"Well, well, and so Mr. Bingley is coming down, sister," (for Mrs. Philips first brought her the news.) "Well, so much the better. Not that I care about it, though. He is nothing to us, you know, and I am sure I never want to see him again. But, however, he is very welcome to come to Netherfield, if he likes it. And who knows what *may* happen? But that is nothing to us. You know, sister, we agreed long ago never to mention a word about it. And so, is it quite certain he is coming?"

"You may depend on it," replied the other, "for Mrs. Nicholls[8] was in Meryton last night; I saw her passing by, and went out myself on purpose to know the truth of it; and she told me that it was certain true. He comes down on Thursday at the latest, very likely on Wednesday. She was going to the butcher's, she told me, on purpose to order in some meat on Wednesday, and she has got three couple of ducks, just fit to be killed."

Miss Bennet had not been able to hear of his coming, without changing colour. It was many months since she had mentioned his name to Elizabeth; but now, as soon as they were alone together, she said,

"I saw you look at me to-day, Lizzy, when my aunt told us of the present report; and I know I appeared distressed. But don't imagine it was from any silly cause. I was only confused for the moment, because I felt that I *should* be looked at. I do assure you, that the news does not affect me either with pleasure or pain. I am glad of one thing, that he comes alone; because we shall see the less of him. Not that I am afraid of *myself*, but I dread other people's remarks."[9]

Elizabeth did not know what to make of it. Had she not seen him in Derbyshire, she might have supposed him capable of coming there, with no other view than what was acknowledged;

5. *spiritless*: depressed.

6. It is now around the middle of September (see chronology, p. 719). The season for shooting game started September 1.

7. *in the fidgets*: in a state of nervous excitement, one marked by fidgeting.

8. *Mrs. Nicholls*: the housekeeper at Netherfield. Bingley, her employer, called her just "Nicholls," but Mrs. Philips, as a stranger, speaks of her more formally. A similar phenomenon is evident in the case of Darcy's and the Bennets' housekeepers, called only by their last name by characters who knew them but identified with a "Mrs." by the narrator.

Mrs. Nicholls has obviously been staying at Netherfield while Bingley has been away: this was the normal procedure for housekeepers, one also seen with Mrs. Reynolds at Pemberley. Generally, servants whose work pertained specifically to the maintenance of a residence, including housemaids and cooks, would tend to remain with it even when it was unoccupied; in contrast, servants whose job was to attend to the persons of their employers, like lady's maids or valets, would accompany the latter when they traveled.

9. Jane will continue to insist on her indifference about Bingley, almost all the way up to her accepting him in marriage, even though others will easily perceive her feelings for him. This demonstrates her lack of discernment and self-knowledge compared to Elizabeth.

but she still thought him partial to Jane, and she wavered as to the greater probability of his coming there *with* his friend's permission, or being bold enough to come without it.

"Yet it is hard," she sometimes thought, "that this poor man cannot come to a house, which he has legally hired, without raising all this speculation! I *will* leave him to himself."

In spite of what her sister declared, and really believed to be her feelings, in the expectation of his arrival, Elizabeth could easily perceive that her spirits were affected by it. They were more disturbed, more unequal,[10] than she had often seen them.

The subject which had been so warmly canvassed[11] between their parents, about a twelvemonth ago, was now brought forward again.

"As soon as ever Mr. Bingley comes, my dear," said Mrs. Bennet, "you will wait on[12] him of course."

"No, no. You forced me into visiting him last year, and promised if I went to see him, he should marry one of my daughters. But it ended in nothing, and I will not be sent on a fool's errand again."

His wife represented to him how absolutely necessary such an attention would be from all the neighbouring gentlemen, on his returning to Netherfield.

"'Tis an etiquette I despise," said he. "If he wants our society, let him seek it. He knows where we live. I will not spend *my* hours in running after my neighbours every time they go away, and come back again."

"Well, all I know is, that it will be abominably rude if you do not wait on him. But, however,[13] that shan't prevent my asking him to dine here, I am determined. We must have Mrs. Long and the Gouldings soon. That will make thirteen with ourselves, so there will be just room at table for him."

Consoled by this resolution, she was the better able to bear her husband's incivility; though it was very mortifying to know that her neighbours might all see Mr. Bingley in consequence of it, before *they* did. As the day of his arrival drew near,

"I begin to be sorry that he comes at all," said Jane to her sister.

10. *unequal:* variable, uneven.

11. *canvassed:* discussed in detail.

12. *wait on:* call upon.

13. *But, however:* this redundant phrase is used on numerous occasions by Mrs. Bennet; she says it three times in this chapter. The only other person in the novel to employ it is Lydia, who takes after her mother in so many ways. In both cases, the phrase indicates mental shallowness.

"It would be nothing; I could see him with perfect indifference, but I can hardly bear to hear it thus perpetually talked of. My mother means well; but she does not know, no one can know how much I suffer from what she says. Happy shall I be, when his stay at Netherfield is over!"

"I wish I could say any thing to comfort you," replied Elizabeth; "but it is wholly out of my power. You must feel it; and the usual satisfaction of preaching patience to a sufferer is denied me, because you have always so much."

Mr. Bingley arrived. Mrs. Bennet, through the assistance of servants, contrived to have the earliest tidings of it, that the period of anxiety and fretfulness on her side, might be as long as it could. She counted the days that must intervene before their invitation could be sent; hopeless of seeing him before. But on the third morning after his arrival in Hertfordshire, she saw him from her dressing-room window, enter the paddock,[14] and ride towards the house.

Her daughters were eagerly called to partake of her joy. Jane resolutely kept her place at the table; but Elizabeth, to satisfy her mother, went to the window—she looked,—she saw Mr. Darcy with him, and sat down again by her sister.

"There is a gentleman with him, mamma," said Kitty; "who can it be?"

"Some acquaintance or other, my dear, I suppose; I am sure I do not know."

"La!" replied Kitty, "it looks just like that man that used to be with him before. Mr. what's his name. That tall, proud man."

"Good gracious! Mr. Darcy!—and so it does I vow. Well, any friend of Mr. Bingley's will always be welcome here to be sure; but else I must say that I hate the very sight of him."

Jane looked at Elizabeth with surprise and concern. She knew but little of their meeting in Derbyshire,[15] and therefore felt for the awkwardness which must attend her sister, in seeing him almost for the first time after receiving his explanatory letter. Both sisters were uncomfortable enough. Each felt for the other, and of course for themselves; and their mother talked on, of her dislike of Mr. Darcy, and her resolution to be civil to him only as

14. *paddock:* enclosed field or lawn next to a house.

15. Thus Elizabeth has told her sister little of all that happened at Pemberley and Lambton. This is partly because the affair of Lydia and Wickham has distracted everyone's attention; it is also due to reasons Elizabeth will explain when she tells Jane of her engagement to Darcy (see p. 682, and p. 683, note 12).

Mr. Bingley's friend, without being heard by either of them. But Elizabeth had sources of uneasiness which could not be suspected by Jane, to whom she had never yet had courage to shew Mrs. Gardiner's letter, or to relate her own change of sentiment towards him. To Jane, he could be only a man whose proposals she had refused, and whose merit she had undervalued; but to her own more extensive information, he was the person, to whom the whole family were indebted for the first of benefits, and whom she regarded herself with an interest, if not quite so tender, at least as reasonable and just, as what Jane felt for Bingley. Her astonishment at his coming—at his coming to Netherfield, to Longbourn, and voluntarily seeking her again, was almost equal to what she had known on first witnessing his altered behaviour in Derbyshire.

The colour which had been driven from her face, returned for half a minute with an additional glow, and a smile of delight added lustre to her eyes, as she thought for that space of time, that his affection and wishes must still be unshaken. But she would not be secure.[16]

"Let me first see how he behaves," said she; "it will then be early enough for expectation."[17]

She sat intently at work,[18] striving to be composed, and without daring to lift up her eyes, till anxious curiosity carried them to the face of her sister, as the servant was approaching the door.[19] Jane looked a little paler than usual, but more sedate[20] than Elizabeth had expected. On the gentlemen's appearing, her colour increased; yet she received them with tolerable ease, and with a propriety of behaviour equally free from any symptom of resentment, or any unnecessary complaisance.[21]

Elizabeth said as little to either as civility would allow, and sat down again to her work, with an eagerness which it did not often command.[22] She had ventured only one glance at Darcy. He looked serious as usual; and she thought, more as he had been used to look in Hertfordshire, than as she had seen him at Pemberley. But, perhaps he could not in her mother's presence be what he was before her uncle and aunt. It was a painful, but not an improbable, conjecture.

16. *secure:* certain or confident (about Darcy's continued affection).

17. *expectation:* expectation of more that might ensue, such as Darcy's renewed attentions to Elizabeth.

18. *at work:* engaged in needlework.

19. The servant would be answering and opening the door.

20. *sedate:* composed.

21. *complaisance:* obligingness, desire to please.

22. An indication that, while Elizabeth engages in the almost universal feminine activity of needlework, she normally does not pursue it with any zeal.

Bingley, she had likewise seen for an instant, and in that short period saw him looking both pleased and embarrassed. He was received by Mrs. Bennet with a degree of civility, which made her two daughters ashamed,[23] especially when contrasted with the cold and ceremonious politeness of her curtsey and address to his friend.

Elizabeth particularly, who knew that her mother owed to the latter the preservation of her favourite daughter from irremediable infamy, was hurt and distressed to a most painful degree by a distinction so ill applied.[24]

Darcy, after enquiring of her how Mr. and Mrs. Gardiner did, a question which she could not answer without confusion, said scarcely any thing. He was not seated by her; perhaps that was the reason of his silence; but it had not been so in Derbyshire. There he had talked to her friends, when he could not to herself. But now several minutes elapsed, without bringing the sound of his voice; and when occasionally, unable to resist the impulse of curiosity, she raised her eyes to his face, she as often found him looking at Jane,[25] as at herself, and frequently on no object but the ground. More thoughtfulness, and less anxiety to please than when they last met, were plainly expressed. She was disappointed, and angry with herself for being so.[26]

"Could I expect it to be otherwise!" said she. "Yet why did he come?"

She was in no humour[27] for conversation with any one but himself; and to him she had hardly courage to speak.

She enquired after his sister, but could do no more.

"It is a long time, Mr. Bingley, since you went away," said Mrs. Bennet.

He readily agreed to it.

"I began to be afraid you would never come back again. People *did* say, you meant to quit the place entirely at Michaelmas;[28] but, however, I hope it is not true. A great many changes have happened in the neighbourhood, since you went away. Miss Lucas is married and settled. And one of my own daughters. I suppose you have heard of it; indeed, you must have seen it in the papers. It was in the Times and the Courier,[29] I know; though it was not put

23. The implication is that the "degree of civility" was excessive.

24. That is, Mrs. Bennet has distinguished or selected out Darcy in a negative sense, by coldness toward him, instead of distinguishing him in a positive sense as she should.

25. Darcy will eventually reveal the reasons for both his silence and his observation of Jane; see pp. 694, 696.

26. Meaning that she was angry with herself for having expected more attention and affection from him than she reasonably could have expected.

27. *humour:* mood.

28. *at Michaelmas:* since he came last year just before Michaelmas (September 29), it would be logical to leave Netherfield then (assuming he had a year's lease).

29. *the Times and the Courier:* the two leading daily London newspapers of the time; they both had a circulation of around 5,000. The *Times* was a morning paper, and the *Courier* an evening one, which may be why the announcement appeared in both. London newspapers did circulate in the provinces, especially in nearby counties like Hertfordshire, though there is no necessary reason to assume that the Bennets regularly got one. Newspapers, which were very expensive because of high stamp taxes placed on them, were regularly shared around, so Mrs. Bennet could easily have read others' copies.

in as it ought to be. It was only said, 'Lately, George Wickham, Esq.[30] to Miss Lydia Bennet,' without there being a syllable said of her father, or the place where she lived, or any thing. It was my brother Gardiner's drawing up too, and I wonder how he came to make such an awkward business of it.[31] Did you see it?"

Bingley replied that he did, and made his congratulations. Elizabeth dared not lift up her eyes. How Mr. Darcy looked, therefore, she could not tell.

"It is a delightful thing, to be sure, to have a daughter well married," continued her mother, "but at the same time, Mr. Bingley, it is very hard to have her taken such a way from me. They are gone down to Newcastle, a place quite northward, it seems,[32] and there they are to stay, I do not know how long. His regiment is there; for I suppose you have heard of his leaving the ——shire, and of his being gone into the regulars. Thank Heaven! he has *some* friends, though perhaps not so many as he deserves."

Elizabeth, who knew this to be levelled at[33] Mr. Darcy, was in such misery of shame, that she could hardly keep her seat. It drew from her, however, the exertion of speaking, which nothing else had so effectually done before; and she asked Bingley, whether he meant to make any stay in the country at present. A few weeks, he believed.

"When you have killed all your own birds, Mr. Bingley," said her mother, "I beg you will come here, and shoot as many as you please, on Mr. Bennet's manor. I am sure he will be vastly[34] happy to oblige you, and will save all the best of the covies[35] for you."

Elizabeth's misery increased, at such unnecessary, such officious attention![36] Were the same fair prospect to arise at present, as had flattered them a year ago, every thing, she was persuaded, would be hastening to the same vexatious conclusion. At that instant she felt, that years of happiness could not make Jane or herself amends, for moments of such painful confusion.

"The first wish of my heart," said she to herself, "is never more to be in company with either of them. Their society can afford no pleasure, that will atone for such wretchedness as this! Let me never see either one or the other again!"[37]

30. *Esq.*: an abbreviation for esquire, a title often added to a man's name in formal settings, such as a newspaper announcement, to signify status as a gentleman. Wickham's being an army officer allows him to claim that status. Esquire derives from squire, a term used earlier for the attendant of a knight and used in this period for someone, generally a member of the landed gentry like Darcy or Mr. Bennet, who was of high social standing but untitled. All gentlemen were considered esquires, if they did not have a superior title, though not all gentlemen actually used the designation. In addressing letters to some of her relatives Jane Austen affixes "Esq." to their name. In one to a nephew who has just finished school, and therefore can now be considered an adult gentleman, she says, "One reason for my writing to you now, is that I may have the pleasure of directing to you *Esqre*" (Dec. 16, 1816).

31. Mr. Gardiner would wish to draw minimal attention to their wedding, since it occurred under the cloud of their cohabitation before marriage.

32. Mrs. Bennet shows a feeble command of geography by being so uncertain about the location of Newcastle, which was a major industrial and coal-mining center and one of the largest cities in England at the time.

33. *levelled at*: directed or aimed at (the term was often used to refer to the aiming of a weapon, so it suggests hostility).

34. *vastly*: extremely. "Vastly," a popular word in the eighteenth century, was by this point declining in use. It is generally used by less educated or intelligent characters in Jane Austen's novels.

35. *covies*: broods of partridges. Partridges were the principal game bird of southern England at the time, though changes in hunting practices during this period—particularly the movement away from the older method of stalking game over open countryside and toward a new method of having birds driven toward shooters—were causing partridges to be displaced in popularity by pheasants, which were more suited to the new method.

36. Part of the reason Mrs. Bennet's offer is so officious is that guns at this time, despite some recent innovations, were fairly inaccurate; being muzzle (i.e., front) loaders, they were also slow to reload. This meant that hunters would be able to shoot only limited numbers of birds. Thus it is unlikely that Bingley would kill all his own birds and need to use someone else's land, especially since, given the apparent grandeur of Netherfield House, he probably has the use of an ample property. In making the offer, Mrs. Bennet is seeking any way possible to be generous and polite to Bingley, but is in fact only making herself ridiculous.

37. It is probable that Elizabeth's uncertainty and disappointment concerning Darcy's silent behavior helps inspire this angry wish.

Yet the misery, for which years of happiness were to offer no compensation, received soon afterwards material relief, from observing how much the beauty of her sister re-kindled the admiration of her former lover. When first he came in, he had spoken to her but little; but every five minutes seemed to be giving her more of his attention. He found her as handsome as she had been last year; as good natured, and as unaffected, though not quite so chatty. Jane was anxious that no difference should be perceived in her at all, and was really persuaded that she talked as much as ever. But her mind was so busily engaged, that she did not always know when she was silent.

When the gentlemen rose to go away, Mrs. Bennet was mindful of her intended civility, and they were invited and engaged to dine at Longbourn in a few days time.

"You are quite a visit in my debt, Mr. Bingley," she added, "for when you went to town last winter, you promised to take a family dinner with us, as soon as you returned. I have not forgot, you see; and I assure you, I was very much disappointed that you did not come back and keep your engagement."

Bingley looked a little silly at this reflection,[38] and said something of his concern, at having been prevented by business. They then went away.

Mrs. Bennet had been strongly inclined to ask them to stay and dine there, that day; but, though she always kept a very good table, she did not think any thing less than two courses, could be good enough for a man, on whom she had such anxious designs, or satisfy the appetite and pride of one who had ten thousand a year.

38. He looks silly because of Mrs. Bennet's silliness in making such a point of a simple and vague promise offered almost a year ago.

Chapter Twelve

As soon as they were gone, Elizabeth walked out to recover her spirits; or in other words, to dwell without interruption on those subjects that must deaden them more.[1] Mr. Darcy's behaviour astonished and vexed her.

"Why, if he came only to be silent, grave, and indifferent," said she, "did he come at all?"

She could settle it in no way that gave her pleasure.

"He could be still amiable, still pleasing, to my uncle and aunt, when he was in town; and why not to me? If he fears me, why come hither? If he no longer cares for me, why silent? Teazing, teazing,[2] man! I will think no more about him."

Her resolution was for a short time involuntarily kept by the approach of her sister,[3] who joined her with a cheerful look, which shewed her better satisfied with their visitors, than Elizabeth.

"Now," said she, "that this first meeting is over, I feel perfectly easy. I know my own strength, and I shall never be embarrassed again by his coming. I am glad he dines here on Tuesday. It will then be publicly seen, that on both sides, we meet only as common and indifferent acquaintance."

"Yes, very indifferent indeed," said Elizabeth, laughingly. "Oh, Jane, take care."

"My dear Lizzy, you cannot think me so weak, as to be in danger now."

"I think you are in very great danger of making him as much in love with you as ever."

———

They did not see the gentlemen again till Tuesday; and Mrs. Bennet, in the meanwhile, was giving way to all the happy

1. This is not the only time in the novel when people are presented as unable to resist pursuing subjects of thought that may only make them unhappy. This passage, like others in this section, also shows the author directing a greater degree of irony toward Elizabeth than at other times in the book, for Elizabeth is now acting and thinking in a less clear-headed way because of her strong feelings for Darcy.

2. *teazing:* irritating.

3. That is, the distraction of her sister's presence causes Elizabeth, without her willing it, to maintain temporarily her resolution to think no more of Darcy. The phrasing of the passage suggests that this resolution will not be kept for long, since external distractions will not always be present to bolster her resolve.

schemes, which the good humour, and common politeness of Bingley, in half an hour's visit, had revived.

On Tuesday there was a large party assembled at Longbourn; and the two, who were most anxiously expected, to the credit of their punctuality as sportsmen,[4] were in very good time. When they repaired to[5] the dining-room, Elizabeth eagerly watched to see whether Bingley would take the place, which, in all their former parties, had belonged to him, by her sister. Her prudent mother, occupied by the same ideas, forbore to invite him to sit by herself. On entering the room, he seemed to hesitate; but Jane happened to look round, and happened to smile: it was decided. He placed himself by her.

Elizabeth, with a triumphant sensation, looked towards his friend.[6] He bore it with noble indifference, and she would have imagined that Bingley had received his sanction to be happy, had she not seen his eyes likewise turned towards Mr. Darcy, with an expression of half-laughing alarm.

His behaviour to her sister was such, during dinner time, as shewed an admiration of her, which, though more guarded than formerly, persuaded Elizabeth, that if left wholly to himself, Jane's happiness, and his own, would be speedily secured. Though she dared not depend upon the consequence, she yet received pleasure from observing his behaviour. It gave her all the animation that her spirits could boast; for she was in no cheerful humour. Mr. Darcy was almost as far from her, as the table could divide them. He was on one side of her mother. She knew how little such a situation would give pleasure to either, or make either appear to advantage. She was not near enough to hear any of their discourse, but she could see how seldom they spoke to each other, and how formal and cold was their manner, whenever they did. Her mother's ungraciousness, made the sense of what they owed him more painful to Elizabeth's mind; and she would, at times, have given any thing to be privileged to tell him, that his kindness was neither unknown nor unfelt by the whole of the family.[7]

She was in hopes that the evening would afford some opportunity of bringing them together; that the whole of the visit would

4. *punctuality as sportsmen:* their punctuality in finishing their sport (i.e., shooting).

5. *repaired to:* moved into. The guests would have been received initially in another room.

6. The implication is that Elizabeth still suspects Darcy to harbor snobbish reservations toward a marriage between Bingley and Jane, despite Elizabeth's experience of Darcy's improved behavior at Pemberley and her knowledge of his actions with regard to Lydia.

7. Elizabeth's inability at this juncture to communicate with Darcy or to learn his true thoughts constitutes another ordeal for her and a further test of her feelings for him.

not pass away without enabling them to enter into something more of conversation, than the mere ceremonious salutation attending his entrance. Anxious and uneasy, the period which passed in the drawing-room, before the gentlemen came, was wearisome and dull to a degree, that almost made her uncivil.[8] She looked forward to their entrance, as the point on which all her chance of pleasure for the evening must depend.

"If he does not come to me, *then*," said she, "I shall give him up for ever."[9]

The gentlemen came; and she thought he looked as if he would have answered her hopes; but, alas! the ladies had crowded round the table, where Miss Bennet was making tea, and Elizabeth pouring out the coffee, in so close a confederacy,[10] that there was not a single vacancy near her, which would admit of a chair. And on the gentlemen's approaching, one of the girls moved closer to her than ever, and said, in a whisper,

"The men shan't come and part us, I am determined. We want none of them; do we?"

Darcy had walked away to another part of the room. She followed him with her eyes, envied every one to whom he spoke, had scarcely patience enough to help anybody to coffee; and then was enraged against herself for being so silly!

"A man who has once been refused! How could I ever be foolish enough to expect a renewal of his love? Is there one among the sex, who would not protest against such a weakness as a second proposal to the same woman? There is no indignity so abhorrent to their feelings!"

She was a little revived, however, by his bringing back his coffee cup himself; and she seized the opportunity of saying,

"Is your sister at Pemberley still?"

"Yes, she will remain there till Christmas."

"And quite alone? Have all her friends left her?"

"Mrs. Annesley is with her. The others have been gone on to Scarborough,[11] these three weeks."[12]

She could think of nothing more to say; but if he wished to converse with her, he might have better success. He stood by her,

8. Commentators of the time would often describe this period when the ladies waited for the men as one of boredom for them. The implication of this sentence is that it is even more tedious than usual for Elizabeth now.

9. Elizabeth's making such a silly resolution is a sign of how much Darcy is affecting her emotionally, and causing her to be less the confident and often sardonic person that she was earlier.

Showing such confusion or irrationality in Elizabeth is one way for the author to reveal, in the absence of actual love scenes, the growing strength of Elizabeth's love for Darcy.

10. *confederacy:* league or union. The terms suggests that the ladies are, at least to Elizabeth's mind, almost conspiring to prevent Darcy from talking to her.

11. *Scarborough:* a town on the northeast coast of England (see map, p. 742); it was a popular spa and seaside resort, the largest of such resorts outside the vicinity of London. For people already in Derbyshire, it would be closer than the resorts on the southern coast. "The others" probably refers to, at the least, Miss Bingley and the Hursts.

12. *these three weeks:* for the last three weeks.

however, for some minutes, in silence; and, at last, on the young lady's whispering to Elizabeth again, he walked away.

When the tea-things were removed, and the card tables placed, the ladies all rose, and Elizabeth was then hoping to be soon joined by him, when all her views[13] were overthrown, by seeing him fall a victim to her mother's rapacity for whist players,[14] and in a few moments after seated with the rest of the party. She now lost every expectation of pleasure. They were confined for the evening at different tables, and she had nothing to hope, but that his eyes were so often turned towards her side of the room, as to make him play as unsuccessfully as herself.

Mrs. Bennet had designed to keep the two Netherfield gentlemen to supper;[15] but their carriage was unluckily ordered before any of the others, and she had no opportunity of detaining them.

"Well girls," said she, as soon as they were left to themselves, "What say you to the day? I think every thing has passed off uncommonly well, I assure you. The dinner was as well dressed as any I ever saw. The venison[16] was roasted to a turn[17]—and everybody said, they never saw so fat a haunch. The soup was fifty times better than what we had at the Lucas's last week; and even Mr. Darcy acknowledged, that the partridges were remarkably well done;[18] and I suppose he has two or three French cooks[19] at least. And, my dear Jane, I never saw you look in greater beauty. Mrs. Long said so too, for I asked her whether you did not. And what do you think she said besides? 'Ah! Mrs. Bennet, we shall have her at Netherfield at last.' She did indeed. I do think Mrs. Long is as good a creature as ever lived—and her nieces are very pretty behaved girls,[20] and not at all handsome: I like them prodigiously."

Mrs. Bennet, in short, was in very great spirits; she had seen enough of Bingley's behaviour to Jane, to be convinced that she would get him at last; and her expectations of advantage to her family, when in a happy humour, were so far beyond reason, that she was quite disappointed at not seeing him there again the next day, to make his proposals.

"It has been a very agreeable day," said Miss Bennet to Elizabeth.

13. *views:* expectations.

14. Since whist is a card game requiring four players for each group, a hostess would often need to recruit additional players in order to make sure each potential group of four was complete.

15. Jane Austen herself commented on the issue of Mrs. Bennet's suppers; see p. 627, note 14.

16. *venison:* this, and other game such as partridges (also served at this dinner), would be in season at this time. Because restrictions on hunting and selling game made it difficult to procure, serving it was a mark of status, as Mrs. Bennet would certainly know. According to one authority on rural life (E. W. Bovill), "In the shooting season no dinner party with any pretension to smartness was complete without a game course." Venison was especially prestigious, for the rarity of deer in England meant that obtaining it required either the possession of extensive lands or an acquaintance with someone who possessed such lands.

Serving two different kinds of meat, in this case venison and partridges, at the same dinner was not at all unusual for the time, for those who could afford it had a heavily meat-based diet. Sample menus for formal dinners from the time show a great variety of meats or meat dishes being served.

17. *to a turn:* to the exact proper degree.

18. Darcy's willingness to offer such a compliment, and to someone as annoying and as impolite to him as Mrs. Bennet, indicates his improvement in courtesy and sociability.

19. *French cooks:* often hired by the wealthy, for by this time French cuisine had become more prestigious; French cooking was also more prevalent in towns than in the countryside. One of Jane Austen's brothers hired a French cook.

20. *pretty behaved:* pleasingly or properly behaved.

"The party seemed so well selected, so suitable one with the other. I hope we may often meet again."

Elizabeth smiled.

"Lizzy, you must not do so. You must not suspect me. It mortifies me. I assure you that I have now learnt to enjoy his conversation as an agreeable and sensible young man, without having a wish beyond it. I am perfectly satisfied from what his manners now are, that he never had any design of engaging my affection. It is only that he is blessed with greater sweetness of address,[21] and a stronger desire of generally pleasing than any other man."[22]

"You are very cruel," said her sister, "you will not let me smile, and are provoking me to it every moment."

"How hard it is in some cases to be believed!"

"And how impossible in others!"[23]

"But why should you wish to persuade me that I feel more than I acknowledge?"

"That is a question which I hardly know how to answer. We all love to instruct, though we can teach only what is not worth knowing. Forgive me; and if you persist in indifference, do not make *me* your confidante."

21. *address:* way of speaking, or bearing in conversation.

22. After first saying that she harbors no special regard for Bingley, Jane then exalts him above all other men. This indicates both the strength of her feelings for him, and her continued inability or unwillingness to acknowledge these feelings.

23. This line and the previous line were printed as one line, and thus as utterances of the same speaker, in initial editions of the novel. Jane Austen noticed this in a letter written when the novel first appeared, calling it "the greatest blunder in the Printing that I have met with" (Feb. 4, 1813).

Chapter Thirteen

A few days after this visit, Mr. Bingley called again, and alone. His friend had left him that morning for London, but was to return home[1] in ten days time. He sat with them above an hour, and was in remarkably good spirits. Mrs. Bennet invited him to dine with them; but, with many expressions of concern, he confessed himself engaged elsewhere.

"Next time you call," said she, "I hope we shall be more lucky."

He should be particularly happy at any time, &c. &c.;[2] and if she would give him leave, would take an early opportunity of waiting on[3] them.

"Can you come to-morrow?"

Yes, he had no engagement at all for to-morrow; and her invitation was accepted with alacrity.

He came, and in such very good time, that the ladies were none of them dressed. In ran Mrs. Bennet to her daughter's room, in her dressing gown, and with her hair half finished, crying out,

"My dear Jane, make haste and hurry down. He is come—Mr. Bingley is come.—He is, indeed. Make haste, make haste. Here, Sarah,[4] come to Miss Bennet this moment, and help her on with her gown. Never mind Miss Lizzy's hair."[5]

"We will be down as soon as we can," said Jane; "but I dare say Kitty is forwarder[6] than either of us, for she went up stairs half an hour ago."[7]

"Oh! hang Kitty! what has she to do with it? Come be quick, be quick! where is your sash my dear?"

But when her mother was gone, Jane would not be prevailed on to go down without one of her sisters.[8]

The same anxiety to get them by themselves, was visible again in the evening. After tea, Mr. Bennet retired to the library, as was his custom, and Mary went up stairs to her instrument.[9] Two

1. *home*: this, as is revealed later, means Bingley's home of Netherfield, rather than Darcy's own home of Pemberley. Of course, it is returning to the former that will allow him to resume seeing Elizabeth.

2. *&c. &c.*: etc., etc. This is a way of indicating that Bingley is going on to express standard phrases of polite gratitude. In other places this abbreviation appears to be something used by a character in the novel in a letter or note; here it seems to be employed by the author herself to avoid relating unnecessary details of a conversation.

3. *waiting on*: calling upon.

4. *Sarah*: a maid; use of her first name indicates low status.

5. Sarah is helping the girls to dress and fix their hair. In contrast to Bingley's sisters, the Bennet daughters do not each have a separate maid, so Sarah has to turn from Elizabeth to Jane. It would also seem that Sarah was already attending Elizabeth in the same room where Jane was dressing, which implies that the two sisters share a bedroom (the phrase in the preceding paragraph "her daughter's room" was written as "her daughters' room" in one of the early editions of the novel; in any case, even in the singular form it does not indicate necessarily that the room was not Elizabeth's as well). Earlier (on p. 216) there is in fact a reference to "their [Elizabeth and Jane's] own room." This sharing of a room would indicate Elizabeth and Jane's closeness.

6. *forwarder*: more prompt, or more advanced in her preparations.

7. This probably means that Kitty went to her room to start dressing half an hour ago, and thus is further along. This in turn suggests the existence of at least three floors in the Bennets' house: Jane's talk of coming down indicates that she is not on the ground floor, while the phrase "went up stairs" implies that Kitty's action involved ascending to one floor above Jane, rather than simply reaching the same floor. This higher floor could be a less significant one, where Kitty, and perhaps Mary, have their rooms (lower priority being given to younger daughters); the servants' rooms might also be on this floor.

8. Jane, in her disinclination to go down alone in order to be with Bingley, is exhibiting some of the female modesty that was highly praised at the time and that Mr. Collins mentioned in his proposal to Elizabeth. Of course, the modesty that keeps one from throwing oneself at a man is hardly the same as the extravagant modesty of directly refusing an offer of marriage that one actually desired, a modesty that Mr. Collins claimed was standard.

9. *instrument*: musical instrument, i.e., the piano.

obstacles of the five being thus removed, Mrs. Bennet sat looking and winking at Elizabeth and Catherine for a considerable time, without making any impression on them. Elizabeth would not observe her; and when at last Kitty did, she very innocently said, "What is the matter mamma? What do you keep winking at me for? What am I to do?"

"Nothing child, nothing. I did not wink at you." She then sat still five minutes longer; but unable to waste such a precious occasion, she suddenly got up, and saying to Kitty,

"Come here, my love, I want to speak to you," took her out of the room. Jane instantly gave a look at Elizabeth, which spoke[10] her distress at such premeditation, and her intreaty that *she* would not give into it. In a few minutes, Mrs. Bennet half opened the door and called out,

"Lizzy, my dear, I want to speak with you."

Elizabeth was forced to go.

"We may as well leave them by themselves you know;" said her mother as soon as she was in the hall. "Kitty and I are going up stairs to sit in my dressing room."[11]

Elizabeth made no attempt to reason with her mother, but remained quietly in the hall, till she and Kitty were out of sight, then returned into the drawing room.[12]

Mrs. Bennet's schemes for this day were ineffectual. Bingley was every thing that was charming, except the professed lover of her daughter. His ease and cheerfulness rendered him a most agreeable addition to their evening party; and he bore with the ill-judged officiousness of the mother, and heard all her silly remarks with a forbearance and command of countenance, particularly grateful to the daughter.

He scarcely needed an invitation to stay[13] supper;[14] and before he went away, an engagement was formed, chiefly through his own and Mrs. Bennet's means, for his coming next morning to shoot with her husband.

After this day, Jane said no more of her indifference. Not a word passed between the sisters concerning Bingley; but Elizabeth went to bed in the happy belief that all must speedily be concluded,

10. *spoke*: indicated, revealed.

11. *dressing room*: often the dressing room of the mistress of the house was a sitting room as well. Jane Austen's letters refer to the dressing room being used for various family purposes; in one she says, "We live entirely in the dressing-room now" (Dec. 1, 1798). Her hyphenation of "dressing room" in the letter, but not in the novel, is an example of the inconsistency in spelling that can be frequently found in Jane Austen's writings, as well as in other writings of the time.

12. That is, to where Jane and Bingley still were.

13. *stay*: stay for.

14. The supper offered here, along with the one in the last chapter that Mrs. Bennet had hoped to serve Bingley and Darcy, sparked Jane Austen's only criticism on a specific point of her novel. In a letter she confided that, "There might as well have been no suppers at Longbourn, but I suppose it was the remains of Mrs. Bennet's old Meryton habits" (Feb. 4, 1813). The reason for this criticism is that the gradual latening of the dinner hour was causing supper to go out of fashion, especially among the wealthy (see p. 139, note 44). If supper was served it would only be a light meal or snack taken among those staying in the house—one such supper was mentioned at Netherfield. In contrast, suppers continued to be a standard, and often substantial, meal among those at a lower social level. Mrs. Bennet's suppers, being significant enough to intend for guests, are not what would usually be found in a wealthy landowning family of the time, which is why Jane Austen refers in her letter to Mrs. Bennet's old Meryton habits, i.e., her habits when she was growing up as the daughter of a simple attorney in Meryton. Earlier her sister Mrs. Philips, now the wife of an attorney in Meryton, was shown offering an ample hot supper.

It is possible that the Longbourn suppers are actually a legacy of the first version of the novel—written fifteen years earlier when supper was still more usual among the wealthy—that Jane Austen neglected to revise when she created the final version. In that case, having noticed the mistake when it was too late (for the above letter was written just after the novel had been published), she attempted to rationalize it with the suggestion regarding Mrs. Bennet's Meryton habits.

unless Mr. Darcy returned within the stated time. Seriously, however, she felt tolerably persuaded that all this must have taken place with that gentleman's concurrence.

Bingley was punctual to his appointment; and he and Mr. Bennet spent the morning[15] together, as had been agreed on. The latter was much more agreeable than his companion expected. There was nothing of presumption or folly in Bingley, that could provoke his ridicule, or disgust him into silence; and he was more communicative, and less eccentric than the other had ever seen him. Bingley of course returned with him to dinner; and in the evening Mrs. Bennet's invention[16] was again at work to get every body away from him and her daughter. Elizabeth, who had a letter to write, went into the breakfast room for that purpose soon after tea; for as the others were all going to sit down to cards, she could not be wanted to counteract her mother's schemes.[17]

But on returning to the drawing room, when her letter was finished, she saw, to her infinite surprise, there was reason to fear that her mother had been too ingenious for her. On opening the door, she perceived her sister and Bingley standing together over the hearth, as if engaged in earnest conversation; and had this led to no suspicion, the faces of both as they hastily turned round, and moved away from each other, would have told it all. *Their* situation was awkward enough; but *her's* she thought was still worse. Not a syllable was uttered by either;[18] and Elizabeth was on the point of going away again, when Bingley, who as well as the others[19] had sat down, suddenly rose, and whispering a few words to her sister, ran out of the room.

Jane could have no reserves[20] from Elizabeth, where confidence[21] would give pleasure; and instantly embracing her, acknowledged, with the liveliest emotion, that she was the happiest creature in the world.

"'Tis too much!" she added, "by far too much. I do not deserve it. Oh! why is not every body as happy?"

Elizabeth's congratulations were given with a sincerity, a warmth, a delight, which words could but poorly express. Every sentence of kindness was a fresh source of happiness to Jane. But

15. *morning:* most of the day.

16. *invention:* inventiveness, ingenuity.

17. In other words, Elizabeth believes it safe not to remain in the room with Jane and Bingley, for others will be in that room playing cards, and thus Jane and Bingley, as Jane wishes, will not be alone.

18. *either:* the word could refer just to Bingley and Jane, since they were the ones who would be expected to speak to explain what had happened, or it could refer as well to Elizabeth (and thus mean "either party"), since she thinks her situation even more awkward than theirs.

19. *others:* the second and third editions printed this as *other,* which would suggest that only Jane and Bingley, but not Elizabeth, had sat down. Either meaning seems possible.

20. *reserves:* secrets.

21. *confidence:* confiding private matters to another.

she would not allow herself to stay with her sister, or say half that remained to be said, for the present.

"I must go instantly to my mother;" she cried. "I would not on any account trifle with her affectionate solicitude; or allow her to hear it from any one but myself. He is gone to my father already.[22] Oh! Lizzy, to know that what I have to relate will give such pleasure to all my dear family! how shall I bear so much happiness!"

She then hastened away to her mother, who had purposely broken up the card party,[23] and was sitting up stairs with Kitty.

Elizabeth, who was left by herself, now smiled at the rapidity and ease with which an affair was finally settled, that had given them so many previous months of suspense[24] and vexation.

"And this," said she, "is the end of all his friend's anxious circumspection! of all his sister's falsehood and contrivance! the happiest, wisest, most reasonable end!"

In a few minutes she was joined by Bingley, whose conference with her father had been short and to the purpose.

"Where is your sister?" said he hastily, as he opened the door.

"With my mother up stairs. She will be down in a moment I dare say."

He then shut the door, and coming up to her, claimed the good wishes and affection of a sister. Elizabeth honestly and heartily expressed her delight in the prospect of their relationship. They shook hands with great cordiality;[25] and then till her sister came down, she had to listen to all he had to say, of his own happiness, and of Jane's perfections; and in spite of his being a lover, Elizabeth really believed all his expectations of felicity, to be rationally founded, because they had for basis the excellent understanding, and super-excellent disposition of Jane, and a general similarity of feeling and taste between her and himself.[26]

It was an evening of no common delight to them all; the satisfaction of Miss Bennet's mind[27] gave a glow of such sweet animation to her face, as made her look handsomer than ever. Kitty simpered and smiled, and hoped her turn was coming soon. Mrs. Bennet could not give her consent, or speak her approbation in terms warm enough to satisfy her feelings, though she talked to

22. A man who proposed marriage, and was accepted by the woman, was then supposed to talk to her father in order to get his permission.

23. In order to leave Jane and Bingley alone. This is how Mrs. Bennet was too ingenious for Elizabeth. One could argue that this is one case where Mrs. Bennet, in her aggressive efforts to promote a match between Jane and Bingley, is vindicated—though it is highly probable that the match would have happened anyway. The most that Mrs. Bennet did was to accelerate it slightly, while making the participants less comfortable during the process.

24. *suspense:* uncertainty, delay in knowing.

25. *cordiality:* warmth, affection. As with Wickham, Elizabeth can now offer her hand to Bingley since, through his engagement, he has effectively become one of the family (see p. 597, note 68). Bingley, not being the inveterate flatterer Wickham is, simply shakes Elizabeth's hand rather than kissing it.

26. That is, normally one might be skeptical of a lover's professed expectations of happiness since all lovers tend, in their enthusiasm, to profess that; here, however, the expectations have a rational basis. This passage indicates that Jane Austen does not condemn enthusiasm or strong feeling in love as such; what she condemns is love founded solely on such feelings, with no other factors, such as those she mentions for Jane and Bingley, to help sustain it.

27. *mind:* spirit, inner person. "Mind" had a less purely intellectual meaning then.

Bingley of nothing else, for half an hour; and when Mr. Bennet joined them at supper, his voice and manner plainly shewed how really happy he was.

Not a word, however, passed his lips in allusion to it, till their visitor took his leave for the night; but as soon as he was gone, he turned to his daughter and said,

"Jane, I congratulate you. You will be a very happy woman."

Jane went to him instantly, kissed him, and thanked him for his goodness.

"You are a good girl;" he replied, "and I have great pleasure in thinking you will be so happily settled. I have not a doubt of your doing very well together. Your tempers[28] are by no means unlike. You are each of you so complying, that nothing will ever be resolved on; so easy, that every servant will cheat you; and so generous, that you will always exceed your income."[29]

"I hope not so. Imprudence or thoughtlessness in money matters, would be unpardonable in *me*."[30]

"Exceed their income! My dear Mr. Bennet," cried his wife, "what are you talking of? Why, he has four or five thousand a-year, and very likely more."[31] Then addressing her daughter, "Oh! my dear, dear Jane, I am so happy! I am sure I sha'nt get a wink of sleep all night. I knew how it would be. I always said it must be so, at last. I was sure you could not be so beautiful for nothing![32] I remember, as soon as ever I saw him, when he first came into Hertfordshire last year, I thought how likely it was that you should come together. Oh! he is the handsomest young man that ever was seen!"

Wickham, Lydia, were all forgotten. Jane was beyond competition her favourite child. At that moment, she cared for no other. Her youngest[33] sisters soon began to make interest[34] with her for objects of happiness which she might in future be able to dispense.

Mary petitioned for the use of the library at Netherfield; and Kitty begged very hard for a few balls there every winter.

Bingley, from this time, was of course a daily visitor at Longbourn; coming frequently before breakfast, and always remaining till after supper; unless when some barbarous neighbour, who

28. *tempers:* dispositions, characters.

29. In this statement Mr. Bennet shows himself as usual to be both astute, for Jane and Bingley's characters offer much support for his predictions, and callous, for normally one's first words to a daughter after her engagement would be more congratulatory than the harsh words Mr. Bennet offers.

Mr. Bennet's statement, and reminder of Jane and Bingley's limitations, also hints at the limitations of this marriage, compared to the marriage of the even more admirable principals that will close the book.

30. Jane does not explain why financial prudence should be so particularly incumbent on her. It is possible her feeling stems from the great disparity between her own fortune and Bingley's: she could think that any profligacy on her part would mean she was wasting his money, and that she, being unable to contribute much money to their marriage, should contribute thriftiness instead.

31. *very likely more:* no other indication exists in the book to support this supposition of Mrs. Bennet; it is undoubtedly the product of her own foolish enthusiasm. She will say the same thing about Darcy's ten thousand pounds after hearing of Elizabeth's engagement to him.

32. The idea of a woman's beauty as a precious commodity that should procure her some reward, especially a monetary one, is one that often appears in Jane Austen's novels; it reflects many of the prevailing ideas in this society. Jane Bennet herself, however, is clearly an example of someone who does not think this way.

33. *youngest:* the second and third editions changed this to "younger," but that seems less logical since it would imply that Elizabeth was also among those asking Jane for things, which does not appear to be the case. In either case, the word could only apply to the youngest or younger present, since Lydia, the youngest of all, is not there.

34. *make interest:* make a special plea, exercise personal influence.

could not be enough detested,[35] had given him an invitation to dinner, which he thought himself obliged to accept.

Elizabeth had now but little time for conversation with her sister; for while he was present, Jane had no attention to bestow on any one else; but she found herself considerably useful to both of them, in those hours of separation that must sometimes occur. In the absence of Jane, he always attached himself to Elizabeth, for the pleasure of talking of her; and when Bingley was gone, Jane constantly sought the same means of relief.

"He has made me so happy," said she, one evening, "by telling me, that he was totally ignorant of my being in town last spring! I had not believed it possible."

"I suspected as much," replied Elizabeth. "But how did he account for it?"

"It must have been his sisters'[36] doing. They were certainly no friends to his acquaintance with me, which I cannot wonder at, since he might have chosen so much more advantageously in many respects. But when they see, as I trust they will, that their brother is happy with me, they will learn to be contented, and we shall be on good terms again; though we can never be what we once were to each other."

"That is the most unforgiving speech," said Elizabeth, "that I ever heard you utter. Good girl! It would vex me, indeed, to see you again the dupe of Miss Bingley's pretended regard."

"Would you believe it, Lizzy, that when he went to town last November, he really loved me, and nothing but a persuasion of *my* being indifferent, would have prevented his coming down again!"

"He made a little mistake to be sure; but it is to the credit of his modesty."

This naturally introduced a panegyric from Jane on his diffidence,[37] and the little value he put on his own good qualities.[38]

Elizabeth was pleased to find, that he had not betrayed the interference of his friend,[39] for, though Jane had the most generous and forgiving heart in the world, she knew it was a circumstance which must prejudice her against him.

35. Detested and considered barbarous by Mrs. Bennet.

36. *sisters':* this was "sister's" in the original edition, but the subsequent use of "they" implies that the word should be plural. The third edition made that change.

37. *diffidence:* modesty.

38. It is characteristic of Jane that she should consider this to be high praise. Her attitude toward such humble modesty contrasts with Elizabeth's acceptance of certain aspects of Darcy's pride as proper and good.

39. *his friend:* Darcy. In all the early editions this was written as *friends*, but that would make no sense since Darcy is the only friend to have interfered with Bingley's love for Jane ("friends" could also include Bingley's sisters, but their interference has already been suspected by Jane).

"I am certainly the most fortunate creature that ever existed!" cried Jane. "Oh! Lizzy, why am I thus singled from my family, and blessed above them all! If I could but see *you* as happy! If there *were* but such another man for you!"

"If you were to give me forty such men, I never could be so happy as you. Till I have your disposition, your goodness, I never can have your happiness. No, no, let me shift for myself; and, perhaps, if I have very good luck, I may meet with another Mr. Collins in time."

The situation of affairs in the Longbourn family could not be long a secret. Mrs. Bennet was privileged to whisper it to Mrs. Philips, and *she* ventured, without any permission, to do the same by all her neighbours in Meryton.[40]

The Bennets were speedily pronounced to be the luckiest family in the world, though only a few weeks before, when Lydia had first run away, they had been generally proved to be marked out for misfortune.

40. One imagines that Mrs. Bennet, far from requiring her permission to spread the news through the neighborhood, was hoping that Mrs. Philips would do precisely that.

Chapter Fourteen

*O*ne morning, about a week after Bingley's engagement with Jane had been formed, as he and the females of the family were sitting together in the dining room, their attention was suddenly drawn to the window, by the sound of a carriage; and they perceived a chaise and four driving up the lawn. It was too early in the morning for visitors,[1] and besides, the equipage[2] did not answer[3] to that of any of their neighbours. The horses were post;[4] and neither the carriage, nor the livery[5] of the servant who preceded it, were familiar to them. As it was certain, however, that somebody was coming, Bingley instantly prevailed on Miss Bennet to avoid the confinement of such an intrusion, and walk away with him into the shrubbery. They both set off, and the conjectures of the remaining three continued, though with little satisfaction, till the door was thrown open, and their visitor entered. It was Lady Catherine de Bourgh.[6]

They were of course all intending to be surprised; but their astonishment was beyond their expectation; and on the part of Mrs. Bennet and Kitty, though she was perfectly unknown to them, even inferior to what Elizabeth felt.

She entered the room[7] with an air more than usually ungracious, made no other reply to Elizabeth's salutation, than a slight inclination of the head, and sat down without saying a word. Elizabeth had mentioned her name to her mother, on her ladyship's entrance, though no request of introduction had been made.

Mrs. Bennet all amazement, though flattered by having a guest of such high importance, received her with the utmost politeness. After sitting for a moment in silence, she said very stiffly to Elizabeth,

"I hope you are well, Miss Bennet. That lady I suppose is your mother."[8]

1. Current etiquette counseled against visits early in the day (Bingley, who is already at the Bennets, is a different case since he is virtually a family member by now); this visitor's violation of that principle is a sign of rudeness.

2. *equipage*: carriage and horses, and possibly the attendant servants. They would be distinctive to individual families.

3. *answer*: correspond.

4. *post*: hired. This could be ascertained because post horses were driven by a man riding one of the front horses, rather than by a man seated on the carriage (see illustration of such a method of driving on p. 397). The use of post horses signaled that it was a visitor from farther away, for those traveling locally would use their own horses if they had them. When Elizabeth traveled from Kent her carriage as well as her horses were hired; in this case, the carriage may be owned by the traveler, which would indicate greater wealth.

5. *livery*: uniform; they would identify the family employing the servants.

6. Lady Catherine's visit, and her exchange with Elizabeth, is one of the most dramatic episodes in the novel. It serves a number of purposes: it advances the story, specifically by precipitating Elizabeth and Darcy's marriage (though one imagines that this would have happened eventually in any case); it gives further evidence of Elizabeth's intelligence and strength of character, and gives a sense that after marrying Darcy she will not be intimidated by associating with people of a higher rank than she had known; it allows Lady Catherine, one of the most distinctive characters in the novel, to enter the story once more; and finally, it vividly presents, in the person of Lady Catherine, a caricature of the very pride that is central to the theme of the novel, and that Darcy needed to acknowledge and to curb in himself.

7. *room*: the text gives mixed clues as to the identity of this room. The chapter's first sentence indentifies it as the dining room, but on the next page Lady Catherine calls it a sitting room. She is then described as inspecting a separate "dining-parlour." The last would be the room where formal dinners occur; this is indicated by its location next to the entrance hall on the ground floor, and its proximity to the drawing room, the room where people withdrew after a formal dinner. The room where they are now may be an informal dining room that is also a sitting room; it could even be the breakfast room mentioned elsewhere, which seems to serve such dual functions.

8. As the one who is superior in social position, it would be up to Lady Catherine to decide whether and when to initiate conversation with those she does not know. That is why Elizabeth sat silently and did not introduce her mother on her own initiative.

Elizabeth replied very concisely that she was.

"And *that* I suppose is one of your sisters."

"Yes, madam," said Mrs. Bennet, delighted to speak to a Lady Catherine.[9] "She is my youngest girl but one. My youngest of all, is lately married, and my eldest is some-where about the grounds, walking with a young man, who I believe will soon become a part of the family."

"You have a very small park[10] here," returned Lady Catherine after a short silence.[11]

"It is nothing in comparison of Rosings, my lady, I dare say; but I assure you it is much larger than Sir William Lucas's."

"This must be a most inconvenient sitting room for the evening, in summer; the windows are full west."

Mrs. Bennet assured her that they never sat there after dinner, and then added,

"May I take the liberty of asking your ladyship whether you left Mr. and Mrs. Collins well."

"Yes, very well. I saw them the night before last."[12]

Elizabeth now expected that she would produce a letter for her from Charlotte, as it seemed the only probable motive for her calling. But no letter appeared, and she was completely puzzled.

Mrs. Bennet, with great civility, begged her ladyship to take some refreshment; but Lady Catherine very resolutely, and not very politely, declined eating any thing; and then rising up, said to Elizabeth,

"Miss Bennet, there seemed to be a prettyish kind of a little wilderness[13] on one side of your lawn. I should be glad to take a turn in it, if you will favour me with your company."

"Go, my dear," cried her mother, "and shew her ladyship about the different walks. I think she will be pleased with the hermitage."[14]

Elizabeth obeyed, and running into her own room for her parasol,[15] attended her noble guest down stairs. As they passed through the hall, Lady Catherine opened the doors into the dining-parlour and drawing-room, and pronouncing them, after a short survey, to be decent looking rooms, walked on.

9. Now that Mrs. Bennet has been introduced, and Lady Catherine has asked another question, Mrs. Bennet is free, according to the conventions of the day, to speak to her.

10. *park*: grounds, especially for pleasure, around a home. Having one was a sign of status, which is why, after Lady Catherine belittles this park, Mrs. Bennet eagerly asserts its superiority to the Lucases'.

11. Lady Catherine's brief silence suggests that she was not pleased with Mrs. Bennet's entrance into the conversation.

12. This statement hints at the origin of the report that Lady Catherine will shortly say reached her two days ago.

13. *wilderness*: term for a wooded area arranged in an elaborate pattern. Wildernesses had been very popular in the seventeenth and early eighteenth centuries, but from the middle of the eighteenth century they had been gradually superceded by shrubberies. The main difference between the two—for both terms could refer to areas involving trees as well as undergrowth—is that wildernesses tended to be arranged in a highly geometric pattern, whereas shrubberies were usually formed in the more serpentine and irregular style that had become popular by Jane Austen's time (see also p. 463, note 64). In *Mansfield Park* a wilderness is described by the author as being "laid out with too much regularity." Thus it is probable that Lady Catherine, who has already denigrated the Bennets' park as very small, means to imply a slight insult by describing their wooded area as a wilderness; immediately below the same area is described by the narrator as "the copse," a completely neutral term. That this could be Lady Catherine's intent is suggested by her calling the area "a prettyish kind of a little wilderness."

14. *hermitage*: the dwelling of a hermit or monk. During the eighteenth century the movement toward landscapes and gardens that were more natural and primitive, along with the increasing interest in the medieval and Gothic, led to the frequent construction of mock hermitages on the grounds of estates. They would be built to appear as simple and rustic as possible, and were, if possible, placed in remote or wooded areas. In a few cases, in order to make them as realistic as possible, people were hired to inhabit them as full-time hermits, with the stipulation that they live with monkish austerity and not cut their hair or nails; the extravagance of these requirements generally kept the experiments from succeeding. In other cases, wax hermits were installed in hermitages to make them look more real.

15. *parasol*: a parasol was considered essential for a lady when walking outdoors, especially during warmer months, in order to keep her from getting tanned.

Her carriage remained at the door, and Elizabeth saw that her waiting-woman was in it. They proceeded in silence along the gravel walk that led to the copse; Elizabeth was determined to make no effort for conversation with a woman, who was now more than usually insolent and disagreeable.

"How could I ever think her like her nephew?" said she, as she looked in her face.[16]

As soon as they entered the copse, Lady Catherine began in the following manner:—

"You can be at no loss, Miss Bennet, to understand the reason of my journey hither. Your own heart, your own conscience, must tell you why I come."

Elizabeth looked with unaffected astonishment.

"Indeed, you are mistaken, Madam. I have not been at all able to account for the honour of seeing you here."

"Miss Bennet," replied her ladyship, in an angry tone, "you ought to know, that I am not to be trifled with. But however insincere *you* may choose to be, you shall not find *me* so. My character has ever been celebrated for its sincerity and frankness,[17] and in a cause of such moment as this, I shall certainly not depart from it. A report of a most alarming nature, reached me two days ago.[18] I was told, that not only your sister was on the point of being most advantageously married, but that *you*, that Miss Elizabeth Bennet, would, in all likelihood, be soon afterwards united to my nephew, my own nephew, Mr. Darcy. Though I *know* it must be a scandalous falsehood; though I would not injure him so much[19] as to suppose the truth of it possible, I instantly resolved on setting off for this place, that I might make my sentiments known to you."[20]

"If you believed it impossible to be true," said Elizabeth, colouring with astonishment and disdain, "I wonder you took the trouble of coming so far. What could your ladyship propose by it?"

"At once to insist upon having such a report universally contradicted."

"Your coming to Longbourn, to see me and my family," said Elizabeth coolly, "will be rather a confirmation of it; if, indeed, such a report is in existence."

16. Thus Lady Catherine helps give Elizabeth a renewed appreciation for Darcy, for even in his worst moments he was never as disagreeable as his aunt.

17. A boast similar to one made by Darcy earlier. An early sketch of Jane Austen's, "Letter the Third," contains an aristocratic lady, arrogant and unpleasant like Lady Catherine, who also boasts repeatedly of her frankness as she issues insulting words to a young woman of lower social rank.

18. The source of this report is revealed shortly (see p. 660). It also turns out that Lady Catherine heard the report in the evening, which meant that it was too late for her to leave immediately. This is why, despite her hurry, she has only arrived two days later; it is possible that she reached the Bennets' vicinity on the day she set out, which would allow her to visit them early the following morning.

19. *injure him so much:* do him such an injustice, malign him so much.

20. Lady Catherine's hurry in coming has already been indicated by her arrival in a chaise, rather than the barouche she spoke of traveling in earlier. The latter carriage would normally be preferable since it was more luxurious and it displayed one's wealth more conspicuously; a chaise, however, was faster. For illustrations of the two carriages, see pp. 389 and 397.

"If! do you then pretend to be ignorant of it? Has it not been industriously circulated by yourselves? Do you not know that such a report is spread abroad?"[21]

"I never heard that it was."

"And can you likewise declare, that there is no *foundation* for it?"

"I do not pretend to possess equal frankness with your ladyship. *You* may ask questions, which *I* shall not choose to answer."

"This is not to be borne. Miss Bennet, I insist on being satisfied. Has he, has my nephew, made you an offer of marriage?"

"Your ladyship has declared it to be impossible."[22]

"It ought to be so; it must be so, while he retains the use of his reason. But *your* arts and allurements may, in a moment of infatuation, have made him forget what he owes to himself and to all his family.[23] You may have drawn him in."[24]

"If I have, I shall be the last person to confess it."

"Miss Bennet, do you know who I am? I have not been accustomed to such language as this. I am almost the nearest relation he has in the world, and am entitled to know all his dearest concerns."

"But you are not entitled to know *mine*; nor will such behaviour as this, ever induce me to be explicit."

"Let me be rightly understood. This match, to which you have the presumption to aspire, can never take place. No, never. Mr. Darcy is engaged to *my daughter*. Now what have you to say?"

"Only this; that if he is so, you can have no reason to suppose he will make an offer to me."

Lady Catherine hesitated for a moment, and then replied,

"The engagement between them is of a peculiar kind.[25] From their infancy, they have been intended for each other. It was the favourite wish of *his* mother, as well as of her's. While in their cradles, we planned the union: and now, at the moment when the wishes of both sisters would be accomplished, in their marriage, to be prevented by a young woman of inferior birth, of no importance in the world,[26] and wholly unallied to the family![27] Do you pay no regard to the wishes of his friends? To his tacit engagement

21. *abroad*: widely, or outside of one's home. Lady Catherine's supposition is that the Bennets have purposely circulated the rumor in order to make a marriage between Darcy and Elizabeth more likely. Since it was considered dishonorable for a man to break an engagement, making people in general believe that an engagement existed could be one means of pressuring a man to marry a woman.

22. Elizabeth avoids answering the question directly, for if she were to answer directly she would either have to lie or to tell Lady Catherine of Darcy's earlier proposal.

23. That is, his obligation to his family to marry someone of a suitable social position. This was considered a very important obligation at the time, especially for someone of high social rank.

24. The idea of a woman drawing a man in, especially with her "arts and allurements," was a common one at the time. Jane Austen, drawing on earlier literary examples, presents a title character who is an expert at seducing and gulling men in the unfinished novel, *Lady Susan*.

25. What is peculiar, i.e. special or distinctive, about the engagement is that it was formed in the plans of Darcy's mother and Lady Catherine, rather than by Darcy and Miss De Bourgh themselves. Since this is not a society in which arranged marriages occur (even though parents are expected to have a say in their children's marriage), parental plans like that in no way constitute a real engagement.

26. *no importance in the world*: no social significance or rank.

27. Marriages among the upper classes frequently involved people whose families were related, or allied, in some way, for such marriages could further strengthen the family ties that were so crucial in this society in determining power, wealth, and position, especially among the upper classes. This is a critical reason why first cousin marriages, such as that envisioned here, were tolerated, and why Lady Catherine and her sister would have been concerned to plan a marriage while their children were still in their cradles. Their incentive to match the two children would have been strengthened by the knowledge that both were heirs of wealthy estates, which means that a union of the two would greatly enrich each of their families.

with Miss De Bourgh? Are you lost to every feeling of propriety and delicacy?[28] Have you not heard me say, that from his earliest hours he was destined for his cousin?"

"Yes, and I had heard it before. But what is that to me? If there is no other objection to my marrying your nephew, I shall certainly not be kept from it, by knowing that his mother and aunt wished him to marry Miss De Bourgh. You both did as much as you could, in planning the marriage. Its completion depended on others. If Mr. Darcy is neither by honour[29] nor inclination confined to his cousin, why is not he to make another choice? And if I am that choice, why may not I accept him?"

"Because honour, decorum, prudence, nay, interest, forbid it. Yes, Miss Bennet, interest; for do not expect to be noticed[30] by his family or friends, if you wilfully act against the inclinations of all. You will be censured, slighted, and despised, by every one connected with him. Your alliance[31] will be a disgrace; your name will never even be mentioned by any of us."

"These are heavy misfortunes," replied Elizabeth. "But the wife of Mr. Darcy must have such extraordinary sources of happiness necessarily attached to her situation, that she could, upon the whole, have no cause to repine."

"Obstinate, headstrong girl! I am ashamed of you! Is this your gratitude for my attentions to you last spring?[32] Is nothing due to me on that score?

"Let us sit down. You are to understand, Miss Bennet, that I came here with the determined resolution of carrying my purpose; nor will I be dissuaded from it. I have not been used to submit to any person's whims.[33] I have not been in the habit of brooking disappointment."

"*That* will make your ladyship's situation at present more pitiable; but it will have no effect on *me*."

"I will not be interrupted. Hear me in silence. My daughter and my nephew are formed for each other. They are descended on the maternal side, from the same noble line;[34] and, on the father's, from respectable, honourable, and ancient, though untitled families.[35] Their fortune on both sides is splendid. They are

28. *delicacy*: moral sensitivity and refinement.

29. *by honour*: because of an agreement he himself made, and therefore is obliged by honor to follow.

30. *noticed*: acknowledged, accepted.

31. *alliance*: marriage.

32. That is, Lady Catherine's invitations to dinner and to tea, which she apparently considers such tremendous favors that they confer a strong obligation in return from Elizabeth.

33. There has already been much evidence of this, and it is itself part of Lady Catherine's problem. Having always been able to dictate to others, and having apparently never benefited from the type of lesson in humility that Elizabeth administered to Darcy, she neither knows how to persuade by argument someone who is not under her power, nor how to reconcile herself to being unable to change another person's mind.

34. *noble line*: in this case, a line of earls.

35. Being a long-established family, as the Darcys apparently are, would be a distinction even if the family had no title. The sentence also implies that Miss De Bourgh comes from an untitled family on her father's side, which suggests that Sir Lewis de Bourgh was a knight rather than a baronet (the latter status, because it is inherited, would make the family a titled one).

destined for each other by the voice of every member of their respective houses;[36] and what is to divide them? The upstart pretensions of a young woman without family, connections,[37] or fortune. Is this to be endured! But it must not, shall not be. If you were sensible of your own good, you would not wish to quit the sphere, in which you have been brought up."

"In marrying your nephew, I should not consider myself as quitting that sphere. He is a gentleman; I am a gentleman's daughter; so far we are equal."[38]

"True. You *are* a gentleman's daughter. But who was your mother? Who are your uncles and aunts? Do not imagine me ignorant of their condition."

"Whatever my connections may be," said Elizabeth, "if your nephew does not object to them, they can be nothing to *you*."[39]

"Tell me once for all, are you engaged to him?"

Though Elizabeth would not, for the mere purpose of obliging Lady Catherine, have answered this question; she could not but say, after a moment's deliberation,

"I am not."

Lady Catherine seemed pleased.

"And will you promise me, never to enter into such an engagement?"

"I will make no promise of the kind."

"Miss Bennet I am shocked and astonished. I expected to find a more reasonable young woman. But do not deceive yourself into a belief that I will ever recede. I shall not go away, till you have given me the assurance I require."

"And I certainly *never* shall give it. I am not to be intimidated into anything so wholly unreasonable. Your ladyship wants Mr. Darcy to marry your daughter; but would my giving you the wished-for promise, make *their* marriage at all more probable? Supposing him to be attached to me, would *my* refusing to accept his hand, make him wish to bestow it on his cousin? Allow me to say, Lady Catherine, that the arguments with which you have supported this extraordinary application,[40] have been as frivolous as the application was ill-judged. You have widely mistaken my

36. Of course, the only actual voices Lady Catherine has referred to are those of herself and of Darcy's mother, now deceased.

37. *connections:* family ties. By using the word after "family" Lady Catherine may be intending to designate more distant relations, or she may simply be trying to reinforce her point.

38. Elizabeth shows her consciousness of her own social position. Though her father is much less wealthy than Darcy, he is in the same broad category of gentleman.

39. Here Elizabeth does not refute Lady Catherine directly, for she knows that in fact her mother's family is on a lower social level.

40. *application:* appeal, request.

character, if you think I can be worked on[41] by such persuasions as these. How far your nephew might approve of your interference in *his* affairs, I cannot tell; but you have certainly no right to concern yourself in mine. I must beg, therefore, to be importuned no farther on the subject."

"Not so hasty, if you please. I have by no means done. To all the objections I have already urged, I have still another to add. I am no stranger to the particulars of your youngest sister's infamous elopement. I know it all; that the young man's marrying her, was a patched-up business,[42] at the expence of your father and uncles.[43] And is *such* a girl to be my nephew's sister? Is *her* husband, is the son of his late father's steward,[44] to be his brother? Heaven and earth!—of what are you thinking? Are the shades of Pemberley to be thus polluted?"[45]

"You can *now* have nothing farther to say," she resentfully answered. "You have insulted me, in every possible method. I must beg to return to the house."

And she rose as she spoke. Lady Catherine rose also, and they turned back. Her ladyship was highly incensed.

"You have no regard, then, for the honour and credit[46] of my nephew! Unfeeling, selfish girl! Do you not consider that a connection with you, must disgrace him in the eyes of everybody?"

"Lady Catherine, I have nothing farther to say. You know my sentiments."

"You are then resolved to have him?"

"I have said no such thing. I am only resolved to act in that manner, which will, in my own opinion, constitute my happiness, without reference to *you*, or to any person so wholly unconnected with me."

"It is well. You refuse, then, to oblige me. You refuse to obey the claims of duty, honour, and gratitude. You are determined to ruin him in the opinion of all his friends, and make him the contempt of the world."

"Neither duty, nor honour, nor gratitude," replied Elizabeth, "have any possible claim on me, in the present instance. No principle of either, would be violated by my marriage with Mr. Darcy.

41. *worked on:* influenced, persuaded.

42. *patched-up business:* business or arrangement put together hastily or clumsily.

43. *uncles:* of course, it was only one uncle, Mr. Gardiner, who was involved, and it was someone else, Darcy, who bore this expense. But Lady Catherine, who would not know the details of the affair, is probably just assuming that both Lydia's uncles, along with her father, would have acted in the affair.

44. *steward:* an inferior position socially; see p. 151, note 53.

45. By shades Lady Catherine probably means grounds, which would include many shades (or pieces of ground shadowed by trees, a then-current meaning of "shade"). The pollution would come from having people of inferior birth traverse those grounds as guests and members of the family; such "pollution" is mentioned at the very end of the novel.

Some have suggested that shades could mean ancestors, i.e., ghosts. Shade was used in that sense then, but only occasionally and usually in reference to the shades supposed to inhabit the underworld in ancient mythology. It was not really used to signify the general spirit of a dead person, and thus the sort of entity that could be harmed or polluted in a symbolic way by dishonor to the family. As for the idea of actual ghosts who might inhabit a house and could be affected by changes in it, such an idea had for at least a century been regarded as foolish superstition and would never be employed in serious argument by an intelligent and educated person like Lady Catherine.

46. *credit:* reputation, public standing.

And with regard to the resentment of his family, or the indigna-tion of the world, if the former *were* excited by his marrying me, it would not give me one moment's concern—and the world in general would have too much sense to join in the scorn."

"And this is your real opinion! This is your final resolve! Very well. I shall now know how to act. Do not imagine, Miss Bennet, that your ambition will ever be gratified. I came to try you. I hoped to find you reasonable; but depend upon it I will carry my point."

In this manner Lady Catherine talked on, till they were at the door of the carriage, when turning hastily round, she added,

"I take no leave of you, Miss Bennet. I send no compliments to your mother. You deserve no such attention.[47] I am most seriously displeased."

Elizabeth made no answer; and without attempting to per-suade her ladyship to return into the house, walked quietly into it herself. She heard the carriage drive away as she proceeded up stairs. Her mother impatiently met her at the door of the dressing-room, to ask why Lady Catherine would not come in again and rest herself.

"She did not choose it," said her daughter, "she would go."

"She is a very fine-looking woman! and her calling here was prodigiously civil! for she only came, I suppose, to tell us the Collinses were well. She is on her road somewhere, I dare say, and so passing through Meryton, thought she might as well call on you. I suppose she had nothing particular to say to you, Lizzy?"

Elizabeth was forced to give into a little falsehood here; for to acknowledge the substance of their conversation was impossible.

47. It would be standard form to send compliments after a visit, if one did not actually say good-bye to the person in question.

Chapter Fifteen

*T*he discomposure of spirits, which this extraordinary visit threw Elizabeth into, could not be easily overcome; nor could she for many hours, learn to think of it less than incessantly. Lady Catherine it appeared, had actually taken the trouble of this journey from Rosings, for the sole purpose of breaking off her supposed engagement with Mr. Darcy. It was a rational scheme to be sure! but from what the report of their engagement could originate, Elizabeth was at a loss to imagine; till she recollected that *his* being the intimate friend of Bingley, and *her* being the sister of Jane, was enough, at a time when the expectation of one wedding, made every body eager for another, to supply the idea. She had not herself forgotten to feel that the marriage of her sister must bring them more frequently together. And her neighbours at Lucas Lodge, therefore, (for through their communication with the Collinses, the report she concluded had reached Lady Catherine) had only set *that* down, as almost certain and immediate, which *she* had looked forward to as possible, at some future time.[1]

In revolving[2] Lady Catherine's expressions,[3] however, she could not help feeling some uneasiness as to the possible consequence of her persisting in this interference. From what she had said of her resolution to prevent their marriage, it occurred to Elizabeth that she must meditate[4] an application to her nephew; and how *he* might take a similar representation of the evils attached to a connection with her, she dared not pronounce. She knew not the exact degree of his affection for his aunt, or his dependence on her judgment, but it was natural to suppose that he thought much higher of her ladyship than *she* could do; and it was certain, that in enumerating the miseries of a marriage with *one*, whose immediate connections were so unequal to his own,

654

1.   Elizabeth's speculations about the source of Lady Catherine's idea will shortly be confirmed by Mr. Bennet. It is highly doubtful that any general rumor about Elizabeth and Darcy had been circulating in the neighborhood, for if so, such lovers of gossip as Mrs. Bennet and her sister Mrs. Philips would surely have heard of it. The Lucases, however, could easily have come up with the idea on their own. Earlier at the Netherfield Ball, Sir William Lucas, when complimenting Elizabeth and Darcy on their excellent dancing, anticipated their meeting often after Jane and Bingley were married. Now Sir William, who would relish the idea of a close acquaintance of his being married to someone of high rank like Darcy, could easily leap to the idea of Elizabeth's marriage, especially after Darcy had accompanied Bingley in their recent visit. Furthermore, Charlotte had already suspected, when Elizabeth was visiting her, a tie between Darcy and Elizabeth and could have mentioned this idea to her family, either at that time or later. In a society where speculations about marriages, especially advantageous ones, were a constant subject of talk and communication, even a hint like that could have inspired the Lucases to imagine an impending marriage of Elizabeth and Darcy. It is also possible that they had only the germ of the idea, and that it was then elaborated further by Charlotte or Mr. Collins.

2.   *revolving*: considering, pondering.

3.   *expressions*: utterances.

4.   *meditate*: intend, plan.

his aunt would address him on his weakest side. With his notions of dignity, he would probably feel that the arguments, which to Elizabeth had appeared weak and ridiculous, contained much good sense and solid reasoning.

If he had been wavering before, as to what he should do, which had often seemed likely, the advice and intreaty of so near a relation might settle every doubt, and determine him at once to be as happy, as dignity unblemished could make him.[5] In that case he would return no more. Lady Catherine might see him in her way through town;[6] and his engagement to Bingley of coming again to Netherfield must give way.

"If, therefore, an excuse for not keeping his promise, should come to his friend within a few days," she added, "I shall know how to understand it. I shall then give over every expectation, every wish of his constancy. If he is satisfied with only regretting me, when he might have obtained my affections and hand, I shall soon cease to regret him at all."[7]

The surprise of the rest of the family, on hearing who their visitor had been, was very great; but they obligingly satisfied it, with the same kind of supposition, which had appeased Mrs. Bennet's curiosity; and Elizabeth was spared from much teazing on the subject.

The next morning, as she was going down stairs, she was met by her father, who came out of his library with a letter in his hand.

"Lizzy," said he, "I was going to look for you; come into my room."

She followed him thither; and her curiosity to know what he had to tell her, was heightened by the supposition of its being in some manner connected with the letter he held. It suddenly struck her that it might be from Lady Catherine; and she anticipated with dismay all the consequent explanations.

She followed her father to the fire place, and they both sat down. He then said,

5.   That is, such a course (shunning Elizabeth) would give him the happiness of not having harmed the family dignity, though it would not give him the happiness of having Elizabeth as a wife.

6.   *town:* London.

7.   Of course, all that has happened recently indicates that Elizabeth, if Darcy did stay away from her, would regret him greatly and for a long time. Clearly her reflections are an attempt to inoculate herself against possible disappointment, and to keep under some control the strong emotions concerning Darcy that are currently buffeting her.

"I have received a letter this morning that has astonished me exceedingly. As it principally concerns yourself, you ought to know its contents. I did not know before, that I had *two* daughters on the brink of matrimony. Let me congratulate you, on a very important conquest."

The colour now rushed into Elizabeth's cheeks in the instantaneous conviction of its being a letter from the nephew, instead of the aunt; and she was undetermined whether most to be pleased that he explained himself at all, or offended that his letter was not rather addressed to herself;[8] when her father continued,

"You look conscious.[9] Young ladies have great penetration in such matters as these; but I think I may defy even *your* sagacity, to discover the name of your admirer. This letter is from Mr. Collins."

"From Mr. Collins! and what can *he* have to say?"

"Something very much to the purpose of course. He begins with congratulations on the approaching nuptials of my eldest daughter, of which it seems he has been told, by some of the good-natured, gossiping Lucases. I shall not sport[10] with your impatience, by reading what he says on that point. What relates to yourself, is as follows. "Having thus offered you the sincere congratulations of Mrs. Collins and myself on this happy event, let me now add a short hint on the subject of another; of which we have been advertised[11] by the same authority.[12] Your daughter Elizabeth, it is presumed, will not long bear the name of Bennet, after her elder sister has resigned it, and the chosen partner of her fate, may be reasonably looked up to, as one of the most illustrious personages in this land."

"Can you possibly guess, Lizzy, who is meant by this?" "This young gentleman is blessed in a peculiar[13] way, with every thing the heart of mortal can most desire,—splendid property, noble kindred, and extensive patronage.[14] Yet in spite of all these temptations, let me warn my cousin Elizabeth, and yourself, of what evils you may incur, by a precipitate closure with this gentleman's proposals, which, of course, you will be inclined to take immediate advantage of."

8.   Normally a man would not ask the father first if he wished to propose. In some cases, when pursuing a very sheltered daughter, he might ask the father's permission before he began courting her, but Elizabeth is certainly not such a daughter.

9.   *conscious*: aware or cognizant of something.

10.   *sport*: amuse myself.

11.   *advertised*: notified, warned.

12.   *same authority*: the Lucases, already identified by Mr. Bennet as the source of Mr. Collins's knowledge of Jane's marriage.

13.   *peculiar*: distinctive, unique.

14.   Mr. Collins's list of "every thing the heart of mortal can most desire" is revealing.

"Have you any idea, Lizzy, who this gentleman is? But now it comes out."

"My motive for cautioning you, is as follows. We have reason to imagine that his aunt, Lady Catherine de Bourgh, does not look on the match with a friendly eye."

"*Mr. Darcy*, you see, is the man! Now, Lizzy, I think I *have* surprised you. Could he, or the Lucases, have pitched on any man, within the circle of our acquaintance, whose name would have given the lie more effectually to what they related? Mr. Darcy, who never looks at any woman but to see a blemish, and who probably never looked at *you* in his life! It is admirable!"[15]

Elizabeth tried to join in her father's pleasantry, but could only force one most reluctant smile. Never had his wit been directed in a manner so little agreeable to her.[16]

"Are you not diverted?"

"Oh! yes. Pray read on."

"After mentioning the likelihood of this marriage to her ladyship last night, she immediately, with her usual condescension,[17] expressed what she felt on the occasion; when it became apparent, that on the score of some family objections on the part of my cousin, she would never give her consent to what she termed so disgraceful a match. I thought it my duty to give the speediest intelligence of this to my cousin, that she and her noble admirer may be aware of what they are about, and not run hastily into a marriage which has not been properly sanctioned." "Mr. Collins moreover adds," "I am truly rejoiced that my cousin Lydia's sad business has been so well hushed up, and am only concerned that their living together before the marriage took place, should be so generally known.[18] I must not, however, neglect the duties of my station,[19] or refrain from declaring my amazement, at hearing that you received the young couple into your house as soon as they were married. It was an encouragement of vice; and had I been the rector of Longbourn, I should very strenuously have opposed it. You ought certainly to forgive them as a christian, but never to admit them in your sight, or allow their names to be mentioned in your hearing." "*That* is his notion of christian forgiveness! The rest

15. *admirable*: astonishing, extraordinary.

16. Elizabeth's discomfort, and her subsequent anxiety about the possible truth of her father's assertions, represents one final penance for her before Darcy's proposal. It is a particularly appropriate one, for her father's belief in Darcy's indifference results in part from Elizabeth's own denunciations of Darcy, while her father's behavior, subjecting her to his sharp wit and raillery, is giving her an unpleasant taste of the same medicine that she herself administered so freely to Darcy.

17. *condescension*: friendliness and attention toward inferiors. Mr. Collins means this as a term of praise.

18. The irony of Mr. Collins's concern about discretion is that he himself was the one who informed Lady Catherine of the affair when it first occurred (see p. 540), and Lady Catherine seems like one who would not hesitate to spread such news. In any case, his concern here stems not from worries about the effects of public knowledge on Lydia herself, for he shortly reveals that he cares nothing for her; most likely he is worried about the reputation of the family, which is something that might affect himself, at least a little.

19. *my station*: my position as a clergyman.

of his letter is only about his dear Charlotte's situation, and his expectation of a young olive-branch.[20] But, Lizzy, you look as if you did not enjoy it. You are not going to be *Missish*,[21] I hope, and pretend to be affronted at an idle report. For what do we live, but to make sport for our neighbours, and laugh at them in our turn?"[22]

"Oh!" cried Elizabeth, "I am excessively diverted.[23] But it is so strange!"

"Yes—*that* is what makes it amusing. Had they fixed on any other man it would have been nothing; but *his* perfect indifference, and *your* pointed dislike, make it so delightfully absurd! Much as I abominate writing, I would not give up Mr. Collins's correspondence for any consideration. Nay, when I read a letter of his, I cannot help giving him the preference even over Wickham, much as I value the impudence[24] and hypocrisy of my son-in-law.[25] And pray, Lizzy, what said Lady Catherine about this report? Did she call to refuse her consent?"

To this question his daughter replied only with a laugh; and as it had been asked without the least suspicion, she was not distressed by his repeating it.[26] Elizabeth had never been more at a loss to make her feelings appear what they were not. It was necessary to laugh, when she would rather have cried. Her father had most cruelly mortified her, by what he said of Mr. Darcy's indifference, and she could do nothing but wonder at such a want of penetration,[27] or fear that perhaps, instead of his seeing too *little*, she might have fancied too *much*.

20. *olive-branch:* a child. Hence Charlotte is pregnant; that also may be what is meant by "Charlotte's situation." The use of olive-branch to mean offspring derives from Psalm 128, Verse 3: "Thy wife shall be as a fruitful vine by the sides of thine house; thy children like olive plants round about thy table." Such an allusion, one both pedantic and biblical, is appropriate for Mr. Collins.

21. *Missish:* affectedly prim or squeamish; hence inclined to take offense easily.

22. Probably Mr. Bennet's best summation of his philosophy of life.

23. *excessively diverted:* Elizabeth's use of such a hyperbolic expression, when in fact she is not diverted at all, indicates her confusion of mind as well as her wish to prevent her father from guessing the true state of her feelings.

24. *impudence:* effrontery, shamelessness.

25. He means valuing these qualities of Wickham, just as he values those of Mr. Collins, as a source of amusement.

26. Here Elizabeth is helped by her father's tendency to treat everything as a joke. Were he more serious, a little reflection might cause him to perceive that Lady Catherine, alerted by the Collinses, could have called to speak to Elizabeth about Darcy.

27. *want of penetration:* lack of penetration or discernment (on Mr. Bennet's part regarding Elizabeth and Darcy's relationship).

Chapter Sixteen

*I*nstead of receiving any such letter of excuse from his friend, as Elizabeth half expected Mr. Bingley to do, he was able to bring Darcy with him to Longbourn before many days had passed after Lady Catherine's visit. The gentlemen arrived early; and, before Mrs. Bennet had time to tell him of their having seen his aunt, of which her daughter sat in momentary dread, Bingley, who wanted to be alone with Jane, proposed their all walking out. It was agreed to. Mrs. Bennet was not in the habit of walking, Mary could never spare time, but the remaining five set off together. Bingley and Jane, however, soon allowed the others to outstrip them. They lagged behind, while Elizabeth, Kitty, and Darcy, were to entertain each other. Very little was said by either; Kitty was too much afraid of him to talk; Elizabeth was secretly forming a desperate resolution; and perhaps he might be doing the same.[1]

They walked towards the Lucases, because Kitty wished to call upon Maria; and as Elizabeth saw no occasion for making it a general concern, when Kitty left them, she went boldly on with him alone. Now was the moment for her resolution to be executed, and, while her courage was high, she immediately said,

"Mr. Darcy, I am a very selfish creature; and, for the sake of giving relief to my own feelings, care not how much I may be wounding your's. I can no longer help thanking you for your unexampled kindness to my poor sister. Ever since I have known it, I have been most anxious to acknowledge to you how gratefully I feel it. Were it known to the rest of my family, I should not have merely my own gratitude to express."

"I am sorry, exceedingly sorry," replied Darcy, in a tone of surprise and emotion, "that you have ever been informed of what may, in a mistaken light, have given you uneasiness. I did not think Mrs. Gardiner was so little to be trusted."[2]

1. His resolution could be to propose to her. Hers we see, and it could be made with the idea of provoking such a response in him.

2. Darcy has already shown how much he wishes to keep Elizabeth from learning of his assistance to Lydia, for which purpose he extracted strict promises of secrecy from the Gardiners and from Wickham and Lydia. Now he indicates the reason: fear of making her uneasy. What he probably feared most was that she would interpret his actions as an attempt to make her feel obliged to marry him in return; he may even have feared that she would actually feel such an obligation. Many in this society would consider themselves, or someone like Elizabeth, to be under such an obligation in this case: in one of Jane Austen's favorite novels, Fanny Burney's *Camilla*, the heroine is considered by her sisters to be morally obliged to marry a man, even though she does not wish to, after he gives critical financial assistance to her brother. Darcy, of course, would not want Elizabeth to be made uncomfortable in this way, nor to resent him because of what she might believe was manipulation on his part. Finally, as much as he wishes Elizabeth to marry him, he does not want her to do so out of a sense of obligation.

"You must not blame my aunt. Lydia's thoughtlessness first betrayed to me that you had been concerned in the matter; and, of course, I could not rest till I knew the particulars. Let me thank you again and again, in the name of all my family, for that generous compassion which induced you to take so much trouble, and bear so many mortifications, for the sake of discovering them."

"If you *will* thank me," he replied, "let it be for yourself alone. That the wish of giving happiness to you, might add force to the other inducements which led me on, I shall not attempt to deny. But your *family* owe me nothing. Much as I respect them, I believe, I thought only of *you*."

Elizabeth was too much embarrassed to say a word. After a short pause, her companion added, "You are too generous to trifle with me. If your feelings are still what they were last April, tell me so at once. *My* affections and wishes are unchanged, but one word from you will silence me on this subject for ever."

Elizabeth feeling all the more than common awkwardness and anxiety of his situation, now forced herself to speak; and immediately, though not very fluently, gave him to understand, that her sentiments had undergone so material a change, since the period to which he alluded, as to make her receive with gratitude and pleasure, his present assurances. The happiness which this reply produced, was such as he had probably never felt before; and he expressed himself on the occasion as sensibly[3] and as warmly as a man violently in love can be supposed to do.[4] Had Elizabeth been able to encounter his eye, she might have seen how well the expression of heartfelt delight, diffused over his face, became him; but, though she could not look, she could listen, and he told her of feelings, which, in proving of what importance she was to him, made his affection every moment more valuable.

They walked on, without knowing in what direction. There was too much to be thought, and felt, and said, for attention to any other objects. She soon learnt that they were indebted for their present good understanding to the efforts of his aunt, who *did* call on him in her return through London, and there relate her journey to Longbourn, its motive, and the substance of her

3. *sensibly:* vehemently, fervently. It is possible that "sensibly" is being used in the sense of rationally or with good sense, in which case the logical meaning would be that Darcy is not showing much reason or good sense (since that is what would be expected from a man violently in love). But this seems unlikely. While at this time the adjective "sensible" was already being used to mean rational or level-headed (as it is at points in this novel), the adverb form does not seem to have adopted a comparable meaning until later. "Sensibly" continued to mean acutely or with aroused feeling; that it meant such in this instance is indicated by its being paired with warmly.

4. As in other novels, Jane Austen only provides a general summary of what is said in a successful proposal. She always avoids relating enthusiastic lovers' talk (except when she ridicules foolish examples of it). In this scene she only returns to direct dialogue when the characters have resumed speaking in more analytical or ironic tones, the tones that are most congenial to Jane Austen.

conversation with Elizabeth; dwelling emphatically on every expression of the latter, which, in her ladyship's apprehension,[5] peculiarly[6] denoted her perverseness and assurance,[7] in the belief that such a relation[8] must assist her endeavours to obtain that promise from her nephew, which *she* had refused to give. But, unluckily for her ladyship, its effect had been exactly contrariwise.

"It taught me to hope," said he, "as I had scarcely ever allowed myself to hope before.[9] I knew enough of your disposition to be certain, that, had you been absolutely, irrevocably decided against me, you would have acknowledged it to Lady Catherine, frankly and openly."

Elizabeth coloured[10] and laughed as she replied, "Yes, you know enough of my *frankness* to believe me capable of *that*. After abusing you so abominably to your face, I could have no scruple in abusing you to all your relations."

"What did you say of me, that I did not deserve? For, though your accusations were ill-founded, formed on mistaken premises, my behaviour to you at the time, had merited the severest reproof. It was unpardonable. I cannot think of it without abhorrence."

"We will not quarrel for the greater share of blame annexed to that evening," said Elizabeth. "The conduct of neither, if strictly examined, will be irreproachable; but since then, we have both, I hope, improved in civility."[11]

"I cannot be so easily reconciled to myself. The recollection of what I then said, of my conduct, my manners, my expressions during the whole of it, is now, and has been many months, inexpressibly painful to me. Your reproof, so well applied, I shall never forget: 'had you behaved in a more gentleman-like manner.' Those were your words. You know not, you can scarcely conceive, how they have tortured me;[12]—though it was some time, I confess, before I was reasonable enough to allow their justice."

"I was certainly very far from expecting them to make so strong an impression. I had not the smallest idea of their being ever felt in such a way."

"I can easily believe it. You thought me then devoid of every proper feeling, I am sure you did. The turn of your countenance[13]

5. *apprehension:* conception, view.

6. *peculiarly:* particularly.

7. *assurance:* audacity, impudence.

8. *relation:* account, i.e., relation of events.

9. Darcy's reluctance at this stage to be too hopeful about Elizabeth's willingness to accept him stands in contrast to his arrogant certainty before his first proposal.

10. *coloured:* blushed.

11. Both Darcy and Elizabeth are admitting their past wrongs, but they do so in different manners. She is more likely to look on it calmly and laugh about it. He, who has always tried to be so scrupulous in acting rightly and has prided himself on his success, is more severe, unable to think lightheartedly about occasions when he failed in that endeavor. He also is inclined to reproach only himself, rather than to call them both at fault as she does. Thus, even as both have genuinely changed in important respects, they continue to display certain characteristic traits.

12. Darcy was shown starting at her words when she uttered them. For him failure to act like a gentleman would be the greatest catastrophe, and this was probably one of the only, if not the only, time in his adult life when he was directly accused of that (at least by someone whose opinion he valued).

13. *turn of your countenance:* manner or character of your facial expression.

I shall never forget, as you said that I could not have addressed[14] you in any possible way, that would induce you to accept me."

"Oh! do not repeat what I then said. These recollections will not do at all. I assure you, that I have long been most heartily ashamed of it."

Darcy mentioned his letter. "Did it," said he, "did it *soon* make you think better of me? Did you, on reading it, give any credit to its contents?"

She explained what its effect on her had been, and how gradually all her former prejudices had been removed.

"I knew," said he, "that what I wrote must give you pain, but it was necessary. I hope you have destroyed the letter. There was one part especially, the opening of it, which I should dread your having the power of reading again. I can remember some expressions[15] which might justly make you hate me."[16]

"The letter shall certainly be burnt, if you believe it essential to the preservation of my regard; but, though we have both reason to think my opinions not entirely unalterable, they are not, I hope, quite so easily changed as that implies."[17]

"When I wrote that letter," replied Darcy, "I believed myself perfectly calm and cool, but I am since convinced that it was written in a dreadful bitterness of spirit."

"The letter, perhaps, began in bitterness, but it did not end so. The adieu is charity itself. But think no more of the letter. The feelings of the person who wrote, and the person who received it, are now so widely different from what they were then, that every unpleasant circumstance attending it, ought to be forgotten. You must learn some of my philosophy. Think only of the past as its remembrance gives you pleasure."[18]

"I cannot give you credit for any philosophy of the kind. *Your* retrospections must be so totally void of reproach, that the contentment arising from them, is not of philosophy, but what is much better, of ignorance.[19] But with *me*, it is not so. Painful recollections will intrude, which cannot, which ought not to be repelled. I have been a selfish being all my life, in practice, though not in principle.[20] As a child I was taught what was *right*, but I was not taught to correct my temper.[21] I was given good

14. *addressed*: proposed to, courted.

15. *expressions*: statements, choices of words.

16. It was the opening of the letter where Darcy displayed his resentment at her rejection, as well as his remaining pride. At the same time, it was not so bad as to make someone likely to hate the writer—Darcy is again showing his tendency to hold himself up to the strictest possible standards.

17. That is, Elizabeth—once more introducing an element of playfulness into Darcy's solemn reflections—asserts, with a slight tone of mock offense, that he should trust that her feelings are not so changeable that they would be turned against him by a simple rereading of his letter.

18. Elizabeth's stated philosophy here stands in contradiction to her own earlier behavior, when she engaged in many painful reflections on her mistakes and faulty conduct. Her change to a more lighthearted perspective could reflect her happier condition now that Darcy has proposed; in other words, she, like many people, is only inclined to reproach herself for errors while she is actually suffering their ill effects. It is also possible she is simply responding to Darcy: she sees him inclined to dwell, more than she thinks he should, on his own errors, and she wishes to divert his thoughts from that. If so, her action would form an early example of the "ease and liveliness" she has already identified as a principal benefit she could impart to Darcy in the event of their union.

19. In other words, Darcy says that because Elizabeth, unlike himself, has acted so well, she can simply ignore or not think about her past deeds, which means she has no need of any special philosophy in order to feel contented.

20. One commentator (Lord David Cecil) has described Darcy as confessing to "the besetting weakness of all men who, though conscientious and unegotistic, are accustomed to have their own way." Such characteristics, though they undoubtedly could be found anywhere, may have abounded particularly among upper-class males of this society, who tended to be educated in strict principles while also being accorded high status and endowed with great power over others. Jane Austen probably observed a number of examples of this herself.

21. *temper*: disposition. Meaning that he was not taught to be more friendly and affable toward others.

principles, but left to follow them in pride and conceit. Unfortunately an only son, (for many years an only *child*)[22] I was spoilt by
my parents, who though good themselves, (my father particularly,
all that was benevolent and amiable,) allowed, encouraged,
almost taught me to be selfish and overbearing, to care for none
beyond my own family circle, to think meanly[23] of all the rest of
the world, to *wish* at least to think meanly of their sense and worth
compared with my own.[24] Such I was, from eight to eight and
twenty;[25] and such I might still have been but for you, dearest,
loveliest Elizabeth![26] What do I not owe you! You taught me a lesson, hard indeed at first, but most advantageous. By you, I was
properly humbled. I came to you without a doubt of my reception. You shewed me how insufficient were all my pretensions to
please a woman worthy of being pleased."

"Had you then persuaded yourself that I should?"

"Indeed I had. What will you think of my vanity? I believed
you to be wishing, expecting my addresses."

"My manners must have been in fault, but not intentionally I
assure you. I never meant to deceive you, but my spirits[27] might
often lead me wrong. How you must have hated me after *that*
evening?"

"Hate you! I was angry perhaps at first, but my anger soon
began to take a proper direction."

"I am almost afraid of asking what you thought of me; when we
met at Pemberley. You blamed me for coming?"

"No indeed; I felt nothing but surprise."[28]

"Your surprise could not be greater than *mine* in being noticed
by you. My conscience told me that I deserved no extraordinary
politeness, and I confess that I did not expect to receive *more* than
my due."[29]

"My object *then*," replied Darcy, "was to shew you, by every
civility in my power, that I was not so mean[30] as to resent the past;
and I hoped to obtain your forgiveness, to lessen your ill opinion,
by letting you see that your reproofs had been attended to. How
soon any other wishes introduced themselves I can hardly tell,
but I believe in about half an hour after I had seen you."[31]

22. Darcy is 28, while his sister is only 16, so he would have been an only child for his first twelve years.

23. *meanly*: disdainfully.

24. This account of Darcy as a child differs from the laudatory one of the housekeeper at Pemberley (p. 452). One possible explanation for the discrepancy is that the housekeeper judged Darcy mainly by his behavior to those within the family circle, possibly including family servants, and they are the ones Darcy says he did care about. Another possible explanation is that one or both of their accounts are biased, with either the housekeeper being inclined to praise her master excessively or Darcy being inclined to condemn himself excessively—which he might wish to do at this time since he is describing the badness of the habits that Elizabeth forced him to confront and reform.

25. *eight to eight and twenty*: Darcy presumably chooses the age of eight because it corresponds neatly to his present age and because it would be the age around when he would have become old enough to develop the attitude he describes.

26. This is the first time Darcy has called her Elizabeth. In a society where first names are only used when speaking to family members or to intimate acquaintances, its use here is significant, especially for someone as formal as Darcy. It is partly through such small gestures that Jane Austen is able to convey romantic feeling even while omitting passionate declarations of love.

27. *spirits*: liveliness or vivacity. Earlier incidents suggested that Elizabeth's spirited teasing of Darcy, precisely because of her vivacious and playful manner, could have been interpreted as flirtation rather than as serious indications of dislike. As Elizabeth acknowledges, his pride alone was not to blame for his mistaken expectations about her response to his proposal.

28. The reader is finally given an account of what Darcy has been thinking and feeling since his proposal. This account must come now since throughout the latter part of the novel only Elizabeth's perspective is given. Delaying the account of Darcy's feelings—and Jane Austen usually does this with her male protagonists—keeps the narrative more focused, and increases the suspense about what he will decide, but it also means that the changes in him are not presented and analyzed as vividly and thoroughly as the changes in her, and that many crucial developments can only be fully explained later.

29. That is, Elizabeth expected to receive the standard politeness due to any guest at Pemberley; she did not expect, or believe she deserved, the special consideration she actually received.

30. *mean*: ungenerous, small-minded.

31. The other wishes are those of winning her love. The extent of Darcy's feeling for Elizabeth is revealed by the rapidity with which his romantic hopes were rekindled.

He then told her of Georgiana's delight in her acquaintance, and of her disappointment at its sudden interruption; which naturally leading to the cause of that interruption, she soon learnt that his resolution of following her from Derbyshire in quest of her sister, had been formed before he quitted the inn, and that his gravity and thoughtfulness there, had arisen from no other struggles than what such a purpose must comprehend.[32]

She expressed her gratitude again, but it was too painful a subject to each, to be dwelt on farther.

After walking several miles in a leisurely manner, and too busy to know any thing about it, they found at last, on examining their watches, that it was time to be at home.

"What could become of Mr. Bingley and Jane!" was a wonder which introduced the discussion of *their* affairs. Darcy was delighted with their engagement; his friend had given him the earliest information of it.

"I must ask whether you were surprised?" said Elizabeth.

"Not at all. When I went away, I felt that it would soon happen."

"That is to say, you had given your permission. I guessed as much." And though he exclaimed at[33] the term, she found that it had been pretty much the case.

"On the evening before my going to London," said he "I made a confession to him, which I believe I ought to have made long ago. I told him of all that had occurred to make my former interference in his affairs, absurd and impertinent.[34] His surprise was great. He had never had the slightest suspicion. I told him, moreover, that I believed myself mistaken in supposing, as I had done, that your sister was indifferent to him; and as I could easily perceive that his attachment to her was unabated, I felt no doubt of their happiness together."

Elizabeth could not help smiling at his easy manner of directing his friend.

"Did you speak from your own observation," said she, "when you told him that my sister loved him, or merely from my information last spring?"

"From the former. I had narrowly observed her during the two

32. That is, all that the pursuit of her sister must involve. Darcy is here revealing the reasons for his pensiveness after Elizabeth told him the news about Lydia (see p. 504).

33. *exclaimed at:* protested against.

34. *impertinent:* intrusive, meddlesome; in other words, interfering in matters where one does not belong.

visits which I had lately made her here; and I was convinced of her affection."

"And your assurance of it, I suppose, carried immediate conviction to him."

"It did. Bingley is most unaffectedly modest. His diffidence had prevented his depending on his own judgment in so anxious a case, but his reliance on mine, made every thing easy.[35] I was obliged to confess one thing, which for a time, and not unjustly, offended him. I could not allow myself to conceal that your sister had been in town three months last winter, that I had known it, and purposely kept it from him. He was angry.[36] But his anger, I am persuaded, lasted no longer than he remained in any doubt of your sister's sentiments. He has heartily forgiven me now."

Elizabeth longed to observe that Mr. Bingley had been a most delightful friend; so easily guided that his worth was invaluable; but she checked herself. She remembered that he had yet to learn to be laught at, and it was rather too early to begin.[37] In anticipating the happiness of Bingley, which of course was to be inferior only to his own, he continued the conversation till they reached the house.[38] In the hall they parted.

35. How quickly Bingley was persuaded is indicated by his actions, for it was the very morning that Darcy left for London that Bingley began courting Jane assiduously (see p. 624).

36. Darcy's account also helps explain why he left for London at that point: in addition to giving Bingley a chance to complete his wooing and to propose, he probably also wished to give Bingley's anger a chance to cool.

37. Elizabeth's restraint is significant. It signals that she has learned to check her banter and playfulness when it is not appropriate, and to avoid always seeking a spur to her wit—as much as her instincts make her wish to joke and to tease right now.

38. This willingness to talk so extensively about Bingley and Jane at such a crucial time for themselves demonstrates the unselfish character of both Darcy and Elizabeth. It also corresponds to the view of marriage Jane Austen consistently asserts, which is that rather than being simply a union of two individuals, it is a condition in which the couple will continue to be connected to a variety of other people. The remaining chapters will show Elizabeth and Darcy taking the trouble, even when they find it unpleasant, to accommodate and maintain good relations with other family members and acquaintances. The romantic notion of lovers isolated from, or even hostile to, the rest of the world is never Jane Austen's ideal. She satirizes a version of it in "Love and Friendship" when she has the foolish sentimental heroine declare: "In the Society of my Edward & this Amiable Pair, I passed the happiest moments of my Life: Our time was most delightfully spent, in mutual Protestations of Freindship [sic], and in vows of unalterable Love, in which we were secure from being interrupted, by intruding & disagreeable Visitors, as Augustus & Sophia had on their first Entrance in the Neighbourhood, taken due care to inform the surrounding Families, that as their Happiness centered wholly in themselves, they wished for no other society."

Chapter Seventeen

My dear Lizzy, where can you have been walking to?" was a question which Elizabeth received from Jane as soon as she entered the room, and from all the others when they sat down to table. She had only to say in reply, that they had wandered about, till she was beyond her own knowledge. She coloured as she spoke; but neither that, nor any thing else, awakened a suspicion of the truth.

The evening passd quietly, unmarked by any thing extraordinary. The acknowledged lovers talked and laughed, the unacknowledged were silent. Darcy was not of a disposition in which happiness overflows in mirth; and Elizabeth, agitated and confused, rather *knew* that she was happy, than *felt* herself to be so; for, besides the immediate embarrassment, there were other evils[1] before her. She anticipated what would be felt in the family when her situation became known; she was aware that no one liked him but Jane; and even feared that with the others it was a *dislike* which not all his fortune and consequence[2] might do away.[3]

At night she opened her heart to Jane. Though suspicion[4] was very far from Miss Bennet's general habits, she was absolutely incredulous here.

"You are joking, Lizzy. This cannot be!—engaged to Mr. Darcy! No, no, you shall not deceive me. I know it to be impossible."[5]

"This is a wretched beginning indeed! My sole dependence was on you; and I am sure nobody else will believe me, if you do not. Yet, indeed, I am in earnest. I speak nothing but the truth. He still loves me, and we are engaged."

Jane looked at her doubtingly. "Oh, Lizzy! it cannot be. I know how much you dislike him."

1. *evils*: painful difficulties.

2. *consequence*: high social position.

3. Of course, this dislike of Darcy is partly Elizabeth's own doing, as is, to an even greater degree, her family's belief in her hostility to him.

4. *suspicion*: suspicion of others' truthfulness, inclination not to believe someone.

5. Jane's astonishment has parallels with Elizabeth's earlier astonishment at hearing of Charlotte's engagement. The surprise in the two cases, however, stems from different sources. In the earlier case it came from Elizabeth's misunderstanding of Charlotte; in the present instance, it stems from Jane's prior ignorance of the important facts concerning Elizabeth and Darcy from the time of their encounter at Pemberley. As discussed below, Elizabeth said little to Jane about that encounter, nor did she inform Jane about Darcy's actions regarding Lydia and Wickham. Jane did hear Lydia's accidental revelation about Darcy's presence at her wedding, but she had no basis for connecting that with Darcy's feelings for Elizabeth. In fact, Jane's general lack of suspicion about other people means that she would be one of the last to guess a difficult secret; she would be especially unlikely to suspect that her own favorite sister, with whom she was generally so intimate, would have been harboring a strong romantic passion and keeping it from everyone.

"You know nothing of the matter. *That* is all to be forgot. Perhaps I did not always love him so well as I do now. But in such cases as these, a good memory is unpardonable. This is the last time I shall ever remember it myself."

Miss Bennet still looked all amazement. Elizabeth again, and more seriously assured her of its truth.

"Good Heaven! can it be really so! Yet now I must believe you," cried Jane. "My dear, dear Lizzy, I would—I do congratulate you—but are you certain? forgive the question—are you quite certain that you can be happy with him?"

"There can be no doubt of that. It is settled between us already, that we are to be the happiest couple in the world. But are you pleased, Jane? Shall you like to have such a brother?"

"Very, very much. Nothing could give either Bingley or myself more delight. But we considered it, we talked of it as impossible. And do you really love him quite well enough? Oh, Lizzy! do any thing rather than marry without affection.[6] Are you quite sure that you feel what you ought to do?"

"Oh, yes! You will only think I feel *more* than I ought to do, when I tell you all."

"What do you mean?"

"Why, I must confess, that I love him better than I do Bingley. I am afraid you will be angry."

"My dearest sister, now *be* be[7] serious. I want to talk very seriously. Let me know every thing that I am to know, without delay. Will you tell me how long you have loved him?"

"It has been coming on so gradually, that I hardly know when it began. But I believe I must date it from my first seeing his beautiful grounds at Pemberley."[8]

Another intreaty that she would be serious, however, produced the desired effect; and she soon satisfied Jane by her solemn assurances of attachment. When convinced on that article, Miss Bennet had nothing farther to wish.

"Now I am quite happy," said she, "for you will be as happy as myself. I always had a value[9] for him. Were it for nothing but his love of you, I must always have esteemed him; but now, as Bingley's

6.   A statement expressing Jane Austen's own deepest feelings. In a letter to her niece Fanny (see cover) discussing marriage, she declares, "Anything is to be preferred or endured rather than marrying without Affection" (Nov. 18, 1814). It is also a sentiment appropriate to place in the mouth of Jane Bennet, one of the most affectionate of the author's characters.

7.   *be be*: this repetition appears in the original. If intentional, rather than a printing error, it would be meant to convey Jane's earnestness.

8.   Some commentators, including Sir Walter Scott in an early commentary on the novel, have seen this statement as a revelation of Elizabeth's true motives (i.e., mercenary ones) in accepting Darcy. That the statement, however, is meant primarily as a joke — and throughout this exchange Elizabeth is resorting to humor to lighten what is obviously a difficult ordeal — is indicated by Jane's subsequent entreaty to be serious. The germ of truth it does contain is that Elizabeth had, when visiting Pemberley, reflected on the advantages of being its mistress. But this was due less to its wealth, as impressive as that was, than to her perception of how much good someone in charge of it could do, and of what the beauties of Pemberley revealed about the taste and judgment of its proprietor.

9.   *value*: liking, regard.

friend and your husband, there can be only Bingley and yourself more dear to me. But Lizzy, you have been very sly, very reserved[10] with me. How little did you tell me of what passed at Pemberley and Lambton! I owe all that I know of it, to another,[11] not to you."

Elizabeth told her the motives of her secrecy. She had been unwilling to mention Bingley;[12] and the unsettled state of her own feelings had made her equally avoid the name of his friend. But now she would no longer conceal from her, his share in Lydia's marriage. All was acknowledged, and half the night spent in conversation.

"Good gracious!" cried Mrs. Bennet, as she stood at a window the next morning, "if that disagreeable Mr. Darcy is not coming here again with our dear Bingley! What can he mean by being so tiresome as to be always coming here? I had no notion but he would go a shooting, or something or other, and not disturb us with his company. What shall we do with him? Lizzy, you must walk out with him again, that he may not be in Bingley's way."

Elizabeth could hardly help laughing at so convenient a proposal; yet was really vexed that her mother should be always giving him such an epithet.

As soon as they entered, Bingley looked at her so expressively, and shook hands with such warmth, as left no doubt of his good information; [13]and he soon afterwards said aloud, "Mr. Bennet,[14] have you no more lanes hereabouts in which Lizzy may lose her way again to-day?"

"I advise Mr. Darcy, and Lizzy, and Kitty," said Mrs. Bennet, "to walk to Oakham Mount this morning. It is a nice long walk, and Mr. Darcy has never seen the view."

"It may do very well for the others," replied Mr. Bingley; "but I am sure it will be too much for Kitty. Won't it, Kitty?"[15]

Kitty owned[16] that she had rather stay at home. Darcy professed a great curiosity to see the view from the Mount, and Elizabeth silently consented. As she went up stairs to get ready, Mrs. Bennet followed her, saying,

10. *sly . . . reserved:* secretive; the words have a similar meaning. Jane's redundant use of both words suggests how much she has been surprised by Elizabeth's uncharacteristic secrecy.

11. *another:* Bingley, who would naturally have told Jane about his earlier encounter with Elizabeth and the Gardiners. Of course, Bingley had only a brief experience of seeing Elizabeth and Darcy together at that juncture, so he would not have had much to share with Jane about them.

12. She presumably did not mention Bingley to Jane because she feared that this might lead to describing Bingley's continued affection for Jane, which in turn might have raised Jane's hopes at a time when no one could know if Bingley would ever pursue Jane again.

13. *information:* knowledge of the matter.

14. *Mr. Bennet:* this was Mr. Bennet in the original edition, but it probably should be Mrs. Bennet since it is she who replies; Mr. Bennet normally seems to be in the library when visitors call.

15. It is possible that Bingley's obvious contriving to get Elizabeth and Darcy together, something that might embarrass Darcy a little, represents intentional teasing of Darcy, and a slight revenge on Bingley's part for Darcy's interference with his love life.

16. *owned:* acknowledged.

"I am quite sorry, Lizzy, that you should be forced to have that disagreeable man all to yourself. But I hope you will not mind it: it is all for Jane's sake, you know; and there is no occasion for talking to him, except just now and then. So, do not put yourself to inconvenience."

During their walk, it was resolved that Mr. Bennet's consent should be asked in the course of the evening. Elizabeth reserved to herself the application for her mother's. She could not determine how her mother would take it; sometimes doubting whether all his wealth and grandeur would be enough to overcome her abhorrence of the man. But whether she were violently set against the match, or violently delighted with it, it was certain that her manner would be equally ill adapted to do credit to her sense; and she could no more bear that Mr. Darcy should hear the first raptures of her joy, than the first vehemence of her disapprobation.

———

In the evening, soon after Mr. Bennet withdrew to the library, she saw Mr. Darcy rise also and follow him, and her agitation on seeing it was extreme. She did not fear her father's opposition, but he was going to be made unhappy, and that it should be through her means, that *she*, his favourite child, should be distressing him by her choice, should be filling him with fears and regrets in disposing of her, was a wretched reflection, and she sat in misery till Mr. Darcy appeared again, when, looking at him, she was a little relieved by his smile. In a few minutes he approached the table where she was sitting with Kitty; and, while pretending to admire her work,[17] said in a whisper, "Go to your father, he wants you in the library." She was gone directly.

Her father was walking about the room, looking grave and anxious. "Lizzy," said he, "what are you doing? Are you out of your senses, to be accepting this man? Have not you always hated him?"

How earnestly did she then wish that her former opinions had been more reasonable, her expressions[18] more moderate! It would have spared her from explanations and professions which

17. *her work*: her needlework.

18. *expressions*: utterances, choices of words.

it was exceedingly awkward to give; but they were now necessary, and she assured him with some confusion, of her attachment to Mr. Darcy.

"Or in other words, you are determined to have him. He is rich, to be sure, and you may have more fine clothes and fine carriages than Jane. But will they make you happy?"

"Have you any other objection," said Elizabeth, "than your belief of my indifference?"

"None at all. We all know him to be a proud, unpleasant sort of man; but this would be nothing if you really liked him."

"I do, I do like him," she replied, with tears in her eyes, "I love him. Indeed he has no improper pride.[19] He is perfectly amiable.[20] You do not know what he really is; then pray do not pain me by speaking of him in such terms."

"Lizzy," said her father, "I have given him my consent. He is the kind of man, indeed, to whom I should never dare refuse any thing, which he condescended to ask. I now give it to *you*, if you are resolved on having him. But let me advise you to think better of it. I know your disposition, Lizzy. I know that you could be neither happy nor respectable, unless you truly esteemed your husband; unless you looked up to him as a superior.[21] Your lively talents would place you in the greatest danger in an unequal marriage. You could scarcely escape discredit and misery. My child, let me not have the grief of seeing *you* unable to respect your partner in life.[22] You know not what you are about."

Elizabeth, still more affected, was earnest and solemn in her reply; and at length, by repeated assurances that Mr. Darcy was really the object of her choice, by explaining the gradual change which her estimation of him had undergone, relating her absolute certainty that his affection was not the work of a day, but had stood the test of many months suspense,[23] and enumerating with energy all his good qualities, she did conquer her father's incredulity, and reconcile him to the match.

"Well, my dear," said he, when she ceased speaking, "I have no more to say. If this be the case, he deserves you. I could not have parted with you, my Lizzy, to any one less worthy."

19. *no improper pride:* Elizabeth's choice of words is significant. At earlier points she had questioned whether any degree of pride could be good or justified. She has now accepted some of Darcy's defense of pride—even as he has come to acknowledge the excessive and unjustified nature of the pride he actually did have.

20. *amiable:* kind, good natured, worthy of being loved.

21. A statement that is in line with this society's ideal of ultimate male primacy in marriage. Elizabeth does not directly respond to the statement, so it is impossible to know her view (or Jane Austen's view, for that matter). This lack of a rebuttal could signal that she, even with her clear desire for a man who will respect her and be willing to be teased by her, accepts this prevailing ideal, or it could result simply from her concern with more immediate matters during this conversation.

22. The most poignant words Mr. Bennet utters. Their poignancy is only increased by their contrast with his usual cynicism. He clearly is thinking of himself and his own tragic mistake in choosing a marriage partner. He is too indolent and too resigned to try to correct any of the damage in his own case, but, temporarily abandoning his customary sarcasm and banter, he expresses a fervent wish that his favorite child avoid the same error. His fervor may be increased by his knowledge that she, as a woman and thus the one who would be legally and socially weaker under prevailing marital arrangements, could suffer even more from a bad partner than he has.

23. *suspense:* state or period of waiting to learn about something, often involving anxiety and uncertainty.

To complete the favourable impression, she then told him what Mr. Darcy had voluntarily done for Lydia. He heard her with astonishment.

"This is an evening of wonders, indeed! And so, Darcy did every thing; made up the match, gave the money, paid the fellow's debts, and got him his commission! So much the better. It will save me a world of trouble and economy.[24] Had it been your uncle's doing, I must and *would* have paid him; but these violent young lovers carry every thing their own way. I shall offer to pay him to-morrow; he will rant and storm about his love for you, and there will be an end of the matter."

He then recollected her embarrassment a few days before, on his reading Mr. Collins's letter; and after laughing at her some time, allowed her at last to go—saying, as she quitted the room, "If any young men come for Mary or Kitty, send them in, for I am quite at leisure."

Elizabeth's mind was now relieved from a very heavy weight; and, after half an hour's quiet reflection in her own room, she was able to join the others with tolerable composure. Every thing was too recent for gaiety, but the evening passed tranquilly away; there was no longer any thing material to be dreaded, and the comfort of ease and familiarity would come in time.

When her mother went up to her dressing-room at night, she followed her, and made the important communication. Its effect was most extraordinary; for on first hearing it, Mrs. Bennet sat quite still, and unable to utter a syllable. Nor was it under many, many minutes, that she could comprehend what she heard; though not in general backward[25] to credit what was for the advantage of her family, or that came in the shape of a lover to any of them. She began at length to recover, to fidget about in her chair, get up, sit down again, wonder, and bless herself.

"Good gracious! Lord bless me! only think! dear me! Mr. Darcy! Who would have thought it! And is it really true? Oh! my sweetest Lizzy! how rich and how great[26] you will be! What pin-money,[27] what jewels, what carriages you will have! Jane's is nothing to it—nothing at all. I am so pleased—so happy. Such a

24. *economy*: exercise of frugality; this would be to accumulate money in order to repay Mr. Gardiner.

25. *backward*: reluctant, hesitant.

26. *great*: important or high-ranking socially.

27. *pin-money*: regular allowance given to a married woman for clothes and other private expenses (the term originated from the traditional importance of pins in clothing). The annual amount was often guaranteed as part of the settlements drawn up before marriage.

charming man!—so handsome! so tall!—Oh, my dear Lizzy! pray apologise for my having disliked him so much before. I hope he will overlook it. Dear, dear Lizzy. A house in town![28] Every thing that is charming! Three daughters married! Ten thousand a year! Oh, Lord! What will become of me. I shall go distracted."[29]

This was enough to prove that her approbation need not be doubted: and Elizabeth, rejoicing that such an effusion was heard only by herself, soon went away. But before she had been three minutes in her own room, her mother followed her.

"My dearest child," she cried, "I can think of nothing else! Ten thousand a year, and very likely more! 'Tis as good as a Lord![30] And a special licence.[31] You must and shall be married by a special licence. But my dearest love, tell me what dish Mr. Darcy is particularly fond of, that I may have it to-morrow."

This was a sad omen of what her mother's behaviour to the gentleman himself might be; and Elizabeth found, that though in the certain possession of his warmest affection, and secure of her relations' consent, there was still something to be wished for. But the morrow passed off much better than she expected; for Mrs. Bennet luckily stood in such awe of her intended son-in-law, that she ventured not to speak to him, unless it was in her power to offer him any attention, or mark her deference for his opinion.

Elizabeth had the satisfaction of seeing her father taking pains to get acquainted with him; and Mr. Bennet soon assured her that he was rising every hour in his esteem.

"I admire all my three sons-in-law highly," said he. "Wickham, perhaps, is my favourite; but I think I shall like *your* husband quite as well as Jane's."[32]

28. Darcy has already been described as having a house in London (see p. 44). Maintaining a house there, in addition to one in the country, was normal for very wealthy people.

29. *distracted*: mad, frantic.

30. In fact, Darcy's wealth is comparable to that of a Lord (meaning a titled aristocrat).

31. *special licence*: a marriage license granted by the Archbishop of Canterbury, the head of the English church, that allowed a couple to marry whenever and wherever they wished. Only wealthy and prominent people would be able to procure such a license, so it carried great social prestige. In addition, a special license allowed one to marry in a home or private building—in contrast to a regular license, which, in addition to specifying the parish, required marriage in a chapel or church. Thus marriage by special license offered the maximum possible privacy, something that had become highly valued in weddings during this period.

It is uncertain whether in the end Darcy and Elizabeth bother with a special license: it turns out that they get married on the same day as Bingley and Jane (presumably as part of the same ceremony), and nothing is ever said about a special license for the latter two.

32. This statement could be interpreted in more than one way. Clearly Mr. Bennet does not value Wickham in the same way he values Bingley and Darcy. The question is whether he is being purely sarcastic, because he despises Wickham, or whether he is being sincere in a way, because he values Wickham in the same way as he values Mr. Collins, i.e., as someone to laugh at. On the one hand, he recently referred to Wickham's impudence and hypocrisy and compared those qualities as sources of amusement to Mr. Collins's absurdity; on the other hand, Wickham is not someone who can be continually laughed at like Mr. Collins, and in contrast to the other man Wickham has caused Mr. Bennet the only genuine distress he has experienced over the course of the book. The question is thus not easy to answer. It is possible there is an element of both meanings in Mr. Bennet's words.

Chapter Eighteen

*E*lizabeth's spirits soon rising to playfulness again, she wanted Mr. Darcy to account for his having ever fallen in love with her. "How could you begin?" said she. "I can comprehend your going on charmingly, when you had once made a beginning; but what could set you off in the first place?"

"I cannot fix on the hour, or the spot, or the look, or the words, which laid the foundation. It is too long ago. I was in the middle before I knew that I *had* begun."

"My beauty you had early withstood, and as for my manners—my behaviour to *you* was at least always bordering on the uncivil, and I never spoke to you without rather wishing to give you pain than not. Now be sincere; did you admire me for my impertinence?"

"For the liveliness[1] of your mind,[2] I did."

"You may as well call it impertinence at once. It was very little less. The fact is, that you were sick of civility, of deference, of officious attention. You were disgusted with the women who were always speaking and looking, and thinking for *your* approbation alone. I roused, and interested you, because I was so unlike *them*.[3] Had you not been really amiable you would have hated me for it; but in spite of the pains you took to disguise yourself, your feelings were always noble and just; and in your heart, you thoroughly despised the persons who so assiduously courted you. There—I have saved you the trouble of accounting for it; and really, all things considered, I begin to think it perfectly reasonable. To be sure, you know[4] no actual good of me—but nobody thinks of *that* when they fall in love."

"Was there no good in your affectionate behaviour to Jane, while she was ill at Netherfield?"[5]

"Dearest Jane! who could have done less for her? But make a virtue of it by all means. My good qualities are under your

1. *liveliness:* thus Darcy has recognized the basic quality in Elizabeth that is so opposed to his character—though it is possible that Darcy, in using the term, is thinking of its meaning of energy and vigor as well as its meaning of playfulness and lightheartedness.

2. *mind:* character.

3. Miss Bingley is the obvious example of this, and Darcy's disgust with her was generally apparent. It is also probable there were others like her, for a man of his wealth and social standing would be considered such a catch that many women of an ambitious and flattering kind could seek to ingratiate themselves as Miss Bingley did.

4. *know:* this could be a printer's error since "knew" seems more logical.

5. Darcy's response is wholly serious; even as he praises Elizabeth's liveliness, he maintains his characteristic gravity and does not reciprocate her playfulness.

protection, and you are to exaggerate them as much as possible; and, in return, it belongs to me to find occasions for teazing and quarrelling with you as often as may be; and I shall begin directly by asking you what made you so unwilling to come to the point at last. What made you so shy of me, when you first called, and afterwards dined here?[6] Why, especially, when you called, did you look as if you did not care about me?"

"Because you were grave and silent, and gave me no encouragement."

"But I was embarrassed."

"And so was I."

"You might have talked to me more when you came to dinner."

"A man who had felt less, might."[7]

"How unlucky that you should have a reasonable answer to give, and that I should be so reasonable as to admit it! But I wonder how long you *would* have gone on, if you had been left to yourself. I wonder when you *would* have spoken, if I had not asked you! My resolution of thanking you for your kindness to Lydia had certainly great effect. *Too much*, I am afraid; for what becomes of the moral, if our comfort[8] springs from a breach of promise, for I ought not to have mentioned the subject?[9] This will never do."

"You need not distress yourself. The moral will be perfectly fair. Lady Catherine's unjustifiable endeavours to separate us, were the means of removing all my doubts. I am not indebted for my present happiness to your eager desire of expressing your gratitude. I was not in a humour[10] to wait for any opening of your's. My aunt's intelligence[11] had given me hope, and I was determined at once to know every thing."[12]

"Lady Catherine has been of infinite use, which ought to make her happy, for she loves to be of use. But tell me, what did you come down to Netherfield for? Was it merely to ride to Longbourn and be embarrassed? or had you intended any more serious consequence?"

"My real purpose was to see *you*, and to judge, if I could, whether I might ever hope to make you love me. My avowed one, or what I avowed to myself, was to see whether your sister were

6. This would be when he and Bingley had returned to Netherfield.

7. Darcy's silence toward Elizabeth because of his strong feelings forms the complete contrast with someone like Mr. Collins, who could propose to Elizabeth without hesitation precisely because no genuine feelings existed to interfere.

8. *comfort*: happiness.

9. In other words, it would seem a bad moral for their story if they owed their marriage to Elizabeth's having spoken to him about a subject that she should never have known about (since Lydia had committed a breach of confidence by revealing to Elizabeth the secret of Darcy's presence at her wedding).

10. *humour*: mood.

11. *intelligence*: information (regarding her confrontation with Elizabeth).

12. Darcy and Elizabeth's ability to talk sensibly and objectively about their love, and how it developed, indicates the rational character of their love. While they feel strongly for one another, those feelings do not prevent their thinking clearly.

still partial to Bingley, and if she were, to make the confession to him which I have since made."

"Shall you ever have courage to announce to Lady Catherine, what is to befall her?"

"I am more likely to want[13] time than courage, Elizabeth.[14] But it ought to be done, and if you will give me a sheet of paper, it shall be done directly."[15]

"And if I had not a letter to write myself, I might sit by you, and admire the evenness of your writing, as another young lady once did. But I have an aunt, too, who must not be longer neglected."

From an unwillingness to confess how much her intimacy with Mr. Darcy had been over-rated, Elizabeth had never yet answered Mrs. Gardiner's long letter, but now, having *that* to communicate which she knew would be most welcome, she was almost ashamed to find, that her uncle and aunt had already lost three days of happiness, and immediately wrote as follows:

I would have thanked you before, my dear aunt, as I ought to have done, for your long, kind, satisfactory, detail of particulars; but to say the truth, I was too cross to write. You supposed more than really existed.[16] But now suppose as much as you chuse; give a loose[17] to your fancy, indulge your imagination in every possible flight which the subject will afford, and unless you believe me actually married, you cannot greatly err. You must write again very soon, and praise him a great deal more than you did in your last. I thank you, again and again, for not going to the Lakes. How could I be so silly as to wish it![18] Your idea of the ponies is delightful. We will go round the Park every day. I am the happiest creature in the world. Perhaps other people have said so before, but not one with such justice. I am happier even than Jane; she only smiles, I laugh. Mr. Darcy sends you all the love in the world, that he can spare from me. You are all to come to Pemberley at Christmas. Your's, &c.

Mr. Darcy's letter to Lady Catherine, was in a different style; and still different from either, was what Mr. Bennet sent to Mr. Collins, in reply to his last.

13. *want*: lack, need.

14. *Elizabeth*: this is the second time Darcy has called Elizabeth by her first name. It is a further sign of affection and intimacy, and it is fitting that it occurs in the last line that Darcy speaks to Elizabeth in the novel.

15. *directly*: immediately.

16. That is, more than really existed at that time between Elizabeth and Darcy, at least as regards an understanding between them—it was not more than really existed as regards the two lovers', especially Darcy's, feelings. This is why Elizabeth says she was cross. Of course, the Gardiners' guesses were fully justified in the end.

17. *give a loose*: give full vent.

18. Since her wish of going to the Lakes stemmed in part from her general, and somewhat peevish, disgust with humanity, it is appropriate that the decision to go elsewhere is what has ultimately provided her with such means to be happy with everyone.

DEAR SIR,

I must trouble you once more for congratulations. Elizabeth will soon be the wife of Mr. Darcy. Console Lady Catherine as well as you can. But, if I were you, I would stand by the nephew. He has more to give.[19]

Your's sincerely, &c.[20]

Miss Bingley's congratulations to her brother, on his approaching marriage, were all that was affectionate and insincere. She wrote even to Jane on the occasion, to express her delight, and repeat all her former professions of regard. Jane was not deceived, but she was affected; and though feeling no reliance on her, could not help writing her a much kinder answer than she knew was deserved.

The joy which Miss Darcy expressed on receiving similar information, was as sincere as her brother's in sending it. Four sides of paper were insufficient to contain all her delight, and all her earnest desire of being loved by her sister.[21]

Before any answer could arrive from Mr. Collins, or any congratulations to Elizabeth, from his wife, the Longbourn family heard that the Collinses were come themselves to Lucas Lodge. The reason of this sudden removal was soon evident. Lady Catherine had been rendered so exceedingly angry by the contents of her nephew's letter, that Charlotte, really rejoicing in the match, was anxious to get away till the storm was blown over.[22] At such a moment, the arrival of her friend was a sincere pleasure to Elizabeth, though in the course of their meetings she must sometimes think the pleasure dearly bought, when she saw Mr. Darcy exposed to all the parading[23] and obsequious civility of her husband. He bore it however with admirable calmness.[24] He could even listen to Sir William Lucas, when he complimented him on carrying away the brightest jewel of the country,[25] and expressed his hopes of their all meeting frequently at St. James's,[26] with very decent composure. If he did shrug his shoulders, it was not till Sir William was out of sight.

19. A reference presumably to Darcy's power of patronage in the Church. Mr. Bennet obviously knows what will most influence Mr. Collins.

20. This is the only letter we actually see by Mr. Bennet, the man who has always avowed his hatred of writing. It is thus not surprising that the letter is as short as possible.

21. As a girl who seems to have lost her mother at an early age, and who has otherwise only had a father and a brother for her immediate family, she would undoubtedly like to have a close female relation (one doubts Lady Catherine or Anne de Bourgh would fill that gap).

22. If Mr. Collins has taken Mr. Bennet's words of advice to heart, he might also wish to come to the place where he could curry favor with the person who has more to give in the way of patronage.

23. *parading*: ostentatious show.

24. The advantages of Darcy's reserve become apparent here, though his calmness has presumably been assisted by his having learned under Elizabeth's influence to curb his pride and lack of sociability.

25. *country*: county, area.

26. Sir William's idea is presumably that Darcy, thanks to his rank and aristocratic connections, would frequently attend the royal court of St. James, where Sir William always likes to imagine himself as a regular even though he has been there only once.

Mrs. Philips's vulgarity was another, and perhaps a greater tax[27] on his forbearance; and though Mrs. Philips, as well as her sister, stood in too much awe of him to speak with the familiarity which Bingley's good humour encouraged, yet, whenever she *did* speak, she must be vulgar. Nor was her respect for him, though it made her more quiet, at all likely to make her more elegant. Elizabeth did all she could, to shield him from the frequent notice of either, and was ever anxious to keep him to herself, and to those of her family with whom he might converse without mortification; and though the uncomfortable feelings arising from all this took from the season of courtship much of its pleasure, it added to the hope of the future; and she looked forward with delight to the time when they should be removed from society so little pleasing to either, to all the comfort and elegance of their family party at Pemberley.

27. *tax*: imposition, strain.

Chapter Nineteen[1]

*H*appy for all her maternal feelings was the day on which Mrs. Bennet got rid of her two most deserving daughters.[2] With what delighted pride she afterwards visited Mrs. Bingley and talked of Mrs. Darcy may be guessed.[3] I wish I could say, for the sake of her family, that the accomplishment of her earnest desire in the establishment[4] of so many of her children, produced so happy an effect as to make her a sensible, amiable, well-informed woman for the rest of her life; though perhaps it was lucky for her husband, who might not have relished domestic felicity in so unusual a form,[5] that she still was occasionally nervous[6] and invariably silly.

Mr. Bennet missed his second daughter exceedingly; his affection for her drew him oftener from home than any thing else could do. He delighted in going to Pemberley, especially when he was least expected.

Mr. Bingley and Jane remained at Netherfield only a twelve-month. So near a vicinity to her mother and Meryton relations was not desirable even to *his* easy temper, or *her* affectionate heart. The darling wish of his sisters was then gratified; he bought an estate in a neighbouring county to Derbyshire, and Jane and Elizabeth, in addition to every other source of happiness, were within thirty miles of each other.[7]

Kitty, to her very material advantage, spent the chief[8] of her time with her two elder sisters. In society so superior to what she had generally known, her improvement was great. She was not of so ungovernable a temper as Lydia, and, removed from the influence of Lydia's example, she became, by proper attention and management, less irritable, less ignorant, and less insipid. From the farther disadvantage of Lydia's society she was of course carefully kept, and though Mrs. Wickham frequently invited her to

1. Jane Austen generally ends her novels with a summing up of the fates of her characters. These fates are meted out according to a sense of moral justice, with everyone generally getting what they deserve, though their future course and actions are still made consistent with what has already been shown of their natures.

2. This implies that they married on the same day; that would make sense, given the closeness of both the brides and the grooms.

3. Mrs. Bingley can be visited because she is at Netherfield; Mrs. Darcy, now far away at Pemberly, can only be talked of.

4. *establishment*: marriage.

5. That is, felicity that came from enjoying the sensible qualities of his wife rather than from laughing at her foolish ones.

6. *nervous*: afflicted with nervous disorders (at least in her perception).

7. Thus Elizabeth and Jane are depicted as enjoying an almost ideal condition as wives. This is always the fate toward which everything in Jane Austen's novels leads, for the heroines as well as for most other female characters (she does not present any examples of young women happily choosing the single life she herself lived). The prominence in her thinking of this matrimonial fate for her characters is suggested by a letter in which she discusses looking for pictures of Elizabeth and Jane at a gallery, for in the letter she refers to them as Mrs. Darcy and Mrs. Bingley rather than by the names they are called throughout the novel.

8. *chief*: greater part.

come and stay with her, with the promise of balls and young men, her father would never consent to her going.

Mary was the only daughter who remained at home; and she was necessarily drawn from the pursuit of accomplishments by Mrs. Bennet's being quite unable to sit alone. Mary was obliged to mix more with the world, but she could still moralize over every morning visit; and as she was no longer mortified by comparisons between her sisters' beauty and her own, it was suspected by her father that she submitted to the change without much reluctance.[9]

As for Wickham and Lydia, their characters suffered no revolution[10] from the marriage of her sisters. He bore with philosophy the conviction that Elizabeth must now become acquainted with whatever of his ingratitude and falsehood had before been unknown to her; and in spite of every thing, was not wholly without hope that Darcy might yet be prevailed on to make his fortune. The congratulatory letter which Elizabeth received from Lydia on her marriage, explained to her that, by his wife at least, if not by himself, such a hope was cherished. The letter was to this effect:

My Dear Lizzy,

   I wish you joy. If you love Mr. Darcy half as well as I do my dear Wickham, you must be very happy. It is a great comfort to have you so rich, and when you have nothing else to do, I hope you will think of us. I am sure Wickham would like a place at court[11] very much, and I do not think we shall have quite money enough to live upon without some help. Any place would do, of about three or four hundred a year; but, however, do not speak to Mr. Darcy about it, if you had rather not.

                                  Your's, &c.

As it happened that Elizabeth had *much* rather not, she endeavoured in her answer to put an end to every intreaty and expectation of the kind. Such relief, however, as it was in her power to afford, by the practice of what might be called economy in her own private expences,[12] she frequently sent them. It had

9. According to a later memoir by her nephew, Jane Austen did reveal her vision of the future fates of Kitty and Mary: "Kitty Bennet was satisfactorily married to a clergyman near Pemberley, while Mary obtained nothing higher than one of her uncle Philips's clerks, and was content to be considered a star in the society of Meryton."

10. *suffered no revolution:* experienced no great change or reversal.

11. *place at court:* certain army units were attached to the court. These units were generally more prestigious and better paid.

12. This probably refers to her pin-money, the allowance she has to spend on things for herself; it would be out of this sum that Elizabeth would try to save.

always been evident to her that such an income as theirs,[13] under the direction of two persons so extravagant in their wants, and heedless of the future, must be very insufficient to their support; and whenever they changed their quarters, either Jane or herself were sure of being applied to, for some little assistance towards discharging their bills. Their manner of living, even when the restoration of peace dismissed them to a home,[14] was unsettled in the extreme. They were always moving from place to place in quest of a cheap situation,[15] and always spending more than they ought. His affection for her soon sunk into indifference; her's lasted a little longer; and in spite of her youth and her manners, she retained all the claims to reputation which her marriage had given her.[16]

Though Darcy could never receive *him* at Pemberley, yet, for Elizabeth's sake, he assisted him farther in his profession. Lydia was occasionally a visitor there, when her husband was gone to enjoy himself in London or Bath;[17] and with the Bingleys they both of them frequently staid so long, that even Bingley's good humour was overcome, and he proceeded so far as to *talk* of giving them a hint to be gone.

Miss Bingley was very deeply mortified by Darcy's marriage; but as she thought it advisable to retain the right of visiting at Pemberley, she dropt all her resentment; was fonder than ever of Georgiana, almost as attentive to Darcy as heretofore, and paid off every arrear of civility[18] to Elizabeth.

Pemberley was now Georgiana's home; and the attachment of the sisters was exactly what Darcy had hoped to see. They were able to love each other, even as well as they intended.[19] Georgiana had the highest opinion in the world of Elizabeth; though at first she often listened with an astonishment bordering on alarm, at her lively, sportive, manner of talking to her brother. He, who had always inspired in herself a respect which almost overcame her affection, she now saw the object of open pleasantry.[20] Her mind received knowledge which had never before fallen in her way. By Elizabeth's instructions she began to comprehend that a woman may take liberties with her husband, which a brother will not always allow in a sister more than ten years younger than himself.

13. The pay for an ensign in the army, Wickham's rank when they were married, was around 95 pounds. This would be a very small amount to live on. In fact, lower officers were in a particularly difficult position because they were still expected to live like gentlemen, which involved expense, despite their meager salaries.

14. The specific reference here has been disputed. The first version of the novel was written in the 1790s, and some have argued that the novel, even when revised later, was still set in this period. If so, "restoration of peace" would refer to the brief period of peace between England and France in 1802–03. More likely, Jane Austen intended the novel to be set around the time she completed it, in 1811–12, and was here referring to an eventual end of the current war with France. In fact, most of the fighting ended in 1814, a year after the publication of the novel, and the war terminated completely in 1815.

15. *situation*: residence, living situation.

16. Being married would by itself add to a woman's public standing, and since Wickham was a military officer, a position of prestige, Lydia would be able to assume a reasonably prominent position in society.

17. *Bath*: a town in southeastern England that was a spa and popular vacation destination (see map, p. 742). Jane Austen lived in Bath and set large parts of two of her novels there.

18. *arrear of civility*: debt or obligation of civility. The wording of the passage suggests the nature of Miss Bingley's civility: she returns Elizabeth's politeness not from genuine good will or graciousness, but from a wish to square accounts, to avoid being in debt to Elizabeth and thus at a disadvantage.

19. The implication is that in many cases, if not most, people do not manage to love a new relation as well as they intend at the outset.

20. A description that hints that Elizabeth's playfulness and liveliness continue to be prominent after her marriage.

Lady Catherine was extremely indignant on the marriage of her nephew; and as she gave way to all the genuine frankness of her character, in her reply to the letter which announced its arrangement, she sent him language so very abusive, especially of Elizabeth, that for some time all intercourse was at an end.[21] But at length, by Elizabeth's persuasion, he was prevailed on to overlook the offence, and seek a reconciliation;[22] and, after a little farther resistance on the part of his aunt, her resentment gave way, either to her affection for him, or her curiosity to see how his wife conducted herself; and she condescended to wait on[23] them at Pemberley, in spite of that pollution which its woods had received, not merely from the presence of such a mistress, but the visits of her uncle and aunt from the city.[24]

With the Gardiners, they were always on the most intimate terms. Darcy, as well as Elizabeth, really loved them;[25] and they were both ever sensible of the warmest gratitude towards the persons who, by bringing her into Derbyshire, had been the means of uniting them.[26]

21. Lady Catherine's abuse of Elizabeth has affinities with a lengthy episode in Samuel Richarson's *Pamela,* in which the sister of the hero harshly castigates and attacks the less socially elevated heroine after she marries the hero.

22. Elizabeth's efforts here with Darcy, despite having herself been the main object of Lady Catherine's abuse, are an example of the role she envisioned for herself as his wife, that of softening him. It also shows Darcy eschewing the tendency toward resentment he had avowed to Elizabeth, and that she had found so objectionable.

23. *wait on:* visit.

24. Lady Catherine had earlier warned of the pollution its shades or woods would receive in the event of Elizabeth's marriage to Darcy (see p. 650, and p. 651, note 45), although she referred specifically then to visits by Wickham and Lydia.

25. Thus Darcy drops some of his social snobbery out of appreciation for the Gardiners' good qualities.

26. In listing the future situations and actions of the various characters, Jane Austen ends up saying little about the actual relationship of Elizabeth and Darcy. It is possible that she considered that the whole story had already given the reader a strong sense of what their marriage would be like. Jane Austen does, however, give one hint of her thoughts on the subject in the letter, mentioned in note 7 above, that describes her search for pictures on public display that resemble Jane and Elizabeth. She laments that she could find none that matched her idea of "Mrs. D." [i.e., Elizabeth]. Speaking as if her characters were real people, she concludes, "I can only imagine that Mr. D. prizes any Picture of her too much to like it should be exposed to the public eye. — I can imagine he w^d have that sort [of] feeling — that mixture of Love, Pride & Delicacy" (May 24, 1813).

Note on the Text of the Novel

The first edition of *Pride and Prejudice* came out in early 1813. Jane Austen herself checked over this edition, something indicated by a letter complaining of two speeches being made into one (see p. 623). It is uncertain if she examined it thoroughly enough to identify any changes she wished to make in spelling, capitalization, or punctuation. A second edition appeared later in 1813, a third in 1817. Each of these editions made slight changes to the text.

All subsequent editions have been based on one of these initial editions. Some recent versions have modernized the punctuation and spelling, and eliminated inconsistencies in the latter. This has made the text read more easily in places, but at the cost of historical accuracy. Moreover, some of the alterations, especially of punctuation, have created subtle shifts in meaning, thus obscuring a little of what Jane Austen intends to say.

The most important exception to this tendency is the 1923 edition of R. W. Chapman (the most authoritative edition of the novel, it is available as part of *The Oxford Illustrated Jane Austen*). Chapman essentially reproduces the original 1813 edition, making only a tiny number of changes where he believes there was a clear mistake in printing. Chapman also provides an invaluable set of notes indicating where changes were made in the second and third editions of the novel, and explaining the reasons behind any of his decisions to depart from the first edition.

The text used for this annotation also follows faithfully the first edition of the novel (even rejecting a few of the changes to that edition made by Chapman). The aim is to bring the reader as close as possible to what Jane Austen wrote in her own draft of the novel, however odd or awkward this may make certain passages seem. The one exception made is in the spelling or capitalization of proper names, where consistency has been maintained even when that meant departing from the original edition.

Chronology

VOLUME II

Elizabeth (p. 248), and Mr. Collins's departure being mentioned after that.

Sat., Dec. 21	Mr. Collins ends second visit	258
Mon., Dec. 23	The Gardiners arrive for Christmas	258
Mon., Dec. 30	The Gardiners leave, with Jane	268

The Gardiners are said to have "staid a week" at Longbourn (p. 264).

Early Jan.	Mr. Collins arrives to stay with the Lucases	268
Tues., Jan. 7	Jane visits Miss Bingley in London	270, 272

A probable date: Jane is described as writing to Elizabeth after "a week in town" (which would be around Jan. 6), and of intending to call on Miss Bingley the next day.

Wed., Jan. 8	Charlotte says goodbye to Elizabeth	268

The day is identified in the text; the date is not certain, but is probable. Mr. Collins is described as arriving at the Lucases "soon after" the Gardiners and Jane left, with the marriage "fast approaching." An interval of nine days from the Gardiners' departure, rather than one of either two or sixteen days, seems logical.

Thurs., Jan. 9	Marriage of Mr. Collins and Charlotte	270
Early Feb.	Miss Bingley returns visit to Jane	272

Described as an interval of four weeks.

Late March (1st day)	Elizabeth, Sir William, and Maria depart	278

See essay below for why it should be late March.

Late March (2nd day)	The travelers arrive at the Collinses	286
Late March (3rd day)	Visit of Miss De Bourgh	290, 292
Late March (4th day)	First dinner at Rosings	294

Invitation (p. 292) is for "next day."

Late March, Early April	Sir William leaves the Collinses	308

Said to be "a week" after their arrival.

Early to Mid-April	Darcy and Col. Fitzwilliam arrive at Rosings	310

This happens two weeks, and possibly a few days, after Elizabeth's arrival in the area. It may occur on a Monday, since on Sunday Darcy is said to have been there "almost a week" (p. 316).

VOLUME III   PAGE

*In the following section most dates are too uncertain to be given. But, unless
stated otherwise, each day mentioned is the first of those days to fall after the
previous day mentioned.*

*probably written the same day, and it quickly leads
to Mrs. Gardiner's writing back on Sept. 6 (at least
a week after the wedding).*

Sun.–Tues., Sept. 6.	Mrs. Gardiner replies to Elizabeth *See essay below for uncertainty of the calendar.*	582
Mon.–Wed.	Elizabeth receives letter	582
Wed.–Fri.	Lydia and Wickham depart *Said to be "soon" after he and Elizabeth talk, which was the same day as the letter (p. 592).*	598
Mid-Sept.	Mrs. Bennet hears of Bingley's return *Said to happen "shortly" after Lydia has gone, and to be "a day or two" before next event.*	600
Wed. or Thur., Mid-Sept.	Bingley arrives at Netherfield *The day is given on p. 600; it would be approximately a week after the departure of Lydia and Wickham.*	604
Sat. or Sun.	Bingley and Darcy call on the Bennets *This is three days after Bingley's arrival.*	604
Tuesday	Bingley and Darcy dine at Longbourn	616
Wed. or Thur.	Darcy's confession to Bingley *Described as occurring the day before Darcy's departure (see next note).*	674
Thur. or Fri.	Darcy leaves; Bingley sees the Bennets *Said to be "a few days" after the dinner at Longbourn; two or three days seems most likely.*	624
Fri. or Sat.	Bingley comes again, and stays all day *The day after above, and day before below.*	624
Sat. or Sun.	Bingley returns, proposes to Jane *By this point it would be late September.*	628

*Neither exact calendar dates nor days of the week can be supplied for the final
sequence of events, but the events generally can be placed in definite order.
They would happen during the beginning of October (for Day Three falls
"about a week after Bingley's engagement with Jane"—p. 638), with the first
day or two possibly falling in September.*

Day One	Lady Catherine hears a rumor that Elizabeth is engaged to Darcy *Lady Catherine says this occurred two days before her visit (p. 642).*	642

Day Two	Mr. Collins writes to warn Mr. Bennet *Mr. Collins says that he told Lady Catherine of the* *rumor "last night."*	660
Day Three	Lady Catherine's visit to Elizabeth	638
Day Four	Mr. Collins's letter arrives, and is read to Elizabeth by Mr. Bennet	656, 658
Day Six or *Seven*	Darcy visits and proposes to Elizabeth *This is said to take place "before many days had* *passed after Lady Catherine's visit." Three or four* *days later seems the most likely period.*	664, 666
Day Seven or *Eight*	Darcy and Elizabeth walk again The Bennets are told of the engagement	682, 684
Day Eight or *Nine*	Darcy dines at the Bennets	690
Day Eleven or *Twelve*	Elizabeth and Darcy talk further Elizabeth writes to Mrs. Gardiner *Elizabeth has delayed "three days" to tell Mrs.* *Gardiner of the engagement.*	692 696
Later in the *Year*	Double wedding of Elizabeth and Darcy, and Jane and Bingley *Elizabeth, in her letter to Mrs. Gardiner, speaks of* *their coming to Pemberley at Christmas, so the* *wedding would presumably be before then.*	702
One Year *Later*	Bingley and Jane leave Netherfield, and find a home not far from Pemberley.	702

The issue of *Pride and Prejudice*'s chronology has sparked differing interpretations, for the dates provided in the novel are not all compatible. The novel mentions three specific dates along with their days: Monday, Nov. 18, Tuesday, Nov. 26, and Monday, Aug. 2 (of the following year). The first two days are compatible; furthermore, since 1811 would have contained both days, and Jane Austen composed the final version of the novel in 1811 and 1812, many have supposed that she followed the calendars for those years when preparing the manuscript. Unfortunately, 1812 did not contain a Monday, August 2, nor would any year that succeeded a year containing a Monday, November 18 and Tuesday, November 26. This has left anyone wishing to date the novel with a dilemma.

The solution adopted by R. W. Chapman in his notes to *The Oxford Illustrated Jane Austen*, the leading scholarly edition of the novels and the one whose chronology is frequently followed here, is to argue that the novel is nonetheless set in 1811–1812. His argument is founded on the correct assertion that Monday, Aug. 2—the date put on the express letter by Mr. Gardiner informing the Bennets of Lydia's engagement—is a mistake; in fact, the letter must have been written approximately two weeks later (see p. 549, note 10). Chapman postulates that Jane Austen confused the date of Mr. Gardiner's letter with the date of the express sent to the Bennets telling them of Lydia's running away, which was on Sunday, Aug. 2 if the novel was aligned with the 1812 calendar.

Chapman's theory, however, suffers from a fatal flaw. One other specific day mentioned in the novel is Easter (p. 316), which occurs at the midpoint of Elizabeth's six-week visit to the Collinses (see above and p. 310). In 1812 Easter fell early, on March 29. This would make Elizabeth's visit last from early March until late April. But when Elizabeth returns home, after she has stayed with the Gardiners in London for "a few days," it is said to be "the second week of May," i.e., sometime between May 8 and May 14 (see above and pp. 400 and 402). That would not have been possible if Elizabeth had left in late April. Chapman notices this problem but tries to resolve it by arguing that Jane Austen must have been mistaken in describing the visit to the Gardiners as lasting a few days. Instead he proposes that the visit lasted approximately three weeks (he does not propose that the statement that Elizabeth returned in the second week of May was mistaken, for a much earlier return would be incompatible with the description of later events).

This attempted solution, in addition to supposing that the normally scrupulous Jane Austen would make such a flagrant error in describing the length of the visit to the Gardiners, runs into other serious problems. The most glaring is that a week before Elizabeth leaves the Collinses Lady Catherine talks of traveling to London herself a month after their departure, and says that will be in early June (p. 390)—such a statement would not make sense if Elizabeth were leaving in late April. In addition, a visit of only a few days to the Gardiners is more logical, for a number of reasons. First, as Chapman himself acknowledges, it is only after Elizabeth has stayed with the Gardiners and returned home that she tells Jane of Darcy's proposal— this subject is described as a secret that "had weighed on her for a fortnight" (pp. 416 and 418). But since Darcy's proposal occurred almost two weeks before Elizabeth left the Collinses, it could not still be a fortnight unless she had stopped for only a brief time at the Gardiners; it is also hard to imagine Elizabeth keeping such important news from Jane over the course of a three-week stay at the Gardiners. Second, Elizabeth is said to have little opportunity to talk to Jane during the visit because of the various engagements Mrs. Gardiner has arranged for them, something far more plausible for a short visit than a long one. Third, it would not really make sense for Jane, who has been staying with the Gardiners for four months, and Elizabeth, who will see them again for an extended vacation in the summer, to remain with the Gardiners for such a long time. It would make even less sense for Maria Lucas—who has no connection with the Gardiners and seems to be close to neither Jane nor Elizabeth—to continue accompanying Elizabeth as she does, rather than returning to her nearby family in Hertfordshire, if Elizabeth were stopping in London for three weeks.

This leaves two possibilities. The first is that Jane Austen did not use calendars at all, or at least not any from a specific pair of years. She could have used an 1811 calendar for the action in the first part of the novel, the part with the most precise sequence of events, and then not bothered with a calendar for the remainder of the action. Or she could have dispensed with calendars altogether: having arbitrarily chosen November 18 as the date of Mr. Collins's Monday arrival at the Bennets, she could easily have calculated the need to make Tuesday of the next week November 26, and she could have then plotted the remaining sequence of days from the first part of the novel without any reference to calendar dates. In either case, she could have planned the rest of the novel with a purely imaginary year in mind, one in which Easter fell in the middle of April, as it often does. As for the remaining exact date of Monday, August 2, since it is certainly wrong it is impossible to know how it was derived.

Supporters of the idea that Jane Austen used specific calendars in this novel have pointed to some evidence that she used one in *Mansfield Park*, but even for that novel the evidence is not certain, and the other novels do not provide any clear indication of the use of a calendar. In fact, in the case of *Persuasion*, in which the action is stated to occur in 1814–15, the one exact day indicated—Monday, February 1—is wrong by the calendar.

The second possibility is that *Pride and Prejudice*, which does involve a more precise sequence of days than in her other novels, is based on the 1811 and 1812 calendars, but that at the time Jane Austen was writing the passages set in the spring, she did not check the date of Easter and see that it was at the end of March. A similar error occurs in *Mansfield Park*, if in fact it was composed with reference to exact calendars. The one exact date in that novel is Thursday, December 22; it also refers, for the following spring, to a "particularly late" Easter; but any year close to the time Jane Austen was writing *Mansfield Park* that included a Thursday, December 22 was followed by a year in which Easter was early.

As for the possibility that she could have envisaged another specific pair of years besides 1811–12, a possibility suggested by Jane Austen's having composed an initial version of *Pride and Prejudice* many years earlier, that is excluded by the days and dates related to Lydia's wedding. As mentioned above, the wedding must have occurred on one of the last days of August; the wedding is also specified as happening on Monday. But a year in which November 26 is a Tuesday is followed by a year in which the last Monday in August is the 25th, unless the second year is a leap year. In that case the last Monday is August 31; this of course would work for the novel, but during Jane Austen's lifetime there were no leap years following a year with a Tuesday, November 26, except for the already discussed 1812.

All this means that no specific year can be identified as the clearly appropriate one for the' novel's chronology, and that the safest course, except for the early part of the novel, is to be precise when possible about the sequence of days, without ever assigning specific calendar dates.

References

Andrews, P. B. S., "The Date of *Pride and Prejudice*," *Notes and Queries* 213 (1968): 338–342.

Chapman, R. W., "The Chronology of *Pride and Prejudice*," in *The Oxford Illustrated Jane Austen*, Vol. II (Oxford, 1988)

Modert, Jo, "Chronology within the Novels," in *The Jane Austen Companion*, ed. J. David Grey (New York, 1986)

Nash, Ralph, "The Time Scheme for *Pride and Prejudice*," *English Language Notes* 4 (1966–67): 194–198.

Bibliography

WORKS BY JANE AUSTEN

Jane Austen's Letters, ed. by Deirdre Le Faye (Oxford, 1995)
Jane Austen's "Sir Charles Grandison," ed. by Brian Southam (Oxford, 1980)
The Oxford Illustrated Jane Austen, 6 Vols., ed. by R. W. Chapman (Oxford, 1988)

WORKS RELATING TO JANE AUSTEN

Biographical

Austen, Caroline, *Reminiscences of Caroline Austen* (Guildford, 1986)
Austen-Leigh, J. E., *A Memoir of Jane Austen and Other Family Recollections* (Oxford, 2002; originally published 1871)
Austen-Leigh, William and Richard Arthur Austen-Leigh, *Jane Austen: A Family Record*, revised and enlarged by Deirdre Le Faye (Boston, 1989)
Cecil, Lord David, *A Portrait of Jane Austen* (New York, 1979)
Honan, Park, *Jane Austen: Her Life* (New York, 1989)
Jenkins, Elizabeth, *Jane Austen* (New York, 1949)
Laski, Marghanita, *Jane Austen and Her World* (New York, 1969)
Le Faye, Deirdre, *Jane Austen: The World of Her Novels* (New York, 2002)
Myer, Valerie Grosvener, *Jane Austen: Obstinate Heart* (New York, 1997)
Nokes, David, *Jane Austen: A Life* (New York, 1997)
Ross, Josephine, *Jane Austen: A Companion* (New Brunswick, NJ, 2003)
Tomalin, Claire, *Jane Austen: A Life* (New York, 1997)

Critical

Babb, Howard S., *Jane Austen's Novels: The Fabric of Dialogue* (Columbus, OH, 1962)
Bloom, Allan, *Love and Friendship* (New York, 1993)
Bush, Douglas, *Jane Austen* (New York, 1975)
Butler, Marilyn, *Jane Austen and the War of Ideas* (Oxford, 1975)

Copeland, Edward and Juliet McMaster, eds., *The Cambridge Companion to Jane Austen* (Cambridge, 1997)

Craik, W. A., *Jane Austen: The Six Novels* (London, 1965)

Duckworth, Alistair M., *The Improvement of the Estate: A Study of Jane Austen's Novels* (Baltimore, 1971)

Fergus, Jan, *Jane Austen and the Didactic Novel: "Northanger Abbey," "Sense and Sensibility" and "Pride and Prejudice"* (Totowa, NJ, 1983)

Gard, Roger, *Jane Austen's Novels: The Art of Clarity* (New Haven, 1992)

Gooneratne, Yasmine, *Jane Austen* (Cambridge, 1970)

Grey, J. David, ed., *The Jane Austen Companion* (New York, 1986)

Halperin, John, ed., *Jane Austen: Bicentenary Essays* (Cambridge, 1975)

Hammond, M. C., *Relating to Jane: Studies on the Life and Novels of Jane Austen with a Life of her Niece Elizabeth Austen-Knight* (London, 1998)

Hardy, John, *Jane Austen's Heroines: Intimacy in Human Relationships* (London, 1984)

Jones, Vivien, *How to Study a Jane Austen Novel* (Basingstoke, Hampshire, 1987)

Kaye-Smith, Sheila and G. B. Stern, *Speaking of Jane Austen* (New York, 1944)

——, *More About Jane Austen* (New York, 1949)

Kennedy, Margaret, *Jane Austen* (London, 1950)

Konigsberg, Ira, *Narrative Technique in the English Novel: Defoe to Austen* (Hamden, CT, 1985)

Kroeber, Karl, *Styles in Fictional Structure: The Art of Jane Austen, Charlotte Brontë, George Eliot* (Princeton, 1971)

Lascelles, Mary, *Jane Austen and Her Art* (Oxford, 1939)

Liddell, Robert, *The Novels of Jane Austen* (London, 1963)

Mansell, Darrel, *The Novels of Jane Austen: An Interpretation* (London, 1973)

McMaster, Juliet, ed., *Jane Austen's Achievement* (New York, 1976)

Moler, Kenneth L., *Jane Austen's Art of Illusion* (Lincoln, Nebraska, 1968)
    "Pride and Prejudice": A Study in Artistic Economy (Boston, 1989)

Mooneyham, Laura, *Romance, Language and Education in Jane Austen's Novels* (New York, 1988)

Morris, Ivor, *Jane Austen and the Interplay of Character* (London, 1999)

Nardin, Jane, *Those Elegant Decorums: The Concept of Propriety in Jane Austen's Novels* (Albany, NY, 1973)

Page, Norman, *The Language of Jane Austen* (Oxford, 1972)

Pinion, F. B., *A Jane Austen Companion* (London, 1973)

Rubinstein, E., ed., *Twentieth-Century Interpretations of "Pride and Prejudice"* (Englewood Cliffs, NJ, 1969)

Roberts, Warren, *Jane Austen and the French Revolution* (New York, 1979)

Sherry, Norman, *Jane Austen* (New York, 1969)

Southam, B. C., ed., *Jane Austen: The Critical Heritage*, 2 Vols. (London, 1968–1987)

Stovel, Bruce and Lynn Weinlos Gregg, *The Talk in Jane Austen* (Alberta, 2002)

Sutherland, John, *Who Betrays Elizabeth Bennet?: Further Puzzles in Classic Fiction* (Oxford, 1999)

Tave, Stuart, *Some Words of Jane Austen* (Chicago, 1973)

Ten Harmsel, Henrietta, *Jane Austen: A Study in Fictional Conventions* (The Hague, 1964)

Todd, Janet, ed., *Jane Austen: New Perspectives* (New York, 1983)

Waldron, Mary, *Jane Austen and the Fiction of Her Time* (Cambridge, 1999)

Watt, Ian, ed., *Jane Austen: A Collection of Critical Essays* (Englewood Cliffs, NJ, 1963)

Weinsheimer, Joel, *Jane Austen Today* (Athens, GA, 1975)

Weisenfarth, Joseph, *The Errand of Form: An Assay of Jane Austen's Art* (New York, 1967)

WORKS OF HISTORICAL BACKGROUND

General Histories and Reference

Encyclopaedia Britannica; or, A Dictionary of Arts, Sciences, and Miscellaneous Literature, 3rd ed. (Edinburgh, 1797), and 4th ed. (Edinburgh, 1810)

Halevy, Elie, *A History of the English People in the Nineteenth Century*, Vol. I: *England in 1815*, translated by E. I. Watkin and D. A. Barker. 2nd ed. (London, 1949)

Hay, Douglas and Nicholas Rogers, *Eighteenth-Century English Society: Shuttles and Swords* (Oxford, 1997)

Langford, Paul, *A Polite and Commercial People: England 1727–1783* (Oxford, 1989)

Marshall, Dorothy, *English People in the Eighteenth Century* (London, 1956) *Industrial England, 1776–1851* (New York, 1973)

Perkin, Harold, *The Origins of Modern English Society, 1780–1880* (London, 1969)

Porter, Roy, *English Society in the Eighteenth Century.* Rev. ed. (London, 1990)

Rule, John, *Albion's People: English Society, 1714–1815* (London, 1992)

Language of the Period

Blair, Hugh, *Lectures on Rhetoric and Belles Lettres*, 3 Vols. (New York, 1970; reprint of 1785 ed.)

The Compact Edition of the Oxford English Dictionary (Oxford, 1971)

Crabb, George, *English Synonymes Explained, in Alphabetical Order; with Copious Illustrations and Examples Drawn from the Best Writers* (London, 1816)

Empson, William, *The Structure of Complex Words* (London, 1951)

Johnson, Samuel, *Dictionary of the English Language*, ed. by Alexander Chalmers (London, 1994; reprint of 1843 ed.)

Phillipps, K. C., *Jane Austen's English* (London, 1970)

Room, Adrian, *Dictionary of Changes in Meaning* (New York, 1986)

Schapera, I., *Kinship Terminology in Jane Austen's Novels* (London, 1977)

Stokes, Myra, *The Language of Jane Austen: A Study of Some Aspects of Her Vocabulary* (New York, 1991)

Tucker, Susie, *Protean Shape: A Study in Eighteenth-Century Vocabulary and Usage* (London, 1967)

Cultural and Literary Background

Bradbrook, Frank W., *Jane Austen and her Predecessors* (Cambridge, 1966)

Brewer, John, *The Pleasures of the Imagination: English Culture in the Eighteenth Century* (New York, 1997)

Porter, Roy, *The Creation of the Modern World: The Untold Story of the British Enlightenment* (New York, 2000)

Watt, Ian, *The Rise of the Novel: Studies in Defoe, Richardson, and Fielding* (Berkeley, 1957)

Everyday Life

Burton, Elizabeth, *The Pageant of Georgian England* (New York, 1967)

Craik, W. A., *Jane Austen in Her Time* (London, 1969)

Hole, Christina, *English Home-Life, 1500–1800* (London, 1947)

Olsen, Kirstin, *Daily Life in 18th-Century England* (Westport, CT, 1999)

Turberville, A. S., ed., *Johnson's England: An Account of the Life and Manners of His Age*, Vols. I and II (Oxford, 1933)

White, R. J., *Life in Regency England* (London, 1963)

Marriage and the Family

Gillis, John R., *For Better, For Worse: British Marriages, 1600 to the Present* (New York, 1985)

Laslett, Peter, *The World We Have Lost: England Before the Industrial Age.* 2nd ed. (New York, 1971)

Outhwaite, R. B., *Clandestine Marriage in England, 1500–1850* (London, 1995)

Parker, Stephen, *Informal Marriage, Cohabitation and the Law, 1750–1989* (London, 1990)

Stone, Lawrence, *The Family, Sex and Marriage in England, 1500–1800.* (London, 1977)

——, *The Road to Divorce: England 1530–1987* (Oxford, 1990)

Tadmor, Naomi, *Family and Friends in Eighteenth-Century England: Household, Kinship, and Patronage* (Cambridge, 2001)

The Position of Women

Hayley, William, A *philosophical, historical, and moral essay on old maids. By a friend to the sisterhood.* 3 Vols. (London, 1786)

Hill, Bridget, *Women Alone: Spinsters in England, 1660–1850* (New Haven, 2001)

Randall, Rona, *The Model Wife, Nineteenth-Century Style* (London, 1989)

Shoemaker, Robert B., *Gender in English Society, 1650–1850: The Emergence of Separate Spheres?* (London, 1998)

Vickery, Amanda, *The Gentleman's Daughter: Women's Lives in Georgian England* (London, 1998)

Female Education

Bayne-Powell, Rosamond, *The English Child in the Eighteenth Century* (New York, 1939)

Gardiner, Dorothy, *English Girlhood at School: A Study of Women's Education Through Twelve Centuries* (London, 1929)

Hans, Nicholas, *New Trends in Education in the Eighteenth Century* (London, 1951)

Kamm, Josephine, *Hope Deferred: Girls' Education in English History* (London, 1965)

Entails and Settlements

English, Barbara and John Saville, *Strict Settlement: A Guide for Historians* (Hull, 1983)

Habakkuk, John, *Marriage, Debt and the Estates System: English Landownership, 1650–1950* (Oxford, 1994)

Spring, Eileen, *Law, Land, and Family: Aristocratic Inheritance in England, 1300 to 1800* (Chapel Hill, 1993)

Staves, Susan, *Married Women's Separate Property in England, 1660–1833* (Cambridge, MA, 1990)

Money and Finance

Burnett, John, *A History of the Cost of Living* (Harmondsworth, Middlesex, 1969)

Homer, Sidney and Richard Sylla, *A History of Interest Rates.* 3rd ed. (New Brunswick, NJ, 1991)

Landed Society

Baugh, Daniel A., ed., *Aristocratic Government and Society in Eighteenth-Century England: The Foundations of Stability* (New York, 1975)

Beckett, J. V. *The Aristocracy in England, 1660–1914* (Oxford, 1986)

Book of the Ranks and Dignities of British Society, attributed to Charles Lamb (London, 1805; reprinted 1924)

Greene, D. J., "Jane Austen and the Peerage," *PMLA* 68 (1953): 1017–1031.

Mingay, G. E., *English Landed Society in the Eighteenth Century* (London, 1963)

——, *The Gentry: The Rise and Fall of a Ruling Class* (New York, 1976)

Stone, Lawrence and Jeanne C. Fawtier Stone, *An Open Elite: England 1540–1880* (Oxford, 1984)

Thompson, F. M. L., *English Landed Society in the Nineteenth Century* (London, 1963)

Trumbach, Randolph, *The Rise of the Egalitarian Family: Aristocratic Kinship and Domestic Relations in Eighteenth-Century England* (New York, 1978)

Housekeeping and Servants

Bayne-Powell, Rosamond, *Housekeeping in the Eighteenth Century* (London, 1956)

Hardyment, Christina, *Home Comfort: A History of Domestic Arrangements* (Chicago, 1992)

Hecht, J. Jean, *The Domestic Servant Class in Eighteenth-Century England* (London, 1956)

Hill, Bridget, *Servants: English Domestics in the Eighteenth Century* (Oxford, 1996)

The Rural World

Bayne-Powell, Rosamond, *English Country Life in the Eighteenth Century* (London, 1935)

Bovill, E.W., *English Country Life, 1780–1830* (London, 1962)

Eastwood, David, *Governing Rural England: Tradition and Transformation in Local Government, 1780–1840* (Oxford, 1994)

Everett, Alan, "Kentish Family Portrait," in *Rural Change and Urban Growth: Essays in Regional History in Honour of W. G. Hoskins,* ed. by Chalklin, C. W. and M. A. Havinden (London, 1974)

Horn, Pamela, *The Rural World, 1780–1850: Social Change in the English Countryside* (New York, 1980)

Keith-Lucas, Brian, *The Unreformed Local Government System* (London, 1980)

Mitford, Mary, *Our Village,* 2 Vols. (London, 1865; originally published in 5 vols., 1824–1832)

Urban Life

Borsay, Peter, ed. *The Eighteenth-Century Town: A Reader in English Urban History, 1680–1820* (London, 1990)

Corfield, P. J., *The Impact of English Towns, 1700–1800* (Oxford, 1982)

Girouard, Mark, *The English Town: A History of Urban Life* (New Haven, 1990)

Mui, Hoh-Cheung and Lorna H. Mui, *Shops and Shopkeeping in Eighteenth-Century England* (Kingston, Ontario, 1989)

London

The A to Z of Regency London (London, 1985)

George, M. Dorothy, *London Life in the Eighteenth Century.* 2nd ed. (London, 1966)

Picard, Liza, *Dr. Johnson's London* (New York, 2000)

Porter, Roy, *London: A Social History* (Cambridge, MA, 1994)

Schwartz, Richard B., *Daily Life in Johnson's London* (Madison, WI, 1983)

Sheppard, Francis, *London: A History* (New York, 1998)

The Professions

Corfield, Penelope J., *Power and the Professions in Britain, 1700–1850* (New York, 1995)

Reader, W. J., *Professional Men: The Rise of the Professional Classes in Nineteenth-Century England* (London, 1966)

The Church and the Clergy

Collins, Irene, *Jane Austen and the Clergy* (London, 1994)

Evans, Eric J., *The Contentious Tithe: The Tithe Problem and English Agriculture, 1750–1850* (London, 1976)

Francis Brown, C. K., *A History of The English Clergy, 1800–1900* (London, 1953)

Hart, A. Tindal, *The Country Priest in English History* (London, 1959)

Sykes, Norman, *Church and State in England in the XVIIIth Century* (Hamden, CT, 1962)

Virgin, Peter, *The Church in an Age of Negligence: Ecclesiastical Structure and Problems of Church Reform, 1700–1840* (Cambridge, 1989)

The Army

Beckett, Ian F. W., *The Amateur Military Tradition, 1558–1945* (Manchester, 1991)

Bruce, Anthony, *The Purchase System in the British Army, 1660–1871* (London, 1980)

Emsley, Clive, *British Society and the French Wars, 1793–1815* (London, 1979)

Glover, Richard, *Peninsular Preparation: The Reform of the British Army* (Cambridge, 1963)

Haythornthwaite, Philip J., *The Armies of Wellington* (New York, 1994)

Myerly, Scott Hughes, *British Military Spectacle: From the Napoleonic Wars through the Crimea* (Cambridge, MA, 1996)

Western, John R., *The English Militia in the Eighteenth Century: The Story of a Political Issue, 1660–1802* (London, 1965)

Law and Lawyers

Baker, J. H., *An Introduction to English Legal History*. 2nd Ed. (London, 1979)

Birks, Michael, *Gentlemen of the Law* (London, 1960)

Duman, Daniel, *The Judicial Bench in England, 1727–1875: The Reshaping of a Professional Elite* (London, 1982)

Robson, Robert, *The Attorney in Eighteenth-Century England* (Cambridge, 1959)

Medicine

Porter, Roy, ed., *The Cambridge Illustrated History of Medicine* (New York, 1996)

Porter, Roy and Dorothy Porter, *In Sickness and in Health: The British Experience, 1650–1850* (New York, 1989)

Rousseau, G. S., "Towards a Semiotics of the Nerve: The Social History of Language in a New Key," in *Language, Self, and Society: A Social History of Language*, ed. by Peter Burke and Roy Porter (Cambridge, 1991)

Trotter, Thomas, *A View of the Nervous Temperament* (Troy, NY, 1808; originally published, London, 1807)

Higher Education

Ashton, T. S., ed., *History of the University of Oxford*
Vol. V: *The Eighteenth Century*, ed. by L. S. Sutherland and L. G. Mitchell (Oxford, 1986)
Vol. VI: *Nineteenth-Century Oxford, Part 1*, ed. by M. G. Brock and M. C. Curthoys (Oxford, 1997)

Searby, Peter, *A History of the University of Cambridge, Vol. III: 1750–1870* (Cambridge, 1997)

Winstanley, D. A., *Unreformed Cambridge: A Study of Certain Aspects of the University in the Eighteenth Century* (Cambridge, 1935)

Books and Publishing

Altick, Robert, *The English Common Reader: A Social History of the Mass Reading Public, 1800–1900* (Chicago, 1957)

Bronson, Bertrand H., *Printing as an Index of Taste in Eighteenth-Century England* (New York, 1958)

Feather, John, *The Provincial Book Trade in Eighteenth-Century England* (Cambridge, 1985)

Orcutt, William Dana, *Master Makers of the Book: Being a Consecutive Story of the Book from a Century before the Invention of Printing through the Era of the Doves Press* (New York, 1928)

Libraries

Hamlyn, H. M., "Eighteenth-Century Circulating Libraries in England," *Library*, Fifth Series I (1947), pp. 197–218.

Kaufman, Paul, *The Community Library: A Chapter in English Social History* (Philadelphia, 1967)

Varma, Devendra P., *The Evergreen Tree of Diabolical Knowledge* (Washington, DC, 1972)

The Press

Barker, Hannah, *Newspapers, Politics and English Society, 1695–1855* (Harlow, Essex, 2000)

Christie, Ian, "British Newspapers in the Later Georgian Age," in *Myth and Reality in Late-Eighteenth-Century British Politics and Other Papers* (Berkeley, 1970)

Cranfield, G. A., *The Press and Society: From Caxton to Northcliffe* (London, 1978)

Writing

Complete Letter Writer, or Polite English Secretary (London, 1792). No author; many editions.

Barton, David and Nigel Hall, eds., *Letter Writing as a Social Practice* (Philadelphia, 2000)

Finlay, Michael, *Western Writing Implements in the Age of the Quill Pen* (Carlisle, Cumbria, 1990)

Whalley, Joyce Irene, *English Handwriting, 1540–1853* (London, 1969)

Writing Implements and Accessories: From the Roman Stylus to the Typewriter (Newton Abbot, Devon, 1975)

The Postal Service

Kay, F. George, *Royal Mail: The Story of the Posts in England from the Time of Edward IVth to the Present Day* (London, 1951)

Robinson, Howard, *The British Post Office: A History* (Princeton, 1948)

Transportation

Copeland, John, *Roads and Their Traffic* (Newton Abbot, Devon, 1968)

McCausland, Hugh, *The English Carriage* (London, 1948)

Pawson, Eric, *Transport and Economy: The Turnpike Roads of Eighteenth Century Britain* (New York, 1977)

Sparkes, Ivan, *Stagecoaches and Carriages* (Bourne End, 1975)
Stratton, Ezra, *World on Wheels* (New York, 1972; reprint of 1878 ed.)
Tarr, Laszlo, *A History of the Carriage* (New York, 1969)

Leisure and Amusement

Hole, Christina, *English Sports and Pastimes* (Freeport, NY, 1949)
Pimlott, J.A.R., *The Englishman's Christmas: A Social History* (Atlantic Highlands, NJ, 1998)
Plumb, J.H., *Georgian Delights* (Boston, 1980)
Selwyn, David, *Jane Austen and Leisure* (London, 1999)

Music and Dance

The Jane Austen Collection (CD), Concert Royal (2001)
Loesser, Arthur, *Men, Women and Pianos: A Social History* (New York, 1954)
Piggott, Patrick, *The Innocent Diversion: A Study of Music in the Life and Writings of Jane Austen* (London, 1979)
Richardson, Philip J. S., *The Social Dances of the Nineteenth Century in England* (London, 1960)
Wilson, Thomas, dancing master, *The Complete System of English Country Dancing* (London, 1820)

The Theatre

Donohue, Joseph W., *Theatre in the Age of Keen* (Oxford, 1975)
Hogan, Charles Beecher, *The London Stage, 1776–1800: A Critical Introduction* (Carbondale, IL, 1968)
Trussler, Simon, *The Cambridge Illustrated History of British Theatre* (Cambridge, 1994)

Cards

Hoyle's Games Improved, Consisting of Practical Treatises on Whist, Quadrille, Piquet, etc., revised and corrected by Charles Jones, Esq. (London, 1800)
Parlett, David, *A Dictionary of Card Games* (New York, 1992)
——, *A History of Card Games* (New York, 1991)

Hunting

Leopold, Aldo, *Game Management* (New York, 1933)
Longrigg, Roger, *The English Squire and His Sport* (New York, 1977)
Trench, Charles Chenevix, *A History of Markmanship* (Norwich, 1972)

Tourism

Leapman, Michael, ed., *Eyewitness Travel Portrait of Britain* (New York, 1999)

MacKinnon, Honourable Mr. Justice (F. D.), "Topography and Travel in Jane Austen's Novels," *The Cornhill Magazine*, series 3, Vol. 59 (1925): 184–199.

Moir, Esther, *The Discovery of Britain: The English Tourists* (London, 1964)

Ousby, Ian, *The Englishman's England: Taste, Travel and the Rise of Tourism* (Cambridge, 1990)

Tinniswood, Adrian, *A History of Country House Visiting: Five Centuries of Tourism and Taste* (Oxford, 1989)

Withey, Lynne, *Grand Tour & Cook's Tours: A History of Leisure Travel, 1750 to 1915* (New York, 1997)

Contemporary Travel Writings

Dibdin, Charles, *Observations on a Tour through almost the whole of England, and a considerable part of Scotland*, 2 Vols. (London, 1801)

Michaelis-Jena, Ruth and Willy Merson, trans. and ed., *A Lady Travels: Journeys in England and Scotland from the Diaries of Joanna Schopenhauer* (London, 1988; based on 2nd ed. of 1816)

Silliman, Benjamin, *Journal of Travels in England, Holland, and Scotland, . . . In the Years 1805 and 1806* (New Haven, 1820)

Simond, Louis, *An American in Regency England. Journal of a Tour in 1810–1811*, ed. by Christopher Hibbert (London, 1968)

The Seaside

Lencek, Lena and Gideon Bosker, *The Beach: The History of Paradise on Earth* (New York, 1998)

Walton, John K., *The English Seaside Resort: A Social History, 1750–1914* (New York, 1983)

The Idea of the Picturesque

Andrews, Malcolm, *The Search for the Picturesque: Landscape, Aesthetics and Tourism in Britain, 1760–1800* (Stanford, 1989)

Batey, Mavis, *Jane Austen and the English Landscape* (Chicago, 1996)

Gilpin, William, *Observations, on Several Parts of England, particularly the Mountains and Lakes of Cumberland and Westmoreland, relative chiefly to Picturesque Beauty, made in the year 1772*. 3rd ed. (London, 1802)

Remarks on Forest Scenery and other Woodland Views (London, 1791)

Hussey, Christopher, *The Picturesque: Studies in a Point of View* (London, 1927; reprint 1967)

Gardens and Landscaping

Coffin, David, *The English Garden: Meditation and Memorial* (Princeton, 1994)

Forsyth, William, *A treatise on the culture and management of fruit trees; in which a new method of pruning and training is fully described* (London, 1802)

Hobhouse, Penelope, *Gardening Through the Ages* (New York, 1992)

Jacques, David, *Georgian Gardens: The Reign of Nature* (Portland, OR., 1984)

Laird, Mark, *The Flowering of the Landscape Garden: English Pleasure Grounds, 1720–1800* (Philadelphia, 1999)

Lasdun, Suan, *The English Park: Royal, Private and Public* (London, 1991)

Quest-Ritson, Charles, *The English Garden: A Social History* (London, 2001)

Stuart, David, *The Kitchen Garden: A Historical Guide to Traditional Crops* (London, 1984)

Thacker, Christopher, *The History of Gardens* (Berkeley, 1979)

Williamson, Tom, *Polite Landscapes: Gardens and Society in Eighteenth-Century England* (Baltimore, 1995)

Country Houses

Arnold, Dana, ed., *The Georgian Country House: Architecture, Landscape and Society* (Stroud, Gloucestershire, 1998)

Clemenson, Heather, *English Country Houses and Landed Estates* (New York, 1982)

Girouard, Mark, *Life in the English Country House: A Social and Architectural History* (New Haven, 1978)

Pevsner, Nikolaus, "The Architectural Setting of Jane Austen's Novels," *Journal of the Warburg and Courtauld Institutes* 31 (1968): 404–422.

Wilson, Richard and Alan Mackley, *Creating Paradise: The Building of the English Country House, 1660–1880* (London, 2000)

Interior Decoration

Edwards, Ralph and L. G. G. Ramsey, *The Connoiseur Period Guides to the Houses, Decoration, Furnishing and Chattels of the Classic Periods*, Vol. 4: *The Late Georgian Period, 1760–1810*, Vol. 5: *The Regency Period, 1810–1830* (London, 1958)

Gloag, John, *Georgian Grace: A Social History of Design from 1660 to 1830* (London, 1956)

Harrison, Molly, *People and Furniture: A Social Background to the English Home* (London, 1971)

Pilcher, Donald, *The Regency Style, 1800 to 1830* (New York, 1948)

Richards, Sarah, *Eighteenth-Century Ceramics: Products for a Civilised Society* (New York, 1999)

Female Decorative Activities

Allen, B. Sprague, *Tides in English Taste (1690–1800): A Background for the Study of Literature*, Vol. I (New York, 1958)

Beck, Thomasina, *The Embroiderer's Story: Needlework from the Renaissance to the Present Day* (Devon, 1995)

Bermingham, Ann, *Learning to Draw: Studies in the Cultural History of a Polite and Useful Art* (New Haven, 2000)

Gandee, B. F., *The Artist, or Young Ladies Instructor in Ornamental Painting, Drawing, &c.* (London, 1835)

Harrower, Dorothy, *Decoupage: A Limitless World in Decoration* (New York, 1958)

The Ladies Amusement, or, Whole Art of Japanning Made Easy (London, 1762; facsimile ed. of 1959)

Robertson, Hannah, *The Young Ladies School of Arts* (York, 1777)

Wing, Frances S., *The Complete Book of Decoupage* (New York, 1970)

Dress

Ashelford, Jane, *The Art of Dress: Clothes and Society, 1500–1914* (New York, 1996)

Buck, Anne, *Dress in Eighteenth-Century England* (London, 1979)

Byrde, Penelope, *A Frivolous Distinction: Fashion and Needlework in the Works of Jane Austen* (Bristol, 1979)

Ewing, Elizabeth, *Everyday Dress, 1650–1900* (London, 1984)

Food and Drink

Black, Maggie and Deirdre Le Faye, *The Jane Austen Cookbook* (Chicago, 1995)

Grigson, Jane, *English Food* (London, 1992)

Hickman, Peggy, *A Jane Austen Household Book, with Martha Lloyd's Recipes* (North Pomfret, VT, 1977)

Johnson, Hugh, *Vintage: The Story of Wine* (New York, 1989)

Lane, Maggie, *Jane Austen and Food* (London, 1995)

Mennell, Stephen, *All Manners of Food: Eating and Taste in England and France from the Middle Ages to the Present* (Oxford, 1985)

Palmer, Arnold, *Movable Feasts* (New York, 1952)

Paston-Williams, Sara, *The Art of Dining: A History of Cooking and Eating* (London, 1993)

Wilson, C. Anne, *Food and Drink in Britain: From the Stone Age to Recent Times* (London, 1973)

Etiquette

Fritzer, Penelope Joan, *Jane Austen and Eighteenth-Century Courtesy Books* (Westport, CT, 1997)

Morgan, Marjorie, *Manners, Morals and Class in England, 1774–1858* (New York, 1994)

Wildeblood, Joan, *The Polite World: A Guide to the Deportment of the English in Former Times* (London, 1973)

Female Conduct Books

Advice of a Mother to her Daughter, by the Marchioness of Lambert; *A Father's Legacy to his Daughters*, by Dr. Gregory; *The Lady's New Year's Gift, or, Advice to a Daughter*, by Lord Halifax, in *Angelica's Ladies Library* (London, 1794)

Burton, John, *Lectures on Female Education and Manners* (London, 1793; reprint ed., New York, 1970)

Chapone, Hester, *Letters on the Improvement of the Mind* (Walpole, NH, 1802; first published London, 1773)

Fordyce, James, *Sermons to Young Women* (New York, 1809 — 3rd U.S. ed. from 12th London ed.)

Gisborne, Thomas, *An Enquiry into the Duties of the Female Sex* (London, 1796)

Lady of Distinction, *The Mirror of Graces; or, The English Lady's Costume* (London, 1811)

Murry, Ann, *Mentoria, or, the young ladies instructor* (London, 1785)

Pennington, Sarah, *An Unfortunate Mother's Advice to her Absent Daughters* (London, 1770)

Trusler, Rev. Dr. John, *Principles of Politeness, and of Knowing the World, in Two Parts* (London, 1800)

Ideas of the Gentleman

Carter, Philip, *Men and the Emergence of Polite Society, Britain 1660–1800* (Harlow, Essex, 2001)

Castronovo, David, *The English Gentleman: Images and Ideals in Literature and Society* (New York, 1987)

Dueling

Baldick, Robert, *The Duel: A History of Dueling* (London, 1965)

Kiernan, V. G., *The Duel in European History: Honour and the Reign of Aristocracy* (Oxford, 1988)

Fashionable Society

Erickson, Carolly, *Our Tempestuous Day: A History of Regency England* (New York, 1986)

Foreman, Amanda, *Georgiana: Duchess of Devonshire* (New York, 1999)

Green, William, *Essay on Gaming* (London, 1788)

Laudermilk, Sharon H. and Teresa L. Hamlin, *The Regency Companion* (New York, 1989)

Murray, Venetia, *An Elegant Madness: High Society in Regency England* (New York, 1999)

Maps

ENGLAND

Places mentioned in the novel; see following pages for maps of Derbyshire and the Southeast, and information on all places identified on the maps.

Gretna Green: where English couples eloping to Scotland marry.

Lake District: the original destination in the northern tour planned by Elizabeth and the Gardiners.

Newcastle: the location of Wickham's new regiment.

Scarborough: the resort where Darcy's friends go after Pemberley.

York: the place, according to Mrs. Bennet, the Bennet family might as well be, for all that Elizabeth cares for them.

Liverpool: where Miss King is sent while Wickham is pursuing her.

Oxford, Blenheim, Warwick, Kenilworth, and *Birmingham*: places Elizabeth and the Gardiners visit during their vacation.

Bath: where Wickham sometimes vacations after his marriage.

DERBYSHIRE (Old County Lines)

Tourist sites mentioned as part of Elizabeth and the Gardiners' tour. Of these sites, Bakewell is probably the one closest to Darcy's home of Pemberley.

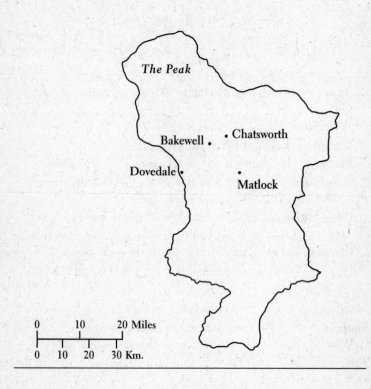

The Peak

Bakewell •   • Chatsworth

Dovedale •

• Matlock

0   10   20 Miles

0   10   20   30 Km.

SOUTHEASTERN ENGLAND

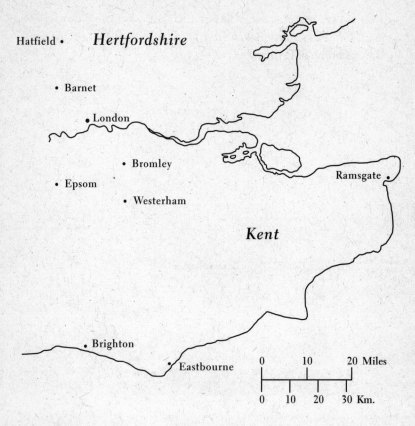

Hertfordshire: the county in which the Bennets live.

Hatfield and *Barnet*: the towns Colonel Forster searched in case
Wickham and Lydia stopped there on the way to Scotland.

Epsom: the last place Wickham and Lydia changed horses on the
way to London.

Bromley: where to change horses between Westerham and London.

Westerham: the town closest to Lady Catherine's residence.

Ramsgate: where Wickham tried to seduce Georgiana Darcy.

Brighton: where Lydia runs away with Wickham.

Eastbourne (or East Bourne): the closest to Brighton Mr. Bennet says
he will allow Kitty.

JANE AUSTEN

Available in beautiful and
elegant hardcover editions from

EVERYMAN'S LIBRARY

publishers of the most extensive and distinguished library of our time

These beautiful and enduring Everyman's Library editions feature original introductions, an up-to-date bibliography, and a complete chronology of Jane Austen's life and works. These are classically designed books printed on acid-free paper, with Smyth-sewn signatures, full-cloth cases with two-color stamping, decorative endpapers, silk ribbon markers, and European-style half-round spines.

EMMA

The most perfect of Jane Austen's perfect novels begins with twenty-one-year-old Emma Woodhouse comfortably dominating the social order in the village of Highbury, convinced that she has both the understanding and the right to manage other people's lives—for their own good, of course. Her well-meant interfering centers on the aloof Jane Fairfax, the dangerously attractive Frank Churchill, the foolish if appealing Harriet Smith, and the ambitious young vicar Mr. Elton—and ends with her complacency shattered, her mind awakened to some of life's more intractable dilemmas, and her happiness assured.

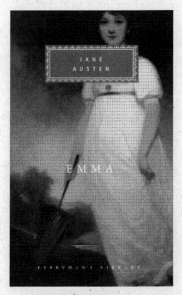

FICTION | LITERATURE
978-0-679-40581-8

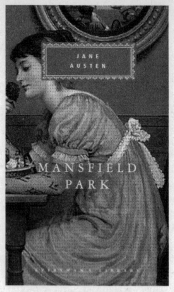

FICTION | LITERATURE
978-0-679-41269-4

MANSFIELD PARK

Mansfield Park is the longest and most measured of Jane Austen's novels, giving us her largest cast of characters and her most dramatic narrative. At its center is Fanny Price—brought as a child to Mansfield Park by the rich Sir Thomas Bertram and his wife as an act of charity. As she grows, modest and with a loving heart, Fanny watches her cousins engage in dangerous flirtations (and worse), and as she herself resists the advantages of marriage, her seeming austerity grows in appeal and makes clear why she was Jane Austen's own favorite among her heroines.

NORTHANGER ABBEY

Northanger Abbey is both a perfectly aimed literary parody and a withering satire of marriage. But most of all, it is the story of Catherine Morland, a willing victim of the contemporary craze for Gothic literature who is determined to see herself as the heroine of a dark and thrilling romance. When she is invited to Northanger Abbey, the grand though forbidding ancestral seat of her suitor, Henry Tilney, she finds herself embroiled in a real drama of misapprehension, mistreatment, and mortfication, until common sense and humor—and a crucial clarification of Catherine's financial status—resolve her problems and win her the approval of Henry's formidable father.

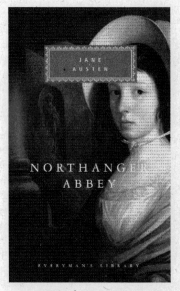

FICTION | LITERATURE
978-0-679-41715-6

FICTION | LITERATURE
978-0-679-40986-1

PERSUASION

When Anne Elliott was nineteen, she fell in love with—and was engaged to—a naval officer, the fearless and headstrong Captain Wentworth. But the young man had no fortune, and Anne was persuaded to give him up. Now, at twenty-seven, Anne learns that Captain Wentworth has returned to the neighborhood, a rich man and still unwed. Anne's love is muffled by her pride, and Wentworth seems cold and unforgiving. What happens as the two are thrown back together in the social world of Bath is touchingly and wittily told in a masterpiece that is also one of the most entrancing novels in the English language.

PRIDE AND PREJUDICE

No novel in English has given more pleasure than *Pride and Prejudice* with its wonderfully charming and intelligent heroine, Elizabeth Bennet. Everyone is held fast not only by the novel's romantic suspense but also by the fascinations of the world it portrays. The life of the English country gentry at the turn of the nineteenth century is made as real to us as our own, not only by the author's wit and feeling but by her subtle observation of the way people behave in society and how we are true or treacherous to each other and to ourselves.

FICTION | LITERATURE
978-0-679-40542-9

SANDITON
AND OTHER STORIES

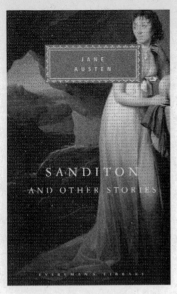

Collected here are the marvelous manuscripts Jane Austen left unpublished (and some unfinished) at her death. In *Sanditon*, a colorful cast of characters collides at a seaside resort. *The Watsons* tells the story of a young woman raised by a rich aunt who then finds herself back in the comparative poverty of her own family. The novella *Lady Susan* is a miniature masterpiece, featuring Austen's only villainous protagonist. The collection also includes tiny novels, the enchantingly funny *Love and Freindship*, comic fragments, and a (very) partial history of England.

SENSE AND SENSIBILITY

Sense and Sensibility is the answer to those critics who believe that Jane Austen's novels lack strong feeling. Its two heroines both experience great suffering when they are separated from the men they love. Impetuous Marianne falls into paroxysms of grief when she is rejected by the dashing John Willoughby; while her self-controlled sister, Elinor, masks her despair when it appears that Edward Ferrars has chosen another woman. All, of course, ends happily—but not until Elinor's "sense" and Marianne's "sensibility" have equally worked to reveal the profound emotional life that runs beneath the surface of Jane Austen's immaculate and irresistible art.

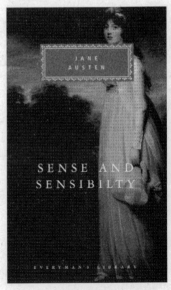

Build Your Own Library At: